HEAVY LOSSES

HEAVY LOSSES

*The Dangerous
Decline of
American Defense*

BY JAMES COATES
AND MICHAEL KILIAN

Viking

VIKING
Viking Penguin Inc., 40 West 23rd Street, New York, New York 10010, U.S.A.
Penguin Books Ltd, Harmondsworth, Middlesex, England
Penguin Books Australia Ltd, Ringwood, Victoria, Australia
Penguin Books Canada Limited, 2801 John Street, Markham, Ontario, Canada L3R 1B4
Penguin Books (N.Z.) Ltd, 182–190 Wairau Road, Auckland 10, New Zealand

First published in 1985 by Viking Penguin Inc.
Published simultaneously in Canada

LIBRARY OF CONGRESS CATALOGING IN PUBLICATION DATA
Coates, James, 1943–
    Heavy losses.
    Bibliography: p.
    Includes index.
    1. United States—Defenses.   2. United States—Military policy.
3. United States—Armed Forces.   I. Kilian, Michael.   II. Title.
UA23.C567 1985   355′.033073   84-26985
ISBN 0-670-80484-3

A selection from this book appeared originally in *Penthouse*.

Grateful acknowledgment is made to the following for permission to reprint copyrighted
material:
Air University Review: From *Air University Review*, Volume XXXII, Number 5, July–
August 1981, pages 101–113.
Doubleday & Company, Inc.: An excerpt, "archy the cockroach," from *archy's life of
mehitabel,* by don marquis. Copyright 1927, 1933 by Doubleday & Company, Inc.
Alfred A. Knopf, Inc.: An excerpt from *Resistance, Rebellion and Death*, by Albert
Camus, translated by Justin O'Brien. Copyright © 1960 by Alfred A. Knopf, Inc.
Reprinted by permission of the publisher.
Warner Bros. Music: Portions of lyrics from "Army Song," by K. Weill and B. Brecht.
Copyright 1928 by Universal Edition. Copyright renewed and assigned to Weill-Brecht-
Harms Co., Inc. Copyright 1951 by Weill-Brecht-Harms Co., Inc. All rights reserved.
Westview Press, Boulder, Colorado: An excerpt from *Thinking About National Security:
Defense and Foreign Policy in a Dangerous World*, by Harold Brown. Copyright © 1983
by Westview Press.

Printed in the United States of America by
R. R. Donnelley & Sons Company, Harrisonburg, Virginia
Set in Times Roman
Designed by Barbara DuPree Knowles

For Dieter; he gave his life for his country,
and no one knew.
And for John S. D. Eisenhower,
officer, gentleman, and a shining example for
those who would serve their country.

"The big, fat Republic that is afraid of
nothing because nothing up to the present date has
happened to make her afraid, is as unprotected as a
jellyfish."

RUDYARD KIPLING, *American Notes*

Contents

HEAVY LOSSES

Introduction

THE AMERICAN WAY

> *It has long been a grave question whether any government, not too strong for the liberties of its people, can be strong enough to maintain its existence in great emergencies.*
> —ABRAHAM LINCOLN, NOVEMBER 10, 1864

The United States of America hates war. Antimilitarism and isolationism loom among its most driving traditions. Yet the United States of America is one of the two mightiest military powers on earth. And now it is embroiled in a bitter internal debate over whether that should be so, or any longer can be so.

The seeds of this uniquely American contradiction were sown in 1784, when the first act of the post–Revolutionary War Continental Congress was to disband the army and send it home. Despite the many dangers faced by the new nation, the congress sold off the national navy and reduced the army's strength to eighty enlisted men—just enough to defend the arsenals at West Point and Fort Pitt—and a handful of officers, none above the rank of captain.

"Standing armies in time of peace," the congress proclaimed, "are inconsistent with the principles of republican governments."

This was the republican way, the democratic way, and was to be the American way. If troops were needed, they would not be summoned until combat was at hand. Instead of trained professionals, the nation would rely on the militia, the same sort of citizen soldiers who fought the Revolutionary War, men who would bear arms for brief periods to repel invaders or meet a military emergency and then go home.

George Washington, who was father of the American military as much as he was of his country, thought this would suffice. To maintain a standing army comparable to those of Europe, he said, would cause "great oppression of the people." To fortify the coastline would be "impracticable, at any rate, amazingly expensive. The militia of this country must be considered as the palladium of our security and the first effective resort in case of hostility."

For most of the nation's history, this continued to be the American way. In 1860, the U.S. government possessed an army of 16,215 men. Five years and a bloody civil war later, the Union had 1,062,848 men under arms. A year after that, in 1866, there were only 76,749 left, and General George Armstrong Custer was reduced to a lieutenant colonel because far fewer general officers were needed. So it went with the War of 1812, the Mexican War, the Spanish-American War, and World Wars I and II. In 1939, American military strength was 334,473. In 1944, it was 12,123,455. By July 1947, that huge force had been reduced to 1,582,999.

Korea was the turning point. That nasty Asian "police action" had been brought on by a bewildering set of circumstances, including Secretary of State Dean Acheson's unfortunately inviting "defense perimeter" speech and a disastrous miscalculation of American strength, intent, and resolve by the North Koreans. Unlike the later conflict in Vietnam, an Asian land war it otherwise much resembled, the Korean conflict was fought on a narrow peninsula that allowed the United States to bring massive sea and air power to bear and achieve a static front. It ended only after newly elected President Dwight Eisenhower quietly threatened to use tactical atomic weapons. He deployed atomic artillery in Korea, stockpiled nuclear shells in staging areas, and allowed Chinese military intelligence to discover the fact. He also warned he might turn the Nationalist Chinese of Taiwan loose for military actions against the Chinese mainland. Korea was an extremely unpopular war, and American support for it probably would have diminished greatly had Eisenhower not ended it when he did.

But Korea changed American thinking. The lofty republican ideals of the Founding Fathers were abandoned to deal with what was perceived as a long-term global menace. Thereafter, the United States would never again scrap its navies, send its armies home, and retreat into an insular "Fortress America." It would maintain its forces at a close approximation of a war footing. This least military of nations would do whatever was necessary to remain the greatest military power in the history of mankind, whatever the cost. Or so it was promised.

With wrenching dislocations still not adequately understood—or adequately dealt with—the antimilitary and fiercely libertarian United States of America has been engaging in all-out competition with the Soviet Union, one of the most regimented and oppressive societies on the planet and certainly the most menacing opponent any power has faced in the history of warfare.

"We face a hostile ideology—global in scope, atheistic in character, ruthless in purpose, and insidious in method," President Eisenhower told the nation in his televised farewell address in 1961, a few months short of the United States's initial reinforcement of advisor forces in Vietnam.

> Unhappily the danger it poses promises to be of indefinite duration. To meet it successfully, there is called for, not so much the emotional and transitory sacrifices of crisis, but rather those which enable us to carry forward steadily, surely, and without complaint the burdens of a prolonged and complex struggle—with liberty the stake. Only thus shall we remain, despite every provocation, on our charted course toward permanent peace and human betterment.

This was the same speech more remembered for Eisenhower's warning of the

> acquisition of unwarranted influence, whether sought or unsought, by the military-industrial complex. The potential for the disastrous rise of misplaced power exists and will persist.
>
> We must never let the weight of this combination endanger our liberties or democratic processes. We should take nothing for granted. Only an alert and knowledgeable citizenry can compel the proper meshing of the huge industrial and military machinery of defense with our peaceful methods and goals, so that security and liberty may prosper together.

Eisenhower stated the essence of the dilemma facing the United States in the remaining decades of this century. These are the principal questions to be dealt with in this book: Can a constitutional democracy with America's traditions compete indefinitely in a worldwide struggle with a totalitarian, imperialist, and yet revolutionary military power as immense as the Union of Soviet Socialist Republics? Can it do so without injuring its democratic and economic institutions and cherished way of life? Can it do so at all?

The answer to these questions, as matters currently stand, is unfortunately no.

As this book will make clear, American defense simply does not work. Its record since Korea has been one of fecklessness and failure. Korea, at least, was a stalemate snatched from probable disaster. Vietnam was an unredeemed disaster. The *Mayaguez* and the Desert One Iranian rescue raids were bizarre black comedies. The Reagan administration's military misadventure in Lebanon was a grisly tragedy.

The only "success" of the American military since Eisenhower was the 1983 storming of the tiny Caribbean island of Grenada, in which American rangers and Marines managed to defeat perhaps six hundred Cubans and a ragtag army of locals whose resistance to the invasion amounted mostly to stripping to their underwear and running off into the hills. Though they outnumbered the Cubans by more than three to one, U.S. forces suffered 18 killed to the Cubans' 25 and in a few short minutes lost nine helicopters.

The U.S. military must function amid a tangle of alliances with friends who all too often act as enemies, who fail to carry their fair share of the mutual defense burden, and who pursue their own policies and ambitions, no matter what the effect on collective security.

American defense has become at once dangerously costly and dangerously weak. It suffers from the lack of any clear-cut, agreed-upon strategy for the protection of American interests around the globe, and a lack of the combat strength, equipment, training, and tactics needed to carry out such a strategy. Its policy-making suffers from timidity, a dispersion of responsibility, and a craving for the status quo. Its top-heavy officer corps is made up increasingly of bureaucrats and its all-volunteer enlisted force continues to depend disproportionately on the poor to fill its ranks.

To compensate for this weakness in the face of the Soviet Union's and other adversaries' superior forces, American defense has turned to high-technology weapons that cost increasingly extravagant sums, are produced in ever decreasing numbers, and—to a frightening degree—don't work. Such wonder weapons as the York air defense gun are considered by many military professionals to be more dangerous to their users than to the enemy.

The military-industrial complex has proved every bit as dangerous to America's best interests as Eisenhower so sternly warned. To produce its arsenal of junk, it is consuming American resources at a rate not seen since the Vietnam War—a rate that will increase geometrically as the final production costs of the ballooning weapons projects come due. In the process, it is helping to produce unprecedented federal deficits and a national debt that pose the greatest threat to the nation's economic health since the Arabs imposed the oil embargo in 1973.

By the end of his first term, Reagan had pushed defense spending up to the $300-billion-a-year mark. In constant dollars adjusted for inflation, this compares with a defense budget authority of $244 billion for 1969 at the height of the buildup for the Vietnam War. With Defense Secretary Caspar Weinberger asking for $334 billion at the outset of the second term, estimates were that defense spending could easily exceed $400 billion in adjusted constant dollars by 1989.

Nearly two thirds of this would go for personnel costs associated with maintaining the all-volunteer military and paying for the weapons already ordered in the first Reagan term. Except for the Navy, which was building itself a fleet of $4 billion aircraft carriers protected by $1 billion destroyers, the actual number of weapons would steadily shrink as their costs rose dramatically. Dr. William Kaufmann of the Brookings Institution observed, "What is not generally recognized is that we are a bit more than midway on the road to building a much more expensive permanent military establishment. These expenditures are just going to explode."

The military-industrial complex is also sapping American military strength through corruption of our officer corps. Officers are not only turning away from combat to pursue bureaucratic ambitions; they are advancing their careers according to the size and cost of their weapons programs. They influence decisions on weapons procurement while looking forward to cushy post-retirement jobs with the defense contractors who make those weapons.

In turn, the contractors infiltrate their own executives into powerful and influential government positions within the civilian administration of the Pentagon. They gain further advantage by having their people on important advisory boards or in defense-oriented think tanks. Using government money, and sometimes uniformed officers, they lobby Congress shamelessly, abetted by powerful committee chairmen who view weapons contracts as juicy official plunder for their home states and districts.

The contractors and their wasteful, incestuous methods flourish under a system that allows contracts to be awarded without competitive bidding on a cost-plus-profit basis that encourages companies to make the cost as great as possible. This system produces such absurdities as the Air Force mindlessly paying $9,600 for 17-cent Allen wrenches.

American defense suffers from the benign and all too often malicious neglect of a civilian populace that tries as hard as possible to ignore it and the dangers its existence represents. Though the United States still faces the "hostile ideology" of Eisenhower's warning, ostensibly vital missile projects can be halted by the lawsuits of Western developers, not for reasons of policy or principle but because the projects would consume too much water. We have become a nation in which college students can find moral principle in opposing a requirement that they comply with the draft-registration law as a condition of receiving federal student loans. We are a nation in which a president and Congress can initiate the greatest rearmament program since World War II, not only without asking the American public to pay for it, but while actually cutting federal income taxes by 25 percent to make the burden completely painless—until the national debt begins to mushroom uncontrollably.

The American armed services are not merely subservient to civilian authority, as is proper; they have civilian bureaucrats operating at command levels throughout the system. A Congress often at quarrelsome odds with itself as well as with the executive branch has power over every aspect and function of the military—down to whether an American advisor can carry a weapon in Central America or whether a midshipman can keep cowboy boots at Annapolis. The Joint Chiefs of Staff have a restricted, ineffective function and preside over a weak approximation of a general staff woefully inferior to that of other militaries, most notably the Russians'. With their internecine rivalries, the individual services are often as hostile to one another as they are to any enemy, willing to sabotage and steal from each other no matter what the ultimate cost to national security.

None of this is to say that American defense is run by fools and traitors. For the most part, the people in the U.S. military are as well intentioned as Americans could hope. The men and women serving throughout the far-flung American defense empire, in and out of uniform, do their duty as they see it with the best interests of American security at heart. To the extent that the American defense establishment has become monstrous—dangerously expensive, and out of control— it has been the result of its attempt to meet Eisenhower's dictates, to cope with the greatest military menace this nation has ever known without endangering its institutions or disturbing its way of life, and to put and keep the country on a war footing through a prolonged period of so-called peace. But it is failing to meet that challenge.

The question logically obtains: how could a nation so poorly defended so long survive? Shouldn't the American military be considered a success? Middle Eastern oil still flows. Western Europe is still free. The United States and its institutions survive. We of the planet Earth, as of this writing, still live. No matter how much any general, admiral, or service secretary may argue the contrary, this success is *not* due to American military genius, industrial resilience, capacity for suffering and sacrifice, or technological expertise—save in one area.

As it has been since 1945, the United States remains the most powerful nuclear power on this planet, possessing a nuclear arsenal ranging from Army artillery shells to mammoth ICBMs capable of erasing entire cities. It is here that the competition with the Soviets is the keenest. In President Reagan's first term, spending on strategic weapons rose more than 80 percent, while the increase for conventional forces was less than 30 percent. It is this that stays the hand of those who would wage a major war against the United States. It is this that makes it possible for the heirs of the Founding Fathers to reconcile the contradictory demands of war and peace.

Yet as the United States pursues this excellence in nuclear war fighting, as it expands its technological capability in this area and perforce becomes more militarily dependent upon it—as it allows itself to indulge in the fruits of peacetime by placing its military burden increasingly on nuclear weapons—it runs the risk of a terrifying irony.

Excellence in and increasing dependence on nuclear war fighting inexorably make its use more likely. The massively destructive intermediate-range nuclear missiles deployed by both the Soviets and the Americans in Europe were put there for tactical purposes, not merely political ones—not simply for deterrence. Because of the vast array of tactical nuclear weapons now available to field commanders on both sides, because of the cruise missiles now being deployed on the surface and the submarine fleets on all the seas, the distinction between strategic and tactical nuclear weapons has been completely blurred. It has led some military officers to refer to even the 1,200-mile-range Pershing II nuclear missile in Western Europe as a "conventional weapon," because it would be used against Soviet tank formations in Eastern Europe. With the rationales for the use of nuclear weapons now including the protection of infantry, the nuclear threshold has never been lower. American troops in Europe now carry nuclear "demolition" weapons in backpacks.

War is often inescapably necessary. The alternative to war is seldom peace. As the history of this century attests, the alternative to war is most often an international version of robbery, subjugation, rape, and murder.

But if nuclear war becomes the only form of war we are capable of successfully waging and it continues to be our only effective means of keeping the peace, then the peace the United States is enjoying is in reality a condition hurrying it to war. The worst kind of war.

Generous reference is made in this book to Sun Tzu, author of *The Art of War,* the fifth-century B.C. Chinese military genius whose strategies and tactics would be used so devastatingly in Asia against the West twenty-five centuries later, and Karl von Clausewitz, author of *On War,* the Napoleonic-era Prussian general and reformer given much of the credit for the creation of the general staff and the modern army.

The two are often quoted in military works, for good reason—and for bad. Sun Tzu is often read by Western military thinkers (though not enough during the Vietnam War) as the prophet of The Enemy. Mao Tse-tung drew much of his military thinking from Sun Tzu, as is evident in such works of Mao's as *On Guerrilla Warfare.* The North

Vietnamese general Vo Nguyen Giap, mastermind of both the French and American defeats in Vietnam, read both Sun Tzu and Mao. Clausewitz helped transform the Prussian army from an instrument of soldier-kings like Frederick the Great to a powerful and enduring national institution. As he helped create the modern army, he laid down the formulas for the modern war it would fight.

Both are celebrated in American military circles for their ruthlessness. Sun Tzu had the three favorite concubines of his king decapitated to demonstrate a point of drill. In combat, he employed every "dishonorable" means of warfare imaginable.

Clausewitz, who commanded Russian troops against Napoleon after his native Prussia fell to the French, described war as an extension of politics. His "brutal force" maxims are often cited by American military thinkers who advocate swift, massive, "thinkable," and, if necessary, surprise use of nuclear weapons. He has been taken to heart by Kremlin marshals for similar reasons, though his theories were disdained in the days of Lenin and Stalin.

But Sun Tzu and Clausewitz were so effective because they were principally realists. Their works have survived so well because they formalized plain common sense. They argued that the primary goal of war is to disarm an enemy, not destroy him. Sun Tzu believed in confusing, subverting, isolating, and demoralizing his enemy before resorting to combat. If the enemy could not be overcome by these means, only then should there be recourse to armed force.

Sun Tzu's tactics were diabolical, but they emphasized that battle should be waged for "the shortest possible time; at the least possible cost in lives and effort; with infliction on the enemy of the fewest possible casualties."

Clausewitz saw the need to wage wars for the people's purposes, not merely the king's, and the need for armies to be national armies—not bribed mercenaries such as are attracted to all-volunteer forces. Clausewitz said, "War does not consist of a single instantaneous blow. . . . the result in war is never absolute . . . war is not pastime; no mere passion for venturing and winning, no work of a free enthusiasm; it is a serious means for a serious object."

Both Sun Tzu and Clausewitz would have been appalled at such timid and inept projections of American military power as those attempted by Presidents Carter and Reagan in the Mideast. Sun Tzu would have applauded the genius of Syria's strategy and tactics in the 1983 Lebanon fighting. And in Europe, a strategy that depended on the massive use of tactical nuclear weapons would have been incomprehensible to Clausewitz. Such mass destruction would be inimical to his concept of the purpose of war. It would not be the extension of politics, but the utter abandonment of them.

This book contains a number of recommendations for change, some the ideas of more recognized authorities, some those of the authors. Obviously, the complexity of the vast American military and the problems it faces in this changing and dangerous world do not invite simple solutions. The authors have no intention of suggesting sweeping remedies that would lead to an American approximation of the military and social system that opposes it or of the system that produced one of the most effective armies in the history of warfare—the Wehrmacht of World War II. Nor would we wish upon the American military any of the oft-proposed utopian reforms and restraints that would render it even more impotent.

We realize that much of what we recommend is more theoretically than politically possible. But reform *is* possible, and we feel it is urgently needed. It is a conceit of the authors that Sun Tzu and Clausewitz might well approve and agree, for so much of what is needed is grounded simply in common sense.

It is a reflex of the American defense establishment to dismiss its critics as uninformed, biased, and, frequently, leftist, as in the term *peace creep*. The authors are not peace creeps. James Coates was a Pentagon correspondent for the *Chicago Tribune* from 1974 to 1984. He was a lecturer at the United States Military Academy at West Point for Senior Conference XX, an annual meeting of top Army experts, in 1982. President Reagan presented him with the Raymond Clapper Award for journalistic excellence at the 1982 White House Correspondents Dinner for his contribution to a series on military procurement. He also won this award in 1980 and the Edward Scott Beck Award that year for reporting on problems with the manufacture and testing of nuclear weapons.

Michael D. Kilian is a member of the *Chicago Tribune* editorial board, specializing in military affairs, and is a *Tribune* Washington columnist. He served as a draftee with the Eighth Army in Korea and with the Eighty-second Airborne Division at Fort Bragg, North Carolina. He is a captain in the U.S. Air Force Civil Air Patrol, and a member of the Air Force Association. His reporting has included coverage of the war in Northern Ireland, the 1975–1976 Anglo-Icelandic "cod war," NATO, and the Soviet Union. He has taken part in conferences on national security whose participants have included former

Secretary of State Dean Rusk, General Edward Rowny, Admiral Bobby Ray Inman, and Assistant Secretary of Defense Richard Perle.

The motivation for this book is in large part one of moment. The neglect of the military by the Carter administration and the excesses in the other direction of the Reagan administration have served to focus public and political question on the military preparedness issue as never before. The remaining years of this century will be marked by a vigorous national debate on American defense—in terms of both policy and arms procurement. This book is intended as a contribution to that debate.

It is a matter of moment in another sense. The ruinous policies and practices that have put the United States in this serious predicament cannot long continue. The nation is moving too close to war and too far from strength.

Too often, public comment on American defense has had all the impact of tossing a rose petal into the Grand Canyon and waiting for the echo. But it is the authors' feeling that two more voices cannot hurt. Certainly nothing at this critical juncture justifies silence.

chapter one

DEATH
IN A BRIEFCASE

> *Weapons change but man who uses them changes
> not at all. To win battles you do not beat weapons;
> you beat the soul of man of the enemy man.*
> —LETTER FROM GENERAL GEORGE S. PATTON
> TO HIS SON

Any discussion of American defense must first take cognizance of the fact that it is a human thing, comprising not only ICBMs and supersonic bombers and aircraft carriers but more than 2.1 million American men and women. It has a human face, and not simply that of the scowling, cigar-chomping, medal-laden four-star fiends of the editorial cartoons or the goldbricking Beetle Bailey of the comic strips. Most usually, it is the face of someone next door, someone like Air Force Colonel Christopher I. Branch.

During Colonel Branch's most recent tour of duty at the Pentagon, he went to work with a briefcase like nearly all his neighbors in the northern Virginia suburbs. He kissed his wife good-bye and hugged his two children on his return. But unlike his neighbors, when he went to work every day, he went to war. And the war he went to was World War III.

With the responsibilities of today's officers ranging from the care of the feet of recruits in basic training to satellite monitoring of the Ural Mountain missile ranges, it is difficult to point to any one of them as typical of the entire military. Branch can at least be called typical of the high-tech Pentagon breed—the kind of officers who have the most to do with running the military establishment and who have the best hope of becoming generals.

Now on field assignment, an important command at a huge Minuteman missile base in the West, Branch served two tours at the Pentagon and looks forward to returning for another. His title during his last Pentagon tour was chief of the Force Analyses Division of Air Force Studies and Analysis. His job and that of his expert team was not merely to think about a nuclear conflict with the Soviet Union, but, with the aid of computers and other electronic war-waging tools, actually fight one, day in and day out, in every way imaginable.

If the Joint Chiefs of Staff wanted to know what the resulting effect of removing two hundred B-52s from service or deploying three additional Trident submarines in the Indian Ocean would be on a nuclear conflict, Branch's team and its computers could tell them.

Though Branch's unit worked principally for the Air Force high command, it provided information to others with the proper clearances and need to know. These could include the president and his national security advisor, arms control negotiators, and even United States senators planning amendments to treaties.

It functioned less like a combat unit responding instantly to commands than, say, an advertising agency or management-consultant firm working through methods of its own device to solve its clients' problems. It snapped to when told "I want this yesterday" and, with a sharp salute, delivered. But it roamed the myriad possibilities of nuclear war fighting quite freely, offering to the brass/clients data, information, and conclusions they might not otherwise have considered. It had a very important job.

The team not only had top security but was one of the very, very few in the entire military service with any real working knowledge of what nuclear war might be like. One curious aspect of the team's work was that it never declared a winner in any of the war games it fought with such regularity. "There was no one useful measure of winning or losing," Branch said. "We just gave them [the decision makers] the whole menu of what would have been destroyed, what would be left, and what weapons were left. We never gave the answer."

Editorial-page cartoonists would not be happy with Branch as a symbol of the Pentagon. A boyish, athletic sort of man in his middle forties, he has missile models serving as andirons in his fireplace but, while serving at the Pentagon, often came to the door of his suburban home clutching, if not a stuffed animal, at least his small son, Christopher.

In civvies, Branch looked much like any other Washington commuter, and in fact more resembled a stockbroker or account executive than he did the public's conception of a nuclear thinker. But instead of carrying *Business Week* or *Advertising Age,* he'd be more likely to have some research paper or scientific journal on the blast effects of atmospheric nuclear explosions. The briefcase he set down on the sidewalk when he greeted his daughter, Morgan, upon coming home from the office often contained, if only in statistical form, millions of deaths.

An exceptionally bright superachiever, Branch was born in Honolulu, Hawaii, in 1939, just a few weeks before World War II broke out in Europe. His father, then Lieutenant Irving "Twig" Branch, was a fighter pilot stationed at Hickam Field. Lieutenant Branch's family left Hawaii in time to miss the Japanese attack on Pearl Harbor, but he remained, flying everything from P-40s to B-17s against the Japanese in locales extending from the mid-Pacific to the Burma-China theater with the famous Fourteenth Air Force and Flying Tiger leader Claire Chennault. Much decorated, Twig Branch became one of the most acclaimed and skilled pilots in the service, rising ultimately to the rank of major general and the job of commander of the Edwards Air Force Base Flight Test Center—the base that figured so prominently in the X-1 and X-15 rocket aircraft program and in the best-selling book *The Right Stuff*. General Branch was killed while flying a T-38 jet trainer from Edwards to Washington State in 1966. The airplane crashed in Puget Sound in bad weather. He was fifty-two years old and one of the best-known men in the Air Force.

His son Christopher was fortunate (for a military dependent) to be able to remain in the same Virginia suburb of Washington for all four of his high school years. Before that, his family had traveled as most military families do, living variously in New York, Florida, Maryland, Colorado, New Mexico, and Germany, the latter posting allowing him to go to summer camp in Switzerland. "It was a neat childhood," he says.

It did not incline him toward a career in the service, however. Upon graduating as class president from Fairfax High School, he entered Stanford University in 1957 as an engineering major with plans for a civilian career. But the draft was a fixture of American life in that era. With military service a certainty upon his graduation from Stanford in 1961, he elected to do his time as an officer and applied for Air Force Officers Training School.

He was only seventh in his class when he learned that the speaker at the graduation ceremonies would be his own father. He began cramming with the ferocity sufficient to elevate him to first in the class by the Big Day. Twig Branch was the one to pin on his second lieutenant's bars. (Christopher returned the favor when his father won his second general's star two years later.)

Young Branch's first duty assignment was as deputy commander of a missile combat crew in Texas, but a large part of his first hitch was taken up earning his master's degree at Stanford in an Air Force studies program. By then, he was as committed to the Air Force as any Academy man. Returning to the field, he served as a maintenance officer on Minuteman I missiles in North Dakota. His principal task was aiming missiles. Now performed electronically, the delicate task was then done with manual controls.

From there, Branch was transferred to Strategic Air Command (SAC) headquarters at Offut Air Force Base in Nebraska, where he was part of the team that perfected the reliability of the Minuteman II and Minuteman III warheads. There he met and married Stephanie Barrett, a curator at a local art museum and the daughter of Navy Captain Ernest Barrett, a nuclear-missile submarine commander who was at Offut as the senior naval representative on the Joint Strategic Target Planning Staff.

A major by 1970, Branch was then sent to Armed Forces Staff College for a year. His academic portfolio also includes studies at Squadron Officers School, the Air War College, the Industrial College of the Armed Services, the elite National War College, and the National Defense University, where he was a senior research fellow. In the modern military, officers spend considerable time at school.

From 1971 to 1975, he put in his first tour at the Pentagon, working for the deputy chief of staff for research and development on the MX missile project. Branch specialized in feasibility studies of launching the missile from airplanes, a scheme later rejected by Congress though highly favored by the Reagan White House. He worked on other projects as well and was part of the group responsible for doing away with the requirement that both officers on duty at each missile-launch console stay awake throughout their twenty-four-hour shifts. Grogginess is not a virtue in missile-firing situations.

"You look misty-eyed back on those days, when you were an action officer at the Pentagon," he said. "We were manipulators; we used to go around and manipulate millions of dollars in missile money. If you knew where the power centers were, who controlled this and who controlled that, it was really fun. We got things done. We were left relatively alone. Missiles were an arcane field in those days. We were in a world of our own. We got a lot of programs and modifications put into effect that have served the Air Force for years."

One of Branch's associates, then Lieutenant Colonel Joseph Mc-Glinchey, got one assignment because he was the only one in the group at that moment with nothing much to do. The project he was given ultimately resulted in the concept of "fratricide," the strategic-theory-turned-MX-deployment-plan based on the premise that a barrage of enemy nuclear missiles fired at an American missile base will defeat their own purpose by destroying each other instead of the American missiles underground.

Branch said McGlinchey had a leg up on this project. He was one of only three men in the section, including Branch, who had actual operational missile experience. "The rest were R and D guys. They knew money and programs, but they didn't have the missile experience."

As Senator Barry Goldwater has complained for a decade or more, actual "missile experience" is nearly impossible to come by. Because of treaties and engineering problems, the United States has never fired a live missile from any of its more than one thousand silos. In the mid-1960s, the Air Force stopped all engine tests at the silos for fear a bad launch could explode a test missile in a populated area. Still, Branch's years in North Dakota prepared him far better than most to deal with missile issues—particularly the chilling theoretical work performed by the analyses division, which usually starts with the premise that the missiles will work when the launch keys are turned.

While he was assigned to the Pentagon, the Branches bought their first real home, a town house in the Virginia suburb of McLean. Their neighbors included Stuart Knight, director of the Secret Service; Senator Paul Laxalt; several congressmen; and a great many colonels, generals, admirals, and foreign service officers. They had their first child while there, Morgan, in 1974, and were extremely happy with their lives. But advancement does not hurry to those who sit and wait for it.

Deciding he needed to get out into the field again, Branch wrote to SAC and asked for additional missile duty. He ended up with a much respected general for a sponsor and an assignment as a missile-squadron commander at a missile base at Minot, North Dakota—not one of the most popular installations in the Air Force.

They were not extremely happy with their lives during that tour at Minot. As many may not know, or want to know, missiles are always "on"—their electrical systems kept humming so they can be launched at an instant's notice. Maintenance officers are responsible for keeping them "running" and finely tuned. The slightest fault could mean the difference between taking out the oil fields at Baku or wasting a missile on a useless explosion. The job is essentially a twenty-four-hour-a-day one.

"It was very, very tough on family life," Branch said. "There was tremendous pressure on all of us. I'd come home, Stevie would make me a nice dinner, she'd put Morgan to bed, and stay out of my way."

In 1978, after a brief stint as a staff officer with the Fifty-seventh Air Division at Minot, Branch was transferred back to the Pentagon and given a job in the analysis division that fought World War III with computers. He shortly thereafter became a full colonel and head of that division.

As a Pentagon officer, his day usually began at 5:45 a.m. He made his own breakfast and left the house in time to be at his office by 7:00 or 7:15 a.m. Washington traffic on the major arteries leading to the Pentagon is surprisingly heavy at this hour. As a division chief, he was allowed to park his small Audi in a "nearby" location—three quarters of a mile away and just the other side of a major interstate highway from the nearest Pentagon entrance. To get a better place among the 9,849 spaces available, he would have to be promoted again or join a car pool.

"All the really good parking spaces go to senior department secretaries, generals, and janitors," he said. Probably the best, just down the steps from the Pentagon's front door, belong to the press.

Branch's office was in one of the Pentagon's better locations. The building consists of five concentric rings—A through E—with a five-acre park in the center. The secretary of defense, the department secretaries, the Joint Chiefs of Staff, and other top brass have their offices in the E ring, the outer ring with expansive views of the Potomac River and downtown Washington. The building has 7,748 windows, but those in the inner ring are appreciated only for the light, for the views out of most of them are about as sweeping as those from one of the cells in Moscow's Lubyanka Prison. (Actually, when construction started on the Pentagon in August 1941, plans called for the structure to have no windows. Franklin Roosevelt, harshly criticized for constructing a major federal office building outside the District of Columbia, disingenuously promised to convert it into a records warehouse "after the emergency.")

Working at the Pentagon "Death Factory," as many Washingtonians call it, takes a psychic toll on some, especially civilian Defense Department workers. Military personnel are transferred in and out, but civilians serve long terms. In 1983, one of them set fire to the defense secretary's stained-glass "meditation room" originally installed by Melvin Laird, and another, leaving a note saying he could no longer cope, killed his wife, three children, and himself. He reportedly had money problems, and the Washington area is one of the most expensive duty stations in the military, for civilians and uniformed personnel alike.

Pay is a sore issue for some in Branch's situation. Though the base pay of a colonel with twenty years' service is better than $40,000 a year, plus allowances, he can double his income or better simply by retiring and taking a job in the private sector—most often a company associated with the Pentagon. Branch's father-in-law, Captain Barrett, actually drew more on pension than Branch, of equal rank, did as a serving officer. Barrett's wife, a former Metropolitan Opera singer who abandoned her career to become a Navy wife, augmented that generous pension with her income from the boutique she ran in their retirement home in Annapolis. Automatic cost-of-living adjustments in military pensions have for years outstripped active-duty pay raises. Financial problems are nearly always present for Pentagon officers who, on the income of a good plumber, must move in a world of high-priced lawyers, lobbyists, diplomats, and corporate executives. A young major assigned to Pentagon duty for the first time can get murdered just trying to find a decent place to live.

Branch's office was in the D ring of the Pentagon, just off one of the main corridors. The Pentagon is not a terribly secure place. Guided tours for the public are conducted throughout the day, a privilege not allowed in the Kremlin. Probably 90 percent of the offices are not secured—or "vaulted," in Pentagon terminology—and passers-by have ample opportunity to wander by and riffle through papers, though these would most likely have to do with personnel transfers or purchases of truck parts. The biggest security hazard for many Pentagon workers is being caught sitting around doing nothing.

But this was definitely not the case in Branch's section. After signing in at a checkpoint protected by a guard and closed-circuit television in the morning, Branch would have to undo two alarm systems, six switches, and two combination locks before he could open up shop. Once inside, he had to dead-bolt the door.

Branch's office was on the first floor, another advantage in the five-story Pentagon. Though there are 19 escalators and 13 elevators, located generally in unhandy places, most of the floor-to-floor coming and going is by ramp or one of the 150 stairways.

For Branch, there was a lot of coming and going. As with any executive, even an executive whose section daily obliterates entire oil fields, a major part of his workaday life was taken up by meetings—meetings with his own staff, with Air Force colleagues and other service counterparts, with intelligence officers, and with superiors up to Air Force chief of staff and above. He organized briefings and went out to other briefings. He attended study groups and defense councils. "Otherwise, my days were reasonably my own."

He was to a large degree a deskman. However grisly the details they contained, he viewed the analyses he and his staff developed as a product, and managed their production as might the manager of one of Detroit's automobile factories.

He coordinated the analysis needs of his superiors and designed the most suitable kinds of analysis to match—the station wagon for this market, the convertible for that. He constantly reviewed and refined the product, turning his researchers from one statistical direction to a more profitable course: "No, they're not interested in this; they'll like that." He dealt with an endless succession of charts and graphs, computer printouts and piles of reports. Assisted by two secretaries, he wrote or helped write reports and transmittal papers that went to the chief of staff and the service secretaries. He had to file progress reports on all his division's activities every two weeks.

He was a briefcase man, not a swagger stick man, but he was a commanding officer too. As with any officer in the field, he had to deal with the personal problems of his people—family illnesses, emergency leaves, whatever arose. He had to look out for them in the jungle fighting of the Pentagon. And he had to let them do their jobs as best they could, even if it meant their going off by themselves for days at a time.

Just as a ship captain almost never touches the helm or trains a gun with his own hands, Branch stayed off his section's computers. "I did that on purpose. Two thirds of my staff spent their days in front of video display terminals, but that was their job, not mine. I didn't interfere."

The computer printouts that came before him on any given day would look like mathematical gibberish to those uninitiated into the mysterious methodology of nuclear war fighting—mostly long columns of seemingly unrelated numbers. But when finally translated into ordinary English for the purposes of, say, a congressional report, the processed information might read something like this:

Case	Attack Cases	Population Posture	Percent of Fatalities	
			HIGH	LOW
3	Attack on U.S. ICBMs	In-place	1–3	8–10
	Attack on Soviet ICBMs	In-place	1	1–4
	Attack on U.S. CF	In-place	1–5	7–11
		Evac.	—	5–7
	Attack on Soviet CF	In-place	1	1–5
		Evac.	—	1–2

"I had a lot of stress on that job. The Air Force was worried about a lot of things, and we had to be absolutely right. What we did would direct the course of strategic programs. We had to be very careful with our emphasis. Not too much; not too little.

"I've always dealt with stress. It's not from fear of nuclear war. That doesn't weigh on you. I don't think about holocaust all the time. It's that I have an important job. But the stress, I found a way to deal with it."

He found it in the Pentagon gym. It would seem there would be sufficient exercise to be had just walking about in a building with 6.5 million square feet of floor space and 17.5 miles of corridors. But like a great many officers at the Pentagon, he was a compulsive user of its huge complex of athletic facilities. These include an enormous gymnasium; handball, paddleball, and badminton courts; swimming pool; and weight room. For an hour and a half every day, usually in place of lunch, he put his body through a punishing routine. He also ran five to six miles a day around the Washington area or in suburban McLean.

Though Branch exercised primarily to relieve stress, it's a valuable Pentagon habit for other reasons than health and fitness. A great many of the service secretaries and ranking brass are runners and users of the athletic facilities. The workouts also function as social gatherings and there is a highly developed old-boy network of gym users that has proved quite helpful for those seeking promotion, transfer, or shortcuts in achieving missions.

The gym is also one place where individuals not close together in grade can mingle. Otherwise, a stringent caste system operates. In the building's ubiquitous coffee shops, snack bars, and cafeterias, you will see captains and majors together, majors and lieutenant colonels, and lieutenant colonels and colonels, but you seldom see colonels fraternizing with captains. You almost never see generals fraternizing with anyone. One colonel, upon being promoted to general, tried hanging out with his old lieutenant colonel and major friends for about a week, and then got the word that this was a gross violation of coffee-shop protocol. Generals are to be found in generals' messes, not in snack bars, and not with junior officers. Some civilians get to eat there, too, though not all are welcome. (A. Ernest Fitzgerald, the abrasive Pentagon whistle-blower who won his job back despite the best efforts of the White House and the high command to squash him, was entitled to eat in generals' messes as a top-grade civilian—and did so regularly with great glee, just to observe all the discomfiture he caused.)

Pentagon duty can be hard on the egos of intermediate-level officers, especially Army ones. Out in the field, a colonel can find himself treated as a minor deity. In the Pentagon, colonels go around saying "sir" all the time.

A lot of face used to be saved by wearing street clothes instead of a uniform to work. Fearful that Washington was beginning to look like an armed camp, President Eisenhower instructed officers to wear uniforms only once a week. More than two decades later, upset that Washington did not look military enough, the Reagan administration ordered the uniforms back on again, startling a great many real civilians the first day the order went into effect. It was almost as if there had been a coup.

The predominance of higher rank in the Pentagon has been very obvious since then. On any stroll now through the building's maze of corridors, lieutenant colonels, majors, Navy commanders, and captains abound, while lower grades are rarely seen. Many of the people sent to the Pentagon are on their last tour of duty, assigned to Washington at the end of their careers and hopeful that the excellent connections they can make will mean comfortable jobs in civilian life.

Some veteran Pentagon observers complain that many colonels there do the work of captains—and sergeants that of privates—and contend that a primary function of the building is to provide jobs for personnel promoted beyond actual staffing needs.

It is certainly an easy place in which to become lost physically as well as administratively. With office door plates offering such inscrutable identifications as "OASD-(PA)" and a corridor numbering system that would confound CIA cryptologists (and sometimes does), it's not unusual to see people with twelve years in the building asking directions.

Display cases on a number of corridor walls contain want ads for available jobs—"Supervisor Sports Specialist, GS-9, Fort Stewart, Ga."—for those inspired by such accompanying mottos as "Be all you can be." And the Pentagon remains perhaps the best place in the country to get an honest deal on a used car. Hundreds are advertised on bulletin boards every day. The prices are reasonable and the cars generally come in the condition promised. After all, it's less than prudent to stick a superior officer, or someone who might become a superior officer, with a lemon.

While the high command has its secret mountain hideaways in Maryland and the Virginia Blue Ridge to flee to if it receives sufficient warning of an enemy missile launch, neither the Pentagon building nor the top secret war room deep inside it are "hardened" against nuclear attack. One of the more disconcerting (if otherwise pleasant) experiences to be had at the "Death Factory" is to stroll out into the magnolia-lined five-acre park in the middle and walk to the gazebo-like hamburger stand at the very center—home, incidentally, of the Pentaburger. This is ground zero for perhaps a dozen Russian missiles, the bull's-eye of what would likely be the first strike of a surprise Soviet attack.

In warm weather, military bands and popular music groups often entertain those who take their lunch out on the bull's-eye. During the Vietnam War, one tune heard quite frequently was "Where Have All the Flowers Gone?"

Colonel Branch usually left the Pentagon in time to get home to his McLean town house by 5:30 or 6:00 p.m., though special requests from top brass could keep him at his office until well into the early hours of the morning. He also received special assignments, such as investigating a Titan missile accident in Kansas and flying to Argentina and Brazil to confer with Latin American military officers. Often, having left the house at 6:00 a.m., he would return twelve hours later having flown by Air Force jet transport out to some far-flung SAC base for a meeting and back.

To make up for the hard times in North Dakota, he tried to spend as much time as possible with his family, which had grown to four members with the birth of his son, Christopher, in 1978. But for officers of Branch's rank, the military has a requisite and rigorous social life— a schedule of cocktail parties, receptions, banquets, and teas as full as any diplomat's, with a protocol to match.

Whatever the demands on his time, Branch made a point of taking his daughter, Morgan, out for a special activity of some kind every week, come what may. His son, who suffered from a digestive disorder during infancy, received a full measure of attention as well, as did a number of the neighborhood children. Among other things, it was part of dealing with the stress.

"I tried not to take the work home with me, to make some family time. In North Dakota, that can be impossible. You have to eat, sleep, and breathe the job. A malfunction in a missile test can keep you busy for days. In Washington, it was easier. You could put your work out of your mind."

As the crowded bars at northern Virginia officers clubs attest, there are traditional ways of dealing with the pressures that afflicted Branch. Most seek whatever works. Army Chief of Staff Edward C. Meyer told one of the authors over drinks at a West Point seminar shortly before his retirement that he went home after a hard day of war planning and budget fighting and assumed the role of an Air Force officer. Getting out his Atari machine, he'd play his favorite video game, Missile Command, and sometimes for an hour or more would joyfully shoot down enemy missiles before they could destroy his cities. It was very therapeutic for an Army man.

Fighting World War III every day, Branch appreciated a spot of R and R whenever possible. Generally, the only military diversion he indulged in was watching a rerun of *M*A*S*H* over one or two beers upon coming home. When he read, it was seldom war novels or military history but technical and engineering books and magazines or, occasionally, spy thrillers. Though he greatly enjoyed classical music, he was just as fond of fiddling with the stereo that played it. He installed the stereo in his Audi and attended to many of its more major mechanical problems by himself. He did the restoration work on his old Lotus Elan sports car. He installed the ceiling fans in his house, hand-built a new room in his basement, and spent endless hours sawing and grinding away in his workshop. When there was nothing else to do, he'd mow his own lawn and those of neighbors with a hand mower.

Though not a military pilot, he is a licensed general aviation one and active with the Experimental Aircraft Association. He has played tournament-class croquet, and, at the age of forty, took up sailing. Ever the superachiever, he labored hard at the skills required "to get my ticket," only to be amazed and aghast to learn that no license was required for sailing and that people were allowed to go out in boats without first having to score points on a test—without having to achieve.

When in 1981 Branch was selected as a student at the National War College at Fort McNair, just across the Potomac, it was a signal honor, as important as a combat tour in Vietnam was in the 1960s—in Air Force terms, more so. The college is something like the Harvard of the military, and the academic credential counts for much in a service ostensibly run by technological geniuses. It is also an arena where a superior performance is well noticed. And it is a place where contacts and friendships of the most influential sort are made, often to last for life. The college is attended not only by military officers but by high-ranking State Department officials and CIA intelligence officers as well. Alumni have formed old-boy networks every bit as strong as those maintained by classmates at the academies.

The year at the college would be a significant advantage to Branch in overcoming a major obstacle to his hopes of becoming a general like his father—his lack of a military pilot's background. A small number of nonflying missile men have become general officers, but more than 90 percent of Air Force officers wearing stars also wear wings. With more than twenty years' service, Branch could retire now on a comfortable pension while at the same time hiring out to private industry at a handsome salary. Engineering experts of his caliber and experience are hard to find. But he intends to pursue his goal of a general's star as long as there's a chance. "The funnel narrows," he said, "but if you can keep on track and stay in jobs where you can compete, it's still possible."

Few realize how narrow the funnel can get. Of the 581,000 men and women in the Air Force, by act of Congress only 343 can be generals.

From his present position, he's likely to return to the Pentagon as high-level brass in strategic-nuclear-policy planning and analysis, with offices not far from the generals' mess. "I would love to come back to the Pentagon," he said, much as Hemingway might have spoken about a return to Paris.

Branch was asked the obligatory questions for a man who has aimed nuclear missiles with his bare hands, who has worked long into the night making it ever more certain that multiple warheads will perform as catastrophically as intended, who has been a runner in the nuclear arms race virtually every day of his military life. How does he cope? How does he deal with such awesome destruction? How does he feel about all the death in his briefcase?

"I have different feelings," he said, "but mainly it's a feeling of obligation. Service people come equipped with a capacity for that, with a sense of patriotism. Their job is a calling. It's important to themselves, to their families, and to the nation. It's a tremendous responsibility, and somebody's got to do it. We realize out here in the boondocks that we're dealing with the machinery of deterrence, that which keeps the free world free.

"We're a bunch of firemen, and firemen are the last people who would want to start fires. But if we have a fire, we want to be able to deal with it with the best possible equipment, in the most effective way.

"If war starts, you know, we're the target. It's my family, my house, that's going to be hit.

"Most guys in the military think this way. The answer is, it's our responsibility."

chapter two

THE MEANEST
SONOFABITCH
IN THE VALLEY?

> *Yea, though I walk through the valley of the shadow of death, I will fear no evil, for I am the meanest sonofabitch in the valley.*
> —VIETNAM WAR RENDERING OF THE
> TWENTY-THIRD PSALM

The most appropriate measure of the strength—or weakness—of any military force is its ability to inflict death. Armed forces do not occupy territory, achieve objectives, restore governments, project power, or keep the peace. They kill, maim, and destroy. That is their function. What purpose might be made of that function is a matter for others, but that is what armies, air forces, and navies do. The sixteen-inch guns of the battleship *New Jersey* worked the same off the shores of Japanese-held Pacific islands as they did off Vietnam and later off Lebanon. If the rounds fired into the Lebanese hills accomplished nothing, it was not for want of trying. Killing and maiming is the ultimate business of every person in the military. Like it or not, think about it or not, every supply sergeant, file clerk, mess attendant, and uniformed Pentagon bureaucrat is as much in the butcher's game as the axmen and archers of Attila's hordes.

In these terms, the strength of the American military is absolute, beyond quantifying, if only in one regard. The United States has the power to kill every man, woman, and child on Earth, with the action required taking a relative instant. That is the ultimate that can be asked of any military and the United States's supplies the maximum.

It also has the ability to parcel out mass death in an almost infinite variety of ways. It can in a trice inflict upon the Soviet Union the same 20 million fatalities that country suffered in World War II. Or it can change plans and inflict 40 million casualties. It can create the same firestorms in Hamburg with a flick of the finger that British and American bombers took three days and nights to ignite. With the assistance of its extraordinarily capable computer technology, American defense can configure its strategic weaponry to destroy, say, every French-speaking city on the globe—and no other. Employing its strategic weapons in a "conventional" mode, it can transform all of Europe from the outskirts of Paris to the Russian frontier into a continuous battlefield.

The non-nuclear weapons in its arsenal—when they work—can also produce unprecedented devastation. The United States has aircraft equipped with a six-barrel cannon that can fire six thousand shells in a minute—enough to pulverize an entire city block in the time it takes to say "hippopotamus." It has weapons that, on paper at least, can turn the insides of tanks into microwave ovens and others that can render them into something like the interior of an ignited flashbulb. It has aerial bombs that shred victims and others that literally suck out their lungs. It has the capability of creating "death zones" stretching for hundreds of miles.

It has weapons that don't necessarily kill. One bomb contains 182 smaller bombs that can spew flesh-adhering burning chemical particles over an area as large as several football fields. It designed, though held back from production, a laser weapon capable of blinding enemy soldiers who might look toward American positions. Another variety of American bomb hurls clouds of needlelike plastic darts, inflicting awful internal injuries that no field surgeon can detect with an X ray.

Unfortunately, it also has weapons that inflict harm only upon their users because they do not work very well. It has become so committed to an all-volunteer force and so politically opposed to a draft that it has turned to high technology as a replacement for manpower. From the new main battle tank to television-guided antitank weapons to antiaircraft missiles to the latest Navy fighter-bomber, the consequence has been the same. The more complicated and costly the weapon, the less well it seems to perform in tough combat conditions. The Hummer, a clumsy, elongated vehicle the Army intended as a replacement for the hardy Jeep, developed so many problems it became known as the Bummer. It even had its funding frozen by the Senate, an action taken with the frequency of a cut in congressional pay. On a demonstration flight over northern Virginia to impress congressional committee chairmen, the B-1 bomber, an aircraft costing more than one hundred times what a B-17 bomber cost during World War II, had its doors fall off. Navy inspectors found so many flaws and questionable quality-control practices involved in the production of the Phoenix air-to-air missile that the Navy ordered all shipments sent back to the manufacturer and halted further purchase. Similar stories can be found in every corner of the American arsenal.

Any assessment of American military strength has to be made in consideration of a troubling reality. The United States has not won a war since V-J Day. The "death zones" and rapid-fire cannon in Vietnam failed to stop a primitive yet persistent enemy. America's aircraft-carrier battle groups proved as useless in ending the Iranian hostage crisis as the *New Jersey*'s sixteen-inch guns were in restraining the Moslem militants in Lebanon. Libya, Cambodia, North Korea, and other nations have felt no qualms about sinking their teeth into the American ankle.

There are jokes now about the American military. West German army officers reportedly now refer to their American counterparts derisively as "the Italians of the eighties."

Whatever its ultimate worth, the United States does not keep its military to itself. It constitutes an empire as global in scope as the threat it is posed against.

At its center is the Pentagon. It is more than a simple headquarters. The more than thirty thousand service secretaries, generals, admirals, civilian workers, and lesser ranks who labor there preside over the most extensive military organization in the history of mankind, its reach surpassing the wildest ambitions of the great conquerors of antiquity and modern tyrants alike.

Shipwrecked sailors in the Indian Ocean, farmers in Argentina, bikini-clad bathers in Bermuda, caravan drivers in Turkey, seal-hunting Eskimos in the Arctic, and Cuban soldiers on their own territory all encounter barbed-wire and chain-link fences that mean the presence of American defense. Deployed on every continent and on every ocean, it reaches from the bottom of the sea to far out into space. The American president who is in charge of all this often has enormous difficulty getting legislation through a congressional committee or making a bureaucracy budge, but from his desk in the Oval Office he can order military patrols about in Central America or observe auto traffic in Moscow's Dzerzhinsky Square (assuming, of course, that the orbiting spy satellites are working well and that cloud cover is absent over the Russian capital).

And always near, in the next room, in a car just behind the presidential limousine in motorcades, or in the Capitol cloakroom during State of the Union speeches, is the major source of presidential military power—the officer carrying the "football," a deadly black satchel containing the codes to order bomber pilots toward Soviet airspace and missile commanders to launch their ICBMs.

While the vast armies and navies of World War II exceeded the total manpower of today's American defense establishment, which is demonstrably undermanned in terms of the mission given it, no American institution past or present has approached its scope or potential capability.

Constitutional and political limitations have kept the American military subordinate to the three separate, coequal branches of government, but its sheer size and the awesome importance of its mission so dominate the attentions of the executive branch and Congress that it functions in many ways as a fourth branch of government.

It is without question the largest branch of government. Of the some 2 million civilian workers employed by the federal government, 1.1 million are on the Defense Department (DOD) payroll. More than 230,000 others are with the Veterans Administration and another 23,000 are with the National Aeronautics and Space Administration (NASA), both agencies having a military affiliation (NASA's civilian space shuttle is to be used to construct U.S. killer-satellite space stations). The Energy Department (20,000 employees), which makes and tests all nuclear explosives, and the Transportation Department (70,000 employees), which includes the Coast Guard, also have important military functions.

The entire State Department has only about 23,000 employees and the Department of Education only some 6,500.

The Defense Department's civilian payroll is not confined to file clerks and secretaries. DOD employs approximately 1,000 biologists, 3,000 mathematicians, 1,000 surveyors, 1,000 economists, 4,000 social scientists, 9,000 college teachers, 4,000 sales clerks, 4,000 printers, 10,000 dry cleaners, 7,000 painters, 9,000 sawyers, 28,000 transport workers, 11,000 food service workers, 4,000 janitors, 20,000 security guards, and 8,000 laborers.

When the more than 2,100,000 uniformed personnel are added to the total Defense Department workforce, the non-defense portion of the federal payroll seems puny indeed. There is an all-volunteer Army of about 785,000 men and women, organized into 17 divisions and some 40 separate brigades and regiments (the Warsaw Pact armies, of course, have 115 divisions in Europe alone). There are approximately 600,000 people in the U.S. Air Force, and about 570,000 in the Navy. The Marines number about 200,000. Reserves, mostly Army, come to 1,096,000. All told, U.S. uniformed and civilian Defense Department personnel make up about three quarters of the federal payroll. Still, when the Army sought added troops in 1984 to create three new "light divisions" for swift deployment to crisis areas, its request had to be cut to two divisions and the manpower for them was swiped from other units.

Defense consumes nearly 30 percent of the federal budget and the rate of increase is propelling it toward the nearly 50 percent share it enjoyed at the height of the Cold War, in the years following Korea (compared to 20 percent in 1925 and just 10 percent in 1935). That Korean War–era 50 percent was achieved before Social Security, medical assistance, and debt service became major factors in federal spending. Social Security and the federal government's nonmilitary retirement programs consume 25 percent of the budget. Social welfare, which was just 2 percent of the budget in 1955, now comes to 19 percent.

Defense budgets now exceeding $300 billion a year compare with just $27 billion in federal funds for transportation, $13.5 billion for education, $6.7 billion for justice, and $400 million for housing—the latter less than half the cost of a single missile cruiser. A single $50 million F-15 fighter costs twice what the Reagan administration budgeted annually for pollution control on the Great Lakes.

Defense is a major component of many state economies—in some cases *the* major component. In 1982, California received $32.3 billion in defense outlays, about 18 cents of every defense dollar spent in the United States. Virginia that year received $12.1 billion, or $2,274 per capita. Connecticut took in $6.3 billion, or $2,034 per capita. There are a few states like West Virginia, recipient of a paltry $200 million or $104 per capita in 1982, but no fewer than 36 states received $1 billion or more.

In addition to the 1,130,515 civilians on the DOD work staff, military spending supports another 2.4 million civilian jobs in defense industries. The MX missile program entailed major contracts with thirteen different companies. The B-1 bomber project involved four major corporations and hundreds of subcontractors.

But the civilian economy can suffer as well as prosper. According to one survey, capital intensive defense spending of $154 billion in 1981 generated 1.7 million industry jobs, but the same money would have created 3.2 million new civilian jobs if it had simply been left in the hands of the taxpayers to spend on more labor-intensive private industry. The result was a net loss to the economy of 1.5 million jobs. Still, economic stultification has a military use. Absent a national draft, the Pentagon's best friend in acquiring adequate and qualified personnel for the country's huge, high-tech military machine is a recruiter named Sergeant Recession.

Having piled alliance upon alliance since World War II, the United States's military commitment and presence remain global and continue to expand. More than half a million American military serve overseas at 3,000 installations, including 336 major bases in twenty-four countries—with some 324,000 in Europe and 252,000 in West Germany alone (though the number is considered by many commanders to be so small as to invite nuclear war).

In addition to the 3,000 overseas installations, American defense maintains a Rapid Deployment Force of some 200,000 troops, organized into between five and six divisions and based in the United States. In theory, though not yet in practice, they could be carried into action anywhere in the world in a few days on six hundred jumbo jet transports, although getting a fully equipped unit into combat is more likely to take a month and backup support is considered woefully insufficient.

The United States itself is well garrisoned. Whether it's a fort, camp, arsenal, supply depot, or recruiting center, there is a military installation of some kind in every state of the union—and congressmen enough to make sure they stay there. The Washington metropolitan area alone accounts for fourteen installations and 132,000 Defense Department personnel, of whom 56,000 are active-duty military and 30,000 work in the Pentagon.

According to the Treasury Department, which keeps inventory of all federal assets, the Defense Department owns 29.5 million acres within the United States—an area the size of all of New York State. The land was acquired over two centuries at a cost of $39.6 billion. As much of it is in principal cities and along major waterways and seacoasts, its value now is astronomical.

The Army owns its own island in New York harbor, gaining access to Manhattan by means of its own ferryboat line. The superstructure of a Navy Aegis missile cruiser sits somewhat startlingly in a New Jersey cornfield, implanted there to test its radar systems. The Grand Forks missile and bomber base in North Dakota occupies territory the size of New Jersey. Fort Bliss and the adjoining White Sands Missile Range sprawl for 130 miles across two states, Texas and New Mexico.

In addition to the three service academies, the Defense Department operates its own system of colleges and universities, including the National War College, the Air University, the Armed Forces Staff College, the Defense Systems Management School, and the Industrial College of the Armed Services. The latter teaches officers how to manage natural resources and run government agencies and industries in times of national emergency.

The Army's Corps of Engineers, responsible for keeping the nation's navigable waterways clear and for most of its flood and erosion control, has a reach that can put a dam anywhere in the country, as it often seems to be doing.

The Defense Department owns more than seventy industrial plants and factories in its own right, some of them dating back to World War II. The bulk of them are run by independent contractors. DOD's industrial holdings used to approach two hundred plants, but some one hundred were sold back to private industry in an economy program begun in 1961.

Defense also operates or contracts for a worldwide network of department stores (the ubiquitous PX), supermarkets (its commissaries), liquor stores, gasoline stations, restaurants, nightclubs, yacht harbors, toy stores, garden shops, golf courses, riding stables, movie theaters, gambling clubs, resort hotels, libraries, and laundries, nearly all on military bases. It has its own airlines, steamship lines, railroads, trucks, and bus service. Its civilian schools range from kindergarten to adult extension college classes; its medical services, from brain surgery and cardiology to dentists and veterinarians.

It has its own law firms and its own undertakers. A hangar-sized Defense Department mortuary at Dover Air Force Base in Delaware receives the corpses of all Americans, civilian or military, who die abroad and are shipped home. The mortuary is so large that it was only 30 percent occupied when it was used to embalm the 900 followers of Reverend Jim Jones who died in Guyana in the infamous 1978 mass suicide.

The military establishment has a major religious involvement through its chaplain coteries in all four service branches and at the theology departments of the service academies. It has its own army of press agents as well. Thomas Ross, head of Pentagon public affairs in the Carter administration, once estimated that he had seven thousand people working for him in the United States and throughout the world.

The large audio-video section at the Pentagon provides radio and television broadcasts to troops around the globe, via the armed forces networks in Europe, Korea, and elsewhere that rival some of the broadcasting empires in the United States. The audio-video division also provides military assistance to film producers who need an aircraft carrier or a flight of helicopters for their productions. From major epics like 20th Century-Fox's expensive *Tora! Tora! Tora!* to more modest films like *The Swarm,* in which killer bees destroy Kansas, the Pentagon motion-picture liaison office provides troopers and weaponry.

It is a publishing giant that was able to produce 300,000 copies of *Soviet Military Power,* Defense Secretary Caspar Weinberger's highly graphic polemic setting forth the Russian military threat to the United States, virtually overnight. Cost is seldom a question. As they like to say at the Pentagon, "war is not cost-effective."

Neither are interservice rivalries. In recent years, the Air Force has become the richest branch of service in terms of its share of the military procurement budget, but this is chiefly a function of the astronomical cost of the technology it employs. A single fighter wing of two dozen or so aircraft now costs more than $2 billion. The Navy, the "Senior Service," remains the most socially elite and best connected politically and its procurement wealth runs close to the Air Force's, with a single carrier battle group costing $18 billion. Five of the last six presidents, coincidentally, were Navy men.

The Army has suffered continuing neglect since the Vietnam War, with its authorized annual spending requests cut by Congress (as much as 12.5 percent) in every fiscal year but one since 1976. With a combat division costing $5 billion, this has held troop strength far below stated needs. (In the same period, Congress actually increased the Navy's and Air Force's spending requests about half the time.)

Despite the long-ago advent of the missile age, the pilot-dominated Air Force has more than 2,000 combat aircraft, including 241 of the aging B-52 strategic bombers—used mostly as airborne cruise-missile launching platforms now—and another 56 F-111 shorter-range bombers that also carry nuclear warheads. Though delivery dates remain highly speculative, and their ostensible low-level mission may be scrubbed for a less vulnerable and less useful high-altitude one, 100 supersonic B-1 bombers are due to go on line. The Navy has 967 combat aircraft, plus 160 combat helicopters, and the Marines more than 400.

The Navy, whose strength fell from more than 800 combat vessels under Eisenhower to a little more than 400 under Carter, is being built back to an ultimate goal of 600, including nearly 100 nuclear-powered, missile-firing submarines and 190 major combat ships. But the numbers are deceptive as a measure of strength. To keep the ship-building program within budget constraints, the Navy has sometimes had to mothball old vessels to achieve savings toward financing the construction of new ones. Its fiscal 1983 budget called for the retirement of 22 ships alone.

Much of the money has been going into a $7.4 billion new carrier program, adding two nuclear carriers, each carrying ninety high-tech combat planes, to the Navy's extant fleet of thirteen nuclear- and conventionally powered carriers. The two new ships are designed to strengthen the American presence in Middle Eastern waters and carry air power to the Soviets, though retired Admiral Hyman G. Rickover, among others, warned they—and all our other carriers—would survive no more than two days in an all-out war.

According to recent reports, the Army has some 12,000 tanks, including more than 2,000 of the old but reliable M-48s; some 20,000 armored fighting vehicles which serve as troop carriers; and more than 12,000 artillery pieces and tactical missiles, including the 203.2-mm self-propelled howitzer, which uses nuclear ammunition. With all fixed-wing combat aircraft having been put in the charge of the Air Force by act of Congress in 1948, the Army has constructed its own 8,600-aircraft tactical air force, consisting mostly of highly vulnerable helicopters.

A high priority of the Reagan administration was to modernize all this equipment, but the weapons modernization programs of all three major services have produced tragicomic failures. From missiles that attack their own launching sites to new radar missile cruisers so top-heavy that they list in turns to radar systems that are most effective as beacons for enemy missiles, the causes for worry are mitigated only by the knowledge that the Soviets are attempting to copy or otherwise produce many of the same weapons and systems.

The Army has been particularly plagued. Its new M-1 main battle tank, the Bradley Infantry Fighting Vehicle, and even its new combat boot were all initially found in one way or another not to work. The lightweight Viper antitank bazooka, which rose in price from $75 to an astounding $780 apiece during its production, proved so useless in test frontal attacks against Russian armor that the Army redefined the Viper's mission to snipe at enemy tanks' sides and rear after they've gone by. Much of the new equipment works well in tests, but many officers question how well it might perform in the mud, blood, heat, and terror of actual combat.

Most of the weapons work most of the time, however, and when they work well, they can be devastating.

The M-16 rifle, which fires bone-smashing tumbler bullets at the rate of 650 to 800 rounds a minute, is one of the more benign weapons in a conventional war arsenal brimming with terrifying incendiary devices, cluster bombs, napalm canisters, fragmentation grenades and shells that fill the air with thousands of particles, supersonic ground-to-ground missiles, automatic repeating cannons, suffocation grenades, "tank busting" rifles, flamethrowing mortars, mine-laying helicopters, and dozens of other demonic devices unknown in World War II.

RAW, the Rifleman's Assault Weapon designed by the Brunswick Corporation, fires a grenade about the size of one of the company's famous bowling balls that can blast through three feet of concrete, three-quarters inch of steel, and six inches of aluminum. According to its advertisements, it can destroy buildings, railroad trains, and other civilian targets. New improved mortars, replacing the feared flamethrower, can lob phosphorus shells at targets 750 meters away and spray that brutal chemical over an area 50 meters in diameter.

Modern-day mine-laying helicopters and trucks can cover every road in Western Europe with deadly explosives, at least if the Soviets are not shooting at them. A single Huey helicopter, however vulnerable to enemy riflemen, can scatter 160 land mines over an area if given the time. Each mine, when detonated, will spray a 50-meter circle with 700 steel balls.

If there were to be a strictly conventional war between NATO and Warsaw Pact forces in Europe, these high-tech wonder weapons would be expected to assure catastrophic casualties, exceeding even those of the ravenous meat grinder that was the western front in World War I.

A succession of provocative incidents and events have brought the two forces close to such combat a number of times in the last four decades. Flashpoints that could ignite a European conflict are visible in the future. What most prevents that from happening is what has prevented it from occurring in the past forty years—the fearful respect each side has for the enemy's nuclear arsenal. Whatever else might be said about nuclear weapons and the horror they represent, a million or more American military men and women would probably now be dead if they hadn't been invented.

At the end of 1984, U.S. strategic force consisted of 1,948 "nuclear delivery vehicles," including 1,023 intercontinental ballistic missiles (ICBMs); about 296 B-52 and F-111 strategic bombers; and some 40 Trident, Poseidon, and Polaris nuclear submarines carrying about 592 missile launchers. It also had deployed 112 intermediate-range missiles. All told, the United States now has the ability to launch more than 10,000 strategic nuclear warheads in a single sortie, ranging in destructive weight from 170 kilotons to 10 megatons.

In comparison, Soviet strategic nuclear forces included approximately 1,398 ICBMs at the close of 1984, 60 or more submarines carrying 981 launchers, and 290 long-range bombers. Its intermediate-range missile force numbered 602. With three of their newest intercontinental missiles carrying between four and ten warheads each, the Soviet Union now has the capability of firing 7,000 warheads in a single strike.

Descriptions of nuclear inventories, both American and Russian, are usually rendered inadequate if not incomprehensible for the general public by the jabberwocky nuclearspeak practiced by both sides. The Pentagon and the Kremlin talk and think in terms of SLBMs and GLCMs (submarine-launched ballistic missiles, ground-launched cruise missiles), MIRV and ABM (multiple, independently targetable reentry vehicle and anti-ballistic missile). Destructive power is measured in throw weights and fallout in rems, for roentgen equivalent man, a measure of gamma radiation absorbed by body tissue. If one insisted that discussions of nuclear war be carried on in terms of "fried Americans" or "radiated Russians," the terms would quickly become "FAs" and "RRs."

Fatalities from bullet wounds or shrapnel in conventional war are readily understood. Deaths in a nuclear attack come from blast, direct nuclear radiation, thermal radiation, and radioactive fallout. In an attack employing a single one-megaton warhead—a very minor attack by contemporary standards—the blast extending out to three miles from ground zero would be between 10 and 30 pounds per square inch of pressure (psi), generating winds of between 290 and 470 miles an hour. Pressure exceeding 12 pounds per square inch would suffice to topple and pulverize the twin towers of New York's World Trade Center and kill some 98 percent of the people within that radius.

At 4.4 miles from center (the distance from the Boston Common to the center of the city of Revere, Massachusetts), the blast would be 5 psi—enough to demolish almost any two-story house with a force of 180 tons slammed against its exposed wall—and winds would reach 160 miles an hour. Blast fatalities would be 50 percent. At six miles out— three quarters of the way from Chicago's Loop to the North Shore suburb of Evanston—winds would be 95 miles an hour, enough to kill anyone caught in the open.

Direct radiation from a nuclear explosion is intense but more limited in range. Fatality rates would vary according to degrees of exposure and physiological factors, but doses of 600 rem or higher would be probable in areas where inhabitants might survive the blast. Such a dose would cause the death of 90 percent of those exposed within a few weeks. A dose of 450 rem from a blast would create a fatal illness within weeks or months in 50 percent of those exposed. A person exposed to 50 rem would be likely to die of cancer.

The flash from a one-megaton nuclear blast would cause third-degree burns as far as five miles from ground zero, second-degree burns as far as six miles, and first-degree burns equivalent to serious sunburn out to seven miles. The flash blindness from the explosion would be temporary, but retinal burns would occur in victims as far away as thirteen miles in daylight and fifty-three miles on a clear night. Not counting the victims of fires set off by the blast, a one-megaton explosion would easily cause 10,000 burn casualties from flash alone. In the entire United States, there are facilities to treat only about 2,500 burn victims.

The amount of radioactive fallout increases the closer the nuclear explosion is to the ground surface, just as the effect of blast increases the higher the explosion is above ground. The radioactive particles would tend to be blown in a long plume extending hundreds of miles. With a one-megaton explosion detonated at ground surface in downtown Detroit and a 15-mile-an-hour northwest wind, a plume containing radioactive doses of fatal 900 rem would reach all the way across Lake Erie to Cleveland. A 300-rem plume would reach almost to Pittsburgh, and one of 90 rem—causing serious radiation sickness—would reach to the Maryland border.

If the Pentagon had been able to deploy the MX "Peacekeeper" missile in the Utah and Nevada "racetrack" configuration as originally planned—and the Soviets fired 4,600 missiles to strike each of the holes in which the 200 MXs might be deployed—the radioactive plume, given prevailing winds from the west, would stretch all the way across the United States, causing fatalities as far east as Kansas and radiation sickness as far away as Virginia.

A one-megaton nuclear weapon detonated in typical conditions on the Detroit Civic Center would create a 1,000-foot crater and cause 220,000 immediate deaths and 420,000 serious injuries. A one-megaton weapon exploded at 6,000 feet above the city would cause casualties of 470,000 dead and 630,000 wounded, though fallout would be negligible. An airburst of a 25-megaton weapon over Detroit would kill 1,840,000 people instantly and seriously injure 1,360,000 others, leaving 1,100,000 survivors in the metropolitan area to care for them somehow.

Both the United States and the Soviets have the capability of destroying five hundred of each other's cities in this manner several times over. Attacks designed to eliminate both countries' oil-refining capacity would require just ten nuclear warheads in both cases. In passing, much of New York, Philadelphia, Detroit, Chicago, Kansas City, New Orleans, Houston, Dallas, Los Angeles, San Francisco, Moscow, Kaliningrad, Kirishi, Polotsk, Gorki, Perm, Ishimbay, Angars, Grozny, and Baku would be destroyed in the process.

This is the truest reflection of the magnitude of the American defense establishment—and that of its superpower nemesis—in the next to last decade of this millennium.

Supporters of a nuclear freeze and advocates of unilateral disarmament often seize upon such overkill in support of their causes. The Pentagon argues that the Soviets and the United States no longer have any military interest in killing civilian populations. Both have drafted nuclear war plans in which the number of civilians killed in a nuclear exchange is considered a peripheral matter. The Mutual Assured Destruction (MAD) and massive retaliation strategies, which ultimately reached the point where each side possessed the power to kill the entire population of the other nine times over, ceased to be the primary focus of nuclear-war-fighting thinking a quarter century or more ago, when the American defense establishment began adoption of the "no cities" approach. The modern-day nuclear force is primarily targeted at opposing missile installations, other military facilities, and targets essential to the economic survival of the enemy—steel mills, refineries, central banks, electrical power generators and grids, and other strategic targets. In this strategic mind-set, whatever civilian casualties result from an attack on military or economic targets are considered incidental.

A major danger lies in the fact that neither side has been able to test or perfect its long-range nuclear missiles to any satisfactory degree and their pinpoint accuracy—as required with military targets—remains questionable. The unhappy possibility exists that either side might turn to indiscriminate nuclear bombing of population centers simply in frustration at being unable to inflict any other telling kind of damage. Also, there is a growing and unsettling Pentagon interest in launch on warning (LOW) and launch on provocation (LOP) or first-strike techniques that to some minds would lessen the amount of death and destruction the United States would have to suffer in the event of a nuclear confrontation. This would put this country in the business of firing what could prove to be the first nuclear shot, and possibly provoke the Soviets into a preventive nuclear strike.

In any event, the Defense Department is pressing on full blast with expansion of the American nuclear arsenal. In the 1980s, more than 17,000 new warheads were scheduled to be manufactured—11,500 of them to replace old or obsolete weapons and 5,500 more simply to fatten the stockpile. By the end of the decade, the number of nuclear devices at the Pentagon's disposal—counting missile payloads, bombs, and artillery projectiles—will exceed 31,000.

"The United States has got to be the meanest sonofabitch in the valley," said an Air Force colonel, a former bomber pilot now serving as high-ranking brass with the Strategic Air Command. "We have to keep everybody else wondering, worrying about what we might do."

He had been explaining why he had liked the zany antiwar film *Dr. Strangelove, or How I Learned to Stop Worrying and Love the Bomb,* and how he thought it served a useful defense purpose. "A little irrationality," he said, was good for the rest of the world to see.

"I think we *are* the meanest sonofabitch in the valley," he said. "You have to remember, we are the only nation on earth that has ever used the atomic bomb on our fellow human beings."

But 1945 was two generations ago. The number and power of nuclear weapons has increased geometrically since then, but so has the reluctance to use them. The United States is relying increasingly on a weapon it rightly dare not use except in the most extreme provocation—and probably not even then. Nations large and small have engaged the United States in war and lesser combat many, many times since Hiroshima with little fear of nuclear reprisal, with little fear even of America's conventional wonder weapons—especially if their spies have had a look at initial-performance test results.

The United States can no longer call itself the meanest sonofabitch in the valley. As Afghanistan and the Korean-jetliner downing attest, that title belongs to quite another sonofabitch, one West German officers do not joke about.

chapter three

THE RED MENACE

> *There can be no real peace in the world unless a*
> *new relationship is established between the United*
> *States and the Soviet Union.*
>
> —RICHARD M. NIXON,
> *REAL PEACE: A STRATEGY FOR THE WEST*

The engine that drives American military policy is Soviet military policy.

Were it not for the Soviet threat, had World War II ended with just one superpower, had the Nazis somehow destroyed the Russians before they were themselves somehow destroyed by the Western allies, the immense American defense empire of today would be unthinkable. American taxpayers would simply not tolerate it. The larger portion of the United States's eleven hundred generals and admirals and fourteen thousand colonels would be looking for work—with no mammoth defense industry to take them in.

To the American military, the Soviets are a dilemma. They pose an awesome threat, yet even that threat must be exaggerated to persuade the American people of its seriousness. To the extent that it is exaggerated, it becomes that much less credible.

The Soviets are not the "evil empire" of Ronald Reagan's hyperbole, to be blamed for every ill that plagues the world. But they have been to some degree responsible for or exploitive of every military conflict in which the United States has been entangled since World War II. Because they too possess the power to destroy every human being on Earth, they are also the force that in nearly every case has prevented the United States from carrying armed conflict to any useful conclusion. Simply because it exists, the Soviet threat both invites American military action and frustrates it.

Accurately assessing the capabilities and dangers posed by the Soviet military is the most important and most difficult task of any American president. Most aren't very good at it.

History has belatedly honored Eisenhower's genius for directly confronting Soviet ambitions while, by and large, keeping his powder dry. But he had the advantage of an overwhelming American nuclear superiority, which was lost forever in the next decade. As his inaugural address, missile-gap rhetoric, and sometimes terrifying lust for crisis attest, John Kennedy was obsessed with Soviet ambitions. Yet ultimately he was able to counter them successfully only with the reckless gamble of the Cuban missile crisis that for several days had both nations' fingers on the nuclear button, with no room whatsoever for the miscalculation all too common on both sides. Lyndon Johnson, as though trying to prove himself the mightier man, groped for the Russian bear in Vietnam and had his arm torn off, losing both his presidency and much of America's military will in the process.

Richard Nixon understood the Russians and America's predicament much better. Perceiving Vietnam in 1970 as both lost and irrelevant to the U.S.'s principal national security worries and needs, he set about disengaging as politically expeditiously as possible (LBJ had already begun lowering troop levels) and then dealt with the major strategic question by offering the Soviets détente while intimidating them with the United States's embrace of the People's Republic of China. The Ford administration pursued the same productive course.

Jimmy Carter, who had liked to make the boast that no American soldier had been killed in action on his watch (though three were killed in the 1979 Iranian revolution and eight others in the tragic failure of the 1980 Desert One raid), offered the Soviets what they took for indecision and meekness and was treated accordingly in Afghanistan, among several other places. Ronald Reagan struck the opposite pose, lashing out at the Russians with vicious, almost violent rhetoric, grievously miscalculating the Russian reaction. He wielded the "big stick" of American military power with such ineptitude and timidity in Lebanon that he ended up as humiliated as Carter, though that didn't seem to matter to the voters.

Some realities of the Soviet threat are fairly obvious. National Security Council wisdom and presidential rhetoric notwithstanding, the Soviet leadership is not motivated chiefly by ardor to enslave the world and place its teeming billions under the control of one Soviet government. The Kremlin's masters are anxious enough about being able to maintain absolute power in their own increasingly Asiatic country.

As xenophobic as the czars, they have the same military policy: to maintain absolute authority over the motherland, to dominate their neighbors, and to gradually extend their sovereign dominion. And to defeat their enemies.

Like Peter the Great, Catherine the Great, Alexander I, and Nicholas II before them, the Kremlin marshals and party oligarchs also want to be treated with the respect due a global power. They are a global power. In every sense of the term, they and the United States constitute the only global powers extant. This is a respect the United States has persistently refused to accord them. With its policy of containment, its encircling network of missile and bomber bases, surface and submarine fleets, and well-armed hostile armies, the United States has since World War II treated the Soviet Union as a wild beast.

This stern policy has not been without justification, but it has been dangerously provocative in its effect, especially since the United States is now so woefully incapable of enforcing it.

The Prussian military genius and reformer Karl von Clausewitz wrote, "I shall not begin by formulating a crude, journalistic definition of war, but go straight to the heart of the matter, to the duel. War is nothing but a duel on a larger scale. Countless duels go to make up war, but a picture of it as a whole can be formed by imagining a pair of wrestlers."

Though their armed forces have only rarely engaged in direct combat with one another, the United States and the Soviet Union have been locked in a deadly struggle for military advantage since the end of World War II. A better analogy than the duel or a wrestling match might be the brutal dance performed by lumberjacks to enliven payday evenings in north woods' saloons. Gripping each other's forearms, they circle round and round, right feet shod in heavy nailed boots, left feet bare and vulnerable to the crushing stomp. Until one succumbs, they cannot escape one another.

In January 1983, *U.S. News & World Report* commissioned assessments of the American-Soviet military rivalry from former Defense Secretaries James Schlesinger, Donald Rumsfeld, and Harold Brown, and from Senator John Tower, then chairman of the Senate Armed Services Committee.

Schlesinger called any claim that the United States had fallen to Number 2 a distortion of reality, but conceded the Soviets a lead in counterforce missile-strike capability, the ability to take out the other's missiles. Brown, employing a favorite phrase of the Carter administration, described the American military position as "adequate," but warned that a continuation of the trends of the previous fifteen years would ultimately put the United States at a dangerous disadvantage. Tower saw this disadvantage becoming a reality within two or three years.

Rumsfeld said the United States was deficient in conventional capabilities and theater nuclear forces, with the Soviets holding a significant advantage in the destructive power of individual missiles. While the situation did not appear immediately serious, he said, the greatest danger lay in the American public's failure to "recognize the long-term competition that exists with the Soviet Union and the urgent need to proceed with a well-balanced, well-directed defense program" that produces "deterrents across the spectrum."

He stressed that the United States must cease the wasteful and weakening practice of turning "the defense-funding faucet on and off." The cyclical ups and downs, starts and stops in American defense production and posture that occur with every change in Congress and administration must somehow be curtailed.

"A reality of our political system is that leaders are forced to emphasize problems in order to sustain support for programs that ought to be supported on their undramatic merits," he said. "And nuclear age perceptions of the military balance are important. We must tell the truth about the seriousness of our situation and get about the task of fixing it. But we need not frighten our allies and friends into thinking that the U.S. is through as a world power. It is not. And it must not be."

Ronald Reagan's defense secretary, Caspar Weinberger, came to the post with long experience in government but a military background amounting largely to advancing from private to infantry captain in World War II and ultimately serving as one of the sycophants on the staff of General Douglas MacArthur. Critics have charged that, like his president, he has been overly adoring of the military and has swallowed every scare story in the generals' and admirals' vast repertoire, becoming a zealous proselyte of their "blank check" defense-spending gospel and the nation's most credulous exponent of the "Red Menace."

His rationale was contained in the glossy Pentagon broadside *Soviet Military Power,* first published in the early days of the Reagan administration with a printing of 300,000 copies. The hundred-page book, aimed mostly at Congress, was filled with scary pictures of Russian missiles, submarines, tanks, artillery, computers, and combat aircraft. Among all the graphs comparing numbers of MIRVed ICBMs and the like was one showing that the Soviet Typhoon missile submarine was equal in size to the Washington Monument.

"The Soviet defense budget continues to grow to fund this force buildup," Weinberger wrote, "to fund the projection of Soviet power far from Soviet shores and to fund Soviet use of proxy forces to support revolutionary factions and conflict in an increasing threat to international stability."

The Russian response, *Whence the Threat to Peace,* its cover in some editions colored a somewhat radioactive-looking red, was as hyperbolic.

One Soviet illustration made the point that the United States had beaten the USSR to such weapons as the atomic bomb, strategic bomber, nuclear submarine, nuclear carrier, MIRVed warhead, and neutron bomb. It failed to mention how much Russia's subsequent excessive production of some of these weapons had threatened to upset the military balance or how it had itself beaten the United States to development of laser and other directed energy weapons and heavy throw-weight rockets and was rapidly gaining supremacy on the high seas.

In *Soviet Military Power,* Weinberger included a map showing that the huge Russian Nizhniy Tagil tank plant would take up a large part of downtown Washington and dwarf the U.S. tank plant at Lima, Ohio. In *Whence the Threat to Peace,* the Soviets countered with a map showing that the Detroit tank complex would take up even more of downtown Washington and dwarf the Nizhniy plant.

When Weinberger issued his next edition of *Power* in response to *Threat,* the map of Washington with the Nizhniy plant map superimposed over it was deleted. The Russians, at least, won the map race.

The assertions contained in both books are not only painfully self-serving ("We are not seeking military superiority over the West," etc.) but sometimes in error.

Perhaps the most objective and respected assessment of world military strengths is that made in *The Military Balance,* published every year by the International Institute for Strategic Studies (IISS) in London and used by the U.S. Air Force Association in making its annual military strength report to its members.

The Soviets claimed in *Whence the Threat to Peace* that the United States had 40 missile submarines. The IISS count was 32. Weinberger listed 36 Russian cruisers. The IISS listed 34. In the first edition of *Soviet Military Power,* Weinberger made much of the threat of the Soviet T-80 supertank, including a drawing of the monster in action, with a huge cannon extending from an octagonal turret encased in superhard Chobham-grade armor. In the second edition, Weinberger replaced this with a photograph showing a tank with a rounded turret plated with more conventional armor. Though it had been cited as the justification for the costly and problem-plagued M-1 tank, the T-80 was actually an updated version of the Soviets' old T-72 main battle tank. The real competition for the M-1 would be the mightier T-84, to which the M-1, without refitting, was inferior.

The greatest disparity in American and Soviet strength is in troops. The United States has a total military of 2,100,000 and an Army of 785,000 troops, compared to a Soviet military of 5,050,000 and an army of 1,800,000. Because of the Soviet Union's universal military service (approximately 1.4 million of those army troops are conscripts), with a two-year service commitment and call-up liability to fifty years of age,

Soviet reserve strength has been estimated as high as 25 million for all services, with 5 million having been on active duty within the last five years.

With its all-volunteer military, the United States has reserves of 660,000 in the Army, 87,900 in the Navy, 42,000 in the Marines, and 165,400 in the Air Force. The 38,700-strong Coast Guard and 65,000-member Civil Air Patrol are also counted as American paramilitary forces. The Soviet Union has 450,000 paramilitary personnel, of whom 190,000 are KGB border guards and 260,000 internal-security troops. Some 900,000 Soviet soldiers are used as construction and railway workers, largely because they are considered unreliable for more military duty.

In addition to the Soviet military, the six other Warsaw Pact nations—Poland, East Germany, Czechoslovakia, Hungary, Romania, and Bulgaria—have a combined troop strength of 1,169,000. All have conscription.

NATO troop strength, not including the United States, comes to 3,200,000. Of the sixteen NATO countries, Belgium, Denmark, France, West Germany, Greece, Italy, the Netherlands, Norway, Portugal, Spain, and Turkey have conscription. The United States, Britain, Canada, and Luxembourg have no draft. Tiny Iceland (pop. 230,000) has no military save a small coast guard. Its chief contribution to NATO is the important air base at Keflavík.

A strictly numerical comparison, however, is not useful. No ICBM or submarine-launched missile belonging to either side has ever been tested along its intended flight path. No one on either side can say with anything like certainty whether the missiles can reach their targets—especially after flying over the magnetic aberrations of the polar regions—let alone strike them with the pinpoint accuracy required to destroy an enemy missile in its silo. In its first series of tests, the United States's intermediate-range Pershing missile had a failure rate of five out of eighteen flights. Cruise missiles, which now have both strategic and tactical functions, were also initially plagued by troubles and, for all their ground-hugging capability, may shortly prove vulnerable to improved Soviet radar and antimissile defenses.

The United States is a maritime power whose sphere of interest embraces the entire Pacific and whose strategic naval concerns include the defense of Europe, the protection of Persian Gulf oil nations, the maintenance of naval supremacy in Caribbean and Latin American waters, and defense against Soviet missile-firing submarines and surface ships on all the world's oceans. In conventional terms, the American one-and-a-half-ocean Navy is stretched very thin.

Yet, in the age of Exocet and other devastating anti-ship missiles, adding more ships, especially large, costly ships, may only increase the United States's vulnerability, especially if the Aegis cruisers prove as dangerously flawed as some preliminary tests indicated.

In contrast, except for its strategic and antisubmarine naval elements, the Soviet Union's navy has much less of a defensive role to play and is freer to range the world's oceans making mischief and harassing the American Navy. Its huge army, however, is tied down in ways the United States's is not. In addition to United States and NATO forces, it confronts a People's Republic of China military exceeding 4.7 million. Much of the Chinese force is deployed along its Russian border and has been frequently involved in clashes with the Soviet army, which now keeps forty-seven divisions along the Sino-Russian frontier. Another thirty divisions are kept in the central and southern USSR, with duties that include maintaining domestic order. The ninety-nine Soviet divisions deployed in Eastern Europe also share that mission, as do a large proportion of Warsaw Pact troops.

Again, the quantitative difference is not always what counts. The Chinese and North Koreans outnumbered the United States in the Korean War. The United States outnumbered the North Vietnamese army in all but the last stages of American troop withdrawal. American generals who anguish over the size of the Soviet hordes—especially around budget-making time—are always quick to state that as commanders they would not want to trade places with the Kremlin marshals.

There is a fairly significant body of American thought—concentrated in, but not confined to, the political left—that clings to the belief that the Soviet military is rotting from within, that its threat has been deliberately exaggerated and its weaknesses ignored by an American defense establishment seeking to advance its own ends. Probably the most articulate spokesman for this view is New York writer and commentator Andrew Cockburn, author of a book widely celebrated outside American military circles called *The Threat: Inside the Soviet Military Machine*. The book depicts the Soviet military, most particularly the army, not so much as a paper tiger but as a drunken, ill-fed, ill-led, ill-disciplined, and incompetent one.

In painting his disparaging picture of Soviet military capabilities, Cockburn did make use of published reports and interviews with former intelligence officers and other sources, such as Ivan Selin, former head of the strategic division of the Defense Department's Office of Systems Analysis. Selin is famous for saying, "Welcome to the world of strategic analysis, where we program weapons that don't work against threats that don't exist."

Cockburn seized upon such embarrassing case studies as the Pentagon's terrified reaction to the Russian MIG-25 "Foxbat" fighter, which then–Defense Secretary James Schlesinger called so formidable that "we might have to reappraise our entire approach to the strategic technological balance." Congressional appropriations for the F-15 swiftly followed.

In 1976, Cockburn noted, a Russian pilot defected to Japan in a MIG-25, and it was quickly discovered that its combat radius was one third of what intelligence sources had stated. Its top speed was believed to be Mach 3.3, but the pilot said the plane was kept to Mach 2.5 because the turbines might melt at anything faster.

As though to maintain parity, when it was first developed, the F-15 didn't work very well either.

Cockburn's main argument, however, was based largely on interviews with Soviet Jewish refugees who had settled along the East Coast of the United States, most of them in the Brighton Beach section of Brooklyn. Because of universal conscription in the USSR, many of the men had served in the Soviet army and navy, some of them as junior officers. They described living conditions not much better than those in the gulag of Solzhenitsyn's *A Day in the Life of Ivan Denisovich*. According to the immigrants, Soviet troops generally are kept in isolated posts; crowded into crude barracks; fed a diet of potatoes, porridge, dried fish, and salt pork; and worked from dawn to dark.

They said the Soviet army lacked the cadre of well-trained, veteran noncommissioned officers that has been the backbone of the American and West German armies, and that enlisted ranks are largely divided into two groups: green newcomers and the old-timers who beat them up, steal their food, and otherwise prey upon them. The work and duties that would be performed by sergeants and petty officers in Western armies and navies are generally performed by officers in the Soviet military, especially when something important is on the line.

"This policy of playing safe by reserving any important task for officers can be carried to extreme lengths," Cockburn wrote.

> To celebrate the coronation of Queen Elizabeth in 1953, the British arranged a naval parade of warships from many nations. The Soviets dispatched the cruiser *Sverdlovsk*. Western observers were most impressed by the skill and smartness of the crew; what they did not know was that every single one of the 900 men on board was an officer.

Soviet troops from the USSR's Asiatic provinces and the Ukraine, among others, are considered unreliable and hostile to Russians, a complaint Kremlin planners also have about many satellite nation forces. In response to their wretched conditions, harsh discipline, brutal treatment from fellow soldiers, lonely postings, and miserable pay ($6.50 a month), most Soviet soldiers drink whenever possible, Cockburn found. Without the pay to afford decent liquor, they turn to vile home brews and dangerous chemical extracts. More commonly, they sell military parts, gasoline, or personal equipment to buy alcohol. In an emergency alert, his refugee veterans said, officers could find military vehicles immobilized by a lack of wheels and their crews immobilized by drink.

The Threat went on to describe the Soviet officers corps as ridden with ideologues and office politicians, as well as craven bureaucrats whose first duty is to their own behinds. In sum, American fears of the Red Menace were less than fully justified and the Pentagon was being excessively overwrought.

While no one could effectively fault Cockburn's assertions, his book's chief impact was to reinforce the prejudices of liberal intellectuals.

The nucleus of his book was the basis for a Peabody Award–winning television documentary, "The Red Army" (actually, the name was officially changed from the Red Army to the Soviet Army immediately after World War II), but the warmest reception given it in Congress was from liberal Democrats, and it was largely ignored by the Pentagon high command, although many of its points were appreciated by reformers.

It was far easier to accept Cockburn's facts than the book's overall implication. As he himself acknowledged, the Russian army has always *looked* bad. Its comparative quality has not changed markedly in the last two hundred years—or for that matter, since Prince Alexander Nevsky of Novgorod defeated the Teutonic Knights in the Battle of Peipus Lake in 1242. It is much the same kind of shabby but tenacious Russian Army that repeatedly lost to, but ultimately repelled, the great Napoleon, that frustrated the French, British, and Turks in the Crimea, that endured the charnel house of World War I until March 1918, despite a year of revolution, widespread desertions, and the complete collapse of the Russian government at home.

Such a Russian army—only less well-paid, less well-fed, less well-equipped and led by an officer corps decimated by Stalin's paranoid purges—fought and defeated the Nazi war machine in World War II in a grimly tenacious effort duplicated by no other nation, suffering 6.7 million casualties (along with 13 million or more civilian deaths). U.S. combat deaths in the war were 291,557.

Veterans of Vietnam can cite examples of alcohol and drug abuse among American troops as debilitating as those recounted by Cockburn's Brighton Beach Soviet Army veterans. One of the authors can recall similar incidents of brutality, theft, corruption, incompetence, and malingering among American forces in Korea. As recounted elsewhere in this book, the combat readiness of American troops (except for a few elite units like the Eighty-second Airborne Division) has been found wanting—frequently dangerously so—in study after study, with particular weaknesses noted among U.S. forces in Europe. The Navy lacks sufficient crews and the Air Force has chronically been short of qualified maintenance personnel.

If Soviet weapons have their deficiencies (and they have as many deficiencies as Soviet bathroom plumbing and television sets do), they tend to be simpler and more rugged than their American high-tech counterparts. The issue in determining and maintaining a credible American defense is as much a matter of perceptions of American strength as knowledge of Soviet weakness. Soviet strength increases in direct proportion to American weakness. American deterrence decreases with every procurement horror story. As one congressman put it during a recent defense budget debate: "They read all the technical manuals. They know our stuff doesn't work."

Granting the better health, diet, pay, and living conditions of American soldiers, the disparities noted by Cockburn are more between societies than military forces.

The United States is a nation with a gross national product (GNP) in excess of $3 trillion and a per capita income approaching $15,000. Some 30 percent of its government spending goes for the military.

The Soviet Union's gross national product is approximately $1.2 trillion and its per capita income $4,550. According to official figures, its defense expenditures amount to only 5.3 percent of its government spending. These figures likely include only military operating and construction costs and reflect bookkeeping juggling. The actual percentage of government spending is presumed to be much, much higher. In any event, it constitutes a much larger burden imposed on a much poorer economy and standard of living.

But it is an economy and standard of living that has been steadily improving since World War II—and, in fits and starts, since the Bolshevik takeover in 1917. For older Russians, certainly those who lived through the Great Patriotic War, as World War II is known in the Soviet Union, life is comparatively quite comfortable. One hears the frequently repeated, "Today we have hot water and our own apartment. Ten years ago we had only cold water and shared an apartment. Ten years before that we had no plumbing at all."

A concept that seized many in the early days of the Reagan administration, most particularly Defense Secretary Weinberger, was that the arms race in itself could be used as a weapon against the Soviets, because a rapid acceleration of it would put a severe and damaging strain on the staggering Soviet economy. That such competition would put similar strains on the American economy Weinberger saw as a strategic plus.

Of Reagan's initial proposal for dramatic increases in American military spending, Weinberger said in a 1982 interview:

> Rightly or wrongly, it is the index by which the resolution and the will of America is judged. And in this case, because it meant the acquisition of things we urgently needed, and doing it at a time of economic difficulty when we were reducing all of the other departments, practically speaking . . . all of these things at the same time conveyed to the world a picture of a total change in the United States and an astonishing dedication to the idea of regaining strength in the face of what all of the people interested in normal politics would tell you was an impossible set of conditions.

Pursuing this logic—accepting the premise that huge defense budgets are militarily worthwhile not only because of what they might buy but simply because they are big—it is a short hop from the Pentagon maxim "war is not cost-effective" to "military waste is patriotic."

George Bush, considered one of the most knowledgable and pragmatic of the major figures in the Reagan White House, was much less sanguine in a conversation with one of the authors about the efficacy of the United States's waging economic warfare with the Soviets, but thought the USSR was becoming increasingly sensitive to economic pressure.

> Just as the West has had some serious economic recession, sometimes we overlook the fact that the Soviet Union has had some severe economic problems and the [Communist] bloc has had them. There's been an assumption in many quarters, in many quarters in the intelligence community, that given this kind of society the Soviet Union has it can take whatever percentage of its GNP it wants ad infinitum for defense.
>
> I think it's well worth challenging the assumption—and it's been out there a long time—that they can do whatever they want with the GNP. I'm not sure yet that a generational change will find their people as taciturn about that either. I'm not suggesting any great uprising, but I just think you may have a different internal situation, too.
>
> A lot of people have brought this home to me about myself. You know, every time I get introduced, someone will say I was the youngest combat pilot in the Navy. They ask where, and I have to tell them World War II. A lot of people have never heard

of World War II. Or the Korean War. And I expect there's a hell
of a lot of people [in the Soviet Union] who don't remember the
Battle of Leningrad.

New generations are coming along. New economic problems.
I'm not saying they're deviating from their Marxist line or they're
soft or they're not going to be able to do things that a democracy or an open parliamentary system couldn't do, but I'm just not
sure they can do it as much as they have in the past. Or will
want to.

The Soviet Union is not, as Bush observed, a country on the brink
of bread riots. A study prepared by the CIA for the Joint Economic
Committee of Congress and released in December 1982 found that the
Soviet GNP had increased at an annual rate of 4.8 percent over the
last three decades. Most recently, the GNP increase has dropped to 3
percent and less because of poor harvests. The amount of grain produced per capita in the Soviet Union fell from 909 kilograms in 1978
to 590 in 1981. It was 540 kilograms in 1913, in the wretched days of
the czar. Continuing grain purchases from the United States, Canada,
and Argentina have made up the slack.

A CIA report found the annual increase in Soviet defense spending
falling from more than 4 percent to about 2 percent in the early 1980s,
though the Supreme Soviet called for a 12 percent increase in 1985.
The number of major surface ships built fell from as many as twelve
to seven a year, and submarines constructed from eleven or twelve to
nine, but Moscow poured $2.7 billion a year into its stepped-up war in
Afghanistan; it also spent vast sums propping up the economy of Poland
with hard-currency loans, credits, oil, food, raw materials, and manufactured goods. It also spent $100 million, as it does every year, just
on jamming the signals of the BBC.

The average Russian may not have been very happy about this, but
there's been little visible civil unrest on solely economic issues. As a
woman economist in less Marxist Siberia told *The New York Times*'s
Leonard Silk, "I think it is the character of the Russian people. They
will accept anything, put up with anything."

If this is slowly changing, as Bush suggests, it is not likely that the
vast gap separating the stoic, long-suffering Russian from the acquisi-
tive, comfort-loving American will narrow anytime soon. Tolerance of
hardship remains a uniquely Russian strength.

The percentage of the American GNP devoted to military spending
dropped from 7.4 percent in 1970 to 5.2 percent in 1981. The Reagan
administration set a goal of 7.2 percent by fiscal year 1987. As though
calling that small potatoes, Caspar Weinberger has noted that defense

spending was 9.2 percent of the American GNP in 1955 and averaged 8.9 percent from 1954 to 1964.

But the question that obtains is whether the American public would countenance a reduction in government services and standard of living to the levels of 1954. In the ten-year period he cited, the United States underwent a revolutionary change. Its working class rose from the lower class to the middle class, an accomplishment it would not gladly surrender. How many Americans would willingly make the kind of sacrifices suggested by Weinberger's call for "astonishing dedication to the idea of regaining strength," especially if they're aware it means paying $10,137 apiece for antenna clamp alignment tools, one-piece metal gizmos only an inch wide? As one Washington columnist put it, "They'd be rioting in the streets as soon as you took away their video games."

The Reagan administration got away with its huge increases in defense spending because, instead of increasing taxes to pay for them, it simply borrowed the money through $200 billion annual deficits.

In the wretchedness of the Soviet soldier's existence there is much strength, as there is weakness in the relative comfort of the American soldier's life. The brutality endemic in the Soviet ranks may be assessed as an asset. It was the Russian soldier's capacity for hardship and brutality in attack that enabled the Soviets to defeat in World War II one of the finest armies the modern world has ever seen. On the other hand, American soldiers in Vietnam went into combat with cold beer and copies of *Playboy* magazine. They were ultimately defeated by an enemy that lived in vermin-infested holes beneath the ground and wore sandals cut from truck tires.

Many consider the Soviets a fearsome threat mainly because of the Kremlin marshals' ruthless grasp of reality as it concerns their advantages and disadvantages.

Dr. Steven Rosefielde stated in his *False Science: Underestimating the Soviet Arms Buildup* that the Soviet failure to seize the initiative in seeking mutually balanced force reductions

> reveals a great deal about Soviet defense policy preferences.
> Their motives may have been diverse. They may have wanted to enhance their power to police their empire [Poland], to expand their boundaries [Afghanistan], to Finlandize Western Europe, to wield increased influence in the Third World, to launch a preemptive first-strike with their strategic nuclear forces, or, as some still believe, they may have been driven by defensive paranoia, Kremlin fears, and complexes.

In 1983, a working group of some fifty civilians and military officers from West Germany, Norway, Great Britain, and the United States produced for the European Security Study (ESECS) a book-length report entitled *Strengthening Conventional Deterrence in Europe*, which laid out their assessment of Soviet military goals and expectations in Europe coldly:

> To neutralize the West's strategic option by
> * improvements in their own systems;
> * political pressure and propaganda;
> * decoupling the tactical theater option;
> * arms control.
>
> To paralyze, neutralize, or destroy NATO's theater nuclear capabilities by
> * political pressure and propaganda;
> * a balance of nuclear force in their favor, e.g., the SS-20 mobile missile system with three warheads;
> * military preparedness for a conventional phase of the war involving air power, diversionary forces, helicopter assault, sabotage, ground forces;
> * the use of their own preemptive nuclear strikes against NATO if required.
>
> To destroy NATO forces in Western Europe as rapidly as possible before they can be reinforced, thus to avoid a possible stalemate in the land battle which might then escalate to nuclear war, might have an adverse effect on the Warsaw Pact allies, might be a temptation to the Chinese.
>
> To occupy NATO territory in the Central Front.

The word *offense* in discussions of Soviet military spending and preparation seems to recur as frequently as the word *defense* does in the United States's military.

Writing in Isby's *Weapons and Tactics of the Soviet Army,* General V. G. Reznichko described the Russian concept of the term as follows:

> The Soviet offensive has its origins in the offensive thought of the Czarist Army, in the fast moving cavalry forces of the Russian Civil War and Russo-Polish War, and it was highly developed in the decade 1926–36. Much of this was wiped away by the purges, and the Army that met the Wehrmacht in 1941 was inadequate both in weapons and tactics. However, the hastily improvised mass army soon rectified these failings and provided today's Soviet Army with the basis of its offensive thinking, which has been constantly refined and updated since 1945.
>
> That victory comes only from the attack is recognized by all armies, and since the 1920s the Soviet Union has evolved its strategy, operations, tactics, and technology towards the offensive. Surrounded as they are by what they perceive as hostile capitalist

states and potentially unreliable allies, the nightmare of a world
in arms against them has been a "worst case" for military planning
from the founding of the Soviet Union. The impression the Second
World War made on Soviet society as a whole—which cannot be
underestimated—was compounded by the Cold War. The Soviets
will not lose a war, for defeat must mean massacre and enslavement
or, at the very least, the overthrow of everything painstakingly
built since 1917.

The Soviets intend to win, and they intend to win quickly in a
war fought off the soil of the Soviet Union. The way to do that is
to attack quickly and relentlessly, using mechanized combined-
arms forces with the emphasis on tanks. The end of war is victory.
All else is nonsense.

One of the most accurate and chilling assessments of the menace
posed by the Soviets was made recently by Viktor Suvorov, the nom
de plume of a former middle-echelon Russian Army officer now living
in Britain, who for fifteen years served as a troop commander and on
the general staff. In his book, *Inside the Soviet Army*, which includes
a laudatory foreword by Britain's General Sir John Hackett, he cites
many of the same weaknesses noted by Andrew Cockburn, among them
the horrors of Soviet military life.

Though he had somewhat higher respect for the Soviet Army's noncoms than did Cockburn, Suvorov flatly predicted that millions of Soviet
soldiers would surrender almost immediately if war with the West should
break out. He recognized that the USSR's Eastern European satellites
are a military "house of cards" not to be relied upon. All this, he noted,
is very dangerous—to the West.

> The theory that a nuclear war would take a long time to build up
> originated in the West at the beginning of the nuclear age. It is
> incomprehensible and absurd, and it completely mystifies Soviet
> marshals. For a long time there was a secret debate at the highest
> levels of the Soviet government—have the Western politicians and
> generals gone off their heads or are they bluffing? . . .
>
> The philosophy of the Soviet General Staff is no different from
> that of the horsemen whom I had watched riding the desert. "If
> you want to stay alive, kill your enemy. The quicker you finish
> him off, the less chance he will have to use his own gun." In
> essence, this is the whole theoretical basis on which their plans for
> a third world war have been drawn up. . . .
>
> Soviet generals consider, with good reason, that an initial nu-
> clear strike must be unexpected, of short duration and of the great-
> est possible intensity. If it is delayed by as much as an hour, the
> situation of the Soviet Union will deteriorate rapidly.

Former Secretary of Defense Clark Clifford, whose experience with the Cold War goes back to his days as an aide to President Truman, recently said, with former Defense Secretary Schlesinger concurring, "The major task of the president of the United States is to find a way to get along with the Soviet Union."

This was made all the more imperative by two significant developments in the Reagan administration. The division between tactical and strategic nuclear weapons was blurred, with Army units in Europe given command of nuclear missiles with enough range to impact on Russian territory, all in the name of waging limited warfare against troops and tanks. Also, with the deployment of cruise nuclear missiles on both American and Soviet conventional-attack submarines operating in each other's coastal waters, the effective decision time for responding to an enemy nuclear attack was reduced to about six minutes, yet Reagan took several months to decide whether to remove American Marines from Lebanon.

In the face of this grim reality, such terms as *détente, peaceful coexistence,* and *arms control* take on a certain attractiveness. The trouble is, an American president who treats with the Soviets too amiably will always be taken advantage of quite ruthlessly. The Soviets lie and cheat. (So, of course, do the Americans.) Yet an American president who tries himself to treat the Soviets ruthlessly, who rants and raves and shakes a diplomatic fist, produces not a more submissive Russia but an even more cantankerous and intractable one. The Soviets backed down in the 1962 Cuban missile crisis. They swore never to do it again, and they haven't.

After the missile crisis came a number of arms-control agreements, beginning in 1963 with the signing of the first Limited Test Ban Treaty by the United States, the USSR, and 123 other nations. There followed treaties to keep weapons of mass destruction out of outer space (now ignored), and to keep nuclear weapons out of Latin America; the Nuclear Non-Proliferation Treaty, which banned the transfer of weapons from nuclear powers to nonnuclear countries; and a ban on the deployment of nuclear weapons on the ocean floor.

In 1972 came the first Strategic Arms Limitation (SALT) agreement, which for five years kept both sides from increasing the size and throw weight of their missiles and still limits both countries to just one anti-ballistic missile site each.

In 1979, Leonid Brezhnev and President Carter signed the SALT II agreement, which was to limit the number of strategic delivery systems and the number of warheads allowed on each missile, hold each side to just one new type of missile each, and make provisions for unimpaired verification. General Edward Rowny, Carter's chief negotiator, felt the treaty so favored the Soviets that he resigned in protest. Partly as a result, the Senate refused to ratify the treaty.

The Reagan administration took a much more bellicose approach, pushing SALT II aside to pursue its own Strategic Arms Reduction Talks (START). Convinced by its rhetoric and conduct that the White House had no real interest in another arms control treaty, the Kremlin entrenched itself still further in the good opinion of the European peace movement by offering concessions for withdrawal of missiles from Europe that the Reagan administration, predictably, spurned. When Reagan then complicated matters by suddenly offering concessions of his own, vilifying the Soviet Union for its 1983 attack on an unarmed Korean jetliner, and proceeding with deployment of 1,200-mile-range Pershing II missiles in Europe, the Soviets did not rush back to the negotiating table. Instead, they stormed away from it and slammed the door. They took only thiry-five minutes to consider and reject the United States's last offer, and two days later suspended negotiations indefinitely. It was not until after the 1984 election that the Soviets and the Reagan administration agreed to resume arms talks again, and only after it became an issue in the campaign.

The Americans' chief disadvantage in dealing with the Soviets is that the United States is essentially a reactive and defensive power—an inherently conservative power. It cherishes the status quo. It rages most furiously at change. It is tolerant of almost any kind of foreign government, however unpopular its internal policies, as long as that government refrains from threatening regional stability and the world order and supports American interests.

As a consequence, America's policies are dictated by the policies of those powers willing to threaten stability and the world order. Latin American revolutionaries, mischievous megalomaniacs like Libya's Colonel Muammar Qaddafi, and small bands of armed men all over the world have more to say about what the United States will do or how powerful its military strength will be than any general, admiral, service secretary, or congressman.

The Kremlin marshals have even more to say.

No adversary has grappled with the United States so successfully, in so many different places, and over so long a period of time. With relatively small investments in munitions and money, and almost none in manpower, the Soviet Union has made Americans die all over the globe, with often very painful political consequences.

The Korean War may have been a costly mistake on both sides, but it was costly mostly to the two Koreas, the United States, and the

People's Republic of China. For what it did to the U.S. economy, political stability, and will to compete militarily, the Vietnam War was for the Soviet Union as heady a success as any nation could desire.

Soviet contributions to the Arab-Israeli conflict through its client states and terrorist operations have often served to snatch that terrifying dilemma from the prospect of solution. Its Mideastern troublemaking continually threatens Western Europe and Japan with the loss of half their oil. The Soviets have been so successful at this kind of game that they even had President Reagan, a man much fond of his sleep, worrying about the tiny Caribbean island of Grenada.

The Soviets have achieved other successes that were less visible but more meaningful. Though effectively countered in the Far East by the Nixon-Kissinger play of the China card, the Soviets have largely been achieving their agenda in Europe. According to NATO commander General Bernard Rogers, their objectives are to persuade the West to forgo military improvements opposed to the USSR, to enourage Western foreign policies conducive to Soviet ambitions, to secure Western approval of trade and financing agreements vital to the Soviet Union, and to divorce the United States from Western Europe in both political and military terms.

Though the West did proceed with cruise- and Pershing-missile deployment in Western Europe, the Soviets' noisy campaign against the tank-crew-killing neutron bomb succeeded in securing its withdrawal. Many NATO nations are backsliding in their commitment to strengthen their land forces in Europe, allowing those forces to weaken as those of the Warsaw Pact continue to improve.

European participation in America's "punishments" of the Soviets for the Afghanistan invasion and the Korean jetliner-downing was reluctant, truncated, and ineffective. Similarly, European trade embargoes against the USSR have never really worked. The inclination of most Western European countries has been toward East-West trade.

There is a division between the United States and Europe, and the Soviet Union has often been successful in widening it. By loading up its Western marches with intermediate-range nuclear missiles, the USSR both intimidated great numbers of Western Europeans and provoked the American deployment of its intermediate missiles. Prodded by a hyperactive peace movement heavily financed by Moscow, a large segment of European public opinion turned against the American missile deployment.

In its reactive, defensive way, the United States has responded to the Soviets' schemes, initiatives, and exploitation as best it can—squashing offensive regimes in woebegone little places like Grenada, groping for elusive surcease in Central America, sending ancient battleships and ineffectual aircraft carriers to play the popgun role of gunboats in the Eastern Mediterranean and Arabian Sea.

It takes few initiatives of its own, hobbled by an institutionalized body of domestic criticism and a sentiment toward isolationism that has persisted for two centuries. In grappling with the Soviet threat, most of America really is content with "adequacy," with parity, with a mutually ratified status quo. This is the chief difference between the Americans and the Soviets. For, by all evidence, the Kremlin is convinced of a maxim that any American analyst of Soviet capabilities must keep uppermost in mind, and that will plague the United States most grievously unless its military establishment is drastically overhauled.

It is a maxim of Clausewitz's: "An absolute balance of forces cannot bring about a standstill, for if such a balance should exist the initiative would necessarily belong to the side with the positive purpose—the attacker."

chapter four

THE COMMANDER IN CHIEF

The president shall be commander in chief of the army and navy of the United States, and of the militia of the several States, when called into the actual service of the United States.
—SECTION 2, ARTICLE II, U.S. CONSTITUTION

The weakest link in the American military chain of command is the one at the top, and often it is a very weak link indeed. The military challenges and dangers facing the United States are complex and frightening beyond any historical measure, yet the requirements of the Constitution and democracy of necessity place the country's supreme military authority in the hands of haberdashers and movie actors, hustling lawyers and professional politicians—some, like Lyndon Johnson, whose military experience amounted to little more than a single airplane ride over an enemy-occupied island.

When the telephone of anyone else in the defense hierarchy rings, that person may expect orders. The president must expect to give them, no matter how awful or confusing the choices with which he is confronted. In the post–World War II era, they have not been given well. Only one president since 1945 has led and managed the affairs of the military establishment with any brilliance or effectiveness—Dwight D. Eisenhower, a career soldier who came to office having borne the principal managerial, diplomatic, and decision-making burdens of waging total war in Europe, as well as having had the experience of bush warfare in Asia and the military bureaucracy in Washington. His successors have been markedly less competent at military matters, and each was responsible for military disasters both major and minor.

Their misadventures are nothing new. President Madison's frustrating incompetence in the conduct of the War of 1812 reached its nadir when he personally took command of troops defending Washington in the Battle of Bladensburg and presided over a rout that led to the burning of the capital. Democratic President James K. Polk became so paranoid over the presidential ambitions of his Whig Mexican War generals, Zachary Taylor and Winfield Scott, that he deliberately withdrew troops from them to deny them victories—victories they won anyway. But Madison and Polk at least were spared having to exercise their flawed judgment in assessing the risk of nuclear annihilation as little as six minutes away.

As much as presidential military fecklessness has been due to personal flaws and deficiencies, it has also been a result of America's flawed and deficient military system. Though Eisenhower mastered it, even such great war presidents as Abraham Lincoln and Franklin D. Roosevelt would be frustrated trying to deal with the conduct of today's national defense. Napoleon himself might resign in disgust after his first congressional budget or War Powers Act hearing.

What every new president discovers almost immediately is that there are only two circumstances in which the commander in chief has absolute command of the Armed Forces of the United States. One, theoretically at least, is in a nuclear war. The other is in a very small, limited conventional combat operation, such as the Reagan administration's clumsy conquest of the tiny Caribbean island of Grenada in 1983 or the Carter administration's ill-fated "Desert One" Iranian hostage rescue mission.

For all things military between the macro and micro—the inconceivable ultimate in war and the minor action directed by Oval Office telephone—presidential command isn't so easy. Sometimes it's impossible.

Directing a nuclear war can be done by anyone who's ever ordered something from a department store by telephone using a credit card. The president can do it from the Oval Office, the White House Situation Room, his "Doomsday" 747 command plane, any pay phone, or—using a Secret Service radio field phone—from the fourth tee at Augusta.

All he needs is the small, laminated plastic card, not unlike an ordinary credit card, that he keeps with him at all times. Called the Gold Codes card, it contains a list of supersecret numbers and code words. Changed at frequent intervals, their sole purpose is to verify to the uniformed and civilian authorities in the National Military Command Center, better known as the Pentagon war room, that he is in fact the president of the United States and he is indeed about to order a nuclear strike.

The card is probably the most important document in the government. The president keeps it with him at all times. In the event he sees a need for nuclear war, he telephones the war room and reads off the code numbers and words. Once his identity and purpose are established, he gets down to business.

With the card alone, he can order an all-out assault with every weapon in the American nuclear arsenal. Or he can order a nuclear strike but leave it to the powers in the command center to determine the individual targets and strength of the assault.

He also has several hundred other options, but these require the officer with the "football." This officer always holds the rank of major or above or its naval equivalent. The "football" officer travels with the president at all times, even for short jaunts around Washington. The "football" is the large briefcase he or she carries, containing coded Emergency War Orders (EWOs) for initiating various kinds and degrees of nuclear war. It's called the "football" because the EWOs, drawn up by Pentagon and White House planners using computer projections and scenarios, are very much like football plays. The president calls them depending on what the enemy has done or seems likely to do. With so many thousands of nuclear warheads on hand, the targets range from Soviet missile bases and oil fields down to small installations east of the Urals housing fewer than one hundred KGB personnel.

But even nuclear war fighting has its complications. During the Carter administration, the irreverent White House chief of staff, Hamilton Jordan, took to calling the president's "football" officer "Bam Bam." He probably called him something else on the occasion of one of Carter's frequent visits to the United Nations. Pausing in the building lobby, "Bam Bam" set down the "football," only to see Carter hurrying on into an elevator. He dashed to the President's side, not realizing until the elevator was ascending that the "football" was still in the lobby.

A scarier incident occurred on March 30, 1981, when President Reagan was shot and wounded by a would-be assassin as he left the Washington Hilton Hotel. The President was rushed to Washington Hospital and all the important people in his party rushed to the hospital after him.

Except one: Lieutenant Colonel Jose Muratti, Jr., the "football" officer. He was left on the curb. An excellent officer, he realized his place was with the president, or at least with the Gold Codes card— known as the Sealed Authentical System in Pentagonese. Making his way through heavy traffic to the hospital, he arrived to find a new problem. When Reagan was rushed into the emergency room, all his clothes were cut off and dumped in a pile. Inside that pile was the Gold Codes card, and the FBI agents refused to turn it over to Muratti with the argument that it and the cut-up clothing were "evidence." A quarrel ensued, with Muratti and the Secret Service on one side and the stubborn FBI on the other. Finally, the Secret Service prevailed and Muratti was given the card. The system was at last back in working order. It had taken about thirty minutes from the time Reagan was shot, which is the approximate flight time for an ICBM launched from the Soviet Union against the United States.

Actually, even if Muratti was never heard from again, the nation still would have been able to wage nuclear war, as four other people carry Gold Codes cards at all times—in descending order of command precedence, the vice-president, the secretary of defense, the deputy secretary of defense, and the chairman of the Joint Chiefs of Staff. This chain of nuclear-war command has nothing to do with the constitutional line of succession to the presidency. When then–Secretary of State Alexander Haig stumbled into the White House press room to stammer, "I am in control here, here in the White House," he was in error on two counts. The vice-president, the Speaker of the House, and the president pro tempore of the Senate were ahead of him in constitutional succession. In terms of authority over the military, with Vice-President George Bush still en route to Washington in Air Force Two, Defense Secretary Caspar Weinberger was in full command. Haig didn't even have a Gold Codes card.

Though the other four Gold Codes card carriers are subordinate to the president, their possession of the codes gives them the functional authority to stop or prevent a nuclear war. During the height of Watergate, when many in Washington were behaving irrationally, there were legitimate questions raised about the possible misuse of presidential military authority, including that to wage nuclear war.

As then–Defense Secretary James Schlesinger explained later, he had prepared for that eventuality, instructing the members of the Joint Chiefs of Staff and the civilian service secretaries to report to him any "unusual" presidential orders. If a nuclear strike had been ordered, lacking any evidence of a Soviet attack, Schlesinger and the Joint Chiefs would likely not have obeyed it. Their successors today might not obey it, no matter who's president.

Though five seems a large number of people to be carrying around the authority to start nuclear war, all five unfortunately spend most of their time in Washington. The Soviets have among their nuclear-war-fighting plans a "Spasm" missile attack from offshore submarines that could hit the capital in as little as six to ten minutes and obliterate it in one swift, massive strike, leaving the Pentagon and White House molten rock. The United States has its own version of this attack plan for wiping out Moscow, called "Decapitation," but it takes slightly longer.

There are duplicate war rooms in the strategic hideaway at Raven

Rock, Pennsylvania, on the Maryland border; in the Blue Ridge Mountain bastion at Mount Weather, Virginia; and in the "Looking Glass" plane kept constantly aloft. But there would be precious little chance of reaching them or even escaping from Washington in six or even ten minutes.

The president's personal command plane, the "Doomsday" 747 that for years had been stationed at Andrews Air Force Base in Maryland, was moved in 1983. At its new home, Grissom Air Force Base in Indiana, it is out of reach of Soviet submarine missiles, which could be expected to blow up Andrews before the president could get there by helicopter from the White House. The new plan calls for the president to be rushed from the capital by helicopter, in hopes of making a rendezvous with his command plane at a specially designated "marry-up point." Three backup command 747s are also kept in readiness at Offut Air Force Base in Nebraska.

But the chances of even a helicopter escape remain dicey, especially if nuclear war was not considered imminent when the USSR chose to strike. Worried about Soviet "Spasm" attacks, President Carter ordered his White House assistant and cousin, Hugh Carter, to arrange for a surprise test of the escape plan. It proved an utter failure. Cousin Hugh did not inform the Secret Service of the test, and when the Marine helicopter swooped down over the White House south lawn from its nearby base across the Anacostia River, Secret Service men rushed outside and, brandishing automatic weapons, shooed it away.

Should the card holders all be wiped out, the "Looking Glass" plane could direct the nuclear fighting, but the highest-ranking man aboard might well be only a one-star general. Commanders at the big missile bases in the Dakotas and elsewhere would have the capability of firing off their weapons, but would not have the authority to command all strategic forces.

Some have proposed complicating the procedures even more. At a meeting of the International Society for Political Psychology in 1982, Professor Roger Fisher of Harvard University, along with Professor Morton Deutsch of Columbia University, urged that the EWOs be placed not in the "football" but in a plastic capsule surgically implanted in the chest of the "football" officer, appropriately close to the heart. To possess them, the president would have to cut open the "football" officer's chest. The officer would carry a surgical knife for that purpose.

Fisher complained that the nuclear war command system was too antiseptic and clinical, that there was a "psychological distance" between the president and the victims of the nuclear barrage he might order. Deutsch worried further that nuclear weapons were psychologically seductive for presidents, that "they provide a tremendous emotional kick for those with strong power drives."

In urging the chest implant, Fisher asserted, "He, the president, has to look at someone and realize what death is, what an innocent death is. It's really brought home."

There were drawbacks to the idea. "Football" officers now include women. And if Lieutenant Colonel Muratti could be left on the sidewalk, someone might forget to bring the surgical knife. Even in nuclear war, things can go wrong.

Not surprisingly, American presidents much prefer the kind of command associated with minor conventional actions that can bring about glorious victory at a minimal price. Among their other virtues, when they work, these operations permit a president to circumvent the weighty command structure and war-making bureaucracy, not to speak of Congress and the press, and deal with matters directly—with their own bare mouths, if not hands. Yet it is in this pursuit that recent presidents have gotten in the most trouble.

Dwight Eisenhower, formerly supreme allied commander in Europe, was naturally a president very high on staff work and orthodox command procedures and very chary of the use of the military force. Despite the Soviet suppression of the Hungarian revolution in 1956, similar actions against uprisings in Poland and East Germany, the takeover of Cuba by Castro, and countless other provocations, Eisenhower embarked on a major combat operation just once, when he sent a large, quick strike force of soldiers and Marines into Lebanon at the request of President Chamoun in 1958. After they had attained their military objectives—moving deep into the countryside far from the kind of indefensible beachhead in which Ronald Reagan and his commanders trapped U.S. Marines in 1983—and the Chamoun government was deemed secure, Eisenhower took them out, at all times working through the official chain of command.

John F. Kennedy, a Navy PT-boat skipper who lost his vessel in World War II, was certainly a president bent on proving his manhood, whether in wrangles with Nikita Khrushchev in Vienna or his entertainment of young women at nude à deux White House swimming-pool parties. This was also painfully manifest in his military adventuring. He put Eisenhower's Bay of Pigs Cuban invasion plan into action, leaving out the key ingredient of air cover for fear it would too deeply implicate the United States, with disastrous results. He unleashed the CIA on the Congo, Ghana, and other African hot spots and they only grew hotter as a consequence. He undertook a stirring if ineffective response to the building of the Berlin Wall, underwrote a secret CIA war in Laos, and allowed—indeed, caused—the guerrilla strife in Vietnam to get so far out of control that the resort to American troops to help stabilize the situation became inevitable, with horrific consequences.

With the Cuban missile crisis of 1962, Kennedy brought the United States the closest to nuclear war it has ever been since Hiroshima and Nagasaki. Distrustful of dealing solely with the CIA and the Joint Chiefs because of his Bay of Pigs fiasco, he conducted his Cuban blockade and grappled with the crisis in a highly unorthodox manner, forming his own command group—the "Ex Com," for Executive Committee of the National Security Council. Its thirty-four members included Vice-President Johnson; Secretary of State Dean Rusk; Defense Secretary Robert McNamara; General Maxwell Taylor, chairman of the Joint Chiefs of Staff; and other national security officials. But Kennedy also added Treasury Secretary Douglas Dillon, speechwriter Ted Sorensen, a representative of the U.S. Information Agency, U.N. Ambassador Adlai Stevenson, New York banker Robert Lovett, former Secretary of State Dean Acheson, White House appointments secretary Kenneth O'Donnell, and his brother Bobby, the attorney general. Somehow this large and disparate group was able to meet regularly as the crisis built without disrupting normal activities or tipping the public as to what was afoot until a week into the crisis.

The early consensus recommendation of this group was for an air strike against the Cuban missile emplacements, which would have killed a lot of Russians and could have led to a need for the "football" officer. But the Kennedys managed to keep them meeting for four more days and they instead decided on a naval blockade, which killed no one except for an American U-2 pilot shot down over Cuba by a Soviet anti-aircraft missile. The operation proved a success—fortunately, for failure might have meant a nuclear catastrophe. Considering the Cuban missile crisis the finest hour of his presidency, Kennedy had Tiffany's make up thirty-four walnut-mounted silver commemorative calendar pages marking the thirteen days of the trauma, which he gave to each of the Ex Com members.

During the Dominican Republic crisis of April 1965, Lyndon Johnson made himself into an Ex Com of one. Plagued by the accumulating troubles of Vietnam, he found himself distracted by the outbreak of civil war in the Caribbean island republic. Rebel forces, led in large part by Communists and including a number of defecting army units, had risen against the military junta that had ousted the democratically elected president Juan Bosch. There were more than one thousand Americans in the Dominican Republic at that time and there was some concern for their safety.

Johnson abandoned the Oval Office for the White House Associated Press and United Press International Teletypes to follow developments as soon as they were reported on the wire. One report, which later proved to be unfounded, said that rebel forces were decapitating people and impaling their heads on sticks. With that, LBJ's distraction became an obsession. Hovering over the Teletypes, he began issuing military orders. Eventually, aides were able to wean him from the news wires, but by then he had set in motion a military effort that shortly put 21,900 American Marines and soldiers into the republic—nearly as many troops as the United States had in Vietnam at the time.

The mission quickly expanded from one of rescue of American nationals to one of assisting the junta in its repulse of the Communist insurgency. Though few Americans properly understood what was going on, or exactly why, it was a highly successful mission—for Johnson, in more ways than one. Not only was a Castro-style Communist regime kept out of power in an important area of the Caribbean, but, for one of the rare occasions in his long, wartime presidency—standing at the Teletypes and issuing orders—Lyndon Johnson, commander in chief, was actually in command.

Needless to say the same approach could not work with Vietnam. Johnson's military experience in World War II amounted mostly to his having himself made a Navy commander as a Roosevelt protégé in Congress, riding as a passenger in a bomber on an overflight of New Guinea, receiving the Silver Star from Roosevelt as a result, and then returning to Congress on orders—all in a few weeks.

Richard Nixon, who spent World War II as a naval aviation ground officer in the Pacific, was too preoccupied trying to extricate the United States from the Vietnam War and himself from his Watergate troubles to go in much for military adventuring, except for one distracting global alert he called during the 1973 Yom Kippur War.

Gerald Ford, whose World War II combat experience included duty on the carrier U.S.S. *Monterey*, was stuck with being president for the final Vietnam humiliation, but he did manage to rescue the U.S. freighter *Mayaguez* from the Cambodians after the Pol Pot regime seized it in May 1975. This was the first time that the United States had ordered military forces into action since the fall of Saigon a few weeks earlier. That amphibious Marine units were able to recover the ship and its crew from the island of Koh Tang was viewed by Henry Kissinger and others as a symbolic turning point after the impotency brought on by American failure in Vietnam. The cost didn't seem to matter.

Ford and Kissinger dealt with the crisis from the White House basement situation room, while Defense Secretary James Schlesinger operated out of the National Military Command Center in the Pentagon. The three civilians used satellite photos and radio to monitor the movement of the aircraft carrier *Coral Sea* and other American ships. The White House ordered helicopters dispatched hurriedly from Thailand to staging areas in Cambodia to aid in the assault of Koh Tang. In the process, one chopper crashed, killing 23 persons. From twelve thousand miles away, they ordered the island strafed and bombed, including a direct order to use CBU-82 cluster bombs designed to produce the equivalent in blast of a small nuclear explosion.

According to Joseph Laitin, Schlesinger's press secretary, they spoke directly with individual ship captains. Major General A. M. Gray, the Marine commander in charge of the rescue mission, later recalled in an interview how he eventually became so confused by the various orders coming from Washington—which helicopters he was to use, where various ships should proceed, which bombs to drop, and all— that he "just turned the radios off." His successful if costly conclusion of the mission won him another star and proved to be a major highlight of the brief Ford administration.

In 1978, a commission appointed by President Carter to evaluate the high-command function warned that, because modern events have compressed the time in which armies receive orders and carry them out, there was a significant danger that presidents and their aides might add considerable confusion to already chaotic battlefield conditions by attempting to intervene personally. The *Report of the Secretary of Defense on the National Military Command Structure* was released July 9, 1978, by the commission chairman, Richard Steadman. Senator John Culver, among others, found it disturbing:

> It points out that our communications have reached such a degree of sophistication and reliability on a global basis that civilian policymakers can get too intimately involved in the actual operation on the ground, and in a way usurp the appropriate function of the field commander, or the one most immediate to the crisis. That can introduce confusion and complication into a successful operation. Besides having no control, there is also the other side of that; there could be too much control.

That warning would come to haunt Carter two years later after his own spectacularly unsuccessful efforts to direct the units attempting the rescue of the American hostages in Iran.

Carter in the Oval Office and Defense Secretary Brown in the Pentagon worked with military officers for more than a year planning the rescue mission, which was to use six C-130 "Hercules" troop transport planes and six to eight Navy RH-53 helicopters to transport a force of 200 commandos to Tehran, free the hostages, and fly them out of Iran to safety. The plan called for loading enough fuel into a staging area code-named Desert One to enable the choppers to make it to the Iranian capital and back.

Desert One was to collapse in chaos because of mechanical breakdowns, because of the failure of its planners to anticipate the weather conditions and changes peculiar to Iran, and because Carter insisted that only eight helicopters be sent, meaning that, if more than two became inoperative, the mission would have to be called off. A minimum of six of these RH-33s were needed to carry all the commandos and hostages. Carter aides were later to explain that he wanted to use the smallest possible amount of force in the mission because he wanted the world to know afterward that the mission was a "humanitarian" one rather than a punitive assault. He even issued instructions that the raiding force was not to wound or kill its Iranian opponents if possible.

A Special Review Group was formed by the Joint Chiefs of Staff (JCS) to determine why the mission failed. What it found proved to be a textbook example of the fragility of high-technology weaponry in battlefield conditions.

The Desert One helicopters took off on the night of April 24, 1980, from the aircraft carrier *Nimitz* on station off the Iranian coast, heading for the desert staging area six hundred miles away. Two hours later, one of the choppers had to be abandoned because a rotor blade had started to disintegrate. The crew was picked up by another helicopter and the mission continued.

An hour after that, the remaining seven helicopters encountered one of the wild desert sandstorms endemic to the area, which reduced visibility to zero and began to foul navigation equipment and motors. Unfortunately, the helicopters' sand filters had been removed to make the engines run as strongly as possible. The sandstorm knocked out the navigation instrumentation of a second helicopter and it was compelled to return to the *Nimitz*.

Of the remaining helicopters, the JCS report said, "some crews experienced severe spatial disorientation while continuing to penetrate the obscuring dust cloud. It was impossible to maintain formation integrity and airspeed was reduced to enable navigation. Eventually, six of the original eight helicopters, in separate flights, arrived at the refueling site in intervals between approximately 50 minutes and one hour and 25 minutes later than planned," the chiefs said.

But when the badly shaken force arrived at Desert One it was found that the sandstorm had fouled a vital hydraulic pump in one of the copters, leaving the force with only five for the raid—one less than required.

According to one of the C-130 crew members, who wrote about it later in a magazine called *Gung Ho*, the commandos argued with their commander, Army Colonel Charlie Beckwith, that they could pull off the raid with just the five. Several of the commandos volunteered to stay behind in Tehran. But Beckwith broke radio silence and reported the helicopter breakdowns. He was told by the White House to come home.

It was on the subsequent departure from the Desert One staging area that real tragedy struck. As the C-130s and helicopters restarted their engines to take off, the propeller and rotor blades stirred up enormous clouds of dust. Losing all visibility and his sense of equilibrium and direction, one of the helicopter pilots flew into the rear of a C-130 in a fiery crash that killed five in the cargo plane and three in the chopper.

Critics have questioned Carter's decision to call off the effort when he still had five helicopters. It was later disclosed that a second force of American helicopters had also been operating in Iran that night and one of them could have been loaned to Desert One. Another question was raised over the President's reluctance to send more than eight helicopters into that unknown situation, when there was enough fuel aboard the C-130s to serve fifteen helicopters.

Yitzak Rabin, the former Israeli prime minister and army chief of staff who personally supervised some of Israel's most successful commando raids, said of the Desert One failure: "America doesn't have enough helicopters?"

In their report, the Joint Chiefs accepted responsibility for the decision to send only eight helicopters, but Carter's national security advisor, Zbigniew Brzezinski, also acknowledged that military commanders had pressed hard throughout the planning stages for a larger-scale operation.

One of the most damning criticisms of the Desert One tragedy came after it was learned that interservice rivalries had plagued mission planners from the beginning. The raid was originally planned as a joint Army–Air Force operation, with the Air Force supplying the big C-130s and the Army providing the helicopters and commandos. However, as planning proceeded in "the Tank" (the Joint Chiefs' Pentagon meeting room), the Navy and Marine Corps pushed to have their people participate too.

By adding Navy ships and Marine helicopters to the Army–Air Force enterprise, the Joint Chiefs doubled the number of commandos involved in the mission. Despite this clumsy mix of forces, no joint practice was held before the team went into action, as the Special Review Group report admitted.

As *New York Times* senior military analyst Drew Middleton observed later, "Each service had its own methods of training, its own interpretations of tactical doctrine, which it was not willing to relinquish and, as a former Defense Department official recently said, 'On the basis of my experience, each service would want a piece of the action, and simply settling who was to do what, with which and to whom would be a major problem.' "

Thus, with the Marines doing it the Marine way, the Army doing it the Army way, and the Air Force following its own unique operating procedures, there was poor coordination throughout the mission, including among troopers on the ground. The Special Review Group report said that, while communication was "excellent" for top officers and the President, for the units in the field "relationships were less defined and not as well understood."

And thus were Army commandos in an Air Force transport killed by a Marine helicopter.

It's noteworthy that the advisors Carter consulted in the process of this unfortunate undertaking included his wife, Rosalynn; his press secretary, Jody Powell; his advertising man, Gerald Rafshoon; and his pollster, Patrick Cadell.

Ronald Reagan's lust for military adventure surpassed even Kennedy's, though he was much less personally involved and often far less successful. While he slept, American pilots were able to shoot down two Libyan jets over the Gulf of Sidra early in Reagan's term, but his other military initiatives met with frustration, as in Central America and the Persian Gulf—or in catastrophe, as in Lebanon. Again while Reagan slept, during a golfing holiday in Georgia, a single terrorist bomber was able to wipe out 10 percent of the American Marine force in Lebanon—losses that would have gotten a few generals sacked in World War II. The field commanders, subsequently forgiven by Reagan, were largely responsible for the poor security, but it was his policy of using attack force Marines as garrison troops—undermanned and deployed on untenable ground—that led to the debacle and the United States's ultimate retreat from Lebanon.

The Reagan administration's October 1983 Grenada invasion was a success—though never as great a success as the White House's screeching propaganda machine proclaimed—but it courted disaster every step of the way. Troops landed equipped only with vague tourist road maps. They arrived in the wrong places and attacked the wrong objectives. An air attack ordered on an enemy position struck an American one instead. Two helicopters were downed in a collision. Had there actually been as many Cuban soldiers on the island as some intelligence reports had indicated, Reagan might have provided his country with a tragedy. If he had, as with the misadventure in Lebanon, he likely would have absolved the field and planning commanders of any blame, taken full responsibility himself, and then proclaimed a victory, no matter how severe the casualties.

Fortunately, presidents do tend to grow into their commander's role as they continue in office. Jimmy Carter, described by one Washington columnist as he entered office as a "little-known, second-rate governor of a third-rate state," campaigned much on his past experience as a nuclear engineer aboard a nuclear submarine (he styled it "nuclear physicist"), but it was far from the experience of command. A congressman who went to one of Carter's first White House briefings on foreign policy came out shaking his head sadly and saying, "All I learned was that the President of the United States knows absolutely nothing about anything that happened in the world prior to January 1977." Carter's hasty proposal for the withdrawal of American troops from South Korea, which would have destabilized one of the most overarmed and dangerous regions in the world, was perhaps the most compelling example of his lack of historical knowledge and understanding of consequences.

But Carter was a master of detail and a quick study, qualities that came to the fore in the preparation and process of the negotiations that led to the Camp David accords (however impermanent these proved to be). His problem was that added knowledge and experience failed to make him less irresolute in the face of crisis or less willing to bend military needs and realities to political goals.

During the long Iranian crisis, he had on station usually two and at one point three carrier task forces in the Arabian Sea. Yet, as more than one Air Force officer privately pointed out, there was not an aircraft aboard any of those carriers that had the range to reach and fight over any significant Iranian target without complicated and risky in-flight refueling. For their own safety, the carriers had to stay a considerable distance from the Iranian coast. The Iranians knew that. The big, expensive display of force was mostly for domestic consumption—to convince the voters the president was doing something.

Ronald Reagan came to office with foreign-policy experience that, according to his own campaign pronouncements, amounted to two official trips abroad, one for some minor purpose of President Nixon's. During it, according to Reagan, he met the "King of Siam." Siam became Thailand in 1939.

The day he announced his candidacy in November 1979 Reagan was asked on network television how he would get along with Valéry Giscard d'Estaing. Reagan did not know who the man was, let alone that he was president of France. In response to questions of age, he said he would take office younger than the world leaders he would be dealing with. This must have come as quite a surprise to Margaret Thatcher, Pierre Trudeau, and others a decade or more younger than Reagan.

Reagan adopted two strong party lines on national security policy: the Defense Department was to be given whatever it asked and the Soviet Union was to blame for all the crisis situations in the world. He embarked on a reflexive policy of using military force or the demonstrated threat of it in all crisis situations and of heaping abuse and reproach on the Soviet Union whenever possible.

Then he just sat back and let things happen. His belief in his own beliefs was secure against any and all new developments. As one White House aide put it, "He is an optimist. My God, is he an optimist."

Another aide said, "You have to be careful with him. If you had nine bad items to tell him and one good one, he would latch on to the tenth favorable item and discount the other nine. The blind spots are very troubling."

He retreated from disagreeable truths whenever possible, no matter what their source. When in 1982 his chief congressional lobbyist Kenneth Duberstein informed him that even superhawk Representative Trent Lott, the House Republican whip, was calling for restraint in defense spending to help balance the budget, Reagan just shook his head no, and then took a call from astronauts circling the earth in the *Columbia* space shuttle.

Some aides, most notably White House Chief of Staff James Baker, were able to get him to moderate some of his more extreme positions, but only by convincing them that he was shifting political tactics to achieve a policy goal, not retreating from the policy itself. And it often didn't work. When Baker pressed too hard for new excise taxes and defense cuts, Reagan turned to him and said, "If that's what you believe, then what in the hell are you doing here?"

Another aide was quoted as saying, "I have never heard him say, 'I was wrong.' "

Still, Reagan did manage to acquire something of a military education in the presidency. In March 1982 he participated in a war game—the first president to do so since Eisenhower involved himself in one in 1957. Reagan's was a five-day computerized exercise involving hypothetical Russian conventional attacks against American troops in Europe, Korea, and Southwest Asia near Iran. The United States, with former Secretary of State William P. Rogers acting as president as Reagan looked on, responded with conventional force but tried to expand the fighting. The Soviets upped the ante by using a tactical nuclear weapon against the U.S. Navy and resorting to chemical weapons. American field commanders were given permission to retaliate with small-yield nuclear weapons. The Soviet response to that was all-out nuclear war that destroyed Washington and killed the president.

Another participant told *The New York Times*, "After President Reagan watched someone face up to the decision to push the nuclear button, all of a sudden there was a sensitivity that wasn't there before."

The viciousness of the otherwise limited Anglo-Argentine Falkland Islands War was almost as sobering. After both events, Reagan assumed the dominant role in his administration's military affairs. But it was not to impose restraint. American forces were called into action twenty-six times between the end of World War II and the end of 1984. Nine of those occasions were during the Reagan administration.

He attempted to use force wherever useful and possible, as in Grenada. He reportedly became deeply concerned about the inadequacy of America's conventional capability and manpower strength, and accepted the high command's assertion that another $325 billion over the $1.5 trillion Reagan was already allocating for new weapons systems was needed to provide the troop strength necessary to withstand the Soviets and deter an attack.

In May 1982 he signed National Security Decision Directive (NSDD) 32, which called for expanding America's military capability to fight in a multiplicity of combat situations while waging a protracted conventional war against the Soviets. The doctrine that NSDD 32 replaced had called for fighting the Soviets with bullets and artillery shells for a month, then resorting to nuclear arms. NSDD 32 additionally called for strengthening the U.S. nuclear force to the point it could prevail in a nuclear war with the Soviets.

Reagan's move came too late politically. So much money had been soaked up by his bloated weapons programs that the extra $325 billion was not forthcoming. Though he moved to create two new Army "light divisions" in 1984 (the Army had wanted three), there was money enough only to expand Army troop strength by just one thousand men and women. The "light divisions" came largely from cannibalizing other units.

No sensible American citizen would recommend or countenance a constitutional amendment or legislative act that would preclude the right of a lawyer or former movie actor to assume the command of the American military. The Founding Fathers may have had George Washington in mind when they wrote a constitution that made the president commander in chief, but that constitution has served well for two centuries, most particularly in suppressing the kind of domestic military/political ambitions that have been so ruinous to other democracies in the past.

What saves any president—and the Republic—is the quality of his advisors and subordinates, not only in emergencies and command decisions but in the more bureaucratic matters of international commitments, weapons procurement, troop recruitment, combat readiness, intelligence analysis, strategy and tactics, and future planning. There are for all practical purposes no situations in which the president can truly act alone. But there are often times when he could use a better grade of help.

chapter five

THE MEN
IN THE MIDDLE

> *Between the idea*
> *And the reality*
> *Between the motion*
> *And the act*
> *Falls the Shadow.*
> —T. S. ELIOT

The occupant of the Oval Office deals with the American military through many channels, just as it deals with him. But the principal flow of national-security command decisions downward and intelligence and other national security information upward is through a small, shadowy, weblike bureaucracy headquartered appropriately enough in the White House basement. More a membrane on the organizational charts than a channel or funnel, it's called the National Security Council (NSC), and it involves all the major players in American defense.

When Henry Kissinger was Richard Nixon's national security advisor, backed up by the most professional and experienced NSC staff in memory, the NSC functioned much like a miniature Defense Department and State Department, frequently superseding both agencies and intervening in the regular chain of command whenever Dr. Kissinger thought it necessary. Many a general found drawbacks in this arrangement, but less activist NSCs have too often tended to attract staff who are inexperienced, incompetent, or downright strange.

The NSC is a strange place by its very nature. Consisting of a complicated system of committees—interlocking directorates made up mostly of the same people—the NSC's main membership includes the president, the vice-president, the secretary of state, and the secretary of defense. The director of the Central Intelligence Agency and the chairman of the Joint Chiefs of Staff have advisory roles, although many in Congress have been trying to make the JCS chairman a permanent member of the council. Additional cabinet secretaries and other defense and intelligence officials are invited to join NSC meetings when it is appropriate.

The NSC has a staff of about forty-two analysts, with a much larger support staff, laboring under the direction of the national security advisor (known more formally as the assistant to the president for national security affairs), who in recent years has almost always been an intimate of the president.

Operating as an adjunct to the NSC is the Policy Review Committee (PRC), whose members include the secretary of state, the secretary of defense, the chairman of the JCS, the director of Central Intelligence, and the national security advisor, with the chairman chosen according to the subject under discussion. Others are invited to sit in as needed. The PRC develops the policies the president decides upon and also performs the functions of the now defunct Committee on Foreign Intelligence. Its scope is fairly wide and its mission tends to be long-range.

Working under the PRC are the six interdepartmental groups, which deal with policy and problems in the areas of Africa, Latin America, East Asia, the Middle East and South Asia, Europe, and political-military affairs and are run principally by the State Department.

The NSC also appoints ad hoc groups to deal with special and very specific problems. Who serves on these bodies is determined entirely by the NSC and the president.

The same people on the Policy Review Committee also sit on the Special Coordination Committee (SCC) which is always chaired by the national security advisor and includes the secretary of state, the secretary of defense, the JCS chairman, the Central Intelligence director, and others as desired. The SCC is used principally for overseeing military or covert intelligence operations and crisis management, and is also involved in arms-control matters.

It can sometimes get very confusing. As a member of both the PRC and SCC once put it: "As I run from committee meeting to committee meeting, I have to remind myself what hat I'm wearing and which committee it is, for the same people always seem to be there."

This national-security-by-committee arrangement is what produces the Presidential Review Memorandum (or "prim"), such as the one proposing a switch from Mutual Assured Destruction, or unthinkable nuclear war, to Counterforce, or "thinkable" nuclear war limited largely to military targets. Presidential response to prims comes back in the form of Presidential Directives, such as Carter's PD 59 that produced the large menu of Counterforce nuclear targets.

All national intelligence is supposed to flow to the director of Central Intelligence and then up through the Policy Review Committee and the Special Coordination Committee to the full National Security Council. The NSC, through the PRC, the SCC, and the director of Central

Intelligence, maintains direct control of the CIA, but its relationship to the rest of the intelligence community—defense intelligence, the Drug Enforcement Agency, State Department intelligence, the Federal Bureau of Investigation, the Treasury Department, and the Energy Department—is one of coordinating intelligence rather than supervising the collection of it.

The State Department also has some military functions—the Arms Control and Disarmament Agency comes under its umbrella—but the military is not fond of dealing with it. Then–Secretary of State Cyrus Vance, who opposed the use of military force against Iran in the hostage crisis, was left out of preparations for the Desert One raid and resigned to protest the operation.

The chief flaw of this confusing and sometimes disorganized system is its vulnerability to the foibles, incompetence, or ambitions of individual members of the command team.

Truman restricted his National Security Council to a strictly military advisory role. Eisenhower, fond of staffs, upgraded the NSC's status and mission, but it was completely dominated by the forceful presence of Secretary of State John Foster Dulles. Kennedy, irked by the NSC's contribution to the Bay of Pigs fiasco and preferring more informal groups of advisors, put the NSC back in the closet. Lyndon Johnson promised to let it out again, but it was quickly eclipsed by the "Tuesday lunch" circle of White House advisors who helped him plan the Vietnam War.

Richard Nixon promised to make the NSC a major part of the policy- and decision-making process. He did, with a vengeance. His NSC prospered with the fortunes of his national security advisor, Henry Kissinger, who quickly assumed *the* major role in decision-making. Kissinger filled the NSC with experienced government hands—in nearly every case the best he could find—and the team is generally considered to have been the best ever, before or since. Secretary of State William P. Rogers was overshadowed to the point of humiliation. After Nixon's first term, Kissinger took the secretary of state's job over himself— some say just to keep anyone else from occupying the position—while remaining the president's principal national security guru and maintaining a White House office hard by the Cabinet Room and Oval Office.

It's also interesting to note that Kissinger's assistant and perceptive student was the equally Machiavellian though less brilliant Alexander Haig.

Jimmy Carter was so impressed with this arrangement he tried to duplicate it, hiring his own foreign-born academic, Zbigniew Brzezinski, as an antidote to his Eastern establishment secretary of state, Cyrus Vance, and a counterfoil to his genius secretary of defense, Harold Brown, who was wholly a creature of the Pentagon. Brzezinski proved about as formidable a national security advisor as Carter was a president and Vance was a secretary of state. But the ardent Russophobe was effective enough to blunt if not overturn the policy initiatives of others, and thus contributed to the confusion and paralysis that so often characterized Carter's administration in crisis.

Brzezinski was so satisfied with his role that, in his memoirs, he urged institutionalizing the policy triumvirate by making the national security advisor "Director of National Security," a cabinet officer confirmed by the Senate.

The chief flaw of the NSC system in its present form is that, with no one but the president having charge of everything, it encourages some of the worst bureaucratic sabotage, interoffice warfare, empire building, back stabbing, and all-around power struggling in Washington.

The experience of the first years of the Reagan administration is certainly typical. At first, it seemed that the dominant role in national security would be assumed by his first secretary of state, General Alexander Haig, who by 1981 was able to bring with him the experience and global connections acquired as military commander of NATO and the skills at internecine warfare learned at Kissinger's knee—skills he used to keep Kissinger himself, for a time, at arm's length from the new Republican administration.

Reagan's first national security advisor, Richard Allen, was a man who had spent his Washington years more in pursuit of a successful business career as a consultant than in bureaucratic power. Caspar Weinberger, the mild-mannered secretary of defense, had performed competently in various roles in the Nixon administration but seemed a likely pushover in any struggle with Haig. When Weinberger tried to deploy the neutron bomb in Europe after all the uproar caused by Jimmy Carter's abrupt change of mind on the weapon, Haig, as much Western Europe's ambassador to the United States as he was America's chief diplomat, overruled him with ease.

Reagan did install his closest advisor, William Clark, a man wholly unlettered in foreign affairs, as Haig's deputy to function as a sort of political commissar in the State Department. But Clark quickly became one of Haig's admirers and loyal supporters.

Hubris self-destructs. Haig began to annoy Reagan with his constant whining and quarreling over turf, and that began the slide. First, Vice-President Bush was made White House crisis manager over Haig's howling objections. Then Allen left the NSC and was replaced by Clark, who quickly demonstrated his loyalties belonged primarily to Reagan and began working against Haig when necessary, which was often. Finally, after a year and a half in office, Haig threatened his resignation one time too often and it was snapped up.

His replacement, former Nixon Treasury Secretary George Shultz, proved a cautious, pragmatic, and amiable man who seemed no match for steadfast Reagan loyalist Clark or the surprisingly willful Weinberger, the latter having taken to jetting all over the globe. On a single "defense" trip in 1983, Weinberger met with not only foreign defense ministers but the heads of government of China, Pakistan, and Sri Lanka, and the foreign ministers of Japan, Pakistan, and Italy, as well as Pope John Paul II.

Leaving Shultz to process diplomats' paychecks, the resolutely efficient Clark took to holding overseas meetings on major problems like the Mideast without bothering to consult the secretary of state.

Shultz began making noises that sounded to some like resignation threats, but little came of them, if threats they were. But he ended up top dog anyway, because of three unforeseen developments: Weinberger began to lose face, credibility, and influence on Capitol Hill because of his intransigence on defense spending; Clark tired of the NSA job and leapt at the chance to replace the disgraced James Watt when he was ousted as secretary of the interior; and the hitherto reticent Shultz transformed himself into a towering figure of rage in a one-to-one Oval Office meeting with Reagan in which he reportedly denounced the administration's foreign-policy disarray as "a disgrace." It also helped that he wisely portrayed himself as an outspoken champion of Reagan's hardest-line policy positions, to the point of becoming the administration's most enthusiastic supporter (after Reagan himself) of the 1983 Grenada invasion. When the administration needed a front man to give the President's side of the nuclear-war issue stirred up by the inflammatory 1983 television nuclear-holocaust movie *The Day After*, Shultz got the job.

Shultz even achieved the miracle of having his own highly qualified but quite deferential choice, Robert McFarlane, replace Clark as NSA, knocking aside the candidate of the Republican Party's right wing, United Nations Ambassador Jeane Kirkpatrick. But Shultz acquired this prominence and power the way it's usually done in Washington— by telling the president what he wanted to hear.

As a membrane, the NSC apparat functions as the eardrum of the presidential ear, through which all intelligence and recommendations flow. Consequently, the NSC staff occupies a position of inordinate importance. Its members are usually little known outside of academia and the defense and foreign-policy establishments, and they make many people nervous, including people high up in the CIA and the Pentagon's upper strata. Memos sent to the president collect many thumbprints going through the NSC.

Though a few CIA, Pentagon, and State Department retirees can usually be found on the payroll, NSC staffers have tended to be somewhat younger than most government officials in such a powerful position. Harvard, the Fletcher School of Diplomacy at Tufts, and other venerable Eastern establishment academic institutions turn up consistently in curricula vitae. Eastern European surnames are commonplace. In Reagan's administration, as in many of his predecessors', NSC staff have had frequent opportunity to present their views in person to the President, which most Pentagon, State Department, and CIA officials never get to do.

These can be very interesting views. Harvard's Richard Pipes, a Reagan NSC staffer, held the public opinion that, unless the Soviet Union abandoned its Bolshevism for the ways of the West, war was inevitable. Army Major General Robert L. Schweitzer, who joined the NSC staff under Reagan, made a speech before the Army Association in 1981 in which he asserted there was a "drift toward war" with the Soviet Union. "The Soviets are on the move; they are going to strike," he said. He was fired for making these unsettling public utterances without clearance, but eighteen months later turned up on a Reagan promotion list as a candidate for lieutenant general.

Among those who could count on their memos being read by Reagan was twenty-eight-year-old (in 1984) Paula Dobriansky, the ranking NSC Eastern Europe specialist, who had excellent academic credentials but had never been to Eastern Europe. Colleague John Lenczowski, the ranking Soviet expert and then thirty-three years old, had written a book on Soviet perceptions of U.S. foreign policy, but had never been to the Soviet Union.

The director of Central Intelligence (DCI) has a similar membrane role. While affiliated intelligence organizations such as the National Security Agency (NSA), an independent agency not affiliated with the national security advisor, and the State Department's intelligence branch can find ways to circumvent the DCI—as when then–NSA Director Bobby Ray Inman went directly to the Carter administration with the news that brother Billy had been caught up with Libyans—the CIA must report to the DCI directly. Agency professionals were reportedly less than happy with Reagan's newly installed DCI William Casey when in early 1981 he began dealing cavalierly and sarcastically with intelligence reports that disagreed with the White House policy line, especially as concerned the Soviet Union.

After Casey tried (unsuccessfully) to make New Hampshire sewing-machine dealer and political operative Max Hugel his chief of Human Intelligence or head spy, and Bobby Ray Inman, then deputy DCI, resigned, Congress drew the line. With Republican Senators Richard Lugar and Barry Goldwater the most insistent, it was made clear that the President could name anyone director of intelligence he wished, but the deputy had to be a career professional, like Inman's replacement, John McMahon, and he would be the chief person with whom the Senate and House intelligence committees would deal. The President, of course, preferred dealing with Casey.

Steps can be taken to give future presidents considerably more and better help. Zbigniew Brzezinski was right. The post of national security advisor should be officially upgraded to the supervisory role of policy broker it so often functions as, whether it's called director of national security or not. The unproductive and often dangerous back stabbing and turf fights between the secretaries of state and defense and other policymakers must be brought under control. Someone must coordinate the flow of information, policy proposals, and grabs for the presidential ear from Defense, State, and the intelligence community, and no one is better situated for that role than the national security advisor, who as "director" would certainly have an involvement and prestige warranting the most careful presidential selection and congressional scrutiny. The choice of a national security director ought to be the most important initial appointment a new president makes.

The National Security Council should be upgraded and restructured to include not only the president, vice-president, defense secretary, and secretary of state, but also the national security advisor (functioning as "director," as Brzezinski recommended), Central Intelligence director, and chairman of the Joint Chiefs of Staff. It is here where the civilian-military link ought to be strongest.

It's just as important that the National Security Council staff be expanded and upgraded to that of a major department of government, which it is. Job requirements ought to be instituted to reduce the opportunities for untraveled Eastern Europe scholars in their twenties and assure a staff more like the veteran professionals Kissinger assembled.

It might be well to require attendance in tough security trade schools like the National War College and experience in the field, including if possible military experience.

Don Gregg, a ranking CIA official in Vietnam who emerged from the war with his estimable reputation still intact, was an intelligence officer "of conscience" who went beyond a working knowledge of the political and military realities of the war to learn as much as he could about the essential nature of the Vietnamese people, compiling a knowledge that far exceeded that of many top commanders. Gregg, who went on to serve as national security advisor to Vice-President Bush, would be an excellent prototype of the individual needed for the NSC.

The mission of the upgraded NSC should go beyond analysis, beyond alliance management and crisis management, to at long last deal with crisis prevention. There is much the United States can do to ease its defense burden and reduce the myriad dangers it faces by making a concerted and enlightened high-level effort to remove or alter the circumstances that might lead to crisis long before they reach critical mass.

To avoid the ultimate crisis, it is imperative that means for "getting along with the Soviet Union"—without giving in to the Soviet Union—be established via national-security directive and other mechanisms as a major national-security policy objective and a significant part of NSC operations. Certainly it's vital that, whether through war games such as Reagan participated in or more comprehensive studies and briefings, every White House hierarchy acquires the deepest possible understanding of the Soviet leadership and people and learns to view their own decisions and actions through Russian eyes and against the backdrop of Russian history. Neither Carter nor Reagan nor their closest advisors—except perhaps for George Bush—were quite able to master this.

To its credit, the Reagan administration joined with Congress in late 1983 in agreeing to spend $50 million to encourage and finance Russian studies in the United States and make up what it acknowledged was a dangerous shortage of American Sovietologists.

There are institutional changes that can be made as well. Sovietologists belong at the right hand of the secretary of defense, the secretary of state, and the Central Intelligence director. The national security director's chief lieutenant should be a deputy director for Soviet affairs, in charge of a large NSC directorate. An expert capable of thinking and responding to events like a Russian and making a reasonable assessment of probable Soviet reactions ought to be in attendance at every NSC meeting, every Pentagon war-room gathering, and every White House situation-room emergency session.

Such remedies are, in Washington terms, fairly easy to implement, but their effect would be concentrated largely on the White House. Descending further down the chain of command on the organizational and information flow charts, one comes up against a more massive and intractable problem—centering on a group of individuals in the American defense establishment who all too often come to see themselves as imperial potentates.

For all the power they wield over the American military, they wear no gold braid. They are civilians.

chapter six

THE GENERALISSIMOS IN SUITS

Whose game was empires and whose stakes were thrones,
Whose table earth, whose dice were human bones.
—LORD BYRON

Military complaints about civilian interference in the command of America's armed forces have not always been misplaced. One of the most glaring examples occurred on the eve of the Civil War, a catastrophe the incident played a significant role in bringing about.

Having failed to prevent secession, Lincoln still sought to avoid war by using the deterrent of a strong Union military presence. In keeping with this policy of firmness, he ordered the resupply of the major federal forts and other military installations along the Southern coast, including Fort Sumter. His secretary of the navy, Gideon Welles, carried out his wishes by ordering, on April 5, 1861, Captain Samuel Mercer to take command of the frigate *Powhatan* and lead a naval squadron to the relief of Sumter, showing the newborn Confederacy that Washington meant to enforce the federal writ.

Lincoln's friend and close advisor, Secretary of State William Seward, also wished to avoid war, but thought that end could be accomplished through negotiation. Thinking the resupply mission dangerously provocative, he drew up an order for the President's signature calling off the voyage and turning the *Powhatan* over to a Lieutenant David Porter, who was to take it to Pensacola, Florida, instead. Craftily waiting until the busiest part of Lincoln's office day, Seward slipped the order into a stack of routine papers to be signed. As Seward expected, Lincoln put his name to the order without reading it. Porter took command of the ship just before it was to sail.

Seward's coup at first seemed short-lived. Navy Secretary Welles found out about the inexplicable order and demanded a late-night meeting at the White House at which Seward would be present. The meeting was stormy, but Welles of course prevailed. Lincoln told Seward to telegraph Porter, at the Brooklyn Navy Yard, where the ship was berthed, and countermand the spurious order, letting the flotilla proceed to Sumter under Mercer's command. Seward, doubtless chortling, proceeded to issue such a countermand in his own name. As secretary of state, he of course had no place in the military chain of command and could not issue orders. When a fast tug bearing Seward's dispatch caught up with the *Powhatan* at sea, Porter naturally refused to obey it. He proceeded to Florida, Sumter fell to a confederate siege, and an emboldened South embarked on a military adventure that would become the nation's bloodiest war.

Seward, who remained Lincoln's good friend, was not permitted to involve himself officially in military business again, but the sixteenth president continued to be plagued by civilian troublemakers in his wartime administration. None was as bad, though, as Lincoln's harshminded secretary of war, Edwin M. Stanton.

Some historians contend that Stanton was aware of the John Wilkes Booth assassination plot against Lincoln and actively abetted it—removing Lincoln's trusted military guard from escort duty at Ford's Theater that night and, after the shooting, closing all the escape roads from Washington except the one Booth took. Trials and executions of the conspirators followed with great rapidity, and Stanton took extraordinary steps to keep many of the facts of the case from reaching the public. Using his place in the military chain of command, he afterward functioned as virtual dictator of the country, and was in large part responsible for the savage Reconstruction treatment of the defeated South, which kept the nation divided for so many decades thereafter, and for the attempt to remove the conciliatory Andrew Johnson from the presidency through impeachment.

In the years that followed, cabinet secretaries and other civilians involved with the military included a great many undistinguished people, but they tended to stay out of the military's way. The big trouble began with the National Security Act of 1947, which abolished the War and Navy Departments and replaced them with a vast umbrella bureaucracy called the Department of Defense, replete with separate Army, Navy, and Air Force departments and all-powerful service secretaries to lead them.

Defense never did better than when the great George C. Marshall was its secretary, but it has certainly done worse. In terms of the individual service secretaries, it has done much worse. No matter what their talents or flaws, the system itself has wreaked havoc with the American military, encouraging the interservice rivalries that have proved such a devastating factor in the decline of American defense and extending civilian authority far beyond constitutional command of the military, by sinking civilian officialdom deep into the military's innards. The system is not unlike the proliferation of political commissars throughout the Soviet Army following the Bolshevik revolution, a counterproductive arrangement that almost lost the Reds the Russian civil war, and that the Soviets subsequently abandoned. Today, the pendulum has moved to the other extreme: it is the Soviet military that has become involved in the political apparat.

In the American military, defense and individual service secretaries occupy the place in the chain of command more properly belonging to the chairman of the Joint Chiefs of Staff, and they virtually sit in the laps of the uniformed service chiefs. All too often, both defense and service secretaries come to these positions of power with very little military background. Two defense secretaries—Eisenhower's Charles Wilson and Kennedy's Robert McNamara—were auto executives. Though he had served as a Navy lieutenant in World War II, Cyrus Vance was just another New York Yale lawyer when John Kennedy made him chief counsel of the Defense Department in 1961. A year later, Vance was made secretary of the Army, a role in which he was totally overshadowed by McNamara. He then went on to serve Lyndon Johnson, as deputy secretary of defense and negotiator at the Paris peace talks on Vietnam, and Jimmy Carter as secretary of state. He resigned that post over the Desert One raid.

Another New York lawyer, Clifford Alexander, became Carter's secretary of the Army. As a black, he served an important political purpose by occupying a high-ranking sub-cabinet post. Yet he did not confine himself to any token role. Paying particular attention to the recruitment and occupational training of minority enlistees, he converted much of the Army into what critics charged was a "Job Corps with guns" and a "WPA military."

Given the size of his task—and the policies he had to implement and defend—Melvin Laird was a particularly effective defense secretary, in large part because of his long experience in Congress dealing with defense matters. So, too, was former congressman and Nixon-Ford White House operative Donald Rumsfeld, for much the same reason. The same can be said of former Georgia congressman and Ford Army secretary Bo Calloway.

John Warner came into the job of Navy secretary in the Nixon administration with the reputation of an Eastern establishment pretty boy who had married into the Mellons and functioned more as political appointee than policymaker. But when he finally managed to get himself elected to the U.S. Senate from Virginia, he proved himself one of the Republican party's more knowledgeable and effective spokesmen on defense.

Then there are defense civilians like Ronald S. Lauder, the son of cosmetics matriarch Estée Lauder, a close friend of Nancy Reagan. A

New York fund-raiser for the Republican party and the 1980 Reagan campaign, Lauder was made deputy assistant secretary of defense for NATO and Eastern Europe. He had initially been offered the ambassadorship to Jamaica, but his mother reportedly urged him to hold out for something better. "This seemed to be the right position," he said of his Pentagon job. "It has been on-the-job training, but everyone has that from the Joint Chiefs of Staff down."

As undersecretary of defense for research and engineering, secretary of the Air Force, and secretary of defense, Harold Brown was probably the most efficient, experienced, effective, and brilliant of civilian authorities in the Defense Department. Had it not been for the political compromises the Carter White House forced upon him and that administration's sorry record on defense matters, Brown might have been a figure to stand in history alongside George C. Marshall. He may yet be.

There has been no service secretary in modern times, however, to compare with the extraordinary John F. Lehman, Ronald Reagan's Navy secretary and the man who persuaded Congress to spend billions on the recommission of forty-year-old World War II battleships and aircraft carriers at the height of the worst recession since the Depression. His panache in such a usually transitory and low-profile office was best characterized by his 1983 boast that he wanted "to beat [Soviet] Admiral Gorshkov's record for longevity as head of the Navy."

Only thirty-nine when he became Reagan's Navy secretary, Lehman had begun his career on the staff of the University of Pennsylvania's Foreign Policy Research Institute. In 1969, he became special counsel and senior staff member on Kissinger's National Security Council. In the Ford administration, he served first as delegate to the Mutual Balanced Force Reduction talks in Vienna and then as deputy director of the U.S. Arms Control and Disarmament Agency.

His military experience began with an enlistment in the Air Force Reserve in 1964, but shortly afterward he received a direct commission in the Navy Reserve and eventually became a combat pilot. He left the Navy a commander, a rank he still held in the reserves as Navy secretary.

Academically, he was a match for any defense-establishment intellectual, acquiring a law degree and a master's degree in international law and diplomacy from England's Cambridge University. He also attained a Ph.D. in international relations from the University of Pennsylvania.

During the Carter administration, Lehman worked as a defense consultant and president of Abington Corporation, an arms sales operation.

In sum, he came to the Reagan administration having seen the defense establishment in all its dimensions.

As the new Navy secretary, he struck quickly and hard, accomplishing what the Navy brass had been attempting in vain for decades—the firing of the almighty Admiral Hyman Rickover, the father of the nuclear-submarine program, who had been kept on active duty by his many allies in Congress over the Navy brass' protests well into his eighties.

With the old admiral's blood on the deck, people in and out of dress whites began saluting Commander Lehman smartly. In short order came the big programs for a 600-ship fleet by 1989, the recommissioning of World War II battleships, billion-dollar cruisers and destroyers, and the Navy's own space program. He also brought several defense contractors, including the giant General Dynamics, to heel on questions of production quality by threatening to take Navy business to European firms. He was arguably a more commanding figure in the defense hierarchy than Defense Secretary Weinberger himself.

Until January 1983, that is, when LTV Corporation chairman Paul Thayer took over as deputy secretary of defense, a job to which Lehman had himself aspired. It had by then become clear that Congress was putting an end to the administration's "blank check" defense spending and that the Navy had been getting the largest share of the defense budget for too long. Army General John W. Vessey, chairman of the JCS, complained the Army had been getting too little for too long and urged some large infusions of cash to improve the flexibility and mobility of combat troops. Thayer agreed. In the Defense Resources Board meetings that summer, he argued for an $8 billion cut in Navy shipbuilding funds over five years and a $10 billion cut in naval aviation spending, with much of the savings to go to strengthening the Army. Richard DeLauer, undersecretary of defense for research and engineering, backed Thayer fully, feeling Lehman's aircraft carrier–heavy Navy was going to be too vulnerable to Soviet attack in an era when billion-dollar ships could be sunk with $200,000 missiles.

Lehman struck back with a vengeance, playing on his own connections to the White House, the Republican party, and the far-flung reaches of the defense establishment, but also hitting Capitol Hill with a lobbying campaign on behalf of his programs so fiercely one would have thought he was struggling against the Red Menace, and not his own boss. He warned Republican congressmen of dangerous "senior defense officials" in the Pentagon who were undermining American defense.

"What I am trying to do is simply counter the guerrilla warfare by these defense officials who don't seem to understand what the President's program is all about," he said.

"This place isn't big enough for both of us," Thayer told Weinberger, who had the unhappy responsibility of ending this intradepartmental civil war.

In his mild-mannered way, Weinberger rebuked Lehman for his public displays of insubordination and enforced the point that defense-budget decisions would continue to be made by the Defense Resources Board, and not by individual service secretaries. But Lehman's efforts in Congress and elsewhere worked, and when Thayer came under investigation, as yet unresolved, in late 1983 by the Securities and Exchange Commission over questions about past financial matters, he went over the side in a hurry. Lehman pushed merrily ahead with a program to build some 26 Aegis cruisers and as many as 60 Aegis destroyers—at a total cost of more than $80 billion—even though early testing showed the vessels to be highly vulnerable to wave-skimming Exocet-type missiles. Lehman became so arrogant that at a very public defense seminar in 1984, he dismissed the Air Force and Army as "garrison troops" who had only a very subordinate role compared to the nation's first line of defense, the U.S. Navy. Lehman deserves credit for rescuing the Navy, but condemnation for doing it at the expense of the rest of the American military. If the other service secretaries were as forceful, the result would have been havoc.

The extraordinary, snarling dispute between Lehman and Thayer was a painful experience for Caspar Weinberger, who had been used to dealing with his realm as head of a happy household. His appointment as secretary of defense in January 1981 serves to demonstrate the weakness of the present system as little else can.

A small, quiet-spoken Californian whose ancestry includes Jewish immigrants and who disturbed Israelis with what one called "a hang-up" about being Jewish, Weinberger was a man much taken with establishments. He went to Harvard on a scholarship, won the presidency of the prestigious *Harvard Crimson*, and graduated magna cum laude. Weinberger enlisted in World War II, won the Bronze Star in combat, and ended the war an officer on the staff of General Douglas MacArthur. He became a partner in one of California's biggest law firms and treasurer of the Episcopal archdiocese of California. He adopted the life-style and manners of an English aristocrat, having English ancestors as well.

Though he served Governor Reagan as state finance director between

1968 and 1970, he was, like most establishment Republicans, rather a moderate. He had a moderate record as a state legislator from 1952 to 1958 and as chairman of the California Republican Central Committee. He was an active member of the same Trilateral Commission that the right-wing radicals used to bludgeon George Bush with in the 1980 New Hampshire primary.

In the Nixon administration, he was an inoffensive chairman of the Federal Trade Commission and a moderate secretary of health, education, and welfare. Given a much different brief as deputy director and then director of the Office of Management and Budget, he acquired the nickname "Cap the Knife," a hard man on waste in government.

But as secretary of defense, he quickly became known as "Cap the Ladle." The generals and Dr. Strangeloves quickly convinced him of the Soviet threat, which is quite real, and the need for a Pentagon high-tech weapons program for dealing with it, which is bizarrely unreal. Without hesitation, he bought both. After a number of Pentagon briefings, he said:

> I was astounded. Their buildup had gone so far and so fast and all of it was in offensive, not defensive, weapons. . . . It was like running down a hill trying to catch up with a long, long runaway train. You come into this office and on your first day you find your in-basket full of decisions you have to make today. And, on top of this, you have to impose a new long-range policy, and people won't listen to you.

Such prestigious defense experts as Dr. William Kaufmann of MIT complained that, instead of making hard decisions, Weinberger simply "stapled together all the budget requests" of the individual services. Whatever they wanted just had to be vital for national defense.

When Congress began to get restless about the unquestioned amounts of Reagan defense spending in early 1983, Weinberger dug in his heels, insisting on everything the administration had asked for.

> I can cut this budget easily. I can decommission two divisions. I can wipe out two aircraft carriers. It's easy to cut the defense budget. But when the time comes when we need them, it will cost us a lot more. . . . You're making a terrible mistake if you try to adjust your defense budget to food stamps, harbor dredging, and highways. It's the threat that makes the budget. You've got to build your budget on the Russian budget.

But war is not won with budgets; it's won with weapons, machines, systems, strategy, tactics, and combat techniques and manpower deployment that work. Weinberger took the word of everyone in the Pentagon who claimed that the trillions could translate into things that worked. Hence his acceptance of the proposal that the MX missile be hung from balloons or aircraft. Often during Weinberger's tenure at Defense, the flow of authority in the chain of command seemed to go backward.

His adoration for the military began during World War II. Having been rejected for pilot training because of poor depth perception, Weinberger enlisted as a private, but managed to get sent to Officers Candidate School at Fort Benning. By war's end, he had won a Bronze Star in the Pacific and been promoted to captain. Like most on the staff, he was devoted to Douglas MacArthur.

President Eisenhower, however, was not devoted to General MacArthur. Eisenhower, who knew the military inside and out, never once tolerated the kind of excesses that have characterized presidential command of the military under his successors. He was able to make his "military-industrial complex" speech without any qualms about injuring national security. Eisenhower would not have had a Caspar Weinberger as his secretary of defense.

According to Air Force Chief of Staff General Charles Gabriel, in recent years it's been the civilians in the military high command who've been the most hawkish.

"I think you'll find today in all the war games we run, that the military are by far the more cautious of any of the players," he said. "The civilians are more aggressive than the military when it comes to playing a scenario involving escalation."

As the president has many other things to do than serve as commander in chief of the American military, the position of secretary of defense is not one to be eliminated. But, as shall be outlined in later chapters, there are steps that can be taken to improve its function as the bridge between military-policy formulation and execution.

Before anything else, however, the civilian posts of secretary of the Army, Navy, and Air Force should be abolished, and their civilian bureaucracies removed from the innards of the individual services. The positions should be reestablished as part of the overall Department of Defense civilian administration, principally with a liaison function. New job descriptions as undersecretaries of defense for the Army, Navy, and Air Force could be established, serving directly under the secretary and deputy secretary as civilian lieutenants. In their liaison role, they would share the same rank as the undersecretaries for policy and research and engineering. The days of service-secretary warlords such as Reagan's irrepressible John Lehman would be ended.

Former Defense Secretary Brown said of abolishing such posts, "I think it might well make sense as part of a larger package of change."

Perhaps nothing described the problems and dangers of Pentagon empire building and interservice rivalries so well as a letter written by President Eisenhower to Everett Hazlett, a close friend, in 1956. In it, he said:

> My most frustrating domestic problem is that of attempting to achieve any real coordination among the Services. Time and again I have had the high Defense officials in conference—with all the senior military and their civilian bosses present—and have achieved what has seemed to me general agreement on policy and function— but there always came the breakup. The kindest interpretation that can be put on some of these developments is that each service is so utterly confident that it alone can assure the nation's security, that it feels justified in going before the Congress or the public and urging fantastic programs. . . .
>
> I patiently explain over and over again that American strength is a combination of its economic, moral and military force. If we demand too much in taxes in order to build planes and ships, we will tend to dry up the accumulations of capital that are necessary to provide jobs for the million or more new workers that we must absorb each year. . . .
>
> Based on this kind of thinking, [the Chiefs] habitually, when with me, give the impression that they are going to work out arrangements that will keep the military appropriations within manageable proportions and do it in a spirit of good will and of give and take.
>
> Yet when each Service puts down its minimum requirements for its own military budget for the following year, and I add up the total, I find that they mount at a fantastic rate. There is seem- ingly no end to all of this. Yet merely "getting tough" on my part is not an answer. I simply must find men who have the breadth of understanding and devotion to their country rather than to a single Service that will bring about better solutions than I get now. . . .
>
> I do not maintain that putting all these people in one uniform would cure this difficulty—at least not quickly. But some day there is going to be a man sitting in my present chair who has not been raised in the military services and who will have little understanding of where slashes in their estimates can be made with little or no damage. If that should happen while we still have the state of tension that now exists in the world, I shudder to think of what could happen to this country.

chapter seven

THE HILL

A little group of willful men, representing no opinion but their own, have rendered the great Government of the United States helpless and contemptible.
—PRESIDENT WOODROW WILSON, COMMENTING ON A FILIBUSTER WAGED BY ELEVEN SENATORS AGAINST A BILL TO ARM AMERICAN MERCHANT VESSELS IN 1917

The major share of military decision-making power in the United States is not located in the Oval Office or the White House Situation Room, where Reagan listened as his troops used filling-station road maps to seek out their foes on the tiny island of Grenada. Nor is it concentrated in the Pentagon war room. The real military power center is located sixteen blocks to the east of the Executive Mansion, on Capitol Hill.

In the absence of an all-out war when only he can push the dreaded button, the president's every move—from buying foot powder for the infantry to deploying a new generation of nuclear weaponry—must be approved by the warlords of Congress. Even when troops are going into action, the chief executive must cope with the often paralyzing participation of the people's representatives. The Congress is a sticky web through which the commander in chief must reach even when dealing with his generals, and vice versa. As every new president learns, little if anything can be done from 1600 Pennsylvania Avenue without the advice and consent of the real commander in chief, the chairmen of the eight powerful committees: the Senate Armed Services, Appropriations, and Foreign Relations committees; the House Armed Services, Foreign Affairs, and Appropriations committees; plus the Select Committees on Intelligence of both.

These power centers operate in Capitol Hill marbled palaces far grander than anything else in the government—massive office buildings, including three named for the most powerful of the warlords in recent memory: Senator Richard Russell of Georgia, Senator Everett Dirksen of Illinois, and House Speaker Sam Rayburn of Texas, all masterful teachers of presidential humility. Adding to the congressional grip is the expansive network of subcommittees, frequently chaired by men and women emboldened by the Vietnam experience to demonstrate their idea of the limits of presidential authority. There are also a significant number of individual senators and congressmen who do not chair committees or subcommittees but have learned how to attract and manipulate media attention and focus public opinion on an issue.

Presidents can start wars and Pentagon generals can order weapons systems, but they can do so only with the permission of Congress, which frequently doesn't give it or foists some idea of its own upon the military process instead.

Some 150 men and women members of Congress wield specific power over the military on these committees and subcommittees. They are backed up by "professional staffs" totalling more than 350. These staff people are employed as personal representatives of each of the committee members. Their duties include safeguarding the political fortunes of their bosses on military issues and dealing with the complex paperwork required of all congressional committees.

Too often, the staff have even fewer credentials than their bosses for comprehending the highly technical and intimidating details of military policy and procurement. If they are competent, they are fearful to express their views. Most understand that their continued employment is a function of how well they press at staff meetings for such interests of their congressional employer as more military business for the defense contractors in the home state or district. They serve at the pleasure of some of the most self-obsessed and tyrannical bosses in the world. By act of Congress, there is no civil-service protection on Capitol Hill. The "professional staff" aide who dares to tell his or her master that his or her latest idea for a new military base in a home county is cockamamie faces a swift fall of the ax.

Some of the mighty are mightier than others. Senator John Tower, as chairman of Senate Armed Services, was so powerful that his reach extended into the footlockers at Annapolis. Tower, a petty officer in the Naval Reserve and for years the only enlisted reservist in the Congress, received a letter from a Texas midshipman at the naval academy who had been told his off-duty cowboy boots were "inappropriate civilian attire" and not to be worn on the academy's sacred grounds. Chief Petty Officer Tower, a diminutive man known for shiny suits and old-fashioned celluloid collars, had worn cowboy boots on shipboard during World War II in the fighting for Saipan. He wrote a very pointed note to the admiral commanding Annapolis, reminding him that the commander in chief of all the United States's armed forces at the time, Ronald Reagan, wore cowboy boots when he was off duty, and sometimes when he was on duty. The admiral immediately relented. The midshipman was permitted to keep his boots, provided he kept them properly shined.

Congress lacks no access to knowledge. Four-star generals, admirals, and service secretaries are constantly being summoned to the Hill to give humble testimony before committees. As Chief of Naval Operations Admiral James Watkins noted to one congressional panel, "In this calendar year, my staff has prepared and submitted to Congress more than 2,900 responses to requests for information, provided 245 briefings, and submitted in excess of 4,500 responses to questions for the record that emanated out of 110 hearings."

In addition to the eight aforementioned committees, the American military also must report to the government operations committees of both houses and Congress's Military Reform Caucus, which began scheduling private and public hearings in 1981.

God sees every sparrow fall. The Congress has its eye on the military's every bullet, canteen cap, and ladle of creamed chipped beef. Whether it's to alter America's nuclear-defense strategy or to change the style of combat boots, Congress can reach into every nook, cranny, and secret war room of the military and work its will. Consequently, everyone with an interest in affecting military policy works through Congress. The White House does it. Foreign governments attempting to interfere with U.S. military policy, including the Russians (whose agents frequently sit in on committee hearings and have been known to ask for copies of congressional reports under the Freedom of Information Act) do it as well. The defense industry pulls the levers and limbs of Congress shamelessly. So does the American military itself.

The Defense Department has 265 people ranking from generals and admirals down to Coast Guardsmen and civilian aides working the Hill, about one "liaison" for every two members of Congress. These usually uniformed lobbyists are more than willing to provide advice and other assistance to the ill-equipped committee staffs. The military liaison operations are, of course, financed by the annual Pentagon budget approved by Congress.

A number of members of Congress are military men themselves. Senate war heroes Robert Dole and Daniel Inouye receive Army pensions. Senator Barry Goldwater is a pensioned Air Force general. Senator Jeremiah Denton, the famous Vietnam War Navy POW, and Senator John Glenn, the Marine colonel turned astronaut, serve in Congress as retired fliers. Even the patrician Senator Claiborne Pell receives a pension from the Coast Guard.

Many more are active in the reserves. When Senator Gary Hart first began pondering a run for the presidency, he discreetly made a point of joining the Navy Reserve as a lieutenant j.g. at the age of forty-three, though he declined to get a regulation haircut. He had wanted to be made a full commander, but was turned down. The closest he had to previous military experience was running Senator George McGovern's antiwar presidential campaign in 1972. Hart went on to become a forceful advocate of such controversial proposals as building a large force of small aircraft carriers.

Military people even become members of congressional staffs themselves. When Senator Roger Jepsen was chairman of the Senate Armed Services Committee subcommittee on manpower and personnel, he was roundly criticized in 1983 when it was discovered he had an active-duty Marine colonel on his senatorial staff handling home-state military pork-barrel projects. Colonel Dennis Sharon retired from the Air Force Capitol Hill liaison office to become Goldwater's "special assistant." While still in uniform, Colonel Sharon had frequently accompanied the senator on trips back to Arizona aboard Air Force planes to inspect military facilities and perform other missions. The flights also conveniently gave the senator a free ride home—though sometimes he did the flying himself.

It was the anguish over the Vietnam War that provided the impetus and leverage for Congress to assert itself. Its members have not relented since. The War Powers Act of 1974 gave Congress virtual veto power over any presidential decision to send troops into action. New congressional committees were formed with sweeping powers over the CIA and other intelligence agencies that had been used in the past to wage "secret wars" for presidents. Subcommittees acquired their own staffs and subpoena powers to the point where they rivaled full committees. And a swarm of ambitious and politically adept junior members seized much of the power that had traditionally been wielded only by the most senior members of the "world's most exclusive club."

The net effect of this has sometimes been beneficial, as when President Carter was persuaded to rescind his hasty and near disastrous decision to pull American combat troops out of South Korea. Congress also stayed the hand of Henry Kissinger, who was moving us toward involvement in the Angolan civil war—an action the American people would not then have tolerated. This all-powerful Congress does provide a measurement of what the military high command has learned to insist a president must have before undertaking a military adventure—public support. But it has also imposed an almost automatic paralysis on American military-policy initiatives, which screech to a halt because of the collision of opposing ideological interests, or because of congressional political acumen.

Because of the American public's distaste for the El Salvadoran government's past bloody-minded and bloody-handed methods and fears of another Vietnam, Congress was fearful of letting the Reagan administration expand American involvement in the brutal civil war in El Salvador. Yet it was also leery of ending American commitment and withdrawing American personnel from that country because it might be blamed for any subsequent deterioration in the situation there or damage to American interests.

So it tried to take a safe middle ground, by allowing the presence of American military advisors but limiting their number to a precise 55. Clearly, more were needed if the feckless El Salvadoran army was to be whipped into adequate shape for the task before it. Congress kept the United States committed to the administration's policy goal, but deprived it of the means to achieve it. The same "beached whale" syndrome obtained with Congress's response to administration initiatives in Lebanon. Vice-President George Bush said:

> I have been concerned about the proliferation of emerging secretaries of state. There's an awful lot of people who focus on a specific area or concern, who do not have to be burdened as the President is with broader concerns . . . and will be able to set a major foreign-policy direction out of a subcommittee. You might say that's a prerogative of Congress. But the prerogative of setting foreign policy is really the President's under the Constitution, and the Congress should be controlling the funds and all of that.
>
> I'm somewhat disturbed by it. Everybody when they get to this side of the fence longs for the old bipartisan days. Well, our hands aren't clean. We weren't totally bipartisan when we were against SALT II, so I don't think it's fair to say that anybody who differs with us is something less than, you know, playing by the rules, but I must say, there seems to me an increasing amount of . . . incidents where a subcommittee chairman will make a major policy pronouncement, through controlling funds or putting demands on funding, so you can't do it the way the administration wants.

The problem is not simply one of partisanship. During a crucial vote on the Reagan administration's 1983 Turkish aid bill, Republican Senator Larry Pressler not only walked out of the committee meeting, but he left his proxy with Democrat Paul Sarbanes of Maryland.

"I didn't like it a bit," Bush said. "Has the man a right to do it? Sure, he's got a right to do that. But that gets into a whole other question about some degree of fidelity to your own president and helping him accomplish his ends as he was elected to do."

Before the Vietnam revolt, congressional authority over military matters was the province of a relative handful of crusty and autocratic committee chairmen—elderly men who had risen through a seniority system based on the idea that a lifetime of loyalty to the top dogs would ultimately be rewarded, if not with the chairmanship itself, at least with generosity on military contracts and other political largesse.

Those almighty curmudgeons included such legends as Senator Allen J. Ellender, who served as Appropriations chairman until he was well into his eighties; Representative F. Edward Herbert, another Louisiana Democrat who controlled the House Armed Services Committee until he was seventy-four; and Senator John O. Stennis, who was dislodged as chairman of the Senate Armed Services Committee at age seventy-nine, but only because the Republicans, somewhat tenuously, won the Senate. Stennis remained the committee's ranking Democrat. Representative Mendel Rivers was so outrageously flagrant with his penchant for costly junkets and pork-barrel generosity to friends and allies that he became one of the major preoccupations of muckraking Washington columnist Drew Pearson. But he survived.

Such autocrats held such vast power for so long because they sat atop a still extant system dictated by the Constitution, in which two separate sets of legislation are required for every weapon the military buys, every base it opens or closes, and every armed expedition it sends abroad. Before anything else, the armed services committees of both houses must pass "defense authorization" bills, specifying which items may be purchased and which military operations launched. Then, to obtain the money necessary for such projects, the companion appropriations committees in both the Senate and House must "obligate" funds. The appropriations panels may not add any programs but they may vote to deny money, thereby killing procurement projects, diplomatic initiatives, and even troop movements. The president and the Defense Department are forbidden by statute to initiate any unauthorized program or to continue one once it has lapsed.

For decades the seniority system assured that the four men who rose to the chairmanships of these panels would be the equal of presidents on military matters. But, beginning in the mid-1970s, a number of lesser figures started to muscle in. Representative Joseph Addabbo, chairman of the military subcommittee of House Appropriations, defied his chairman, Representative Jamie Whitten, and pressed to kill numerous weapons projects Whitten supported. In the Senate, appropriations military subcommittee chairman Ted Stevens took away prerogatives from Appropriations Chairman Mark Hatfield that such predecessors as Ellender would have commanded without question.

When the Ninety-eighth Congress convened in January 1983, things really got scary for the Old Guard. Two congressmen the military considered dangerous pests, Representatives Les Aspin and Ronald Dellums, achieved enough seniority to become eligible for subcommittee chairmanships—Aspin that of oversights and investigations, which has the power to haul generals and admirals in the dock to explain 1,000 percent cost overruns, and Dellums the subcommittee on personnel.

Aspin had been harassing Pentagon brass for years and his staff was largely responsible for exposing the scandalous cost overruns of the C-5A jumbo transport and the Trident submarine. Dellums, an active member of the congressional black caucus and an unapologetic liberal, was an outspoken nuclear-freeze advocate and keenly interested in Pentagon racial policies.

The Old Guard managed to head them off by employing a cloakroom maneuver. Two of the most senior members of House Appropriations, Representatives Samuel Stratton, sixty-eight, and Charles Bennett, seventy-two, suddenly announced they would both compete for Stratton's all-powerful military procurement subcommittee chairmanship, thus keeping the relatively young Aspin from being considered for the job. Stratton retained the procurement post by a vote of 16 to 13, and Bennett was placed in charge of the coveted seapower subcommittee. Aspin ended up with the personnel chair instead of Dellums, a black. Dellums found himself in charge of military bases.

After the November 1984 elections came a day that had the Pentagon rocking on its very foundations. House Democrats, finally ready to fight the administration's gargantuan defense spending, overruled Speaker Tip O'Neill and voted to dump aging House Armed Services Chairman Melvin Price and replace him with Aspin! Generals turned the color of their uniforms.

A revolution born of Vietnam and the Watergate scandal led to members of Congress assuming an unprecedented role in the exercise of American power abroad. In blocking American involvement in Angola in 1976, Senator Dick Clark was the first to make real use of the War Powers Act, a Vietnam-inspired reform requiring the president to notify members of Congress when even one American soldier is sent into hostile situations and to remove American forces from any such situation in sixty to ninety days, unless the Congress gives its approval.

The congressional reach is just as strong from the right. American military commitments to South Korea and Taiwan were kept strong through the efforts of Representative Edward Derwinski and a few other Republicans, despite the Carter administration's ardent desire to change policy. As a ranking member of the Senate Foreign Relations Committee, Senator Jesse Helms worked at subverting Democratic administration policy all over the globe, with particular attention to southern Africa. His operatives came close to upsetting the Carter-supported British settlement of the Rhodesian struggle by exhorting white leader Ian Smith not to make concessions.

In 1974, after Turkey invaded Cyprus, Congress embargoed arms shipments to the Turks, notwithstanding their crucial status as "the right flank of NATO" and protests from the State Department that the embargo ran counter to existing diplomatic strategy. Also in 1974, Congress passed the Nelson-Bingham Amendment, which gave it the power to veto all but the smallest of arms sales abroad. The Hughes-Ryan Amendment subsequently required presidents to notify several committee and subcommittee chairmen of all covert activities by organizations like the CIA.

In 1976, Congress passed legislation sponsored by Senator Clark that prohibited American involvement in Angola. The 1978 Nuclear Non-Proliferation Act restricted the export of nuclear weapons and materials. Congress also has imposed restrictions on military aid to more than thirty countries and voted bans on assistance to any nation that expropriated United States property, gave refuge to terrorists, violated human rights, and neglected to pay United Nations dues (although the United States itself was later to withhold portions of its contribution to protest U.N. actions it didn't like).

In 1982, when the United States sent arms and advisors to anti-Sandinista guerrillas operating from Honduras and Costa Rica as a means of interdicting Nicaraguan military supplies to leftist guerrillas in El Salvador, Congress responded to this "secret war" with a "secret amendment." Sponsored by Representative Edward Boland, it forbade the Reagan administration to sponsor any such military activity designed to overthrow the Sandinista government of Nicaragua.

After CIA Director William Casey blew the cover on the "secret war" by inviting *New York Times* reporter Philip Taubman out to CIA headquarters at Langley to reveal that the United States was after Nicaraguan supplies to El Salvador, though certainly not attempting to overthrow the Nicaraguan government, Boland made his "secret amendment" very public and the administration was called on the congressional carpet.

Casey had been compelled to make his spy agency's private war public in an administration effort to circumvent the restrictions placed on the White House by Boland, calculating that the *New York Times* interview with Casey would serve later as evidence that the United States had not plotted to overthrow the Sandinistas.

For whatever the purpose, it's clearly a problem when a senator or congressman elected by a relatively small fraction of Americans is able to hobble or dictate to a president who has constitutional charge of national security and who was elected from a broad national base. But it cannot be entirely rectified without sweeping changes that would be difficult to enact or in violation of the constitution. Congress remains the body through which the American public can best keep control of its military. Severe restraints upon Congress's constitutional powers to impose checks and balances would hamper its many good offices and efforts, such as when it slowed the Reagan-Weinberger spending binge, kept national attention and concern focused on the misuse of Marines in Lebanon, and provided valuable public forums for whistle-blowers and military reformers. The dangerously poor levels of combat readiness that persisted in all the services despite four years of record defense-spending increases under Reagan were brought to the public's attention by Congress, not by the Pentagon.

But Congress must be made more accountable and responsible in making defense decisions, and that means strengthening its leadership and decreasing the number of members directly involved with those defense decisions.

The reforms that swept Capitol Hill after Watergate and Vietnam have actually reformed little. The seniority system and other autocratic institutions were weakened as subcommittees were strengthened. But this did not diminish the power of the old congressional bosses so much as it created a plethora of new bosses. The new power structure provided fertile ground for opportunists, more concerned with their own interests than those of the nation. Congress needs a recaucusing, restoring authority over defense matters to those who should be held the most accountable—the Speaker of the House, the Senate majority leader, and the full Armed Services and Appropriations committees.

House and Senate staff, who do most of the work and lay nearly all the groundwork for congressional defense decisions, have improved in recent years but need to be improved much more. If every staff member were of the caliber of Representative Aspin's Warren Nelson on the Democratic side or Representative Denny Smith's John Heubush on the Republican, defense policy and procurement decisions would be much more intelligent, pragmatic, and principled. A staff member surely should be required to have academic and professional credentials beyond the raw clout of their sponsors.

But whatever might be done to restore more rational balance to the policy-making power structure, an equally grave problem must be addressed. Congress's tightest stranglehold on the military is not on security policy but on the procurement and appropriations process. While a handful of congressmen and senators pursue ideological or philosophical beliefs for some pet corner of the world or another, most of their peers are far more interested in what the military establishment can bring to their home states and districts in the form of defense contracts. The Appropriations and Armed Services committee chairmen and the rising stars in the subcommittee chairs constitute one leg of what defense analyst Gordon Adams calls the "Iron Triangle," a nexus of Congress, the Pentagon (and its White House leadership), and the corporations and contractors referred to by President Eisenhower in his "military-industrial complex" speech.

Longevity makes the congressional leg the strongest. The five senior members of the Senate Armed Services Committee in the first Reagan administration had been on the panel during the Kennedy administration. All had long been friends of the Pentagon. Aside from Tower and the aging Goldwater, they were the septuagenarian Strom Thurmond, the late Henry Jackson, who died in 1983, and the elderly Stennis. House Armed Services Chairman Melvin Price was first elected to Congress in 1943 while on active duty as a soldier. It was not until the Ford administration that he became committee chairman. In an era when the last president to complete a full eight-year term was Eisenhower, the staying power of such congressional leaders has become particularly significant.

It takes years and years to design, manufacture, and deploy weapons systems. A president might produce legislation to build an aircraft carrier or new bomber, but he might well be dead or long retired before the ship ever sails or the airplane flies its first training mission. It takes at least eight years to build and float an aircraft carrier; a decade to produce a new bomber. When President Reagan commissioned the carrier USS *Vinson* in 1982, he was adding a ship to the fleet that had been budgeted during the Nixon administration.

While the president is certain to be long gone before one of his major weapons projects is ever completed, chances are good that the congressional committee members who approved it will almost all still be there. Chances are also good that a "dove" president like Jimmy Carter who persuades Congress to agree to his killing of a costly weapons program will watch from retirement as the same Congress reinstates the program.

The $40 billion B-1 bomber proposal that Carter canceled was brought back four years later as one of the top priorities of the Reagan administration, and at a far higher price. The two committee chairmen involved, Stennis in the Senate and Price in the House, had simply stuck away some money from Carter's budgets to continue research and development on the B-1. Then they waited for their good friend and ally, time, to remove Carter. Meanwhile, the R & D money allowed the B-1s prime contractor, Rockwell International Corporation, to keep its engineers and factory workers on hand in the expectation that Carter would go the way of most contemporary presidents. As a result of refinements produced by that R & D, and because of inflation, the resurrected "B-1-B" cost more than $200 billion instead of the Carter-era estimate of $40 billion.

Analysts have been warning for several years now that the exercise of such staying power in Congress was responsible for both gargantuan cost overruns and the fact that American defense was producing ever smaller numbers of weapons for more and more money. A major cause of these high costs is the discovery by defense contractors that they can get far better results by lobbying in Congress than by submitting bids to whatever administration is in power. Congressional leaders have encouraged this end-run strategy by passing legislation to allow contractors to include "congressional liaison"—i.e., lobbying—costs in the price of contracts. In 1984, one Defense Contract Audit Agency study found that twenty-eight defense contractors had billed the taxpayers $1.5 million for expense-account lunches, parties, advertising, and even art exhibits.

Senator William Roth documented in a 1983 study that in the Reagan administration's rearm America program 70 percent of all contracts were being approved by Congress on a "sole source" basis, in which no competing bids were sought or received. Nuclear submarines, guided missiles, metal mess-hall trays, jet fighters, and flashlights alike were all supplied by single companies that set the price without fear of being underbid by more competitive rivals. In each case, the Pentagon simply awarded contracts and sent the bills to Congress for approval, which was usually forthcoming. Meanwhile, the companies were able to raise their prices in later years with certain prospect of little or no complaint. This lack of competitiveness is the major reason that the defense industry has atrophied so alarmingly in recent years. For example, by 1980, there was just one manufacturer of a basic fighter-aircraft landing gear in the country and only two of vital ball bearings for military aircraft.

A senator with hawkish views and constituencies, like Texas's Tower, can press for all the big arms deals he likes and please the folks in Dallas–Fort Worth. Meanwhile, Hatfield can play to his dovish constituents in Oregon by complaining about military cost overruns—but he abides by a rule of the club in not blaming the problem specifically on Tower and by a rule of political survival by not voting against any major contracts headed for his state.

When the big push came for holding back defense spending levels in early 1983, with a major recession on and deficits reaching $200 billion, Tower counterattacked with a "dear colleague" letter that asked all senators, but most especially the outspoken doves, to "volunteer" defense projects in their own states that should be cut from the budget.

He received just one immediate response, from David Pryor of Arkansas, who for years had been trying to get a $158 million chemical-warfare weapons operation out of his state and had urged abolishing all chemical weapons entirely.Tower had written to his colleagues:

> It has never ceased to amaze me that the same senators who stand on the floor and argue against [defense] increases are just as likely to call me aside and ask my personal support for projects or programs of interest in their states. In my twenty-two years in the Senate, I do not recall any senator ever volunteering a budget reduction in his state.

There is, in fact, little to be gained and much to be lost by making an enemy of a Tower or Price or Goldwater. The lawmaker who would rage on about defense cost overruns also knows that they take place only after a majority of Congress approves them. So instead, he is likely to lay the blame at the door of the faceless bureaucrats at the Pentagon.

Jacques Gansler, a former deputy assistant defense secretary for weapons acquisition and now a paid government consultant, feels strongly that the "sole source" contract and pervasive overruns significantly weaken the American military. "Well over 90 percent of defense contract dollars are not awarded on the basis of price competition or in the presence of any incentives that would drive down the costs," he said. "The result is that equipment costs rise continuously, significantly above the rate attributable to inflation." At the same time, he said, the number of planes, ships, and other equipment acquired decreases dramatically, leaving the country with a smaller arsenal of weapons.

Some members of Congress have howled about the bidless bounty, but never has the biblical injunction about being without sin before throwing the first stone been more applicable. For example, the Senate's leading liberal, Edward Kennedy of Massachusetts, has proved loath to attack the bidless contracts delivered to the Boston Navy Yard. California Democrat Allan Cranston, who opened his presidential campaign in 1983 with a call for nuclear disarmament, was curiously silent when his home state's Rockwell International won a long series of contracts for the B-1 bomber and the space shuttle, both part of strategic weapons programs, without an opposing bid in sight.

One of the more dramatic examples of this phenomenon occurred when then-Representative Bella Abzug, an outspoken opponent of defense spending, and a large group of fellow liberals came out strongly in favor of an amendment to forbid the Pentagon from shutting down any military base in the country. The installations Abzug fought for included New York's vital Watervliet Arsenal and Fort Drumm.

She and the others found themselves opposed by the equally liberal Aspin, whose home district's lack of defense industries has allowed him to become a leading critic of Pentagon spending and a not always beloved member of the club.

Pentagon whistle-blower A. Ernest Fitzgerald calls this syndrome "space age feudalism." He has become a folk hero to the legions of Defense Department critics who have argued from both the left and the right that Pentagon spending is wildly out of control. Fitzgerald, a silver-haired Southerner with a gift of phrase, first came to national prominence in 1968, when, as an official Air Force spokesman, he defied the Nixon administration by appearing at a televised hearing chaired by Senator William Proxmire and admitting that the Air Force had underestimated the cost of its new gigantic C-5A cargo and troop-transport jet by 50 percent. Nixon declared, "I want that sonofabitch fired." A decade later, after making a national issue of protecting those in government who come forward with details of fraud, waste, and other abuse, Fitzgerald was finally reinstated in his Pentagon job during the Reagan administration. He was almost immediately embroiled in controversy, this time over whether the government should buy fifty C-5B cargo jets. This contretemps proved to be one of the most surprising chapters in the history of defense procurement.

In the summer of 1982, two of America's defense giants—the Boeing Company and Lockheed Corporation—broke the cardinal rule of the Iron Triangle: they engaged in direct, cutthroat competition for the same contract. This was not, however, a textbook capitalist battle of two sellers trying to undercut the other's prices. It was a Machiavellian struggle in the corridors of the Capitol between lawmakers with big Boeing operations at home in states like Kansas and Washington and those from states like Georgia and California, where Lockheed held sway. At stake was a whopping $10 billion contract for fifty or more giant transport planes needed for the ambitious new plan to create a Rapid Deployment Force (RDF), for what Marine General Paul Xavier "PX" Kelley called "forcible insertion" of U.S. troops in the far-flung theaters in the Mideast and Southeast Asia.

Boeing was first to break the covenant against competition. The giant airplane manufacturer had six unsold 747 jumbo jets sitting in hangars in Everett, Washington, and elsewhere, with dismal prospects for airline customers in a worldwide recession. Worse, Braniff Airlines had just gone bankrupt, dumping 747s and other big jets on the market at cut-rate prices.

Boeing's boasts of big expected profits from its new 757 and 767 wide-bodied smaller jets had proved empty. The heavily subsidized European Airbus was muscling into this market. Desperate, Boeing, maker of AWACS radar planes, nuclear cruise missiles, airborne-refueling tanker planes, as well as most of the U.S. commercial air fleet, decided to go after the "forcible insertion" contract with a vengeance.

Originally, the Air Force and, more important, the Army, had wanted to buy the McDonnell-Douglas C-17, a smaller jumbo that could jet troops and materiel close up to any action the RDF might encounter. By the time Boeing decided to push its way into the act, the Air Force had switched to Lockheed's C-5B, persuaded finally that bigger was better. Although not convinced of this, the Army went along with the Air Force meekly, as it often does in aircraft matters. Boeing could point out that the 747 had originally been designed in the 1960s, with Air Force research and development funds, as a military cargo aircraft. When the Pentagon had bought the early-model Lockheed C-5A instead, Boeing had converted the 747 into a civilian aircraft.

But what mattered was not so much Boeing's argument as the man they brought forth to make it, Henry "Scoop" Jackson, known for two decades as "the senator from Boeing." During two losing presidential campaigns, in 1972 and 1976, Jackson and his partisans had bristled at the sobriquet and left it to his fellow lawmakers from Washington State to press for military projects. But with Boeing on the ropes and the White House the most distant of prospects for Jackson, the aging senator baldly approached his Senate colleagues with a plan to shove Lockheed aside. Other members from states with a stake in the outcome joined the Jackson effort, including Nancy Kassebaum of Kansas, well aware of Boeing's big factories near Wichita, and both Missouri senators, Democrat Thomas Eagleton and Republican John Danforth. The Missourians were bitter because of the Air Force's decision to buy C-5s instead of their state's McDonnell-Douglas C-17s. Jackson found another ally in Wisconsin's William Proxmire, who appreciated the apparent cost savings the 747 represented.

Supplied by Boeing's formidable Washington, D.C., lobbying office with convincing four-color charts, computer printouts, and slide shows depicting the C-5A's horrendous cost growth, the Jackson group quickly began to win support in the Senate, showing also that 747 production lines were still open and functioning while Lockheed hadn't turned out a C-5 since the early 1970s. The Boeing persuaders reminded colleagues that Lockheed had billed the government $2 billion more than they had promised to for the C-5, and that another $1.2 billion had to be spent fixing the aircraft's weak wings. Experts testified that nearly every airport in the world had built facilities to handle 747s, while C-5s could use only a few dozen specially adapted military facilities. They pleaded that the 747 would be a boon to ailing domestic airlines who could sell their spare 747s to the government for RDF conversion and receive a vital infusion of cash. Best of all, the Pentagon could buy the 747s it would need for $5.5 billion, half what it would pay for C-5s under the military procurement system. Because of rigid military specifications written into the C-5 contracts, the government was being charged $1 each for rivets that on a civilian plane cost 5 cents.

Jackson began pushing his Boeing deal in March 1982 and by May had won Senate approval. But Lockheed was weighing in with massive retaliation, its arm-twisting arsenal including a team of uniformed Air Force lobbyists. These "blue suits" were led by Major General Guy Hecker, a trim, glib public relations expert who had won his second star selling the MX missile. He had spent some two years living in Holiday Inns in Nevada and Utah as he appeared at public hearings called "scoping sessions" in which he attempted to sell locals on the idea of having 4,600 Soviet ICBMs targeted on missile holes near their farms and ranches. He was more persuasive than Air Force Chief of Staff Lew Allen, who told the locals they were to serve as a "nuclear sponge" to soak up Russian warheads, but not persuasive enough.

On the hill, Hecker, Lockheed, and the Air Force were more than persuasive. Their methods in winning the day for the C-5B after all were not the stuff that usually sees the public print, but details were provided to influential members of the press by a group of defense establishment insiders known by friend and foe alike as the "reformers."

One was Dina Rasor, head of a reform group called the Project on Military Procurement, a frequent conduit between the reformers and the news media, who called a handful of reporters and offered them a computer printout removed from a Pentagon office where Hecker, other Air Force brass, and Lockheed officials had planned and carried out a lobbying blitz that beat the veteran Boeing advocates at their own game. Her fan-folded computer sheets were a textbook of pork-barrel politics at their ultimate.

At Hecker's urging, Lockheed went to work in those congressional districts throughout the country where Lockheed had subcontractors for its many arms projects and recruited these companies to pressure their local congressmen in favor of the C-5B. The printout noted delightfully that there were forty subcontractors in particular who could call in important IOUs. The computer sheets, labeled "action plan," listed businesses in 260 of the 435 House districts that could lose money and jobs if Boeing won instead of Lockheed.

The biggest of these was General Electric (GE), which was to make the engines for the C-5. GE lobbyists put the arm on sixty lawmakers from such major states as Massachusetts, Florida, and New York, where it had major operations. Colt Industries was assigned to go after forty-six congressmen. Air Force base commanders around the country, themselves big local employers, were also pressed into service. The computer printout assigned the commander of Altus Air Force Base in Oklahoma, for example, to contact the local congressman, Dave McCurdy. The Lockheed/Air Force team even pressed the firm's insurance broker, Marsh and McLennan, to have its employees and executives call up House members on behalf of the C-5B.

In the Senate, Sam Nunn, a bright and relatively young hawk who ironically had risen to power on the Armed Services Committee as a protégé of Jackson's, quickly became known as "the senator from Lockheed." He prepared the groundwork for the effort on the Senate side of the Capitol that would be needed once the House voted for the C-5 and threw the final decision into a House-Senate conference committee.

How could the Air Force and a congressional majority go against a faithful member of the club like Boeing when it was making the least expensive offer? Spokesmen for both the Air Force and Lockheed said they felt they were particularly convincing in arguing that the 747 could not carry the outsized loads the C-5 could, including entire asphalt factories, bakeries, and other major facilities a full-scale army might need in the field.

Rasor, speaking for many of the reformers, also noted that Boeing had broken the rules of the club by going after a contract out of turn.

Indeed, Lockheed's flamboyant chairman, Roy A. Anderson, had marked out his company's claim to be next in line by announcing it would stop production of its L-1011 civilian airliner. Lockheed stock immediately jumped in value as market analysts presumed this meant it had the C-5 deal wired.

Lockheed's C-5B contract meant five thousand jobs in and around Marietta, Georgia, but it also meant that after Lockheed won, the nation's taxpayers paid several billions of dollars more for planes to carry its RDF in. Congress had once again opted for the highest sticker price in sight. Lockheed had simply been able to reach into more congressional districts than Boeing could.

Jackson got a consolation prize, however. The final legislation that awarded Lockheed a contract for fifty jumbos also called for the acquisition of at least two surplus 747s, at a cost of $150 million, even though the Air Force stated publicly that it did not want them and would undoubtedly turn them over to reserve units.

The final irony came in the spring of 1984, when the Air Force decided that the Army had been right after all and asked for a fleet of the smaller C-17s—220 of them! They were not wanted, of course, until after the 50 C-5Bs were delivered.

The General Accounting Office (GAO), which employs five thousand auditors, investigators, and support staff working directly for the Congress, investigated and concluded that the Air Force broke the law by using defense funds to lobby Congress to appropriate more defense funds. The GAO also noted that both Lockheed and Boeing intended to bill the U.S. government for their lobbying costs.

Lockheed had been made eligible for $287,840 in reimbursements for its C-5B lobbying effort, the GAO found, and Boeing was due $28,000. The taxpayers were also paying for the efforts of the Air Force "blue suits." The GAO found that Hecker had spent $69,000 flying a C-5A loaded with helicopters and armored personnel carriers from Dover Air Force Base in Delaware to Andrews Air Force Base in nearby Maryland to demonstrate the plane's capabilities to congressmen and staff. Boeing, lacking such Air Force support, was unable to put on such a dog and pony show.

A more typical example of "by-the-club-rules" defense contract lobbying was the drive by the Grumman Corporation to keep the Navy from cutting back in its purchases of Grumman's $51-million-each F-14 Tomcat jet fighter and buying $31 million F/A-18s instead. Grumman, headquartered on Long Island, was able to enlist such congressional allies as New York Representative Addabbo, chairman of the House defense appropriations subcommittee. A group of thirty-five subcontractors led by General Electric of Massachusetts, Hughes Aircraft of Arizona, and United Technologies of Connecticut went after powerful senators like Kennedy, Lowell Weicker, and Goldwater. Others in the high-powered lobbying effort included Teledyne Inc. of California, Honeywell Ordnance Company of Minnesota, and Brunswick of Illinois.

Grumman Chairman John C. Bierwirth told the company's stock-holders at an annual meeting, "In connection with this critical [F-14] decision, let me assure you that we have marshaled the political clout of our total Long Island and New York State congressional delegation, along with congressmen and senators from other states who support a minimum production rate of thirty-six aircraft per year." The Long Island newspaper *Newsday* estimated that more than twenty thousand people were persuaded to write to their congressional representatives demanding more $51 million F-14s instead of the cheaper F/A-18s.

Bierwirth dramatically described the cost to taxpayers, saying, "At issue is how many carriers and carrier aircraft the country needs. That debate obviously can affect the business outlook of the company that has produced the finest carrier aircraft for over forty years."

Since he spoke, the Congress agreed to a naval expansion program that includes six new carriers built through largely "sole source" con-tracts by the Newport News Shipbuilding and Dry Dock Company of Virginia at a cost of more than $3.5 billion each. The congressmen who sided with Grumman over the objections of the White House made it necessary for the government to commit itself to an expensive program of building carriers to accommodate the Grumman aircraft.

The big difference between the Boeing-Lockheed fight and the F-14 deal is that there were no losers in the Grumman affair. While voting for the F-14s, Congress also authorized buying the same number of F/A-18s from McDonnell-Douglas of Missouri and Northrop of Cali-fornia.

The Pentagon's own bookkeepers at the Defense Contract Audit Agency (DCAA) complain bitterly about the amounts of defense money spent subsidizing contractors' lobbying efforts. The New York–based public-interest group, the Council on Economic Priorities, obtained extensive data from DCAA documenting this kind of "the buck stops there" cost shifting. In one three-year period, Rockwell International billed the taxpayers for $6.5 million of $7.3 million it spent lobbying for the B-1 bomber, the DCAA said. Audits detailed how Rockwell used Pentagon money to marshal some three thousand subcontractors in their lobbying effort, and how their lobbyists Ralph J. "Doc" Watson and Anne Genevieve Allen were able to make substantial inroads with doves Senators Cranston and Howard Metzenbaum. Common Cause, a public-interest lobby, noted that GE planned to make the B-1's en-gines in Metzenbaum's Ohio and that Rockwell was based in Cranston's home state.

While Congress does its share of holding up a leg of the Iron Triangle, the industrial sector reciprocates by providing the campaign contributions so useful and often crucial to keeping a friendly member in the club. The contractors forge their links to Congress with their political action committees (PACs), "voluntary" groups formed inside nearly every defense company to collect donations from employees and pass them along as campaign contributions to congressional and presidential candidates most likely to work for a company's interests. PACs were made possible by post-Watergate campaign financing reform legislation passed in 1974 and expanded in 1976, and in less than a decade they have become the single most significant means of financing congressional reelection efforts. Disclosure requirements in the reform laws do ensure at least that a public accounting is made of the sources and recipients of PAC money.

In the spring and summer of 1982, the twenty largest defense contractors distributed $1.76 million to 250 members of Congress. With a legal limit of $5,000 to any one candidate, no company gave vast sums to individual congressmen, as Litton Industries, Lockheed, and International Telephone and Telegraph did for Richard Nixon's 1972 campaign, but, all combined, the funds from the Iron Triangle's corporate leg have made a big difference.

Reports filed by Boeing's PAC, named the Boeing Civic Pledge Program, and Lockheed's Good Government Program, illustrate the Iron Triangle's clubbiness. Despite the fact that Jackson was appearing daily on the Senate floor trying to keep $11 billion in contracts from going to Lockheed, the company and its subcontractors continued their long-established practice of giving to Scoop's campaign fund, contributing $1,300 during the debate. GE, the C-5 engine manufacturer, gave Jackson another $2,000. Boeing donated $3,600 to his campaign in the same period.

Representative Norman Dicks of Washington state, the leader of the Boeing forces in the House, who bluntly accused Lockheed of criminality in using Air Force computers to lobby for the C-5B, nevertheless accepted $1,600 in donations from Lockheed's PAC. He took another $2,000 from GE's PAC.

Stennis of Mississippi picked up in excess of $60,000 from the top twenty defense industry PACs in the spring and summer of 1982. Congressman Addabbo, the faithful Grumman friend, received $5,000 from them in that six-month period, along with $5,000 from General Dynamics, the nation's biggest defense company, $1,350 from Lockheed, and $1,000 from Boeing. On the average, the top defense PACs each doled out $88,000 to congressmen during the 1982 campaigns.

Tenneco, the big submarine producer, gave out $155,000, including $10,000 to then-Representative Paul Trible. Then representing the de-

fense contract rich Tidewater section of Virginia, Trible ran for the
Senate that year in an expensive campaign that featured him wearing
a pilot's jump suit and sitting in the cockpit of a jet fighter.

The military runs a private VIP airline for the benefit of Congress
and top government officials—the thirty-two-plane Eighty-ninth Military Airlift Wing—spending $2 million a year in taxpayers' money to
fly lawmakers and other government civilians virtually anywhere in a
style to which they have become most accustomed. This includes first-
class food and liquor as well as bellhop and chauffeur service by stewards
assigned to the VIP airlift unit.

The Eighty-ninth flew Representative James Quillen from Tennessee
to Washington, just so that the congressman could fly *back* to Tennessee
with President Reagan for the opening of the Knoxville World's Fair.
Senate Minority Leader Robert Byrd was flown from Beckley to Fair-
mount, West Virginia, about 150 miles, to dedicate an $825,000 Army
Reserve center he had obtained federal funds for. His flight cost $1,497
in federal funds. Senator Paul Laxalt, a Reagan intimate most important
to the military, was flown to Europe on an Air Force version of the
Boeing 707 at a cost of nearly $124,000, along with three other senators
and their wives and seven staff members. Their first stop was the Basque
region of France, Laxalt's ancestral homeland, and the rest of their
$25,000 itinerary included the ballet, balloon exhibitions, and fireworks.
They did stop in Rome, Budapest, and London for military briefings
and they wrote a report on their return.

Club members benefit greatly from the congressional liaison offices
the Pentagon operates on Capitol Hill in every Senate and House office
building. The civilians and uniformed personnel who work in these
outposts provide a variety of services, such as handling the casework
for a lawmaker when constituents call or write about a problem involving the military. Casework on Social Security problems, in contrast,
is paid for out of the congressman's own office budget.

The Defense Department itself has a liaison staff of 33. Another 56
work for the Navy and Marines, 46 work for the Air Force, and 10 for
the Coast Guard. The Army, despite—or because of—its runt-of-the-
litter status, has a liaison staff of 61.

The military-liaison staffs also help congressional staff workers write
speeches, perform research, and provide technical advice on how to
write legislation. The Eighty-ninth's luxury jets are probably the most
valuable service the liaison group provides. On each trip, the liaison
staff sends a military "escort officer" to accompany congressional passengers, running all manner of errands and picking up the tab for

incidental expenses, with a supply of local currency, if necessary, often carried in a satchel (in the Pentagon, these are called "black bag jobs").

Recent newspaper exposés of this practice have revealed military officers paying for scuba lessons, theater tickets, and even grandfather clocks. To ease the heat, Congress cut off much of these "walking around" funds, but the Pentagon still allots about $1 million every year for incidental travel expenses from its Emergencies and Extraordinary Affairs account.

In a newspaper interview, the director of the Navy's Senate liaison office, Captain Ingolf Kiland, Jr., recalled calling up a C-135 VIP passenger jet when Senator Tower decided he wanted to head a delegation of three colleagues to London for a seven-day "exchange program" with the British House of Commons defense committee. It cost $48,000 to fly the four lawmakers, a Navy liaison officer, and crew and staff across the Atlantic and back.

Liaison staff help disseminate the "good news" when a big defense contract is awarded to a congressional district or state, contacting local newspapers and radio and TV stations. They call this making "procurement drops." With twenty-three thousand contracting companies in the country and annual weapons budgets in the billions, the drops are rather like World War II "carpet bombing" saturation missions. Only much costlier.

The abuses of the Iron Triangle in military procurement are draining the strength of America both economically and militarily at a rate that poses more of a threat to national security than all the ships in the Russian fleet. The chaotic mess Congress now routinely makes of the policy-making and implementing process has encouraged the United States's enemies to considerable mischief. Change is imperative, but difficult. Tinkering with congressional power means tinkering with the Constitution. Sweeping reforms along the lines of the War Powers Act have all too often backfired.

But some things can be improved. The Pentagon practice of assigning officers on permanent duty on Capitol Hill to lobby influential congressmen on behalf of various expensive weapons systems must be drastically curtailed. Some military expertise is of course required, but not in such egregious volume. Funding for these operations could be substantially cut with far less difficulty than accompanied passage of the 1974 and 1976 Election Reform Acts, the Freedom of Information Act, or any of the other post-Watergate reforms. Similarly, the practice of financing corporate lobbying efforts through "public information" accounts written right into the budget for a weapon is ludicrous and can be stopped immediately with legislation.

The use of military aircraft by members of Congress for any purpose other than tours of combat areas or observations of military activities or missions should cease. Attending the Paris Air Show, an extremely popular trip currently, should not qualify.

Those members of Congress who are not co-opted by the defense leg of the Iron Triangle should be encouraged to put a brake on their colleagues who sit on the eight committees dealing with the military and to castigate them for pressing parochial interests to the detriment of American society and security as a whole. The members of the Iron Triangle must be made to pay a public penalty for conduct that has made the United States so vulnerable because of weapons that don't work and the huge fortunes in national treasure squandered in producing them.

Perhaps the most important reform that might be made, though, lies in undoing some of the more disastrous reforms of the past. An excellent example is the series of changes instituted in the post–World War II years to "improve" the United States's military high command. If the White House is the weakest link in the chain of command, the Joint Chiefs of Staff have long been rendered the most useless.

chapter eight

THE HIGH COMMAND

> *Normally, it is not possible for an army simply to dismiss incompetent generals. The very authority which their office bestows upon generals is the first reason for this. Moreover, the generals form a clique, tenaciously supporting each other, all convinced that they are the best possible representatives of the army. But we can at least give them capable assistants. Thus the General Staff officers are those who support incompetent generals, providing the talents that might otherwise be wanting among leaders and commanders.*
>
> —GENERAL GERHARD VON SCHARNHORST,
> FATHER OF THE GERMAN GENERAL STAFF

The White House red-phone command line connects to a large room on the third floor of the Pentagon near the offices of the secretary of defense and his principal civilian aides. This chamber is somewhat innocuously called the National Military Command Center, or more commonly, "the war room." It is from here that the commanders of the United States armed forces direct war, although in the prospect of a nuclear conflict, they would be more likely to be found in their similarly appointed underground command centers in Pennsylvania, Virginia, or the Western mountains—if they had time to get there.

The war room's walls are dominated by huge projection and television screens on which can be displayed maps of every location on the planet, along with charts, graphs, and a wealth of other military data. Radio sets connect the chamber via a satellite network with the commanders of the United States's six unified and three specified commands—virtually the entire military. The unified commands, headed by a mix of Army, Air Force, and Navy four-star officers, are European Command, Pacific Command, Atlantic Command, Southern Command, Readiness Command, and Central Command. The specified commands, all run by the Air Force, are Aerospace Command, Strategic Air Command, and Military Airlift Command.

In the event of a crisis, the current state of alert flashes on a red screen similar to a basketball scoreboard in one corner. A second screen shows the level of secret classification of the data being presented at any time. A large digital clock shows the time elapsed since the crisis began. An array of accompanying clocks show the hour in every time zone around the world, along with "Zulu" (Greenwich mean time), the standard used by all U.S. military units in operational situations.

In the center of the room is an oversized T-shaped table. On both sides of the perpendicular of the T sit fourteen "battle officers," representing the unified and specified commands. Along the top of the T sit the members of the Joint Chiefs of Staff, the ranking officers of the Army, Air Force, Navy, and Marines. Flanking the table are two speaking podiums to which any of the officers can go to respond to questions or make reports.

Nearby are the Teletypes and other communications equipment that constitute the Moscow hot line. The United States sends in Russian and the Kremlin sends in English to assure no misinterpretation. The two countries recently agreed to an upgrade of equipment to permit the rapid transmission of maps, printed documents, and other visual aids.

At an elevated console overlooking the table and in full view of the various screens sit the secretary of defense, or his designate, and his top aides. Before the secretary of defense is the red telephone connecting him to the White House and a white phone connecting him to anywhere in the world. At the secretary's left sits the chairman of the Joint Chiefs of Staff, the highest-ranking officer in the American military. It is at this proximity of chairs that the chain of command connecting the civilian authority with the military commanders is most direct. In times of crisis, it is in this manner that the White House and the generals deal with one another.

But there are other ways.

When National Security Advisor Henry Kissinger and his assistant, Alexander Haig, were shuttling mysteriously about Asia arranging the startling American rapprochement with China, there was a young Navy yeoman in their party named Charles Radford. While Kissinger and Haig had their secret talks with Chou En-lai and others, Yeoman Radford took the shorthand, did the typing, and went out for the Chinese equivalent of sandwiches. A straitlaced Mormon, Radford came to the job with excellent references. His principal assignment was in the White House liaison office of the Joint Chiefs of Staff.

In 1974, under what one member of the Joint Chiefs, Admiral Elmo R. Zumwalt, Jr., called "heavy interrogation," Radford admitted he had spied on Kissinger and Haig through the talks and travels. The chief interrogator, W. Donald Stewart, told one of the authors that

Radford revealed how he would wait until Haig had fallen asleep. Radford told Stewart he would slip into the room and, with steno pad in hand, open the general's briefcase and copy the documents inside in shorthand.

According to Stewart, Radford's duties had also included disposing of the daily "burn bag" that was filled with everything from tape-recordings of meetings with Chou En-lai to plans for bombing North Vietnam on Christmas Eve. Nightly, Radford would go through the burn bag before its contents were destroyed. He did these things while back on duty at the White House as well.

To say the least, Radford conducted what was probably the most devastatingly effective spy operation in the history of the United States, working under the noses of the most powerful security officials in the government, and just downstairs from the Oval Office.

Fortunately, Radford was not an agent for the Soviets or any other foreign power. He was apparently an operative for the chairman of the Joint Chiefs of Staff. The secrets he passed along to the country's top officer were of great value to the military side of the government, because Kissinger, using his authority as security advisor, was formulating and executing both military and diplomatic policy and bypassing the traditional command structure.

The information Radford passed back to the Pentagon included documents outlining plans to cut back troop strength in Vietnam and Korea that hadn't been shared with those troops' top commanders. Radford uncovered tentative agreements between Kissinger and South Vietnamese President Nguyen Van Thieu for the staged withdrawal of American forces from the war. He passed along copious notes on Haig's conversations with Cambodian President Lon Nol, which apparently for the first time informed the chiefs of the fact that the White House was planning a military penetration of Cambodia to destroy North Vietnamese sanctuaries.

That the nation's highest-ranking military commanders felt it necessary to infiltrate their commander in chief's inner circle with a spy was a dramatic indication that something was not right in the chain of command. It still isn't. The flaws inherent in the American command system constitute the most vexing problem facing those leaders who hope to reform today's defense establishment.

It is a fiercely held American tradition and constitutional dictate to maintain strict civilian control over the military. After World War II, Americans were so concerned about the evils of the militarist governments of Japan and Germany that all manner of laws were passed restricting the American military's power, as well as its ability to acquire power. Even with the onset of the Cold War, it was widely agreed that the military efficiency which could be had by establishing a strong central-command structure was not worth the risk of creating a military-dominated society.

By the 1980s, many former members of the Joint Chiefs of Staff, such as Air Force General David C. Jones and the Army's Edward C. Meyer, had publicly questioned—after retirement from active duty—whether the vast American military machine could be rationally commanded in a major confrontation today. Choosing their words with great care, the generals argued that the legal restrictions imposed in the wake of World War II were so extensive that the United States might not be able to direct its forces effectively in an era when warfighting decisions that once could be made over days or weeks must be made and implemented in hours or minutes.

Currently, this "time-compression problem" means that almost all of the initial military moves must be made by the civilian president and his advisors without much consultation with the military experts. Bruce Watson, then a Navy lieutenant commander, noted at a 1978 seminar in Washington, D.C., that "in 1941, we had time to take the issue of Pearl Harbor to Congress. During the Mideast War in 1973, Admiral Thomas Moorer, then chairman of the JCS, came back to the Joint Chiefs and told them a decision had already been made to go to DefCon III [a worldwide military alert that includes readying nuclear forces]."

The orders to scramble fighters, get B-52s airborne, and to ready Minutemen missiles and other commands had been issued from the White House to individual military units independent of the President's chief military officers. Jones and Meyer argued that presidents should be much closer to their military advisors under such conditions than is now possible.

In addition to serious worries about the operational capability of today's high command, defense analysts have blamed an ineffectual military leadership for allowing the costly high-tech weapon problem to become as bad as it has.

The Joint Chiefs and other top uniformed commanders play a very small role in determining which weapons are bought and have little say about costs. As General Jones noted in a 1982 post-retirement article in *The New York Times Magazine,* decisions about weapons procurement, costs, and testing are usually made by high-level civilian employees, though military officers have influence and run the weapons programs once under way.

The central role of the Joint Chiefs is to administer the vast military establishment and draft tactical plans for use of forces in actual warfare scenarios. As a result of the virtual exclusion of the chiefs from the procurement side of military policy, today's military operates under a system in which the people who plan the tactics have only a small say in what weapons they will be issued to do their fighting.

Substantial insight into the workings of the Pentagon's high command can be found in *On Watch*, the memoirs of Admiral Zumwalt, the controversial chief of naval operations of the Nixon era. Zumwalt recalled how he had found he had great powers to order such highly publicized initiatives as allowing sailors to wear their hair long and grow beards and serving 3.2 beer aboard ships. But Zumwalt found he had amazingly little to say about how Henry Kissinger deployed ships in the Vietnam War.

While the Joint Chiefs include the chiefs of the four services, the fifth member of the group, the chairman, can come from any one of the service branches. In *On Watch*, Zumwalt remembered the first day he was driven to the River Entrance of the Pentagon building as the new chief of naval operations.

> The setting in which the Joint Chiefs brooded over or debated . . . consequential matters was "the Tank," a big windowless room on the first floor of the Pentagon. There we gathered three times a week, each of us with a name plate, a bowl of rock candy, and a favorite tipple (coffee, tea, or water) in front of him on the rectangular conference table (sixteen feet long, eight feet wide at the middle, and seven feet wide at the ends) and a three star deputy for plans and policy (OpDep) in a chair beside him.
> The first part of each meeting, with the OpDeps, and the director of the Joint Staff and his assistant in attendance, generally was quite formal and was formally recorded. Then, more often than not, the OpDeps, the Joint Staff people, and the reporter [official recorder] left, and we five principals, the four service chiefs and the chairman, conversed in a considerably more informal and candid manner than we cared to in front of others.

It is at sessions like that that the high command develops the strategies the uniformed military side of the Pentagon will use in its continuing battles to influence policy-making. Zumwalt recalled that the "candid" sessions during his watch often dealt with the U.S. commitment to build a military that could fight "one and a half wars" simultaneously. Under that strategy, the military had to prepare to conduct both a regional war on the scale of Vietnam at the same time it was fighting a major one with the Soviets in Europe. Each day, the reports

from the real "half war" in Vietnam that came into the Tank grimly
dramatized how far from the American grasp that war-fighting capability was.

Zumwalt lamented that the chiefs' discussions on such matters rarely
had an impact on the real policymakers because of legal strictures.

> The Joint Staff was almost totally useless as an instrument to mon-
> itor what other parts of the government were doing or thinking.
> Working, as it had to, strictly through the prescribed channels of
> communication and command, it was generally the last to know
> what was happening in Washington's bureaucratic labyrinth. One
> thing my years . . . had taught me was that the most carefully
> constructed position was of little value unless it came before the
> right person at the right time. We all needed help in keeping track
> of those persons and times and I did not find a place to get it in
> the organizational chart of either my own Navy staff or the Joint
> Staff.

The Yeoman Radford affair was a desperate effort to get the chiefs
plugged into the flow of information and power emanating from the
White House. After the Radford story was broken by *Chicago Tribune*
correspondent Jim Squires, the White House reacted not by granting
the Joint Chiefs more access but by expelling the Pentagon's liaison
office from the White House grounds. In subsequent years, the chiefs
have complained frequently—and with some dramatic evidence to support their case—that the country has suffered because presidents
have distanced themselves from the counsel of their top military commanders.

Throughout 1983, the chiefs in their Tank were unanimous in their
feeling that the President was making a very bad mistake in his deployment of Marines in Lebanon. But a subsequent report assessing
blame for the deaths of the 241 Marines killed by the terrorist bombing
of their headquarters at Beirut Airport noted that the Reagan White
House had consulted the JCS only rarely for their views of the Lebanese
situation.

This report, written by retired Admiral L. J. Long, described how
Pentagon leaders had gradually concluded over a year of meetings that
the political situation had changed in Lebanon and that it was no longer
possible to achieve American goals there through the use of troops.
Admiral Long faulted the chiefs for not pushing harder for withdrawal.
Reagan's ultimate decision to pull out of the airport staging ground
came eight months after the chiefs had concluded such a move was
imperative.

Reagan never complained, at least publicly, that the chiefs had not been more forceful on the question. However, other presidents have expressed displeasure at the chiefs for keeping too low a profile in times of crisis. President Kennedy openly chastised the JCS for failing to come forward with their misgivings about the plan to attack Castro forces in Cuba with a landing at the Bay of Pigs. Kennedy later learned that discussions in the Tank had led to the conclusion that the plan couldn't work without air support. Angry because he had never heard that advice, Kennedy established the same Joint Chiefs liaison office at the White House that was later abolished over the Radford scandal.

Actually, the JCS and its chairman have traditionally been dutifully obedient, sometimes to a fault. When plans for the B-1 bomber were coming off the drawing boards, JCS Chairman David C. Jones—one of that service's most highly regarded general officers—was a forthright spokesman for its need. When Carter abruptly (if in vain) cancelled the project, General Jones supported the decision, citing its lack of need. When Reagan came in and revived the B-1, Jones spoke again of its necessity.

When members of the JCS do stand up, they often regret it. Although set aside from the direct chain of command, the JCS and its chairman are supposed to function as the president's most expert military counselors. But they are frequently brusquely dismissed.

Although publicly silent, the Joint Chiefs were privately apoplectic about Carter's call for removing U.S. troops from South Korea, which was viewed in military circles as an irresponsible act that could have ignited another round of war on the peninsula. Carter ignored them. He ultimately succumbed to the outspoken criticism of the Eighth Army's General John Singlaub, who eventually had to resign from the service, but who won his point when Carter gave in.

Two years into office, the ostensibly pro-military Reagan administration came under severe public attack from a number of powerful congressmen for ignoring the advice of the JCS. "There appears to be an alarming lack of consultation with the [JCS] prior to major defense spending decisions," said Norman Dicks, a member of the House Appropriations defense subcommittee. "The Congress has learned of their opinions only after the fact, and then often by accident."

He disclosed that the JCS had opposed the Reagan-Weinberger "dense-pack" deployment mode for the MX missile, arguing among other things that its reliability had not been proven.

When General Meyer left as chief of staff of the Army in 1983, he let administrations and congresses, past and present, have it with both barrels. "If we were trying to convince an enemy that we were able to go to war with a system that works like this, he would laugh," Meyer said.

He complained that the Reagan administration and Congress had failed to reach basic agreement on strategy and uses for the American armed forces, obstructing any rational approach to developing a viable military policy. He said Congress had run amok on weapons procurement, focusing on individual systems instead of developing a broad budget policy.

Meyer also stated that the administration and Congress were pursuing policies that ignored the major lesson of Vietnam: that military campaigns cannot be waged without sustained public support. "Soldiers should not go off to war without having the nation behind them," he said, emphasizing the application of this doctrine to Central America.

When Meyer left, the only member of the JCS who had served in World War II was General Vessey, the chairman. The others were officers out of Korea and Vietnam, tempered by that kind of frustration and failure, and consequently more cautious.

Ignored, rebuffed, or embarrassed—such as when Reagan failed to consult with Caribbean command headquarters in Key West when he launched his 1983 invasion of Grenada—the military high command salutes and does its duty. There has yet to be another MacArthur-Truman contretemps.

"Do I feel that, if something is decided here, the Pentagon is responsive?" Vice-President Bush said. "I think the top echelons are. I can't tell you I don't feel that at some point, somewhere along the line, somewhere in the vast bureaucracy here, at State, there in the Pentagon, that someone won't drag their feet or try to build backfires on things. There's some of that goes on in a bureaucracy. What you gotta do is try to ferret it out."

Asked whether, as White House crisis manager, he was ever troubled by a lack of military responsiveness, Bush said, "No, . . . you say we've got to do this, that, and that, then I think the machinery has responded superbly. I am confident that in that kind of situation, where a determination is made, and something has to happen, things will happen."

But that's not enough. The chairman of the JCS simply has to be moved to a more authoritative position in the national-security pecking order. Until a change is implemented, the five four-stars in the Tank will continue to ponder cosmic issues and fret over their inability to influence them, while presidents move military forces about the globe with the sort of results encountered from the Bay of Pigs to Beirut. As constituted today, life in the Tank is a bureaucratic absurdity worthy of Dickens at his glummest.

While the Joint Chiefs sit with their rock candies and tipples pondering bureaucratic nuances, the work actually accomplished by the JCS is left largely to the four "OpDeps" (Deputies for Plans and Policy), one for each service, who sit by each chief at the formal meetings. The OpDeps, who are three-star generals (or admirals), are assisted by a staff of officers, usually with ranks of major or above. These officers draft the various position papers, nuclear-weapons target lists, procurement proposals, posture statements, and general reports to the White House and Congress that constitute the bulk of JCS paperwork. Not only is their number frozen at a maximum of one hundred per service regardless of changing world conditions and tensions, but these officers serving the high command are in large part kept from gaining much expertise at command.

By law, a staff officer may serve in the Tank for only three years, and after that must return to his or her original service branch. The law was written specifically to keep the U.S. high command from evolving into a Prussian-style general staff. It serves that end perhaps too well. It assures that the best talent in each military service will avoid duty with the JCS. Ambitious officers seeking promotion have little to gain by taking themselves out of the running for three years to work with officers of other services on JCS projects.

In their absences, promotions are likely to go to rivals and colleagues serving closer to the advancement funnel. Also, the three-year requirement forces those officers who do join the Joint Staff to leave the JCS just as they are mastering the intricacies of one of history's most complex military organizations.

The Joint Staff thus usually serves as a prestigious graveyard for officers who are passed over for other promotions but who have enough residual influence to secure a final tour of duty in Washington. During those three years in the Tank, such officers can acquire the contacts they'll need to find good civilian jobs after retirement. Abolishing the three-year rule would be a relatively painless fix for at least one small but important part of a serious command problem.

The Tank is also the end of the road for officers like Zumwalt, who rise to service chief but come just short of the very top. The law allows a chief of staff to serve for four years, after which he must step aside. It allows a chairman to serve only two years, but the president can grant him an unlimited number of two-year extensions provided the Senate consents each time.

Veterans of the Joint Staff system ranging from General Jones to Lieutenant Colonel Tyrus W. Cobb, now on the faculty at West Point, have observed that almost none of the work done at the Tank is very innovative because of yet another requirement of the law that is also a longstanding high command tradition. The chiefs do not reach their decisions by the normal committee process in which a vote is taken and the majority prevails. Instead, the JCS do everything through consensus. When the Joint Chiefs are asked to give the president advice on, say, the MX missile or the dispatch of troops to the Persian Gulf, the request is first discussed at one of the formal meetings Zumwalt described. Each chief then assigns his OpDep to prepare a paper on his service branch's view of the situation. The 100 officers reporting to each OpDep then prepare a report on a piece of ordinary onionskin paper, or flimsy.

With each member of the JCS referring to his own flimsy, the group discusses the topic. Then, the three-stars are sent back to prepare a summary of the compromises reached. A report of each service's individual understanding of this compromise is written on tan paper. After another round of discussion by the Joint Chiefs, the "tans" are redrafted into a "green" and this draft is placed before the JCS for final approval. If it gets it, this final report is designated a "purple" and it is marked with a distinctive diagonal red stripe on each page signifying that the comments contained therein are the joint opinion of the Joint Chiefs. "Purples" go on to the president, the secretary of defense, and other civilian officials.

Lieutenant Colonel Cobb warned in a paper on the command structure that this consensus process makes for bland reading at best and a dangerous inability to react quickly to developing crises at the worst.

> Planning in the Pentagon often consists of reworking countless documents each year, inserting a few well-phrased items reflecting the current wisdom, changing "happy" to "glad," securing numerous "chops" (approvals) from superiors, and "crashing" to get the final product on the street in the allotted time frame. A premium is placed on accomplishing the task rather than innovative thinking.

John Collins, a military specialist for the Congressional Research Service of the Library of Congress, complained about the chiefs' output in similar vein. "Their compromise papers on complex problems are banal, ambiguous, and short on substance," he said.

That is a chilling condemnation, in that the primary function of the

Joint Chiefs is the constant updating of the Single Integrated Operations Plan (SIOP) for U.S. forces in nuclear war and lesser situations, in accordance with the most recent information provided by the United States's huge network of intelligence services.

Key to implementing the SIOP are two civilian units within the Pentagon, the Defense Resources Board (DRB) and the Defense Science Board. The DRB is made up of presidentially appointed assistant secretaries of defense and is chaired by either the secretary himself or his deputy. Its mission is to determine what threats to the United States exist throughout the world and how the government should prepare its forces to meet them. A civilian service secretary represents each of the four branches at DRB meetings.

Historically, the Navy secretary will push for more ships; the Army secretary will urge more troops, tanks, and artillery; and the Air Force secretary will ask for bigger and better (more expensive) planes and missiles.

The JCS is supposed to provide less parochial "purple" advice to the Resources Board about how the overall military can be better posed to deal with various world situations. Typically, the DRB is called upon to make such decisions as whether to emphasize nuclear weapons or tactical forces in the next budget or whether it would be more useful to add to the fleet or expand the army or find more technicians and maintenance crew for the Air Force.

The Defense Science Board (DSB) is a civilian panel that includes scientists from both leading defense contractors and academia. The DSB is supposed to determine whether the weapons proposed to meet various threats will work as intended—or at all.

Provided with information and recommendations from both the DRB and the DSB, the Joint Chiefs are supposed to develop a military position on each question and prepare a detailed plan to meet each threat. But, too often, as Zumwalt noted, the chiefs find it impossible to take such an ecumenical view of national military needs because those are precisely the questions that determine which branch of service gets what.

The flaws in the high command's bureaucratic structure were amply dealt with in *Thinking About National Security,* the memoirs of Harold Brown, secretary of defense in the Carter administration. He compared running American defense to managing one of the country's larger corporations, noting that the Pentagon budget is twice as large as that of Exxon, the largest corporation on the Fortune 500 list. But unlike Exxon, where a few autocratic managers exercise nearly absolute control over operations, the defense establishment works according to written formal rules that cover every step its managers take from the bottom to the top.

In testimony before the House Armed Services Committee, Brown outlined how virtually every working moment of the high command is taken up fulfilling some bureaucratic requirement. The workdays of the chiefs and other top commanders are dominated by endless cycles of paperwork and meetings—all required by law. The forms, reports, and even the meetings themselves are identified by sets of initials in Pentagonese.

There are initials for the process of bureaucratic requirements itself—PPBS, for Planning, Programming and Budgeting System. The procedures required for the PPBS to work are compiled in a two-volume tome entitled, of course, *PPBS*.

The PPBS ritual begins every January when a memorandum called the DG, for Defense Guidance, is sent from the defense secretary to the chiefs. This document outlines the administration's marching orders for the service branches for the immediate future. In the DG prepared for 1984 by Defense Secretary Caspar Weinberger, the chiefs were ordered to prepare for nuclear war lasting several months, to strengthen conventional forces, to coordinate Navy and Air Force units in order to better defend naval fleets from Soviet attack, and to add bolder "maneuver warfare" tactics to the Army's war plans.

The system calls for the JCS to respond to the DG with a Joint Strategic Planning Document (JSPD). The chiefs responded to the 1984 Weinberger DG with a JSPD that warned that the costs of implementing the plan would cost $500 billion more than the $1.6 trillion Reagan had demanded for his arms buildup.

The Defense Resources Board, assisted by the Defense Science Board, then steps in to resolve conflicts between the DG and the JSPD, making certain that any proposed plans are technically feasible as well as strategically desirable.

Each chief then prepares documents for his individual service branch called POMs, for Program Objectives Memoranda. A POM is a five-year plan for the individual service's development. It specifies which weapons are considered desirable, sets out goals for personnel strength, and outlines which missions each service branch wants assigned to it.

The chiefs then meet to review each other's POMs and to produce yet another acronym, the JPAM (pronounced jap-am in the Pentagon), for Joint Program Assessment Memorandum. It outlines the chiefs' joint view of how their individual POMs meet the requirements outlined in the original DG.

Then, if the DRB decides the JPAM meets the DG, a budget request is drafted for the White House. As Lieutenant Colonel Cobb pointed out during a seminar at West Point in 1982, the entrenched bureaucracy in the Pentagon deals with the continuing stream of alphabet paperwork in a fashion not unlike that of the local zoning board in a small town. The Pentagon simply recasts last year's document every new year—changing "happy" to "glad," as Cobb put it in a paper presented at the seminar. The ultimate work product is predictably inane.

As such defense veterans as Representative Samuel Stratton have noted, the chiefs much prefer to delegate most of the form-filling and meeting attendance to the OpDeps and lesser staff and to concentrate instead on the more rewarding duties of running their individual service branches.

They meet just three times a week as the JCS. Naturally, fierce loyalty to one's service branch is a requisite to reaching the top of it, and JCS sessions often are given over to officers pressing parochial demands.

Every major decision hurts one branch and helps another. A decision to build toward a 600-ship Navy carries with it a decision not to build as many airplanes or tanks, or to field as many divisions as might otherwise be possible. In the Tank, also known as "the Gold Room" because of the color of the thick draperies, the chiefs urge one another to think "purple" while coping with personal dilemmas over subordinating their service's needs to the overall military's.

A frequently mentioned solution to the problem is the creation of a permanent, elite American general staff that would concentrate the best expertise and intelligence at the top advisory level and whose officers would owe loyalty to the general staff, not to any particular branch of service.

The Prussian general staff created by Scharnhorst, Clausewitz, Gneisenau, and other Napoleonic-era Prussian reformers became the standard toward which most modern military organizations aspired. Curiously, the Prussian military was much like the American in that it did not participate in domestic government (unlike the Soviets) and was ruled absolutely by the civilian authority—king, kaiser, chancellor.

Unlike the American Joint Chiefs, the Prussian (later German) general staff did not administer service branches or command armies. It was concerned with planning for wars with all potential enemies, analyzing intelligence, maintaining operational readiness, preparing manpower mobilization systems to provide large numbers of replacements in the event of war, and coordinating military activities. It played a supervisory role only when there was a breakdown in efficiency and expert help was required.

But this general staff came to rule the Prussian and later the German military because it provided the data and recommendations on which the civilian authority and top commanders based their decisions, and because it was a quasi-autonomous elite.

As Colonel T. N. Dupuy wrote in his book *A Genius for War:*

> If the King was a gifted general, like Frederick the Great, his talent would be enhanced by the availability of such a staff. If he was essentially a civilian ruler, with little military ability, he could rely on this staff to perform the functions of generalship, and to provide him with the military advice needed for political and politico-military decisions.

The great generals of the Prussian and German armies all rose through this general staff system. Entrance to it for junior officers was by means of the most exacting and intense competitive examinations. Once an officer had attained the distinctive red trouser stripe of the general staff, he could keep it for the rest of his career, and it was considered a very high honor.

The United States's chain of command was specifically set up to avoid this kind of general staff.

President Truman tried briefly after World War II to create a powerful chief of staff to take command of the entire military establishment. The job of "unified chief of the services" was offered to Truman's Navy secretary, James V. Forrestal. But Forrestal declined the opportunity, warning against letting the military have so much power. In 1947, Truman, Secretary of War Henry L. Stimson, and Secretary of State General George C. Marshall decided instead upon a plan to eliminate the War and Navy departments as separate entities and combine them in a civilian-run Department of Defense, with a Joint Chiefs of Staff made up of the ranking officer from each service. From a command standpoint, the JCS arrangement was somewhat similar to that which had evolved with the allied forces in Europe.

This system was approved by Congress with passage of the National Security Act of 1947—the same legislation that gave the CIA its interesting charter. The first secretary of defense was Forrestal. To maintain the maximum civilian control, the act placed a civilian service secretary over each uniformed chief of staff.

From the beginning, Forrestal, in failing health and exhausted from his labors in World War II, had complained that he had no power in the new system and that the uniformed JCS—there were then just three members and no chairman—was too powerful. In 1948, the system was changed to allow the Air Force to become independent of the Army.

On May 22, 1949, Forrestal jumped to his death from a window at the Bethesda Naval Hospital, where he was under treatment for nervous exhaustion. That same year, Congress passed a law that created the post of chairman of the JCS, to be drawn from one of the individual services, and established the rules that required the chiefs to reach their decisions by consensus.

In 1958, largely because President Eisenhower was convinced that interservice feuding between the various rocket-program managers in the Army and Navy had allowed the Russians to get into space first with their *Sputnik* satellite, the Defense Reorganization Act was passed, removing substantial power from the Joint Chiefs and giving it to the defense secretary.

That act allowed the president to issue orders directly to field units, either by going through the defense secretary or by issuing commands himself directly through the chief of whichever service was involved. Instead of working through the chairman and the full JCS, the president could order the Army chief of staff to issue commands to individual combat units. This is the system that was used in the Carter administration's abortive Iranian desert raid, and in many other White House military operations in recent years.

At a seminar held by the American Enterprise Institute, General Maxwell Taylor, the chairman of the JCS during the Johnson administration, recounted his dismay over laws passed in 1947, 1952, and 1958 that directed the president to issue his orders to individual units through the civilian defense secretary (rather than through the top generals, as had been the case in World War II). With the JCS confined largely to an advisory role, Taylor said the president can use today's supersophisticated communications directly to give orders to small operational units. "The Joint Chiefs cannot command anybody," he said, "unless they're lucky enough to have a stenographer. They can give [a stenographer] direct orders."

The Joint Chiefs have occasionally given Pentagon correspondents tours of the war room. The projection screens, computers, radio communications, and the rest of the equipment are run by a crew of engineers and technicians seated in a glass-windowed control booth just behind the row of service chiefs. Behind the control booth is an immense support area called the Current Actions Center, containing the hot line apparatus connecting the Pentagon to the Kremlin. When there is no need to communicate, both machines churn out a continuous stream of test transmissions—excerpts from encyclopedias, recipes, trigonometric tables, and the like. The Soviet transmissions received in the war room are flashed to the White House and to the better-protected command centers outside Washington. Also, there is an airborne command post—the communications-packed, specially modified Boeing 707 code-named Looking Glass, which can remain aloft out of reach of enemy nuclear weapons for approximately seventy-five hours.

The modern communications available has strengthened civilian control even further, depriving the uniformed brass of the traditional "hands on" command authority they traditionally enjoyed.

General George S. Brown, who headed the JCS during the Ford administration, said Defense Secretary Donald Rumsfeld had attempted to issue orders personally from Washington to the commander of the small rescue party used to retrieve the bodies of the two American Army officers killed by the North Koreans in the infamous "tree cutting" incident along the DMZ. "We had to remind him that he had agreed to the worldwide military-command control system, whereby we would only provide communication to the task force commander, not to an individual fellow on a ship or in an airplane or holding a weapon on the ground, even though we have the communications to do that today," Brown said.

Citing the virtues of the Prussian general staff may seem jarring. It was the abhorrence of all things German that led to the reorganization of the armed services into the Defense Department in 1947. But it was not the German general staff that brought on the horrors of World Wars I and II, it was the German civilian leadership: a vain and indecisive Kaiser Wilhelm and a madman politician named Adolf Hitler, who came to power through democratic elections.

However the Prussian-style general staff was misused by the civilian German command, it was the most educated, efficient, effective, useful, and brilliant military organization of its kind in history. Too often the American system has been just the opposite. A cautious establishment of an American approximation of the Prussian "red stripes" is the best chance remaining for creating a rational command structure for the United States. The military is now so thoroughly dominated by civilian politicians and bureaucrats from top to bottom that the prospect of a sudden shift to military domination of the American government is hardly possible under any foreseeable circumstance, no matter how much military command is strengthened within the Defense Department.

The chairman of the JCS should be transformed from the president's principal uniformed military advisor to the supreme uniformed military commander of all the armed services, sitting atop the Pentagon chain of command and reporting directly to both the president, in his role of civilian commander in chief, and the secretary of defense. Legislation to permit this has been attracting increasing support in the Congress.

The JCS chairman would be the immediate superior of the commanders of the individual unified and specified commands, although the president would continue to exercise the right to command them himself directly if the need arose. The JCS chairman would also command the branches of service through the individual chiefs of staff, as well as the general staff through the JCS functioning as an administrative body.

In testimony before Congress, JCS Chairman Vessey; former Undersecretary of the Army Norman Augustine; General Paul Gorman, commander of the Southern Command; General Louis Wilson, retired commandant of the Marine Corps; and General Bernard Rogers, the much-respected NATO commander, gave strong support to making the JCS chairman commander of the uniformed military and a member of the NSC. Roger said:

> Placing the chairman of the Joint Chiefs of Staff in the chain of command, making the chairman . . . a member of the National Security Council, having a deputy chairman to insure the presence in Washington at all times of a cross-service spokesman, removing the restrictions on the size and tenure of the Joint Staff, and formalizing the interface of the commanders-in-chief with the Defense Resources Board. Those are the five actions I think are necessary . . . and key to the security arrangements of this country.

Former Defense Secretaries Harold Brown and James Schlesinger were for this kind of reform. Schlesinger said:

> Without [structural] reform, the United States will obtain neither the best military advice, nor the effective execution of military plans, nor the provision of military capabilities commensurate with the fiscal resources provided, nor the most advantageous deterrence and defense posture available to the nation. . . . The central weakness of the existing system lies in the structure of the Joint Chiefs of Staff.

Caspar Weinberger disagreed, saying, "The more formal those [JCS] structures are, the more cumbersome they become." Navy Secretary Lehman attacked the Prussian nature of such a reformed JCS, though his chief complaint seemed to be that he was fearful of any reform that would diminish service secretaries' power.

It's imperative that the Joint Chiefs of Staff and its personnel be restructured into a large, more inclusive, more permanent, and elite general staff, whether civilian service emperors like Lehman like it or not. An American general staff should have jurisdiction over the preparation and recommendation of all planning, strategy, tactics, weapons development and acquisition, manpower recruitment, and combat readiness. It should continue to be commanded by the Joint Chiefs of Staff, who should also continue to serve as an advisory body and function as the administrative heads of their individual services.

But the chiefs should be augmented and supported by a powerful and collegial body of vice-chiefs of staff, who would be assigned the hands-on leadership of the general staff. This general staff should be greatly expanded from the present size of the JSC staff and it should absorb many powers now buried in the Pentagon bureaucracy. It should become a prestigious body and a career goal, rather than the dead end or temporary sideline seat it all too often functions as now.

The emphasis should be on creating a homogenous, collegial, mutually supportive elite corps dedicated to the concerns of total national security rather than those of the service from which these officers would be drawn. Once established as a desirable, career-advancement post, a slot on the Joint Staff should attract the best officers from the different branches. The educational requirements would be the highest in the American military. As with the old Prussian "red stripes," the officers chosen for this elite would be run through as many schools and staff colleges as possible.

As constituted today, the National War College provides an excellent starting point for building a competent military command. Viewed as a graduate school for officers who have passed through the military academies or collegiate Reserve Officers Training Corps (ROTC) programs, the war colleges maintained by each service branch are also natural places to develop a revitalized officer corps.

Unlike so many in the present Pentagon bureaucracy, the new generation of general staff should be assigned field experience as much as possible. They should also be made to serve assignments with different branches of service, thereby increasing the homogeneity and unity of purpose of the general staff. Such mixing, advocated by former JCS chairman General Jones, would help reduce today's horrendously debilitating and obstructive interservice rivalries. These changes are vital. Today's military leadership has become a cauldron of quarreling chauvinists, each loyal to a single service branch and often blinded by that loyalty to the needs of the country as a whole.

In fact, the American military has evolved into a quarrelsome assemblage of Marines, sailors, soldiers, and airmen whose continual infighting produces inefficient weapons, drives defense costs to impossible levels, and makes a mockery of coherent policy. Perhaps the most important benefit to be gained would be to finally put an end to this feuding, which has reduced national defense to what can best be called a brotherhood of rivals.

chapter nine

A BROTHERHOOD OF RIVALS

> *i have noticed that when chickens quit quarreling over their food they often find that there is enough for all of them*
>
> —ARCHY THE COCKROACH,
> *ARCHY'S LIFE OF MEHITABEL,*
> BY DON MARQUIS

Perhaps the greatest flaw in the American military system is the freedom given to the three main branches of service to compete with each other instead of the enemy. Even with such strong secretaries of defense as Melvin Laird, Harold Brown, and Donald Rumsfeld, these exorbitantly costly interservice rivalries have seriously damaged American security. With weaker secretaries, such as Caspar Weinberger, who allow the services to run amok with procurement budgets, the damage to national security can be immense.

But what must be viewed as the most alarming consequence of this enduring rivalry was first discovered near the end of the Eisenhower administration, as Ike prepared to turn power over to newly elected John F. Kennedy shortly after the 1960 election. Eisenhower sent his White House science advisor, George Kistiakowsky, on a secret mission to Omaha, Nebraska, to lay the groundwork for the transfer of control of the vast U.S. nuclear arsenal to the new administration. Kistiakowsky's task was to prepare a report for Eisenhower so the President could advise Kennedy which Soviet cities and military facilities were targeted by which elements of the U.S. nuclear forces—data the new commander in chief would need immediately. To compile that information, Kistiakowsky met at Omaha with Air Force and Navy commanders summoned to Offutt Air Force Base to report on their respective target selections. As Kistiakowsky recalled later, he had to report to a dismayed Eisenhower that, over the fifteen years the American military had possessed nuclear weapons, there had been virtually no coordination between the Air Force and the Navy over which Soviet cities and military targets were to be annihilated. The science advisor found that each of the two service branches had become an awesome nuclear power in its own right. The Air Force had built its Strategic Air Command (SAC) armada with wing upon wing of then shiny new B-52 bombers, nicknamed "Stratofortresses" at the time. The Navy, with its newly commissioned fleet of Polaris nuclear submarines and carrier-based nuclear bombers, possessed an arsenal as potentially destructive as SAC's.

The nuclear-war-fighting plans laid out by Curtis LeMay and other Air Force representatives called for flattening, among many other things, the Moscow-Gorki area with aircraft based in Maine, striking the Leningrad district with bombers flying from Labrador, and hitting the Volga and Donets basins with planes stationed in England. B-52s were assigned to attack the Caucasus oil fields from Air Force bases in the Azores and to strike the Vladivostok/Irkutsk military complexes with bombers flying from the big SAC base on Guam.

To his amazement, Kistiakowsky discovered that the Navy had its own plans to take out exactly the same targets with its own nuclear weapons. In sum, more than two hundred Soviet cities, ports, industries, and other facilities had been targeted simultaneously by the Navy and Air Force without any coordination between the two.

The official history published by the Joint Chiefs of Staff covering that period observed that there was duplication and even triplication of targets by competing service commands. Kistiakowsky, who related the details of his Omaha findings in an interview with Peter Pringle and William Arkin for their book *SIOP*, warned Eisenhower that the lack of coordination created by continual interservice rivalries was causing the United States to acquire many more nuclear weapons than it needed.

As an example of this devastating overkill, he noted that both the Navy and Air Force planned independently to hit the Ural Mountain city of Sverdlovsk, which could easily be taken out with a small, Hiroshima-sized bomb. The four weapons that the Navy and Air Force would in aggregate use against Sverdlovsk amounted to 400 times the destructive power of that 13 kiloton weapon. Kistiakowsky blamed powerful Air Force and Navy officers like General Curtis LeMay and Admiral Arleigh Burke for using their sizable influence to pry needlessly duplicative nuclear weapons from the civilian factories run by the Atomic Energy Commission. This arms race between two American military services ultimately accelerated the arms race between the United States and the USSR.

Interservice rivalry is certainly no nuclear-age phenomenon. In 1842, Commodore Thomas Ap Catesby Jones, commander of the Navy's Pacific squadron, landed a force at Monterey and claimed California for the United States, acting in the belief that war with Mexico was imminent. The Army and the White House thought differently, and Jones had to apologetically withdraw. War was not declared for another four years, and it was brought on in part because the Mexicans had stopped all negotiations after Jones's naval "conquest."

In World War I, the tiny Army Air Service, under the stiff thumb of an Army high command largely educated by veterans of the Civil War, was keen on a new invention called the parachute. It was being used by the Germans, who realized the priceless value of seasoned pilots who had survived the two or three weeks of aerial combat in which most green pilots succumbed. To Berlin, an aerial genius like Oswald Boelcke, who died in a mid-air collision early in the war because parachutes had not then been developed, was worth a hundred airplanes, no matter how expensive.

The hidebound U.S. Army high command, consisting of cavalry, artillery, and infantry theoreticians and allied with the penny-pinching Senate, felt that giving American flyers parachutes would encourage them to cowardice and the abandonment of valuable aircraft. As a result, a number of perfectly brave American pilots died needlessly. Ironically, the war ended with thousands of combat aircraft, which had failed to get shipped across the ocean in time, sitting uselessly on American airfields.

This was the same Army high command, dominated by a number of ex–cavalry officers and polo players like Douglas MacArthur and George Patton, that required American fliers to wear spurs well into the 1930s.

The Navy pompously resisted the evangelistic crusade of Army Air Service Colonel Billy Mitchell to convince the high command that flimsy little airplanes could destroy big naval dreadnoughts, saying it simply could not be done. Finally, in 1921, Mitchell led his bomber squadrons on a sortie over an old captured German warship off the Virginia capes, and the little biplanes sank the vessel with dispatch. That same year, the Navy suddenly found occasion to convert an old collier into a rudimentary form of aircraft carrier.

In his *New York Times Magazine* article retired Air Force General Jones described the progress of American military air power after that:

> The continued development of air power could not help but blur the traditional distinction between land and naval warfare, but the nation reacted to this phenomenon in a traditionally bureaucratic manner. Each service developed its own air power (all four services now have their own air force) and protected it with artificial barriers to obscure the costly duplications. One barrier, established in 1938 (and later rescinded), prohibited any Army Air Corps airplane from flying more than 100 miles out to sea.

Jones went on to say that rivalries were so intense in World War II that to a great extent World War II was fought along service lines.

In the Pacific, the difficulties of integrating the operations of the services resulted in the establishment of two separate theaters: the Southwest Pacific Area, with Gen. Douglas MacArthur reporting to General [George C.] Marshall, and the Pacific Ocean Area, with Adm. Chester W. Nimitz reporting to Adm. Ernest J. King, the Chief of Naval Operations. Split authority and responsibility in the Pacific was a continuing problem, and nearly caused a disaster during the battle of Leyte Gulf.

The lack of coordination between MacArthur's assault force and two separate American fleets which were supposed to engage Japanese Navy units and shell enemy ground positions, put the entire force at risk—the later heroics of the Hollywood version of the operation notwithstanding. But MacArthur's return to the Philippines wasn't the first time a major amphibious operation was imperiled by service rivalries. One of Winston Churchill's finer rhetorical outbursts came in his frustration at Royal Navy refusal to allow the RAF to use its specially trained pilots to fly air cover for a landing on the French coast.

The admiralty insisted that Royal Navy aircraft be used, even though that entailed a greater cost and additional training. A combined operation, the admirals sniffed, "would be entirely against the traditions of the Royal Navy."

Churchill clenched his cigar between his teeth and stormed out. In a moment, he stormed back in again and slammed his fist down on the conference table. "I'll tell you what the traditions of the Royal Navy are," he thundered, "rum, sodomy, and the lash!"

The RAF got to fly the air cover.

In the Pentagon today, the spirit of rivalry even carries to the colors of the walls. The huge building is divided into "countries." "Army Country" is painted an olive yellow. "Navy Country" has a gunmetal blue hue that is close to the color of battleship paint. "Air Force Country" hallways are painted Air Force blue.

In JCS country, the compromise color is gold—gold curtains, gold wall paint, gold rugs, gold furniture trim. The Tank in which the Joint Chiefs meet is also called the "Gold Room." According to one Pentagon story, the original plans had called for using purple, the color used to mark JCS consensus papers and also the color produced when mixing Air Force and Navy blue with Army green. The results were reportedly too putrid for the JCS to contemplate for long.

Each service also decorates its halls with paintings, statues, photographs, and assorted memorabilia of its own heroes. The Army has an entire hallway—the MacArthur Corridor—devoted to displays of such relics as the legendary general's corncob pipe, favorite sidearms, and medals. The Navy has entombed the artifacts of Admiral Chester Nimitz in similar fashon. The Air Force, which didn't exist prior to 1948, has had to settle for portraits of less legendary newcomers like General Hoyt Vandenberg.

The most intense rivalry, of course, is the annual Army-Navy game betwen the cadets of West Point and Annapolis, which has traditionally been played on the neutral ground of Philadelphia. But interservice games with the Air Force Academy are played on its campus at Colorado Springs. In a rare display of unity, the Pentagon likes to schedule conferences out at the Academy the day before the Air Force games with the Army and Navy, so that high-ranking Defense Department civilians and military brass of different services can fly out together.

But the interservice feuding is more often a very serious problem with sometimes disastrous consequences. Time after time, the individual service branches have stolen tactical missions from each other, amassed piles of duplicative new weapons systems, and driven overall defense budgets to astronomical levels, not to meet valid national-defense needs but to foster their own supremacy. As a result, the structure, organization, role assignment, and equipment of the American military today are not the product of a comprehensive plan but of the pattern of victories and defeats established in four decades of internecine Pentagon warfare.

From the nuclear "Triad" of bombers, submarines, and missiles to the composition of small infantry units, the American military has been shaped by the requirements of whichever service happened to be top dog at a given time.

"We need to spend more time on our war-fighting capabilities and less on intramural squabbles for resources," General Jones pleaded in 1982, just before stepping down as chairman of the Joint Chiefs of Staff.

The tragicomic absurdity of the situation is reflected by the little-known fact that the Army possesses more aircraft than the Air Force does. Indeed, as military writer Gregg Easterbrook observed in the small but influential magazine *Washington Monthly,* the Army's air force is numerically second only to the Soviets', with nearly 9,000 aircraft, most of them helicopters.

Unfortunately, as military reformers have repeatedly warned, the helicopter is a slow and highly vulnerable vehicle of war—a modern, expensive weapon that was shot down by the thousands in Vietnam by pajama-clad guerrillas using ordinary Czech-made AK-47 rifles. The Army officially acknowledges a loss of 4,900 choppers in Vietnam.

According to Paul Hoven of Dina Rasor's Project on Military Procurement, the actual total was much greater. Early in the war, Hoven
said in an interview, Army commanders started to disguise their huge
helicopter losses with a highly costly "repair" program. Badly damaged
("totalled" in automobile-repair vernacular) helicopters were worked
on until they could be put back in service when it would have been
much cheaper just to buy new ones. But someone would have noticed.

"If they had a tail left from a burned-out Huey with part of the
number on it, they would build another helicopter around that tail,"
Hoven said.

After the war, the helicopter counts were compared to the notorious
body counts, which the Pentagon was accused of distorting to defuse
criticism of the unpopular conflict. Hoven, who served as an HU-1
Huey pilot in the war, placed the chopper losses at about 10,000, and
other experts agree. "I'm the only guy I know who only got shot down
once," Hoven recalled. "My roommate went down six times, and another guy in our wing lost nine birds."

From the ill-fated aerial attack on the lightly armed group of
Cambodian Khmer Rouge who seized the freighter *Mayaguez* to the
tragic Desert One raid, helicopters have proved a very weak link in
post-Vietnam combat operations as well. Seventeen U.S. soldiers were
shot or drowned when the Cambodians downed three helicopters with
small arms during their approach to the island of Koh Tang. Another
twenty-three servicemen died when a helicopter crashed en route to
fighting over the *Mayaguez*. In total, ten more people died in helicopters
than were rescued in the mission.

As related in Chapter 4, Desert One had to be cancelled because
three of the eight helicopters assigned to the hostage-rescue force broke
down. During the departure from the Iranian desert, eight men were
killed in a ground crash because a helicopter churned up so much sand
and dust.

In the vainglorious invasion of the tiny Caribbean island of Grenada
in October, 1983, American forces quickly lost nine Black Hawk and
Cobra helicopters—two in a collision and seven to enemy ground fire.

Despite Vietnam, the *Mayaguez* incident, Desert One, and Grenada,
the Army has remained stubbornly committed to helicopters, and is
pressing ahead with a new model—the AH-64 Apache—that, with a
$10 million price tag, costs as much as many jet fighters. In a searing
analysis prepared for the Brookings Institution, the much respected
military authority and former presidential advisor Dr. William Kaufmann noted that the Apache's ground-attack mission, especially as it
concerned enemy tanks, was exactly the same as the Air Force's A-10

attack aircraft. If the Army were in charge of tactical air missions as it was in World War II, it would not have asked for the $1.5 billion a year Apache program in the first place.

The Army was put into the helicopter business at the historic conference in 1948 that produced the Agreement on Service Roles and Missions, subsequently codified into law. In drafting the agreement, General Omar Bradley represented the Army, Admiral Louis E. Denfeld spoke for the Navy, and General Vandenberg participated as chief of staff of the newly created Air Force. Defense Secretary Forrestal was the fourth participant.

Vandenberg and his service were then enjoying a high standing with the American public. As the Army Air Corps, the airmen had dropped the atomic bombs on Japan that ended the war and flown the punishing conventional bombing runs over Europe that supposedly had brought Germany to its knees—although captured enemy documents revealed that the German war machine was producing more aircraft in the last full year of Allied bombing attacks than it had been before the precision bombing missions started.

Vandenberg had managed to convince both Forrestal and President Truman that the Air Force should have total control of both tactical and strategic (nuclear-armed) aircraft. The formal agreement signed at Key West gave the Air Force all non-naval "fixed-wing aircraft" heavier than 5,000 pounds. The document also took note of a new type of aircraft with "rotary wings," but had little to say about which service should have control of them.

It was not lost on Vandenberg that helicopters were awkward machines capable of flying only about 150 miles an hour and poorly suited for the types of maneuver used in most aerial and ground support combat. The fact that the rotors must always spin at maximum speed just to keep the craft flying means that the machine burns far more fuel and therefore has substantially less range than an airplane, which can glide at low power. Once a helicopter's engine was hit, it was downed. Because of their gliding ability, fixed-wing aircraft could survive this. As pilots like to say: "Airplanes want to fly. Helicopters want to crash."

The Air Force clashed with the Army from the very beginning. Vandenberg and his successors were obsessed with the modern, high-technology machines of war—the supersonic jet fighters, intercontinental ballistic missiles, and long-range bombers. The Blue Suits were reluctant to allocate budget shares for support of the mud soldiers in Army green who sought ways to defend against enemy tanks from the air.

Instead, Air Force chiefs of staff pressed for war plans that emphasized attacking deep into enemy territory with interdiction bombing rather than the sort of "first echelon" fighting the Army advocated. The interdiction strategy, of course, required the expensive high-tech flying machines favored by Vandenberg and company instead of the workhorse aircraft used so effectively for troop support in World War II.

From the time it was formed as a separate branch of service in 1947 until well into the 1970s, the Air Force did not produce a single close-support airplane. The plane it finally developed to kill tanks and support infantry, the highly effective A-10, was largely shunted aside in the early 1980s in favor of television-guided infrared missiles mounted on highly sophisticated supersonic F-15s and F-16s.

The Air Force was also reluctant to spend its appropriations on the kind of cargo and troop transport plane both the Army and the Marine Corps said they needed to get fighting men and their equipment into combat areas. The cargo transport the Air Force pushed for instead was "the largest airplane in the world," the grievously flawed, ultra-complex C-5A which was too big to bring men and materiel to small airfields near front lines and which produced the largest cost overruns in military history because of reconstruction necessitated by the discovery that the plane's wings were too weak to carry its enormous body aloft.

In the budget battles, the Army was compelled to counter with the helicopter program—Cobras, Hueys, Black Hawks, Kiowas, Chinooks, and others. The machines were touted as capable of missions as diverse as busting Soviet tanks in Eastern European armored combat and flying counterinsurgency combat missions in Southeast Asia.

The Army built a "Sky Cavalry" of the sort immortalized in the film *Apocalypse Now,* sending it to Vietnam for use in "vertical envelopment" tactics, in which infantry squads were dropped into "hot zones" to engage the Communist enemy on his home base—with the disastrous results we've seen. Combat helicopters simply could not carry the sort of armor needed to protect the delicate rotor-turning mechanism and other vital parts from enemy rifle fire. And the choppers operated at such slow speeds that the enemy riflemen had ample time to aim at vulnerable points.

The Army's solution for the 1980s was the Apache, the $10 million machine designed to fly along the "nap of the Earth," rising above ridge lines and treetops only briefly to let loose with its Hellfire antitank missiles and then dropping back into cover, leaving it to infantrymen on the ground to guide the missile to its target. The $10 million cost in part went for added armor for the rotors and engines, which its champions boasted were powerful enough for the Apache to mix in dogfights with fixed-wing aircraft.

Hoven was not so enthusiastic. "They're building a fighter-bomber-cargo plane and you just can't do that."

As Richard Halloran of *The New York Times* observed in a June 1982 article, the interservice lust for aircraft led to a situation in which the taxpayers were supporting four separate tactical air forces. Halloran found that the four service branches had in aggregate thirty production lines manufacturing tactical aircraft.

James Wade, a career Pentagon weapons project manager, attempted—with spectacular lack of success—to get the four service branches to cooperate on a joint aircraft in 1983. He came up with a creature not greatly unlike Hoven's "fighter-bomber-cargo plane"—a craft called the JVX. It was a combination helicopter and airplane with two propellers that stood perpendicular to the ground for takeoff and then rotated to fixed-wing style horizontal alignment once the aircraft was airborne. It was capable of far greater speeds than helicopters and had a much greater range because of the gliding performance of its wings. Best of all, Wade and fellow advocates argued, the JVX would be able to carry twice as many men as the Army's Black Hawk chopper, its primary helicopter troop transport.

The extra passenger capability made it ideal for the Navy and Marines, Wade said, because fewer JVXs would have to be carried aboard ship for amphibious missions. The JVX would spare the Air Force its usual huge outlays of cash because of the savings generated by mass producing it for all services. The Army would benefit because of its longer combat range and greater speeds.

The JVX (for Joint Vertical Experimental) project was initiated through a 1982 agreement signed by the secretaries of the Army, Air Force, and Navy (acting also for the Marines). A year later, after Bell Helicopter Company and Boeing had produced several flying machines, the project collapsed as a joint venture. The helicopter-happy Army dropped out, arguing its funds could better be spent rebuilding and reequipping 436 Chinook helicopters for $3.1 billion. It also was pressing ahead with its own LHX project aimed at producing a long-range, lightweight attack helicopter with the JVX's excellent combat radius. The Navy followed suit. The Air Force announced it might buy a few JVXs for air-sea rescue but would not make purchases in anything like the numbers originally envisioned.

A series of internal Pentagon memos quoted in the October 1982 issue of *Government Executive* magazine documented how the Navy and Army had quarreled from the very beginning over who would control the JVX project. Navy Secretary John Lehman wrote to the director of defense research and engineering, Richard DeLauer, saying, "I certainly endorse the principle proposed in your memorandum suggesting a common solution. The Navy will take the lead in structuring a program for a common vehicle for the Navy, Marine Corps, Army, and Air Force."

An Army memo replied, "A long succession of rotary wing and V/STOL [vertical takeoff and landing] aircraft have been developed under Army leadership. The Army is already heavily committed toward accomplishing Department of Defense's V/STOL mission responsibilities with a fleet of approximately 8,000 aircraft and extensive investment in V/STOL research, development, and acquisition."

Within months all branches but the Marines had dropped out. Before the dropouts, plans had called for building 1,086 of the aircraft for a total cost of $25 billion. With only the Marines left in the project, total production was reduced to just 600 machines but costs dropped only to $20 billion. With all four services in the game, unit cost was figured at $25 million. With only the Marines buying, it jumped to $33 million each.

The damage done to national security by the helicopter fiascos can hardly be overstated. The JVX case illustrates that the feuding and parochial madness which began in 1948 is, if anything, worse today. It should be remembered that the United States in large part lost the war in Vietnam because the helicopter-dependent strategy of vertical envelopment failed to stop an enemy which simply swarmed back into an area after the surviving choppers left. Even those who prefer the hawkish argument that the Army could have won the war if it had been allowed to use the full force of American military might must concede that the reason that additional force was needed lay in the failure of the helicopter scheme.

The artificial constraints that compel the Army to wage war in enormously expensive and dangerous whirlybirds could be eliminated by redrafting the Key West accords—which created the problem in the first place—to give the Army control of fixed-wing tactical aircraft. But the ultimate solution lies in attacking the problem of the interservice rivalry at its roots.

These interservice clashes have not only been disastrous for conventional defense; they have forged the shape, structure, and nature of the country's nuclear forces as well. It started with *Sputnik*.

On October 4, 1957, the Soviet Union became the first nation in history to place a chunk of metal into orbit around the Earth with the launching of *Sputnik I.* That achievement gave the American public its worst Cold War shock since the dismal day in 1949 when the Soviets detonated their first atomic bomb.

For years the American propaganda machine had, with some accuracy, portrayed the Soviet adversary as a country struggling with crude technology in trying to solve the massive problems of feeding and housing a population that, even in the 1950s, was still recovering from the ravages of World War II. How had these people—who lived three families to a Moscow cold-water flat, stood in long lines at grocery stores to buy potatoes, and only dreamed about the automobiles that were parked two-to-a-driveway throughout the United States—accomplished a miracle of technology that still eluded American experts? Didn't the United States have a space program?

People remembered the 20th Century-Fox Movietone newsreels showing American rockets being fired into the stratosphere from gigantic gantries at Huntsville, Alabama, and Cape Canaveral, Florida. Many recalled the articles such as those in *Collier's*'s March 22, 1952, "Space Flight" issue that featured an introduction by Wernher von Braun, the genius of Peenemünde. He wrote of the wonders of the V-2 rockets that had been brought over from Germany—along with two hundred German rocket scientists—to launch the U.S. rocket program. What about all the promises of a space-going future on Walt Disney's 1954 "Man in Space" television show? Americans began to wonder if the U.S. space program really existed.

In fact, America then had not one but three space programs—one run by the Army, another by the Navy, and a third by the Air Force.

For the three services, the space race didn't begin with *Sputnik* in 1957; it began in 1946 as the admirals and generals embarked on a furious competition for the limited number of available scientists, rocket engines, test ranges, and other facilities. Eugene M. Emme noted in his 1965 book, *A History of Space Flight,* how the fighting over rocket programs started immediately after the war when dozens of von Braun's rockets seized at the German missile center at Peenemünde were delivered to the White Sands Proving Grounds in New Mexico. Between 1946 and 1952, rocketry experts from the Army, Navy, and Air Force divided up sixty-six German V-2s and fired them off at their various test ranges with little or no coordination between projects.

Ironically, it was the Air Force that initially was the least aggressive of the three service branches working with rockets. Emme observed that, during the 1950s, the Air Force was far more interested in developing its long- and medium-range bombers as nuclear-weapons delivery vehicles than in putting atomic warheads on rockets. In contrast, the Army and Navy saw rocketry as a means of getting into the nuclear action.

The Army pressed ahead with a rocket project code-named Red Stone while the Navy proceeded with one called Viking. The Air Force's program was for a rocket system called Bumper Wac, which it tested at Cape Canaveral. The Army erected identical testing facilities at White Sands and the Navy put up a third rocket station at its Pacific Missile Range. Each service was adamant about not allowing colleagues in different-colored uniforms to use its facilities.

The absurdity of this wasteful three-way competition was made apparent the day *Sputnik* was launched, when it was learned that the Navy's project Vanguard was working on a satellite effort but had been delayed for several months in 1957 because the Air Force refused to let the Navy use a launching pad at its long-range proving ground at Canaveral. The Cape's geographic position on the Atlantic range was vital to the success of the Navy's project, and it was compelled to duplicate launch facilities at a location with similar advantages.

But the Navy was not a blameless victim. Its operatives in Washington intervened that summer to prevent the Army from launching its own satellite-carrying Orbiter rocket from Cape Canaveral. While the Navy and Army were arguing over Vanguard and Orbiter, the Air Force was proceeding with its Thor project at another Canaveral launching pad.

The national uproar over *Sputnik* did much to alter American life. Aside from the anger and shock at losing the space race to the Russians, there was dismay that the United States had to create what space program it had by relying on a cadre of rocket experts who once were Nazis.

The American educational system was blamed for failing to produce American engineers and scientists to match those emerging from the Soviet Academy of Sciences. Politicians ridiculed educators for offering so many useless Mickey Mouse courses. As space became a national craze as pervasive as the hula hoop and Davy Crockett coonskin caps, sweeping legislation in the form of the National Defense Education Act was passed and there were profound reforms in the space effort.

In one swoop, the rockets, German scientists, launch pads, test ranges, laboratories, and all were taken away from the Army, Navy, and Air Force and turned over to a newly created National Aeronautics and Space Administration (NASA), a civilian agency. Without the interservice quarreling, empire building, resistance to innovation, and prodigious waste of funds endemic to the military, NASA was able to put a man in space within four years and a man on the moon in about a decade.

The military has not changed its ways, however. With the Reagan administration so hot on the military uses of space, the Air Force in the early 1980s went into competition with NASA and began work on its own space center in Colorado. The Navy refused to join in this effort and decided to build its own naval space center at Dahlgren, Virginia.

Sputnik did more than force the creation of a unified civilian U.S. space program. That 184-pound, beep-beeping steel ball made it frighteningly clear to the American high command that, if the Soviets had put an atomic bomb atop their rocket instead of a satellite, they would be in possession of a weapon capable of destroying any city in America. The "missile gap" was born. President Kennedy invoked this threat of Soviet intercontinental ballistic missiles—then an unfamiliar term—throughout his presidential campaign and administration. His vice-president, Lyndon Johnson, set the tone of the American missile crusade in a 1963 Oklahoma City speech, saying, "I do not believe this generation of Americans is willing to resign itself to going to bed each night by the light of a Communist moon."

The Army, Navy, and Air Force then commenced their own missile race. The Air Force pressed for silo-based American ICBMs, while the Navy urged placing ICBMs aboard submarines. For its part, the Army competed with the Air Force for the right to an anti-ballistic missile system that would protect American cities and missile silos from incoming Soviet rockets.

Out of this competition came the "Triad"—the three-legged nuclear strategy and system on which the U.S. has depended for more than two decades. It now consists of the Navy's submarine-launched ballistic missiles (SLBMs), the Air Force's silo-based ICBMs (soon to be supplemented with the MX), and the SAC's manned bomber force. The Army lost out in the missile race, when the first Strategic Arms Limitation Treaty (SALT I) with the Soviets restricted each side to just one ABM site and Congress subsequently decided to close the single ABM facility ever built by the United States, the Safeguard system at Grand Forks Air Force Base in North Dakota. The Army was able to worm its way back into the missile action, however, with the development of the intermediate-range Pershing missile for deployment in Europe.

Critics have long warned against allowing the quarreling services to drive American nuclear policy and strategic planning. Debate continues to rage over whether changing times have now rendered the Triad a dangerous and costly liability rather than an effective nuclear umbrella with which to protect the free world.

Certainly many of the most costly U.S. defense programs and systems scheduled for the next two decades are designed mostly to preserve the Triad. The MX missile—however it's finally deployed—was built not because the existing Minuteman II and III force is wearing out but because the missile theologians successfully argued that more accurate Soviet missiles were making the land-based leg of the Triad obsolete. The Minutemen carry between one and three warheads. The MX has ten warheads and is much more accurate.

To maintain the Triad, planners in the 1970s looked desperately for a means of making land-based missiles "survivable" in a first strike. They argued the silo-based ICBMs were necessary for two reasons. A thousand or more American ICBMs in silos compelled the Soviets to dedicate an equal number of warheads to American missile targets. Also, silo missiles are considerably more accurate than either manned bomber air-to-ground missiles or submarine-based missiles.

Because the silos are in a fixed geographical location, the same sort of ballistic science that allows space engineers at NASA to hit points on the moon or the outer rings of Saturn with pinpoint accuracy can be applied to the silo leg of the nuclear missile, or so its proponents assert. Thus, just as the Soviets theoretically can drop an ICBM "right down the stove pipe" of an American Minuteman complex, so, supposedly, can a Minuteman or MX drop on the Kremlin onion dome of the Pentagon's choice.

Serious questions about this were raised during the national debate over the MX, however. J. Edward Anderson, developer of the inertial guidance systems used in certain Minuteman applications, warned that the Air Force was overstating both the vulnerability of their own silos and the accuracy of their missiles in making their pitch for the billions needed for the MX. Anderson said in an interview that the claims to accuracy were based on computer projections of test data acquired in firing missiles along ranges extending from Vandenberg Air Force Base in California across the Pacific to the Marshall Islands. But in an actual war, the missiles would be fired on a north-to-south trajectory over the North Pole, subjecting the missiles and their multiple warheads to the as-yet-undetermined effects of that region's strong electromagnetic and gravitational forces. He calculated that an error of just three parts per million in mapping the gravitation field of the Earth will cause a guided missile to miss its target by three hundred feet. And, he said, a three-hundred-foot "bias" in the accuracy of Soviet missiles would mean that many of the enemy ICBMs would explode far enough away from the

Minuteman silo "stove pipes" to allow the United States to launch a devastating counterstrike.

As Pentagon consultant Richard Garwin complained in 1980 to author James Fallows in his book, *National Defense,* the Air Force has effectively been taking both sides of the vulnerability question to keep money away from the other service branches.

> It used to be that the Air Force would say that the Minuteman is not vulnerable, to avoid money being spent on ballistic missile defense systems, which would be run by the Army. The Air Force needs the MX. But wait until they start putting the MX in Minuteman silos. Wait till you hear what they say about vulnerability then.

Garwin's prediction came true in 1982, when Defense Secretary Weinberger announced that the United States was dropping its plans to make the MX invulnerable to Soviet attack by moving the new missiles constantly around Western desert "racetracks." Going instead to the fratricide concept of the dense-pack basing mode, which would in theory compel incoming Soviet missiles to blow each other up, he guaranteed that enough missiles would survive to strike back at the USSR.

But no matter how wonderful it claimed dense-packed MXs are, the Air Force still insisted it needed manned bombers to keep up the Triad. In the militarily generous first two years of the Reagan administration, it was able to convince Congress that the hugely expensive B-1 was vital because it could take off faster than the B-52 in the event of a surprise attack and could penetrate Soviet airspace farther because it flew at treetop level, guided by its complex terrain-following system called Tercom.

At the same time, the Navy pressed for its Trident missile submarine program and sea-launched cruise missiles. Each $1.8 billion Trident submarine—one of the most expensive weapons in the U.S. arsenal—carries twenty-four missiles; each has a range of four thousand miles and carries seven or eight warheads, each bearing the explosive force of 100,000 tons of dynamite. The Tridents are replacing the Poseidon submarines, which carry sixteen nine-warhead missiles each. As the Navy frequently boasts, any single Trident or Poseidon sub possesses more explosive power than all the bombs dropped in World Wars I and II combined. Though their missile accuracy is questionable and they're difficult to communicate with, the far-ranging underwater vessels are relatively immune to a Soviet first strike.

The unhappy history of the Triad is replete with examples of obstruction to innovative reforms. During the Carter administration, a number of leading "defense intellectuals," including Garwin, suggested that a common missile be built for both the Air Force land silos and the Navy's Trident launch tubes. Conceivably, the same missile could be carried by bombers and launched aloft. The idea proved predictably unpopular with both the Navy and Air Force. One or the other of the two services would have been compelled to shut down its missile-building operations if a common "bird" was developed.

J. I. Coffey, director of the Center for International Security Studies at the University of Pittsburgh, wrote in 1980 that the Carter administration had been given the option to build three different missiles for the MX project. One would have been 69 inches in diameter with six warheads, one 83 inches in diameter with eight warheads, and one 92 inches across with ten warheads. "Of these," Coffey wrote in an academic paper, "the 69-inch and the 83-inch versions could both be air-launched and the 83-inch one would be compatible with (and in part common with) Trident II." Carter went for the incompatible 92-inch missile as the choice for the MX, a decison that the Reagan administration readily accepted. Coffey said the Pentagon wanted the 92-inch version because it could match the throw weight of a Soviet SS-18 ICBM.

In the 1970s and early 1980s, interservice rivalry kept the Navy from making its Trident and Poseidon missiles far more accurate. The sea launch makes the Trident missiles less accurate than its land-based counterparts, in large part because the passage of the missile through seawater introduces unpredictable changes in its initial trajectory. Also, it's very difficult if not impossible to determine the precise geographical coordinates for a launching point under water.

A program that was initiated by the JCS would have been a godsend in curing this accuracy problem. A joint effort to be funded by the Navy, Army, and Air Force, it was called the NAVSTAR Global Positioning System (GPS). GPS entailed orbiting in space three rings of eighteen satellites, each equipped with cesium atomic clocks and computers that could be used to give an instantaneous navigational "fix" for any ship, aircraft, or missile on the globe.

With NAVSTAR, wrote Senator Hatfield in a 1980 article commissioned by the American Enterprise Institute, a "defense-related user can reportedly determine its position on the earth to better than 10 meters accuracy anywhere in the world at any time, in all weather conditions." Trident missiles could rival the accuracy of land-based systems with NAVSTAR, he concluded.

Hatfield was in fact opposed to installing NAVSTAR, fearing it would make the Trident weapon so formidable it would pose "a paramount first-strike threat in the eyes of Soviet strategists." As with the MX in its racetrack mode, he warned, this Soviet perception could provoke the Kremlin to strike first.

Hatfield had little to worry about. The Navy high command announced it had no interest in adapting its missile force to a joint NAVSTAR program. Thereafter, the separate services progressively reduced funds in their budgets earmarked for the joint project.

The major reason for the Navy's lack of interest in NAVSTAR was that its leadership was pushing hard for the creation of the Naval Space Command. The new Navy space arm was formally established on October 1, 1983 (twenty-six years after *Sputnik* had so stunningly beat the Navy's Vanguard satellite into orbit). Navy Secretary John Lehman said at the time that the plan was to consolidate the Navy's communications, navigation, surveillance, and allied space activities.

But Lehman hadn't taken this independent action until the Air Force had succeeded in attaining control of a newly formed Aerospace Command. Under the legislation that established the new unit, it was certified as a specified command, an important status in the U.S. chain of command that placed it outside any possible control by representatives of rival services and gave the Air Force a substantial advantage.

Unified commands place all the service units in a given theater of military activity—naval fleets, infantry, tactical air, transport, etc.— under the control of a single four-star general or admiral. The European Command, based in Stuttgart, Germany, includes Navy, Air Force, and Army units. The Pacific Command, based in Honolulu, encompasses all service units in the Asian rim. *Specified commands* are supposed to perform universal services for the entire military. The first two specified commands were the Air Force's Strategic Air Command and Military Airlift Command—the former in charge of all nuclear missiles and bombers and the latter providing airlift for the entire military establishment. With the big space-war push of the Reagan administration, Aerospace Command briefly gave the Air Force an important Number 3. In late 1984 Reagan ordered the Air Force and Navy to establish a unified space command.

Both Lehman and Army officials had argued that the space branch should be made a unified command. The Navy secretary explained he had established the Naval Space Command to keep the Navy's hand in space projects and to make certain it wasn't shorted in the services the projects provided. Army Chief of Staff Edward Meyer unhesitatingly offered to place the Army's several space programs—most notably ballistic missile defense—into a unified command.

A unified space command should provide many benefits for the Navy. For one, the Navy's F-14 fighters could be equipped with the same "Star Wars" satellite-killing missiles the Air Force would be getting for its F-15 in its specified-command role.

Under such a unified command, the Army would regain the anti-ballistic missile programs it had lost with the advent of SALT. Without a unified command, antimissile projects such as the controversial "Star Wars" space antimissile defense would belong totally to the Air Force.

As these services went ahead with their own space commands, the military also began to muscle in on NASA, especially its space shuttle program. John H. Gibbons, director of the congressional Office of Technology Assessment, told Congress in 1982 that "the military/intelligence community has been given unambiguous control over [space] policy decisions."

Since 1958, the United States had spent roughly $150 billion on space, about one third of which was for military projects. But in the 1982 fiscal year, the Defense Department's space budget of $6.4 billion surpassed that of NASA for the first time, as Congress allowed the civilian scientists only $5.9 billion. In 1983, the military space projects were accorded $8.5 billion, compared to $6.8 billion for NASA. The General Accounting Office estimated that by 1988, the military space budget would exceed $14 billion while civilian NASA's would drop to $4 billion.

Though the early shuttle flights were cheered as civilian aerospace achievements, the GAO calculated in 1982 that at least 50 percent of all future shuttle missions would be devoted to military work. One of these tasks was to be installation of the Integrated Operational Nuclear Detection System, a satellite setup that would instantly inform the high command below of which American and Soviet cities had been destroyed in the event of a nuclear exchange. This, presumably, would prevent the Air Force and Navy from duplicating the same targets in following strikes.

As the military domination of the once proudly civilian space program illustrates, the service chauvinists have come full circle from the humiliating lessons of *Sputnik* and are once again tripping up one another's space projects in ways the country can ill afford. Garwin, an expert on the impact of internecine quarreling on overall defense, often uses NAVSTAR as an example to show not just that feuding goes on, but how it weakens American military strength. Because NAVSTAR was begun as a "purple" project, financed by funds from each of the service branches' budgets, the admirals and generals have repeatedly cut their contributions to divert more money for their own service's special projects. As a result, navigation-satellite development slipped nearly a decade behind its original schedule. And that is viewed as a tragedy by many Pentagon insiders, especially those with abiding faith in applying high technology to weaponry.

The prospectus for NAVSTAR reads like a dream come true for the weaponry technocrats. Once in place, the satellite system would be available for every serviceman and -woman on the globe. A rifleman deployed in Europe could use NAVSTAR to aim precisely a rocket at an oncoming Soviet tank just as easily as the commander of a Trident submarine could use it to plot his position for missile firing. NAVSTAR would allow an F-16 pilot to land on a foggy runway in Norway just as it would permit a mortar crew to drop a shell on top of a Libyan position in the midst of the Sahara.

NAVSTAR is the type of program that would appeal greatly to the sort of professional general staff recommended for the U.S. military in Chapter 8. More than any other reform, a restructuring of the American command system to create a collegial general staff would alleviate much of the impact of service-branch feuding on national defense. The mission of a general staff is to pull a nation's military resources together to achieve a unified goal. Four separate tactical air forces would have a brief existence in a military dominated by a new breed of general staff.

The chaos wrought by the interservice rivalries calls for strong medicine. The Air Force as presently constituted, with its control over all fixed-wing combat and transport aircraft, should be abolished. It should be replaced in large part by a United States Strategic Force that would be given command of the entire triad of land-based, sea-based, and airborne nuclear missiles, including the multitudinous cruise missiles the Reagan administration scattered all over the world and the European Pershing missiles capable of detonating on Soviet soil.

The Army, Navy, and Marines would assume command of all offensive tactical air units, a move that would allow the Army to junk much of its vulnerable helicopter armada and replace it with more effective fixed-wing aircraft. The Army would take over the Military Airlift Command and would at last again be able to control its own destiny in terms of acquiring and operating support, supply, and transport aircraft most suitable to its combat needs.

The Army would also absorb the various tactical air interceptor units deployed in the air defense of the continental United States. It already has charge of most of the antiaircraft artillery and surface-to-air missiles used for that purpose.

Operationally, the Strategic Force would function as a unified command, having jurisdiction over the submarine missile fleet as well as the B-52s and land-based ICBMs. The Strategic Force would also assume control of all strategic nuclear weapons in Europe, in the Far East, and at sea, including those now generally classified as tactical weapons.

Under both the Carter and Reagan administrations, the once sharp division between tactical and strategic nuclear weapons was increasingly blurred and now has for all practical purposes ceased to exist. With the advent of the Pershing II 1,200-mile intermediate-range missile, surpassing the 500-mile Pershing I, Army field commanders in Europe have at their disposal not only atomic artillery shells but a weapon that the Soviets would treat as a component of an all-out nuclear exchange.

Carter put in motion production programs that ultimately would add some twelve thousand cruise missiles to the nuclear pile. Reagan ordered some 760 Tomahawk cruise missiles with nuclear warheads and a range of 1,500 miles put aboard conventional attack submarines and surface warships—each Tomahawk carrying a 200-kiloton warhead sixteen times as powerful as the Hiroshima bomb. At the present rate, every major air, land, and sea combat unit in the American military will soon have nuclear weapons. By the measure of NATO commander Rogers, the nuclear threshold will be reduced to virtually nothing.

The proliferation of nuclear weapons among the rival service branches must be reversed. The multiplication of deployed nuclear weapons multiplies the chance for accident and unintentional provocation of war. There are already NATO "predelegation" plans in effect, in which Army field officers and Navy submarine commanders may launch these "tactical" weapons under certain circumstances. The rational perception by the Soviets is that the United States now has nuclear warheads in place that can strike Russian cities within six to twelve minutes—without warning. This invites Soviet overreaction, either in the form of preemptive strikes or a panicked response to fears of an impending American attack. Anatoly P. Aleksandrov, head of the Soviet Academy of Sciences, has already warned NATO that, in the event of a perceived American short-range attack, the Soviets would order a counterattack within two to three minutes.

The military advantage of having field armies and attack submarines equipped with 1,500-mile, 200-kiloton nuclear weapons is one the nation can do without. So can the service branches that now possess the weapons. The Pershings and Tomahawks should be taken from field units and placed under the control of the new Strategic Force. This would cost a lot of money. Pulling back all this nuclear weaponry from field units would require a dramatic increase in manpower, armor, and other conventional weaponry deployed in Europe, in order to continue to pose an effective deterrent to Soviet attack or political blackmail. But it would increase the nuclear threshold to a much less threatening level and would be a price well worth paying. Replacing six thousand warheads with six thousand tanks would provide a mighty and much less dangerous deterrent to a Russian conventional attack.

The Soviets, of course, are not all that immune from internecine service rivalries themselves. But there are fundamental differences between the United States and Soviet systems that make the problem much less costly and draining to Moscow. As Andrew Cockburn noted in *The Threat,* the rise of Soviet Defense Minister Dimitri Ustinov indicated that managing a program that gets the lion's share of the military budget in the USSR brings rewards just as it does in the United States.

Ustinov, and his mentor, party chairman Leonid Brezhnev, rose to power leading the Soviet strategic-missile program during the years when both sides were working frantically to build up their ICBM forces. Ustinov replaced Marshal Andrei Grechko, an old-line officer who rose to power not as the proponent of one weapons system over another, but as a leader on the Russian general staff, which essentially produces the officer corps for all divisions of the Soviet Army. Once on the general staff, a Soviet military officer is no longer dependent upon his "native" service branch—the Army, the rocket corps, the Navy, etc.— for advancement.

The United States's horribly unworkable system has produced a defense establishment dominated by people whose individual careers are driven not by the need to defend the country but by their need to defend their bureaucratic empires—especially by keeping individual weapons projects well funded. Careers now are not even made according to how efficiently someone builds a weapon or how well it works, but simply on how large an undertaking it becomes—how many people become involved on such a project and how much a share of the total defense budget it absorbs.

In the absence of war—in which military officers can rise by courageous performances on the battlefield or by drafting brilliant strategy, as Eisenhower did as a mere colonel on the eve of World War II—the uniformed defenders of America have evolved into a bureaucratic elite of procurement officers. They support the interservice rivalries and other weakening flaws of American defense because they have flourished as a result of them.

chapter ten

THE PROCUREMENT
ELITE

> *How are the mighty fallen,*
> *and the weapons of war perished!*
> —II SAMUEL 1:27

Of 394 courses offered at the United States Military Academy at West Point, 17 are in electrical engineering, 26 in mathematics, and 5 in the application of science to the design of military hardware.

There are just 16 courses in military history and, of those, a future Army officer is required to take only two.

Similarly, at the Air Force Academy, there are a scant 5 courses (one required) in military history, compared with 22 in electrical engineering and 16 in management techniques. The solitary required course in military history at the Naval Academy at Annapolis in 1980 was called "American Naval Heritage."

In surveying the course catalogues of the three institutions that produce the bulk of America's military officers, longtime congressional defense analyst Jeffrey Record complained the academies were turning out men and women indoctrinated in the methodology of procuring weapons but with little grasp of how to use them in war.

The elite corps of American military leaders emerging from the academies or rising through the ranks without benefit of a military school ring increasingly has become a cadre of procurement specialists, steeped in the lore of the business college, ever more distant from the study of war.

This procurement elite numbers in its ranks thousands of men and women whose careers rise or fall as a function of the "success" of the weapons project to which they're assigned. As a weapon's cost rises and more and more staff are added to the project, the officers in charge find ready promotions.

Conversely, in the few cases where an officer finds a way to reduce costs and cut staff, the result can be a failure to receive a promotion. And, in the higher ranks, an officer who doesn't move up moves out.

Making a weapons project efficient can lead to the end of an otherwise promising career in the Alice-in-Wonderland world of military procurement.

For nearly a decade Colonel Robert Dilger headed the Air Force project to acquire "tank-busting" projectiles for its A-10 fighters. Eventually, Dilger was able to rid the project of costly bureaucratic rules and persuade two different companies to bid competitively on the ammunition contract—driving costs down dramatically. Dilger recalled in an interview with one of the authors that, when he took over the project, there were military officers assigned to such absurd tasks as measuring the distance of work benches from factory walls to make certain they met military specifications. These specs, he recalled, included such minutiae as the direction in which factory windows faced and, for no reason Dilger could determine, the thickness of the east walls of each building. He found that Army, Air Force, and civilian Defense Department bureaucrats responsible for the ammunition project had created "one thousand pages of rules for just that one bullet."

Dilger said he decided to "throw out the book." He contacted the Aerojet Ordnance Company and the Honeywell Ordnance Company and offered each company a deal where the only military specification would be the requirement that the shell fit the gun pod of an A-10 attack fighter and penetrate 2.11 inches of armor from a distance of 4,000 feet. The arrangement also stipulated that whichever company made the lowest bid would get 65 percent of the business, with the other bidder getting 35 percent. Bids were to be taken each year. That guaranteed, according to Dilger, that the two companies would try to outperform each other to gain the big part of the contract. Giving the loser a 35 percent share of the business assured that he would be around the next year for a fresh round of bidding.

The process produced a fiendish weapon, a foot-long shell with a uranium tip twice as heavy as lead that could rip through Soviet tanks and fill their interiors with molten metal. The shell was named GAU-8. It was designed for a Gattling repeating cannon carried by the A-10 that had a firing rate of 4,200 rounds a minute—70 a second. (The A-10 actually carried only about 1,100 shells, which were fired in bursts of several dozen at a time.) At tests conducted at Nellis Air Force Base against Soviet tanks captured in the Middle East, the A-10/GAU-8 system scored an impressive 80 percent success rate.

The bidding scheme was a great success as well. The budgeted cost of the shell dropped from $80 a round to $13 a round. Dilger was able to decrease dramatically the number of Defense Department personnel

THE PROCUREMENT ELITE 155

assigned to his payroll, and he turned back to the Pentagon $144 million in appropriated funds he hadn't needed to spend.

When his name came up for possible promotion to general, Dilger was passed over in favor of officers who had risen to their colonelcies on projects involving high-technology guided missiles—in Pentagon terms, more glamorous projects than his high-efficiency tank-killing weapon.

Today, Dilger runs a pig farm in Ohio. The Air Force has canceled the A-10 project, replacing the $13 A-10 shell with a $40,000, television-guided, heat-seeking Maverick missile.

The Maverick was first used in Vietnam. Its computer-guidance system was designed to interpret a black-and-white television picture of the combat area to distinguish an enemy tank from nearby rocks, trees, or small buildings. This interpretation involved having the device choose between objects of varying shades of gray. Such an elaborate TV-computer setup was deemed necessary if the Maverick was to be fired from a high-speed jet fighter instead of from the comparatively lumbering—but highly effective—A-10 war-horses. The high speed of planes such as the F-15 made it much more difficult to see targets on the ground.

The missile had worked well in Air Force tests in the laboratory-perfect conditions of the White Sands Proving Grounds in New Mexico. There, the computer had no trouble distinguishing among the various shades of gray presented to the television camera by tanks standing out starkly against their barren surroundings.

But the missile failed miserably in Vietnam. Anthony Battista of the House Armed Services Committee staff and other investigators found that because the Maverick was color-blind, the computer couldn't discern tanks when they were painted green to match surrounding scenery or when humidity caused the cameras to blur the distinctions between grays. The tests that the Maverick had passed with such flying colors had subjected it to nothing more trying than identifying and striking a black tank parked on a white sand dune.

To correct the failures experienced in Vietnam, the Air Force set out to produce the IR/Maverick, an infrared version that was supposed to find tanks by the heat they emitted. It proved prone to hitting hot rocks and telephone poles on the sides that faced the sun. Critics observed that if an enemy tank were sighted near a burning bush, the Maverick would almost certainly attack the bush. They warned that the IR/Maverick would be practically useless in a major tank battle with burning vehicles strewn about the field of action and burning buildings and other heat sources present.

The failures and criticisms caused several delays in the Maverick program but, even though the project had suffered cost overruns exceeding $2.5 billion between 1975 and 1983, the Pentagon went ahead with the dud.

In a 1980 speech to the American Defense Preparedness Association, Dilger warned that the bright young officers who replaced him had little grasp of the harsh combat problems the complicated and delicate Maverick faced, even if they were able to cure it of its habit of killing bushes and telephone poles.

He pointed out that it required only a six-member ground crew to load the A-10 with 1,174 rounds of tank-busting bullets. But it took seventy people to load just four Mavericks. He also noted that a C-130 cargo plane could carry enough A-10 ammunition to make 520 firing passes, but could accommodate only enough Mavericks to make 60 passes. The A-10 crew needed only fifteen minutes to reload while a Maverick crew required seventy-five minutes.

Dilger's bitter experience was seized upon by congressional critics of Pentagon cost overruns to illustrate the ills of the procurement system. The case demonstrates how a weapon system, just like a member of Congress, develops an enduring constituency. As ever more people are employed on a weapons project and ever larger amounts of money are spent on it, the program becomes difficult if not impossible to cancel, no matter how badly the weapon itself performs.

While fewer than two hundred people ever worked on producing Dilger's GAU-8 shells for the A-10, those employed on the Maverick project numbered well into the thousands. The Maverick production line at the Hughes Aircraft plant in Tucson, Arizona, became that city's largest employer and one of the largest sources of jobs in the entire state. And the reason that so many jobs were created was the complexity of the weapon. Trained technicians were needed to develop the ultrasophisticated computer components that were to guide the missile. Every time a Pentagon procurement officer came up with a new idea to make the Maverick more elaborate, additional jobs were created. Each design change increased the number of people dependent upon the Maverick project for their livelihoods. The missile had its own constituency and that constituency wasn't interested in hearing arguments that a $13 bullet could outperform their $40,000 missile. Tragically, the constituency also was uninterested in hearing arguments that replacing an effective antitank weapon with a failure-prone one posed immense threats to national security.

Along with the constituency came the abuses so common in Pentagon weapons buying. Whenever the missile performed poorly in one of its many operational tests—hitting trees instead of trucks—there was always a Pentagon official available to explain away the problem. Significantly, the same procurement officers whose jobs depended on the survival of the project were placed in charge of tests and evaluation. And when there were test failures, they often led to a growth in the Maverick constituency, because Hughes was forced to hire still more people to correct them.

A 1984 investigation by the Senate Government Affairs Committee disclosed that many of the Pentagon officers who oversaw tests of the Maverick missile were subsequently hired by Hughes and often were assigned to Tucson to work on the Maverick project itself.

John Long, a reporter for the *Tucson Daily Star,* filed a federal Freedom of Information Act request and learned that, in 1982 alone, 102 officers with the rank of major or above had left the Pentagon for Hughes. Each of the 102 had disclosed their crossovers from the Pentagon to Hughes on government form "22-RO 288," the "Report of DOD and Defense Related Employment as Required by Public Law 91–121." Long's investigation also found that many of the thousands of persons hired at the Hughes assembly line were idle for much of the workday, and used their spare time for diversions as trivial as building cable television receivers with electronic missile components and watching pornographic movies during their shifts. Senator Percy, who directed the Senate investigation into Long's findings, discovered that while the assembly lines were idle the company was billing the Pentagon for seventeen times the estimated hourly assembly costs originally promised for the missile.

The Percy investigation of the Hughes missile project, conducted by staff members Alan Mertz and William Strauss, found that the Justice Department had never prosecuted anybody under existing conflict in interest statutes. Existing laws flatly forbid officers from leaving the military and then engaging in business with their former sections. Other statutes require a one-year "cooling off" period before a former Defense Department official can join a company that does business with the department. "The laws just were never enforced," Mertz said in an interview.

The Maverick was hardly the only bizarre mistake made by the purchasing-agent officer corps.

One of the costliest was the decision to replace the Army's $80,000 M-113 armored personnel carrier with a new vehicle named after the late General Omar Nelson Bradley, the Eisenhower protégé famous in World War II as "the GI's general" for his concern over the safety and welfare of his troops. The mission of armored personnel carriers is to

carry infantrymen safely forward through areas where tanks and machine guns are being used. The M-113 was a boxy vehicle with steel
plating, a single machine gun on its flat roof, and room inside for eleven
soldiers—an infantry squad. At just $80,000 each, the M-113 was one
of the most useful and widely used pieces of hardware deployed in the
Vietnam war, sparing thousands of U.S. soldiers and Marines from
enemy rifle and machine-gun fire as they advanced.

The procurement elite decided to "improve" upon the M-113. They
installed a 25-mm cannon, two wire-guided antitank missile launchers,
a smoke-grenade launcher, a 500-horsepower engine, and a turret. To
compensate for the big engine and the other heavy add-ons, the armor
was made of lightweight aluminum. The turret made the Bradley ten
feet tall—two feet higher than the M-1 tank it's supposed to accompany.
Although light, the aluminum armor is so thick it has to be removed
before the Bradley can be loaded through the door of the C-141 cargo
jet in which it's supposed to be carried. The weight and huge engine
give it a fuel economy of just two miles a gallon. Because the added
weaponry takes up so much space, the Bradley can carry only six infantrymen as passengers instead of the eleven the M-113 accommo-
dated.

The worst flaw, according to critics like Paul Hoven, is that the
vehicle becomes a death trap if the enemy uses incendiary rounds against
it. The aluminum armor repels machine-gun fire and land-mine frag-
ments but actually provides fuel to burn the people inside when hit by
such weapons as a $2 phosphorous grenade, which is designed to burn
through metal. In a Bradley pierced by a heat round, the aluminum
first begins to vaporize and then ignites, horribly. "Everybody dies,"
Hoven said. The $80,000 M-113 was virtually impervious to heat rounds,
while the Bradley costs some $1.6 million apiece.

Instead of efficiency and workability, the goal of procurement has
become high-technology miracle machines. Projects are transformed
into Pentagon empires, and the officers in charge overspend the country
into impotency.

The Viper shoulder-fired antitank rocket was "improved" by its project officers until the cost rose from $78 to $787 a round. By changing
the type of propellant used, the designers created a weapon so loud
that it causes temporary deafness to the person firing it.

The procurement elite even turned to the old reliable combat boot,
deciding it had to be replaced because its smooth, shiny surface gave
off a gleam that could be detected by infrared sniper scopes at night.
The new tan, shineless boot they came up with instead could not, but
initially it did soak up water and drench infantrymen's feet.

Pentagon developers of the Tercom guidance system for the cruise missiles were greeted with a nasty surprise. The system employed radar to track the ground contours passing below in flight and compare them with computer maps preprogrammed in the missile's memory banks. They discovered that the ground contours as perceived by the radar changed markedly if there was snow on the ground or leaves were gone from trees.

One of the most scandalous procurement horror stories brought to light the military's ludicrous practice whereby personnel were required to order spare parts from big contracting companies from lists that specified parts numbers and prices, but contained no description of what the actual part was. As a result, the Pentagon was discovered to be paying outrageous prices for the most mundane of items.

An Air Force sergeant noticed that a plastic cap was missing from one of the legs of the small stool used by the navigator of one of the B-52 bombers stationed at Tinker Air Force Base in Oklahoma. The sergeant went to a supply clerk and ordered a replacement cap by its number. The clerk typed the order into a computer terminal and the part was shipped from the aircraft's manufacturer, the Boeing company. By a fluke, the sergeant received an invoice that showed the price paid. Boeing was charging the Air Force $1,118 for the plastic cap. The same order included a washer for the B-52's landing gear. Boeing charged $609 for that.

Outraged, the sergeant made a formal complaint, which ultimately led to a Senate investigation. Confronted with one of the worst military-waste scandals of modern times, the Reagan administration gave the sergeant a commendation and tried to take credit for the disclosure, but the flagrant abuse was part of a system it—and previous administrations—had indulgently tolerated.

It was also discovered that the Navy's F/A-18 project officers were paying $435 each for ordinary claw hammers that cost $15 at Sears. They were paying $437 for steel measuring tapes that cost $8 at Ace hardware stores and $109 each for diodes available for 4 cents apiece at any Radio Shack store.

In a system where careers are made as a direct function of how much a project officer spends, there is great incentive to allow prices to rise to such absurd levels. An investigation by the Defense Department's inspector general found that the price of a turbine air seal made for the F-111 fighter-bomber by the Pratt and Whitney subsidiary of United Technologies rose from $16 to $3,032 in a single year. Of fifteen thousand different kinds of engine parts purchased between 1980 and 1982, the prices for four thousand of them rose by more than 500 percent and some increased by more than 1,000 percent.

There were reforms. After Air Force analysts decided the plastic stool cap should have cost about 25 cents, the Pentagon switched suppliers, reducing the price to just $4 a cap. Waving the offending item in the air, Senator Charles Grassley, a hard-line conservative and one of the Reagan administration's strongest supporters, took to the Senate floor to demand whether B-52s and other prime pieces of military hardware cost so much simply because contractors were gouging the government.

Responding to the bad publicity it received for charging the Navy $435 for a claw hammer, the Sperry-Rand Corporation explained that it computed those prices using the military procurement regulations drafted by Pentagon project officers. Sperry executives said they had followed the rules scrupulously in arriving at their prices. Defense Secretary Caspar Weinberger acknowledged that the company had indeed only followed military procedures.

These rules allow a contractor to pass along its overhead—items such as the office Christmas party, the factory light bill, and the cost of buying retirees their gold watches—as a percentage of each item sold to the Pentagon. Through what are called cost-plus contracts, the rules allow a company to charge the Defense Department a profit computed as a percentage of the overall cost of producing a given item. The higher the overhead charged, the larger the profit the company can demand. Private sector businesses, at least in theory, operate by doing exactly the opposite, deducting overhead costs from profits.

Sperry representatives explained that the bizarre prices were put on inexpensive items like the claw hammer because the company had averaged all its overhead charges and tacked them on to the cost of each unit sold the Pentagon, whether that unit was an ordinary hammer or an exotic jet-engine component. The Defense Department's Inspector General Joseph Sherick responded, "I can understand that explanation. I just can't buy it." But Weinberger, until confronted by major scandal, did.

In a prepared statement, Weinberger said, "The investigation further revealed that, although item prices were grossly inflated, there appeared to be no violation of criminal fraud statutes on the part of Gould [a Sperry subcontractor]."

The secretary was chagrined to find that many of the military-waste outrages were attributable to a system in which procurement officers work closely with counterparts at the various defense contractors, who themselves are former military procurement officers. Harmony becomes more desirable than economy, especially when the serving officer hopes one day to take his comfortable military pension and move to a lucrative job with the company in question.

A fraternity has evolved in which members often progress from their military jobs to the outside firms they once dealt with as project officers—the "revolving door" phenomenon. Often, the door turns full circle. Many a career has taken a procurement officer from the Pentagon into a defense company and then back into the Pentagon as a top civilian appointee.

This revolving door syndrome was wonderfully illustrated by Gregg Easterbrook in an *Atlantic Monthly* article about the machinations behind construction of DIVAD. DIVAD, which was a project to mount a computer-aimed automatic cannon on the chassis of a battle tank as a means of protecting infantry from Soviet aerial strafing during a war in Europe, stood for Division Air Defense gun.

Easterbrook's article (confirmed by independent interviews with major sources who requested anonymity) followed the efforts of Army planners after they decided the U.S. needed such an ultramodern gun following the capture by Israeli soldiers of a Soviet weapon called the Shilka in the 1973 Yom Kippur War with Egypt. The Shilka was a radar-aimed, computer-fired cannon mounted on track—a combination then lacking in the U.S. arsenal. Army planners summoned representatives from Ford Aerospace, General Dynamics (GD), General Electric, Raytheon, and Sperry-Rand. The general project was outlined at a session at the Army's Rock Island Arsenal in Illinois. A year later the Army approved designs offered by GD and Ford for the weapon.

Between 1977 and 1980 the two companies built their DIVADs— GD using cannons which fired the 35-mm Bofors shells available to most European NATO units and Ford employing custom-made ammunition that would fit only its gun. As the early prototype tests were conducted, Army officers assigned to the project found it was possible to mount the same radars used in F-16 fighters in the DIVADs and that the guns could kick out dozens of rounds a minute with the crew simply pushing a red switch when the computer flashed a "fire now" message on its screen. But the automatic-fire control system did not work against maneuvering aircraft. It simply could not hit a moving target if the pilot took the most rudimentary evasive action. The Army then redefined the mission of DIVAD, saying that its purpose would thereafter be only to defend against hovering helicopters instead of strafing airplanes. The Shilka also had been unable to hit maneuvering planes in tests conducted by U.S. and Israeli experts.

Ford and GD then took their respective guns to a testing range in

Texas for a "shoot-off" to determine which would receive the contract. Each company was in charge of testing its own gun. Observers of the test interviewed by Easterbrook and one of the authors confirmed that the GD weapon hit twice as many targets as the Ford gun and that GD officials left the testing grounds convinced that they had the contract in their pocket.

But a team hired by Ford and its subcontractors was to work behind the scenes in the months that followed to transform GD's successes to failures. The stunning turnabout came when the Army's Ballistics Research Laboratory (BRL) subjected the test results to "computer interpretation" as it does on all field test results. First, the computer experts ruled that, if the Ford gun had been firing proximity rounds designed to explode in the air and send shrapnel flying in all directions, it would have hit many more of the targets than those for which it was credited. Similar credit, the computer analysts said, had to be denied the GD weapon because the fuses mounted on GD's proximity shells did not meet federal regulations. Thus, BRL ruled that even though GD had actually shot down twice as many target helicopters, aircraft, and drones than Ford did, the Ford gun was the winner. In May 1981 the Army awarded the contract for DIVAD to Ford. The gun that couldn't hit a moving target was named after the most celebrated marksman of World War I. It entered the arsenal with the name Sergeant York.

Throughout the period when the guns were designed, tested, and then so curiously reevaluated, a number of key players moved through the revolving door between Ford and the Pentagon. Two former deputy commanders of DARCOM, the Army's procurement command, Lieutenant Generals Eugene D'Ambrosio and Robert Baer, retired in the late spring of 1980. D'Ambrosio became chairman of the board of Day and Zimmermann, one of the DIVAD subcontractors, and Baer became vice-president at XMCO, a consulting engineering firm with contracts from Ford. Also showing up on the Ford team were retired Lieutenant Generals Howard Cooksey and C. J. LeVan. LeVan, who was employed by Ford's subcontractor R & D Associates after leaving the Pentagon, had been involved in setting many of the specifications for the Sergeant York, including a requirement that the weapon be able to detect an enemy and fire on it within eight seconds.

By the time the Army finally signed its contract with Ford to produce DIVAD, President Reagan had appointed as undersecretary of the Army James Ambrose, formerly vice-president for technical affairs on the DIVAD project at Ford Aerospace. Ambrose declined requests to discuss his role in the project, but was known to have been the highest-ranking Army official present at the meeting of the Defense Systems

Acquisition Review Council (DSARC) the day the panel approved the project for Ford. Ironically, in 1985, Ambrose, as Army undersecretary, was to order an investigation into whether the four generals were guilty of conflict of interest for their roles in using computer simulations to give the contract to Ford Aerospace instead of GD, whose entry had won the field competition.

The four three-star generals involved in the DIVAD affair are among thousands of officers who continually pass through the revolving doors, selling their inside experience and contacts to make careers for themselves after earning military retirement. As the executive staffs of defense contractors become increasingly made up of former military officers, the industry comes to resemble another branch of the Pentagon, a place much less likely to produce the kind of innovative mavericks who flourish in a competitive marketplace. And questions are always raised as to whether the majors, colonels, generals, and others who cross the street make use of their insiders' knowledge of the complex defense procurement system further to increase the profits of their corporate second homes.

Such questions were raised in the case of former General Alton B. Slay, who retired as chief procurement officer for the Air Force to become a consultant serving both Pratt and Whitney and the Pentagon on the question of whether too much was being spent on spare parts. Slay sided with the industry and recommended that an additional $4 billion be spent for spare parts.

Senator William Proxmire told the *St. Louis Post-Dispatch* in 1983: "A lot of people who work in the Pentagon expect to go to work for defense contractors later. The prospect may be greater if they make a decision that can mean hundreds of millions of dollars for a company. The temptation is obvious."

The *Post-Dispatch* had published a series called The Defense Lobby, which followed the activities of former Representative Richard A. Ichord, a Missouri Democrat who had left the chairmanship of a House defense subcommittee on research and development to hire out as a lobbyist for large arms manufacturers. Ichord's clients included eleven of the thirteen largest defense contractors, most particularly McDonnell-Douglas, the Missouri-based prime manufacturer of jet fighters and giant tanker planes. As subcommittee chairman, Ichord had led the push for many of the weapons built by the companies that later hired him. But the newspaper also found a number of military officers in the same game.

Reporter Bob Adams discovered that Lieutenant General Kelley Burke, who had replaced General Slay as top Air Force procurement officer, had later teamed up in a consulting firm, which had important defense-company clients, with former astronaut Thomas Stafford, a three-star general who had also been an important Air Force weapons purchaser. A third member of that consulting team was Major General Guy Hecker, who had been the project officer in charge of promoting the MX missile and had served briefly as the chief Air Force liaison officer with Congress. The firm of Burke, Stafford, and Hecker signed up six of the top ten defense-industry firms in its first year, Burke boasted to Adams in an interview.

The Council on Economic Priorities devoted a year to documenting the mass exodus from high-level Pentagon slots to big corporate jobs. It found that between 1980 and 1983 a minimum of 1,800 officers with the rank of major (lieutenant commander in the Navy) or above became executives in the defense industry.

Between 1970 and 1979, some 270 defense industry executives joined the Nixon, Ford, or Carter administrations as high-ranking civilian Defense Department officials.

The Reagan administration's first director of defense research and engineering, Richard DeLauer, was an executive at defense contractor TRW before taking one of the most influential procurement jobs at the Pentagon. Paul Thayer, board chairman at LTV Corporation, became deputy secretary of defense when Frank Carlucci left to go into the private sector.

Three Boeing officials given important government posts early on in the Reagan administration quickly became the subjects of a Justice Department conflict of interest investigation. The most visible was T. K. Jones, who left the aerospace giant as its program and product evaluation manager in 1981 to become deputy undersecretary of defense for strategic nuclear forces. As a contractor on the Minuteman nuclear missile force, the air-launched cruise missile, and other strategic nuclear weapons, Boeing has a large stake in the Pentagon's planning for its nuclear force and Jones's appointment raised questions as to whether his large severance paycheck from Boeing amounted to an advance payment for favors yet to come. The investigation was in large part prompted by press reports disclosing that Jones had been through the revolving door before. In 1971 he left a job as a deputy program manager at Boeing to join the Nixon administration as a deputy director of defense for research and engineering. In 1974, he returned to Boeing with a promotion to program and products manager.

The other two Boeing executives were vice-presidents Melvin Paisley and Herbert Reynolds. Paisley became director of research for the Navy and Reynolds was placed in an unspecified defense intelligence post.

The Justice Department announced in 1982 that it found no impropriety on the part of any of the Boeing executives.

The Council on Economic Priorities study documented that Jones had been among 453 executives who moved back and forth between Boeing and the Pentagon in a decade. Similar passages were documented for other contractors: 360 involving Lockheed, 287 for General Dynamics, 278 for McDonnell-Douglas, 269 involving Rockwell International, and 89 for United Technologies.

Defense companies insist that the people they hire from the Pentagon are indispensable for dealing with the confusing and complex military procurement bureaucracy. As Wallace Solberg, an executive with Northrop Corporation's combat aircraft electronics branch in suburban Chicago, likes to point out, the "simple" instruction book for Defense Department procurement regulations consists of thirty-two volumes and takes up six feet of shelf space. The people who wrote those rules, naturally, understand them best.

Nevertheless, others worry that the temptation to lay the groundwork for a lucrative civilian job bedevils any Pentagon officer or bureaucrat as he goes about deciding how much government money to spend and where to spend it.

Did General Slay know he was going to be hired by Pratt and Whitney when he was signing contracts to buy jet engines and spare parts from the aviation giant? Did General Burke know he was going to McDonnell-Douglas when he was deciding whether to buy the company's F-15 jet fighter for the Air Force at a cost of $51 million each? Did General Hecker look forward to the day he would be on a corporate payroll as he flew about the Western desert trying to persuade the people of Utah and Nevada to accept the MX missile?

Many of these officers admit to planning for future jobs in the private sector. But they insist they are blameless of any wrongdoing. Instead they argue that their expertise is vital to the defense of the United States. Burke, for example, told the *Post-Dispatch*, "I have a fairly comprehensive understanding of the military requirements, of the decision-making process, of the evolving technology." He added, "It is always possible to cast it in a nefarious and sinister light," but he noted that the military system forces hundreds of colonels—and even some lieutenant generals—to retire while at their professional peak because of the long-standing "up or out" promotion practice. If an officer is passed over for promotion three times, no matter what the reason, he is virtually forced to retire.

This has cost the armed services thousands of officers who are perfectly competent for the jobs they are holding, not to speak of highly valuable ones like Colonel Dilger. It has also created a destabilizing and unproductive officer turnover and placed an enormous burden on American taxpayers, who must support the gargantuan military pension program. The Pentagon argues that this "up or out" system assures the removal of deadwood and infusions of fresh blood. There is no such system in the West German military, which may have slightly older officers but which has much better unit cohesion and has far outperformed the American military in NATO tests and exercises.

"I don't know what the alternative [to taking a corporate job] is," said Burke. "I guess you could shoot guys when they reach retirement."

Some analysts, including Jeffrey Record, now a private consultant and once a key congressional staff aide on the Senate Armed Services Committee, have blamed the lure of comfy civilian defense-industry jobs for drastically weakening the ability of the American military to perform the mission for which the nation, after all, maintains a national defense—fighting wars.

Aside from the lack of military history courses at the service academies, another symptom of the rush to join the procurement elite is the rate at which ambitious young colonels have turned down opportunities to take actual command of troops. During the early 1980s, roughly one in six officers offered field commands turned them down in favor of desk jobs in various administrative areas, a phenomenon that top commanders such as former Army Chief of Staff Edward Meyer warned was weakening the force.

Until relatively recently, the surest route to promotion from colonel to brigadier general has been to command a brigade of troops. However, as it became apparent that the promotions were clearly going to the bright, younger officers in charge of weapons projects, the number of colonels seeking actual field command began to drop. The only solution Meyer could suggest was to try to restore the unit pride that had wedded officers to their units in the past by dropping rules written in the Vietnam era that moved most commanders from outfit to outfit every six months.

Thomas Etzold, professor of strategy at the United States Naval War College, and other critics have warned that the lure of civilian jobs will continue to pull not only brass but lesser ranks through the revolving door in increasing numbers. While the Council on Economic Priorities keeps track of those above major who join defense companies, nobody counts the tens of thousands of captains, lieutenants, and noncoms who leave the Pentagon to serve as engineers, junior project executives, technicians, and clerks for private companies. Etzold noted that the newspapers read most faithfully by junior officers—*Army Times, Navy Times,* and *Air Force Times*—are crowded each week with ads from firms seeking people who know how to deal with the military system. In his book, *Defense or Delusion?,* Etzold wrote, "The *Navy Times* of June 2, 1980, carried a typical series of ads soliciting helicopter pilots, aircraft technicians, electronics technicians, computer operators, facilities engineers, boilermen, nuclear technicians."

Etzold blamed the departures on relatively poor pay schedules for military executives compared with their counterparts in civilian enterprises—a theme sounded by many officers in interviews with the authors. The war college expert said it was also significant that many of the best people who move through the military ranks are rewarded with transfers to Washington and the Pentagon, where high living costs often provide the final impetus to push an otherwise committed military careerist through the revolving door.

A sympathetic but highly critical description of the process was written in a privately circulated memorandum given to the authors by Thomas Amlie, formerly technical director of the Navy's supersecret China Lake Weapons Center, a missile testing ground.

> The officers who get Washington duty tours just prior to retirement are big winners because their future employment prospects are greatly enhanced. Timing is important. An officer who spends early tours in Washington and the rest of his career in the field has a real problem; he misses out on the early duty assignments which teach him his military trade and he loses his contacts in Washington with the passage of time. Most careers are arranged so that the later tours are in Washington.

Key to the problem, Amlie continued, is that the people in question are products of a military system in which junior officers are trained to follow orders from their seniors without question. "Most are clannish and strongly anti-civilian," said Amlie, himself a former naval officer.

> During his younger years, he is very much under the control of the system and does exactly what he is told. If, for example, a retired general, now retained by the Ajax Corporation, remarks to one of his friends while golfing that young Lt. Col. Smith, who is managing a contract with Ajax, is too picky about overruns and quality control, it is a good bet that Smith will be either less picky or transferred. To their everlasting credit, many young officers have not given in and have suffered the consequences.
>
> It is when an officer reaches his forties that his real problems begin. Like his civilian counterpart, his expenses are at a maximum with mortgage, children in college, etc. . . . He realizes that he

will not make colonel—general, chief of staff—and that he will
have to find employment to keep up his standard of living. In
addition, there is the problem of "psychic income." He is at the
peak of his powers, works very long hours, is emotionally involved
in what he is doing, and doesn't want to quit. Yet, for reasons
beyond his control, he will be forced out. These officers are honorable and decent men, yet they are forced into supporting the
present system which provides post-retirement employment for
them.

The military is a closed society which takes care of its own. If
a retired general representing a client goes in to see an old classmate still on active duty or a more junior man who was once in
his squadron, he will get a very attentive hearing. The officers on
active duty are also thinking ahead. Fighting the system gets one
blackballed and future employment prospects are bleak.

It is an inherently corrupt system and must change, Amlie, who
worked for Reagan Air Force Secretary Verne Orr, concluded. Amlie
urged that in the future military officers simply not be allowed to serve
as the government's program managers for defense contracts. Instead,
he said, those duties should be handled by career civil servants who
are free of the rigid military chain of command and its accompanying
mentality, and spared the insecurity that comes with the "up or out"
system.

Many companies themselves are aware of the unworkability and
other flaws of the system and have set up separate subsidiaries to deal
with the Pentagon to shield their other operations from the corrupting
influence of doing business with the procurement corps. The DIVAD
gun, for example, was made not by the parent Ford Motor Company
but by a subdivision, Ford Aerospace. Similarly, United Technologies
sold its inflated spare parts to the Pentagon through its Pratt and Whitney Government Products Division in West Palm Beach, Florida.

It was executives working out of this Florida office who submitted—
and received initial approval for—bills for spare parts in which the cost
of rivets incorporated the overhead expenses.

The incestuous interplay between company and military brass is not
always a matter of the official order of business. A corporate executive
who helped develop the General Dynamics version of DIVAD said in
an interview he had "gossiped about building a tracked antiaircraft
cannon at the country club and barroom" with Pentagon officials in
1974. The executive, who spoke only on the condition that his name
not be divulged, said his personal security clearances allowed him to
visit officers doing the early DIVAD planning and that, because he was

cleared for secret material, the officers were willing to discuss plans for the gun though they were still official secrets. While the GD man was using his access, so were his competitors from Ford, Sperry, and the other companies that expressed interest in the project—all long before the government formally called for bids.

The incomprehensible procurement regulations to be found in the aforementioned thirty-two volumes and the cumbersome processes that companies must follow to adhere to them are part of what is called the military's "requirement system." It revolves around an alphabet soup of panels, committees, boards, and other agencies created over four decades in the pursuit of buying bigger and better lemons.

The system starts with the Defense Resources Board, a panel of civilian officials and military commanders who meet each summer to discuss what weapons will be needed in the future (see page 123). It was the DRBs of the mid-1970s, for instance, that decided the country needed a means to defend its tanks in Europe from Soviet ground-support air power and proposed the development of DIVADs. This led to the next step in the system—the Mission Element Need Statement (MENS).

The MENS becomes the first requirement—or "milestone"—in the weapon-buying process. It is prepared by the secretary of defense and is supposed to state both the purpose of a weapon and whether it is major or minor. The rules specify that any weapon that costs less than $75 million for research, testing, development, and evaluation is a "minor" project. Any project calling for spending less than $300 million to produce the weapon is also "minor." At an estimated cost of $8.5 million each for 618 guns, DIVAD was considered a major system.

The next step is forming a Defense Systems Acquisition Review Council (DSARC), which is headed by the undersecretary of defense for research and engineering. It checks each milestone to make certain the item is meeting the military specifications called for in the contract. This is where engineers and outside consultants hired by the Pentagon come forth to determine whether ultrasophisticated weaponry can perform as promised. And here is where much of the cost growth begins.

Engineers on the DIVAD project were told that the gun must be able to detect a target, decide whether it is friend or foe, and fire its first round within eight seconds. Engineers were easily able to build a device that would do all of that in twelve or fourteen seconds, but encountered massive problems bringing the time down to eight seconds.

"We heard nothing but eight seconds, eight seconds, eight seconds," the GD gun designer said in an interview. "I don't know how many extra tens of millions those extra four seconds cost."

He expressed a frequent engineers' complaint. Often, as one sonar designer commented, as much will be spent meeting the last 10 percent of a project's milestone requirement as on the first 90 percent.

The sonar designer illustrated his point with a hypothetical case in which a firm might spend $100 million to build sonar gear that could detect Soviet ships one thousand miles away. "We could give them something that would read at nine hundred miles for $50 million," he said.

After repeated meetings in which the DSARC reviews research and development and performance of prototypes, the project then reaches what is called OT/DT—Operational Testing/Developmental Testing. Operational Testing is when the company that built the machine is placed in charge of determining through its own tests whether the weapon is meeting the requirements. In the DIVAD tests, each drone target had the exact same flight path in every pass. Then comes the Developmental Testing—checks made on selected weapons taken off production lines. These tests frequently reveal the flaws that are concealed in the Operational tests, but the bad news comes too late, because by this time the Pentagon has already spent hundreds of millions or billions on the weapon and Congress is reluctant to cut off funds.

It was in the Developmental Testing stages that the Army learned that its M-1 main battle tank was burning more than four gallons of fuel to move a single mile, producing so much heat through its exhaust that troops could not walk behind it and otherwise proving a $20 billion problem. (See page 262 for a further discussion.)

Deputy Defense Secretary Thayer defended the practice of not involving the Pentagon in earlier testing stages by saying repeated reworkings of the weapons could delay production to the point that the weapons might be obsolete by the time they were deployed.

The military's own tests are sometimes no better than the manufacturer's. In 1983, Senator Barry Goldwater was assured by the Air Force that the troublesome Maverick missile had passed reliability tests with flying colors. He subsequently discovered that the tests consisted of attaching five Mavericks to aircraft wings and flying them around for a total of 103 hours. They were never fired at anything.

In his paper, Amlie concluded:

> This "requirements" process is to blame for more poor equipment and costly overruns than all other causes combined. The concept is faulty which holds that a group of uniformed people, no matter how well motivated, can define exactly the performance required of a piece of equipment to be delivered six to ten years hence,

basing their decision solely on a contractor's promises rather than solid data.

The major problem is that the requirement document gains a life of its own and drives the entire program. Everyone is afraid to challenge any of its provisions even if they can't be met, are obviously unnecessary, or will double the cost or schedule. Also, new components, techniques, or inventions are discouraged because everything is driven by the "requirement." A little reflection will show that the requirement process is essential to keeping the system operating the way it does and the present players in power.

It is to this world that the service academy heirs to Grant and Lee, MacArthur, Eisenhower, and Bradley now flock.

These people who now dominate the American defense establishment must be transformed from a procurement elite into what they once were and must be again, a corps of officers schooled in the science of warfare—masters of tactics and strategy and not buyers of hardware who compete for promotions by seeing who can spend the most money.

The military academies must change and strengthen their curricula. They should toss out some of the courses on cost accounting and add ones on Clausewitz. The study of technology should be augmented with lessons or tactics, maneuver, and surprise. No one should be allowed to wear a full colonel's eagles until he or she has commanded living, breathing troops. These improvements could be implemented simply with an order from those in command of the several service branches.

The revolving door must be shut if the abuses sapping America's military strength are to stop. Actually, many of the people who leave the Pentagon for jobs with the same contractors with whom they dealt while in uniform are violating federal laws already on the books.

As we have noted earlier, existing laws flatly forbid officers from leaving the military and then engaging in business with their former sections. A president could simply instruct the attorney general to enforce these statutes.

There's also a need for stricter rules. The cases of DIVAD and Maverick illustrate all too well how contract officers fail to test hardware impartially, approve costly design changes, and otherwise thwart the best interests of national security. Perhaps the biggest reason that serving officers end up passing through the revolving door lies with personnel policies that make the move so lucrative.

Military personnel are eligible for retirement after twenty years in the service. That means an officer with a degree from a service academy can move on to private industry at the age of forty-one or forty-two and begin what amounts to a second career with a defense contractor.

The retiree's military pension, coupled with a generous executive salary from his civilian employer, make the move hard to resist. And, as we've seen, for a colonel or Navy captain wondering if he's ever going to make general or admiral, there's always the fear of the "up or out" rule to impel him through the revolving door.

Much abuse could be stopped by eliminating military retirement after twenty years and instead requiring officers to adhere to the same retirement rules governing civilian federal executives—calling for thirty years of service and a minimum age of fifty-five. Doing away with twenty-year retirement would require legislation, and it doesn't take much imagination to picture the howling uproar among the procurement elite's friends on Capitol Hill over that. But a simple presidential order could eliminate "up or out" overnight.

A president and his defense secretary could also work wonders by replacing uniformed officers wherever possible with civilian executives at many stages of the procurement process. Critics like A. Ernest Fitzgerald have argued for years that putting civilians in charge of weaponry buying would eliminate the "up or out" problem.

A big factor that Fitzgerald and others cite is the job security that civilians enjoy under civil service, but nervous colonels—as Dilger's case shows (see page 153)—do not. This protection saved Fitzgerald's career at the Pentagon despite strong efforts by the establishment, which were only temporarily successful, to fire him for a decade and a half. It is the lack of job security more than anything else that compels uniformed procurement officers to tread gently when dealing with defense contractors while they are still working in the Defense Department. If they take post-retirement jobs with contractors, they are then even more at the mercy of their corporate sponsors and more inclined to use their influence with former brother officers still inside on behalf of the company. Few civil servants would want to trade their security for such pressure, tension, and anxiety, Fitzgerald argues.

Having to wait thirty years for retirement would provide less temptation for an officer to cross the street. The professional soldiery, especially those with active experience in combat arms, should be guaranteed a strong say, however, in defining missions and the weapons capability needed to fulfill it.

Colonel Dilger's highly successful experiment in allowing at least two companies to share in a production contract—with the lowest bidder getting the largest share, but the other guaranteed enough of the project to stay in business—should be expanded and adapted for use throughout Pentagon procurement programs. In 1984, the Air Force, happily, established such an arrangement with aviation engine giants Pratt and

Whitney and General Electric. That year, GE was awarded 75 percent of a $14 billion Air Force jet-engine contract and Pratt and Whitney received the other 25 percent. The Navy has begun a program of rewarding shipbuilders with cash incentives for work done under budget and ahead of schedule, and stiff penalties for late work done over budget. It saved $1.8 billion this way on just sixty-four contracts.

Certainly valuable officers like Dilger should not be retired off through the "up or out" system to run pig farms because they are able to produce more effective weapons with smaller programs and at less cost, thus stepping on empire builders' toes.

Friends of Dilger have speculated with some justification that by reducing the staff on the GAU-8 ammunition program to fewer than 200, he forced his own retirement as a colonel because a general commands far larger numbers of people. The troubled Maverick missile program that replaced the GAU-8/A-10 system requires so many people to keep it going that a general of necessity must command them.

Amlie urged with some success that a system of bonuses be created to reward both innovators like Dilger and individuals who blow the whistle on charging the taxpayers more than $1,000 for a plastic stool cap and similar outrages. The procurement system also needs inventory lists in plain English that accurately describe items instead of just noting their computer codes.

Weapons testing should be taken out of the control of arms manufacturers and their military allies in the Pentagon. An independent testing office is urgently needed. Congress attempted to establish such an office in the Pentagon in 1984, but was thwarted by some canny bureaucratic maneuvering in which administration officials neatly changed the definition of the term "testing" to limit the new agency strictly to weapons already in production. The procurement elite managed to keep control over testing of weapons during developmental stages.

Opposition to these reforms will be rough to overcome. There are too many savvy Pentagon brass hats and bureaucrats who stand to lose too much. Consider the efforts by Representative Mark Andrews, who persuaded his colleagues to pass legislation in late 1983 requiring the Defense Department to obtain a guarantee from the contractor that each weapon it buys will work. This Weapons Warranty Act went into effect in early 1984, but Deputy Defense Secretary William Howard Taft, who by then had replaced Thayer in the Number 2 job, issued an authorization allowing waivers of the requirement.

Pentagon lobbyists had persuaded conservative Republican Andrews and his patriotic colleagues to include language in the legislation that would allow the defense secretary to bypass the law for reasons of national security. Taft invoked this national-security clause the first time anyone tried to press for a warranty. Congress must try again. People whose lives are on the line deserve every bit of the same consumer protection as civilian automobile or appliance buyers, and it is shameful that the well-meaning Andrews was sabotaged in trying to give it to them.

The siren song of newer and more complicated technology must be muted. The pursuit of new technology for its own sake must be seriously questioned at every turn. It should be kept constantly in mind that each time the level of technology is raised, the cost goes up and the constituency for the weapon expands dramatically, though the effectiveness often declines.

Retired General John S. D. Eisenhower stated the case with particular poignancy. Speaking with one of the authors of the aircraft carrier named for his late father, he said:

> Never confuse accomplishment with usefulness. I went to visit the carrier *Eisenhower*. It's a tremendous accomplishment. All those people have a right to be terribly proud. But that doesn't mean it's necessarily useful. The thought applies also to the manned bomber and equally to the bayonet. No weapon is justified simply because it takes a lot of skill and guts to man it.

It takes an awful lot of skill and guts to man the weapons and equipment of the modern American military. As with the procurement elite who dominate the officer corps, there's a serious question whether enough of those who wear uniforms today are up to it.

chapter eleven

LIFERS

> *Let's all go barmy, live off the army,*
> *See the world we never saw,*
> *When we get feelin' down,*
> *We wander into town,*
> *And if the population,*
> *Should greet us with indignation,*
> *We chop 'em to bits because we like our*
> *hamburgers raw!*
> —"ARMY SONG," BY KURT WEILL AND BERTOLT
> BRECHT, FROM *THE THREEPENNY OPERA*

As staggering as defense budgets have been in recent years, it remains a startling fact that half the money spent goes for personnel costs. This is in part to finance the most generous retirement system in the history of any military, a system that pays retirees in their forties pensions comparable to above-average civilian salaries and that has built up an unfunded liability—a lack of resources to meet future commitments—of more than $500 billion.

But it goes mostly to support—through a system of high pay scales, generous bonuses, and frequent raises—that most dangerous and crippling manifestation of the post-Vietnam syndrome: the all-volunteer military.

Since Richard Nixon moved to end the draft in an attempt to buy the political time necessary to negotiate his way out of the Vietnam War, American presidents and congresses have been willing to pay almost any price to avoid its reinstitution. By the mid-1970s, this meant filling the ranks with any kind of bodies who could somehow be recruited. In the Reagan era, standards improved, but only because of the stick of economic hard times and the carrot of hefty pay and benefit increases. The military continued to have to draw its manpower from the poor and disadvantaged, shunting the duty of restraining the Soviet military onto the lower classes.

It has not worked. Even in the depths of the Reagan recession, the worst since the Great Depression, shortages of the skilled and experienced personnel needed to run and maintain increasingly complex weapons systems continued to plague all of the services (though the Air Force and Navy have certainly fared better than the Army). The Pentagon argues that it has continued to meet all of its recruiting goals, but its goals suit a political purpose; they do not answer the real needs caused by the threats facing the United States. The troop numbers needed to counter the full Soviet combat potential have not been there either. The Soviet Army continues to outman the American by a ratio of more than 2 to 1. Reserves for all services in the Soviet Union outnumber American reserves by 5 to 1 in terms of veterans no more than five years from active duty, and 25 to 1 in terms of all those subject to call-up.

Despite the European NATO nations' numerical superiority over their Eastern European Warsaw Pact counterparts, overall conventional strength comparisons increasingly favor the Soviet Bloc. Reliance by the West on nuclear weapons in Europe has reduced the nuclear threshold there to an all-time low. In Asia, as the Soviets arm their territorial borders with Japan and Korea to the teeth, the U.S. presence is so inadequate that there are not even combat forces in Japan with which to reinforce American troops in South Korea should the North Koreans attack. The June 1950 rout of Americans with which the North Koreans began the Korean War was stemmed only because MacArthur was able to get an infantry division across the Straits of Japan in time. Now American troops in Korea would have to flee into the sea.

There are myriad other weaknesses. The obsessive reliance on complex high-tech weapons has been driven mostly by a desire to spare American peacetime warriors the risk of death and injury in potential combat. The unworkability and exorbitant cost of these systems are rationalized as excusable and justified by the pursuit of this elusive goal. The volunteer nature of the military has led to misuse of recruiting for social ends that have little to do with the needs of national security. Women, because of their remarkable willingness to volunteer, have been turned to increasingly, though they are dangerously ill suited for combat roles and cause a number of other serious problems through no fault of their own.

As George Washington, Napoleon, and Clausewitz well understood, a military carrying out not a king's but a nation's purposes must be a people's military—its ranks reflecting a wide cross-section of the entire population. The all-volunteer American military demonstrably does not. Much of middle America is isolated from its military, and vice versa, and has little perceivable part in the conduct of its country's defense.

The true strength (or weakness) of the American military cannot be shown by Pentagon briefing charts or the bottom lines of congressional appropriations bills. It is to be found beyond the walls of the Pentagon, among recruit privates drilling in the dust of Georgia, Navy radar specialists hunched over computer screens in Iceland, women doctors tending to the injuries of the Eighty-second Airborne in North Carolina, supply officers lacing their guts nightly with tax-free gin in Korea as they await the early retirement that follows too many failures at promotion.

Nothing is more key to the indefinite struggle Eisenhower warned would be required against the Soviets than the quality and quantity of America's military manpower pool. Nothing has fluctuated more. Nothing has been more subject to the injurious cycles of defense boom and bust, hawks and doves, war and peace. Whether because of Nixon's political abandonment of the draft, Carter's deliberate neglect, or Reagan's obsessive pursuit of hardware and technology, no component of America's military deterrent has suffered more since the Vietnam War.

In the summer of 1963, one of the authors of this book, serving as a twenty-four-year-old draftee in the Army, spent a hot afternoon working in a rifle range target pit at Ford Ord, California, with a seventeen-year-old recruit who had volunteered for military service.

The two tried to pass the time with conversation. The seventeen-year-old's sole contribution was a recitation of the bodies of water he had swum in during his life. He could think of only five, but he repeated their names over and over, for most of the afternoon.

A few days later, the young volunteer was discharged for being mentally deficient. The author, a college man like many of the draftees in his platoon, served his two years. He had been a television writer in civilian life and consequently was made a Signal Corps radio technician by the Army, serving with the Eighth Army in Korea and the Eighty-second Airborne Division in North Carolina. He was honorably discharged as an Sp/4, the equivalent of corporal. His experience was typical of a draftee's, just as he was fairly typical of the draftees who manned the ranks of the highly technical Signal Corps.

By the late 1970s, with the draft gone and America's military policies dictated by the Carter administration, things had greatly changed. The draft had been ended in 1972. In the all-volunteer military of Carter's last year in office, only 1.5 percent of enlisted men were college graduates. In the "cannon fodder" draft year of 1967, 2.2 percent were, despite the plethora of exemptions, deferments, and other opportunities for draft dodging. In the draft year 1964, fully 56 percent of new soldiers scored above average on intelligence and aptitude tests. By 1980, that had fallen to 27 percent. Mental deficients like the seventeen-year-old in the target pit were being accepted.

The Carter period marked the lowest point to which American military manpower had sunk since before World War II. The all-volunteer Army had been given more than half a decade to prove itself, and it had proved itself a disaster.

In 1965, the first year of the Vietnam "cannon fodder" draft, 28 percent of Army draftees lacked a high school diploma. By 1980, no less than 46 percent of Army recruits were high school dropouts. Nearly 40 percent of the Army's enlisted personnel could not read at the fifth-grade level. Though the high command was foisting increasingly sophisticated weapons and gear on them, many could not comprehend operation and maintenance manuals. The Army had to resort to using comic books to teach complex radar repair techniques.

A confidential 1980 Army report found that of the ten infantry divisions stationed in the continental United States ("CONUS"), six were unfit for combat and three others had major deficiencies. Only the elite Eighty-second Airborne was rated fully fit for combat and even it was found to have some minor deficiencies.

Sixty percent of American tank crews in Europe could not operate their weapons' battle sights. In NATO competitions, American gunnery crews finished dead last almost every time—in one exercise, failing to make a single hit, while allied gun crews scored 70 percent or better. A 1980 test of nuclear weapons personnel dismayed commanders when nine out of every ten soldiers assigned to atomic weapons in Europe flunked tests of basic military skills. Six thousand sergeants in Europe and 900 in Korea had to be sent home to try to improve the troop quality stateside. Thirty-five percent of all recruits were leaving the Army before their three-year enlistment was up. The departure rate among those without high school diplomas was 49 percent. A large number of enlisted men were applying for food stamps. Amidst cries that he was turning the Army into a WPA and an armed Job Corps, Army Secretary Clifford Alexander ordered intelligence scores removed from enlisted men's personnel files so they would not interfere with their career advancement. Generals complained bitterly in private—and sometimes in public. Even Army Chief of Staff Edward C. Meyer admitted to Congress that the Army was "hollow." Meyer turned down a chance to be chairman of the Joint Chiefs to devote his time to rebuilding the Army.

Nor were the other services much better off. Though Carter allowed the Navy to shrink to 423 ships, Navy personnel shortages were such

that a support ship that had in 1979 won the Navy's most prestigious award for most efficient vessel had to refuse sailing orders in
1980 because it lacked sufficient trained crew. More than 60 percent of
sailors screened for drugs at the Norfolk, Virginia, carrier base were
found to have traces of marijuana in their bloodstream. The Navy
was losing 21,000 trained petty officers a year, men who were needed
to operate the huge array of technical equipment on ships. The
Air Force was losing trained mechanics at a similar rate. A 1980
readiness test of the First Tactical Fighter Wing at Langley Air Force
Base found only 23 of the unit's 66 F-15 fighters were "mission
capable."

The Reagan administration was supposed to change all that. Initially,
it did. By 1983, some 59 percent of new recruits were scoring better
than the national average on intelligence and aptitude tests. Fully 91
percent of new recruits were high school graduates, including 88 percent
of Army volunteers. (Only 75 percent of children in the nation as a
whole graduate from high school.) A higher percentage of black enlistees had high school diplomas than whites. The percentage of college
graduates in the enlisted ranks increased to 1.9 percent, and those who
had had at least one year of college stood at 248,000, or 18.8 percent
of the total, compared to 15.2 percent in 1981 (though the figure had
been 21.5 percent in the draft year of 1967).

More important to the high command, the first-term reenlistment
rate for all services was 52 percent, a substantial increase from the 39
percent of Carter's last year. Total paid reserves, including the Army
Reserve, Army National Guard, Naval Reserve, Marine Corps Reserve, Air National Guard, and Air Force Reserve, came to 953,256
in 1964. In 1978, they were down to 787,767. By 1984, they were over
one million. All services were achieving their recruiting goals.

According to Lawrence Korb, assistant secretary of defense for manpower, reserve affairs, and logistics, the Defense Department could
easily have signed up another 60,000 new recruits, but didn't need to
because so many people had reenlisted. Immediately after the 1983
bombing of the Marine barracks in Beirut, there was a 10 percent
increase in the number of applicants for entrance examinations for the
Marine Corps, Korb said.

The Pentagon attributed its recruitment success to "increases in pay
and the total compensation package, increases in recruiting resources,
better recruiting management, a variety of training and assignment
options, enhanced educational benefits, and the growing support and
appreciation of the American public for our young men and women in
uniform." Caspar Weinberger said:

This is our all-volunteer force. These are the men and women who have freely accepted the danger, hardship, and discipline of military life, the family separations and long hours without over-time pay, the mud, the jungle, the desert, the heat, and the bone chilling cold. America has never been protected by a finer military. . . . Part at least of the criticism levelled against our all-volunteer force was really just a smokescreen. Behind that smokescreen was a basic unwillingness to pay the price of giv-ing our armed forces a decent compensation for their contribution to their nation's security.

The Reagan administration did substantially raise pay—by 11.7 per-cent in 1981, 14.3 percent in 1982, and 4 percent in 1983. Starting enlisted pay is now $10,500 a year, and it rises to $12,500 after two years. Starting pay was two $20 bills for a recruit's first month in 1963. Studies by both the Congressional Budget Office and the General Ac-counting Office in 1983 found that military personnel in all ranks were substantially better paid, had more fringe benefits, and had better re-tirement programs than their civilian counterparts in the government. An Army lieutenant colonel or Navy commander with twenty years' service earned $37,400 a year, compared to $29,500 for a civilian gov-ernment employee at the same job level. Everyone in the military can retire after twenty years' service and is guaranteed thirty days' vacation every year.

There have been a number of other inducements and incentives established for the all-volunteer military. Army recruits sign up for between two- and six-year hitches and are offered their choice of train-ing courses or worldwide assignments, with enlistment bonuses ranging from $1,500 to $5,000. In all branches of the service, reenlistment bonuses are as high as $16,000 after the first hitch, and the Navy will pay up to $20,000 to nuclear personnel who re-up.

All four services emphasize education, offering more rapid promo-tion to recruits with high school diplomas and some college and to those who continue their education while in uniform. All four provide a wide variety of college degree programs for both enlisted men and officers, with the military either paying personnel to be full-time students or supporting them with loans, scholarships, and paid tuition fees for studies undertaken in addition to regular duty.

"Area beautification," KP, garbage collection, and other menial "Beetle Bailey" details are generally performed by enlisted personnel only during basic training, with DOD civilians now doing much of that sort of labor. Beer is allowed in barracks, which are a vast improvement over the wooden tinderboxes of a generation ago, and, in 3.2 form, on once-dry Navy ships.

The military also continues to rely on a hard-sell $170-million-a-year advertising campaign—$60 million for the Army alone—to pitch young people on service careers. The outlay is certainly comparable to a large corporate advertiser's and works out to about $500 a recruit. Using the theme of "Be All You Can Be" and employing barrages of TV commercials during pro football games, the Army says its campaign is aimed at "higher mental categories."

But for all the alluring incentives and slick advertising, the fact remains that the principal motivation for these higher-caliber enlistees is hard times. Pentagon officials like Weinberger and Korb may talk of pay and patriotism as they might, but the reality is that civilians who become soldiers merely to find jobs tend to prefer civilian life to "the mud, the jungle, the desert, the heat, and the bone chilling cold," and it shows clearly in the numbers.

In fiscal year 1978, the reenlistment rate was 54.4 percent and 73.7 percent of recruits were high school graduates. The unemployment rate was 6 percent.

In fiscal year 1979, reenlistment was 50.5 percent and high school graduates made up 64.1 percent of recruits. The unemployment rate was 5.9 percent.

In 1981, the reenlistment rate was up to 60.8 percent and the percentage of high school graduates among recruits was up to 80.3 percent. The unemployment rate was at 8.8 percent in December of that year.

Fiscal year 1982 saw the reenlistment rate rise to 68.3 percent and the percentage of high school graduate recruits to 86 percent. Unemployment reached 10.1 percent—a rate achieved despite the Reagan administration's dubious new practice of counting military personnel in the nation's statistical work force.

In 1983, the reenlistment rate was 68 percent and the percentage of high school graduates 91 percent. Unemployment stayed well above 10 percent for much of the year.

The unemployment rate began to drop substantially late in 1983, to 8.6 percent that November, and this was reflected in another interesting statistic. The overall first-term reenlistment rate that year dropped slightly from 53 to 52 percent. First-term reenlistments dropped from 34 to 33 percent in the Marines. In the Army, always the quickest to show recruiting trends, the rate of first-term reenlistments fell sharply from 59 to 45 percent. In the last quarter of 1983, Army recruiting posts reported a 22 percent drop in applications from the same period the year before. By the end of fiscal year 1984, total reenlistment for all services were declining from 68 to 67 percent.

A statistic that made Pentagon manpower experts particularly happy in the Reagan "success" years of the all-volunteer military was the one showing a marked decrease in the number of black recruits accepted for service. They were happy not because they were racists, but because the all-volunteer military has long been accused of using a disproportionate number of blacks recruited from the slums as cannon fodder to fill large gaps in the ranks. In 1979, when black recruitment was actively being discussed as a viable means of getting unemployed ghetto youths off the street, blacks constituted 36.7 percent of new recruits, some three times their proportion in the general population. By 1983, this had been reduced to 24.6 percent, through a deliberate policy of tightening standards and rejecting high school dropouts whenever possible. Some 700 recruiting centers were relocated to suburbs or were opened there.

"It may not be good for urban inner-city America," one Army official was quoted as saying, "but it certainly is good for the defense of the United States of America."

According to recent manpower reports, blacks constitute some 29.3 percent of Army strength, 19.6 of the Marines, 14.8 percent of the Air Force, and 11.4 percent of the Navy, the service in which they were allowed to be only cooks and servants until well into World War II. They are 22.1 percent of all enlisted personnel and 19.7 percent of the entire military. (Hispanics make up 3.6 percent of the armed services, and American Indians, native Alaskans, and Pacific Islanders constitute 4 percent.)

Blacks make up 22.1 percent of those in the E-1, or lowest, enlisted pay grade in the military, but only 13 percent of the E-9, or highest, enlisted pay grade. Blacks are only 8.1 percent of all Army commissioned officers, 4.8 percent of Air Force, 3.7 percent of Marines, and 2.6 of Navy, or 5.3 percent of all service commissioned officers. They constitute 5.8 percent of Army generals, 3.2 percent of Air Force generals, 1.5 percent of Marine generals, and only 0.8 percent of Navy commodores and admirals.

Where the statistics are the most disproportionate is with black troop strength in infantry units. Of stateside outfits, they constitute 26 percent of the Eighty-second Airborne Division, 33.8 percent of the 101st Airborne, 38.2 percent of the First Cavalry, 40.5 percent of the Twenty-fourth Infantry Division, and 51.8 percent of the 197th Infantry Brigade.

Overseas, they are 41.1 percent of the Second Infantry Division stationed in South Korea, the United States's principal fighting force along the DMZ. In Europe, they constitute at least 30 percent of every armored or infantry division, brigade, or regiment, including 34.2 percent of the Third Armored, 34 percent of the Eighth Infantry, and 31.6 percent of the Berlin brigade.

If war were to break out in Korea, one of the likeliest spots for such an eventuality, it's anticipated that blacks would suffer at least 40 percent of the early casualties. With war in Europe, which would involve an immediate clash of armored and mechanized infantry units, easily a third of the early casualties would be black. If a Rapid Deployment Force was sent to the Persian Gulf, at least a quarter of the initial casualties would be blacks.

Women have posed a different problem for the Pentagon. Technically, everyone in the service—from aging generals to clerk-typist privates—is secondarily combat personnel, supposedly prepared to shoulder a rifle in extremis. Women do not possess the same combat proficiency as men, especially as concerns physical skills, and are by law and regulation barred from a large number of combat and combat-related military occupational specialties, although they were put into combat positions four days after the first landings in the 1983 invasion of Grenada. There has been increasing pressure over the last decade or so to expand women's roles and opportunities in the military. Many generals, not to speak of sergeants, feel this will do the military no great good, but the high command feels obliged to accommodate this demand as gracefully as possible.

There has long been resistance to women serving in any but the most mundane support roles. General William Westmoreland told a congressional committee, "No man with gumption wants a woman to fight our country's battles." A spokesman for President Reagan said he opposed the draft or draft registration of women "at any time"; he "supports women serving in the armed forces but does not approve of their serving in combat." Films ranging from Goldie Hawn's comedy *Private Benjamin* to the deadly serious documentary *Soldier Girls* have stressed the female's incompatibility with military life—*Private Benjamin* through silliness, *Soldier Girls* by focusing on the physical rigors and mental brutality of female recruit training.

Antonia Handler Chayes, undersecretary of the Air Force in the Carter administration, disagreed, saying, "We are going to need women as well as men to fight the next war. It isn't sensible to shut out 50

percent of a dwindling manpower pool." She was wrong. Women have
hurt rather than helped American combat proficiency, which declined
badly in the all-volunteer military even before women began shouldering M-16s.

There were at last count some 198,908 enlisted women in the American military, 9.4 percent of the total, and 27,531 female officers, 9.2
percent of all officers. The bulk of them are in the Army and the Air
Force. About 5 percent of enlisted women make E-6, compared to 12
or 13 percent of men.

Of the female officers, by the second year of the Reagan administration there were two women generals in the Army, two in the Air
Force, and none in the Marines, and two female admirals in the Navy.
There had been a woman major general in the Air Force in the Carter
administration, but by 1982, no woman held more than one-star rank.
Though there are some 23,000 pilot slots in the Air Force, it is graduating about only 100 female pilots a year, none of them authorized
for combat aircraft. The Navy has 185 women officers and about 3,000
enlisted women serving aboard thirty ships, none of them combat vessels. About 2 percent of women serve in Army infantry units, while 40
percent are in functional support and administration (supply clerks,
clerk-typists). In the Marine Corps, less than 1 percent are in the infantry and 42 percent are in support.

More women than men in the service have high school diplomas,
some college, and college degrees. Only a third as many women as men
are high school dropouts. Except for the top enlisted grade in the Air
Force, Navy, and Marines, women consistently serve a shorter time
than men before promotion. They consistently score better than men
on intelligence and aptitude tests. It should be noted, however, that
with the much smaller number of women being accepted into the military, recruiters can apply higher standards.

Little of this translates into combat effectiveness, however. The basic
problem of the female soldier is a lack of strength, especially upper-
body strength. It is largely that which has produced the lower combat
proficiency scores, held back basic-training-unit performance, driven
drill sergeants to rage, and made the kind of punishments meted out
in *Soldier Girls* so painful. It was this that led the Army in 1982 to
discontinue joint male-female basic training courses. According to one
Army report, male black recruits routinely reject orders given them by
women, particularly white women.

There was a shipboard incident in 1982 that reflected part of the
problem, when a female Navy ensign who'd been harassed by male
crew found herself trapped in a watertight compartment. Men at each

door had simply "dogged the hatch," using their full strength. The less powerful woman was unable to open either door.

In 1982, the Army proposed subjecting all recruits, male and female, to a strength test that involved lifting 100 pounds. (Troops in Vietnam sometimes had to carry as much as 120 pounds in the field.) Those who could not were to be barred from some 76 percent of Army jobs, at a time when 94 percent of them were open to women. Army tests showed that only 11 percent of women could pass the test. In addition to the 100-pound test, the Army also proposed closing another twenty-three job categories to women, because such job assignments could involve combat zones.

When he took office, Reagan ordered the number of women in the Army frozen at the 65,000 it had reached in Carter's last year, up from 12,000 in 1977. Carter had wanted 87,500 women in the Army by 1986.

In late 1983, Weinberger and Korb backed down under pressure from women in and out of the service. Enforcement of the 100-pound strength-test rule was deferred. Instead, recruits were to be divided administratively into those who could lift 80 pounds and those who could not. Tests show 20 percent of Army women can lift 80 pounds. Also, failure to lift 80 pounds would not disqualify a woman for a job that required that kind of strength, but the recruit would be warned she stood a good chance of failure in the position and would be happier somewhere else.

The military has rightly been much worried by the differences in men and women. In its FM 21-20 Physical Readiness Training manual, it noted that the percentage of muscle mass compared to total body weight is 50 percent greater in the male soldier. Even if the female soldier is the same size as her male counterpart, she will be only 80 percent as strong as the male. Men accumulate body fat primarily on the back, chest, and abdomen. Women accumulate fat on the waist, arms, and thighs, and have to overcome more resistance in activities requiring lower-body movement. Females have less bone mass than males, but their pelvic structure is wider. This gives the male soldier an advantage when running, because he does not sway as much from side to side. The female's heart is 25 percent smaller than the male's.

The biggest Pentagon hang-up about females is sex, with good reason. Sexual harassment is pervasive in the American military. It ranges from catcalls, whistles, leers, and obscene remarks to physical abuse and rape. It can even take a very official form. The following is from a memo from one Navy command to another entitled "Subj: Shipboard Energy Conservation Program; Reduced Flow Hand Held Showers."

All ships have ordered hand held shower installations to commence the program. . . . As a practical matter, can you just picture a tattooed, Buddha-bellied, 20-year veteran using a hand-held shower on a ship taking 20 degree rolls? His bending, stretching, and twisting gyrations in pursuit of the objective rivals the foolishness of this program. And who would want to be next in line at the trough knowing the instrument had the potential of coming in contact with his private parts? . . . On the positive side there could be a water savings if the Navy adopted the buddy system with hand held showers. Though this might not be suitable for major combatants it would fit nicely on ships with mixed crews. Not only would there be a substantial water savings in hosing each other down but the excitement generated by the procedure would undoubtedly lead to a self sustaining Navy population. Money would thereby be saved in recruiting and could be put to good use in establishment of necessary day care centers.

During a field exercise by a Signal Corps Battalion in Germany, the commander ordered some half dozen women soldiers to share a tent with men because of a shortage of shelters. A haphazard partition was strung up down the middle, but the women complained it offered ample opportunity for the men on the opposite side to peek around it. They charged the tent shortage was contrived by noncoms looking for some fun. Two of the women were married, and their husbands, also soldiers, objected bitterly.

In January 1984 the Army refused to pay damages to a woman soldier who had been raped and beaten while being confined in a barracks at Ford Ord, after returning to the post absent without leave. In dismissing her claim, the Army said such rapes and beatings were "incident to service."

According to another Army report, at any given time, 10 percent of all women in the military are pregnant, and a surprising number of them obtain sick-bay abortions. On the Navy support ship USS *Yellowstone,* carrying a crew of 1,000, of whom 100 were women, 23 of the women became pregnant within a year. Pregnancy is officially listed as a medical disability. Pregnant military women remain in the service unless they request a discharge or release to inactive duty, following usual hardship/dependency or sole parenthood procedures. In the Navy, women must return to shipboard duty six months after their babies are born.

Families are a great strength of the all-volunteer military and a great weakness of American combat readiness. More than half of all military personnel are married. Whether single, married to military spouses, or heads of traditional dependent families, they are parents of more than 1.5 million children. All told, the 2.1 million men and women in the military support 2.7 million dependents.

More than 80 percent of them reside in the continental United States, but more than 400,000 of them live in or near military installations abroad—about 340,000 in Europe and most of these in West Germany. Though their families often live in near-poverty, having their dependents with them is presumed to ease the lot of the soldiers facing the tanks and armies of the Soviets, and serves as an inducement to their remaining in service. But the arrangement has a serious flaw. Many soldiers in Europe have said that if the Russians attack, their first act will be to remove their dependents to safety. Then they will return to duty.

But that safety will be hard to come by. In the swift, ferocious, mass-produced destruction of the kind of combat envisioned in the conventional war-fighting scenarios for a European conflict, the combat zones will be quickly extended deep into NATO territory and casualties will be heavy—military and civilian alike.

And those military casualties are going to include a great many women. In the massive "Reforger" exercise in Germany, which involved flying in units from the United States, about 10 percent of those taking part were women. Men of gumption may not like it, but American women are in the direct line of fire in Germany, whether they're shouldering a rifle, driving a truck, or working in a field hospital. Should the Soviets attack, thousands of the bullet-torn, burned, and butchered bodies in Army green sacrificed all over the German landscape to slow the Russian advance will be female. And the number of women in the Army now stands at 76,461.

The American military is one top-heavy with officers. In June 1945 there were more than 12 million Americans in uniform, of whom slightly more than one million were officers. The ratio of officer to enlisted man was 1 to 11.6. Now there are just 2,150,000 under arms and about 300,000 are officers, for a ratio of 1 to 7. There were 15,000 colonels in 1945. There are now about 14,600, though they serve a military one sixth the World War II size. The German army in World War II, one of the best in history, had an officer-to-enlisted-man ratio of 1 to 35.

In 1945, that 12-million-strong American military was commanded by 2,068 generals and admirals—a ratio of 1 for every 5,319 enlisted men. In 1984, there were 1,073 general and admiral slots—more than half the World War II figure—with a ratio of 1 for every 1,724 enlisted men.

In terms of combat force, these brass hats have much less to command. In 1945, the 1,221 Army generals led eighty-nine active divisions, a ratio of 14 generals for every division. Now, 395 Army generals—one third the World War II contingent—command just sixteen divisions. That's 25 generals a division.

In 1945, the Air Force, then part of the Army, had 298 generals in charge of 72,726 aircraft—most of them combat types—a ratio of 1 general to every 244 airplanes. By 1984, the Air Force had 338 generals, but only 7,194 airplanes, of which only 3,336 were fighters and bombers. That made a ratio of 1 general for every 21 aircraft and 1 per only 10 combat aircraft. As a squadron usually consists of 24 planes, that means more than one general for every squadron.

At the end of World War II, 470 Navy admirals were in charge of a fleet of 61,045 ships. The fleet has shrunk to fewer than 600 ships (depending on how many are mothballed to pay for newly commissioned ships), of which some 412 are warships. Now there are 252 admirals. The 1945 ratio of 1 admiral for every 130 ships has become 1 admiral for every 2 ships—in terms of warships, 1 for every 1.6 ships.

The same phenomenon has occurred in the lower officer grades, with the same sort of promotion inflation. In 1945, the most numerous officer ranks in the Air Force were first and second lieutenants; now they're captains and majors. The same officer grades are now the most numerous in the Army and Navy. The Marine Corps had five times as many second lieutenants as majors in 1945; now it has more majors than second lieutenants.

Despite all this, the Pentagon continues to seek more general and admiral slots. After the Vietnam War, the Congress reduced the number of generals and admirals from 1,214 to a maximum ceiling of 1,073. Worse for the Pentagon, it imposed a fixed ratio—allowing only 15 percent of the generals and admirals to hold three-star or above rank. Of that group, only 25 percent could be four-stars.

This ratio stuck the Air Force with a quota of 12¾ four-stars in 1983, meaning a usable quota of 12. When it wanted to play a little high command wheelie-dealie—moving the heir apparent for chief of staff out for some command experience in the Pacific before moving him up to the top—the ratio got in the way. The heir was a four-star and the Pacific job was a three-star slot. Yet the heir had to be replaced in the chain of command by a four-star. It was a game of musical chairs with too many chairs and not enough four-stars.

To pull off this transfer, and also make room for the Navy to let one of its three-stars move out of the chain of command to serve in the Central Intelligence Agency, the Pentagon tried this scheme on the

Congress: simply increase the number of flag and star (admiral and general) ranks by twenty-seven, and the ratio would automatically produce the extra two slots! Legislation to accomplish this was put through but fortunately snagged by Representative Les Aspin and his military expert, Warren Nelson. A compromise was reached under which the Air Force was temporarily allowed to increase its four-star quota from 12¾ to 13, and the Navy was allowed an additional three-star for as long as it had a three-star serving with the CIA.

But the Pentagon wasn't satisfied. It was shortly back with a bill seeking sixty more admirals and generals.

The Pentagon argues that officer inflation is natural in a peacetime military in order to maintain a cadre of leaders to command the sudden influx of recruits who would come into service with the outbreak of war. But that doesn't wash either. In 1936, when the American military consisted almost entirely of such a cadre, the ratio of officers to enlisted men was 1 to 11.

Another argument is that modern military combat has become so technical that more highly qualified—and thus highly ranked—leaders are necessary. But in fact the chief reason for the disproportion of officers to planes, ships, and guns is that recent generations of officers have been turning *away* from combat-related fields.

To be sure, fighting skills and combat leadership are still honored. General Meyer, the retired Army chief of staff, holds the Combat Infantryman's Badge, the Master Parachutists Badge, the Silver Star with Oak Leaf cluster, the Legion of Merit with two Oak Leaf clusters, the Distinguished Flying Cross, the Bronze Star with two Oak Leaf clusters, the Air Medal, the Army Commendation Medal, and the Purple Heart.

There are still West Point cadets like Jim Nagel, who said:

> I came to the military academy for many reasons. The first would be education and the next, football. But I gave up varsity football because I'm more concerned about becoming a military officer. I plan to go infantry. As a platoon leader, I'll have 40 people behind me. If I think hard about it, it's really frightening. Because on one occasion I might have to say, "OK, let's go." And what I do may wind up getting people killed. And I'm responsible for my men.

But for every Nagel, there are too many others bent on becoming technocrats and bureaucrats. In keeping with the trend outlined in Chapter 10, the Army has a goal that 70 percent of all new officers hold science, engineering, or business degrees. It highly prizes young officers with political skills. The Pentagon, among a great many other

military installations, is aswarm with black-striped, gold-braided ac-
countants, lawyers, public-relations men, lobbyists, inventory clerks,
actuaries, and office managers. Especially office managers.

They have swelled the ranks of the officer corps beyond reason,
performing jobs that DOD civilians could perform at less cost, while
the cadres needed for combat leadership and readiness, strategy and
tactics, languish. Their housing allowance, subsistence allowance, moving compensation, supplementary training, educational assistance, and
other untaxed military benefits lift a middle echelon or higher officer's
total compensation significantly above his or her civilian DOD em-
ployee's. Add free medical care, subsidized food and liquor, and other
benefits, and the disparity increases. In hearings on military pay and
retirement, the House Budget Committee was surprised to discover
that, in terms of disposable income, the job of a lieutenant colonel was
more lucrative than that of a congressman or the secretary of the Army.
A full colonel was better off than the secretary of state.

These subsidized, uniformed civilians have expanded niches into empires in the best bureaucratic manner. Promotions are handed out freely
among these nonwarriors almost as an additional fringe benefit, ostensibly as part of efforts to retain experienced officers in the service.
Hence the "Pentagon syndrome" of colonels doing captains' work, and
captains doing second lieutenants'—or sergeants'. Some colonels spend
much of their time running movie projectors. Many add no more to
American military strength and vitality than the file clerks down at
Housing and Urban Development.

"The military has become civilianized in the sense of emulating, at
higher cost, things the civilians can do better," said analyst Edward
Luttwak, "but not concentrating on the things the civilians cannot do,
which are to train combat leaders, to study tactics, and to prepare
strategies."

The higher-ranking officers no longer live in the style of Oriental
pashas, as they did before the Vietnam era. Generals and admirals in
command positions on military bases are accorded mansions—rent-
free—but others, especially at the Pentagon, must make do renting
suburban houses or apartments on housing allowances of $700 or so.
The schools that trained enlisted servants for generals and admirals—
there were more than twenty thousand laboring for Army generals at
one point—have been closed since 1973, but some generals still have
cooks, "aides" to pick up their cleaning, and drivers, though many now
have to drive themselves.

One of the most burdensome costs to the taxpayers—more than $18
billion a year—is for military personnel who perform no duties at all,

even though in the civilian world they'd be considered to have many years of useful work in them. As we have seen, members of the armed services can retire at half pay (with generous, automatic cost-of-living increases) after only twenty years. If they retire after thirty years, when most are still in their fifties, they receive 75 percent of their final pay.

They receive this whether or not they take a full-time civilian job after retirement. They continue to receive it when they become eligible for Social Security and when they start receiving civilian pensions. They make no contributions to the military pension fund while still in service. After retirement, they're still eligible for such active-duty benefits as lifetime free health care and privileges at military commissaries and PXs. Many retired officers are not only better off than when they were on active duty, but are receiving more income than officers of the same rank who are still on active duty.

The most common retirement age for officers is forty-three. For enlisted men, it's thirty-nine. Of the 1.3 million military personnel now on retirement, 87 percent are under sixty-five.

The military retirement fund's unfunded liability—a projection of anticipated outlays against estimated revenues to cover them—of $560 billion is an amount equal to a third of the national debt in 1984. Annual retirement costs are now about 8 percent of the defense budget.

Weinberger defended the system, as he has defended every defense excess, by calling it vital to the strength of the military.

> The retirement system helps meet our manpower management goal of maintaining an orderly flow of members throughout the ranks, allowing sufficient incentives through promotions, and supports our retention efforts. This permits us to maintain the age, experience, and skill mix in the active force compatible with military personnel and defense requirements. At the same time, the retirement system provides a foundation for the strong institutional support of members.

Few "retention efforts" offer such wonderful inducement to quit working.

It is too often forgotten that the term *American military* does not mean a few evil-minded editorial-cartoon generals but more than two million individual human beings—men and women as decent, hardworking, and law-abiding as any in civilian society, and in many cases considerably more dedicated, motivated, and willing to sacrifice. They work in an endeavor whose ultimate end is to kill other human beings and which puts them at that same ultimate risk, yet amazingly they manage to make ordinary lives for themselves.

But they can be very different lives. Perhaps the most extreme example was expressed in the comments of Lieutenant Colonel Wesley B. Taylor, commander of the "Black Beret" First Battalion, Seventy-fifth Rangers, upon its return from the invasion of Grenada: "Our job is to kill people and destroy things. . . . Our mission is to go any place, any time, very quickly. We're either packed or repacking. . . . We're killers, not trainers."

Army Rangers lead hell-hole lives. In their initial training, each unit is given a goat as a mascot. Most mascots eventually get eaten. When in the field, Rangers eat anything—small mammals, frogs, and lizards. They sleep on the ground, not in tents. Though they live better than Rangers, the Airborne units have similar traits of toughness, as do the long-famous Marines.

The Green Beret Special Forces are more sophisticated—they speak many languages and are highly skilled at counterinsurgency tasks ranging from demolition to psychology—but they have the same killer instincts. Increased by Reagan to a strength of 5,000 from a low of 3,600 under Carter, the Green Berets are now drawn from the top 3 percent of Army volunteers and score on the average far better on Army aptitude tests than do soldiers who qualify for Officers Candidate School. Unlike Rangers, Marines, and Airborne (who tore up bars in Fayetteville, North Carolina, to celebrate their victorious return from the nearly shotless 1965 campaign in the Dominican Republic), the Special Forces are supremely professional. "Our soldiers know they don't have to go clean out a bar to prove themselves," said Colonel Joseph Cincotti, director of the Special Forces School at Fort Bragg. Humiliated and abused because of the Vietnam disaster (though some tacticians feel the American cause might have been more successful if U.S. combat activity had been confined to Green Beret operations from the outset), the Special Forces are now trying to redeem themselves in training work in Central America.

If the Green Berets are the ultimate soldiers, most Americans in uniform demonstrably are not. Such high standards do not apply to the hundreds of thousands of men and women in the nonelite infantry and armored units, and certainly not to the multitude of supply officers, microwave technicians, cooks, pharmacists, mechanics, file clerks, and kindred support personnel who populate so much of the military. They are not killers, but neither are they simply civilians in uniform. They are military, a separate subspecies of *Homo sapiens*. If they do not themselves feel distinct and different from civilians, many at least feel that civilians feel distinct from them. This might not be so obvious at a big Southern post such as Fort Bragg or Camp Lejeune, but it's very obvious at installations like the Great Lakes Naval Station and Fort Sheridan, located amid the richest North Shore suburbs of Chicago. It's obvious even in the Washington area, despite the military's enormous presence there.

There is good reason. The realities of American military life are starkly unreal to the average civilian, especially since there has not been a draft for more than a decade.

A major difference from civilian life is that the American military is one of the most highly developed examples of totalitarian socialism in the world. Everything is provided by the government—food, clothing, housing, medical care, recreation. What is not free is heavily subsidized—liquor, entertainment, appliances, laundry, education, transportation.

Military society is thoroughly regimented. One's place in it, one's rank, is determined by the state, or military apparat. Everyone in ranks above that, no matter how individually inferior, is to be obeyed and exalted. Everyone beneath can be considered vermin, especially as concerns the relationship of officers to enlisted men. The state decides the work the individual shall perform and where the individual shall live. The state reserves the right to search the individual's belongings without warrant, to restrict the individual's movements and free speech. The state dictates how the individual shall dress. Indeed, the soldier's job is one of very few where people can be sent to jail for having their shoes untied.

This may be no big thing for a lizard-eating Ranger, but it's quite something else for a Signal Corps sergeant who goes home to a wife, two children, and a lot of unpaid bills every night.

The improvements in pay have lifted the lower enlisted ranks from poverty, but not by all that much. House trailers and small, cramped apartments are still commonplace domiciles. Automobiles are commonly secondhand. Even well-heeled colonels' and admirals' wives can be seen loading up on the cut-rate goods at the commissary, hosting cocktail parties with government whiskey, avoiding civilian costs whenever possible—and considering it their due.

And avoiding civilians. The rigorous social life of officers and spouses is mandatory, and leaves little time for fraternization with outsiders. There's usually little inclination for it. Military bases are self-sufficient universes unto themselves—life revolves around officers' and NCOs' clubs, the commissary, the PX, the military day care center, the post movie. They have their own newspapers, with self-help articles concentrating on such subjects as loneliness, stress, and battle fatigue, and editorials on complex world affairs that sound as though they were written by generals (as many are).

Civilians are all too often viewed as selfish, uncaring, overly comfortable ingrates. Every congressional budget cut is muttered about as another civilian attempt to get at the military. So is every increase in Pentagon parking fees.

If there is a barrier between the military and civilian world, there is another between the military personnel of the individual services. The hard-knuckle fighting between the components of the high command at budget time is reflected lower down by such comments as "the Army works on the assumption that most soldiers are stupid"—that from a high-ranking Air Force officer with three college degrees. The Navy struggles to maintain its tradition of social superiority to the other services. Marines refer to Army soldiers as "doggies." Soldiers in hardship posts like Korea look upon Air Force types as sissies and quasi-civilians. What counts is how well such hostility can be set aside, or turned against an enemy in the event of combat.

This is an altogether different military than that of the Vietnam era—on paper, a substantially more effective one. Shipboard life may be much the same, but Navy warships now carry enough supersophisticated radar gear and missile weaponry, when they work, to have blown the Japanese Pearl Harbor task force to molecules before it came within a thousand miles of Hawaii. Bridge banter between officers and enlisted men is likely to involve technical and engineering subjects that only scientists discussed a decade or more ago.

Each soldier now carries around the neck not only a dogtag but a plastic computer chip containing his or her entire records. In battle, monitors are supposed to wander the battlefield with portable computers, inserting the dogchips to give an instant reading on troop dispositions. Troops ride in tanks that, when they work, can zoom along at sixty miles an hour while firing (if an expressway is handy). Combat training not only includes games of king of the hill, but special pamphlets printed up by the Army to teach soldiers *how to play* king of the hill.

It has often been said of peacetime militaries that all they need to be transformed into an effective fighting force is a good war. The best the United States has provided its military recently was the Grenada invasion. It proved to be an extraordinary gathering of heroes. The campaign lasted one week in combat terms and cost the United States 18 dead and 116 wounded, some by friendly fire. For this triumph, the Pentagon issued 8,612 medals, though only about 7,000 American troops actually set foot on the island and a substantially smaller number were actually involved in any fighting. A sizable number of decorations went to troops who stayed behind at Fort Bragg and other installations, and some 50 medals went to people who got no closer to the combat than the Pentagon. Grenada wasn't Normandy, but it was treated as such. Creating 8,612 instant "heroes" did nothing to create an effective fighting force.

Though the Pentagon has been laboring mightily and extravagantly to expand its maritime force beyond what has long been a one-and-one-half-ocean Navy, its Army and Marines still constitute what is effectively a one-and-a-half-war fighting force. It is enough, theoretically, to fight a major conflict in Europe and a brushfire war—as Vietnam once was—somewhere else in the world.

Whether even that can prove true depends on this new high-technology weaponry, which is designed both to protect the fighting man (and woman) as much as possible and maximize his firepower to compensate for his comparatively small numbers. As is amply discussed elsewhere in this book, too much of this weaponry doesn't work.

But the United States is threatened not only by a one-and-a-half-war situation involving its manpower in Europe and, say, Thailand, but by a whole range of scenarios that could certainly also include having to fight in the Mideast and Korea at the same time—a situation well beyond its immediate manpower capacity to cope with. The all-volunteer military, combined with the Pentagon–White House mania for diverting defense dollars to hardware, simply has not provided the amount of troops needed to protect American interests around the globe. It cannot.

The Carter administration tried to retreat from the Pacific basin. The Reagan administration saw the terrible danger in that and set about reinforcing the American presence there. By 1984, the U.S. had 120,000 military personnel in the region, stretching from Fiji to Australia to Thailand and up the Asian coast to the Japanese-Soviet frontier. Of these, there were still just 40,000 in the front-line nation of South Korea, and another 45,000 in Japan, few of them combat troops.

The Soviets had fifty-one divisions in the area, or 460,000 troops, enough to fight a major war in the theater while waging one in Europe as well. The North Koreans had more than 700,000 troops in line.

In 1984, the Army produced a new war-fighting doctrine for Europe called Airland 2000, which plans for not only an all-out defensive struggle fought in Germany and eastern France but long-range penetration of Eastern Europe and the Soviet Union. But it hasn't the manpower to wage even an adequate defensive battle.

America's failure properly to man its military has also hurt its combat readiness. There simply aren't the personnel needed to keep the modernized Army up to combat standard—to operate and maintain the wonder weapons and the "flying-computer" aircraft—not to speak of a 600-ship Navy. Internal Defense Department documents made public in March 1984 found that despite the Reagan administration's huge increases in defense spending and massive arms buildup, there were 25 percent fewer Army units certified as combat ready than there were in 1980. Air Force units "fully or substantially" combat ready fell by 15 percent in the same period. Combat readiness of naval air units decreased from 86 to 83 percent.

A subsequent House Government Operations Committee report found that the Navy's readiness findings were inaccurate and misleading. Aircraft that for one reason or another could perform only one function— say, fire an air-to-air missile—were counted as combat ready even though their primary mission was ground support.

A General Accounting Office report issued at the time revealed that the same military that had so many colonels and captains performing civilian jobs in the Pentagon was relying on as many as six thousand contractors and other civilians to run sophisticated weapons and communications systems on ships and at bases in front-line areas around the world. These people were under no strictures to remain at their posts in the event of hostilities. The GAO said the Worldwide Military Command and Control System, through which the president and Pentagon operate the military, would collapse within a week if the civilian employees working for it from the Honeywell Corporation alone left their jobs. Assistant Secretary Korb said he thought the country could depend on their "patriotism."

Much is made of reliance on reserves to meet manpower problems, even by reformers like Congressman Aspin. Reservists cannot crew carrier task forces in the Pacific or forward-line armored units in Bavaria. The Army's 951,455 reservists and National Guardsmen could be called up to replace the horrendous casualties expected in a Warsaw Pact attack on Western Europe, but they would be on the wrong side of the Atlantic. And after they were called up, the United States would have nothing left.

If they could be called up. A 1984 GAO study revealed that, because of missing or incorrect telephone numbers or addresses, fully 22 percent of Army reservists and guardsmen could not be reached within seventy-two hours of an emergency.

The peacetime draft must be reinstated. Pentagon officers dealing with or having had experience with combat arms acknowledge this, if under their breath. So do forthright members of Congress such as Senator Fritz Hollings. Many in the military regard Jimmy Carter as a wimp, but he had the courage to reinstitute draft registration. Ronald Reagan sought stiff punishments for draft-age men who refused to register, but hypocritically denounced the draft as unnecessary. Most officers and many in Congress view it as inevitable, but presume it will take a serious war to get civilian America to agree to it. The trouble with serious wars in this era is that they are likely to be over in a few days, especially if "conventional" nuclear weapons are employed. The manpower, intelligence, and technical capability a draft would provide are needed now.

As even Pentagon champions of the all-volunteer military concede, the last of the baby boom young men are passing beyond recruitment age and the manpower pool is beginning to diminish significantly—expected to fall by 15 percent from 1984 levels by 1990.

A draft involving a year's service, as was the case with the 1941 peacetime draft, could be fairly implemented. It would have no exemptions or deferments except the traditional ones of hardship and sole support of dependents. There could be a form of alternative public service for conscientious objectors, also lasting one year. This would make possible a compulsory national service for women as well—one not involving combat arms.

Though the relatively short period of active duty would not be sufficient to train inductees for highly technical jobs, it would certainly suffice for basic and advanced infantry training and the attainment of some rudimentary technical skills. It would serve to create an expanded, self-replenishing backup pool of trained fighting men to be called on as the reserves are called up.

As it has in the past, the draft would induce many to enlist for a two- or three-year hitch in some technical field (thus avoiding being drafted into the infantry). It would also encourage officer training and enlistment in the reserves.

Whether blacks enlist at a rate of only twice their proportion of the total population, as in the Reagan years, or three times, as under Jimmy Carter, the all-volunteer military can never be fair as long as the economic underclasses of the country are made to bear most of the burden. If the United States is to have a strong military—and it seems a consensus of the American public that it should—no one who benefits from that protection should be exempt from helping to provide it. The risk of battle death should be shared by all, and not hypocritically made a condition of American poverty.

To have all classes, including the best educated, serve in the military

is healthy for the armed services, healthy for the citizenry, and healthy
for the nation. A republic with the traditions and principles of the
United States should always have a "national army." It is imperative
if the citizenry is to be wed to any vital military purpose. It is important
if the military high command is to be adequately prudent in its use of
manpower resources. If it had been 241 *draftees* killed in a single bombing of an American headquarters in Beirut, including the sons of the
powerful and prominent, there would have been a more swift and
thoroughgoing reassessment.

To judge by interviews, some of the strongest opposition to the draft,
aside from that in the student population, comes from the officer corps,
especially those in comfy Pentagon jobs living in the expensive Washington, D.C., area. They fear that reinstatement of the draft would
mean a curtailment of the generous military pay increases and other
benefits (or bribes) used to attract recruits and officer candidates. Consequently, the retention inducements they've come to enjoy since the
draft was ended at the close of the Vietnam War might also be curtailed.
"Bring back the draft and I'd have to give up my house," said one
high-ranking Pentagon naval officer.

It is true that the United States is not at war, but neither is it at
peace, and, in our lifetime, it may never be at peace.

The draft has been replaced, not so much by the all-volunteer military
as by the nuclear device. If one can believe in the efficacy and surviv-
ability of a limited nuclear war, then this is acceptable. If one cannot,
then one must come to the grim conclusion that there are too many
young American men and women walking around in civilian clothes
who should be in uniform, just as there are too many scientists working
in the depths of the Pentagon and its far-flung empire of laboratories
and consultancies developing more deadly and more "thinkable" nuclear weapons.

chapter twelve

INSIDE BRAINS

There is no way of judging with any confidence what the process of fighting a nuclear war would be like.

—HAROLD BROWN,
THINKING ABOUT NATIONAL SECURITY

As each new president moves into 1600 Pennsylvania Avenue, a new scientist usually moves into Room 3E 1008 at the Pentagon—the work space assigned to each administration's "Dr. Strangelove," better known as the director of defense research and engineering (DDR&E). The initials DDR&E inspire awe, respect, and fear throughout the American defense establishment. From this office just down the yellow-painted circular hall from the secretary of defense's quarters, the DDR&E directs a vast network of scientists, design experts, university thinkers and strategists specializing in both nuclear and conventional war, and engineers in both military uniform and corporate mufti. He is chief of an intellectual empire, the apparat of a science dedicated to death.

The product of the DDR&E and his elaborate team is each generation's nightmares. It is these usually quite brilliant people who conceive, design, and see to the building of thermonuclear warheads, uranium-tipped bullets, deadlier napalm, space death rays, binary nerve gas projectiles, plastic dart grenades, infrared sniper rifles, Teflon-coated commando throwing knives, eye-frying microwave devices, and other horrors and wonders of the modern American arsenal. James Canan, a longtime Pentagon specialist for *Business Week* magazine, called the DDR&E and his domain "the exchequer of the evocative."

Pentagon research and development projects range from the awesome to the absurd, from drafting the latest and most destructive nuclear-war-fighting plans to designing combat boots whose soles are molded to leave in the ground prints of someone walking barefoot.

In secret laboratories in such far-flung locations as Moundsville, Ohio; Pinellas, Florida; Denver; and Seattle, the weapons of the nuclear apocalypse are created. In places like Natick, Massachusetts; Albuquerque, New Mexico; Rock Island, Illinois; and Leavenworth, Kansas, resident geniuses pursue less devastating ends.

At Natick, for example, a Pentagon laboratory created the air-conditioned underwear—garments woven of tiny hollow tubes containing coolant—which proved to be necessary if crews of the trouble-plagued new Abrams M-1 main battle tank were to survive in its superheated interior long (see page 263 for a further discussion). A spokesman for the Natick lab also described the "barefoot" boots as "definitely a covert operation."

Senator William Proxmire once awarded one of his Golden Fleece Awards to Natick, after discovering the Army had used the expensive facility for a study of ways to make Worcestershire sauce bottles meet rigid military specifications.

The public exposure given their more absurd creations by critics like Proxmire have never diminished the inside brains' zeal for the extraordinary. Unspecified millions were spent during the Carter years on deadly serious research projects seeking ways to use fortune-tellers and other psychics to locate Soviet missile silos and other secret installations. When news reports of these strange pursuits surfaced in early 1984, Pentagon spokesmen flatly denied that "so much as a nickel" was spent on seers. However, Admiral Stansfield Turner, former CIA director for Carter, told one of the authors in 1977 that the administration indeed had studied the possibility of using psychics, albeit without any luck. Turner said that officials showed one psychic pictures of Soviet locales and asked him to tell them what was going on there at that time. But, said Turner, "He died, and we haven't heard from him since."

Whether it's work on psychic phenomena, doomsday devices, or Army-way steak sauce containers, it's all controlled by one man, the DDR&E. He is the ultimate Pentagon "inside brain," paid a mere civil-service wage to think the unthinkable and ponder the imponderable, to do the devil's work and yet play God.

He is master not only of his Defense Department scientists and engineers but their counterparts in major corporations, universities, and colleges, and in the myriad consulting firms housed in the archipelago of gleaming new office buildings that circles Washington on either side of Interstate 495, the Capital Beltway. Hence their endearing nickname: the Beltway Bandits.

The nexus between the DDR&E's "inside brains" and that multifaceted array of "outside brains" has produced the larger part of today's most complex weaponry and continues even more chilling scholarship into bigger and better ways to fight nuclear war. In this secret establishment was born the Mutually Assured Destruction theory, which almost religiously held that the prospect of global nuclear destruction would keep the United States and the Soviets from firing off their missiles.

It was here that MAD evolved into the "no-cities" or Counterforce strategy, which opted instead for concentrating solely on military targets in hopes of keeping destruction at "acceptable" levels, and making nuclear war "thinkable."

As "Dr. Strangelove," the DDR&E is the third-highest official in the Defense Department, just below the deputy secretary and the secretary himself. From the time the job was first created in 1958 to the last year of the first Reagan term, it has been held by only six men. All came from the tight fraternity that is the industrial-academic-military complex.

The first DDR&E, Dr. Herbert York, left the post before cinema audiences everywhere developed nuclear angst from Terry Southern's chillingly hilarious black comedy screenplay for Stanley Kubrick's movie, *Dr. Strangelove, Or How I Learned to Stop Worrying and Love the Bomb*. The movie saddled all future DDR&Es with the sobriquet of "Strangelove." Like his next two successors, Harold Brown and John Foster, York was a nuclear weapons expert who had served as director of the Lawrence Livermore Radiation Laboratories in the mountains east of San Francisco, one of the two complexes established by the Atomic Energy Commission (AEC) to design nuclear weapons and study their prospective uses.

That there were two such institutions resulted from a feud between Dr. Edward Teller, known as the father of the hydrogen bomb, and Dr. J. Robert Oppenheimer, the chief physicist in the World War II Manhattan Project that produced the atomic bomb. Oppenheimer clashed violently with Teller over the need for an H-bomb, prompting the AEC to keep them apart but still working for the government by setting Oppenheimer up in a weapons laboratory outside Los Alamos, New Mexico, and installing Teller in similar facilities at Livermore.

York, Brown, and Foster were all intellectual partisans of Teller's position. Brown, a child prodigy who earned his bachelor's degree at eighteen and a Ph.D. in physics at twenty-two, was credited with much of the early work that made the H-bomb possible. York and Brown were also key architects of the MAD Single Integrated Operations Plan (SIOP) that assumed that both the United States and the USSR would unleash their entire nuclear arsenals once either was attacked with a nuclear weapon—a SIOP remaining in effect for more than fifteen years. It was phased out under the stewardship of James Schlesinger, who served as Richard Nixon's last defense secretary, and Brown himself, when he became defense secretary under Carter.

After leaving the post with the advent of the Kennedy administration in 1961, York wrote an angry book called *Race to Oblivion,* which generally damned the weapons culture, but he continued to earn his living from the defense industry by serving as a consultant to a variety of companies and think tanks, operating from a headquarters in San Diego.

Brown took over as DDR&E at a time when Kennedy's defense secretary, former Ford president Robert McNamara, was attempting to impose the same management techniques and efficiencies he had practiced running the giant auto manufacturer on a Pentagon that was the antithesis of such methodology. His effort proved feeble, but one McNamara reform that continues to the present was his strengthening of the powers of the DDR&E. As one of McNamara's whiz kids, Brown set about doing away with such pet military projects as the quickly obsolete Nike Zeus antiaircraft missile, deployed in unlikely places like the parks along Chicago's lakefront, and the controversial B-70 bomber, precursor of today's controversial B-1.

After Johnson became president, Brown ascended to secretary of the Air Force and was a key planner in the monumentally ineffective air war in Vietnam. He's been given the major credit for the largely useless aerial defoliation of Vietnamese jungles and the development of "smart" bombs that aim themselves while falling toward the ground. When not employed in the Pentagon, Brown has worked for academic institutions with large defense consulting contracts, including the California Institute of Technology and Johns Hopkins University—reportedly for quite sizable salaries.

Replacing Brown as DDR&E in 1965, Livermore's John Foster remained in the post for eight years, under both Johnson and Nixon. An extremely popular man with a quick wit, Foster served at a time when an actual war was on and the Pentagon was less fixated on research and development. Nonetheless, Foster was responsible for most of the work that led to making U.S. missiles capable of firing multiple, independently targetable warheads (MIRVs), and to the development of the nation's spy satellite system.

During Foster's tenure, Richard DeLauer was in charge of missile and satellite systems for TRW Incorporated, which produced much of the government's equipment of that sort. When DeLauer became Ronald Reagan's first DDR&E, Foster was TRW's vice-president for missiles. He was also made a member of a panel of the Defense Science Board that reviewed the MX missile and many satellite weapons projects.

As DDR&E, Foster was more concerned with how to use weapons than with how to build them. It was under Foster that Pentagon scientists worked up the many thousands of computer scenarios predicting the probable outcomes of limited or "theater" nuclear exchanges between the United States and the Soviets, as well as those involving such smaller nuclear powers as France, Britain, India, and China. Foster's targeting studies became the basis for National Security Decision Memorandum Number 242, the so-called flexible option plan that replaced MAD as the operational nuclear-war-fighting strategy in the Nixon era.

This plan required the development of a variety of tactical nuclear weapons that could be used in small theater engagements in both Europe and Asia. This meant a great many new contracts for defense companies, as well as a profound change in U.S. war thinking, which hitherto had visualized just two types of war—conventional and nuclear. That concept had become so entrenched that the word *tactical* had come to mean non-nuclear weapons. Foster changed all that, with the help of such Flexible Response Doctrine advocates as Schlesinger, whose background had included service as director of the CIA and as a thinker for the Air Force's principal think tank, the RAND Corporation.

Foster was succeeded in 1973 by Malcom Currie, a hardware-oriented former Navy flier who had worked at Hughes Aircraft and later for Beckman Industries of Fullerton, California. Currie had been in charge of the laboratory at Hughes where Dr. Theodore Maiman built the first operational laser, the weapon that would later become the centerpiece of Reagan's "Star Wars" space militarization program. When he became the DDR&E, Currie personally held nine patents stemming from his engineering work, and had several others pending. His tenure saw an explosion of new weapons systems come off the drawing boards— the B-1, the MX, the M-1 tank, the Copperhead laser-guided missile, the TOW missile, and billions of dollars' worth of others.

When Gerald Ford took over from the disgraced Nixon, Currie sent Congress, on the new president's behalf, a massive package of sixty-four new major weapons systems and spending requests for underwriting more than twenty thousand research and exploratory technology projects. As the Vietnam War wound down, Currie seemed bent on winding up a frantic R & D technology race. After Ford lost to Carter, Currie went back to Hughes Aircraft and its laser development program. After Reagan took over and launched the "Star Wars" space race, Currie served on the same Defense Science Board as Foster.

When Carter made Brown defense secretary, Brown recruited William Perry, a San Francisco defense contractor who owned his own company, to serve as DDR&E. Unlike the hardware-oriented Currie, Perry displayed an analyst's bent for rethinking many policies of the past. He joined forces with Brown to scrap the B-1 bomber project that Currie had championed. He advocated restraint in the numbers of new weapons programs that the Ford Pentagon had begun at Currie's urging. A friend and intellectual soul mate of Brown, with a genius IQ to match, Perry was also a savvy businessman, and something of a mysterious figure. His California consulting firm, ESL Incorporated, specialized in electronic reconnaissance devices and in using computers to analyze reconnaissance data. ESL obtained several Pentagon contracts for the study of the accuracy of both U.S. guided missiles and their Soviet counterparts.

Perry received an Army medal for top secret work that was described in the citation only as "the development of systems for the collection of vitally important intelligence through the use of advanced electronics." But if Perry was antagonistic to big hardware projects like the B-1, Carter's Strangelove became a passionate advocate of the granddaddy of all modern military hardware extravaganzas, the plan to build 200 MX missiles and hide them among 4,600 firing sites along a racetrack base occupying much of Nevada and Utah.

Christopher Payne of the American Federation of Scientists was later to tell writer Michael Parfit, author of *The Boys Behind the Bomb,* that Perry, while still with ESL, had himself prepared much of the scientific research that had persuaded Carter to press for the MX. ESL was the developer of the American techniques used to monitor Soviet missile tests and calculate how accurately the Russian rockets hit their targets. Using ESL methodology, U.S. analysts concluded that the Soviet ICBMs of the mid-1970s were so accurate their warheads could strike U.S. Minuteman silos with precision enough to wipe out most if not all of the land leg of the American Triad in a first strike. This Minuteman "vulnerability" was the driving force behind arguments for the MX.

While Perry was pushing for the MX, he was also helping Brown devise the new nuclear weapons strategy that Carter eventually implemented in Presidential Directive 59, which replaced the Flexible Response Doctrine. PD 59 established a descending order of Soviet military and civilian targets and then specified various mixes of U.S. nuclear weapons to be used against each other.

Military targets were designated Counterforce and civilian targets Countervalue. The strategy, which Brown, Perry, and company named "countervailing," served to increase greatly the number of nuclear targets for U.S. weapons because of the numerous scenarios of Soviet action that would have to be dealt with. One entire set of weapons would be earmarked for use in the event of a Soviet "Spasm" attack from submarines off the U.S. Atlantic coast against Washington—an attack designed to kill the president and other government and military leaders in the first six to ten minutes of war. Other U.S. responses prepared under PD 59 included coping with a Soviet attack that took out several major American cities but left Washington intact so that there'd be a president and government left to negotiate a cease-fire or surrender—the so-called blackmail scenario.

When Reagan replaced Carter, DeLauer moved into Room 3E 1008 and Perry went back to San Francisco, joining the merchant bank of Hambrecht and Quist, a financial institution with numerous defense companies and high-tech firms as clients.

DeLauer, who left the post after the 1984 election, came aboard as an affable guided missile genius in his sixties who had risen to the board of directors at TRW, the Southern California firm involved in the design of almost the entire American ICBM force. DeLauer was instrumental in the creation of the Minuteman's three-warhead multiple reentry vehicle system that Foster later took over—a system that made it possible for one rocket to destroy three cities hundreds of miles apart.

As Reagan's weapons engineering chief, DeLauer found himself presiding over the most ambitious arms building program in modern American military history. His scientists hit upon the modified "deep basing" scheme for the MX that finally gave Congress enough of a rationale for approving the missile. They pressed ahead with Carter's supposedly radar-proof Stealth bomber and revived the B-1 bomber that the Stealth was believed to render obsolete.

DeLauer was the Strangelove who directed the nuclear arms race into the high frontier of space with the "Star Wars" death ray program that initially called for spending $27 billion on research and development and eventually some $500 billion to $1 trillion to orbit laser beams over the Earth.

It also fell to DeLauer to defend all the new and controversial weapons against critics who charged the nation was building a dangerously hollow force of fragile machines that would break down under wartime stresses. As with his fellow scientist predecessors, DeLauer was able to draw on hitherto unnoticed bureaucratic skills to make himself a potent in-house advocate for the defense industry from whence he came.

Like so much of the modern American defense establishment, the office of the DDR&E derived its power and mission from the national trauma that followed the Soviets' launching of *Sputnik* in 1957. The surge of hurried legislation that created the National Aeronautics and Space Administration, streamlined the Joint Chiefs of Staff, and strengthened the power of the secretary of defense and other civilians over the Pentagon also gave Pentagon research chiefs and their corporate cousins virtual control over the purse strings of high-tech development—with predictable results.

The Directorate for Defense Research and Engineering was established in 1958 by amendments to the 1947 National Security Act as a means of placing the competing R & D projects of the rival service branches under centralized—and civilian—authority. The DDR&E was given jurisdiction over the newly created Advanced Projects Research Agency (ARPA), which dealt with the Pentagon's most futuristic research. Other directorates that the DDR&E oversaw were acquisition management, plans and assessment, strategic and space systems, tactical warfare programs, and test and evaluation. Beneath all these headings was a vast weapons bureaucracy, one that has grown ever larger.

The Tactical Warfare Program alone is divided into branches specializing in air warfare, combat support, international programs, land warfare, and ocean control, and also includes the Weapons Systems Evaluation Group and elements of the Institute for Defense Analyses, a group of academics from within and outside the government who study the management of war.

The DDR&E's most crucial role in the fortunes of the big corporations' building weaponry has to do with his companion powers as chairman of dozens of ad hoc Defense Systems Acquisition Review Councils (DSARCs), mentioned earlier. A DSARC—"dee sark" in Pentagonese—is empaneled for every tank, airplane, missile, bomb, and rifle the Pentagon wants developed. Each DSARC includes both career engineering experts from the civilian bureaucracy and representatives of whichever service branch secretary is to get the new weapon. In theory, the DSARC gives the managers at the Pentagon the opportunity to cancel weapons when they don't work or when they prove too costly or otherwise unsuitable. In practice, only a handful of weapons projects have ever been killed by DSARCs.

There are many reasons for the failure to eliminate lemons. The major one is the little-noticed but government-chartered Defense Science Board (DSB). It consists of a chairman and thirty colleagues, all appointed from the private sector. Their function is to make the decisions about whether a proposed weapon is feasible and then later to evaluate the finished product to determine if it works as advertised. As with the DSARCs, the DSB operates by forming individual task forces for each item under consideration.

Travel, computer time, scientific research, and other requirements are all paid for from the Pentagon budget. U.S. law requires that the board publish notice of its planned topics in the Federal Register and that minutes of meetings be kept in both classified and unclassified versions. This outsiders' board also has the authority to use taxpayers' money to hire consultants to assist with studies.

A 1983 report by the Pentagon's own inspector general (IG) documented how the DSB has become an old-boy network. Its members frequently moved in and out of the Pentagon and to and from big jobs with contractors—many of whose weapons they evaluated as board members. Former DDR&Es Currie and Foster were prime examples. DeLauer, as we have noted, was a major TRW executive before becoming Reagan's DDR&E. The chairman of the Defense Science Board at the time of the IG report, Norman Augustine, was a vice-president at Martin Marietta, a major contractor on the MX missile and on several other projects evaluated by DSB task forces, and a former Pentagon official as well.

The IG report on such incest was one of the first projects of the independent inspector general operation installed that year, despite long opposition from Republican and Democratic defense secretaries alike. The report found that board members had repeatedly served on task forces where they had a clear conflict of interest and that members routinely refused to fill out the required financial disclosure forms that are supposed to indicate whether members hold stock or other interest in projects under their domain.

"Reviews for conflict of interest that were being conducted appeared to us to be of a superficial nature," the report concluded.

Critics of the process, including economist Gordon Adams, contend the major flaw of the DSB is not so much the conflict involved with weapons projects already under way but with the board's powerful role in setting the direction of future weapons programs. Board members have pivotal roles in decisions as to whether Navy needs should be emphasized or Air Force space programs should take precedence.

As Adams noted, board members are able as a result of knowledge gained from these and other matters under study to advise their corporate colleagues on what projects to suggest to the Pentagon. As a result, companies know long before Congress what sort of weapons projects are likely to be approved by the president. The IG report noted that between 1978 and 1982 the science board had dealt with topics like "Cruise Missiles, High Energy Lasers, Naval Surface Ship

Vulnerability, Review of the Defense Department Space-Based Laser Weapons Study, Closely Spaced Basing for MX, and Water Support for the Rapid Deployment Joint Task Force in Southwest Asia." Each project was subsequently ordered, resulting in hundreds of billions in new contracts.

The Pentagon IG's study of the DSB followed charges by Representative Jack Brooks that a majority of members of a task force on computer procurement had financial interests in companies that would directly benefit from the panel's recommendations.

Brooks took action after the General Accounting Office found that the Defense Science Board had convened a task force of eleven members to study prospects of standardizing Pentagon computers and that seven of the eleven had financial ties to computer companies supplying the Defense Department. Comptroller General Charles Bowsher, head of the GAO, told Brooks's Government Operations Committee that the stakes in that DSB recommendation were enormous, since the Pentagon would be spending an estimated $38 billion a year on computers by 1990. The DSB task force recommended that, instead of buying machines directly from the country's highly efficient domestic computer industry, the Pentagon should develop its own. However, the task force called for the hiring of outside companies to design computers to military specifications—an old and costly refrain.

The American Electronics Association, the Computer and Communications Industry Association, and other of the industry's major trade groups told Brooks's committee that the task force recommendation would lock the military into owning thousands and perhaps millions of computers that would rapidly become obsolete. Spokesmen for the groups said the American computer industry avoided this problem by following practices antithetical to those advocated by the science board. Big corporations tended to lease their computer systems, they said, and these had to be constantly upgraded if the computer firms were to keep their hold on the business. On the other hand, the task force had recommended that the Defense Department acquire only computers whose designs it had developed or to which it held full ownership rights. It also wanted restrictions that would limit the bidding to firms preselected by the Pentagon.

Bowsher said the GAO had found that the companies most heavily engaged in selling computers to the military had virtually no commercial customers. "It obviously is advantageous to such firms for the Defense Department to establish a policy of standardization on their computer lines," he told the Brooks committee.

"The commercial computer industry continues to lead the world in technical innovation and marketing," said Brooks. "The federal government, particularly the Defense Department, should be applauding the success, not trying to undermine it."

But DeLauer wasn't clapping. The all-powerful DDR&E launched a counterattack, beginning with an angry letter to the IG team's supervisors, complaining about the inquiry's having been made public. DeLauer questioned "the appropriateness of this report, done in response to an internal request for a review, being distributed outside the department. It appears that the credibility of, and indeed the usefulness of your office to the DoD will be eroded if this practice persists— review assistance is unlikely to be requested knowing the result could be external dissemination and use of your reports in a destructive way."

The DDR&E was particularly critical of one passage of the IG report that noted that the same vice-president of TRW had headed two different task forces on space-based lasers, a project in which TRW was deeply involved. DeLauer didn't mention that he also was a former top TRW executive, but did say that the report was "biased" and the "worst example" of this was its criticism of the unnamed TRW executive.

According to the IG report, the laser task force was made up entirely of persons who had openly advocated expansion of military laser operations into space. The report noted that TRW "was a major contractor in DoD's research and development efforts regarding laser/space technology."

The laser task force recommendation, made after a year of study, was for further research and development—to no one's surprise. As DeLauer noted, however, it recommended against ordering a full-scale, space-based laser weapon, even though a TRW executive headed the panel.

Yet shortly afterward, acting on the advice of, among others, another frequent DSB member, Dr. Edward Teller, President Reagan came forth with his call for a massive national effort to put the American military in space, this "Star Wars" undertaking so similar in size and scope to the Apollo moon landing effort it was immediately dubbed "Apollo II."

It meant the development of space death technology and other wonder-weapon wizardry limited only by the scientists' and engineers' imagination and the American taxpayers' willingness to pay. For years to come, the Dr. Strangeloves moving in and out of Room 3E 1008 would have whole new worlds to conquer—though no one could guarantee what would happen to this one, or how many years there might be left for it.

All that was guaranteed was that, whatever happened, Dr. Strangeloves would, like the Peter Sellers character, be there to see. They may go from inside brains to outside brains, but they never go away.

chapter thirteen

OUTSIDE BRAINS

> *Between the acting of a dreadful thing*
> *And the first motion, all the interim is*
> *Like a phantasma, or a hideous dream:*
> *The Genius and the mortal instruments*
> *Are then in council.*
> —WILLIAM SHAKESPEARE,
> *JULIUS CAESAR*, ACT II, SCENE I

They know that they are an elite. They are the "outside brains," the brilliant minds drawn from industry and academia to advise the "inside brains" within the Pentagon on what weapons to buy, which to invent, and what to do with them. They would shrink from the term Dr. Strangelove. Instead, they sometimes call themselves "the Jasons."

Well into the 1970s, the government money for this exterior advice was tucked away in the accounts of the Pentagon's director of defense research and engineering under the Institute for Defense Analyses. One line item, with no further explanation, simply read "Jason."

The Jason account, which was held under $1 million a year, financed the travel, meetings, and research of some forty to fifty of the best American scientists specializing in theoretical physics, mathematics, and strategy.

They took their name from the Jason of Greek mythology. Jason and his Argonauts, of course, sought the Golden Fleece in hopes of weaving armor that would make the warriors who wore it invulnerable, a quest not unlike a lot of modern-day weapons development at which the outside brains have labored. Those outside scientists who took the name tended to have much less hawkish mind-sets than their fellow intellectuals on the inside at the Pentagon.

The Jasons first gathered in 1959 at the Atomic Energy Commission's Los Alamos scientific laboratories in New Mexico, which had been headed by the iconoclastic genius J. Robert Oppenheimer.

Oppenheimer, the son of a wealthy Jewish clothing importer, grew up in a New York apartment graced with three van Goghs, a Picasso, and a Renoir. After graduating from Harvard, he studied at England's Cambridge University and attained his doctorate at the University of

Gottingen in Germany. Until chosen to direct the top secret Manhattan Project, he taught physics at the University of California at Berkeley and the California Institute of Technology. An ardent leftist in the 1930s, he counted many Communists as close friends, including a number of Stalinist sympathizers. Still, he served as chairman of the AEC's general advisory committee from 1946 to 1952.

Edward Teller, a Hungarian refugee who fled to the United States in poverty to escape the Nazis, harbored much hatred and disgust for the same leftist causes Oppenheimer had espoused, especially after the establishment of Soviet tyranny over Eastern Europe.

Both men were brilliant physicists and among the handful on Earth competent to translate Albert Einstein's theoretical advances into a practical means of developing "Fat Man" and "Big Boy," the first American A-bombs. Both, however, had egos to match their abilities. They quarreled constantly while on the same Manhattan Project team. They clashed even more violently after the war, when the defense establishment decided to improve upon the technology that had so dramatically brought victory in the Pacific.

In the months immediately following the end of World War II, as Oppenheimer began discussing his qualms about the nuclear age with President Truman and other leaders, Teller started work on feasibility studies for the construction of a new weapon, the awesomely more powerful fusion or hydrogen bomb.

Oppenheimer opposed this. As he told Truman at the end of the war, "I feel we have blood on our hands." Truman afterward told Secretary of State Dean Acheson, "Don't you bring that fellow around here again. After all, all he did was make the bomb. I'm the guy who fired it off."

Oppenheimer finally was removed from Los Alamos in 1953. After Teller testified against him during congressional hearings on Oppenheimer's Communist associations, the Eisenhower administration had his security clearance taken away. As a consequence, those at the Livermore complex under Teller came to dominate Pentagon weapons projects, as we have seen.

While those who made their careers at Oppenheimer's Los Alamos Laboratories were not exactly doves, they tended to represent different strains of thought from the Livermore group's and were far more innovative. As Jasons, they received federal financing in a government effort to exploit the expertise of scientists whose economic and intellectual resources were less wedded to the entrenched military establishment.

The Jason enterprise started out with the code name Project Sunrise.

Its founders included Marvin Goldberger of Princeton, Keith Bruechner of the University of California at San Diego, Kenneth Watson of Berkeley, and Charles H. Townes, who later won the Nobel Prize in physics for his work advancing the laser beam invented at Hughes Aircraft. Townes was still working as an important outside advisor thirty-two years later, when President Reagan put him in charge of the scientific study group that rejected the Carter administration's racetrack scheme for basing the MX missile in 4,600 holes all over Nevada and Utah. Another founding member was George Kistiakowsky, the Russian émigré physicist who, as President Eisenhower's chief science advisor, had learned that the service branches were not coordinating their nuclear targets.

Goldberger's wife suggested that the group change its name from Sunrise to the Jasons because she thought the first name sounded too much like a brand of orange juice. The Jasons gave their time to government projects largely on a *pro bono* basis. They gathered on weekends and for summer vacations at government expense at scenic retreats, notably La Jolla, California, and Woods Hole and Falmouth, both on Cape Cod in Massachusetts. A favorite summertime meeting place was the Bowdoin College campus in Maine, where family members relaxed on the nearby rocky beaches while the scientists joined together at a hunting lodge to talk about nuclear weapons and killing more North Vietnamese soldiers.

The meetings were always held under heavy security, with armed guards keeping custody of the secret files the scientists brought with them, as well as keeping a wary eye on the scientists' children, in the event enemy agents thought of using kidnapping as a means to force secrets from a Jason. The Jasons' identities are still kept secret because of such fears, though many in the defense establishment speak quite openly about the group.

Richard Garwin, for one, has routinely distributed biographical material on himself to reporters that included references to his time as a Jason. Garwin, a leading outside defense intellectual for three decades, was a longtime executive at IBM's research and development facility and served in faculty posts at both Harvard and Columbia universities.

The Pentagon had other fears than kidnapping in mind in keeping the Jasons hidden. The group became the driving force involved with a number of controversial research projects during the Vietnam War, including a study about whether the United States could win by using small or "tactical" nuclear weapons. In 1968, *The Nation* disclosed that four well-known scientists had written a report on nuclear weapons use in Vietnam, a document called IDA Report HQ-66-5220. The Jasons who prepared the report were Freeman Dyson of the Princeton Institute for Advanced Study, S. Courtenay Wright and Robert Gomer of the University of Chicago, and Harvard's Steven Weinberg.

The Nation disclosed that these four eminent physicists had dispatched yet another expert, Garwin, to Vietnam to perform the needed field research. It was later learned that the Jasons had recommended against the use of nuclear weapons in the war. They advocated instead using some fiendishly deadly new antipersonnel weapons. While in Vietnam, Garwin had among other things studied the feasibility of the so-called electronic barrier that Defense Secretary Robert McNamara had suggested erecting across the Demilitarized Zone between North and South Vietnam. Along with this project, dubbed "McNamara's Wall," the Jasons dreamed up an arsenal of fantastic new killer weapons every bit as horrible as anything ever created by the Pentagon's research and engineering section.

In 1973, *Science* magazine told how the idea of creating a high-technology death zone between the two Vietnams was conceived by Harvard Law Dean Roger Fisher. In a letter to McNamara aide John McNaughton, Fisher suggested calling on a number of leading scientists to conduct the project. As a result of the Fisher letter, a Jason session was held at the Dana Hall School for Girls in Wellesley, Massachusetts.

Leading the session were McNaughton, Maxwell Taylor, and John Foster, the DDR&E. At that meeting and in successive conferences, the Jasons developed a plan for sowing sensors and deadly "bomblets" across a strip of Vietnam eighty miles long and fifteen miles wide. A similar strip would be laid out along the border between Vietnam and Laos at the mouth of the Ho Chi Minh Trail. The apparatus was designed so that, when an enemy soldier set foot on the ground, the vibration would be detected by a sensor and explode a nearby "bomblet" mine, which would fill the air with a blizzard of shrapnel and gravel. At the same time, the sensor would automatically call in an air or artillery strike on the position—the first "automated" combat.

In its revelations, *Science* magazine noted that the Army and Air Force were locked in fierce disagreement over which branch of service would control the death zones, and the project was implemented only piecemeal because of this territorial imperative.

Their sudden notoriety within the scientific community over their role in planning for the Vietnam effort led many to drop their affiliation with the Jasons. By the early 1970s, the project was being financed through the Pentagon's Defense Advanced Research Projects Agency (DARPA), (the new name for the Advanced Research Projects Agency), with much of the funds channeled through the Stanford Research Institute in Menlo Park, California.

To build their automated battlefield, the Jasons had called upon a great number of more traditional government consultants to help in the development work. RCA designed and built the Command Mike III, an ultrasensitive audio microphone that was to serve as a ground sensor. Sandia Laboratories, the designer of much of the equipment in the Bell System, furnished Air Delivered Seismic Intrusion Detectors, which could pick up the softest enemy footfall. Honeywell's Magnetic Intrusion Detector provided backup to call in strikes against any effort to penetrate the "Wall" with rapidly moving vehicles. In the 1980s, American military personnel hundreds of miles away were still picking up signals from these sensors, left behind more than a decade before. The CIA learned of Vietnamese plans to invade Cambodia in 1978 and 1979 as a result of such signals, which indicated large Vietnamese troop movements.

While the Jasons have tried to operate in secret, there is no effort to hide most of the consultants hired by the Pentagon to do much of its thinking. The most visible of the think tanks serving the military is the RAND Corporation of California, formed by the Air Force after World War II to bring expertise in both the physical and social sciences to bear in the study of war.

RAND scientists have never built anything. Their product is confined to reports, as the name "R and D" implies—blue with a diagonal red stripe for classified ones and gray with the RAND logo for unclassified studies. Early employees liked to joke that the company's initials stood for "research and no development." Housed in a complex of pink and yellow buildings adjoining a sliver of beach in Santa Monica, California, RAND thinkers have provided much of the mental effort depended upon by Pentagon planners in drafting U.S. nuclear strategy since World War II.

Working out of four rented rooms at the Douglas Aircraft Corporation plant, RAND's experts produced its first report on May 2, 1946, entitled "Preliminary Design of an Experimental World-Circling Spaceship." The report was nothing less than a prediction of the launching of *Sputnik*. RAND prophesied that such a satellite launching "would inflame the imagination of mankind, and would probably produce repercussions in the world comparable to the explosion of the atomic bomb." During those eleven intervening years before *Sputnik* was launched, RAND was often ridiculed for preparing its first Air Force report on a subject that had nothing to do with airplanes.

As with defense corporations, defense think tanks function as part of the revolving door. Many important figures moved back and forth between the Pentagon and RAND. James Schlesinger, defense secretary in the Nixon and Ford administrations, worked at RAND developing plans for new nuclear weapon targets before crossing through the revolving door. At RAND, the pipe-smoking Schlesinger, who counted among his other interests bird-watching and reading the works of Lutheran theologians, had been director of the Strategic Studies Division.

He had conducted a number of studies for the Air Force that came up with varying menus of Soviet targets to fit different kinds of big-power confrontations. When he joined the Nixon cabinet, he was quick to bring forth a new nuclear strategy that increased the weapons at the Air Force's disposal. This was the "flexible options plan" implemented as the nation's Single Integrated Operations Plan. The package called for the development and production of a new manned strategic bomber (the B-1) and a much more accurate ICBM (the MX).

Schlesinger came into the Pentagon just as a big fight was raging between the Air Force and Navy over which would get new nuclear weapons. The Navy had argued its fleet of Polaris submarines was aging and needed replacing by modern and much more costly Poseidon and Trident subs. With the Schlesinger doctrine in place, there were enough targets for both an expanded Navy as well as a modernized Air Force.

It was another thinker hired from time to time by RAND, the Massachusetts Institute of Technology's highly respected William Kaufmann, who came forward with the nuclear philosophy in which the United States would target its forces against Soviet military installations and resources rather than cities, which he called "Countervalue" targets. Thinking the unthinkable, Kaufmann argued the efficacy of hitting military or "Counterforce" targets, but noted this mode of nuclear war required the kind of missile accuracy obtainable from land-based ICBMs but not submarines. Kaufmann reigned as one of the defense establishment's leading intellectuals from the Eisenhower era to the Reagan years and won many converts to his theories.

In 1975, while president of the California Institute of Technology, Harold Brown made a speech in which he said that only the threat of Mutually Assured Destruction (MAD) would prevent a U.S.-Soviet nuclear war. He recanted belief in gradual escalation of nuclear strikes against military targets and "economic objectives" (cities). But when he became secretary of defense in early 1977, he retained Kaufmann as a consultant on nuclear strategy and eventually was persuaded that a mix of military targets and cities—the so-called countervailing strategy—was best. The centerpiece of this strategy was the highly accurate new MX missile, carrying ten independently targetable warheads. The Schlesinger-Nixon Presidential Directive 242 was replaced by Carter's now famous PD 59, and the countervailing nuclear theology became gospel.

These presidential directives carry the highest possible security classification and contain long lists of nuclear targets, along with lists of options available for each likely Soviet response and counterresponse. The PDs also incorporate plans for establishing martial law during prewar phases, stipulate which federal records are to be saved for use by post–nuclear war government, and even include provisions for rewriting U.S. laws to accommodate the changed conditions that would follow nuclear war. Much of the work that has gone into these PDs was done by RAND and other outside think tanks.

But RAND also deals with less lofty matters. A 1982 RAND study considered "the economics of strikes and revolts during early space colonization," and concluded that, if the United States sent workers into space to build a gigantic solar-energy station, the workers would likely lose their sense of identity with the United States and would be tempted to revolt and seize the space station. The report observed that "if the initial seizure were successful, the obvious U.S. counter strategy would be to threaten to destroy the colony and its inhabitants unless the seized assets were returned unharmed."

The think tank was also paid $75,000 in 1982 to read back issues of the French newspaper *Le Monde* and the British magazine *The Economist* to determine how the two publications had "projected the strategic arms balance" between the East and West since 1979.

RAND, among whose most recent chairmen is former defense secretary and Reagan administration Mideast coordinator Donald Rumsfeld, is one of less than a dozen institutions designated Federal Contract Research Centers and is considered the elite among think tanks. A number of universities with large defense Research, Development, Testing, and Evaluation (RDT&E) contracts are designated as Federal Contract Research Centers, conferring a special status on their work and increasing the likelihood they will qualify for future projects. The number of schools so designated fluctuates, but over the years there have been five major academic think tanks concerned with warfare: the Applied Physics Laboratory at Johns Hopkins University, the Pennsylvania State University Ordnance Research Laboratory, the University of Washington Applied Physics Laboratory, MIT's Lincoln Laboratory, and the Stanford Research Institute. Stanford absorbed much of the work started in the 1970s by the Jasons.

Other think tanks with more tenuous academic ties include the large MITRE Corporation of Bedford, Massachusetts; Batelle National Laboratories of Ohio; and Sandia Laboratories of New Mexico. There are hundreds and hundreds of think tanks in less elite and less highly funded categories, ranging down to two- and three-employee companies with a single Pentagon research project and a one-room office along the Capital Beltway.

Many of the smaller research firms have come under intense criticism for alleged conflicts of interest and profiteering, because they so often accept large sums of government money for producing studies of little or no use. A major investigative series by *Washington Post* reporters Jonathan Neumann and Ted Gup examined some two hundred companies with offices around the Capital Beltway and documented how the small fish move through the revolving door every bit as easily as the Browns, Curries, Schlesingers, and Fosters.

Gup and Neumann used the case of Sam Shimomura and Russ Long to illustrate the situation. Shimomura had been with a consulting company called ManTech, which had a contract with the Navy to determine whether naval sonar systems were performing within military specifications. Long was the civilian Navy official in charge of the Sea Systems Command office that had hired Shimomura for the job. The two men told the *Post* in interviews that they had become close friends—lunching together, sharing family outings, dining at each other's home. In the two years that ManTech worked on the sonar project Shimomura became dissatisfied with his private-sector job because of the company's strict travel allowance policy. Meanwhile, Long reached retirement age at the Navy and left his job. Shimomura quit ManTech and went to work for the Navy on the sonar project at Sea Systems Command. Long was then hired by ManTech as a "permanent part-time consultant." A 1981 GAO study indicated that the Long/Shimomura case was just one of thousands in which Pentagon officials retire and hire out as consultants to the same military projects they once directed. Of 256 consulting contracts selected by the GAO at random, the agency found that 131 were obtained by contractors that had former military and civilian employees of the Defense Department "in capacities of top management as well as various technical levels." The GAO also found that 102 contracts had resulted from unsolicited proposals—former Pentagon officials suggesting projects to old colleagues still on the DOD payroll.

A sonar engineer who worked with ManTech complained that the work the consultants performed on their $199,000 Navy contract served to drive up the overall costs for sonar sets.

Every time we came down to Washington, we had to meet with Navy guys and consultants who always had some kind of design change to order. Every change drove the cost up higher. They [the consultants] had to suggest changes or they wouldn't get more contracts, so there was no way they would accept whatever we built.

Nearly every major hardware project of the Pentagon's is subjected to study by outside hired consultants, a factor long cited by Admiral Hyman Rickover as a major source of cost overruns in weapons projects. Often, the big defense companies will themselves complain about these changes.

In testimony before the Joint Economic Committee of Congress, which was his last official appearance before going into the retirement forced upon him by the Reagan administration, Rickover told of some of the more absurd extremes of the practice.

The use of consultants often impedes, rather than facilitates, action by government agencies. For the past two decades, consultants and systems analysts have endlessly studied and debated the relative merits of nuclear and non-nuclear ships, and the proper composition of our future Navy. Contracts for studies frequently waste the time of agency personnel who often must educate the so-called experts doing the study, assist them in gathering the data, and then respond to their reports and recommendations—which often defy common sense.

Rickover, whose tyrannical management style and intolerance for human weakness became a national legend, had been kept from the chopping block by powerful friends and allies on Capitol Hill. From 1949 to 1977, they had intervened forcefully to keep presidents from firing him. After January 1977 he had one of his own disciples as president, but with the ascendancy of Reagan, his luck as well as his disciples' ran out.

In the 1960s and 1970s, Rickover had been targeted frequently by a succession of defense secretaries and Navy superiors because of his recurring complaints about cost overruns in contracts from mammoth ship-building companies including General Dynamics, Lockheed, Litton Industries, and Tenneco. Rickover charged that the firms used consultants to persuade the Navy to order changes in vessels while they were under construction. The firms then wrote off the added costs to the Navy, thereby increasing profits, which were figured as a percentage of cost. Rickover charged that often these change orders were part of the strategy the companies used to make money out of contracts gained by unrealistically low bids, the practice known as "buying in."

Rickover said that General Dynamics filed unrealistically low bids to build Trident submarines, counting on later change orders to cover the actual costs. The scheme was an effort, he said, to take business away from the Newport News Shipbuilding and Dry Dock Company. During the 1970s, the Navy awarded contracts for twenty submarines to General Dynamics and only twelve to Newport News, in large part because GD had submitted lower bids. But, Rickover said, "because the Navy was unable to enforce the contract it ended up paying Electric Boat [General Dynamics] more for these ships than it had to pay for comparable ships bought from Newport News, and the Newport News ships have been delivered far earlier."

In his valedictory 1982 testimony, Rickover blamed numerous ills of the military establishment on the outside brains. The crusty admiral singled out Pentagon policy regarding independent research and development (IR&D) as a major source of the problems with complex weapons projects. IR&D contracts allow big companies like General Dynamics, Hughes, Lockheed, and others to write off huge research and development bills as part of their operating costs—just as they write off gas, lights, raw materials, and the like.

Rickover said he considers this IR&D process unacceptable because the military has virtually no say about what sort of research these companies might undertake. As a result, he charged, companies often use Pentagon-financed IR&D projects to develop ideas with no military applications. He also complained to the Joint Economic Committee of Congress that the IR&D operations often retain control of patents even though they were developed at government expense.

Without mentioning specific company names, Rickover said that the Navy had covered the costs for one of its contractors to develop and build automatic welding machines used at shipyards under a government IR&D contract. He said that after the machines were installed at a Navy shipyard, the company began charging the Navy royalties for using the machines on government jobs.

The admiral also complained that IR&D money often goes either for frivolous projects or to finance research that bolsters a company's commercial operations instead of its military projects. He said that companies themselves are allowed to decide whether a given project has possible military applications. He said:

> I cannot envision a project that could not be defended as having a potential military relationship. What is to prevent a turbine manufacturer from studying fruit flies since fruit is eaten by the piccolo player of a military band? What if the contractor decides to develop

a new blend of coffee—obviously this would have a potential relationship with the eating habits of the military.

The contractors contend this independent research has created much
of today's highly efficient killer weaponry. In fact, many of the weapons
on today's fat procurement lists were developed in the futuristic design
bureaus of the major arms contractors, notably the famous "Skunk
Works" at Lockheed, where the U-2 and other spy planes were created;
the laser shops of Hughes Aircraft Corporation; the robot airplane
laboratories at Teledyne Inc.; and Northrop Corporation, where civilian
scientists built remotely piloted vehicles (RPVs) which are guided by
Apple computers bolted into their tiny cockpits. The RPVs, designed
to perform the artillery spotter role that once belonged to light Army
aircraft, came in overweight, late, and some $2 billion over the original
target price of about $600 million.

By the 1980s, the Pentagon budget contained more than $3 billion
annually for IR&D, and projects ranged from efforts to train dolphins
to plant mines on the hulls of enemy ships to experimenting with ways
to use microwave guns to create ovenlike temperatures inside enemy
tanks.

While he was serving in the Dr. Strangelove seat at the Pentagon,
Dr. Malcolm Currie asked industry friends to conduct a study of which
weapons had been dreamed up as IR&D projects and then sold to the
military as unsolicited bids for new weapons projects. At the same time,
Currie ordered the Defense Science Board to make a similar study.
The inside and outside brains agreed that the IR&D efforts were crucial
to the national security. Certainly Currie would find some merit in
IR&D because his former company, Hughes Aircraft, had used such
funds to develop the laser.

In response to Currie's request, three trade associations from the
arms industry—the Aerospace Industries Association, the National Security Industrial Association, and the Electronics Industries Association—prepared a list of dozens of weapons and technologies that had
come out of the IR&D shops. At the top of the list, to no surprise,
was the laser. Other wonders coming out of the "Skunk Works" and
similar plants were the integrated circuitry for home computers; sonars
capable of sensing Soviet ships at Vladivostok from as far away as San
Diego; the Huey and other helicopters using jet engines to turn their
rotor blades; short take-off airplanes such as the jump jet Harriers that
proved so useful in the Falklands War; radar altimeters; and the Har-
poon missile, a much faster and more sophisticated version of the French
Exocet missile that proved so dangerous in the Falklands. (Ironically,

an investigation by the GAO faulted the IR&D programs for dwelling too much on devices with benign civilian applications rather than concentrating on more devastating weapons of war. The deadliest systems have come largely from the military's DDR&E and DARPA projects.)

Progress in this growth field continues apace. There have been spectacular breakthroughs from IR&D in the design of air-carried machine guns and cannon capable of firing staggering volumes of rounds per second. The General Electric 7.62-mm "minigun" is a six-barrel cluster weapon that kicks out bullets at rates as high as 6,000 rounds a minute— 100 a second.

As Tom Gervasi said in his book *Arsenal of Democracy,* that's about the length of time it takes to say the word "hippopotamus."

A smaller cousin to the "minigun," the 5.56-mm XM-214 produced by General Electric, was developed for use on ground vehicles, where it can be set for adjustable rates of fire ranging from 400 to 6,000 rounds a minute. Also developed through GE IR&D is the M-61A1 Vulcan 20-mm aerial cannon suitable for strafing buildings and vehicles with firing rates as fast as 6,000 rounds a minute. Only the AC-130, a modified version of the Lockheed C-130 cargo plane, can carry enough ammo to fire more than a minute, however—as one did in the Grenada invasion, causing such violent casualties among enemy forces that piles of severed feet were found afterward.

The civilian weapons designers have made great strides in conventional bombs as well. Instead of the massively destructive and crude blockbusters used against London and Hamburg in World War II, the modern-day bomb arsenal runs to more effective antipersonnel devices. The M-36 incendiary cluster bomb carries 182 separate two-pound magnesium thermite bombs in a sheet-metal case that breaks apart in the air, spreading the small individual bombs over several hundred yards and creating far more heat and spewing more flesh-adhering burning particles than was possible with the napalm bombs of the Vietnam era.

A major triumph of Air Force IR&D has been the "fuel air munitions" developed by major chemical companies also too late for use in Vietnam. These weapons release a large cloud of extremely volatile gases like ethylene oxide methylacetlyene and propadiene, which are then ignited to create blast effects rivaling the concussive powers of atomic bombs.

One version of this weapon, CBU-82, was used to kill an unspecified number of Cambodians on the island of Koh Tang during the Ford administration's rescue of the *Mayaguez* crew. The CBU-82—the CBU nomenclature stands for cluster bomb—drops three 100-pound cannisters that produce a cloud fifty-six feet in diameter and nine feet high, which then explodes with a force five times greater than a charge of dynamite with the same dimensions would produce. The force of the blast creates a massive vacuum, which then draws in air for miles around, sucking it up in a dust cloud very much like the atomic bomb's infamous mushroom cloud.

The CBU-82 is particularly effective where the enemy has sought refuge in bunkers or tunnels underground. A Marine who went ashore at Koh Tang after CBU-82 was used there said of the victims, "It sucked their lungs right through their noses. It was ugly."

In the Vietnam era, the practice of using university laboratories, faculty, and graduate students to invent and refine such weapons became extremely unpopular and was dramatically curtailed. Trustees at the University of California rejected further defense work at Berkeley and similar cutbacks were ordered at the Massachusetts Institute of Technology and even at Johns Hopkins, where scientists and engineers had long been deeply involved in Navy projects.

By the end of the Carter administration, however, the campuses were once again major participants in designing the weapons of war and laying plans for their use. In fiscal year 1981, the thirteenth largest recipient of RDT&E funds was Johns Hopkins, where substantial research was under way into aspects of the shaky Aegis cruiser project and other weapons programs. At thirteenth, the Maryland institution better known for its superb medical school received just slightly less than Honeywell, and slightly more than IBM. All the companies with bigger arms research grants than Johns Hopkins are blue-chip weapons contractors.

In 1981, Johns Hopkins received $184 million in RDT&E funds from the Pentagon, compared with $884 million for first-ranked Martin Marietta. MIT, with $163 million from the military, was fifteenth on the list.

Other higher education institutions receiving Pentagon money included the Illinois Institute of Technology, $36 million; University of California, $29 million; Georgia Tech Research Institute, $18.2 million; Stanford University, $18 million; and Pennsylvania State University, $15 million.

According to the House Armed Services Committee, university RDT&E contracts increased by 70 percent in the first three years of the Carter administration, and the trend continued at full swing into the 1980s. This resurgence of academic involvement in defense programs came with virtually no protest from the traditional antiwar quarters, which seemed more concerned with draft registration and nuclear freeze movements, or with finding jobs after graduation.

While the high-tech cadre of inside and outside brains has been criticized for saddling the military with an arsenal of costly computerized "hanger queens" too delicate for actual warfare, these thinkers of the unthinkable can hardly be faulted for lacking imaginative genius, or for lacking the zeal to apply that imagination to the ponderous tasks at hand. Of all the grand visions that the alchemists of Armageddon have transformed from the dross of the drawing board to cold reality, the most spectacular of all came forth in the late 1970s and early 1980s. It was then that the world learned that the human brains in American national defense were well down the road to replacing themselves with a wholly new kind of defense thinker—an electronic brain. A brain not yet much good at designing new weapons systems, but more than capable of its principal mission—starting wars.

chapter fourteen

ELECTRONIC BRAINS

"SHALL WE PLAY A GAME?"
—INVITATION EXTENDED BY A COMPUTER IN THE
MOTION PICTURE *WARGAMES*

On one side of Cheyenne Mountain is the Colorado Springs city zoo, a happy gathering place for a population that includes the personnel of the nearby United States Air Force Academy. It is a place for rejoicing in living things, including the many elk, deer, moose, bear, and mountain lions brought to the zoo from the surrounding Rockies.

On the other side of the mountain, closed off by fences far more impenetrable than those used to restrain the lions, is the entrance to a large underground city. Its principal inhabitant, on which the federal government spends billions, is a machine—a complex of computers that each year becomes more and more like a living creature itself. Its name is Wimex, for Worldwide Military Command and Control System (WWMCCS).

Among its habits is reading *The New York Times*. Among its capabilities is scrambling B-52 bombers for nuclear strikes against the Soviet Union—all by itself.

To err is human. It is also electronic. Wimex, called by some "the electronic president," has made some mistakes. On several occasions in the last few years it has sent flights of jet fighters into the air after nonexistent Soviet bombers, scrambled B-52s for a retaliatory strike against Russia in response to a Soviet missile launch that hadn't happened, summoned American missile launch officers to their battle stations, and otherwise frazzled the nerves of Strategic Air Command chiefs.

The most unnerving such incident occurred in November 1979, when a lieutenant colonel at the Colorado Mountain underground complex incorrectly loaded a set of taped instructions into Wimex that were supposed to be used only in war games. The tape simulated a situation in which three American "chalet" geosynchronous satellites, set in stationary orbit twenty-five thousand miles over fixed points on earth, detect waves of missile launches from both inside the Soviet Union and sectors of the world's oceans where Russian guided missile submarines frequently patrol. Wimex, not equipped to discern between real signals sent from spy satellites and tape recordings, pondered this sudden threat and—on the basis of preprogrammed instructions—decided to declare a worldwide alert at the level code-named Cocked Pistol, a state of war preparedness also referred to as DefCon IV. (Alert status is measured on a scale of five to one; one is the most serious.) F-15 jet fighters in British Columbia, Missouri, and Oregon were hurried into the air to counter the waves of Soviet Backfire and Badger bombers that Wimex expected to penetrate U.S. airspace. At Minuteman and Titan ICBM bases missile-firing crews were summoned to their launching keyboards by flashing lights and buzzers. Radio signals were beamed by the computer to civilian radar operators at twenty regional centers operated by the Federal Aviation Administration (FAA), ordering them to suspend takeoffs and divert approaching aircraft to make way for military traffic.

The civilian world first learned about Wimex and its strange ways because Susan Baer, a reporter from the now defunct *Washington Star,* was in the FAA air control center at Leesburg, Virginia, just outside Washington, working on a story about air controllers' stomach ulcers. When the Wimex alarms sounded, she was ordered to leave for "reasons of national security." Within days, congressional investigators made inquiries and, through checks made by *Star* reporters, learned that the Defense Department had moved with little public or congressional notice toward creating an "electronic president"—a computer brain with spy satellites for eyes and much of the world's knowledge of war, history, diplomacy, and even religion and poetry in its memory, along with constantly updated newspaper files.

Subsequent investigations of Wimex by various House and Senate committees, the General Accounting Office, and the Congressional Office of Technology Assessment showed that the Joint Chiefs of Staff had gone a long way toward computerizing the agonizing decision-making process that would have to be completed within minutes or seconds by commanders—most particularly by the one in the White House—if American satellites, perimeter radars, and other sensors should detect a Soviet nuclear attack.

They discovered that Wimex had been programmed to respond automatically to a variety of warnings and potential threats. The computer was empowered to order DefCon V and DefCon IV alerts on its own, though it was required to consult human beings before DefCon III or worse was declared.

Among the alert conditions it could call were "Cocked Pistol," "Apple Jack," "Lemon Juice," "Snow Man," and "Big Noise." Human consultation was required before moving to "Fast Pace," "Round House," "Double Take," and, most ominously, "Fade Out."

In "Big Noise," Wimex notifies the constantly airborne Air Force command plane "Looking Glass" that a change in alert status is required. Upon receiving the "Big Noise" warning, the pilot of the "Looking Glass" plane immediately puts a black patch over his left eye. Then, according to the war plans fed into Wimex, if a nuclear explosion should blind the pilot's uncovered eye, he need only remove the patch and continue with his mission.

A Senate Armed Services Committee report on Wimex made by Senator Gary Hart found that in eighteen months the giant computer had moved up and down the alert ladder 3,703 times, including 151 occasions when U.S. satellites had registered launches of Soviet rockets on their orbiting infrared energy detecting sensors. In one case, Wimex responded to the launch of four missiles from a Soviet submarine north of Japan near the Kuril Islands. They followed the most likely flight path for a Soviet sneak attack. The launch turned out to be a test, but Wimex alerted the Joint Chiefs of Staff directly. Another time, Wimex detected a Soviet rocket burning up as it reentered the atmosphere from a test flight and sent out a war warning. On yet another occasion, it mistook forest fires in the Ural Mountains for missile launches and pulled the cord.

In addition to using the United States's three "chalet" geosynchronous satellites, which sense the heat given off by Soviet missile firings, Wimex also receives data from a network of satellites called Vela, which detect the distinctive flash of light that is produced when a nuclear device is exploded in the atmosphere.

It was Vela that, two weeks before Wimex was loaded with the wargames tape, picked up the famous flash in the South Atlantic that the CIA, Defense Intelligence Agency, and Navy ultimately concluded was a nuclear bomb detonated by South Africa in collaboration with Israel and possibly Taiwan. Senator John Glenn noted at the time that Vela had detected forty-one nuclear blasts since the first of the satellites was deployed in 1961 and that intelligence agencies in each case had verified that an actual nuclear weapon had been detonated.

The White House Office of Science and Technology, along with other scientific bodies, held in the South Atlantic incident that Vela had simply made a mistake. They contended that an incoming micrometeor smaller than a grain of sand had knocked a chip of paint off the satellite and sent it spinning in front of its lens. The brilliant sunlight reflecting from the speck produced a reading identical to the "distinctive" flash of a real bomb, they argued.

Many in Congress found neither theory comforting.

The drive toward computerization of the nuclear-war-fighting process surged with the advent of the Reagan administration. President Reagan put hundreds of executives from high-tech firms into high-ranking positions in the Pentagon and elsewhere in the defense establishment. Far more comfortable with computer-age jargon and technology than their predecessors in the Carter and Ford administrations, they quickly moved things along to the point where the computer-research budget was increased from $50 million to $250 million a year. Reagan boasted to the nation that the United States was going to win the race to the supercomputer.

He put Robert Cooper, head of the Pentagon's Defense Advanced Research Projects Agency (DARPA), in charge of an effort to create an American "fifth generation" computer capable of simulating human thought. In testimony before Congress, Cooper described his mission as "to jump orders of magnitude ahead in military capability." A "fifth generation" computer would "emulate the human brain" and produce not just the sort of "smart bombs" used in Vietnam but "brilliant weapons," Cooper enthused.

DARPA, supported with a $1 billion war chest, moved forward on three fronts: building ever smaller computer chips containing ever greater memory; designing ways to make millions of the tiny chips work in tandem (computer architecture); and, finally, searching for an electronic means of using this vast new combined computing power to make actual "knowledge-based" decisions. Cooper described the goal as creating artificial intelligence.

At the same time the DARPA project got under way, a consortium of high-tech government contractors launched a private sector drive toward the same target. Former Admiral Bobby Ray Inman, longtime director of the ultrasecret National Security Agency and later deputy director of the CIA, took charge of a new company called Microelectronics and Computer Technology Corporation, a consortium of Univac, Control Data Corporation, and Digital Equipment Corporation, normally three of the most bloodthirsty competitors in an industry famous for ruthless free enterprise.

This American Big Three were impelled to cooperation by a Japanese announcement of plans to leapfrog over American third-generation computer technology and get to the fifth generation first. Inman was chosen as leader because, as National Security Agency director, he had commanded the most extensive array of secret computer equipment in the U.S. electronic arsenal—devices used by the spy agency to monitor worldwide telephone traffic, evaluate satellite data, conduct war games, observe Soviet rocket tests, and perform other extraordinary functions. The NSA was reported to own the largest computer complex on earth. Inman's predecessor, General Marshall S. Carter, once told an interviewer that, while most federal agencies measured their computer wealth in square footage, NSA measured its in acres. "I had five and a half when I was there," he said.

In its 1984 budget message to Congress, DARPA asked for a big boost in funds for human voice computer research: "Work in speech will focus on the development of a system which can handle real-time continuous speech with a large vocabulary. Special attention will be paid to speech in a fighter aircraft environment and over telephone lines."

The ultimate goal, DARPA suggested, was to build a jet aircraft which a pilot could fly by such simple voice commands as "take off," "fire," or "land." Similarly, a president might one day ask a machine, "What should I do about the Russian MIGs in Pakistan?"

To achieve such electronic miracles, the computer brass devised a plan to create a parallel system of many computers, each equal to or faster and better than the most powerful computing device of the present period, the Cray 1. Like a team of plow horses harnessed together, the integrated computers would be able to duplicate and digest a complete set of the Single Integrated Operations Plan (SIOP), the Pentagon war plans.

According to sources among the very few who have seen it, the NSA Cray 1 is a machine that occupies only seventy square feet of all that acreage at the NSA's underground complex. Each machine weighs five tons, but much of the weight is an ultraefficient air-conditioning system necessitated by the enormous heat generated by the tons of microchips and other state-of-the-art components. Designed and built by Seymour Cray, the reclusive founder of Cray Research of Mendota Heights, Minnesota, the first Cray 1 installed at the spy agency's complex virtually doubled its computer strength when it was delivered in 1976. It was able, for example, to scan 320 million words a second, the equivalent of reading roughly 900 books each as long as *Gone with the Wind* in that instant. Its data-storage discs held 30 billion words, and the machine could extract any one of them in a flash of time measured in millionths of a second.

NSA has added other Cray 1s to its system. By harnessing rows of them together—a technique computer technicians call "daisy chaining"—ever more miraculous feats should be possible.

The final piece of research necessary for producing an electronic brain capable of plotting strategy with the president and the Joint Chiefs of Staff is the Military Planning and Advising Project at DARPA. This grew out of the war-games studies that began in 1964, when DARPA tried to create a computer model of the "internal revolutionary conflict" in Vietnam.

Undertaken by Abt Associates of Cambridge, Massachusetts, the project made a war game out of efforts by belligerents and friendly forces to gain and retain the loyalty of the inhabitants of twenty Vietnamese villages selected from case histories. Code-named AGILE-COIN and played entirely within the computer, the game had players on one side manipulate food supplies, weaponry, and martial-law measures to keep control of the villages, while the opposing forces made a similar effort to wrest it away.

The rules were that the insurgents won the game if they could hold the loyalty of 40 percent of the villagers for three consecutive rounds of play, while succeeding in getting 20 percent of the villagers to join their forces as fighters. The friendly forces—the Americans in Southeast Asia—won if they could retain the loyalty of 80 percent of the villagers while causing less loss of life among them than the opposition did.

Abt Associates constructed a computer model that projected the consequences of each action—such as shooting the village elders—by having dozens of CIA, State Department, and military experts freshly returned from the war play a noncomputer version of the game, using the actual case histories to determine the outcome of actions whenever possible. The game was later adopted by the Army's Special Forces schools to train officers in counterinsurgency tactics. Commanders in the field were very high on AGILE-COIN because it taught "the political consequences of military actions." To win the game, participants simply implemented actions that the State Department role players had said worked in the field.

Probably the longest-running computer game at the Pentagon is one called TEMPER (Technological, Economic, Military, Political Evaluation Routine). This computer model of the world political-military situation attempts to predict how roughly forty to forty-five Cold War scenarios will turn out if various actions are taken by the player. Originally designed in 1962 by Raytheon Company, TEMPER divides the globe into twenty "conflict regions" and deals with everything from the global effect of deploying particular weapons systems to the political dynamics of military budgeting. TEMPER projects for each of the twenty regions how greatly domestic needs will affect military spending and how much arms purchases will cut into foreign aid, world trade, and other vital activities. As the computer generates a variety of military and diplomatic crises for the players to grapple with, it projects the results of the actions they take. If a player abolishes the bomber leg of the nuclear triad, builds or does not build an MX missile, or deploys a new battle tank, TEMPER instantly shows how the world situation changes as a consequence.

An increasing number of field officers take a large measure of their training on a computer code-named Janus, which is capable of producing an elaborately detailed contour map of any piece of terrain on Earth—thanks to the Defense Mapping Agencies' extraordinarily accurate photo satellites—and then calculating the effect of any weapon in the U.S. arsenal on whatever enemy force might be operating there. Designed by the Lawrence Livermore nuclear warfare laboratory in California, Janus was particularly appreciated by senior instructors at the Army War College in Carlisle, Pennsylvania. It enabled them to discover that younger commanders invariably underestimated the degree of devastation that atomic weapons would cause and were therefore too prone to use them. Further training with Janus made them much more judicious.

These computer systems are largely operated by the Joint War Games Agency of the Joint Chiefs of Staff. The agency has three divisions— General War, Limited War, and Cold War. They help to generate the policies, responses, and war plans that occasionally surface in the news media when Wimex or another system goes wrong. Alert levels from "Apple Jack" all the way up to "Fade Out" call for military moves and responses determined by human strategists, but these humans increasingly draw their conclusions from the information, intelligence, and judgments of the Pentagon's computer systems.

DARPA scientists predict that leaders in the future will rely more and more on computer-generated scenarios and projections to make decisions. Ultimately, as the horrible decision to pull the nuclear hair trigger must be made in progressively shorter periods of time (for humans), Wimex or its descendants will have to assume much of the burden of command.

That prediction comes not as a guess but from a Pentagon computer.

To some, such prospects are not particularly rosy. There have been complaints from within and outside the defense establishment that the same old cycle of cost overruns, equipment failure, and political opposition and interference that plagued other ambitious high-command schemes will make the creation of anything resembling the supercomputer brain impossible.

Investigations initiated by Representative Jack Brooks, chairman of the House Government Operations Committee, and the General Accounting Office found that the Pentagon has ordered computer systems with little coordination, and that procurement bureaucrats with little working knowledge of the ultracomplex technology they've been buying have allowed vendors to charge the government prices far in excess of going commercial rates.

The GAO found, for example, that the Wimex failures were largely attributable to the Joint Chiefs of Staff's insistence that the computer systems be bought from long-time government computer supplier Honeywell, instead of allowing the Air Force to buy other equipment that GAO said was more suited to the project.

Defense Department technicians tried to compensate for Wimex's many hardware weaknesses by writing programs (software) that filled the gap. The GAO found that it cost some $3 million a year to write these programs—and they didn't seem to work anyway.

It was discovered that the Pentagon had a $2 billion item in its budget for computer program writing. Investigations by Brooks and others revealed that much of this excess cost was due to the fact that the various computer contractors each used a different language in their computer programming and operation. Overall, the defense/national security sector was employing as many as a thousand different computer languages in their systems. The computer routines in the "black boxes" that run an F-15 fighter were totally incompatible with and incomprehensible to the ones in the fire control computers of the F-16 fighter. The Pentagon's Wang word processors couldn't talk to its Hewlett-Packard models. The result has been electronic babel.

By 1983, the Pentagon finally developed its own computer Esperanto, a "high level" language called Ada which was supposed to become the single tongue for all future military computer systems. It cost $25 million to write the language and copies were quickly distributed to the hundreds of companies that sell the Pentagon computer hardware and software.

But, even as its supporters were boasting of Ada as the solution to the language problem, DARPA announced it was diverting unspecified millions toward producing ROSIE, a computer language designed "for implementing expert systems," especially the Cray 1 hookup.

As the drive toward more complicated computer systems and languages continues apace with the record of failures, the Pentagon has begun to raise fears and doubts about the effort to produce an electronic general staff.

In one of its most comprehensive reviews on a single topic in its history, the GAO has issued more than two hundred reports documenting shortcomings of various Pentagon computer schemes. One of the Wimex-related studies noted that one part of the system or another had malfunctioned during every major American military crisis from the fall of Saigon in 1975 to the failed Desert One mission to rescue American hostages in Iran in 1980. The GAO found that the communications link broke down while U.S. troops were en route to Guyana to take charge of the removal of the 900-some bodies of the victims of the Jonestown cult mass suicide.

A Pentagon survey of 272 of its top commanders in 1981 found that a majority said they did not trust the Wimex system. The minority who expressed faith in the computer said they believed that there were sufficient checks in the system whereby humans could intervene to prevent disaster.

"That logic is largely true," acknowledged Dr. Kosta Tsipis, a leading high-tech weapons analyst at MIT. "But," he added, "the very fact that you have to use it again and again is the problem. If it cries 'wolf' too much, you won't trust it anymore."

But having military commanders lose faith in electronic brains is not what disturbs most people upon learning just how far the defense establishment has gone toward placing the American military—particularly its nuclear forces—increasingly under the control of a computer in chief instead of a human commander in chief. There is far more to worry about if the officers and the politicians elect to trust it too much.

Despite all the brilliantly conceived war games written and played by Abt Laboratories and the Joint Chiefs during the Vietnam years, Americans never learned how to capture the hearts and minds of the Vietnamese villagers. And despite all the precautions and sophisticated hardware that has gone into Wimex, the computer piled up a dismal performance record even as more and more circuitry and silicon chips were added to increase its powers to order various units into action.

The work toward producing electronic military brains is still in early stages. That means that the defense establishment has a rare opportunity to avoid many of the problems that have beset other of its high technology projects. In particular, the pursuit of artificial intelligence should include a clear-eyed jugment about whether the technocrats are promising far more than they can deliver. Will the final product simply be another faulty machine produced after years of cost overruns and prone to failure just when needed most? Artificial intelligence threatens to be the ultimate high-tech folly if the American arsenal is placed even further in the control of fallible circuitry.

The electronic-brain project raises questions even more complex than whether the technology exists to produce it. The computer brain represents a sea change in how a nation prepares for war. Wimex evolved as the players of computer war games realized that they could program the machine to do more than conduct the millions of simulations of responses in various worldwide scenarios. They could also program the machine to issue the orders to carry out those computer-generated moves. Wimex, therefore, became a battery of computers linked to the worldwide "command, communications, and control" network of satellites, telephone lines, radio, television, microwave, and other facilities available to gather intelligence and issue orders to units in the field.

Wimex was built because computers proved far more proficient than humans in examining the likely impact of a given action on whatever scenario was being considered. In any game, no matter how complex, the machine never forgets a prior move. And as the game progresses, it never forgets a single predrafted contingency plan to react to whatever move an opponent makes next. Of course, its lightning-quick ability to make decisions and implement them without emotion made it superior to humans who were playing the games themselves. In turn, the outcome of each war game determined the strategy adopted by Pentagon commanders as they prepared for events in the real world. If the computer game indicated that the best response to detecting a wave of Soviet rocket launches off the Atlantic coast of the United States would be a total launch of the American missile strike force, then the command computer would not hesitate to order the launch.

The blending of these two roles in a machine—drafting plans through war games and then ordering their implementation through electronic command, communications, and control systems—makes it imperative that deep consideration be given to the impact the electronic brain will have on the military establishment.

As noted earlier, the experience with the Janus computer project, which allowed young officers to try out different combinations of conventional and nuclear weapons to meet various simulated Soviet threats and actions, indicated that humans—at least while playing the game— were more likely to fall back on nuclear weapons than would be a machine. But what would happen in a real confrontation, when the human military officer was faced with the awesome moral question of whether to be the first to cross the threshold and use an atomic weapon?

While the computer has been less ready to open the gates of hell in the games, there is no question that it would do so precisely—and without emotion—the moment the computer-drafted scenarios called for it. Isn't there a very real danger that as officers train more and more according to computer-drafted scenarios using computer-derived responses, human judgment will be blunted? Will the human plod along, acting as a slow imitation of a computer instead of exercising the comprehension and imagination that even the most devout technocrats acknowledge is beyond the realm of artificial intelligence?

Wimex, of course, is not yet the electronic president. But the machine clearly is the foot in the door that presages such a role for its descendants in the near future. The implications of such a future must be considered while Wimex is still an adolescent with a bad reputation for crying wolf.

As Wimex matures and one day stops shouting wolf, it may pause as human beings do and wonder where it came from. Unlike its human counterparts, it was produced by a system—the same system that gave American defense both the Wright brothers' military Flyer and the space shuttle, but also the erratic Maverick missile and superheated M-1 tank. It's the same system that saw unscrupulous suppliers of Civil War arms and equipment add the word "shoddy" to the dictionary. It is a system which has much to do with greed and profit, but precious little to do with free enterprise. It is the system by which the American military acquires its weaponry from the "makers," the defense industries who are probably the most important component of American defense—and all too often the most flawed.

chapter fifteen

THE MAKERS

> *You couldn't find a better time to have high priority government contracts. For the stability of the company, you can't beat government business in hard times.*
>
> —DAVID LEWIS, $700,000-A-YEAR-PLUS
> PRESIDENT OF GENERAL DYNAMICS

On September 3, 1908, the United States government bought its first airplane—a lumbering wood, canvas, and metal contraption built by the celebrated Orville and Wilbur Wright. The contract was let, without competitive bidding, by the U.S. Army Signal Corps. Unlike the brothers' first airplane, which had cost about $800 to construct, mostly out of bicycle parts, the Flyer was designed to meet Army specifications. The cost, including $5,000 in bonus payments to the Wrights for meeting specified deadlines, ultimately ran to $30,000—for an aircraft not that much more advanced than the one that made history at Kitty Hawk.

The contract called for a flying machine capable of carrying two people with a combined weight of 350 pounds for one hour. The plane also had to carry enough fuel to travel 125 miles. A final military specification was that, during tests, it had to complete a ten-mile course at an average speed of forty miles an hour.

On September 17, two weeks into tests being conducted near Arlington Cemetery, just across the river from Washington, D.C., the Flyer crashed with Orville Wright at the controls. He was badly injured and his military passenger, Army observer Lieutenant Thomas Selfridge, was killed.

A marker near the Fort Meyer, Virginia, crash site notes that Lieutenant Selfridge was "the first Army officer to pay the supreme sacrifice in an effort to aid man's endeavor to fly." The Pentagon has yet to erect a monument commemorating its first aviation cost overrun.

A notable successor to the $30,000 Wright Flyer is the $23 million F-16 jet fighter built in Texas by the giant General Dynamics Company. There are no fewer than twenty thousand American firms with defense contracts, and General Dynamics is the largest. A megafirm that evolved from a Chicago-based concrete company called Material Services Corporation, GD is a major supplier to all the military service branches and could outfit any country bent on making war.

It produces jet fighters and bombers—F-16s and F-111s—in Fort Worth, Texas. At other plants as far-flung as California, Michigan, Connecticut, and Florida, the company builds the Army's M-1 main battle tank, the Navy's Trident submarine, the Marine Corps' Stinger missile, and dozens of other major weapons.

The company happily provides tours of its plants to defense writers and other outsiders. One of the most frequently visited GD facilities is the enormous aircraft factory at Fort Worth. According to P. L. Chik of the company's marketing department, an average of 1,578 visitors from the Pentagon and elsewhere come to the red-brick F-16 plant there each week. On one such tour, those in the crowd of some two hundred visitors included two newspaper reporters, several hard-eyed Israeli fighter pilots there to train in computerized F-16 flight simulators, and a group of Egyptians who came to watch the factory turn out the next six jets on order for Egypt's air force. There were also a group of Belgian engineers from the European factories that produce a NATO version of the F-16 and a half-dozen Japanese sent from Tokyo to observe the performance of robots their company had sold GD. They reluctantly left their cameras with guards at the front desk.

Behind the Japanese came a contingent of blue-suited U.S. Air Force colonels, in the charge of Brigadier General George Monahan, commander of the thousands of Air Force personnel assigned to the F-16 program.

Well-trained GD tour guides smoothly led the visitors through the gates—keeping the Israelis separated from the Egyptians, apologizing to the Japanese for the temporary confiscation of their cameras, and politely steering the Europeans to their destinations.

Rob Mack, GD's public-relations man at Fort Worth, explained that the reason there are so many foreigners at the top secret war plant is that GD, in common with many other major American defense contractors, is deeply committed to U.S. efforts to sell friendly countries the same military hardware used by the United States—a practice defended as a way of keeping down the unit cost of weapons to the American military.

Dozens of F-16s were sold to both Israel and Egypt. They were useful to American diplomats as bargaining chips in negotiations with both countries, but also produced added profits for GD while keeping costs to the Pentagon less unreasonable than they otherwise would have been.

Mass visitations like that to GD's Fort Worth plant are made every day in every state in the country, their numbers and diversity just one indication of the immense scope of the defense industry and its role in the American economy.

Each year, the Pentagon publishes directories listing the top one hundred companies receiving Defense Department contracts. The information is broken out in a variety of ways to help the industry and its friends show the public how government money flows out to the states. The Directorate for Information Operations and Reports (DIOR), the bureaucracy created to promote goodwill by informing civilians about the armaments pork barrel coming their way, provides information on defense money flow by city, region, company, types of companies, and—of course—by congressional district.

The same group of roughly twenty companies heads the list each year. Depending on the ebb and flow of contracts, the megafirms move in and out of first place, but most years either General Dynamics or the St. Louis–based McDonnell-Douglas Corporation can be found at the top of the pile.

McDonnell-Douglas, called "Mack Cee Dee" by its Pentagon friends, dominates the high-cost fighter aircraft market, most lately by producing the Air Force's F-15 top-of-the-line fighter, the popular F-4 Phantom now also used by friendly countries like Israel, and the F/A-18, the highly complex computerized fighter-bomber built mostly for deployment on aircraft carriers.

The typical ranking of these arms giants in contract worth would be General Dynamics, McDonnell-Douglas, United Technologies, General Electric, Boeing, Lockheed, Hughes Aircraft, Raytheon, Grumman, Litton Industries, Martin Marietta, Tenneco, Rockwell International, Westinghouse, FMC, Honeywell, and Northrop.

The top twenty firms account for nearly every major weapon the Pentagon purchases. Each corporation can count on business ranging between $1 billion and $4 billion annually from the government. These companies have dominated the field for nearly two decades. The 1968 list of 100 top firms was led by Lockheed, and followed by General Electric, General Dynamics, McDonnell-Douglas, United Technologies, American Telephone and Telegraph, Rockwell International, and Boeing.

Conservative economist Murray Weidenbaum, who served as chairman of the White House Council of Economic Advisers in the first term of the Reagan administration, was warning in the mid-1960s that the concentration of business with the same few companies would create unnecessarily high costs and lead to waste and inefficiency. In a highly prophetic 1966 study of concentration and retrenchment among firms selling to the Air Force, Weidenbaum noted that four companies were selling 86 percent of all airplane engines and that General Electric and United Technologies—then called United Aircraft—had between them 65 percent of all engine contracts. Weidenbaum found that because these companies as sole sources were able to set their prices free of competition and were producing much of the weaponry with government-supplied machines, the defense giants were enjoying a 17.5 percent return on their investment at a time when nonmilitary industries high on the Fortune 500 list were averaging 10 percent profits.

Just behind the military hardware giants in the rankings are the major oil companies, which supply the fuel for everything from Jeeps to diesel cruisers to nuclear aircraft carriers, as well as heating oil for military bases and other energy products. Philbro Corporation usually heads the energy giant list, followed by Exxon and Standard Oil of California. Philbro was the thirteenth-largest defense contractor in 1981, solely through sales of petroleum.

Profiles of the companies make for interesting prospectus reading.

Boeing, the nation's biggest airplane manufacturer, successfully markets many of its civilian aircraft to the Pentagon in military versions, such as the 707 passenger jet that was converted into the Air Force's Advanced Warning and Control System plane (AWACS). With its windows removed and tanks installed, the 707 also serves as the Air Force's KC-135 refueling tanker.

Headed by T. A. Wilson, who draws an annual salary in excess of $500,000, Boeing has reaped lucrative contracts for the Minutemen missiles now in one thousand silos around the United States, the booster rockets for the space shuttle, the Army's Chinook helicopter, the Strategic Air Command's B-52 bomber fleet, and hydrofoil missile ships for the Navy.

Because both Lockheed and McDonnell-Douglas have virtually abandoned the civilian passenger jet market, Boeing dominates that field, but it remains dependent on defense contracts to maintain profit margins.

Boeing spokesmen acknowledge that the company hopes to keep its Pentagon and NASA contracts at about 30 percent of total business and thus tide it over periods when demand for civilian jets is soft.

United Technologies, a Connecticut-based conglomerate, is made up of a number of old-line arms companies, including Pratt and Whitney Aircraft Group, the nation's preeminent aircraft engine manufacturer; the Sikorsky Aircraft Division; and Norden Systems, the famous maker of the bombsights that were credited with the success of American daylight precision bombing in Europe during World War II.

The second-largest defense contractor in 1981 with $4 billion in military sales, United Technologies (UT) also does substantial civilian business, thanks to its acquisition of such blue-chip outfits as Otis Corporation (elevators), Carrier Corporation (air-conditioning equipment), and Essex International (hotels). In the late 1970s and early 1980s, the company was doing roughly 30 percent of its annual business with the Defense Department and NASA, for whom UT is the major designer and producer of space suits and rocket engines.

Presided over by Harry J. Gray, at an annual salary exceeding $800,000, the company's present major arms contracts are for the F-100 jet engine used in both the F-15 and F-16, as well as engines for several Navy carrier-based jets and the AWACS planes of the Air Force. The company produces the Black Hawk helicopter for the Army and the Sea Stallion heavy-lift copter for the Navy.

In 1980, UT hired Alexander M. Haig, Jr., as its president and chief operating officer, after he stepped down as NATO supreme commander in Europe. Haig, formerly Richard Nixon's controversial Watergate-era chief of staff, then left to serve as President Reagan's secretary of state.

With corporate headquarters in Burbank, California, Lockheed is a $5-billion-a-year defense company that has had a full share of the negative publicity associated with the industry.

It was Lockheed that in 1971 became the first defense company to be bailed out by the government, when Congress had to arrange $250 million in loans to keep it from going bankrupt.

Lockheed's gargantuan cost overruns on the C-5A project produced the first major scandal on ballooning defense costs. When its secret computer printouts detailing its arm-twisting efforts in Congress were made public in the early 1980s, it won notoriety for lobbying tactics that are practiced throughout the industry.

In 1975, the company attracted even more public scorn when congressional committees and the Securities and Exchange Commission accused its executives of paying more than $200 million in bribes to obtain business abroad. Though Lockheed took the heat, many other companies were later found to have made the same kind of payments.

Its chief executive officer, Roy A. Anderson, makes an annual salary of $350,000. The company has had the contracts for the Trident and Polaris missile systems, the P-3 Orion submarine-hunting planes, the C-141 Starlifter cargo jet, a number of space vehicles, amphibious assault ships, and the propeller-driven C-130 troop and cargo plane that is greatly sought by armed services around the world for its ability to operate from small airfields.

In a 1982 interview, Anderson said he planned to operate the company "90 percent military to 10 percent civilian."

General Dynamics has also all but abandoned the civilian sector for Pentagon contracts. The last passenger aircraft it made—the Convair 880 and 990 jets—have long been out of production.

Instead, GD's corporate strategists have plotted some of the biggest arms deals ever made. It drove Chrysler from Number 10 among defense contractors all the way off the list in 1982, by buying out the troubled automaker's contracts to produce the M-1 main battle tank. At least 90 percent of GD's sales are now to the Pentagon, compared to just 45 percent in 1976.

That 1976 nadir was chiefly the result of the continuing crashes and disastrous cost overruns of the company's swept-wing F-111 fighter-bomber. At the same time, the company's Electric Boat Division was sued by the Navy because of massive cost increases in its SSN 668 attack-submarine program. *Business Week* described GD, with its passenger aircraft gone and its overrun troubles, as "a prime candidate for extinction."

Chicago industrialist Henry Crown took over as chief stockholder and hired David Lewis away from McDonnell-Douglas to become GD's president at an annual salary of about $700,000. In short order, the firm was at the top of the arms heap.

For the visitors at GD's Fort Worth plant that morning, the times looked very good indeed. Public-relations man Mack ushered the two newsmen into an office suite decorated, as are other executive areas of the facility, with photos of the company's jets streaking through cloud-puffed azure skies.

The factory is the second-largest aircraft assembly in the United States and the free world. The only one larger is the immense structure at Everett, Washington, where Boeing assembles its 747s. Said Mack with quiet pride, "Of course, they're private and we're GOCO."

This acronym stands for "government-owned, contractor-operated." It means that the government of the United States furnished General Dynamics with its factory and much of the machinery used to build the highly profitable F-16s. Similarly, Lockheed turns out its $206 million C-5Bs at a GOCO factory in Marietta, Georgia.

The GD factory, with its 6.5 million square feet of work space, is listed on the U.S. Treasury books as Air Force Plant 4. Lockheed's is designated Plant 5. Similar federally supplied facilities are used by firms throughout the military-industrial complex to produce the items they sell to government.

Rockwell International Corporation produces the plutonium triggers for hydrogen bombs at a GOCO installation just outside Denver, and Honeywell makes ammunition for the Air Force's A-10 tank-killer plane in a federal arsenal near Minneapolis. The Defense Department estimates that it has turned over facilities worth more than $100 billion to private firms in this manner since World War II. Nearly all of these free factories are in the hands of the top two dozen defense contractors.

Whistle-blower A. Ernest Fitzgerald observed in an essay entitled "Space Age Feudalism" that the most vocal critics of social welfare programs for the poor become the staunchest supporters of "welfare capitalism."

"They can grow livid at the waste of a couple of hundred dollars resulting from bureaucratic stupidity such as lodging a welfare mother in the Waldorf," he said, "then open the money sack at both ends for corporate incompetents."

A number of senior defense analysts have concluded that major corporations are affected by welfare much as ordinary people are—it saps their initiative by discouraging efforts to get off the dole. A company with a GOCO factory has little incentive to use any of its profits to build more and better production lines. As these would of necessity bring down unit costs, the taxpayer is doubly docked—first to pay for the GOCO factory and then to cover the high cost of turning out modern weapons in increasingly obsolete and inefficient facilities.

This welfare capitalism virtually ensures that no aggressive new companies (in the best storybook capitalist fashion) will be able to wrest contracts away from the old establishment, because the newcomers can't afford the front-end costs of building the kind of factories that the defense industry establishment got for nothing.

Defense contractors are not a new problem, as the records of the 1934 Special Committee on Investigation of the Munitions Industry, named the Nye Commission after its chairman, Senator Gerald P. Nye of North Dakota, attest. The group was formed after General Douglas MacArthur, then Army chief of staff, and Socialist Norman Thomas, among others, joined forces to warn that profiteering was rampant in the dealings between a few favored companies and the War Department. The companies, critics said, were overcharging the military for ships and munitions, were overpaying their top executives, and were profiting from weapons sales all over the globe. The committee concluded these sales were dangerous to world peace. In one passage particularly relevant to today's profligate peddling of billions of the most sophisticated armaments abroad, the panel wrote in its 1937 final report:

> While the evidence before this committee does not show that wars have been started solely because of the activities of munitions makers and their agents, it is also true that wars rarely have a single cause, and the committee finds it to be against the peace of the world for selfishly interested organizations to be left free to goad and frighten nations into military activity.

The Nye Commission made reference to firms still doing a big defense business. In cautioning against sales to participants in the Sino-Japanese War that was raging in the middle 1930s, the panel noted that Lockheed and Douglas Aircraft Corporation (precursor of McDonnell-Douglas) were selling planes to Japan's puppet government in Manchukuo. Sperry Gyroscope and DuPont were selling aviation instruments and munitions to Japan and both Boeing and United Aircraft (precursor of United Technologies) were selling aircraft to China.

At the same time, United Aircraft, Sperry Gyroscope, DuPont, and the Electric Boat Company (now part of GD) were doing business with Germany and Italy.

The Nye Commission's warning was little heeded. By 1980, many of these same companies were closing deals that pushed overseas arms sales to more than $17 billion a year, with some $9 billion going to Third World countries alone. Between 1976 and 1980, the United States's top customer in arms purchases—ahead of Britain, West Germany, and South Korea, among others—was Iran.

The arms companies that helped so many nations prepare for World War II were in an excellent position once it broke out and American rearmament began. Enriched with military contracts exceeding their wildest Depression-era dreams, they also, as part of national mobilization, acquired many of the GOCO plants they operate today.

In addition to the more than $100 billion in free factories it has turned over to private firms since the war, the government has also provided for free $10 billion in machinery ranging from expensive foundry presses to motor test stands.

Former Pentagon official Jacques Gansler, now an outside consultant on acquisition matters, told Congress that Defense Department welfare capitalism has weakened the national defense by encouraging the same old players to continue the same inefficient practices in the same aging factories, confident that each year's profit will be the same—adjusted for inflation, of course. Testifying before the Joint Economic Committee in 1981, he said companies continued to use obsolete facilities, producing ever smaller numbers of weapons, because it was easier to simply increase the unit cost in each year's contract than install the expensive, modern machinery and other factory improvements that eventually would bring unit costs down.

"In the 1950s, the United States bought over 3,000 fighter planes per year," he said. "In the 1960s, this went down to 1,000 planes per year, and in the 1970s down to 300 planes per year. Yet the structure of the aircraft industry remained largely the same, with essentially the same number of plants."

Fitzgerald observed in "Space Age Feudalism" that the corporations play favored medieval dukes to the Pentagon's generous king. His proposed solution was to dismantle the system entirely and put the GOCO factories up for sale under competitive bidding. "The suggestion that a changing economic climate demands that dinosaur companies adapt or die breeds panic," he said.

Defenders of the system argue that a few government factories in the hands of major corporations serve as the hub of an industrial complex that creates millions of jobs throughout the economy. In times of recession, weapons production becomes crucial to keeping the national industrial base functioning, they say.

GD's Mack and his staff have prepared hundreds of press releases proudly outlining how the company reaches out from the Fort Worth GOCO factory to hire more than four thousand subcontractors to produce the components for just one fighter plane.

Mack's lists note that the engines for the F-16 are built by Pratt and Whitney of Hartford, Connecticut, while a small firm in Oxnard, California, called Abex makes hydraulic pumps for the plane. Goodyear Aerospace makes the spare tires for the fighter in Akron, Ohio, while the Singer-Kearfort Company of Little Falls, New Jersey, supplies navigation equipment. The nose of the F-16 is supplied by the Brunswick Company of Skokie, Illinois, and a company called Texstar in Grand Prairie, Texas, makes the transparent canopies. The ejection seat is made by McDonnell-Douglas, while the airspeed indicator is manufactured by one of the smallest, Systron-Donner of Concord, California.

By the early 1980s, analysts noted that the system by which revenues trickled down from megacompanies to mom-and-pop weapons subcontractors was beginning to unravel. Gansler prepared a study for the Joint Economics Committee showing that hundreds of small contractors—"lower-tier suppliers" in Pentagon lingo—had dropped out of military work because they couldn't take the cycle of feast and famine typified by the lush Vietnam years and the lean peace that followed. Small contractors would invest in machinery, add workers, and incur other costs to fill thousands of orders one year and then have only a

THE MAKERS 245

few to fill the next. Lacking a government-supplied factory, the small operators collapsed, Gansler said.

Another problem for the small firms—who, unlike many of the defense giants, also produce for the civilian economy—is the requirement that they meet stringent military specifications.

Sears, Roebuck and Company, the giant civilian merchandiser that often functioned as a small contractor selling appliances and the like to the military, found government specifications and restrictions too demanding even for a company of its size. In 1981, the firm withdrew from Pentagon business, complaining that the cost and bother were not worth the effort. Philip Knox, a Sears vice-president, said that the company made the decision after the federal Office of Contract Compliance complained that the merchandising giant had not properly filled out the required forms called for under the Pentagon's "mil-specs," or military specifications. The instruction book for those forms, as noted earlier, fills thirty-two volumes and thirty thousand pages.

In a study for the Small Business Administration, economist Gail Garfield Schwartz noted that the Pentagon had tried to stem the defections of thousands of small subcontractors by producing a book called *Selling to the Military* that attempted to reduce the thirty thousand pages of often incomprehensible mil-specs to a much more manageable number of simplified instructions.

These included discussions of items the Pentagon wanted, which Pentagon officials should be contacted by companies wanting to do business, how to make a Pentagon sales pitch, how to fill out the required federal forms, and how to write the required and complex contract proposals. Schwartz applauded the Pentagon for trying to remedy the problem but warned it is a basically unhealthy situation when a buyer (the Pentagon) has to court salesmen to come calling.

The shortage of small contractors can prove ruinously expensive, because the big firms often then produce the small parts themselves. The consequences of this were dramatically illustrated when a federal whistle-blower named George Spaunton came forward to disclose the scandalously high prices that Pratt and Whitney was charging the Defense Department for spare parts it needed to repair older jet engines. It was found that the company had sold the Air Force several hundred thousand rivets at a cost of $1 each, when similar rivets used in civilian aircraft manufacturing cost only 24 cents. Reporters obtained a memo written by an Air Force civilian executive, Robert Hancock, which listed thirty-two items ranging from the rivets to engine cowling parts for which the company had marked up prices by 300 percent and more.

All told, according to Hancock and others, the firm had jacked up the price of spare parts by $140 million in a single year.

The company defended the huge markup by saying that the added expenses were the result of having to retool to make the small parts. But it was disclosed that a substantial part of the cost increases were write-offs of company parties, foreign travel, and other frivolities. Auditors for the Defense Contract Audit Agency found that the cost-plus contracts given to the large companies allowed executives to charge such indulgences as "morale" expenses and the like. Small contractors who win single contracts rarely are allowed the cost-plus terms enjoyed by the big operators.

Perhaps the most damning critique of what these contracting abuses mean to national security came from Dr. Hans Mark, former secretary of the Air Force and deputy administrator of the National Aeronautics and Space Administration. Mark, a no-nonsense engineer, told a Defense Industrial Base Conference in Boston in 1983 that the industry was rapidly pricing itself out of the business and making it ever more difficult for the country to obtain the numbers of weapons it needed to defend itself. He told the conference:

> In 1943 a Lockheed P-38 fighter aircraft cost the government about $125,000. The P-38 was a highly sophisticated airplane with two powerful reciprocating engines, the latest in electronic detection and navigation gear, and a formidable arsenal of weapons. Today's equivalent is the McDonnell-Douglas F-15, which is also a highly sophisticated twin engined fighter aircraft with a fearsome array of weapons and a very capable package of electronic equipment.

Mark asked his audience, "What does an F-15 cost? The last figure I can get from the Air Force is about $23.7 million apiece" (now $51 million). That, Mark told a room full of increasingly uncomfortable industrialists, means that the F-15 is more expensive than the P-38 by a factor of two hundred. Inflation between 1943 and 1983 increased by a factor of only five.

> That is, a dollar today will buy about what twenty cents bought in 1943 in equivalent commodities. I looked at the cost of many other commodities and only in the area of sophisticated weaponry could I find factors that came close to two hundred for the increase in cost during the last four decades.

Mark noted further that in World War II the United States produced 9,257 P-38s but will produce at the most only 1,395 of the F-15s. He also observed that it took five times as long to design and develop the F-15.

Thus, the same industrial leaders who are repeatedly invited to address the American Legion and other patriotic groups are responsible for a system that grows ever more inefficient at maintaining a national defense while sapping larger and larger amounts of national treasure that could be used to rebuild the nation's collapsing infrastructure of roads and bridges, among other vital needs. The numerical loss in weapons strength in recent years has been awesome. In 1956, the Air Force had 24,000 airplanes; today, it has 7,000. It had 1,900 long-range strategic bombers then compared to just over 400 in the mid-1980s.

Also in 1956, the Air Force possessed 3,480 "air superiority" jet fighters, but in 1983 had only 661—the F-15s and F-16s. The Navy in 1956 had 1,300 ships but only 453 when the Reagan administration took office. The Army bought 10,000 tanks in 1956. By the 1980s, tank production was about 750 a year.

Advocates of present-day defense policy have argued that today's weaponry, despite its small numbers, is so far superior to that of the past that numerical differences are unimportant. A growing number of experts including Mark counter that the flaws in the system are so severe that the argument over whether large numbers of relatively unsophisticated weapons can be defeated by a few advanced ones is becoming irrelevant.

The defense industry is producing an American defense the nation cannot afford—militarily as well as financially. As unlikely a critic of big business as Republican Senator Bill Roth of DuPont-dominated Delaware has charged that corporate America's greed is bringing about "gold-plated unilateral disarmament." The central reason that the number of weapons in the arsenal has dwindled so dramatically is the huge cost overruns that have become an institutional part of defense industry methods. The overrun is so commonplace today that news stories about the latest outrage now are usually consigned to the back of the paper or the tail end of the broadcast, if they make it at all. When they were first discovered, they made for banner headlines.

The arithmetic of the cause and effect is starkly simple. If the U.S. has $7 billion to buy tanks and tanks cost $1 million, then the country can afford a credible force of 7,000 tanks. But if the tanks end up costing $3 million each, as does the M-1 (until the price goes up again), the country can acquire only 2,100 machines. The Soviets have 40,000 or more.

Cost overruns are produced by many of the systemic flaws dealt with earlier in this book. Members of the uniformed services' procurement elite remain ever eager to increase the costs of their projects in hopes of more bureaucratic power and promotion. Design changes are ordered throughout the process of a weapon's development, each change increasing the number of persons associated with the project and its cost. Battalions of technology-enamored think-tank sages stand by to suggest ever more elaborate (and costly) alterations in projects. Industrial leaders take jobs in the Pentagon and use them to press for projects back at the plant. Procurement officers rubber-stamp cost increases, with an eye to future industry jobs after retirement. Congressional advocates keep the cash flowing despite public outrage at the soaring costs. Presidents foster the system out of a reluctance to alienate even small pockets of voters dependent on defense industry jobs.

But the overrun process starts with the companies, and the time-honored buying-in tactic. The companies almost universally submit bids for the weapons contracts which they know are unrealistically low. They know that, as it always has, Congress will be standing by to vote the increased funds needed to cover the overrun and true cost. The low bid buys in to the project.

This has outraged critics ranging from iconoclasts like Fitzgerald to establishment figures like tycoon J. Peter Grace, who excoriated his industrial peers and pals for using the buy-in practice in his Grace Commission report on government cost-cutting prepared at the request of President Reagan. In his final report, Grace told the President:

> The problem with government weapons procurement is that the system protects the suppliers instead of the taxpayers. After a weapons manufacturer wins a contract from the military—sometimes by "under bidding" with unrealistically low amounts—the manufacturer can become the sole source for 20 years, at which time costs are typically doubled and tripled in the absence of competition.

Grace quoted research done by Senator Roth to show the impact. "Cost estimates for 25 major weapons systems initiated between 1971 and 1978 have increased 323 percent," he complained. At the outset, noted the archconservative Grace, the companies had promised to build the weapons for only $105 billion, but when the actual bills came in, they demanded $339 billion and delivered far fewer copies of each weapon than had originally been promised.

Grace, the head of one of the country's biggest chemical companies and himself a big Pentagon contractor, cited the "Charlie Brown" syndrome as typical of buy-ins—an allusion to all the *Peanuts* comic strips in which Lucy keeps promising to hold a football for Charlie Brown, only to pull it away at the last instant every time the kid tries to kick it. Grace told Reagan:

Prior performance—specifically with respect to a source's past record of sticking to cost estimates—is given insufficient weight in the weapons contracting procedure. Sources with poor performance records can still obtain a contract by "under bidding" with unrealistically low numbers, with the hope, of course, of bidding up subsequent negotiated contracts.

Shelves at the congressional General Accounting Office are jammed with blue-covered reports outlining how the buy-ins cited by Grace and others sap national strength and drain away the public treasure. The GAO noted in one report how United Technologies had promised to deliver Black Hawk helicopters to the Army for only $2.8 million apiece in the late 1970s, but then jacked up the price to $4.7 million each when the deliveries started. The higher costs compelled the Army to buy fewer helicopters. In 1979, instead of obtaining 129 Black Hawks as planned, the Army could afford only 92 of them. The next year, costs went up again and the Army was able to acquire 94 instead of its planned 145, despite generals' claims that the higher numbers were desperately needed to replace the helicopter armadas lost in the Vietnam War.

General Dynamics promised to supply 2,250 antitank Stinger missiles in 1980 for $36,000 apiece, but then pleaded cost-growth problems and delivered only 900 at a cost of $70,000 apiece, the GAO found. Once again, the company got more money than bargained for and the military, fewer weapons. And so it went—fewer F-15s at higher unit cost, half the number of M-1 tanks at twice the cost, overruns exceeding 200 percent with the Maverick missile, $235 million for a B-1 bomber instead of an originally promised $35 million. When it's pumpkin-headed Charlie Brown hitting the ground with a shuddering *thump*, it's funny. When it's taxpayers and national security taking the fall, the humor fades.

Grace angrily demanded that past performances be held against his fellow arms capitalists. A company with a history of overruns should not be allowed to get further government business, he said.

A number of reform efforts already have been announced by officials now smarting at disclosures of so many outrages. An office was set up inside the Pentagon to oversee buying of spare parts to eliminate any further "gold-plating." Another office was created to supervise some of the future weapons testing done by the Pentagon. The ability of the Defense Department to investigate abuses has been increased by beefing up the in-house Inspector General apparatuses. But most needed are the sort of reforms that address the flawed nature of the system, not just add more watchdog bureaucracies to the already nightmarish mishmash of special Pentagon offices. Indeed, many of the extant Pentagon subgroups, such as the DSARCs and DRBs we've mentioned, were created to solve problems that arose in simpler eras.

American defense must become cost effective—and at once. Legislation must be passed to accomplish what defense secretaries from Robert S. MacNamara to Harold Brown could not achieve with their so carefully crafted executive directives and orders—ending the practice of buy-ins by requiring a firm, fixed price. The system of penalties and incentives employed by the Navy on some contracts should be used throughout the entire system. If a megafirm like Lockheed should fall for failing to meet requirements, the national security will be well served by that collapse. Effective legislation toward this end would bar all additional appropriations to cover the ballooning "out year" cost growth that inevitably occurs in the latter phases of production or company-induced project changes. This would compel firms to use accurate inflation projections and make honest assessments of true costs, instead of attempting to delude the Congress with artificially low initial bids.

To assist companies in making more honest and less costly proposals, there should be implementation of reforms urged by Weinberger and his former deputy, Frank Carlucci, to allow contractors to buy raw materials on a multiyear rather than single-year basis. By stocking up initially on enough basic supplies to last the better part of the project, a great deal of inflation can be kept out of the total cost, especially with immense Pentagon hardware projects.

In the event a contractor runs into an actual, legitimate emergency which threatens it with bankruptcy, a government receivership mechanism, similar to the Mutual Assistance Corporation ("Big Mac") that rescued New York City in the 1970s, could be put in place to keep production going while the responsible management is replaced and a "go/no-go" decision is made. Those who fail should be fired—in corporate board rooms as well as military command.

Also, the government could help establish defense industry risk-sharing consortiums, similar to those formed for offshore oil drilling and deep seabed mining, to deal with financial reverses encountered in undertaking problematical military projects (such as building a new nuclear missile).

All the government-owned but contractor-operated factories should be put up for sale—at market prices. By providing these facilities for a few "in" contractor-operators, the Pentagon is subsidizing their ability to undercut healthy competition in bidding. All bidders should be put on an equal footing.

Colonel Robert Dilger's highly successful experiment—in allowing at least two companies to share in a production contract (see page

154)—later emulated by the Air Force in splitting jet engine work between General Electric and Pratt and Whitney (see page 172)—with the lowest bidder getting the largest share but the other receiving enough work to stay in business and competition, should be expanded and adapted for use throughout the Pentagon.

Above all, the country should begin to utilize a little-noticed resource: an ever growing group of insiders at the Pentagon and the CIA, on Capitol Hill, and elsewhere, who are genuinely worried about the prospects for American survival and who have the expertise to cure the procurement sickness that is eating away at the defense arsenal these companies are supposed to be replenishing. The defense establishment must finally bring itself to listen to the reformers.

chapter sixteen

THE REFORMERS

> *There are occasions when the commands of the*
> *sovereign need not be obeyed.*
> —SUN TZU, THE ART OF WAR

Not everyone in the American defense establishment accepts a system that has nearly bankrupted the federal treasury while dangerously weakening the U.S. military. Opposed to it is a steadfast group working from within. They like to call themselves the "Christians." They are more commonly known as the "reformers." Some brass hats in the Pentagon call them by unprintable names. One of them—as many like him—works for the Central Intelligence Agency.

He is one of the most respected defense analysts in Washington. His office is in one of the many gleaming new high rises in the Virginia suburb of Rosslyn, directly across the Potomac River from Washington. An armed guard sits at a reception desk in front of the office and the office door is opened with a combination lock. A peephole and a closed-circuit television camera are in place to scan visitors.

Behind the door, the analyst's work load includes pondering computer projections of the outcome of a conventional war with the Soviets. He and his fellow analysts in the CIA, the Pentagon, and elsewhere in the defense establishment have made a major science of such things. He studies, as chemists do formulas, "exchange ratios"—combat results that are a function of manpower totals, the elements of surprise and initiative, and the current estimates of equipment breakdown and failure rates in both U.S. and Soviet weapons systems. A macabre calculus of death allows these experts to reduce the numerical outcome of battle to a decimal point on a dotted line glowing on the screens of their computer terminals.

On a recent afternoon, the analyst—a "supergrade" civil servant whose career has been spent at a variety of tasks for both the CIA and the Pentagon—pushed a cardboard carton filled with computer printouts from a chair and told one of the authors how the reform movement had begun.

As the nation entered the 1980s, with the Soviets apparently more powerful than ever before and the Third World growing ever more impoverished (and thus resentful of the United States), a group of patriotic men and women in the uniformed, civilian, and private-sector sections of the defense establishment decided the time had come to go public with a long-brewing but secret controversy. They called themselves the "Christians" because, in a very real sense, they risked a martyrdom akin to that suffered by the inmates of Rome's catacombs. They could be expelled from their careers and forever blackballed from the only world most had ever known.

They thought that what they were about to do was worth the risk. In positions of responsibility in both the Pentagon and at CIA headquarters at Langley in Virginia, they had grown increasingly worried about the results of their computer projections. In scenario after scenario, the analysis pointed to a U.S. defeat. The "Christians" became convinced that the U.S. military was being ravaged from within, degenerating deeper and deeper into weakness as generation after generation of military officers inflicted increasingly complicated, expensive, and unworkable weapons systems on the Army, Navy, Air Force, and Marine Corps.

This underground group—many of whose members remained anonymous even to those elsewhere in government and the news media who helped them in their crusade—realized that, as weapons became more complex, they also became far more expensive than earlier generations of ships, bombers, missiles, fighters, tanks, and guns had been. Higher costs meant fewer weapons. Increased complexity meant decreased reliability. In the computers, as probably on the battlefield, it meant defeat.

Unlike traditional critics of the military, whose opposition to big defense spending lies in the ideological complaint that it cruelly saps programs for the poor and hungry or will lead to nuclear war, the reformers were pleased when the Reagan administration called for readjusting the budget balance (shortly to be an imbalance) in the military's favor. Few if any of them could remotely be called a liberal, let alone leftist.

Lieutenant Colonel Walter Kross, a critic of the reformers, described them as follows in the *Air University Review*:

> Their professed purpose is to change U.S. military strategy, planning, tactics, and force structure in order to fight and win a modern theater war. They would markedly alter the way DOD prepares for war, establish significantly different war-fighting concepts and attendant force structure, and change the way weapons are developed and procured. Their motivation is simple: they are patriots

who believe the United States will lose the next war unless their ideas are adopted. . . .

These defense critics have survived through several administrations. Last spring [1981], their influence grew widespread because they were able to seize upon the major initiative of the Reagan administration: large increases in defense spending. Turning the issue to their advantage, the Reformers argue that blind increases in defense spending will not guarantee greater military capability. Instead, they say more spending could yield even less capability if we continue to buy expensive, complex, vulnerable weapons that are costly to operate. Our military leaders, they assert, are transfixed on a losers' game: attrition warfare.

The Reformers suggest a different approach to modern war. First, military operations should rely on maneuver, deception, decentralized C³ [command, control, and communications systems] and exploitation of the enemy's weaknesses. Second, force structure should be recast to emphasize simpler, cheaper, more easily supportable weapons that really work in combat. In this way, the Reformers hold out the promise of more capability for less cost. There it is—more or less—a fiscal aphrodisiac guaranteed to gain widespread support, both inside government and with the public.

Steeped in military lore, converts to the wisdom and philosophies of Sun Tzu and Karl von Clausewitz, the reformers worried about the efficacy of modern weapons in the mud, heat, confusion, and terror of battle. Over glasses of ouzo in their favorite Greek restaurant down the road from the Pentagon, they worried about how the people who fly planes, drive tanks, and command infantry in the present era have had no personal experience of war and no real grasp of the central fact of war—that a brilliant use of tactics and a completely unexpected maneuver can be far more potent and destructive than a weapon wielded by a soldier, pilot, or ship captain who acts predictably, as so many operating computer-driven weaponry must.

As the reformers talked—and plotted—engineers from big defense contractors were telling official Washington that ultrasophisticated new weaponry was so good that "one of ours" could easily destroy three, five, fifty, or even one hundred of "theirs."

Navy commanders brought members of congressional committees aboard their billion-dollar Aegis-class battle cruiser, *Ticonderoga*, and assured them that the ship's computer-run rockets, guns, and cannons could shoot any incoming enemy missile out of the air before it could strike either the cruiser or the $3.5 billion aircraft carrier it was designed to protect. Boeing and its subcontractors spun other yarns about the magical AWACS plane, which could be flying three hundred miles away from a battlefield and still use its omniscient radars to detect every enemy fighter, tank, and ship, directing U.S. fighter pilots, tank gunners, ship captains, and artillery officers in firing upon the enemy with dazzling accuracy.

The reformers knew better. They had reviewed the secret performance reports about the wonder weapons. They had figures showing massive problems with breakdowns in even the most favorable operating conditions. They passed among themselves studies revealing that the Pentagon could not afford to buy spare parts because the systems they were to go in cost so much. They obtained reports listing failures in operational test after operational test that had been glossed over to keep the money flowing from Congress.

Gradually, they compiled a brief about each of the magic weapons that reinforced and increased their own fears and flatly contradicted the rosy declarations of the Pentagon procurement elite and the manufacturers. Then, working through a group on Capitol Hill that came to be known as the Military Reform Caucus, the reformers began letting the damning details reach the glaring light of public scrutiny. Adding enormous weight to their arguments was the fact that they were based on the same resources, data, and access used by the government, including those agencies for whom they worked. Their conclusions were devastating.

The F-15, the "air superiority fighter" that cost the Air Force $51 million apiece, was tested at Nellis Air Force Base outside Las Vegas in mock dogfights with the much cheaper and simpler F-4 and F-5 jets made by Northrop and widely sold to smaller countries that cannot afford more expensive U.S. aircraft. Robert Fay, the retired fighter pilot who designed the tests, found that the F-5 pilots were able to defeat the sophisticated F-15s with such crude but effective tricks as employing an ordinary "fuzz buster" radar detector of the kind sold to heavy-footed motorists who want warning of highway patrol radars. Because the much larger F-15 is so loaded with electronics and gives off so many radar signals, the Vietnam era air aces flying the F-5s waited until the fuzz buster picked up an F-15 radar signal and then used a telescopic rifle sight to pick the F-15 out of the blue Nevada sky. Then the pilot would fire off a cheap Sidewinder missile at the F-15. Because of the disparity in sizes, the pilot in the small F-5 almost always could see a big F-15 before being sighted himself.

Fay showed one of the authors an unclassified photograph of the highly complex instrument panel of an F-15, replete with digital readouts, gauges, multiple radar screens, and endless control switches, toggles, and levers, and asked him to imagine sitting in the cockpit trying to fire and guide six Phoenix air-to-air missiles at six different Soviet

MIGs while checking radar screens and other warning sensors, flying the aircraft, and listening to radio guidance from a distant AWACS.

"You are going to become damned confused," Fay said. "You are going to give up on your instruments and do what fighter pilots have always done—look out the window."

When an F-15 pilot does that, according to Fay, longtime fighter designer Pierre Sprey, and other experts, his aircraft and the F-5 are weapons platforms with virtually the same capabilities. But the United States could buy eight F-5s for every F-15, and one hundred Sidewinder missiles for every Phoenix. The United States planned to acquire nearly 1,500 F-15s over the presumed twenty-year life span of the program. For the same money, the Air Force could equip itself with an armada of twelve thousand F-5s.

And numbers, Fay's tests showed, can be everything. His final report found that, in cases where the F-15 went one-on-one with an F-5, it won. But when four F-5s took on one F-15, the bigger, more expensive airplane usually lost. Even when four F-15s were posed against four F-5s, they ran into serious combat problems. Before their radar gear could sort out the attacking F-5s, the little plane's simple fuzz buster/Sidewinder system was firing away.

Fay, who flew combat missions in both Korea and Vietnam, said F-15 pilots found the aircraft's incredible speed a disadvantage in combat because of the great volumes of fuel required to reach that speed. Not one second of flight time at Mach 2 or even Mach 1.8 (1.8 times the speed of sound) was logged in the entire Vietnam War. "You get to Mach 2 just in time to run out of fuel," Fay said. Six of the American POWs taken to Hanoi had bailed out of F-4s when they ran out of fuel while pursuing MIGs into North Vietnamese airspace at Mach 1.6.

When the embarrassing results of the F-15/F-5 competition leaked out of the Pentagon, champions of the high-tech fighter complained that the test was unfair because it was limited to firing its missiles at visual targets. In the *Air University Review* article in which he attacked the reformers as "a small group of well-placed civilian analysts who want to recast the United States military in their preferred mode," Lieutenant Colonel Kross asserted that, in a real war, F-15 pilots would be allowed to fire their Phoenix missiles "beyond visual range," and that the radar-laden AWACS planes would be operating nearby to assist F-15s in their aerial battles.

The AWACS aircraft, converted Boeing 707 passenger planes with a distinctive saucer-shaped antenna housing welded on top of the fuselage, cost nearly $250 million apiece with all the radar options. The U.S. fleet consists of 29 AWACS, each packed with hundreds of electronic "black boxes" and complex computer circuitry. The plane's mission is to direct American or NATO pilots in a conventional tactical air war, in Europe or anywhere in the world. It is also used extensively to track Soviet fleet and submarine movements in the North Atlantic.

In one respect—intimidation—the AWACS took over a role formerly performed by battleships and gunboats. When the American hostages were seized in Iran, President Carter deployed an AWACS task force near the area. President Reagan sent AWACS into the Caribbean when things got hot in Central America in 1983, and into Africa to show U.S. displeasure at Colonel Qaddafi's invasion of Chad. Reagan also sold five AWACS planes to Saudi Arabia, in part to further secure its vital friendship and in part to show his displeasure with a then militarily adventurous Israel.

But one of the most disturbing findings the reformers were able to get into the public record was that the AWACS had compiled a history of repeated failures—all very chilling to the fighter pilots who'd been told the superplane could protect them against all comers.

Much of the unhappy AWACS story was divulged by a now-deceased Pentagon engineer who participated in two tests in which the aircraft performed dreadfully. He became one of the in-house converts to the reformers' cause. In the first test, AWACS planes flying above Frankfurt, Germany, ordered accompanying fighter pilots to investigate numerous "low-flying aircraft" active around the city. The low-flying aircraft, detected by the wealth of AWACS radar but badly identified, turned out to be cars whizzing along the autobahn.

More alarming was the second test, held over the Pacific Ocean west of Seattle. Two F-106s, the most primitive fighters in the Air Force arsenal, were able to fly undetected to within 150 feet of an AWACS operating at 40,000 feet.

The now-deceased engineer, who had devoted a lifetime to designing radar-guided devices, had become convinced that the American military was becoming vulnerable because so many of its high-technology weapons depended on sending out powerful radar beams to detect enemies— a vulnerability found to be shared by the AWACS, the Aegis-class cruiser, the F-15, and many, many other weapons.

The powerful radar beam serves as a warning to enemy war machines. In the Pacific test, a twenty-year-old EA-6B Prowler, an antiquated aircraft designed in the early 1960s to detect and jam radars, was flying a mission with the two F-106s, patrolling in a pattern outside the AWACS' maximum sensing range.

The old Prowler then switched to a course converging with the AWACS' with its radar detectors turned on. At the exact second the

Prowler detected the first bleep of incoming AWACS radar signal, its radar jamming equipment was automatically activated, causing the screens aboard the AWACS to "light up like strobe lights," the engineer recalled. In the confusion, as technicians in the AWACS began working frantically to unjam their equipment, the two F-106s closed on the big Boeing to 150 feet.

"At that distance," the engineer said, "we didn't need a missile to kill the AWACS. We could have used a rifle."

Critics of the AWACS project complain that the system was originally designed in the 1960s not as an airborne command center for tactical engagements between jet fighters, but as part of U.S. defenses against manned Soviet bombers attacking American cities.

As designed by Harold Brown, in the days when he was a Defense Department scientist, the AWACS was not intended to go into unfriendly skies filled with enemy fighters. It carries no arms. The AWACS project was predicated on the belief that Soviet bombers would be engaged only after they had moved beyond the range where Soviet fighters could protect them. But the Soviets never built the bomber fleets that the AWACS planners expected. Instead, they opted for a vast force of guided missiles. Despite the change in Soviet planning, the Pentagon was loath to kill the AWACS project; several hundred million dollars had already been budgeted for Boeing and other contractors. So instead of killing a weapon that was no longer needed, the procurement elite changed its mission to mother-henning American fighters in air battles where the foe's own fighters would likely be involved.

The test failures over the Pacific raised fears that, in battle, an enemy could "blind" U.S. fighter pilots by attacking the AWACS first. With the AWACS eliminated the U.S. pilots would not be able to use their missiles beyond visual range.

From the beginning, fighter pilots who would be placing their lives in the hands of some airborne radar operator as far as three hundred miles from the action, and who would have to fire their weapons on radio command at targets they couldn't see while ignoring enemies they could see, have doubted the AWACS' premise. During one series of "Red Flag" tests against mock Soviet fighters staged at Nellis Air Force Base, a roomful of F-15 pilots stood up and booed when the crew of an AWACS flight walked into their briefing room.

The ultimate in American radar weaponry, however, is not AWACS but the cruiser class named Aegis, after the shield used by the mythical god Zeus. Each Aegis ship is designed to serve as the "shield" for an entire naval battle group, comprising aircraft carriers, destroyers, guided missile frigates, and other warships and support vessels, and sometimes including a battleship. A single Aegis cruiser costs more than $1 billion, and the Navy set out to buy 26 of them—despite the serious reservations that arose when, just as the first Aegis cruiser *Ticonderoga* went out on sea trials, Argentinian fighter pilots were able to sink the $50 million British destroyer *Sheffield* with a simple $200,000 French-made "radar sniffing" Exocet missile. The Exocets could skim toward their targets at high speed just ten feet above the water, guided to their victims by the very radar signals used to detect the missiles. The waves they skimmed over created "chaff" on the enemy's missile detection radar, making defense difficult.

The *Ticonderoga* is to ordinary radar what a symphony orchestra is to a piccolo. Atop her command deck are four giant radar antennas rising to one hundred feet above the waterline and covering all points of the compass. Each of the four dishes comprises more than four thousand small radars that send out a myriad of pencil-thin radar beams. A second radar system broadcasts the traditional IFF (international friend or foe) signal used to warn U.S. gunners of friendly craft. A third is used to guide the cruiser's own missiles at targets picked up by its four dishes. The ship is equipped with a computerized weapons control system to direct its antiaircraft weapons, which include 20-mm Phalanx repeating cannons, five-inch deck guns, rocket-launched torpedoes, and other arms. The idea is to throw up such an incredible amount of fire power that attacking enemy aircraft, missiles, submarines, or surface ships will be destroyed, repelled, or discouraged in attempts to get through to the juicy carrier or battleship targets.

Thomas Amlie, onetime technical director of the Navy's China Lake Weapons Center, designer of the American radar-guided Sidewinder missile, and a leading force in the reform movement, wrote in the April 1982 issue of the engineering journal *IEEE Spectrum* that building weapons systems around such "loud" radars was akin to sending an infantryman to the top of the highest hill on the battlefield with a flare to dare the enemy to shoot at him.

> All an enemy need do is deploy low-cost anti-radiation missiles capable of homing in on the radiating antennas of the U.S. radars long before the radar can detect the presence of the enemy. The range of U.S. radar is limited to line of sight and an inexpensive [enemy] radar seeker, using passive sensors that do not radiate any energy, can detect and fire at radar systems from over the horizon.

In short, Amlie charged, the Aegis actually could serve to alert an enemy as to just where a U.S. carrier task force was sailing and then helpfully guide the adversary's weapons to their target.

After the Falklands War ended, Michael Gordon of the prestigious *National Journal* interviewed Rear Admiral Wayne E. Meyer, the project officer for Aegis, and others involved in the ship's development, and found that the vessel had never been tested against the sort of weapons that had been used successfully by the Argentinians against the British. In fact, Gordon reported, most of the Aegis testing had been accomplished with the use of a mock-up of the cruiser's bridge and radar work placed in a cornfield near the New Jersey Turnpike. The radar was made to track civilian passenger aircraft flying in the busy New York area. But because of the many farmers living in the vicinity—not to speak of the motorists on the Turnpike—the engineers at the site were unable to test the Aegis radars against low-flying targets, as enemy fighters and bombers would be in an attack. According to Gordon, Meyer acknowledged that the *Ticonderoga* never faced a target flying lower than 200 feet, though Exocets fly 190 feet below that. In subsequent testing, the *Ticonderoga* was able to down enemy missiles at 50 feet, but then experienced a failure to stop a high-altitude enemy missile.

Also, the Aegis in sea trials never faced more than two or three missiles at one time, even though the vessel is supposed to be capable of tracking and firing at eighteen different targets simultaneously. In its operational tests, required before production funds could be appropriated for more such ships, the eighteen targets were simulated by loading test tapes in the Aegis computers, which then calculated the number of hits that the various shipboard weapons system would likely have made.

The Navy went ahead anyway with a $90 billion ship-building scheme. It wasn't until 1984 that the Aegis was successfully tested against low-flying missiles, and then only because Representative Denny Smith had made a public issue of it.

Smith was the most effective critic of the 26-ship Aegis cruiser and 60-ship Aegis destroyer program. A genuine hero who flew 180 combat missions in Vietnam as an F-4 pilot, Smith was one of the conservatives in the Military Reform Caucus who took the label "cheap hawks" for themselves to emphasize that, while they were adamantly critical of the military establishment, they were more than willing to spend whatever it might take to produce a viable, workable military force. Smith had defeated powerful Oregon Democrat Al Ullman in 1980 by accusing Ullman of being "squishy" on defense.

When he found himself in the company of liberals like Representatives Thomas Downey and Patricia Schroeder in his opposition to
Aegis, Smith still didn't waver. While pressing for a halt to Aegis
funding in the House until the ships were able to pass combat-condition
testing, he used his congressional prerogatives in 1984 to obtain an
invitation to testify before the Senate Armed Services Committee,
overcoming resistance from Senator William Cohen of Maine, whose
state's shipyards have received billions in defense work. Persevering
until he received a public hearing, Smith angrily testified how he had
originally written letters to Navy Secretary Lehman and Admiral Watkins, expressing concern about reports that the celebrated Aegis defense shield had proved so much tissue paper in actual tests. The fighter-
pilot-turned-congressman brandished letters he received from those two
top Navy officials insisting that the ship had passed its tests with flying
colors.

In fact, Smith found, the Navy had given him the same public-
relations blitz it had used against outsiders like Downey and Schroeder.
The Navy, said Smith, tried to conceal repeated failures at sea trials to
halt wave-skimming missiles by combining the results of computer simulations with actual tests—giving the Aegis system a better performance
record. In fact, Smith charged, the Aegis had failed most of its real
sea-trial tests, while passing most of the tests done in the New Jersey
cornfield. Secretary Lehman, who had been hell-bent to rush the
Aegis program into production to build up the $90 billion project's
multistate constituency as soon as possible, got the message. The
program was slowed until the Navy could come up with honest test results assuring that the expensive system was more of a savior than a
killer.

Congressman Smith had zeroed in on one of the biggest flaws in the
procurement system as determined by the "Christians." Because of the
immense pressures created by a weapon's Pentagon, defense industry,
and Capitol Hill constituency, the military establishment frequently and
outrageously jiggers test results if possible or conceals results when they
prove so bad that even jiggering won't fix things.

As noted earlier, when the favored Ford Aerospace version of the
Sergeant York DIVAD antiaircraft gun was badly beaten in tests against
a General Dynamics weapon that was able to use more readily available
European ammunition, the testing people changed the rules to transform the Ford gun from a loser to a winner.

The reformers point out that it is this sort of jiggering in testing that
is filling the American arsenal with duds that could have been cancelled
if the failures had become known in time. The procurement elite knows

well that if they can get a weapon past its testing hurdles, the reigning administration and Congress will feel compelled to keep the project going, in hopes of getting at least something back for the vast sums already invested by that time.

A prime example is the M-1 main battle tank. *Washington Post* columnist Mary McGrory best expressed the reformers' view of the M-1 in 1982, after it was disclosed that the tank could not go into combat without an accompanying bulldozer to dig it into and out of protective ground cover. McGrory speculated what General Patton would have done with it. "He would have slapped it in the face," she said.

Of all the test failures the reformers were able to make public, none was more outrageous than the sorry saga of this Abrams M-1 tank, the supervehicle designed to replace the aging M-60s deployed against the hordes of Warsaw Pact armored units in Europe and stockpiled by the hundreds at nearly every major Army post.

When the Abrams was first delivered in 1981, the Army was committed to purchase 7,058 of the tanks for $21.2 billion between then and 1988. Even as the Abrams were rolling off the assembly lines at plants in Lima, Ohio, and Warren, Michigan, a reformer group called the Project on Military Procurement was passing out to selected journalists the highly damning results of the tank's operational tests.

Patrick Oster and Bruce Ingersoll of the *Chicago Sun-Times* began one story based on leaked documents: "Crewmen testing the Army's tank of the future, the M-1, call it the 'Cadillac of tanks,' but critics fear it is more likely to become an armored Edsel."

That conclusion was inescapable after reading a pile of reports nearly six inches thick passed out to the two *Sun-Times* men and other reporters in the summer of 1981 by the Project on Military Procurement director, Dina Rasor, a primary conduit between concerned Pentagon insiders and newsmen eager for the next exclusive story on weapons fiascoes. The reports on the Abrams, largely prepared by the General Accounting Office and leaked to Rasor by one of her many sources, showed that the Army's Tank Automotive Command (TACOM) had approved its production, even though the vehicle displayed an alarming tendency to break down just when it would be needed in action most and otherwise presented major problems for armored division commanders deploying it in Europe.

The tank's revolutionary diesel turbine engine burned up fuel so fast that it required four gallons to move the Abrams a single mile, making it necessary for the tank in many situations to be accompanied by its own fuel tanker along with the bulldozer.

The engine gave off such tremendous heat that crews had to wear special coolant vests. Infantry were prevented by the unbearable exhaust from marching behind it, though that is a very basic tactic. The heat was so intense that, when tanks stood by idling, they caused fires among nearby shrubbery and trees, requiring the infantrymen to turn from their rifles to fire extinguishers.

Testers also worried that the heat might make the tank a prime target for the wide variety of heat-seeking, infrared weapons at the Soviets' disposal.

The diesel turbine, similar to those used in some aircraft engines, was intended to give the tank speeds of fifty to sixty miles an hour on the battlefields, but testers complained that the vehicle had so many breakdowns it actually became "the slowest tank in the world, not the fastest."

A major reason for these breakdowns was that the air filters essential to keep road dust from the delicate turbine blades frequently became clogged, compelling crews to stop, open the engine assembly with a special wrench, and replace the filters. In addition, the Abrams frequently threw its tracks. In fact, they lasted an average of only 850 miles before breaking off, though they were supposed to last for 2,000 miles. It was found that the Abrams had a cruising range of only 131 miles, not the 275 to 350 miles expected when the contract was let.

There were also major problems with the tank's laser-aimed, computer-fired cannon, which was supposed to enable the crew to fire on the run. Crews discovered that, when they attempted to aim the laser sight in forested areas, it was easily deflected by shiny leaves on trees and that, when the vehicle was moving, the sight bumped up and down, making it difficult for the computer to keep the cannon trained. According to Rasor, in European tests against the West German Leopard tank, American Abrams crews scored their best results by turning off the computer and firing by eye alone.

The tank's large reservoirs of hydraulic fluid—for the suspension system that supposedly was to keep the laser sight level when the vehicle was moving—were highly flammable and a mortal danger to crews. Another flaw test analysts were dismayed to discover was that, after the Army spent millions to develop a new kind of armor called Chobham to protect tank crews against Soviet rounds that burn through plating, the Russians had in turn developed a "kinetic" round capable of crumpling the Chobham simply through brute force.

It was also determined that, at an unprecedented sixty-plus tons, the Abrams was too heavy for many of the key bridges in Europe that can support other tanks. The tank was so heavy that only one could be carried on rail cars on which two M-60 tanks could be carried.

The Abrams cannot be equipped with its own bulldozer blade—as M-60s and virtually every other extant tank can—and so, as noted earlier, must be accompanied by a separate bulldozer. Tanks need protective "hidey holes" from which to fire their weapons and, until the M-I came along, were equipped to dig their own.

Despite having been confronted with nearly two years' worth of such disclosures, Defense Secretary Weinberger still defended the Abrams at a breakfast meeting with reporters. "We have a huge sunk cost in the M-I," he said, noting that it had taken twenty years to design, test, and produce the dangerously flawed weapon. He said that the billions spent in the process would be lost unless more billions were spent buying the tanks. He disclosed that the Army planned to open a new research and development project to design a successor to the Abrams and restore its armor strength and capabilities, but in the meantime would go ahead and buy all seven thousand of the Abrams called for.

Such attitudes are precisely what provoked the high-level defense and intelligence leaks in the first place. The reformers found it maddening that the United States would insist on taking on the dreadful Abrams while the number of Soviet tanks, which are free of nearly all the Abrams's high-tech problems, was increasing rapidly.

As the United States opened full production of the Abrams in 1983, factories were turning out seven hundred a year. But Avco Lycoming, the company with the subcontract for producing the diesel turbine engines, fell so far behind its schedules that the only way the tanks could be test-driven before delivery was to take engines out of already delivered tanks and install them in those coming off the assembly line.

At that same time, the Soviets were delivering twenty-five hundred superbly functioning tanks a year to their armored units. NATO analysts observed that the Soviets were deploying both their highly reliable T-72 models and an updated model produced by making improvements to existing tanks, rather than trying to build an entire new weapon from scratch, as was done with the Abrams.

With more than forty thousand Soviet and Warsaw Pact tanks already pitted against roughly ten thousand NATO tanks, the production imbalance was particularly worrisome to those American senior officers assigned to troop commands instead of procurement projects. A dramatic display of that concern came at Senior Conference XX at West Point. The 1982 session was entitled "The Military Reform Debate."

After three days of discussing the reformers' arguments and disclosures, the group of forty generals, admirals, and lesser officers, two newspaper reporters, and several reformers themselves, including weapons designer Pierre Sprey, gathered for a wrap-up session in a West Point library room filled with memorabilia of the careers of Generals Patton and MacArthur. George Wilson, longtime military correspondent for the *Washington Post*, stood and declared he was "amazed" at the admissions voiced during the session about U.S. shortcomings.

"Surely there is another side," Wilson said. "Won't somebody in this room stand up and say that the U.S. could actually win a war with the Soviets; that our weapons are better than theirs?"

A silence fell over the room. Wilson's challenge went unanswered.

As that silence indicated, many national defense officials at the highest levels had developed grave reservations about the military system by the early 1980s. Many of the participants at the Senior Conference were three-star officers assigned at the time to the Joint Chiefs of Staff as OpDeps. Voicing those reservations, however, was a sure ticket to ending a career, or, in the case of outside consultants, losing the government contracts that kept food on their tables and ouzo in their Greek restaurant glasses. Thus, when the reformers started urging their colleagues to come forward and inform Congress as to how the procurement system had become a form of unilateral disarmament, many found that the safest and most effective way to bring forth their evidence and unhappy conclusions was to work through Dina Rasor.

Rasor started her Project on Military Procurement shortly after Reagan's election in 1980, housing its operations in a building two blocks from the U.S. Senate; there's an aromatic Chinese restaurant on the ground floor and the tiny offices of all manner of "save the world" leftist organizations are located throughout the four-story structure.

At twenty-four, Rasor was attractive, articulate, and tireless in her efforts to gain space and airtime in national newspapers and on radio and television for the reformers' campaign. The daughter of Ned Rasor, an extremely successful high-technology engineer with his own company in California's Silicon Valley, she was at the same time able to win the trust of many of the scientists, engineers, test supervisors, and other Pentagon personnel who were being urged by the reformers to come forward. These science- and technology-oriented specialists often found it difficult to either trust or communicate with the Washington press corps, an assemblage not notable for its grasp of complicated engineering and scientific concepts. Rasor, who had worked briefly for ABC television news, had learned to talk technology literally on her father's knee.

Her group shared space with the National Taxpayers Union (NTU), a probusiness, anti–big government group with great disdain for federal welfare programs. The nexus of Rasor and those she called her "closet patriots" was in large part A. Ernest Fitzgerald, the whistle-blower who had been fired in 1969 by Richard Nixon for divulging that there had been massive cost overruns in the Air Force's C-5A jumbo transport program. Fitzgerald remained active in the NTU, of which he had once been national chairman. Much of NTU's funding came from the Libertarian Party and other rightist groups bent on diminishing if not destroying government's role in American life.

Capitalizing on these right-wing connections, Rasor and Fitzgerald joined forces with the cheap-hawk group of senators and congressmen. The cheap hawks were responsible for forming the Military Reform Caucus, whose members ranged from superwarrior Representative Newt Gingrich to neoliberal Senator Gary Hart.

Among the many lawmakers who eventually associated themselves with the reformers were several of the Republicans who assumed committee and subcommittee chairmanships when their party seized control of the Senate in the 1980 elections after twenty-six years of Democratic rule.

The movement saw rigid conservatives like Senators Charles Grassley, Bill Roth, Gordon Humphrey, and Nancy Kassebaum become foes of the Pentagon establishment. These conservatives joined forces with center-of-the-road Democrats and some moderate Republicans like Senator Mark Hatfield, chairman of the Senate Appropriations Committee. Soon this team of odd bedfellows began scoring some impressive victories.

Working from tips by insiders that cost overruns were exceeding 300 percent in forty-seven Army programs, Roth held a series of devastatingly effective public hearings that dramatized the way companies make false promises of low prices for weapons systems to win contracts, certain that Congress would cover them once they were compelled to rise. The practice had long been a target of Senator William Proxmire of Wisconsin, his House counterpart, Les Aspin, and other liberals, but they had never been able to get their hands on anything like the data Roth was able to obtain from inside the Pentagon.

Roth made a floor speech stating the reformers' credo. "The Russians have in recent years consistently outdone us in terms of weapons produced," he said. "We have, in effect, been engaging in 'gold-plated, unilateral disarmament.' "

Key to the recruitment of such powerful congressional supporters were a series of briefings on Capitol Hill made by three brilliant military experts: Pierre Sprey, John Boyd, and Franklin C. (Chuck) Spinney. Sprey and Boyd had been friends and allies for decades, sharing a common passion for jet fighters. Spinney, a generation younger than Boyd and Sprey, was an analyst who joined forces with the reformers after being assigned by the Defense Secretary to determine the actual costs—devoid of all political rhetoric—of weapons ordered by Congress after cost overruns had taken effect. Spinney found that actual costs were underestimated by 1,000 percent in many cases. He concluded that the nation would find itself unable to afford all the weapons on which its national defense strategy was based.

While Spinney was the group's best cost analyst, Sprey, a trim man in his fifties with salt-and-pepper hair and an urbane manner, was the engineering expert. Boyd, a pilot and master student of air war tactics, was the combat expert. Each man prepared a briefing presentation complete with charts and slides that stated the reformers' case from his particular viewpoint.

Boyd's was the most impassioned exhortation. Pounding the table, gesturing with great sweeps of his arms as the screen showed charts of various combat exchange ratios, Boyd recalled his days as a Korean War fighter pilot flying F-86s against the Soviets' MIG-15s and otherwise presented impressive credentials. After the war, he became tactics instructor at Nellis Air Force Base in Nevada, a prime center for aerial war games. In the 1950s, Boyd authored *Aerial Attack Study,* a manual that became the bible of military analysts who favored the "maneuver" approach to warfare over the "attrition" approach—the Robert E. Lees as opposed to the Ulysses S. Grants.

Boyd used the now long obsolete F-86s and MIG-15s in a parable illustrating the advantages of maneuver. "The MIG was the better airplane," Boyd would boom. "It could climb faster, turn tighter, and out accelerate the '86." But, he said, the F-86 nearly always beat the MIG because, when the Russian fighter was screaming into the attack at maximum speed, the F-86 was able to break away from it in a snap-backward maneuver similar to the World War I Immelman turn and World War II split S that put the American plane in behind the Russian—"coming in at his six."

The lawmakers sat transfixed as Boyd cited the lessons of history—learned in famous battles of antiquity like Marathon, Cannae, Thermopolae—to illustrate how unconventional tactics either turned the course of battle or at least seriously hampered a vastly superior foe. Quoting military prophets Sun Tzu, Clausewitz, and Mao Tse-tung, he drove home the central point that commanders who do the unexpected and create surprise and confusion for the enemy almost always prevail even if badly outnumbered.

The key to maneuver warfare, and the reason the U.S. military is dangerously vulnerable, Boyd argued, is the Clausewitzian concept of "friction."

Clausewitz defined friction as the tendency of carefully planned military operations to collapse in confusion amidst the terror, noise, dirt, mud, blood, and utter chaos of mass combat. In those conditions, Boyd argued, it is the army with the simplest weapons and the crudest transport that enjoys the advantage over an enemy relying on delicate weapons and complex logistics. The Prussians did score impressive victories in the early eastern front campaigns of World War I using then high-tech, high-speed railway trains against the primitive Russian hordes, but the Prussians used their railway network to enhance maneuver, while the Russians fought a murderously costly war of attrition. In World War II, the same Germans plunged on into Russia in an armored blitzkrieg that depended on roads, but were ultimately defeated by a primitive but hardy foe who fought tenaciously in the knowledge that Russia had few roads.

Clausewitz said:

> Everything is very simple in war, but the simplest thing is difficult. These difficulties accumulate and produce a friction which no man can imagine exactly who has not seen war. Friction is the only conception which in a general way corresponds to that which distinguishes real war from war on paper. The military machine, the army and all belonging to it, is in fact simple, and appears on this account easy to manage. But let us reflect that no part of it is in one place, that it is composed entirely of individuals, each of which keeps up on its own friction in all directions.

Robert Fay, the aerial combat expert, had noted before the congressional hearing that airmen invariably become confused when trying to sort out all the various targets on their radar screens and the orders broadcast from battle directors in remote AWACS planes while trying to fly their own sophisticated aircraft at high speed. In an interview in his private consulting office in Las Vegas, Fay likened the F-15 to the heavily armored French knights who fell at Agincourt to the arrows of the largely peasant army of English longbowmen led by Henry V.

Boyd's congressional listeners were fascinated with his recitations of the gospel of Sun Tzu, the legendary Chinese general and tactician of the fifth century B.C. His devastating campaigns on behalf of King Ho-lu of Wu relied on not only reducing his own friction but maximizing the friction of the enemy. Bold enough to behead the king's favorite concubines in a demonstration of the importance of discipline in drill and cunning enough to send an impetuous enemy general a gift of a jade vase full of urine to provoke him into a rash attack, Sun Tzu terrorized enemy troops and made widespread use of deception, assassination, elaborate traps, and other unpredictable and, for the times, dishonorable but highly effective tactics. His principles became the fundamentals of warfare for many military thinkers, including Mao Tsetung. It is interesting that, during World War II, one of Chiang Kaishek's military aides told the noted British historian and theoretician Basil Liddell Hart that, in Chiang's army, Sun Tzu's *The Art of War* was considered a classic but out of date. A few years later, Chiang fell to Sun Tzu's tactics—employed at the hands of Mao.

Boyd's mesmerizing briefing was followed by Sprey's show-and-tell talk, "What 'Quality Versus Quantity' Issue?" Military history, Sprey said, is full of cases of "cheap winners versus expensive losers." From the infantryman's rifle to the most modern fighter plane, Sprey said, attempts to improve upon already effective weapons had disastrous results.

The cheap winner in infantry rifles was a weapon that the United States first wanted nothing to do with—the AR-15, which cost about $75. The expensive loser was the $295 M-14, the semi-to-fully-automatic ferociously kicking rifle used in the earlier and bloodier part of the Vietnam War.

The M-14 was developed by the Army's ordnance corps, which according to Sprey is a heavily bureaucratic organization subject to exactly the same flaws as the rest of the weapons acquisition system. The ordnance corps buys items built—and priced—according to military specifications, and often lets contracts on the basis of powerful congressional constituencies and produces most of its designs by committee.

The M-14 was created in response to studies of combat in World War II. Commanders found that as many as four out of every five American soldiers never fired their semi-automatic M-1 rifles in the heat of battle, because it seemed futile to squeeze off single round after single round while all about them cannons were firing, machine guns were clattering, and fighters were strafing overhead.

The single man in each infantry squad who was issued the Browning Automatic Rifle, which for all practical purposes was a hand-held machine gun, nearly always fired his weapon in the same engagements that the M-1 riflemen did not. There was no sense of futility whatsoever for someone with a weapon that could spray enemy positions with dozens of rounds a minute.

So the Army came up with an ill-conceived compromise, the M-14, a rifle that used the same .30 caliber rounds as the M-1. Because it was so much lighter than the Browning, it bucked wildly when fired automatically, making it difficult to concentrate fire on a given target and bloodying the face of many an infantryman battered by the recoil. In training, soldiers were required to fire the weapon only on semi-automatic, as though it were an M-1. Nevertheless, the M-14 was the principal rifle that went to war with the United States in Vietnam when Americans became directly involved in combat in 1965.

The Armalite Corporation came up with the AR-15 as an alternative to the M-14. It was much lighter than the M-14 but had virtually no kick because it fired light, .22 caliber ammunition. The .22 rounds were designed to tumble in the air, greatly increasing the amount of damage they did to an enemy soldier when they hit. The lack of recoil greatly increased accuracy and the light weight meant that an infantryman could carry three times as many bullets as he could with the M-14, which had just twenty rounds to a clip. Also, the AR-15 was four times cheaper than the M-14 because its parts were stamped out of metal instead of hand-machined, as were the components of the bigger rifle.

The Army refused to buy the AR-15 as offered, but instead went about trying to improve upon its design. What the procurement bureaucracy eventually came up with was the M-16, a rifle that proved a tragic dud for many a soldier because of all the Army's meddling modifications.

For example, the Army added a manual bolt to the rifle, which was splendid for parade-ground drills but which caused repeated jamming in Vietnam when mud got into the mechanism. The degree of tumbling during the bullet's flight was reduced because the Army increased the rifling grooves within the barrel, and a new kind of gunpowder was used in the ammunition which often didn't supply enough energy to make the automatic loading device on the rifle work. It took years to correct these "improvements," but by then the war was over.

Sprey devoted his briefing to many other examples of high-cost losers versus cheap winners. Most of the contracts that produced the weapons he listed were let on a cost-plus basis.

Act Three was Spinney's "Defense Facts of Life," which laid out the cold hard truths of how the procurement system was rupturing the budget and crippling military strength at the same time. It became the best known of the three briefings for Congress, landing Spinney on the cover of *Time* magazine, and was given again before a joint hearing of the Senate Armed Services and Budget committees, over the strenuous objections of Armed Services Chairman John Tower, a great believer in the status quo.

Senators who had become converted to the reformers' cause at private briefings forced the public session on Tower. Led by Grassley and Kassebaum, they threatened to cut Reagan's defense budget requests by 10 percent unless Spinney was heard. Such a move by Republican Budget Committee members would have been devastating and Tower had no choice but to comply. As a result, Spinney, then thirty-seven, not only made *Time* the following week but became a much sought after interview subject by the television networks. His Pentagon bosses transferred him from cost analysis to more restricted duties.

As Spinney spoke throughout that historic session, his boss, David Chu, Secretary Weinberger's chief of analysis, sat grimly at the same table, but his presence was no deterrent. Spinney complained that since World War II the American military had suffered from recurring cycles of feast and famine as the national consensus shifted toward and away from military buildup.

Kennedy succeeded Eisenhower proclaiming a "missile gap," and Congress began spending huge amounts of money on rocketry. Johnson's early presidency had an emphasis on the "war on poverty" and shifted concern from weapons to welfare. The Vietnam War produced huge military budgets but very little commitment to new weapons systems. Nixon and Ford restarted the drive for bigger hardware, and Jimmy Carter stalled it. The Reagan administration won office in part with a pledge to rearm America and set out to buy $1.7 trillion of new weapons in a military spending spree that, in dollars adjusted for inflation, exceeded the military outlays of the Vietnam era.

Spinney's charts showed, however, that even that kind of astronomical budgeting was far too low an estimate of the real costs of those programs Reagan wanted. As he warned, the flaws built into the procurement system would drive the eventual actual costs of that weaponry up by at least 30 percent more than the Reagan administration had projected.

The root of the problem, Spinney said, was that, every time the government sets out on a rearmament binge, it spends money diverted from personnel accounts, training budgets, logistical support, repair facilities, spare parts, and other categories of expenditure needed to maintain and properly operate the new weapons being bought. And, with so much of the complex new weaponry prone to breakdown, more and more of these "operations and maintenance" services are needed—are, indeed, vital.

So, after selling Congress on buying all the new weaponry, the military has to turn around and return much of the money needed to continue the weapons programs to the supply and maintenance accounts, just to keep whatever weapons they've already received serviceable. This back-and-forth game slows down delivery and drives up costs and defense budgets, while continuously shrinking the size of the American military arsenal.

The Reagan arms crusade, like so many others before it, was launched in the hopes of loading up the arsenal as much as possible while the national mood was still receptive. To help keep it receptive, Pentagon budgeteers traditionally have tried to conceal the actual overall costs for the new weapons programs as they will accrue in future years. Instead of budgeting for the kind of cost growth that has occurred in virtually every fiscal year since Korea, the planners instead proceed on the false yet deliberate assumption in their budgets that unit production costs in the latter phases of a program—called "out years"—will actually decline.

The Reagan budget assumed that the unit costs of the $235 million B-1 bomber would drop by 78 percent in the "out years," even though the B-1 program had incurred a substantial cost overrun every year since the project began. Future Congresses dealing not with a 78 percent reduction, but with a quantum increase in B-1 unit costs, will probably want to cancel the program, which was carried out in the full knowledge that the plane would shortly be rendered obsolete. But the "sunk costs" by that time will be so great they'll have to keep the program going.

Spinney predicted the Air Force will probably try to stretch out the B-1 project, buying the bombers over many more years than planned. As a consequence, the country will never receive the big new bomber fleet it was promised.

To keep the total B-1 budget figures down, the bomber's program managers were compelled to allocate 48 percent of the entire budget to building just the first 18 of the 100 bombers to be delivered. To produce the B-1 in the volume and at the prices promised by the Reagan administration, the remaining 82 B-1s will have to be built for only $24 million each—about 10 percent of their present estimated cost and about half the price of a relatively small jet fighter. The real cost of the B-1 by the end of the project is much more likely to be $300 million or more each.

As cheap hawks like Delaware's Senator Roth are quick to point out, the ultimate impact of this kind of devastating cost growth is "gold-plated, unilateral disarmament" achieved by the very people taking the hardest line against the Soviet menace.

Asked if Congress could close the gap with more money, Spinney said: "More money spent the same way could make our problems worse."

With so many converts in the Congress, the reformers have largely been spared the kind of vengeance the Pentagon has traditionally wreaked against such heretics in the past.

Despite the strong objections of Senate allies like Grassley, Chuck Spinney was removed from his job of overall cost analysis by Weinberger and assigned to cost analysis for individual weapons projects, rather than the entire defense budget.

Pierre Sprey continued to work as a consultant to several defense companies and to the Defense Department itself. John Boyd kept his post in the Air Force Tactical Air Programs. Tom Amlie retired from China Lake, but returned to the Pentagon, where he became involved in the effort to make Pratt and Whitney and other contractors pay back overcharges for spare parts for jet engines.

A. Ernest Fitzgerald, as noted earlier, was finally reinstated in his Air Force cost analyst job—at court order—and remained there in spite of being perhaps the most outspoken and grating of the reformers group.

The secret network of sympathizers and operatives in the Pentagon and elsewhere is still in place, supplying Miss Rasor and her operations with a continuing flow of damning and alarming documents.

If, as columnist McGrory suggested, George S. Patton would have slapped the M-1 tank in the face, Clausewitz and Sun Tzu would likely have shipped as many as they could to the enemy—after ascertaining that the enemy would be willing to pay for them. Ronald Reagan and Casper Weinberger were not—choosing instead to finance their wanton arms buildup with the ever expanding federal deficit, until it reached levels of $200 billion a year and all but doubled the national debt in Reagan's first term. No KGB plot could undermine the American government's fiscal well-being more effectively than Reagan and Weinberger have.

Pentagon brass like to assert that the defense budget can't be substantially reduced simply by cutting out big-ticket procurement items. To a degree, that's true. The overall cost is spread out over many years. But cutting out the worst ones will at least help—now, and for those years to come.

Having discovered serious aeronautical deficiencies in the much vaunted Stealth designs, the Air Force has been draining money from

Stealth, B-52 modernization and maintenance, and other strategic aircraft projects to finance its ever growing plans for the B-1 bomber. This aircraft should be eliminated at once, saving a minimum of $20 billion. It is functionally a cruise missile with pilots' seats (although many in the Air Force high command are now interested in turning it into a high-altitude aircraft).

It is more than time to put into effect some of the changes so dramatically advocated by the reformers. As already seen, there are a number of questionably effective and needlessly costly aircraft projects that need no longer crowd the nation's badly strained defense budgets and drain resources from manpower and combat readiness.

Were there any real prospect of a mass Soviet manned-bomber attack against the United States, there might be some rationale for building more highly vulnerable, easily jammed, tactically useless AWACS radar command aircraft, but there isn't—not in an era of six-minute "spasm" missile attacks. The project should be halted, for a savings of some $4 billion at the least. The existing AWACS can continue to be used for what they're most useful—monitoring Russian ship and submarine movements in the North Atlantic.

The intolerably heavy (for its size), limited in range, unwieldy F/A-18 Hornet fighter-bomber, another lamentable Pentagon attempt to build a wonder weapon to do everything, should be junked before one drops into the drink for want of fuel or smashes a hole in a carrier deck on landing—at a savings of $20 billion or more. There has to be a reason the Turkish government preferred the F-16 to the Hornet when it bought a large order of a first-line combat aircraft in the early 1980s.

The short-winded Hornet is just one of many machines where the technocrats have continued adding "bells and whistles" to a weapon until its very sophistication renders it prone to breakdown. The tail assembly cracks that led Navy Secretary Lehman to halt acceptance of the F/A-18 in July 1984 may well have been partly caused by its bad landing characteristics, which are in turn partly the product of the huge load of computer chips it carries.

As soon as possible, the Army's M-1 tank and the Bradley Infantry Fighting Vehicle, both impediments to any ground-fighting success in Europe if not potential death traps, should be phased out in favor of improved versions of older, more reliable, less dangerous models. The $4 billion DIVAD antiaircraft gun should be turned on its creators—though if they started walking briskly, it probably would miss them.

The $90 billion Aegis cruiser and destroyer program should be curtailed if not abolished before it's too late. The risk is simply too great in terms of crew members' lives, the public treasure involved, and the danger the ships pose to the huge and expensive carrier task forces they're supposed to protect. The resurrected World War II battleship program should be mothballed at once. Nothing proved more useless off the coast of Lebanon in 1983–1984 than the USS *New Jersey,* which faced a crew shortage so great it had to call in reservists for relief. Those battleships can require at-sea crews of 1,500, with another 1,000 backing them up in port. The Navy has many other more critical uses for manpower of that magnitude.

The keels for the three remaining Nimitz-class nuclear carriers have already been laid, but the program ought to be reconsidered in light of the enormous advances made in anti-ship missiles and the huge costs involved. Each of these carriers will cost at least $4 billion. And each carrier task force, protected by the dangerous Aegis system, will have a price tag of as much as $30 billion, including aircraft, ordnance, and escort vessels.

Admiral Rickover was not just being cranky when he warned that the survival duration of these ocean-going giants in actual sea war with the Soviets would be "about two days."

Reforms must come in the system that produces these problem weapons in the first place. Members of the congressional Military Reform Caucus have outlined some important "changes in orders" for the military establishment that are easy and simple to implement, but they've been resisted every step of the way by those who created the monster.

Among these is the previously mentioned proposal by Senators Grassley and Roth to remove control of weapons testing from the military officers in charge of weapons projects and turn it over to an independent Pentagon testing agency with no ox to be gored, or fed. Congressman Mark Andrews's idea of requiring Pentagon arms suppliers to furnish the same warranties on a fighter jet that the John Deere factory provides on the tractors Andrews uses on his farm in North Dakota remains vital. Grassley has proposed insightful "creeping capitalism" legislation that would each year reduce the percentage of Pentagon contracts that could be issued on a "sole source" basis.

But often mere passage of a law does little to bring about reform. As we've seen, Pentagon officials found ways to get around Andrews's warranty law by granting exemptions in cases involving national security. Pentagon brass sidestepped the new legislation calling for independent testing by blurring the distinction between "developmental tests" done with computers and "operational tests," which are supposed to utilize actual weapons. Congressional oversight is going to have to be stricter.

It took four decades for today's dangerous system to evolve and degenerate into its present state. The country's best hope now is that those who are trying to institute reforms will persist long enough to bring changes that will stick. All too often, reformers surface, get a lot of attention by raising valid issues and startling horror stories, but then fade away without really changing the ills they were so effective in publicizing. It is frequently pointed out that General Motors is still America's largest automaker while Ralph Nader has been forced to cut back his consumer activities because he no longer attracts the attention that once he commanded with a snap of the fingers—no matter how valid his complaints.

What the American defense establishment must come to realize is that the reformers are not just unhappy insiders but patriots who believe deeply and courageously in the need for the United States to defend itself in a hostile, terrifying world. Unlike so many of the left-wing, pacifist, and violently antimilitary againsters with which the defense establishment has been compelled to deal, the reformers are on the soldiers' side.

chapter seventeen

THE AGAINSTERS

> *Hey hey, LBJ,*
> *how many kids did you kill today?*
>
> —1960S SCHOOL SONG

The American military has always faced strong opposition from large segments of the American public. The Revolutionary War itself was supported by no more than 25 to 30 percent of the colonial population, with a similar number actively opposed. After the final triumph of the Battle of Yorktown, many of the latter fled to Canada, where they helped put down a Canadian revolt against the British crown in 1838.

New Englanders were so opposed to the War of 1812, which they rightly viewed in large part as an attempted land grab of Canada engineered by Henry Clay, John C. Calhoun, and other Western and Southern congressional war hawks while the British were preoccupied with Napoleon, that delegates of the New England states gathered at the Hartford Convention to entertain the idea of seceding from the nation.

The Mexican War, again rightly, was seen by much of the North as an unprincipled war of conquest against a weak neighbor for the purpose of extending not only American territory but the domains of slavery into the southwest. Daniel Webster said of it: "I smell nigger." A then minor Illinois congressman named Abraham Lincoln nagged the Polk administration incessantly with "spot resolutions" demanding proof of Mexican aggression against the United States. The bulk of the troops used in the war came from the South, especially Tennessee, which became known as the Volunteer State as a consequence.

The Civil War saw antidraft riots that far exceeded in bloodshed and violence any of those in the Vietnam era. Proslavery activity and acts of downright treason were rampant in the lower counties of Missouri, Illinois, Indiana, and Ohio.

In World War I, celebrated left-wing intellectuals like Randolph Bourne argued passionately that the United States use its military potential only as leverage to arbitrate an end to the conflict while remaining neutral, and not become a participant in the carnage. Though ostensibly the United States's most popular and patriotic war, World War II saw considerable draft dodging. The Roosevelt administration was bedeviled well into the war by a deep streak of isolationism from Republican conservatives and Midwestern populists alike.

The response of the military and its civilian government sponsors has always been the same: to attack the patriotism and loyalty of the opposition. The antidote to Toryism in the Revolution was the tar and feather, expropriation of property, and, in some rare cases, murder (both sides used Indian allies to this end). The backlash against the Hartford Convention after the War of 1812 was sufficient to kill the Northeastern-based Federalist Party.

Lincoln's congressional constituents hooted him out of office for his "disloyalty" and he never served in Congress again. As president, Lincoln suspended habeas corpus and jailed opposition newspaper editors and politicians. After the United States entered World War I, antiwar utterances could easily get one jailed, often on grounds no more substantial than finger-pointing by vigilante groups like the American Protection League. In World War II, Franklin Roosevelt even contemplated shutting down the powerful *Chicago Tribune* on grounds of aiding the enemy in response to its coverage of the Battle of Midway, which revealed top secret information.

One of the most profound examples of how opposition to the American military can founder on the rock of American patriotism was the experience of the Vietnam War. It is of course the fiercely held belief of those who participated in the antiwar movement of the 1960s and 1970s—most particularly of the students and academics of the period— that they forced the American government to end the war. But the preponderance of evidence indicates just the opposite, that, because of the stridency of their ideology and the mayhem of their methodology, the antiwar protesters alienated so many mainstream American voters and created such a divisive domestic issue with their protests that they actually prolonged the war, or permitted the Nixon administration to do so.

The military still loves to complain about the sabotage done to the war effort by the press, television, and leftist demonstrators, arguing that they made it impossible for the war to be won. It may be true that the uproar rattled some segments of American public opinion and spooked three American presidents. What the military can never explain away with that contention is how a war so supposedly unpopular could have lasted so long—nearly three times as long as World War II and four times as long as another unpopular war, Korea, a war that was brought to a stalemate conclusion because of growing opposition to it. If any-thing, despite widespread feelings against American involvement in Vietnam, the antiwar movement played directly into the hands of the American military and its propagandists. Far from aiding the enemy, as many conservatives complained, Jane Fonda, Tom Hayden, Staughton Lynd, Joan Baez, and their fellows could well have been the Joint Chiefs of Staff's best friends.

To many in the defense establishment, from service secretary down to company commander, the United States's real enemy has always been at home: that part of the American public opinion that opposes the policies and actions of the American defense establishment. In this view, American military might, know-how, and ingenuity will always prevail in war: if only the againsters in American society will let military commanders have their way.

This in part represents the mentality that blamed leftists in the State Department, and not Chiang Kai-shek's corrupt and incompetent war-lords, for the loss of China; and that claimed MacArthur could have won in Korea if only he'd been unleashed, though that egomaniacal incompetent had allowed more than a quarter of a million Chinese to get behind his divided army and trap his forces while they were strung out on two roads facing an oncoming Siberian winter in summer uni-forms.

But it is also a belief held by some of the most intelligent, experi-enced, and respected men in American statecraft. Former Secretary of State Dean Rusk continues to insist that the Vietnam War was lost because of the American news media's spell over the general public. In forums at Washington's Wilson Center and elsewhere he's made the dour prediction that modern television communications has made it impossible for the United States to sustain public support long enough to win another war.

But, even though Walter Cronkite himself came out against the war, in a very essential sense Rusk was wrong. John F. Kennedy was troubled by the inefficacy of the American mission in Southeast Asia and was reportedly pondering the possibility of a pullout shortly before his as-sassination. The angry antiwar protests that swept the nation after the 1968 Tet offensive helped convince Lyndon Johnson that his cause was a political liability and a withdrawal from Vietnam must begin. These protests also goaded Richard Nixon into ending the draft and ultimately negotiating with the Chinese to extricate the United States from the conflict. It can be argued that one of the chief effects of the antiwar movement was to keep the war going years after Kennedy and Johnson wished to end it.

Vietnam was the longest war in American history. For the Vietnamese, it lasted from 1945 to 1975. Americans also died in it from 1945 to 1975; the first U.S. casualty was a CIA colonel sympathetic to Vietnamese nationalists who may well have been murdered by the French. Americans fought in it from 1961 until 1973, although organized combat operations were not begun until 1965.

There were ample grounds on which to question and criticize the conduct of the American participation in the Vietnam War, military grounds far removed from the premises of leftist ideology. The U.S. strategy was reactive, vague, and lacking a clear-cut goal save that of destroying the enemy, though overall policy was firmly opposed to the dangerous steps necessary to destroying the enemy. The heavy-handed combat tactics were clumsy, expedient, and generally ill conceived for what was essentially a guerrilla war—and in their execution too often brutal and counterproductive. For all its occasional brilliance, American military leadership was largely incompetent, as former line officer and author Josiah Bunting and others have made so eloquently clear. The waste of lives, materiel, and treasure for ill-defined, elusive, and quickly abandoned goals was monstrous. The corruption that ran rampant in South Vietnam in the chaos following the American-abetted overthrow and murder of President Diem in 1963 all but destroyed the country. As America chose to fight it after Kennedy's death, the war was unwinnable and the sacrifice of so much blood for so little ultimate purpose unconscionable.

But the antiwar movement, as personified by leftist professors and mobs of shouting students in the streets, attacked the American war effort on ideological and moral grounds, depicting American soldiery as war criminals and attacking as evil the very premise of American values. What many Americans could not fault—the desire to defend the right to self-determination of the South Vietnamese people against Communist totalitarianism—was decried as meddling in a civil war.

Considering the huge size of the opposition, it's a wonder hostilities lasted even a year after Tet. Yet because of the tactics of the protest, they went on for another five, nearly twice as long as the entire unpopular Korean War, allowing Nixon to secure his "honorable" peace.

To the American people, the Vietnam War was never that simple an issue. Had the antiwar movement refrained from its shrillness and violence and let the horrors and frustrations of the conflict speak for themselves, the American public probably would have become fed up with continuing the struggle as quickly as they had wearied of Korea. But the antiwar movement waged too great an assault on traditional

American values and institutions. What was a confusing and frustrating military mistake they depicted as something almost Hitlerian.

At its best, the hard-core antiwar movement included academics and intellectuals with whom mainstream Americans had little in common and for whom they had little affection, war or no. At its worst, as typified by the violent, random rampages of the Weathermen and the bombings that took innocent lives at the University of Wisconsin and elsewhere, it filled most Americans with disgust.

Just as bizarre to ordinary Americans were the erstwhile highly respected academics who came off prestigious campuses like the University of Chicago, Harvard, and Berkeley to seize the podiums of the antiwar movement to preach their existential brand of social anarchism —people who styled themselves more European than American and who hated the American capitalist system passionately.

With the rather egregious exception of Ronald Reagan, actors and actresses have never been a very potent political force in this country— for all their frequent successes as political fund-raisers—and this was certainly true in the Vietnam years. Jane Fonda's multicity tour in the late 1960s, whose purpose was to announce her plan for a network of off-base coffeehouses in which servicemen would be wooed to the antiwar cause with guitar music, espresso, poetry, and Jane-think, was ridiculed in public print and generally viewed as symbolic of the self-indulgent behavior middle-Americans tend to associate with rich, spoiled entertainers. In a 1984 interview, Fonda herself said, "I think the manner in which I opposed the war—not the opposition itself, but the way I went about opposing it . . . probably turned off as many people as I turned on."

As for the hordes of college students whose disruptive protests of the war were certainly in part a protest of their being drafted to serve in it—as Richard Nixon realized in moving to end the draft long before he moved to end the war—they were not warmly received by the middle- and working-class parents of the millions of young men who served in Vietnam as volunteers or draftees without benefit of college exemptions.

The antiwar movement turned student opposition to the conflict into a domestic political issue in itself, one that stirred up a massive backlash and divided the nation. Consider the aftermath of the 1968 Chicago riots during the Democratic Convention, which galvanized the American left for nearly a decade and, via television, treated millions of Americans to the sight of police violence comparable to that of Czar Nicholas.

There was never again a major riot in the city of Chicago, a fact that local organization politicians campaigned upon to great effect. Mayor Richard Daley, opposed by a liberal with the ardent support of the antiwar voters in the city's lakefront neighborhoods, won one of his largest landslides less than two years later, carrying some of those same lakefront wards. Edward Hanrahan, the hard-line right-winger whose police agents later caused a national uproar by gunning down black activist Fred Hampton in 1969, was elected Cook County state's attorney. Adlai Stevenson III, who as of 1968 was supposed to lead the antiwar left in a crusade against the Daley machine, defected to it in September 1969 and won its endorsement for the Senate as a reward.

Antiwar Illinois senatorial candidate William Clark went down in flames in his 1968 challenge of Senator Everett Dirksen, as did antiwar candidates throughout the country. Fully two thirds of those who voted for Senator Eugene McCarthy against Lyndon Johnson in the 1968 New Hampshire primary, according to precinct-by-precinct tallies, turned around and voted for George Wallace and his hawk running mate, retired Air Force General Curtis LeMay, in the fall. According to polls and surveys, their chief complaint against Johnson was his fecklessness in waging the Vietnam War.

The American Bar Association convention in St. Louis in the summer of 1970—after the Kent State massacre—featured an endless succession of politician speakers decrying lawlessness and calling for law and order. They included Hubert Humphrey and Senator Edward Kennedy. One of the most popular speakers there was General William Westmoreland.

At the same time, the Illinois legislature tore into state campus unrest with a "star chamber" investigative session that had one longtime lawmaker saying, "the Declaration of Independence couldn't survive here." State legislatures throughout the country followed suit.

Anyone who seriously believes that the antiwar movement was responsible for ending the Vietnam War must somehow manage to explain how the 1972 antiwar presidential campaign of Senator George McGovern, who for all practical purposes made the election a referendum on the war, resulted in one of the biggest political debacles of the century, carrying fewer states (only Massachusetts and the District of Columbia) than Herbert Hoover did running against Franklin Roosevelt at the height of the Depression.

America did finally turn against its war. Middle America at last put aside its antipathy to all the shouting students with American flags sewn to their jean bottoms and observed instead the mute testimony of too many body bags and government-issue coffins. These sacrifices at last came to be seen as squandered for no perceivable gain. As they did at

Khe Sanh, American forces repeatedly fought bitter battles for "key" positions that, after they were taken or successfully defended, were then abruptly abandoned. Finally, they abandoned one position too many.

In World War II and Korea, the newspapers provided front-page war position maps daily. The enemy territory was rendered in black and the allies' in white. As arrows illustrated armored drives and frontal attacks, Americans could follow the ebb and flow of battle and watch the enemy tide recede. There was tangible evidence of military progress, of value returned for sacrifice.

In Vietnam, there were no such maps. There were just body counts— and body bags. The American public gave the military twelve years to fight that war. The high command should consider itself lucky.

Its challenge now is much more formidable. The opposition to the military has become much better organized and much more sophisticated. It has become much more rational in its behavior and more reasonable in its outlook. Whether seeking a nuclear freeze or merely an end to the drain of public funds into expensive, useless hardware, this opposition has in large part abandoned noise and emotional release for political effectiveness and steady progress toward well-defined goals. Instead of seeking television time through antic or violent street theatrics, it has taken to building coalitions, thus edging into the mainstream of American political thought and activity.

It has in historical terms become remarkably successful. The military can no longer dismiss its members as traitors, subversives, or ignoramuses. The Pentagon must deal with it and has to listen to it. This is of vital importance, for, like those opposed to the Vietnam War for reasons other than leftist ideology, today's loyal opposition has some important things to say. And it is loyal.

Traditionally, even through large parts of the Vietnam experience, American military leadership has been able to function with a relative immunity to outside opposition, working within the secrecy and isolation of its jargon-ridden priesthood and leaving it to the White House to take the heat. But in recent years opponents have become so skilled at marshalling and manipulating the congressional process and public opinion that they've been able to win some remarkable battles, if not all their wars.

For a time, it looked as though the antimilitary movement had actually downed the B-1 bomber. By the mid-1970s, the supersonic bomber project was rattling along toward production, supported strongly on Capitol Hill by a powerful alliance including the Air Force, the 1.5-

million-member International Union of Automobile, Aerospace, and Agricultural Implement Workers of America (UAW), and its principal contractor, Rockwell International, which had one of the most effective lobbying teams working the Hill.

Initially, the chief opposition to the B-1 came from a small bipartisan group of antiwar senators and congressmen organized as the Members of Congress for Peace Through Law (MCPL), which by 1976 numbered 35 senators and 139 congressmen. Some were simply liberal activists looking for something to chew on with the war over. Others, remembering the failures of the B-70 bomber project, which was supposed to replace the B-52 in the early 1960s, were appalled at the short probable operational life-span of the B-1 and its extraordinary cost. When the contract was first awarded to Rockwell International Corporation to build three prototypes in 1970, the unit cost of the bomber was $41 million. By 1977, it had risen to more than $100 million and it kept on going.

It was this last point that began attracting many other congressmen and senators to the MCPL's side of the issue. Congress was trying to extricate the country from the mammoth military spending programs of the war and was looking for a "peace dividend." It was also troubled by the huge cost overruns of the C-5A cargo jet project. However, Congress was used to leaving the major decisions on weapons projects up to defense experts and powerful committee chairmen. On their own, the anti-B-1 congressmen might have failed.

But a large coalition against the project began to form on the outside. First, the pacifist American Friends Service Committee decided to wage a national campaign against it, and was quickly joined by the antiwar Clergy and Laity Concerned. A number of other liberal activist groups came aboard—SANE and the Women's International League for Peace and Freedom, among others. But with them came the more moderate Common Cause and the Federation of American Scientists, which had thirty-five Nobel Prize winners on its board and had recruited former Defense Secretary Clark Clifford—among other prominent Republican and Democratic defense figures—to speak out against the bomber. Environmental Action signed up to protest the B-1 as a symbol of profligate fuel waste.

Most surprising of all, the right-wing National Taxpayers Union joined the crusade, decrying the B-1 as "a weapons system of dubious value, failing the tests of cost, effectiveness, and necessity . . . less a genuine military project than a public works program."

This strange alliance made the B-1 what no weapons systems except the atomic bomb had ever been before—a national issue.

"We took an issue people knew little about and turned it into a controversy," Larry Provance of the American Friends Service Committee told *Congressional Quarterly*. "If people get organized, they can even fight the Pentagon."

After a seesaw battle in both houses, a compromise was reached in 1976 whereby Rockwell could continue building the three prototypes but the Pentagon would be limited to spending no more than $87 million a month on the project until February 1, 1977, after the next president— or the incumbent Ford—had been sworn in.

The next president was Jimmy Carter, who looked to history to judge him a great peacemaker. With the anti-B-1 coalition shifting its efforts to the White House, he cut the number of B-1s to be funded in 1978 from the 8 urged by the Ford administration to 5. In April 1977 the Pentagon reduced its original request for 244 B-1s to 150 planes. On June 30, 1977, after blowing hot and cold but still dropping hints he'd go ahead with the supersonic project, he suddenly announced he was going to kill the B-1. He said of his decision:

> This has been one of the most difficult decisions that I have made since I have been in office. During the last few months, I have done my best to assess all the factors involving production of the B-1 bomber. My decision is that we should not continue with deployment of the B-1, and I am directing that we discontinue plans for production of this weapons system. . . . In the meantime, we should begin deployment of cruise missiles using air-launched platforms, such as our B-52s, modernized as necessary.

The coalition was jubilant. Never before in the history of the military-industrial complex and wheelie-dealie Washington had anything like this happened.

But weapons programs never really die. They just get put away in drawers. In every fiscal year of Carter's presidency, a little money was set aside for some development work on the bomber. In January 1981 Ronald Reagan became president and the Air Force was shortly after notified that it could have its airplane, the costs of which soon surpassed $200 million a copy.

Reagan got away with this because the American people had shown a genuine concern about the post-Vietnam decline in American military strength and because Congress had seen "peacemaker" Carter go down the drain in the 1980 election. But Reagan's bellicose dealings with the Soviets and apparent lust for renewing the nuclear arms race drew the againsters out again, after bigger game than a mere useless bomber, and this time Reagan didn't have it so easy.

At the core of his opposition here were heirs and veterans of both the antiwar movement and the "ban the bomb" crusades of the 1950s and early 1960s. A substantial number of this opposition were bent on unilateral disarmament and the demilitarization of the United States, but for the purposes of their crusade, their goal became a verifiable, bilateral nuclear freeze.

Their argument was perforce quite simple and compelling: the United States and the USSR had the weaponry to destroy each other many times over and, no matter which might start a conflict, both sides would be destroyed.

Though the Soviets had the most powerful warhead arsenal and the largest number of accurate land-based ICBMs, the United States possessed the largest total of all forms of nuclear weapons.

If both sides agreed, it was asserted, a freeze would be verifiable. The movement cited the two countries' array of sophisticated and powerful intelligence-gathering systems, including satellites that reportedly could photograph objects six inches in diameter from space.

If a freeze agreement was reached, both sides would have to stop all testing, all production, and all deployment of new weapons. Eventually, the nuclear arsenals of the two countries would deteriorate into obsolescence and disrepair and the scourge of nuclear war would disappear from the earth.

The Reagan administration reacted predictably, lashing out at the movement as a Soviet Communist front. While this may have been in small part true, the mainstream members of the group included a large number of fairly moderate Americans who had simply become frightened at the prospect of nuclear war—as indicated by the many victories for freeze resolutions in town meetings in essentially conservative states like New Hampshire and Vermont. The backlash to what was denounced as Reagan administration McCarthyism was considerable and won even more publicity and recruits for the freeze cause.

A few of the movement's activities were throwbacks to the antiwar days and downright silly. There were marches replete with grotesquely painted faces and signs saying America: Unite and Disarm. One movement newsletter advertised Nuclear War Prevention Kits (as simple as that) and featured actor Paul Newman and a number of others inexplicably gazing pleasantly from the center of a mushroom cloud. The more militant factions of the movement, such as the Livermore Action Group, urged massive civil disobedience.

But, as with the anti-B-1 crusade, adherents to the cause came largely from the political mainstream. Edward Kennedy assumed leadership of the freeze effort in the Senate and won converts to the cause from both parties. In the House, reliable nose counts showed some 200 of the 435 members supporting a freeze.

The Federation of American Scientists weighed in again, as it had with the B-1, providing large amounts of technical data and propaganda and sponsoring public forums on the subject featuring the likes of former nuclear weapons consultant Richard Garwin and onetime chief SALT negotiator and arms control director Paul Warnke. The dovish Center for Defense Information, a group including many former high-ranking military officers, produced testimony favorable to the cause from retired Admiral Noel Gayler, former director of the National Security Agency, and others, and even dragged arch-conservative columnist James Kilpatrick into the fray, quoting from one of his 1982 *Washington Post* columns that said:

> A point was reached long ago at which both the United States and the Soviet Union had such monstrous arsenals that further accretions became senseless. These have been 37 years of lunacy, of idiots racing against imbeciles, of civilized nations staggering blindly toward a finish line of unspeakable peril. The immediate necessity is to call a truce, to stop the further buildup of nuclear weapons by either side.

The Reagan administration finally got clever. As Congress moved toward a showdown on the freeze in the spring of 1983, the President made a speech before the Los Angeles World Affairs Council that attacked the freeze movement on its own ground:

> The freeze concept is dangerous for many reasons. It would preserve today's high, unequal, and unstable levels of nuclear forces and, by so doing, reduce Soviet incentives to negotiate for real reductions.
>
> It would pull the rug out from under our negotiators in Geneva, as they have testified.
>
> After all, why should the Soviets negotiate if they've already achieved a freeze in a position of advantage to them?

Reagan warned that long-term haggling over verification of maintenance of freeze levels would distract from efforts to negotiate an actual reduction of nuclear weapons, which by then had become the principal thrust of his administration's arms control diplomacy. He also observed that the Soviet role in such an effort might be more meaningful if the Kremlin was under the same public pressure as the freeze movement was putting on the White House. He quoted Carter Defense Secretary Harold Brown, who observed that the freeze would "put pressure on the United States, but not the Soviet Union."

Reagan's final salvo was to point out that the American nuclear missile system was much older than the Soviets', which was the product of a quite recent and massive Kremlin arms buildup, and that, under a freeze, the United States's nuclear defenses would fall apart substantially before the Soviets' did, leaving the United States vulnerable.

Still, indications were that, if a freeze resolution might be stopped in the Republican-controlled Senate, it was still likely to pass the Democratic House, an embarrassment that the White House feared would cost it prestige abroad, unnerve NATO allies, and weaken the hand of United States arms control negotiators.

The administration's greatest worry in all this was the American Catholic Church, with 51 million members the largest single Christian denomination in the U.S. and certainly one of the best disciplined. Since 1981, a powerful group of Catholic prelates organized as the National Conference of Catholic Bishops had been exploring the nuclear weapons issue and was preparing a pastoral letter on war and peace that the White House feared would be an endorsement of the freeze movement and a condemnation of Reagan nuclear arms policy. The much respected Joseph Cardinal Bernardin, archbishop of Chicago, had been elected president of the conference in 1974 and was chairman of the committee that was to draft the letter.

Author Eugene Kennedy, himself a former priest, quoted a White House aide in a *Chicago Tribune Magazine* article who said, "These damn Catholics are causing us trouble everywhere."

As another White House aide disclosed to one of the authors, a high-ranking administration official with a background in intelligence and national security became so concerned about the potential effect of the bishops' effort that he suggested going to Cardinal Bernardin's boss. It was so agreed, and one of the administration's best diplomats met privately shortly afterward with Pope John Paul II in Rome.

A high-ranking member of the State Department told one of the authors a short while later, "The Pope will take care of Bernardin. He'll bring in European cardinals to discuss with Bernardin how the antinuclear movement is being handled by the Church over there, and Bernardin will get the message."

Cardinal Bernardin was summoned to Rome for just such a meeting. The details of what transpired did not become public, but the eventual result was what the administration desired. In May 1983, after a lot of dickering, including an arduous discourse that resulted in changing the "halt" of nuclear arms expansion to "curb," the bishops voted 238 to 9 to endorse a letter that attacked the premises of Reagan's nuclear arms policy but did not exhort Catholics to rise against it. The bishops said instead that "moral judgment in specific cases, while not binding on conscience, is to be given serious attention and consideration" by American Catholics, and conceded that Catholics of goodwill might differ on how the Church's broad moral principles might apply to the complex issue of nuclear weapons.

Though a freeze resolution remained alive in the House, that summer Democratic attempts to bring the issue to a public debate and crucial vote in the Senate Foreign Relations Committee were thwarted and the matter was deferred until September 1983. After the downing of the unarmed Korean jetliner by a Soviet fighter just before Labor Day, the matter was deferred again. The freeze movement's moment of opportunity had passed, and the crusade began to sag like a punctured gasbag.

As Harvard international affairs specialist Samuel Huntington told *U.S. News & World Report,* "Causes like the freeze usually don't last more than two or three years, and the natural sociology is that people drop off as the movement defines its goals more specifically."

Probably the most specific goal of the profreeze and antinuclear movements in recent years has been to stop production and deployment of the MX missile. It was their easiest target and they had little excuse for failing to score a hit. Certainly the Pentagon assisted their cause in every way imaginable.

By the mid-1970s, the Soviets were developing missiles with larger throw weight, more warheads, and, according to Pentagon estimates, sufficient accuracy to destroy American missiles in their silos in a massive preemptive strike that could theoretically wipe out most of the United States's retaliatory deterrent.

This gave birth to the notion of what then–CIA Director Richard Helms dubbed the "window of vulnerability"—a highly dangerous period the United States would pass through until it was able to develop a nuclear countermeasure. In the Pentagon, the "window" was referred to as the "strategic bathtub," after the outline formed by the convergent lines on military charts comparing U.S. and Soviet missile viability.

The remedy decided upon by the Ford administration was the MX— a powerful modern missile equipped with ten warheads and supposedly accurate enough to do unto the Soviets what they might try to do unto the United States. Its "genius," though, lay in its basing mode. Two hundred of these new ICBMs were to be placed in firing holes along a huge racetrack configuration occupying substantial amounts of the territories of Utah and Nevada. There were to be 4,600 holes in all, and the 200 MXs were to be constantly rotated among them. This would make it impossible for the Soviets to succeed with a preemptive strike against the American ICBM force, unless they wished to take the awesome step of firing a massive salvo of 4,600 missiles at the racetrack targets—and even then they could not be certain of success, although they might destroy all of civilization in the process.

In a public forum on the MX issue sponsored by the American Enterprise Institute, Senator Mark Hatfield warned that the basing scheme could prove so devastatingly effective—and give the United States such a substantial nuclear superiority over the Soviets—that the Kremlin might be panicked into attempting a preemptive strike before the MX and its racetrack could be built.

Despite such chilling prospects and a then probable project cost exceeding $20 billion, Jimmy Carter stuck with the MX, to the surprise of many. The profreeze, antinuclear movement began to put together another diverse coalition. The advisory council of the National Campaign to Stop the MX came to include not only such predictable ban-the-bomb names as Dr. Helen Caldicott, president of Physicians for Social Responsibility, and liberal activists Jerome Wiesner and Dr. Benjamin Spock, but also *Cosmos* scientist Carl Sagan, respected defense analyst Herbert Scoville, two retired admirals, a major general, and a colonel. Senator Kennedy assumed his usual leadership role in the Senate fight against the MX, amazed to discover an eventual ally in Senator Daniel Moynihan of New York, a Democrat who had hitherto voted for every military funding bill to come before him.

The biggest recruiter for the anti-MX coalition, however, proved to be the Air Force chief of staff, General Lew Allen, who went out to Utah and Nevada to sell the locals on the missile and its basing scheme personally. He was less than persuasive. In one of the most catastrophic gaffes in the history of public relations, he uttered his famous line that, in the event of a missile fight with the Russians, it would be his audience's role to function as a "nuclear sponge" that would soak up the brunt of the Soviet ICBM assault.

As noted earlier, the good people of Nevada and Utah did not want to be a nuclear sponge. Cattlemen in the two states were already upset by the vast amount of open rangeland the missile project would consume. Developers and farmers in the region were also worried that it might divert and use up whatever additional water resources the West might find in future years. Others were mad that $500 million alone would go for the concrete "roads" the missiles were to be dragged around on, money they felt could be better used on highways serving cars and trucks. "Sponge" slammed the scale down with a loud thud. According to the Air Force's own report, between 70 and 90 percent of those attending the several MX public hearings came away opposed to the project.

By the time Reagan took office, the Pentagon was in retreat and a huge army of right-wing conservatives was joining the anti-MX cause. The Sagebrush Alliance came out against the missile and started an anti-MX newsletter. The usual lure of jobs and money that military installations bring was spurned as eight of the nine Nevada counties it would traverse overwhelmingly approved referenda against the missile deployment. The Mormon Church, not exactly known for antimilitary activism but certainly sensitive to the interests of Utah, came out in opposition. So did Nevada's Senator Paul Laxalt, Reagan's ideological soulmate and closest friend in Congress, thus linking arms with the leftist Dr. Caldicott, who is to nuclear weapons what Carrie Nation was to gin.

Also troubling to the administration were reports of a plan by Westerners to file lawsuits against the MX basing scheme hole by hole for each of the 4,600 firing sites, possibly tying up the project in the courts for years.

Reagan joined the retreat, cutting back the size of the MX force to 100 missiles and cancelling the racetrack plan, proposing instead that the MX be put in existing Minutemen silos. This defused the opposition in the West but outraged many in the Senate, because it was the vulnerability of the Minutemen silos that had originally been used as justification for the MX.

In Congress, meeting halls, and newspaper editorial pages, the struggle ground on. Reagan tried a public-relations coup of his own, naming the MX the "Peacekeeper." The name stuck about as well as the euphemistic "enhanced radiation device" label the Pentagon tried to give the ill-fated neutron bomb. Reagan came in for all manner of ridicule. *New York Times* columnist Russell Baker wondered if the missile's ten warheads should be called "peaceheads."

A much better idea of the administration's, and one that would eventually confound the anti-MX movement, was to link the missile to the arms control process. Having abandoned his initial lack of interest in arms talks for a sweepingly dramatic Strategic Arms Reduction Talks (START) gambit, Reagan pleaded for the MX as a necessary bargaining chip—a weapon that would goad the Russians into negotiating seriously while providing the United States with something of value to give up in the give-and-take. The argument won over a number of neutral or opposition members of Congress and attracted the reluctant but useful support of powerful newspapers like the *Chicago Tribune*, which had been critical of the administration for its "blank check" defense policies.

But the White House was running out of time. The Pentagon was operating on a development and testing schedule for the MX that called for deploying the first operational models of the missile by December 1986. As the debate wound on, the Pentagon found itself having to compress production schedules to the barest minimum, and to take a number of administrative shortcuts as well. There were fears the MX would not get an adequate testing. "With all of the delays, reviews, and reprogrammings in the program, we have never had that initial operational capability date taken off our back," Major General Clifton Wright complained to a House subcommittee.

The problem dogging the administration was where to put the MX once it was built. With the racetrack gone and the Minuteman-hole scheme so unpopular on Capitol Hill, the White House needed something workable fast. The Pentagon was unable to fill that need. Of the thirty-four basing modes it would ultimately propose, some were so laughable as to look as though they'd been suggested by *Times* columnist Baker.

One called for hiding MXs in freighters scattered over the world's oceans. Another was to put them in small, shallow-water submarines (defense analysts countered that the Soviets could roll these subs over with an underwater nuclear blast). Two other proposals were for having the MX ride around on the nation's railroads in trains or on the nation's highways on trucks—both hilarious concepts to veterans of Amtrak or the traffic on the New Jersey Turnpike. Another, dubbed "Roto-Rooter Pack" by one Washington columnist, proposed that MXs be placed in deep mountain tunnels. After the Russians attacked, the MXs would claw their way through the debris at the mouth of the tunnel and then sail on to obliterate the Baku oil works or whatever.

Old Army captain Weinberger was much taken with the idea that the MXs could be lugged around in the skies by continuously airborne aircraft. Only after Air Force flying officers vigorously pressed their unfondness for piloting aircraft in the vicinity of mid-air ICBM launches did he reluctantly back down.

One scheme even called for dangling MX missiles from dirigibles.

What the administration finally settled upon was a form of dense pack, a scheme to site the MXs so close together that incoming Soviet missiles sent to destroy them would instead destroy each other—the first ones to explode blowing up the rockets that followed. This was considered more seriously than the dirigible plan, but not much more. There simply was not enough certainty that the plan could actually work, and certainty was a prime requisite.

Reagan was finally compelled to turn the matter over to a bipartisan blue-ribbon commission led by retired Air Force Lieutenant General Brent Scowcroft, national security advisor in the Ford administration. In the spring of 1983, it came forth with its solution—the old solution of putting 100 MXs into Minuteman silos, but only as a stopgap that would get the MXs into production. In the meantime, the commission said, the Pentagon should work for the development of new small, highly mobile one-warhead missiles (tentatively dubbed "Midgetman") that would present many fewer of the MX's problems.

That September, following the Soviet downing of the Korean jetliner, the Democratic-controlled House, which had been so voluble in its dislike for the MX, voted 266 to 152 for a defense authorization bill that contained funds for the missile.

After a futile two-week filibuster led by Gary Hart, the Senate voted 58 to 41 for the MX package.

The authorization was for only 21 missiles. This was a marked reduction from the originally proposed 200. The anti-MX movement could claim that and the defeat of the elaborate racetrack-basing project. But it wasn't much of a victory. For the generals, 21 was as good as 100 or 200. They had what they had wanted for years. Without the racetrack mode or similar protection, the MX wasn't much good as a deterrent to a Soviet preemptive strike. The powerful, sophisticated missile's chief effectiveness was as a weapon to be fired if the United States felt it was in danger of a Soviet attack.

The generals finally had what the Russians had—a first-strike ICBM.

The ghost of the Vietnam War has been a very effective lobbyist for the antimilitary movement. It was invoked just after the end of the conflict to keep both the American military and the CIA out of Angola, and again a few years later to limit American assistance to the guerrilla-plagued government of Zaire. By 1980, the Vietnam syndrome had become so pervasive that any Third World government that was both in military difficulty and heavily backed by Washington could count on dozens of American television correspondents popping up in safari suits and filing reports which invariably ended with the words "another Vietnam."

The El Salvadoran civil war should have been a natural situation for the specter of Vietnam to work its grim magic—and for a long time it was.

A wretchedly poor little nation with the highest population density in Latin America, El Salvador was governed less by its president, legislature, and courts than by an oligarchy of wealthy landowners supported by military death squads who picked their targets from every walk of life, but had a fondness for murdering labor organizers and activist Roman Catholic clergy.

Those elements of the army who did not function as assassins, brigands, or provincial warlords were well intentioned enough, but tended to be lazy, poorly trained, and ill led. Leftist guerrillas, supplied in part by the Sandinista regime of Nicaragua, Cuba, and the Soviet Union, held strongholds in remote regions of the country and operated with great effect at night and in concentrated raids on key government outposts in the provinces.

This was more than enough rationale for the usual network choruses of "another Vietnam," which came forth in great volume as the Carter administration continued to supply economic and military assistance. The biggest blow to American support for El Salvador, however, came when three nuns and a woman Catholic lay worker were murdered in an ambush outside the capital, San Salvador, on December 4, 1980. The outcry was nationwide and Carter was compelled to suspend assistance.

But the incoming Reagan administration would have no more "no more Vietnams." Throughout the spring of 1981, it did its best to play down the atrocity, to the point of then–Secretary of State Alexander Haig suggesting that the women might somehow have provoked the attack or attempted to run a roadblock. This was about as effective as the administration's attempt to label the nuclear freeze movement a Communist front or renaming the MX "the Peacekeeper."

Television producer Bernard Stone's brilliant film, "A Rose for December," first broadcast on public television in July 1982, provided a more accurate explanation of the incident than either the administration or the El Salvadoran government's own inquiry. High on documentation and low on polemic, unlike most of the antimilitary movement's rhetoric, its gripping footage of the disinterment of the women's corpses from their hasty roadside graves stirred the emotions, while the film firmly established the women's innocence, the military's guilt, and the women's work with the impoverished peasantry as motive. If Carter had still been president, the documentary likely would have served as the *Uncle Tom's Cabin* of El Salvadoran aid.

But Ronald Reagan was not Jimmy Carter. He moved in fifty-five American military advisors (some of them later were found to have participated in combat missions). Democratic liberals in Congress managed to push through a measure freezing the number of advisors at that level, providing a wonderful option for craven lawmakers unwilling to allow the administration to send more American soldiers into the country but fearful of demanding a complete withdrawal that could lead to their being blamed for "losing El Salvador."

The Reagan administration toughed it out. Reasonably free elections were held in March 1982, elections that the leftist guerrillas tried to prevent and the conservatives won. A few democratic and social reforms were gradually being put in place, though the rightists repealed laws permitting the expropriation of land. An even more encouraging development was the subsequent election of centrist José Napoleón Duarte as the country's president.

The American training began to take hold on the El Salvadoran military, and some units of the army were able to go onto the offensive in the interior, employing the latest American counterinsurgency techniques with some success. The guerrillas tried one or two "final offensives," and were beaten back. Though their raids on towns and outposts often succeeded, the war was at the worst a standoff.

The Reagan administration was also able to shatter the simplicity of the "another Vietnam" argument by expanding the controversy—and the conflict—to include Nicaragua. The anti-Sandinista guerrilla forces the administration supported in operations against Nicaragua from bases in Honduras and Costa Rica may have been directed and bankrolled by the CIA, but they were still guerrillas in the style of those in El Salvador, and many of them had fought against the overthrown right-wing regime of Anastasio Somoza. The simplistic El Salvadoran problem became the complex and confusing El Salvadoran–Nicaraguan–Central American problem.

Reagan did get into trouble in April 1984, when his CIA was caught mining the harbors of Nicaragua. This was a certifiable act of war that resulted in the damaging of several neutral ships, but it was still not enough to provide the leverage for the antimilitary movement and its allies in Congress to get the United States out of Central America. In many quarters, people felt comforted. The Mekong Delta had been an almost mythical place, but Texas was closer to El Salvador than it was to Washington. The nation had recently gone through a long-running debate over the future of the Panama Canal that had given a thorough airing to the nature of the United States's problems and vulnerabilities in Central America. That military strife in Mexico might be the end result of the Central American version of the domino theory was a frighteningly compelling argument.

Reagan had to settle for a standoff and was kept from using U.S. military forces in combat in the area, but he had accomplished this victory: the Vietnam syndrome no longer applied as before in Central America.

As it gropes its way to the end of the century, the American defense establishment must cope with the fact that much of the opposition to its policies has become institutional—a functioning part of the Washington power structure. Whatever the turn of international events or American military policy, an array of think tanks, foundations, and other entrenched organizations sits waiting to opine upon it—often with great influence, for they largely represent the political mainstream, and even sometimes very conservative ideologies.

The American Enterprise Institute (AEI) is a great ally of the Republican Party and was a major resource for the Reagan administration and the Pentagon in terms of research and policy formulation. But it has a perverse habit of opening its forums to diverse views, including Senator Hatfield's telling criticisms of MX plans. The AEI's Robert Pranger, a former Pentagon analyst, was critical of Reagan's massive defense budgets and military involvement in El Salvador.

The Brookings Institution, another organization closely associated with government, also has a bent for producing gratuitous—in Pentagon terms—studies and opinions. It came up with the report showing that much of the nation's population would die of radiation sickness if General Allen's "nuclear sponge" theory worked as he said it would. Brookings has always found ways to cut defense spending increases without impairing military strength, eliminating projects dear to the hearts and career plans of procurement officers. It was a 1981 Brookings study that noted that the Soviet Union had used its military forces as an instrument of foreign policy 190 times since World War II—only in 26 cases to expand its territory or gain political influence—while the United States used its military 200 times to assert policy.

Washington and its environs offer an abundance of safe harbors for former officials with independent or critical views on defense policy. After Reagan's victory, former Defense Secretary Harold Brown went to Johns Hopkins' Foreign Policy Institute. Georgetown's Center for Strategic and International Studies is funded with oil-company and Mellon money and can count former National Security Advisor Richard Allen, former Secretary of State Haig, former Defense Secretary and CIA Director James Schlesinger, and Henry Kissinger among past or present associates. But it's also provided a platform for Gary Hart and his nuclear freeze views and made former John Kennedy aide Robert Hunter a senior fellow. Carter mentor Robert Strauss and the AFL-CIO's Lane Kirkland have been appointed to its board.

The National Peace Academy Campaign, headquartered among the activist-crowded brownstones northeast of the Capitol, predictably counted actors Ed Asner and Paul Newman and Jerome Wiesner on its national advisory board. But it also listed former Lieutenant General Andrew J. Goodpaster and Senator Jennings Randolph.

The Center for Defense Information, at the forefront of battles against Reagan defense budgets and the nuclear arms race, is made up entirely of retired senior military officers.

There are dozens of little organizations like the Advanced International Studies Institute, which produce news releases announcing that 110 to 140 million Americans will die in a nuclear war and such—nearly all of them quickly tossed into Washington correspondents' wastebaskets. The right-wing Heritage Foundation, occupying its own eight-story Capitol Hill building, used to be viewed as equally obscure, but came to be used by Reagan as his prime policy resource during the transition between administrations and the early part of his term. Calling for massive increases in defense spending and increased production of nuclear weapons, the foundation was able to *complain* after Reagan's first year in office that he had used *only* about 60 percent of its proposals.

Not long after this, Heritage lashed out at the Pentagon with a stinging criticism of rampant waste, inefficiency, and flawed procurement procedures, which, it charged, were consuming intolerable amounts of taxpayers' money while weakening military readiness and effectiveness.

The extremely promilitary Committee on the Present Danger hectored Jimmy Carter continually for his parsimonious defense spending and SALT II treaty. It was able to count fifty-one past or present board members who served in one capacity or another in the Reagan administration, including Arms Control Director Kenneth Adelman, Undersecretary of Defense for Policy Fred Ikle, U.N. Ambassador Jeane Kirkpatrick, Navy Secretary John Lehman, Chief Arms Control Negotiator Paul Nitze, Secretary of State George Shultz, Assistant Secretary of Defense for International Security Policy Richard Perle, and President Reagan himself.

Naturally, the committee found even Reagan's proposed defense spending increases inadequate. But, in a report issued in late 1982, with the administration in office a year and a half and its policies and programs, as Reagan boasted, firmly in place, the committee also had this to say: "The Committee believes that the most significant defect in American defense policy is the absence of a clear and consistent strategy, with defense programs to support that strategy."

The administration's many global misadventures the following year were to bear that out.

One of the warnings Reagan received from the Joint Chiefs in 1983 was that the high command would have grave reservations about embarking upon a major military commitment in Central America without the support of a substantial segment of United States public opinion.

The impulse of most at the Pentagon, though, remains one of ignoring or trying to delude public opinion, fighting their governmental battles in the back rooms of the Congress and going about their daily military business in a highly insulated vacuum. It will continue to get them in trouble, as many of them realize, but it's the military way.

They make one important exception, however. They work very hard at their dealings with a national institution many of them consider a major component of the antimilitary movement, an institution the defense establishment has come to fear, loathe, and pay constant attention to—the American news media.

chapter eighteen

BAD NEWS

A free press can of course be good or bad, but, most certainly, without freedom it will never be anything but bad.

—ALBERT CAMUS,
RESISTANCE, REBELLION, AND DEATH

The hallowed corridors of the Pentagon honor everyone and everything military from Douglas MacArthur to Walt Disney—or at least the Walt Disney characters used on insignias for World War II Army and Army Air Corps units.

Amazingly, there is even a corridor dedicated to the press.

Located near the E ring second-floor briefing room, where secretaries of defense and their lieutenants struggle mightily to win the hearts and minds of the American public, the Correspondents Corridor is actually an alcove. Dark and drab compared to the emblazoned glory and grand style of the MacArthur hall, its memorabilia include improbable bronzed quotations in praise of the press from the likes of former Defense Secretary Melvin Laird. But it's largely a shrine, devoted to the life, times, and works of a few famous war correspondents of World War II—most particularly the late Richard Tregaskis, author of the much celebrated *Guadalcanal Diary,* and the late Ernie Pyle, who did his vivid reporting of the war from the GI's point of view, and who stopped a Japanese bullet.

"What does all this mean?" a green newsman asked a Pentagon pressroom veteran who was showing him around.

The veteran replied, "It means that the only good reporter is a dead reporter."

The press is the Pentagon's enemy. The press is worse than the againsters: the press makes the againsters possible. The left-wing American Friends Service Committee, the right-wing Project on Military Procurement, and all the others in between would be nothing without the press. Of course, the military brass and civilian overlords make shameless use of the press to manipulate public opinion and Congress or win interservice battles, but with only a few exceptions, they view the news media as a dangerous foe, an evil which may be constitutionally necessary but which the country's national security would be much better off without.

It was not always so. In World Wars I and II, correspondents were considered patriotic members of the team. Drew Middleton of *The New York Times* was one of thirty correspondents briefed by General Eisenhower on the invasion of Sicily fully ten days before it was launched. Likewise, there was little censorship in Korea, and little need for it. Reporters were informed days before of MacArthur's bold amphibious strike at Inchon and they kept the secret well. It was such a surprise it nearly won the war.

In the beginning, the partnership extended to operations in Vietnam. The rationale, policy, strategy, and tactics of the war were accepted largely at face value by the press in the early 1960s. In firefights, reporters were sometimes handed weapons and then helped fight it out like one of the boys. Some correspondents went along on helicopter missions and took potshots at the VC with chopper waist-guns. CBS's Walter Cronkite, the most respected television newsman of his time, went along on a fighter-bomber ground assault run and reported all the thrills.

But then the war began to go wrong, and the press corps in Vietnam that ultimately reached nine hundred began to reach the same conclusion the CIA had a few years earlier—that something seemed terribly wrong with the body counts, enemy "order of battle" inventories, and other optimistic assertions that the high command trotted out at the "five o'clock follies," as its daily Saigon news briefings came to be called.

The mutual feelings of distrust and hostility that grew from this never much diminished. The military's belief in the press's culpability in turning American public opinion against the Vietnam War remains as firm as its belief in Newton's law as applied to artillery trajectories.

Certainly the war correspondents of Vietnam enjoyed less censorship and better communications than their counterparts in World War II. Certainly television made a difference. The "happy talk" movie newsreels of World War II were nothing at all like the grim film or videotape footage of landing-zone firefights and napalm strikes against Vietnamese villages, which were broadcast into so many living rooms in the 1960s and 1970s. (It was not until 1943 that a news photograph showing American World War II dead was allowed to be released.)

But the televised firefights provided no more horrible a picture of war than the *Harper's Weekly* illustrations and first-person accounts of the Civil War. The principal effect of most of that TV footage was one of confusion—blurs of greenery and noise, GIs ("grunts") running through brush or firing at an unseen enemy in distant treelines. As with World War II and Korea (actually America's first "television war"), the most memorable pictures of Vietnam were still photographs—the small girl running down a village road with her clothes burned off by napalm, the villagers lying dead in a row in a ditch at My Lai, the Viet Cong suspect in a checked shirt having his brains blown out by the military police chief of Saigon—though there was some rather gory film footage of these wartime tableaux prepared for television as well.

The on-the-ground print reporting of the war, which tended to attract the best of the country's correspondents, was as honest, courageous, and objective as in the other wars—which may be the military's problem.

Despite hard-nosed reporting, the U.S. high command was not prevented from carrying out its plans—the pacification programs, the invasion of Cambodia, the bombing of North Vietnamese cities. The military was able to fight its war for twelve years. Bad press or no, it had its chance.

Despite extremely vivid footage of continuing atrocities in El Salvador, American public opinion has not compelled U.S. withdrawal from Central America. The grim television scenes of the massacre of Palestinian refugee women and children during the Israeli occupation of Beirut in 1982 did not provoke a break with Israel or fundamentally change American Mideast policy. Neither did the savage bombing of the U.S. Marine headquarters in Beirut in 1983, which wiped out 10 percent of the American peacekeeping force in Lebanon in one vicious explosion.

The news media have evolved into a different beast, one as antithetical to the Pentagon as the "buddy press" of World War II was not. Both print and broadcast media employ space-age technology that provide instant and global communications. The news media's curiosity and expertise in military affairs have increased markedly. The Vietnam syndrome may not be as powerful among the general public anymore, but it has become entrenched as a journalistic cliché. In trying to manipulate or obstruct the media, the Pentagon now faces altogether new challenges—which it has not met well.

Because the nuclear arms race has reached such awesome proportions, because rank and file congressmen no longer meekly accept the dictates and assumptions of the Pentagon and the chairmen of congressional military committees, and because modern weapons individually are so breathtakingly costly, the once arcane debate over nuclear and conventional weapons development has become intense and highly public, and receives news coverage to match.

The dispatch of American military forces to new locales and their conduct once there now undergoes a reflexive scrutiny by the media. When one of the few dozen military advisors first sent to El Salvador was filmed by a television crew carrying an M-16 rifle in violation of his noncombatant status, it caused a national furor. In the very early days of Vietnam, noncombatant military advisors not only carried weapons but sometimes exchanged them in Saigon bars for drinks, all without much public comment.

The most effective of the lobbying organizations seeking to change or obstruct American military policy, both on the right and the left, have become increasingly sophisticated about the news media and have learned to abandon polemic statements and mass demonstrations for facts and figures, studies and reports, that not only justify their conclusions but provide reporters with genuine stories. Military public-information officers must perform as persuasively and, when they're stuck with the likes of the B-1 or the M-1 tank to defend, usually don't.

The newspaper op-ed page, largely an invention of the Vietnam era, has brought before the public debates and discourses heretofore carried on in obscure or esoteric journals like *Foreign Policy, Armed Forces Journal,* and *Defense Week.* Arguments previously confined to the innermost recesses of the defense establishment now rage across the opinion pages of papers read by millions.

A variety of radio and television public affairs programs, with their voracious appetite for material, have fed upon these newspaper debates and brought them before even wider audiences.

The civilian communications satellite system employed so effectively by *Nightline*'s Ted Koppel and by the prime-time network news shows has been an even greater irritation to the Pentagon, in ways that the high command of a generation ago could not have conceived possible. As AWACS planes and a squadron of fighter escorts were dispatched to Chad to stem a Libyan-backed rebel assault that at the least threatened to partition the country, the mad Colonel Muammar Qaddafi himself turned up on *The CBS Evening News* to profess his innocence to anchorman Dan Rather in a live interview—just as he later turned up on *The Today Show,* after a machine gunner in his London Embassy wounded nearly a dozen dissident student protesters and killed a British policewoman in April 1984.

As Marines fell to Druze militia snipers in Beirut during the resurgence of the Lebanese civil war that followed the pullback of Israeli forces in the summer of 1983, Druze leader Walid Jumblatt appeared on *Nightline* to chat about the situation. When the Soviets shot down the unarmed Korean jetliner north of Japan that same year, Kremlin propagandist Vladimir Pozner, a regular guest on the show, took part in the *Nightline* discussion in a satellite hookup live from Moscow. American television cameras were in Havana with Fidel Castro for the return of the Cuban dead and wounded from combat with American Marines and rangers on Grenada.

To career officers who remember Korea and Vietnam and whose fathers served in World War II, this is dumbfounding. How might the jolly Hermann Göring have come across on a live satellite feed explaining the bombing of Rotterdam? Still, Pozner, Jumblatt and company have never been as outrageous to the military as the horrifying television footage of one of the Ayatollah Khomeini's most murderous mullahs putting on public display the burned bodies of the Americans killed in the Desert One raid, for the benefit of both a shrieking anti-American mob and cameras.

Pentagon public information officers have learned to accept this modern phenomenon as something about which they can do little. The major press preoccupation of the Pentagon high command and its career propagandists, however, is not with op-ed page opinion, foreign correspondents, or network anchormen but with the two dozen or so Americans and as many foreign journalists who labor just down the E ring hallway from the Ernie Pyle / Richard Tregaskis shrine. They might be called the "Enemy Within."

The first and last line of defense for the American military in dealing with American public opinion on policy decisions and weapons procurement is the credo that war is much too complex to be left to civilians. The science of war has become a theology, its inner secrets to be divined only by the ordained.

If one complains that the Pentagon's grand civil-defense schemes for nuclear war are absurd in a country with facilities for treating only two thousand burn victims, or that hovering helicopters are vulnerable to rifle fire, or that the Exocet missile may have rendered large warships obsolete, the response is always the same: "You don't understand." Or "It's too complex for you to understand." Or "You couldn't possibly understand; you're a civilian."

This approach has been used to cow general-assignment reporters and more scholarly editorial writers, just as it has to confound congressmen and even sophisticated CIA officials and National Security Council staff. In response, one retired CIA official continues to fume, "Doesn't common sense apply?" If he wasn't a civilian, he would understand. Of course, common sense doesn't apply. It's unmilitary.

But down the hallway on the E ring can be found a group of men and women who have studied the theology, divined the secrets, and come to learn what the Wizard of Oz is really like behind his curtain of Pentagon doublespeak, technical mumbo jumbo, patriotic exhortations, and other obfuscation. They are the correspondents who work out of the Pentagon pressroom on a regular if not daily basis. They are the top priority for the military public-information corps—for attention and for worry. If, ironically, they are the news people with whom the Pentagon gets along best, they are also the Pentagon's problem.

Of the army of thousands of public-information officers that the Defense Department fields to do battle with the nation's press and broadcast media, just five officers man the front lines at the Pentagon pressroom—one for each of the four main service branches and a fifth to handle information from the defense secretary's office. Theirs ranks among the toughest missions at the Pentagon. Consider, from their point of view, what is arrayed against them.

Glancing at the Pentagon pressroom, it wouldn't seem like much. It is a facility out of journalism's past—old office furniture, piles of files and stacks of old press releases and reports, here and there the few souvenirs of serious men—lacking only brass spittoons to complete the ambience.

As with most Washington pressrooms, it is a place of marked routine. There are briefings—sometimes with the secretary of defense, but more often conducted by an underling—every Tuesday and Thursday at 11:30 a.m. "Before the clocks get funny," as one correspondent put it, referring to the Pentagon clocks that show time as 1600 instead of 4:00 p.m. As at the Agriculture Department or HUD, there is a daily outpouring of usually unimportant press releases—called "blue tops" for their distinctive letterhead. There is tedium.

There is sycophancy. It was long said of police reporters that, if you left them on the station-house beat for too long, they would turn into cops. The same can sometimes apply to some Pentagon correspondents, who come to appreciate, admire, and depend upon military brass so much they begin to identify with them.

But there is also enterprise, and that is what terrifies public information officers. Pentagon correspondents fan out into the vast military empire like rangers on a combat patrol. Using their networks of sources and their knowledge of how the place works, they come back with stories—stories that can change policy, derail weapons programs, and truncate careers.

The Pentagon's Early Bird news summary, a daily compilation of significant news stories, editorials, columns, and commentary on military subjects selected from twenty key newspapers around the country, circulates to fifteen thousand civilians and uniformed personnel throughout the defense establishment at the start of every government business day. It is the most avidly read news summary in Washington. The White House summary is often just skimmed, because officials there know that most of the huge White House press corps will be reporting the same story.

No one can ever be sure what Pentagon reporters will be reporting. It could be as many as twenty different major stories. The White House reads the Early Bird, and its following noon edition, as do the major powers on military matters in Congress, the State Department, and the intelligence community.

The Pentagon press corps has a caste system. The elite are the correspondents for *The Washington Post, The New York Times,* and *The Wall Street Journal,* because those papers all circulate daily in Washington. The *Post* is king of them all because it circulates so widely. A survey of senior congressional staff aides found that, of the two and a half hours a day they spent studying various news media, they devoted an average of 31 minutes a day to reading the *Post,* compared to 13 minutes watching *The CBS Evening News,* 12 minutes reading *The New York Times,* 11 minutes reading *The Wall Street Journal,* and 10 minutes watching *NBC Nightly News.*

The generals can be sure that a *Post* story on a flawed weapons system will be read by every staffer on the House Appropriations Committee.

The major publications represented in the Pentagon press corps often use the nice guy / tough guy approach in going after military news. The regular correspondent tends to write the "straight stuff" as he protects his relationships with the Pentagon high command and maintains his network of sources and informants. To dig up the dirt, the big papers deploy investigative specialists who often do not cover the Pentagon full-time and are less vulnerable to reprisals that the brass might take against them.

The networks have the potential for being major forces in the Pentagon. Radio and television news shows accounted for seven of the ten leading news sources for Capitol Hill staffers interviewed in the survey. The staffers also spent more time watching CBS's *60 Minutes* than reading *Newsweek, Time,* or *U.S. News & World Report.*

During times of crisis, the pressroom's sages and graybeards can always be found jammed into the small television room, following events as related by anchormen and their reporting staffs in between forays into the Pentagon labyrinth for information from sources.

But the extremely limited time allocated for most broadcast news stories does not permit much thorough analysis. Stories that should be of paramount importance to the Pentagon receive only cursory attention from the broadcast media—with the significant exception of National Public Radio—if they are too complex, as most are. A detailed broadcast explanation of Maverick missile malfunctioning guidance systems would interfere with at least two commercial breaks.

During the press briefings, the American press corps face the secretary of defense (or his designated hitter) seated according to a pecking order of almost medieval precedence (according to clout). But occupying the "side pews" are a collection of foreign reporters who command almost as much respect. Representing newspapers, wire services, and magazines in Germany, France, Taiwan, China, Japan, Korea, and many other countries, they often ask the hardest and most knowledgeable questions. At every briefing there is always one question from an Israeli reporter of great significance to Jerusalem. The correspondent from the Soviet news agency Tass seldom misses a briefing. He is of great use to the secretary of defense when the administration wants to send a quick message to Moscow.

Though it is the Pentagon's adversary, the press corps readily makes use of its services. The government Voice of America reporters who regularly cover Pentagon briefings provide accurate "fills" for newsmen who miss them. Correspondents whose papers do not circulate widely in Washington court the military editors of the Early Bird to gain exposure there.

In addition to the uniformed information officers representing each of the four service branches and a civilian counterpart representing the secretary of defense's office, the Pentagon also provides "chums," officers assigned to befriend individual correspondents, providing them with tips, stories, and background information and establishing a pair bond. Should a reporter transgress with some story damaging to the Pentagon, however, the chum becomes an instrument of press control, drawing his reporter friend aside and saying "you really let me down."

The chief civilian information officer used to function as something of a chum, but since the position was elevated to the level of assistant secretary of defense in the 1970s, that person has acted considerably less as a servant of the press than as a prime Pentagon official himself. Access to him can be as limited at times as it is to high-ranking military officers. Henry Catto, who held the job until he resigned in September 1983 to become publisher of the *Washington Journalism Review,* responded to the Pentagon's subsequent press blackout of the American invasion of Grenada by saying, "Unhappily, the average Joint Chiefs

of Staff member has all the public-relations sense of Attila the Hun."
Catto seldom spoke that way when he inhabited an E ring office.

For all the infamies of the Saigon "five o'clock follies," the Pentagon
seldom lies. Its principal obfuscation technique is to never volunteer
information and to answer all questions quite literally. A question like
"General, is the Army going to invade North Vietnam?" will draw the
response "No, son, we have no intention whatsoever along those lines."
A veteran Pentagon correspondent will have learned to phrase the
question this way: "Sir, is any element of unified or specified commands
engaged in military action in Southeast Asia?" and thus learn that the
Navy and Air Force are flying bombing missions against North Vietnamese territory.

Another technique of the Pentagon brass is to ask correspondents,
if their questions are "hard," to put them in writing. They then take
two or more days to respond, hoping the intervening time will defuse
the impact of the story.

Massive retaliation is another favored method of countering the press,
with the heavy artillery including flat untruths. John Lehman, perhaps
the most aggressive secretary of the Navy in modern times, responded
harshly to news stories and editorials critical of his administration or
programs with letters to the editor more than suggestive that the newsman or newswoman in question is ignorant or incompetent. In response
to some critical *Time* pieces, he declared, "I have never seen in a major
journal so many bald errors of pure demonstrable fact." When a cheap
Argentine missile sunk an expensive British warship in the Falklands
War, Lehman jumped in to comment before the press had a chance to
print a word on the new combat phenomenon, hastening to tell Pentagon reporters that such a tragedy could not have befallen a big American carrier task force with all its aircraft and elaborate missile defenses.
In fact, he said, the Falklands experience was a demonstration of the
need for big American superships.

When Lehman's $90 billion Aegis cruiser and destroyer program
came under press attack for less than satisfactory test results, the heavi-
est guns were run out. Admiral James Watkins, chief of naval operations, went after the editorial page of the *Chicago Tribune,* questioning
the paper's patriotism and baldly stating that it was incorrect in calling
the Aegis program a $90 billion one. "The 1985 budget request is for
$1.25 billion, not the $90 billion as suggested in your editorial," he
said. "Twenty-six of these fine cruisers plus 29 destroyers will be bought
in the years ahead for a total cost of $47.4 billion."

The *Tribune* never meant to suggest that all the ships in the program
were to be built in a single budget year. The $90 billion figure came

from Pentagon and congressional papers, which described the program
as calling for 26 cruisers, at $1.1 or so billion each, and 60 destroyers,
at an initial cost of $1 billion each. The call for 60 destroyers, rather
than Admiral Watkins's 29, came from Defense Secretary Caspar Weinberger's official report to Congress for fiscal year 1984.

Yet Watkins didn't hesitate to pull out all stops to put down criticism.
He had good political reason. Lehman wanted those keels laid as fast
as possible. Once a weapons program is under way and has built up a
constituency, it becomes more immune to criticism.

The Pentagon probably practices shunning more than any other government agency in Washington—at least more effectively. Capitol Hill
is aswarm in informants and awash in leaked information, with even
the select committees on intelligence adding to the flow. White House
aides sometimes try to get rough on an individual reporter, but the
presidential press corps operates so much as a pack that the individual
is usually unaffected by such muscling. In the Pentagon, reporters depend so much on sources that unanswered telephone calls, rudeness,
and other indications that one is on very bad paper can be chilling
indeed—especially when it carries the connotation that the reporter in
question is being disloyal and harmful to his country.

Sometimes, the Pentagon can get downright nasty. In a September
1983 speech, Air Force Secretary Verne Orr advised aircraft and missile
defense contractors not to advertise in publications that printed articles
critical of American defense policy. "To me, a firm commits corporate
suicide when it advertises in media which denigrate and/or criticize
national defense policies, thereby presenting an unbalanced, inaccurate
view of the product that firm is trying to sell."

The advice didn't take. On a scale not seen since World War II,
arms manufacturers are filling magazine and newspaper pages, frequently encouraged by Pentagon practices that allow them to write off
such advertisements as "overhead" on their weapons contracts. Typical
issues of *Time* and *U.S. News & World Report* contain glossy, sophisticated advertisements for the NAVTAG Naval Tactical Game Training
System, the McDonnell-Douglas magnetic helicopter camera/sensor
mount, the Lockheed S-3 Viking mine-laying jet, the AM General EMS
(Enhanced Mobility System) combat truck, the Lockheed C-5 transport, the Northrop F-20 Tigershark fighter, and the General Electric
Trident submarine and destroyer engine gears—none of them exactly
home consumer items.

The defense establishment also practices the same disinformation
tactics that the Soviet KGB is fond of using. The *Washington Post*'s
George Wilson obtained a government document that had figured largely

in a public controversy between columnists Jack Anderson and Jody Powell over Jimmy Carter's alleged recklessness in planning the ill-fated Desert One hostage rescue raid. Wilson discovered it was a CIA forgery.

Classification of information as secret is a popular Pentagon means of controlling it. Between October 1, 1981, and July 31, 1982, the Defense Department classified 11,691,876 pieces of information, of which 301,355 were labeled top secret. According to the Information Security Oversight Office, a branch of the National Security Council, the growth in the number of classified documents is running at 10 percent a year. There are some 7,000 officials in the government with the authority to classify documents, but they also have the authority to *delegate* that authority, and have given it to 113,000 lesser officials. In one random check, it was found that some 600,000 papers had been classified without proper authority and that another 800,000 had been classified unnecessarily. Here is an excerpt from one Navy document classified secret:

> The Navy must continue to attract and retain sufficient numbers of high quality, skilled and motivated people. Compensation and quality of life improvements must be competitive in the job market. Ways must be found to reduce requirements for administrative functions, reduce personnel turbulence and permanent change of station moves.

In 1983, the Reagan administration issued an executive order requiring at least 110,000 high-level government employees who became exposed to classified material—most of them in the Pentagon—to clear any future writings with government authorities for the rest of their lives. This order quickly ran afoul of civil-liberties groups and became a national controversy. Though presidents and vice-presidents were exempted, it could have prevented Henry Kissinger and many other figures of historical importance from publishing their memoirs.

Also under Reagan, an order was issued authorizing random lie-detector tests, even if the test subjects had done nothing suspicious. Another chilling measure was the requirement that all calls and questions from newsmen be reported to a central authority before being answered—if answered they were to be.

The most egregiously heavy-handed press-control action taken by the Pentagon in recent years was the news blackout of the American invasion of Grenada in October 1983, an excess in which President Reagan and his top White House advisors played a principal role. In attempting to maintain surprise and sustain the myth that the operation was essentially a rescue mission of American medical students on the island, and hide what it really was, a surgical strike to overthrow a pro-Castro Marxist regime, the military refused to inform anyone in the news media of the operation beforehand, refused to let any reporters accompany the invasion force, and refused to allow any reporters on the island for two days after the landings. When three Americans and a British reporter made their way onto Grenada prior to the invasion anyway, they were taken aboard the USS *Guam* to file their stories, only to be told they could neither file any stories nor return to the island. However, another reporter and a photographer who had landed with them had remained on the island and got good stories and photographs—though with little cooperation from the military.

In a news conference, Defense Secretary Weinberger defended the news blackout as necessary for the safety of newsmen, saying they might have been harmed in the action. The same tactic applied to World War II would have seen Ernie Pyle writing the story of GI Joe from the E ring briefing room. Weinberger also said the censorship was the decision of the military commander of the invasion, whose authority Weinberger said he would never think of countermanding. So much for the constitutional dictate that the civilian chief executive control the American military.

A few days later, President Reagan publicly decried "smug know-it-alls" in safe, comfy surroundings who'd been insisting that the American medical students the American invasion was designed to rescue had not been in all that much danger. He asked how many of them would have liked to have traded places with the students. If he was talking about the press, as he seemed to be, more than a hundred had been begging, pleading, and shouting to be put on Grenada from the very first.

"The argument that the safety of journalists was at stake is simply not valid," said Jerry Friedheim, a newspaper executive who had served as chief Defense Department spokesman.

> Journalists have always been willing to take the risks necessary to cover uniformed people in combat. And scores of reporters over the years have lost their lives doing so.
>
> This safety argument is the same one that the Soviet Union makes in United Nations forums and elsewhere when it wishes to close down societies. It says it's not safe for journalists to go where the news is, so no one can report it. To have had U.S. officials arguing the Soviet line was very sad and troubling.
>
> One result of keeping reporters out of Grenada was that the American people were getting reports from Radio Havana—not exactly an ideal situation.

Gloating Pentagon officers talked of how the news blackout was learned from "the lessons of the Falklands," although the heavily censored British reporters were allowed to go ashore with the Falkland invasion force. But the Caribbean resort island of Grenada was hardly the same thing as the far-off, isolated, desolate Falklands. The whole story of the Grenada operation came quickly to the fore—complete with revelations as to the mistaken bombing of a civilian mental hospital, the loss of two helicopters in a collision and seven others to ground fire, the American casualties suffered in an American naval air strike called in against an American position and other mishaps, the overblown enemy-troop-strength figures, the assault against neighboring islands that proved to have no enemy on them, and the fact that American forces were sent into action bearing nothing more accurate than tourist maps.

In terms of domestic politics, strategic goals in the Caribbean, and the Grenadans' own interests, the invasion was, on balance, a success. A *Mouse That Roared* caper or not, the mission and its result were greeted positively in public-opinion polls, indicating that the mission served to vent a great many American frustrations built up since the Vietnam War and the hostage humiliation in Iran. But it cost the administration heavily in terms of condemnation from abroad—including many of the United States's closest allies in Europe and Latin America—and in a severe loss of credibility with the press. The administration put itself on the record as having perpetrated a number of lies. Next time, the press would be gunning for it. A number of White House press aides warned the President of this, and one, Les Janka, was compelled to resign over the matter.

Ultimately, cooler heads in the White House and the Pentagon hit upon the idea of creating a standby pool of trusted, veteran war correspondents who would be taken along on the next military mission. Weinberger also began a series of informal dinners with veteran journalists, including his Harvard classmate Theodore White, CBS's Walter Cronkite and Eric Sevareid, NBC correspondent Jack Reynolds, author James Michener of *Bridges at Toko-Ri* fame, and others. Ostensibly, these medallions of beef and good red wine sessions had the purpose of soliciting advice on press relations from these venerable figures, but they would have been a lot more meaningful if Pentagon beat correspondents were invited.

In a paper prepared for the National War College, Air Force Colonel William Goodyear had a more positive suggestion to make: rather than isolate itself from public opinion, the American military ought to include it as a significant factor in its policy-making and its other key decisions.

Elected officials, anxious to maintain voter support, tend to be more sensitive to the views of the voters than appointed ones, especially if the latter have little or no practical political experience. Certainly the secretary of defense and his top appointees hold politically sensitive positions and are concerned over public opinion.

On the other hand, many defense officials in the lower levels of the policy-making process operate in partial or complete anonymity to the general public. These officials tend to primarily focus on questions related to threat assessment, technical possibilities, and budgetary trade-offs. As a result policy issues are developed and forwarded to senior decision makers in a context that may ignore the views of the general public. . . .

One notable weakness of the current Department of Defense management system is our inability to forecast, monitor, and react to inputs from the general public. In a grand view, we have a responsibility to the democratic process not to use the power, secrecy, and technology of the national security structure to foreclose the vital input that could be provided by a free, questioning, and enlightened public opinion.

In a more practical view, we have a responsibility to the nation we serve not to allow vast sums to be spent on projects that are not in consonance with the perceived need of the American people. It is in this area that the defense policymaker has the greatest problems with potential public opinion. There is a fine line between molding public opinion to gain popular support for certain defense projects and informing the public so that an intelligent democratic decision can be made.

Goodyear's solution was a systematic sampling of public opinion on various defense issues. Though it smacks of advertising agencies and political consultants, such polling might end up providing the most valuable intelligence the American military ever acquires.

chapter nineteen

FRIENDS
AND ENEMIES

> *'Tis our true policy to steer clear of permanent*
> *alliances, with any portion of the foreign world.*
> —GEORGE WASHINGTON, FAREWELL ADDRESS

American defense is confounded not only by the nation's enemies but also by the nation's friends. Sometimes they might as well be enemies.

The United States now has no end of allies. It has *too many* allies. It first broke its long history of peacetime nonentanglement in 1948, when it signed the Rio Pact with the nations of Latin America. One of the more successful such treaties, the pact required all signatories to respect existing national boundaries in the hemisphere. Though the subsequent history of the region was violent, the treaty, which stipulated that an attack on one was an attack upon all, effectively put an end to the bloody border wars that had plagued Latin America for more than a century (Cuba was suspended from membership in 1962). If the insurgencies in Central America, left and right, get out of control, the precedents of the pact could complicate the United States's military activities greatly.

In 1949, with the Cold War a raging blizzard, the United States signed its most important collective-security treaty, the NATO pact. It, too, included a one-for-all, all-for-one article, and now binds Belgium, Britain, Canada, Denmark, France, the Federal Republic of Germany, Greece, Iceland, Italy, Luxembourg, the Netherlands, Norway, Portugal, Spain, the United States, and Turkey to each other's defense.

After that, the United States became a treaty addict. Following the outbreak of war in Korea (which the United States was not obligated to defend), it signed mutual-security treaties in 1951 with Japan and the Philippines and the ANZUS defense treaty the same year with Australia and New Zealand. With another treaty in 1954, it guaranteed the security of Taiwan, which in turn guaranteed it would not unilaterally attack the People's Republic of China.

Also in 1954, the United States, Britain, France, Australia, New Zealand, Pakistan, Thailand, and the Philippines formed the Southeast

Asia Treaty Organization (SEATO), and, in a separate protocol, extended the treaty's protection to South Vietnam, Cambodia, and Laos. Ultimately a colossal failure, foundering over U.S. prosecution of the Vietnam war, SEATO was abandoned in 1977. In 1956, the United States became an associate member of the British-formed Central Treaty Organization (CENTO), a military alliance of Britain, Iran, Pakistan, and Turkey (Iran and Pakistan withdrew in 1979). During the 1962 Berlin crisis, Congress committed the United States to use force, if necessary, to defend the former German capital. The White House that year also made an agreement to defend Thailand. A number of de facto defense agreements subsequently came into being that tied the United States to the security of Israel, Egypt, Saudi Arabia, Oman and other Arabian Gulf states, (Christian) Lebanon, and former American possessions in the Pacific.

In recent years, the United States has made defensive gestures on behalf of Chad, the Sudan, Zaire, and several other African states. It is assumed that the United States would react strongly in some military sense if the Soviet Union were to challenge the sovereignty of Finland, Sweden, Austria, and Yugoslavia.

Alliances imply unity of purpose, and as a consequence are, in historical terms, usually brief. On balance, the United States has been fortunate in long-lasting alliances like NATO, and in its enduring friendships with Britain, France, West Germany, and Japan. But its alliances and friends have also provided the United States with some of its most unhappy moments.

What the White House, the State Department, and the Pentagon regularly fail to appreciate is that America's allies are always looking out for Number 1. Consider the United States's closest ally, Great Britain, and its "I'm all right, Jack" foreign and military policy. A fighting ally of the United States in Korea, under the serendipitous Security Council resolution that declared the war a U.N. police action in the Soviet Union's fortuitous absence, Britain balked at a similar role in Vietnam despite its membership in SEATO. In 1956, Britain joined with France and Israel in a rash assault upon Suez and the Sinai against Egyptian President Nasser that might have led to a major power conflict if the United States and the Soviets hadn't joined forces to order the three to withdraw.

To operate in the Atlantic, the Soviets' gigantic Northern Fleet—based mostly around Russia's Kola Peninsula and comprising 185 nuclear missile and attack submarines and 195 surface warships—must pass through three narrows: the Greenland-Iceland gap, the Iceland–Faeroe Islands gap, and the Faeroes-Scotland gap. The key to NATO's defenses in this vital area is the Keflavík Air Base in Iceland, that small country's lone contribution to NATO and its own defense. Home to AWACS radar planes and P-3 Orion antisubmarine aircraft, it is the command center of a huge and supersecret North Atlantic intelligence and surveillance network that can not only detect the passage of every Soviet submarine but instantly determine which individual Soviet sub it is.

In three bitter "cod wars," Britain sent warships to Iceland's coastal waters in order to bully that nation into letting British trawlers work Iceland's depleted fish stocks there, adhering to a principle described to one of the authors by a British Foreign Office official as follows: "You must understand that Iceland is a very small country." In the last "cod war"—1975-1976—Iceland was so desperate at the prospect of losing its entire export economy and furious at being treated so roughly by a fellow NATO ally that it was prepared to withdraw from its association with NATO and have the Keflavík base dismantled. It would have done so had not Defense Secretary Rumsfeld and others in the Ford administration become alarmed enough to warn the British finally to back off, which they reluctantly did.

In 1982, having embarked on an austerity reduction of the Royal Navy, Britain then withdrew a substantial portion of its North Atlantic fleet in order to wage war against the Argentinians over the barren sheep station in the South Atlantic known as the Falkland Islands. In the process, it lost two vessels to an Exocet missile and a bomb and put all the others at risk. The openings left in NATO defenses had to be covered by the United States.

The United States had tried to dissuade both sides from waging war, but when that failed, weighed in on Britain's side. America provided its ally with 12.5 million gallons of aviation fuel from its military stockpiles, hundreds of Sidewinder missiles, mortar shells, runway netting, and tons of other equipment. It was prepared to lend Britain its helicopter aircraft carrier USS *Guam*. At considerable expense, it moved one of its spy satellites from a northern orbit over the Soviet Union to a southerly one to provide the British fleet accurate intelligence on Argentine ship movements. The British newsmagazine *The Economist* noted that neither Britain's invasion of the Falklands nor its victory would have been possible without the United States.

But when American forces moved into Grenada in 1983 to deal with a rapidly deteriorating situation on that island, London replied with indignation.

Also in 1983, with the United States beset with serious problems in Central America, the Far East, Africa, and the Mideast and its undermanned Navy strained to the point where the battleship *New Jersey* was having to shuttle between the Caribbean and the eastern Mediterranean, the British announced they were taking a Royal Navy task group of ten warships out of NATO waters to show the flag on a seven-month tour of the Indian Ocean, Australia, New Zealand, and the Far East. Other task groups would make similar grand voyages to the same waters, as well as to the South Atlantic and the Caribbean. Yet the British refused to send any additional warships to the eastern Mediterranean, even though it had a peacekeeping force serving in Lebanon. Cutting $360 million from its defense budget in 1983, it curtailed other of its NATO duties as well.

Similarly, France, America's oldest ally, withdrew its military forces from NATO in 1966 and, though remaining technically a member of the alliance, compelled NATO to move its headquarters to Brussels. It has continued to operate its forces—including a growing nuclear arsenal—independently.

The chief leverage the United States has had with the Arab nations in the Mideast has come from its willingness to supply arms. When the United States began to balk at some of the Arabs' arms demands in 1984, the French, as usual, moved in with arms deals to undercut the United States and gain influence in the region for themselves.

Given the dangerously low level of the nuclear threshold in Europe and the continuing buildup of Soviet and Warsaw Pact nuclear and conventional forces, it can safely be said that no NATO ally is making an adequate contribution to the common defense, including the United States.

But at least the United States tries. If some of the larger NATO countries lag behind, the smaller ones don't even try. Despite a right-of-center government, Belgium refused to pay its share of NATO's new Patriot antiaircraft system, complaining of too poor an economy. A large section of the Dutch parliament double-crossed the United States by deciding not to take the contingent of American cruise missiles Holland had earlier decided to accept.

The Greeks and Turks, continuing their bitter quarrel over Cyprus, have become increasingly uncooperative members of the alliance, and their usefulness in a crisis involving their region is much doubted. For a brief time, Denmark had a prime minister whose defense policy amounted to picking up the telephone and saying, "We surrender" in the event of attack, as he made clear in his election campaign. The Danish parliament in 1983 cancelled its share of Pershing and cruise missile support-system costs, and held its increase in defense spending to 0.05 percent annually. There are examples of irresponsibility and cross-purposes with the United States involving nearly every other member of NATO.

The percentage of the American GNP spent on the military has been climbing from 5.5 percent when Reagan took office toward 7 percent, and the Reagan administration laid plans for defense-spending levels of 8 percent of GNP by 1990. To meet the high-technology needs of modern nuclear and conventional war fighting, according to experts like Lieutenant General Andrew Goodpaster, former commander of U.S. forces in Europe, the other NATO countries should increase their spending levels from 3 to 4 percent of their GNP. But by late 1983, half the sixteen NATO nations still weren't spending even 3 percent. West Germany's military spending was 3.2 percent. In 1978, all NATO countries formally agreed to increase annual defense budgets by a minimum of 3 percent. By 1984, their annual increases averaged between only 1 and 1.6 percent, and West Germany's defense budget actually went down, though it subsequently moved to reinstitute annual increases at the 3 percent level.

Canada's military contributions to NATO have long been something of a joke, though it is a largely defenseless country facing the Soviet Union across the Arctic. Japan's U.S.-imposed constitution forbids a standing army, but it has failed to strengthen its permitted defense forces to levels the United States would like to see in one of the most heavily armed corners of the world. With a population of 119 million, Japan supports a defense force of 245,000. South Korea, with a population of 39 million, has 601,600 people in its armed services. Aside from coastal patrol craft, Japan's navy consists of just thirty-three destroyers, sixteen frigates, and fourteen submarines. The bulk of Japan's naval protection comes from the much overworked U.S. Seventh Fleet.

Japan did agree to build a few F-15s under license for its air force, but gained, as always, a commercial advantage from that. It had been preparing to enter the world commercial aircraft market in a big way with passenger jets of its own, and the design techniques it learned from the McDonnell-Douglas F-15 gave this effort a substantial boost. Its planes will compete with new McDonnell-Douglas and Boeing models. The smaller the American firms' share of the world aircraft market, the smaller their nondefense revenue base and the higher the manufacturing costs of American weapons.

When the Reagan administration ordered the cancellation of the troubled Caterpillar Corporation's contract with the Soviet Union for huge pipe-laying tractors needed for its new gas pipeline to Western Europe, the Japanese hurried to Moscow and sold the Russians Komatsu pipe-laying tractors, which also have the capability of loading main battle tanks on railroad flatcars.

Israel is the United States's best friend in the Mideast and, of all its allies, the one that has caused it the most trouble. It has acted with ruthless independence whenever it felt necessary, as when it deliberately attacked the unarmed U.S. reconnaissance ship *Liberty* in the eastern Mediterranean in 1967 and when it launched its bloody invasion of Lebanon in 1982. Its partial withdrawal left the United States, Britain, France, and Italy and their peacekeeping forces around Beirut in great jeopardy.

The United States's foreign friends do not confine their mischief-making to their own areas. They shamelessly exploit the vulnerabilities of the open American political system to their own purposes, especially concerning gaining access to the American defense establishment and policy-making agencies. Israel is probably the most flagrant offender, but they all do it.

There are 143 foreign embassies in Washington, and they do not confine their activities to trade negotiation and cultural exchange. Soviet "journalists" cover important congressional committee meetings on foreign policy and military issues and frequently are able to obtain U.S. government documents through the public process. Sandinista representatives have worked the Hill with the same impunity as the Israelis.

In the days of the Shah, Iranian Ambassador Ardeshir Zahedi had a $25,000-a-month special fund at his disposal just for buying influence in Washington with friendly little gifts, according to a congressional report. His favorite gifts ran to magnums of Dom Pérignon and $200 tins of caviar. He once tried to bestow a $6,000 wristwatch on a network news anchorwoman, but she returned it. All told, 284 Washington news media representatives received major gifts from Zahedi and 386 received lesser ones.

On Capitol Hill, the embassy consistently rated as the most powerful and influential is the Israeli, which maintains a rating system for measuring American publications' loyalty to Israel and has filed huge libel suits against some. Since President Truman recognized the first Israeli government in 1948, it has seldom failed to achieve its major foreign-policy objectives in the United States. One ranking Senate Foreign Relations Committee aide explained:

> No one else is even a close second. The Israelis, partly because of their propaganda and lobbying skills, but also because they really

are our only true friend in the region, always carry the force of
argument. It's persistence, money, and moral standing. When [Jacob]
Javits was in the Senate, no matter if it was the most minor, minute,
irrelevant amendment, he'd invoke the Holocaust at every point.

The power of the Israeli lobby is such that former Senate Foreign
Relations Committee Chairman Charles Percy was compelled to explain
his differences with it as follows: "I don't think anyone can question
my devotion to Israel. But, like many Israelis and many members of
the American Jewish community, I feel that I have an obligation, when
I disagree with the [Israeli] prime minister, to disagree privately at first,
and, if necessary, publicly."

No senator in Mr. Percy's position has ever had to explain his differences with the French president, the West German chancellor, the
Chinese premier, or the Canadian prime minister in that fashion.

The Taiwanese are considered the second most effective foreign
lobbyists. The survival of their country depends entirely on their good
relationship with the White House and Congress, and they comport
themselves accordingly, spending large sums of money entertaining
congressmen, congressional staffs, and, when possible, treating the press
to tours of their country. One congressional aide was invited to Taiwan
seven times. Three staff members of one senator, none of them with
foreign-relations responsibilities, took free trips to Taiwan. Taiwanese
receptions in Washington are frequent and lavish.

Since the Camp David accords, the Egyptians have developed a
formidable lobby in Washington, lining up behind Israel at the military
aid trough and demanding and receiving a proportionate share. The
Saudi Arabians have massive amounts of petrodollars at their disposal
in the United States but employ them for lobbying on a selective basis,
such as their successful effort to win congressional approval of their
request to buy supersecret AWACS planes from the United States.

The Greeks are one of the most potent lobbying forces in Washington—once a year, when the Turkish military aid bill comes up, congressmen suddenly find Greek constituents everywhere. They have failed
in their goal of imposing another military aid embargo on Turkey, but
they keep trying, relentlessly.

The Japanese annually spend millions trying to buy American goodwill, most of it on publications and advertising, though they are also
known as lavish entertainers. They are not articulate persuaders on
individual issues. Though they tend to be successful in winning their
way on trade matters, they have failed to dampen American demands
for a larger Japanese military role in the Far East.

European embassies in general are considered the most professional and knowledgeable of the Capitol Hill operatives, but also the least demanding. As with the Russians, their principal interest is information.

Except for Kenya, which has been consistently skillful at spending and garnering money in Washington, most African lobbies are viewed as incompetent. However, South Africa is constantly applying pressure to Congress wherever it perceives any possible give and runs one of the largest foreign propaganda operations in the United States.

In addition to arms sales and low-interest, long-term loans for arms sales, the United States in 1983 made outright gifts of $720 million in arms around the world. Turkey came in for $230 million worth of free fighter planes, antitank weapons, communications gear, and protective equipment. Portugal received $60 million to help with its antisubmarine force. Morocco and Tunisia each came in for $50 million in free military equipment. The Sudan was granted $60 million; Somalia, $40 million; Kenya, $23 million: and the former American colony Liberia, run by a murderous sergeant named Doe, $13 million. Costa Rica, which has no army, received $2 million in military aid, and Jamaica received $4 million.

Many foreign nations are fortunate in having members of Congress who will do their work for them gratis as a matter of conviction or principle. The late Henry Jackson was as ardent a champion of Israel in the Senate as that country could have invented. Former Representative Paul Findley was just as vigorous in his support of the Palestinian cause, and paid for it by losing his Illinois congressional seat to a Democrat hugely financed with money from American supporters of Israel. His colleague Edward Derwinski, a fierce anti-Communist, became the principal spokesman for Taiwan and South Korea in his two decades in Congress. He was later made one of the top five powers in the State Department.

Senator Jesse Helms's foreign-policy aide John Carbaugh was accused of trying to sabotage Britain's efforts to move Zimbabwe Rhodesia from white to black rule. Democrat Stephen Solarz worked mightily for the British cause in southern Africa and has labored against American military presence and activity all over the globe.

Foreign powers are very fond of using local hired help, which is always in ample supply, especially after elections. In winning its AWACS deal, Saudi Arabia paid $400,000 for the services of the public-relations firm of Cook, Ruef and Associates and $300,000 to Washington lawyer Frederick Dutton. South Africa has used former Ford and Reagan political advisor Stuart Spencer and Taiwan has had Reagan associate and former speechwriter Peter Hannaford on its public-relations payroll.

Robert Gray, who was Dwight Eisenhower's cabinet secretary, Rosemary Woods's party date during Nixon's Watergate troubles, and cochairman of Reagan's inaugural, has counted Turkey, Venezuela, and Haiti among his well-paying clients. After losing his job as head of National Public Radio, former Robert Kennedy and McGovern aide Frank Mankiewicz signed on with Gray to work as a PR man for Canada. The flamboyant Alejandro Orfila, longtime head of the Organization of American States, was found to have been doing some work for Gray while running the OAS, before becoming Gray's leading partner.

According to Justice Department reports, Japan paid $12 million in fees to American agents in 1980. Israel paid $10 million. That same year, Japan had eighty-two paid agents in the United States. Israel had sixteen.

The United States often gets little help, and sometimes a lot of hindrance, from its friends in trying to curb the spread of nuclear arms in the world, even though the nuclear powers on this planet are rapidly assuming the proportions of a crowd.

More than one hundred nations, including the United States, the USSR, and Britain, signed the 1970 Nuclear Non-Proliferation Treaty, which empowered the United Nations's International Atomic Energy Agency to monitor compliance. France did not sign. France does not consult with any power or organization before deploying its nuclear force, which consists of land-based missiles, missile-firing submarines, and strategic bombers and has the capability of destroying at least thirty major Soviet cities.

In the 1970s, French surface testing of nuclear weapons in the South Pacific so angered Australia and New Zealand that they sent naval vessels to station themselves in test areas. The French kept the intruders from harm's way, but persisted with the testing. French President François Mitterrand supported the deployment of intermediate-range Pershing missiles in Europe in 1983, but a major obstacle to a START agreement that might have obviated the necessity of that deployment was the fact that French (and British) missiles were not included in the arms control negotiations, although the Russian missiles opposed to them were. In 1983, the French had 80 warheads at their disposal. By 1992, estimates are that they will have 592.

Another nonsigner, the People's Republic of China, has four intercontinental nuclear missiles, ten intermediate-range missiles, and fifty short-range nuclear missiles in its arsenal, plus ninety nuclear-capable strategic bombers and three missile submarines. Having declared its nuclear weapons strictly defensive, China has refused the Kremlin's entreaties to join a nuclear freeze movement, saying it would reduce its atomic stockpile only when the United States and the USSR reduced theirs by half.

India, which alarmed the world by exploding a nuclear device in 1974 using plutonium from a peaceful nuclear reactor provided it by Canada, is another nonsigner of the treaty. It still lacks a practical delivery system, but has provoked bitter enemy Pakistan, supported by many Moslem nations, to a crusade to produce the Islamic Bomb.

American intelligence credits Israel and South Africa with the bomb. Brazil has the capability to produce one very quickly and Argentina is close to entering that realm. Saudi Arabia has the resources for a bomb. If the Soviet Union decides to press the issue in response to deployment of American Pershings in Europe, Cuba could shortly become a nuclear power. The drive of Third World nations lacking petroleum and coal resources toward nuclear reactors for electrical power is likely to heighten nuclear weapons tensions still further.

But the problems the United States has with friendly and otherwise neutral nations around the world are often caused by itself. Slipping all too easily into the arrogant role of Ugly American, the United States seems sometimes to be deliberately looking for trouble, even when the detriment to its interests is obvious.

Nowhere has this been more true than in the United Nations, of which the United States was a principal founder and remains a principal bankroller. The United States has a considerable investment in the 158-member world body. When the United Nations was created in 1945 with just 51 members, the United States so dominated its affairs that it was able to allow the Soviet Union three votes in the General Assembly (including the Ukraine's and Byelorussia's) without fear of being compromised.

By 1979, the United States had allowed the United Nations to become so exploited by the Soviet Union and its clients that the ground-floor lobby of the General Assembly building on Manhattan's East Side—through which thousands of tourists pass daily—was given over half to poster displays glorifying the Soviet government and half to others vilifying South Africa. The bulk of the negative votes cast in the United Nations have been against South Africa and Israel, though the Soviet Union has repeatedly been guilty of international crimes and such unspeakable governments as those of Pol Pot in Kampuchea (Cambodia) and Idi Amin in Uganda have largely escaped censure. The

United States has regularly lost important votes in the United Nations's General Assembly, where tiny nations like St. Kitts–Nevis (population, 44,404) have the same vote as the major powers. In the Security Council, the United States has regularly suffered embarrassing defeats.

This treatment has periodically given rise to serious calls for the United States to pull out of the United Nations, which would be the ultimate Ugly American stupidity. If exploited properly, the United Nations can be very useful for American interests. The United Nations has generally performed well in the deployment of peacekeeping forces between belligerents, most notably in the Mideast and Cyprus, in marked contrast to the United States's debacle as a peacekeeping force in Lebanon. Brian Urquart, United Nations undersecretary general for politics and an old veteran at international peacekeeping, might have saved the United States the lives of nearly 300 Marines in Lebanon if the White House had sought and heeded his advice.

In its dealings with the world body, the United States suffers too much from idealism and ideology. Career United States diplomats have repeatedly been driven to the point of tears and resignation by the United Nations's sometimes stubborn refusal to behave according to the hopes and standards the United States dreamed up for it, as its member nations adhere to their own hopes and standards. Ideologues such as Senator Patrick Moynihan and academic Jeane Kirkpatrick were so preoccupied with the verbal abuse taken by the United States in the United Nations they spent much of their careers as U.N. ambassadors engaging in counterharangues. According to one European diplomat, Mrs. Kirkpatrick decried one Security Council vote against her on Nicaragua as "a gang rape."

But, as frequently absurd and as unfriendly as is the conduct of the majority of the United Nations's membership, as bloated, expensive, unresponsive, and generally useless as is the United Nations's 20,000-strong bureaucracy, the institution represents reality. The bare minimum of nationhood in many parts of the world may be a flag, a national anthem, and a U.N. delegation, as a frequent U.N. joke goes, but because of that the United Nations in aggregate represents the real world. Whether the United States remains a member of the United Nations or not, it is the world the United States must deal with, and the United Nations can be a very advantageous place to do that. It is so easy to dismiss most U.N. members as small, irrelevant nations, but it should be remembered that El Salvador and the Sudan are small nations, yet objects of considerable U.S. worry and military investment.

Angered by the limp United Nations action on the 1983 Korean jetliner incident, President Reagan did allow some terse anti-U.N. comments to pass administration lips—including his own—but had to scurry back in defense of the United Nations when a frustrated Senate voted by a large margin to reduce the United States's financial support of the body.

Reagan was responsible for the biggest lost American opportunity to put the United Nations to use for its own military purposes. Work on the U.N.-sponsored Law of the Sea Treaty began during the Eisenhower administration and was a favored project of Henry Kissinger, among other prominent Republicans. It came to fruition under the stewardship of Law of the Sea Ambassador Elliot Richardson, a Republican heavyweight retained for the purpose by the Carter administration.

The treaty's negotiating sessions saw the United Nations functioning almost as intended, with countries acting out of national interest but operating through consensus with an emphasis on pluralism, compromise, and pragmatism. Canada and Cuba, for example, voted against the Soviet Union. Every country gave up something, in return for a workable treaty that otherwise provided for most of its maritime desires.

Placing all the world's oceans and seas under the rule of law—70 percent of the Earth's surface—the treaty served to put aside decades of boundary disputes by establishing twelve-mile sovereign seas and two-hundred-mile maritime economic zones. Most pleasing to the Pentagon was the guarantee of the rights of peaceful passage above, upon, and beneath the waters of all the world's key straits, including the English Channel, Gibraltar, Malacca, and the all-important Strait of Hormuz separating the oil-rich Persian Gulf from the Arabian Sea. Convinced that guarantee was worth at least the ocean fleet of ships that would be necessary to protect American maritime rights without a treaty, the Defense Department was a strong supporter of the treaty's acceptance.

But provisions of the treaty governing deep-seabed mining of manganese, copper, and other valuable minerals, which called for all such mining operations to be placed under the jurisdiction of an international authority with taxing and regulatory power, proved more than the Reagan administration could bear, despite the extremely limited nature of such undertakings and the decades it will take before they become profitable.

Kennecott Copper, U.S. Steel, and other American firms involved in deep-seabed-mining consortiums raised hell with administration friends. Though the Pentagon was strongly supportive of the treaty, James Watt's Interior Department reached through the intergovernmental council involved in American treaty negotiation to sabotage the treaty and ultimately withdraw American support from it. It was one of the most shortsighted and militarily dangerous acts in an administration noted for them.

The overwhelming majority of U.N. membership approved of the treaty negotiating text anyway, and subsequently ratified it. But the absence of the United States and a few other key nations among the ratifiers cast a cloud over the pact not unlike that suffered by the League of Nations when the Senate refused to allow the United States to join it. A few months after the U.S. blowup, Iran made threats to close the Strait of Hormuz and the United States was having to use jet fighters to maintain its right of passage through the Gulf of Sidra off the coast of Libya.

U.S. heavy-handed clumsiness has caused it problems elsewhere. The Canadian peace movement would never have been so successful in harrying cruise-missile testing and limiting Canadian defense expenditures if the Reagan administration hadn't riled Canada's populace by adamantly refusing to take any action on the acid rain American power plants were spewing over the border.

In the face of parliamentary opposition to deployment of cruise missiles on Dutch soil, the Dutch government tried to work out a compromise in which at least some of the missiles would be accepted. Caspar Weinberger compromised the compromise by appearing before the Dutch parliament personally and virtually demanding that the Dutch do as the United States bid.

The United States bitterly angered many European governments by suddenly imposing an embargo on technology and equipment for the Soviet–West European gas pipeline, which had been in the works for several years. Its grain embargo against the Soviets over the Afghanistan invasion resulted in little more than the Soviets turning to Argentina and Canada for grain. The U.S. boycott of the 1980 Olympics was similarly provocative and ineffective.

The United States joined in an eight-nation NATO agreement to build an all-NATO, standard-issue frigate for use in the 1990s, then insisted on conditions that gave the United States major control over the technology involved. It angered many European nations by trying to impose U.S. federal law on European manufacturers and dealers in high-tech equipment. It alarmed West Germany, among other NATO countries, by pressing ahead with the Reagan administration's "Star Wars" militarization-of-space program, which the Europeans saw as dangerously destabilizing, probably unworkable, and, with an ultimate price tag of $500 billion or more, an enormous drain on Western military resources needed to deter the Soviets from conventional attack.

The United States also causes some very real trouble for itself through its export of arms. Since the Korean War, arms sales have been the principal means by which the United States has attempted to buy friendship and exert influence with other countries, but it has in many cases bought trouble instead. As Wolfgang Demisch, while working as a defense analyst for the New York brokerage firm of Morgan, Stanley and Company, put it, "We are selling front-line equipment to beggars and murderers and mendicants," adding the warning that one day one of the United States's client nations is going to use this highly potent weaponry to blackmail the United States in some violent fashion.

The Pentagon claims ample justification for its policy. Large-scale arms sales abroad help keep down the unit price of equipment and weapons bought by the American military and keep defense plants operating at a consistent level of output, even when Congress and the White House are in a down cycle on military spending.

It can also be argued, and always is, that if the U.S. didn't supply armament, someone else would—either France, Italy, or Britain, who do a huge overseas business with weapons, or the Soviet Union, which uses arms transfers to buy alliances and generate trouble.

Between 1976 and 1980, 20 percent of all American arms sales went to Iran, which later, under the Ayatollah Khomeini, waged a long, bloody war with Iraq that still threatens to cut off Persian Gulf oil from the West. Another 14 percent went to Israel, which used them in its destabilizing invasion of Lebanon. Saudi Arabia, Jordan, Egypt, Greece, and Turkey also were among the United States's top twenty customers in that period.

The Soviet Union's top customers during those years were Libya and Syria, each of which accounted for 14 percent of Moscow's arms transfers, and Iraq, which acquired 13 percent of the total. Large Soviet arms shipments were also made to India, Vietnam, Ethiopia, Peru, the two Yemens, and Angola.

In the period 1971–1981, the United States supplied 45 percent of all the major weapons sold to the Third World—in 1980 alone, more than $9 billion in weapons transactions to seventy-two countries. The amount in 1970 was $1.8 billion.

The American weapons included the F-16 superfighter, which the United States sold to Venezuela over the protests of neighboring Guyana; laser-guided smart bombs sold to Oman, a desert sultanate with a population of 930,000 people; M-48 and M-60 tanks and F-5 jet fighters to the Sudan; and A-4 attack bombers and Sidewinder missiles, which both Argentina and Britain bought and used against each other in the Falklands.

By 1980, the U.S. had $5.3 trillion worth of its weapons circulating in the world. The Soviet Union had $3.9 trillion worth in foreign hands.

This occurred despite a policy of restraint exercised by the Carter administration up until the Soviet invasion of Afghanistan. The rate was accelerated by the Reagan administration, which had a deliberate policy of increasing arms sales to the Third World and came into office asking a 40 percent increase in global military assistance.

According to a 1981 United Nations report, the Third World accounted for 75 percent of all arms imports in the preceding decade, with one third of the weapons exports going to just five nations—Saudi Arabia, Jordan, Syria, Iraq, and Iran. Of the 25 million people serving in armed forces around the world, fully 38 percent are in Third World military units, nearly the same as those in NATO and Warsaw Pact militaries, who together account for 40 percent of the total.

The financial strain on these countries, many of whom are billions of dollars in debt to U.S. and other Western banks, is staggering, and often then aggravates social and other problems that get these countries into trouble.

In 1983, as the United States prepared to pour more arms into the world caldron, the National Security Council was keeping track of military conflicts around the world. In this year, certainly viewed by most Americans as a time of peace, death was being threatened or brutally inflicted in the following situations:

● War was continuing to rage between Iran and Iraq. A bitter civil war was being fought in Lebanon. Israel, though withdrawn from much of Lebanon, continued to fight an antiguerrilla war against the Palestinian Liberation Organization and other Arab terrorists. Iran, Iraq, Syria, Pakistan, and Turkey used military force to suppress internal terrorism and rebellion. More than 100,000 Soviet troops waged war against rebel forces in Afghanistan. North and South Yemen continued their war.

● In the Far East, civil war continued in Kampuchea, and border clashes continued between Vietnam and China. Indonesia, the Philippines, Laos, Burma, Thailand, and Malaysia all had troops engaged against internal rebellions and guerrilla campaigns. India was confronted first with a bloody religious conflict between Moslems and Hindus in Assam state and later with a rebellion by northern Sikhs.

● In Central America, the United States supported the government of El Salvador against leftist guerrillas, while also supporting guerrilla forces based in Honduras and Costa Rica who were fighting against the leftist Sandinista regime in Nicaragua. Honduras, Guatemala, Colombia, and Peru were all also involved in warfare against leftist guerrilla groups active within their borders.

• In Africa, the longtime civil war in Chad brought French and Libyan troops against each other in combat. In Namibia, South African soldiers fought black nationalist guerrillas for domination of the disputed territory. Moroccan troops fought Polisario Liberation Front guerrillas in the Western Sahara. The Marxist government of Angola was engaged in combat with three guerrilla armies. Ethiopia continued its twenty-year border war with Somalia in the Ogaden while also fighting Eritrean separatist guerrillas. The Sudan was subjected to Libyan-inspired terrorist and other destabilizing efforts. A number of anti-Communist groups in Mozambique fought to topple the regime there. Bitter tribal and guerrilla wars burned across Zimbabwe and Uganda. South African troops fought antigovernment black nationalist groups within their own country.

• In Europe, Basque separatists continued to terrorize northern Spain, while in Northern Ireland, Irish Republican Army terrorists threatened to confront the British and Irish governments with a European version of the Lebanese civil war.

In nearly all of these conflicts, not a few of them serious threats to American national security and stability, American arms were used, part of the great sea of weaponry with which the West and the Soviet bloc has flooded the world. It cannot, of course, be said that any of these conflicts might not have occurred had they not been fueled by all this weaponry. But the world might be a less anxious place if they were fought with machetes and bolt-action rifles instead of laser bombs and aircraft capable of carrying atomic weapons.

With some twenty to twenty-five countries expected to possess some form of nuclear weapon by the end of the century, the United States simply has to elevate its arms control operations from its too minor status within the State Department apparat to a position more in keeping with its true importance. The awesome importance of arms control transcends mere ideology. It certainly requires leadership of more consequence and stature than that provided by the likes of young Kenneth Adelman. The arms control agency ought to have cabinet status, and ought to have jurisdiction over all conventional arms sales abroad as well. Its director also ought to be a party to National Security Council meetings and other high councils. Arms control may likely prove the most important function of our national defense.

If the United States is to derive the maximum benefit from its alliances, it must stop the absurd and aggravating practice of making California car dealers, failed movie actors, failed congressmen, old pals, and generous campaign contributors United States ambassadors.

Not every ambassador should be a career foreign officer. There should always be opportunities for such gifted individuals as former *New York Times* editorial writer William Shannon, who served as ambassador to Ireland, and former Senate Majority Leader Mike Mansfield, who was such a superb ambassador to Japan. But the preponderance of ambassadors should be diplomatic professionals, and all should be required to meet the highest professional standards.

This principle should especially apply to the United Nations. Slam-bang politicos and shrill lecturers like Daniel Moynihan, Andrew Young, and Jeane Kirkpatrick should never again be put in a position where they can cause such damage to U.S. interests, especially when so much can be accomplished with the appointment of a circumspect professional.

Never again should a few U.S. mining concerns and other special interests be allowed to sabotage an enterprise of such global strategic importance to the United States as the Law of the Sea Treaty. No longer should foreign lobbies and their paid American agents be allowed so powerful a grip on the helm of the American ship of state.

All of America's allies and friends must in thoroughgoing manner be reminded of the realities of America's interests. A Canada that depends on the American military for its national survival should not expect American tolerance of cavils against U.S. strategic weaponry or Latin American policies. A Britain so dependent on the United States cannot be allowed to play huffish Queen Victoria with NATO fleets and important if small American allies like strategically key Iceland. Even a centrist, democratic Argentina should not expect continued American economic and military aid if it pursues what should be in the United States view the international crime of becoming a nuclear power. For once, Congress should stand up and loosen Israel's stranglehold on the American political process.

At the same time, the United States should master the differences between itself and its allies, friends, and neighbors. In the United States, Communists are akin to traitors and criminals. In Europe, Communists serve as members of most parliaments and many governments and are viewed not as evil devils but fairly reasonable human beings. Trade with the Soviet Union is often considered irrelevant if not dangerous by many Americans (though not farmers), or at least, American presidents. Europeans see their trade with Russia as highly important, for political and military as well as economic reasons. The United States must learn it can't make all its allies think as it does.

In pressing for greater allied contributions toward European defense, the United States should recognize that its own conventional force there is seriously lacking and that its European allies, for all their faults, still provide 90 percent of the ground forces, 80 percent of the combat aircraft, 80 percent of the tanks, and 70 percent of the warships arrayed against the Soviets, however inadequately.

The operative word is "reality." Whatever principle or purpose drives them, American relationships must be firmly grounded in the real. It must learn to enter every association and situation with its eyes wide open—lest its friends, and its own recklessness and naïveté, do it in.

chapter twenty

SPOOKS

> *It must be evident to every one that it is more praiseworthy for a prince always to maintain good faith, and practice integrity rather than craft and deceit. And yet the experience of our own times has shown that those princes have achieved great things who made small account of good faith, and who understood by cunning to circumvent the intelligence of others; and that in the end they got the better of those whose actions were dictated by loyalty and good faith.*
> —NICCOLÒ MACHIAVELLI, *THE PRINCE*

In an era when war is called peace, when jungle guerrilla conflicts carry the potential for superpower confrontation, when the expenditure of hundreds of billions of dollars turns on often questionable assessments of Soviet intentions and strength, and when serious mistakes risk global devastation, no aspect of American defense is more important than intelligence—most particularly, the Central Intelligence Agency.

Yet no component of the defense establishment has been more abused, misused, misled, misunderstood, corrupted, and compromised by the flaws of the American system. From its creation in 1947 until Eisenhower left office in January 1961, the CIA was consistently effective and often performed brilliantly, its agents and analysts serving as the United States's front-line troops in the darkest days of the Cold War. In the generation that followed, it suffered failure after failure, sometimes through its own fault but more frequently because of the appalling ways in which it was misdirected, or worse, in which it was ignored.

Nowhere was this more evident than in Vietnam.

The calamitous 1961 Bay of Pigs invasion was a CIA operation in which President Kennedy largely followed plans inherited from the Eisenhower administration. He made, of course, one key change. Wishing to keep overt American involvement to a minimum, Kennedy decided to withhold air cover from the landing. As a consequence, he handed himself a tactical disaster, with his free Cuban invaders left pinned down and later mowed down on the beach. Though he publicly and manfully took the blame himself, internally he sought a scapegoat and treated the CIA to withering scorn. The agency's longtime and much respected director, Allen Dulles, subsequently lost his job. After that, agency advice and intelligence often received a frosty welcome in the Oval Office. Possibly, Kennedy might even have given thought to junking or recasting the agency, but with American involvement in Vietnam deepening, he didn't dare.

In July 1963 the Kennedy White House was informed by the CIA station in Saigon that the Vietnamese military was preparing a coup against President Ngo Dinh Diem and his brother, Ngo Dinh Nhu. Kennedy, the nation's first Catholic president, had for months been attacked in *The New York Times* and elsewhere for supporting a Catholic Vietnamese regime so repressive against the Buddhist majority that Buddhist monks had taken to setting themselves on fire as a public protest. Here seemed an opportunity to deal with that political problem for good.

A week later, a CIA report said any successor government to Diem's "might be initially less effective against the Viet Cong, but, given continued support from the U.S., could provide reasonably effective leadership for the government and the war effort."

On August 22, 1963, newly appointed Ambassador Henry Cabot Lodge arrived in Vietnam. Keeping the White House informed of the progress of coup preparations, he urged American support for it and finally, in an August 29, 1963, cable, stated, "There is no turning back because there is no possibility, in my view, that the war can be won under a Diem administration."

A few days later, Lodge cabled his despair that the Vietnamese generals would be able to succeed with a coup. High-ranking State Department officials W. Averell Harriman and Roger Hilsman were opposed to Diem and his brother and pressed for their removal. CIA Director John McCone, who was informed of coup preparations sometime after Kennedy was, raised objections to any such overthrow effort, but given the agency's poor standing in the White House, did not make a major issue of it.

According to Kennedy apologists, by October the President had grown nervous about the coup. Finally informed of it, the American commander in Saigon, General Paul Harkins, had vehemently argued against the move. On October 25, Kennedy sent a message to the Saigon embassy, saying, "while . . . we should not be in position of thwarting coup, we would like to have option of judging and warning on any plan with poor prospects of success." But there was no official word from the White House to call a halt to it. In contact with the CIA, who remained in contact with the White House, the Vietnamese generals made their move on November 1, 1963. Diem and his brother were shot to death the next morning, a fate Kennedy would himself share three weeks later. Diem's notorious sister-in-law, Madame Nhu, fled to exile in Paris.

For all its miseries, Diem's was the last stable government South Vietnam would have until the Communists took over at gunpoint in 1975. Starting in January 1964, when Diem's assassins were in turn overthrown by other generals, coup followed coup. Of a succession of generalissimos and presidents, only Air Marshal Nguyen Cao Ky, who acknowledged he was essentially a pilot with no talent for government, attempted to deal firmly with the black marketeers and corruption that eventually rotted the country from within. He ultimately ended up Number 2 in a largely powerless and exceedingly corrupt government led by Nguyen Van Thieu and maintained only with American money and armed might.

But the worst effects of the coup were military—and immediate. Before the coup, the Vietnamese army controlled most of the country during daylight hours and much of it at night, when the Viet Cong were most active. The United States had fewer than 20,000 troops in the country, most of them in advisory and support roles, with only a few Special Forces units actively engaged in counterinsurgency combat. It had sustained just 47 combat fatalities.

After the coup and collapse of effective government, the Viet Cong overran the country, taking permanent control of some 40 percent of it and assuming tactical control of many other large sections of Vietnam during the night. Ho Chi Minh, astutely recognizing the inherent weaknesses of post-Diem South Vietnamese regimes, began providing the Viet Cong with ever more massive North Vietnamese support. A little more than a year later, the military situation had deteriorated to the point where the United States could not rely on Vietnamese forces to protect even the three coastal-region air bases the U.S. was using. To shore up defenses, 3,500 Marines were landed at Da Nang on March 18, 1965. By summer, there were 72,000 American troops in Vietnam. By the end of the year, there were 200,000. Troop strength ultimately would reach 525,000. Over the years, a total of 8.7 million American men and women would eventually serve in the Southeast Asian war, and 57,702 of them would lose their lives from battle and other causes.

According to one CIA colonel, Diem's government was secretly negotiating with Ho Chi Minh at the time of his assassination. Whether this might have succeeded is a matter for historians' conjecture.

The CIA was certainly correct in its reports on the Vietnamese army's disloyalty to Diem and plots against him. It was wrong in stating that a successor regime could still provide "reasonably effective leadership." Kennedy was wrong in acting on that assessment, but he was wronger still in ignoring the CIA's warning about the help the coup would be to the Viet Cong and in disregarding McCone's objections to it.

The CIA was effective enough running its private little war in Laos, conducting covert missions throughout Southeast Asia, and keeping tabs on the South Vietnamese government—perhaps too effective in keeping tabs on the Diem regime. But in one of its most important missions, assessing the strength of the enemy, it failed miserably, not because it didn't perform well, but because it could not convince the American military command of the accuracy of its figures.

The Army was contemptuous of the CIA for a number of reasons, but principally because it was a *civilian* agency unlearned in the military theology. The enemy order of battle, its troop strength, and other details were supposedly too complex and military a matter for the mere civilian mind to comprehend.

"We told them that a fight at Khe Sanh would be disastrous," said one high-ranking CIA official, who took an early retirement in large part out of frustration in dealing with the military during Vietnam. "They ignored us. Khe Sanh was a disaster."

By the spring of 1967, the Pentagon's hard estimate of the enemy's combat strength was about 270,000, including both North Vietnamese regulars and Viet Cong guerrillas. Estimates on enemy desertions were 100,000 a year and casualties were put at 150,000. At that rate, as an encouraged White House believed, victory would be along shortly.

But the CIA's enemy troop strength estimate was closer to 600,000, a figure more alarming than encouraging. Lower-echelon agency officials tried repeatedly to convince the White House and military command of this, to no avail. Finally, the agency's top leadership reluctantly decided to go along with everyone else—along, and over the cliff. The 270,000 figure was still the official order of battle estimate when the enemy unleashed its vicious Tet offensive in 1968.

Until the creation of the CIA and its more military forerunner, the World War II Office of Strategic Services, American intelligence through most of its history had been circumscribed and amateurish. Prior to and during the Mexican War, President Polk employed private spies paid out of White House contingency funds. Lincoln and his generals relied on cavalry patrols and balloon observers, but also on Pinkerton private detectives. After World War I, Japan, a nominal ally, returned a copy it had obtained of the United States's top secret code—a copy it no doubt copied—bound in a pretty ribbon. For a time, State Department analysts continued to monitor other nations' communications, but the practice was abandoned in 1929 by the Hoover administration with a harrumphing "Gentlemen don't read other gentlemen's mail."

World War II prompted more serious attitudes and the creation of the Office of Strategic Services (OSS), headed by the colorful General William "Wild Bill" Donovan. At the height of its operations in 1944, it had spy bases in London, Dublin, Stockholm, Helsinki, Moscow, Istanbul, Izmir, Ankara, Cyprus, Beirut, Cairo, Naples, Tunis, Algiers, Sardinia, Corsica, Tangier, Gibraltar, Lisbon, Madrid, and Bern. It was not able to penetrate Japan with any agents and had only a few in Germany itself, those under the control of a New York lawyer named William J. Casey, who subsequently became Reagan's intelligence director. The OSS was particularly effective in Greece, Switzerland, and France—it was an OSS unit that talked the Nazi commander of Cherbourg into surrendering, for example. The swiftness of the American advance across Germany prevented Casey's team from carrying out a bizarre plot to kidnap Hitler.

The OSS dealt mostly with low-level intelligence, and was once guilty of unknowingly passing all the way up to Roosevelt faked reports that the Japanese were extending peace feelers. The chief allied intelligence successes of the war were cracking the Japanese and German codes, and keeping the fact that they had done so secret for the duration of hostilities.

President Truman had no wish to keep Donovan and his swashbucklers on after the war, but saw a need for a strong civilian postwar intelligence agency. The National Security Act of 1947, which created the Defense Department, also gave birth to the Central Intelligence Agency and the post of director of central intelligence, which had jurisdiction over the CIA and much of the work done by the rest of what came to be called the "intelligence community."

The community consists of four major parts. The best known is the CIA, which specializes in HUMINT (for Human Intelligence, or spies), as well as scientific research, political analysis, evaluation, research and development, economic research, and other activities. The exact number of personnel employed by the CIA and its annual budget are among the most closely guarded secrets the nation has, though Thomas Bethell of the *Washington Monthly* put personnel at fifteen thousand and the budget is believed to be at least $15 billion. According to Admiral Bobby Ray Inman, former director of the National Security Agency and deputy director of the CIA, the agency in 1982 was only about 40 percent as big as it was in the Cold War days prior to the Vietnam War.

Even less is known about the National Security Agency (NSA), created by a secret order of President Truman's in 1952, except that its staff is believed to be much larger than the CIA's, with at least 3,500 holding top secret clearance. Headquartered in a huge underground complex at Fort Meade, Maryland, about midway between Washington and Baltimore, the NSA is essentially the computer-driven facility that deals with SIGINT (for Signals Intelligence, or electronic eavesdropping) and other top secret operations of ELINT (for Electronic Intelligence). It maintains more than two thousand listening posts around the world. Its computers scan literally hundreds of thousands of radio, telephone, telex, and other communications constantly. Though technically a part of the Defense Department, the NSA operates completely without congressional restriction and has been empowered by the federal courts to eavesdrop on American citizens if it deems this in the interest of national security.

In many respects, the NSA is the actual Big Brother that so many critics have accused the CIA of being. With their principal duty that of code-breaking and surveillance of global communications, NSA staff spend much of their time intercepting telephone traffic, radio messages, television broadcasts, and other communications between and within potentially unfriendly capitals, embassies, military installations, and other facilities. Its computers' great value, aside from decoding secret messages, is in their ability to constantly scan millions of words transmitted around the world for key passages that could bear on American security.

While NSA director, Admiral Inman was compelled to reveal the scope of NSA's capability during a little-noticed byplay of the 1980 Senate investigation into allegations that President Carter's brother Billy illegally accepted bribes from Libya. Inman testified that the NSA had learned about the Libyan affair because its computer monitors had picked up such flag words as "Jimmy Carter," "White House," etc., during routine message interception.

By 1984, the technology for screening tape recordings of telephone calls for key words and phrases had advanced to the stage where companies like Texas Instruments and Atari were selling to home computer users voice synthesizers capable of recognizing—and reproducing—individual spoken words. More sophisticated versions of such devices promised to simplify greatly the work of hundreds of federal agents in the FBI, CIA, Drug Enforcement Administration, and other units, who otherwise would have to review thousands of hours of conversations recorded daily with legal court-ordered wiretaps.

The American public became dramatically aware of the NSA's worldwide eavesdropping network when the Soviets shot down the Korean jetliner north of Japan in 1983. In his bitter statement condemning the attack the following morning, Secretary of State Shultz revealed that the United States had such a capability by telling reporters that American intelligence knew that the Russians had tracked the Korean 747 for two and a half hours. In accompanying remarks to the press, Richard Burt, assistant secretary of state for European affairs, was able to say without hesitation that "the pilot was in constant communication with his ground control, describing and discussing a sequence of movements he was taking to engage, including the arming and firing of the missile."

A transcript and later a recording of the Soviet pilot's conversations with his ground control followed. Within two days, it was known that the United States operated, with the Japanese, a huge Communications Security Group intelligence listening post in northern Hokkaido, which could track and listen to any Russian plane in the area. Using the NSA's elaborate satellite network, it was possible for the White House to listen in on Soviet aircraft transmissions from Washington, 10,000 miles away.

Admiral Inman, interviewed on ABC's *Nightline,* was not alarmed at the disclosure and seemed to view it as useful as a deterrent to Soviet mischief. The use the Reagan administration was able to make of the apparent atrocity as a rhetorical weapon against the Soviets also seemed to justify the publicity the eavesdropping network received.

But the propaganda use the Reagan White House tried to make of the incident in many ways backfired. In strident bombast from Reagan and other administration principals, not to speak of Radio Free Europe and the Voice of America (which have 100 million listeners, including 21 million in the Soviet Union), the White House accused the Soviets of knowingly shooting down a civilian jet without provocation and without warning.

Within a few days, it was compelled to admit that there had been an American spy plane operating in the area that night on a course that intersected that of the Korean jetliner. In another correction, it acknowledged that the Soviet fighter had fired warning shots, which apparently were ignored. Ultimately, it had to concede that the Soviets might not have known they were firing upon a civilian plane with innocent passengers aboard. Polls taken after the incident showed that a majority of Americans harbored doubts about the White House version of events.

Did the much-vaunted NSA listening system fail? The NSA computer that picked up the Soviet radio transmission was able to alert a human being—in this case, a Japanese technician—but the recorded dialogue had to be translated from Russian into Japanese, and then from Japanese into English, and then from pilots' jargon to more comprehensible terminology.

Though the CIA is deeply involved in undercover aerial spy missions, much of the product for PHOTINT (for Photo Intelligence) and imagery services comes from the third section—the Defense Intelligence Agency (DIA) and the separate intelligence units of the Air Force, Army, and Navy. DIA is, of course, not limited to PHOTINT, and is in fact becoming a Pentagon approximation of the CIA, complete with its own shiny new Washington headquarters. Reagan gave it field agents for the first time and a principal role in his "strike first" antiterrorism strike force.

The famous U-2 spy planes of the 1950s and 1960s have been replaced by faster and higher-flying SR-71s. A network of computer-linked geo-synchronous satellites, heat-sensing, light-sensing, and photographic, keep the high command informed of suspected military activities any-where on the planet. The Navy is pursuing space programs concerned with navigation aid and naval reconnaissance. The Army fields covert teams for secret operations, though few so public as its failed Desert One hostage rescue mission in 1980.

The fourth element, the State Department's Bureau of Intelligence and Research, concentrates mostly on analysis and works closely with the CIA, many of whose agents are based in American embassies around the world, to coordinate intelligence gathering with American foreign-policy directives and objectives.

Another player in the American spy network is the Treasury De-partment, which concentrates on gathering economic data and which also operates the elite Secret Service. The Department of Energy per-forms a more minor role, mostly working with the State Department on evaluations of foreign and domestic energy resources and needs.

The FBI is the principal counterintelligence unit operating within the United States, though the CIA and NSA also perform this function. According to reports from the Senate Intelligence Committee, the NSA had twelve hundred Americans under surveillance between 1967 and 1973—with the CIA, DIA, and FBI choosing the targets, mostly be-cause of political activities. The practice was allegedly halted after Con-gress got wind of it.

With narcotics smuggling considered both a threat to national se-curity and a cover for enemy espionage operations, the Drug Enforce-ment Administration functions as a part of the intelligence community.

The community is theoretically, at least, under the direct supervision of the National Security Council. Reporting to this panel is a special coordinating committee chaired by the national security advisor and including the secretary of state, the deputy secretary of defense or the deputy central intelligence director (depending on the issue), and the Joint Chiefs of Staff.

Because of flagrant abuses stemming to a large degree from the paranoia of the Johnson and Nixon administrations, both Presidents Ford and Carter established and expanded watchdog systems for supervising the intelligence community, leading to the creation of an Intelligence Oversight Board, which consists of three private citizens appointed by the president. Their function is to receive reports from internal inspectors general and intelligence counsels on community activities, and in return report questionable ones to the attorney general.

The intelligence community's record has been as varied as the 1948 National Security Council directive authorizing "covert" activities:

> Propaganda; economic warfare; preventive direct action, including sabotage, anti-sabotage, demolition, and evacuation measures; subversion against hostile states, including assistance to underground resistance groups; and support of indigenous anti-Communist elements in the threatened countries of the free world.

In 1953, the CIA was effective in restoring Mohammed Reza Pahlavi, the last shah, to power in Iran, overthrowing the anti-Western Mohammed Mossadegh. In 1954, a CIA operation helped topple the regime of Guatemala's pro-Communist president, Jacobo Arbenz Guzmán, which was replaced by powers friendly enough to the United States to allow their country to be used as a staging area for the Bay of Pigs invasion of 1961.

The Truman White House was extremely pleased with the CIA for its successful efforts to keep Communists from power in Italy in the 1940s, a victory that kept the CIA in large-scale business for decades after.

Eisenhower was delighted with the quality of PHOTINT during his presidency, especially the huge blowups of Russian military installations brought to his office. He was not so pleased when U-2 pilot Gary Powers was shot down in 1960, prompting Ike to first lie about and then confess the nature of Powers's mission.

The American intelligence community has proved very accurate in assessing the strength and intentions of African insurgency movements like the African National Conference guerrilla army operating against the government of South Africa.

In 1982, a CIA NIE (National Intelligence Estimate) provided evidence of widespread Soviet military use of chemical weapons in Afghanistan, Laos, and Cambodia, though some experts argued they had found not chemicals but traces of bee excrement.

The same CIA in 1977 predicted that the Soviet Union would shortly go from oil exporter to oil importer, with the Soviet bloc of nations having to buy 3.5 million barrels of imported oil a day by 1985. Yet, in 1983, the Soviets were selling more than one million barrels of oil a day at cheap prices on the open market. Its prediction of a 34-million-barrels-a-day world demand for OPEC oil by 1980 was off by 20 percent.

In 1983, the CIA released findings casting doubt on its own prediction six years earlier that the Soviet Union would be increasing its military spending at the rate of 3 to 4 percent, settling on 2 percent as a more reliable figure. Predictably, the DIA vigorously disagreed. One of the Pentagon's lesser known flaws is that the military greatly relies on American defense contractors for assessment of Soviet weapons capability and probable cost. That these firms would have incentive to exaggerate Soviet spending estimates as much as possible is blithely dismissed. "If you want to take a look at Soviet engine development," one Air Force spokesman explained, "then it makes sense to contract with Pratt and Whitney or General Electric."

A particularly embarrassing agency bumble involved the death of long-ailing Soviet leader Yuri Andropov in early 1984. None of the CIA's field agents in Moscow reported anything amiss (the State Department went out of its way to shoot down such rumors). Even the CIA's Foreign Broadcast Information Service in Rosslyn, Virginia, which monitors foreign radio broadcasts from all over the world, failed to notice anything unusual. But the *Washingt ~ Post*'s Moscow correspondent noted that Moscow radio had switched to somber classical music, as it had when Leonid Brezhnev died in 1982. Investigating further and observing unusual activity in key Soviet government offices, he reported what American intelligence had not—Andropov was likely dead.

The CIA performed perfectly in making a detailed assessment of the threat posed by Soviet rocketry in the 1962 Cuban missile crisis, allowing Kennedy to act and speak with an authority he had not hitherto enjoyed. But for much of the 1960s, its army of more than three thousand anti-Castro Cubans based in Miami, run by six hundred CIA case officers, accomplished little more than the expenditure of vast amounts of federal money and assassinations of each other. It was in this post-Dulles era that CIA covert-action people were urging the use of such Inspector Clouseau methodology as exploding seashells, poisoned cigars, and beard-removing depilatories to undo Castro.

This was followed by the period in which former CIA operatives Howard Hunt (a Bay of Pigs veteran), G. Gordon Liddy, and James McCord turned up as center-ring clowns in the Watergate circus—Hunt at one point disguising himself in a red wig borrowed from the agency to interview Dita Beard, a lobbyist for ITT, then involved in a campaign contribution scandal, in her hospital room.

Not all CIA operatives are so amusing. Just as the agency must constantly watch for turncoats and double agents in its ranks, it must also cope with those who become free-lancers on the side or outright rogues. The agency functions as a major gunrunner to pro-Western guerrilla forces in many parts of the world, notably the Afghan rebels whom it keeps equipped with Russian and Chinese automatic rifles. The tidy profits to be made from gunrunning for purposes other than flag and country occasionally corrupt American agents—notoriously so in the case of rogue agents Frank Terpil and Edwin Wilson, who went into business for themselves supplying homicidal tyrants Muammar Qaddafi and former Uganda strongman Idi Amin with guns, assassination plots, advice, and other professional niceties. Wilson, who joined the CIA in 1955 as a $70-a-week security guard and was making $20,800 a year as an agent when he was fired from the agency in 1971, became the master of a 2,500-acre estate in the Virginia horse country bordering the farm of Senator John Warner and then-wife Elizabeth Taylor. According to one report, he made some $21.8 million for his services to Libya alone. He was arrested in a government trap in 1982 and is now serving a thirty-two-year sentence for illegally shipping explosives.

Kevin Mulcahy, a former CIA staffer who was a key witness against Wilson and had told federal authorities he had worked for Wilson and Terpil when they were establishing a training camp for Libyan terrorists, was found dead in October 1982, his body lying against the door of a tourist cabin he had rented under mysterious circumstances in Virginia's Blue Ridge Mountains. His death was attributed to "exposure." Waldo Duberstein, an associate of Wilson's and a former CIA analyst with expertise in the Mideast, also died that year from a shotgun blast to the head—attributed to suicide.

Terpil, who paid cash for an elegant home across the road from Ethel Kennedy's Hickory Hill estate in McLean, Virginia, was charged with some of the same crimes as Wilson but remained at large, and was believed to be still operating from Libya. The CIA continues to worry about the surprising number of former agency and military personnel found to have worked for Terpil and Wilson, and about how far inside the agency the two may have penetrated with their enterprises.

Having been handed the files and personnel of the German Gehlen spy network after World War II, along with General Gehlen himself and a treasure trove of information on Soviet agents operating in Europe under the nose of the Allied command, the CIA has long been obsessed with the idea of Russian moles working at the highest levels of the American intelligence community. James Angleton, the spooky, longtime counterintelligence chief who dressed like an undertaker and lunched at a French restaurant featuring waiters on roller skates, was so possessed by this notion that his enemies in American government began circulating the rumor that *he* was the mole. His fixation was sometimes so disruptive that colleagues felt that, if he wasn't the mole, he might as well have been.

At all events, Angleton was much more successful at suppressing Soviet burrowing into his intelligence establishment than his British counterparts, who suffered from an old school, old-boy network of upper-class and often homosexual gentlemen spies in the pay of Moscow (one of them the Queen's own art collector) who have long been a major worry of the agency's.

The CIA uses homosexuals—and anyone else it needs—if necessary, but refuses to hire them as employees and fires those who are found in the closet. In 1982, it dismissed an electronic technician involved in undercover work for this reason and got hit with an American Civil Liberties Union suit as a result. The suit, however, identified the technician only as "John Doe" and the legal proceedings went forth in secret.

The agency has returned to employing journalists, a practice outlawed by then–Central Intelligence Director George Bush in 1976 but restored by successor Casey in 1982. In response to a lawsuit filed under the Freedom of Information Act, Casey was compelled to admit that the organization was using reporters as intelligence agents to recruit local sources, suppress unfavorable news stories, and act as case officers supervising other agents, buying equipment for agents, and distributing their pay. It is a widespread practice. A significant part of the British correspondent corps is believed to be spies. Though they actively work as journalists, frequently filing stories about oppression of American blacks, the thirty-six Soviet correspondents allowed in the United States are considered spies or as good as spies. The CIA will not reveal its estimate of the number of KGB agents among the 1,125 Soviet officials stationed in the United States, but at least 200 of the 411 in Washington are believed to be KGB. The Soviet mission at the United Nations in New York is believed to employ many more.

The CIA operates much differently than the KGB—at least inside the United States. Huge green highway direction signs proclaiming CIA in enormous letters can be found on access roads to its Langley head-quarters in suburban northern Virginia. Though security guards occasionally confiscate film from passengers who chance to snap photographs, public transit buses pull into the complex to board or discharge CIA employees. The agency itself operates a shuttle service of little blue unmarked school buses to transport personnel to and from the Pentagon, White House, Executive Office Building, and other important points in Washington. When the agency wanted to build an annex to its headquarters, it held public hearings to accommodate nearby residents angry over the traffic problems it would generate.

In recent years, the CIA has come to favor using business fronts rather than diplomatic cover for its many operations. These have ranged from the airlines it ran in Southeast Asia during the Vietnam War to Miami boatyards to nondescript export-import firms all over the globe. It finances or has infiltrated a number of internationalist foundations and student associations and is active on American college campuses with recruiting and counterintelligence activities. The federal courts, in response to student Freedom of Information Act suits, have upheld the right of the CIA to neither confirm or deny whether it had operations of this sort on some one hundred campuses.

The CIA and its allied intelligence services own or rent a vast wealth of real estate, ranging from overseas spy stations and luxury high-rise office complexes in Manhattan to topless bars in Washington and an array of safe houses in the Washington suburbs. One, a sixty-two-acre estate with mansion, four-car garage, and outbuildings on Maryland's Eastern Shore, had been used to domicile Soviet double agents, German scientists, Eastern European defectors, and returned U-2 spy plane pilot Gary Powers. Worth at least $1 million, it was put up for sale by the General Services Administration in 1976, but by 1982 had attracted no serious bid higher than $236,600. Perhaps it was the strange noises at night.

As a glance at the stream of Volkswagens and station wagons disgorged by Langley at quitting time will attest, most CIA employees seem fairly typical Washington bureaucrats and civil servants. The agency often recruits in much the same open manner as the military on college campuses, especially graduate schools. Even when filling vacancies in its "dirty tricks" section, the agency has made use of New York advertising agencies and small advertisements in *The New York Times* and other prominent newspapers seeking "special men and women who still have a spirit of adventure" interested in a position requiring them to "withstand hardship, make on-the-spot decisions," and "escape from routine."

Much of the work is routine, however. Photo analysis requires endless hours of hard staring at initially meaningless images. When the CIA proudly presented President Kennedy with its best photographic evidence of Soviet missiles in Cuba in 1962, Kennedy was at once immensely pleased and confused. Looking at the photographs, he couldn't see the missiles. A military intelligence photo interpreter during the Korean War inadvertently caused the bombing of a number of defenseless Korean cemeteries, having mistaken the rounded tombstones and the shadows they threw for mortar emplacements.

Nixon once angrily denounced the CIA as "forty thousand people over there [in Virginia] reading newspapers." The personnel figures were substantially off, but the job description was not. The CIA takes a look at nearly everything published in the world that could possibly be of significance, not to speak of all the mail it opens.

Thousands of other CIA people abroad operate the agency's Foreign Broadcast Information Service, which monitors to the fullest extent possible the myriad radio and television broadcasts of the world, distilling from them its own version of the world news and disseminating the product to an elite network of American government subscribers over its own twenty-four-hour wire service. Recently, the "news" in one of these detailed reports was that a Chinese peasant walking a water buffalo near the Vietnamese border came within three meters of being hit by a Vietnamese bullet.

The intelligence community has long been in the business of diagnosing ailments of world leaders, with particular obsessive attention to every wart and tic of the Soviet Politburo. According to columnist Jack Anderson, the CIA went to elaborate lengths to obtain and examine Nikita Khrushchev's excrement during his 1959 visit to the United States.

It has long been believed in Washington—though never proved—that American intelligence operatives routinely examine such evidence from heads of state quartered in Blair House and other official hostelries. In 1981, then–*Washington Post* columnist Diana McClellan printed an item suggesting that outgoing President Carter and his wife had access to electronic eavesdropping reports on incoming President Reagan and his wife at their transition residence across Pennsylvania Avenue and were angry at learning that Mrs. Reagan wanted them out of the White House early so she could move ahead with extensive redecorating. Carter threatened the *Post* with legal action and, with some uncomfortable embarrassment, the item was eventually retracted—though many Washingtonians still believed McClellan.

Intelligence work can offer as comfy a future as any of the procurement elite of the Pentagon can anticipate. Former CIA Deputy Director

Bobby Inman, seeking the wherewithal to provide his children with the best possible education, stepped down and up to become a major force in one of the best-heeled computer enterprises in the country. Ray S. Cline, another former deputy director, is a wealthy "political risk" consultant to private industry and has included among his clients General Dynamics and the Morgan Guaranty Trust Company. Former central intelligence directors William Colby and Richard Helms have performed similar consulting work.

The CIA is not keen on extracurricular literary efforts by its personnel, as some brutally resolute court cases attest. As late as 1984, former CIA Director Stansfield Turner was trying unsuccessfully to get the CIA publications board to approve the contents of a book manuscript he had written. As one CIA official put it, "He wants to publish secrets!" Still, at least three former CIA agents have become successful, nationally syndicated newspaper columnists, one of them the ubiquitous William F. Buckley.

But the agent's life is not essentially blissful. Because of the extraordinary strains placed on spouses, as well as employees, intelligence personnel have one of the highest divorce rates in the federal government—so much so that bipartisan legislation has been proposed to provide special compensation and a share of pension and other benefits to divorced spouses as payment for their ordeals.

The CIA maintains its own staff of psychiatrists and makes frequent use of private mental-health facilities to deal with recurring staff problems of paranoia, depression, loss of self-identity, marital discord, alcoholism, and drug abuse. It provides counseling services for agency families and includes wives—and husbands—in many agent-training programs.

For more than twenty years, the intelligence community—most particularly the CIA—was in a period of decline—a decline that has only recently been reversed. Admiral Inman dates it from 1964, rather than from the Bay of Pigs, when he claims the Johnson administration decided to help finance the Vietnam War by cutting expenditures for American electronic intelligence equipment and activities. This period also saw a diversion of intelligence gathering efforts from the world at large to the Vietnam effort and the beginnings of substantial cutbacks in staff and global operations. In a speech to nuclear scientists in Illinois in 1982, Inman said that covert operations personnel were reduced by 92 percent between 1964 and 1978.

Furious over apparent CIA involvement in the Watergate scandal and such unpopular covert operations as the bloody overthrow of Chilean Marxist Salvador Allende, a powerful Democratic-controlled Congress dealt some more body blows to the American intelligence community throughout the 1970s. A Senate committee chaired by then-Senator Frank Church and a similar House unit conducted a two-year investigation into CIA activities that found that political assassinations may have been carried out without White House knowledge; the committees initiated successful efforts to put intelligence activities on a congressional leash.

The Senate Select Committee on Intelligence was created as part of this, along with a House counterpart. Its substantial oversight powers ultimately required the CIA to report covert operations within twenty-four hours of their commencement, yield to a case-by-case congressional budgetary review of how covert operation money was spent, and otherwise submit to congressional authority. In short time, the intelligence community found itself having to report to no fewer than eight congressional committees, not all of which were exactly leak-proof. By the Reagan administration, the oversight group was cut back to two committees, but the damage had already been done and some bad congressional habits had taken hold.

The intelligence oversight committees were exempted from House and Senate seniority rules and assignment to them was to be tightly controlled by party leadership to keep indiscreet grandstanders and other unreliable members from having access to the nation's top secrets.

But by 1983 a Republican Senate staffer with top security clearance was complaining that he was receiving telephone calls from a cable-television reporter asking "What happened in the Intelligence Committee today?"

He said he replied "I can't tell you," but received the response "What do you mean? I was told in the House . . ."

The "secret" American-sponsored guerrilla war against the Sandinista regime in Nicaragua was first made public when members of the House oversight committee announced a "secret" resolution that had forbidden secret wars against the Nicaraguans. A House subcommittee in 1982 engaged in a public tussle with the CIA, involving the presence of armed CIA guards at the hearing room, over documents revealing the extent of Saudi Arabian investments in the United States.

In an interview with *The New York Times* in 1983, Senator Malcolm Wallop made this observation:

> There are limits and that's what the oversight function is about. My feeling is that this whole world of oversight is fraught with far fewer abuses than it is with incompetence. Most of intelligence is what you determine from the information you gather. The biggest abuse was the underestimation of the Soviet threat during the 60s

and 70s, which caused us to spend billions of dollars on things we didn't need and not to spend other billions on things that we did need.

In terms of its past strengths and freedoms, the intelligence community was also badly damaged by the election of Jimmy Carter. He decreased spending on technological intelligence collection from an unknown but substantially higher figure to $1 billion a year. He cancelled production of a much needed high-resolution satellite photographic system and reduced the CIA and allied agencies to one satellite launch a year, which they claimed drastically reduced their space-reconnaissance capabilities. He reduced covert operations to two or three a year, compared with twelve to fourteen under the successor Reagan administration.

But his most devastating act was to appoint his Annapolis classmate, Admiral Stansfield Turner, director of central intelligence, compounding an unfortunate trend that had begun with the ouster of Allen Dulles after the Bay of Pigs fiasco. One of Dulles's successors, Richard Helms, later ambassador to the Iran of the Shah, was a professional, but caved in to the Pentagon in the Vietnam order of battle dispute and allowed his agency to be misused by Richard Nixon's Watergate White House. Among those who followed—William Colby, George Bush, Turner, and William Casey—only Bush, an amateur, won the lasting respect of the agency professionals. Turner won undying enmity in many quarters.

Though a highly regarded naval officer, Turner nevertheless managed to reduce CIA morale—and, many say, effectiveness—to an all-time low. In what was billed as a reforming and efficiency-improving housecleaning, Turner with full White House approval reduced undercover operatives, numbering many thousands in the 1960s, to only about three hundred. Some eight hundred high-ranking CIA officials and veteran agents were fired, retired, or reassigned. A short while later, another three hundred staffers—including William Christison, chief of political analysis; Vincent Heyman, chief of the operations center; Sayre Stevens, deputy director of the National Foreign Assessment Center; and much of the agency's intellectual cadre—resigned.

Many of those ousted were old-guard, Eastern establishment, Ivy League types who had dominated American intelligence as a "gentleman's profession" since the 1940s. Their departure made way for a more contemporary, short-haired Pentagon-style generation to assume positions of authority. But, overall, the agency was shell-shocked.

Turner was the seventh military officer of the thirteen men to serve as Central Intelligence director since the office was created. George Bush, an upper-class Easterner turned Texas congressman who carried water for the Nixon and Ford administrations as a failed senatorial candidate, United Nations ambassador, and chief envoy to Communist China, was made Central Intelligence director in 1976 as a strictly political appointment. Indeed, many felt that Donald Rumsfeld, then Ford's principal advisor, had thrown Bush into the post-Watergate CIA hot pot to keep the ambitious rival out of the way and—if possible—in trouble.

But Bush revived the agency and its morale, effectiveness, and image beyond the intelligence professionals' most heartfelt dreams and Rumsfeld found himself being praised for the sagacity of his choice. When Bush announced for the presidency in 1979, two years into Turner's night of the long knives, Bush bumper stickers blossomed all over the Langley area, much to the admiral's irritation.

Worse for Turner, a movement began within the CIA cadre to topple the admiral in a bureaucratic coup. Employing generous leaks to the news media and applying pressure through their friends on Capitol Hill, the conspirators sought to replace Turner with his deputy, Frank Carlucci, a veteran foreign-service officer and bureaucratic infighter who was also one of the few government officials in Washington who could actually claim to have been stabbed in the back (during a diplomatic assignment in Africa). Carlucci balked at the plot (he later became deputy secretary of defense under the Reagan administration).

Reagan troubled many at Langley by turning the agency over to another amateur, his aging campaign manager, William J. Casey, who hadn't run a spy in nearly forty years. The insiders were somewhat mollified when Reagan also named Bobby Inman—the professionals' professional—as Number 2 at the CIA. Even with Inman's careful hand at the controls, Casey quickly got into trouble.

He was scarcely two months in office when high-ranking agency officials were not so discreetly complaining to *U.S. News & World Report*—hardly an organ of the left—that "Casey, CIA director, responds sarcastically when analysts produce conclusions that run counter to the administration foreign policy line. The danger, as these officials see it: Independent analysts will be reluctant to speak their minds."

Casey outraged nearly everyone at Langley, and not a few in Congress, by naming Max Hugel as his chief of covert operations and head spy. Hugel, a close friend of Casey's, was a New Hampshire businessman who ran the Reagan campaign in that state for the crucial 1980 primary. He was quickly dumped after it was charged he had manipulated stock sales.

Casey's own stock dealings kept him in trouble for much of his tenure. Unlike the rest of the Reagan administration leadership, he refused to place his holdings in a blind trust upon taking office. After it was learned that he had made immense profits and had managed to get rid of his oil company stock before the 1980s oil glut reduced its value, there were congressional calls for his resignation. He saved his skin only by finally agreeing to put his investment portfolio aside.

Surprisingly, much of the opposition to Casey came from conservative Republican Senators Barry Goldwater and Richard Lugar. Lugar, a former Navy intelligence officer, had long complained that Casey's intelligence estimates lacked objectivity and competence. "He is not a pro," Goldwater said.

A draft executive order giving Casey and the CIA sweeping powers to spy on American citizens within the United States was sent to the White House in early 1981, but it was hastily withdrawn after being leaked to the press, denounced by Congress, and disavowed by Inman.

Inman suffered Casey as long as possible, but, in 1982, shortly after the inexpert and untutored William Clark was made national security advisor, the admiral abruptly resigned to take over his highly profitable computer enterprise. Goldwater, Lugar, and others in Congress quickly moved to make R. E. Hineman, a CIA expert on Soviet nuclear weapons, head of foreign assessments and thus keep an eye on Casey's intelligence product. Congress also made sure that Reagan replaced Inman with a professional—John McMahon, a longtime agency analyst and administrator.

But Casey established himself as the agency's principal front man, much to the consternation of some of the Reagan administration's best friends.

"Casey is horrible," one Senate Republican said. "He knows who the good guys are and the bad guys are, but he's not an effective spokesman. Inman would come up here and there'd be no doubt about anything he said. Casey could read the same thing Inman said and no one would believe him."

For all that, Casey won many friends among CIA rank and file for delivering on the Reagan promise to restore the agency to the strength it enjoyed before Carter's budget cuts and Turner's firings. Under Casey, the CIA's budget was reportedly increased at a rate of 17 percent a year. In addition to expanding covert operations from two or three to twelve to fourteen, Casey built up the number of covert operatives to

1,000, and hired back as consultants many of the eight hundred agents and officials forced out by Turner. Casey also increased the number of annual National Intelligence Estimates turned out from a dozen or so under Turner to more than fifty.

But matters did not entirely improve.

"Right now," complained the Senate Republican in 1984, "you can't get a good answer from them without a good question. There's just not enough thinking. We get facts, but not thought. One person with good instincts is worth a hundred with good facts.

"The wife of Senator [Richard] Stone [who became Reagan's chief Latin American foreign-policy aide] had a hairdresser who was Nicaraguan. Because of her, he knew more about what was going on there during the Somoza period than the CIA did."

Though acknowledging he wasn't satisfied with his own performance as intelligence chief, Vice-President Bush saw some failings as well.

> I feel very well informed in this job, but I can't tell you I think this system is perfect. Sometimes there's duplication—sometimes you want duplication—but not of collection necessarily. You want duplication of analysis of something, rather than two or three people collecting the same thing.
>
> If you're counting beans, you don't need but one guy to tell you there's three beans there. You don't need four guys to tell you there's three beans. But if it's a question of, hey, are those beans down there, and you need a photo interpretation or you need a department view of whether they're beans that can be shot twenty-five zillion miles into the air or twelve billion, then you need competitive analysis.

The worst failure of the American intelligence community was the Iranian revolution, occurring in the darkest days of the Turner regime. In the 1970s, the United States caused major problems for itself by increasingly relying on the Shah of Iran's secret police, Savak, for intelligence concerning Iran itself. Despite this, the CIA had by early 1976 produced a highly accurate report assessing the strength and nature of the growing opposition to the Shah and correctly identifying the conservative Moslem clergy as the probable leaders of any movement against the Tehran government. It failed to change U.S. policy.

In 1977, the CIA sent Washington another report warning that the White House was giving too much credence to the complacent Savak.

But when the full force of the revolution was unleashed in 1978, the Carter administration was taken completely by surprise. Shocked by the depth and breadth of the uprising, it had no clear idea as to whether the Shah could hold, and later, whether the military could or would intervene to stabilize the situation. After much indecision on Carter's part, when a swift American move might have resolved the matter more advantageously, the Iranian army sat down on its weapons and the revolutionaries swept to power.

During the brief government of moderate Prime Minister Mehdi Barzagan, the CIA made contacts with Abolhassan Bani-Sadr, then a close advisor to the Ayatollah Khomeini, and tried to recruit him as an agent. It failed, and Khomeini seized control of the Iranian government.

In October 1979, when the Carter administration at the behest of Henry Kissinger and others admitted the Shah to the United States for medical treatment, the CIA and State Department passed on serious warnings from moderate Iranian officials that the radicals would use that act to turn the country against the United States. To say the least, they were ignored. Fifty-two Americans—and much of American foreign policy—were held hostage for more than a year. Among the CIA's more painful losses were voluminous embassy files detailing its Iranian operations and its contacts with moderate Iranian politicians.

The CIA was able to eke out only one small victory. Using various disguises, among them that of a motion-picture crew, American intelligence agents were able to get into Tehran and help the Canadians smuggle out six Americans who had eluded capture when the U.S. embassy was seized.

Despite the added money, manpower, and moral support given it during the Reagan administration, American intelligence continued to perform embarrassingly.

In Lebanon, the Navy was able to produce a full target damage report from the air assault on Syrian antiaircraft positions that cost the Navy two planes and the life of a pilot. But no agents were able to report on the damage caused by the long-range shelling by the 16-inch guns of the battleship *New Jersey*—if there was any. The blame for the slaughter of 242 Marines in the 1983 terrorist bombing of their Beirut barracks rests properly with the incompetent military commanders who failed to provide sufficient perimeter security. But, despite the bombing of the American embassy in Beirut a year earlier, there was not sufficient intelligence warning of Iranian terrorist activity in the vicinity. The CIA was able to learn of Iranian plans to attack public places and persons in Washington, however, and thoroughgoing measures were taken to prevent it.

The United States's invasion of Grenada was almost transformed from black comedy to outright tragedy because of poor intelligence. In the previous administration, there had been two CIA operatives on the island, but they were let go because of budget cuts and, subsequently, never replaced. The American invasion force, already hobbled by the chaos caused by all four armed services wanting a piece of the combat, went into action with abysmally poor information about the territory they were invading.

Several Marine units had no maps, and several ships' atlases either made no reference to the island, or showed it simply as a tiny dot. Army units equipped with big three-by-four-foot maps found they came apart in the rain. As mentioned previously, other outfits had only tourist road maps. Yet a few weeks before, President Reagan had gone on national television with detailed satellite photos showing construction work on Grenada's airport.

Two companies of Marines advanced quickly over the island, but the thousands in the Eighty-second Airborne only inched forward because they had been given highly inflated reports of expected opposition. A number of the Navy's elite SEAL commandos drowned because of inaccurate weather forecasting. SEALs who did get ashore to take out the radio station failed because they attacked the wrong building.

The worst time for the CIA in the Reagan era has been in Central America, where the White House claimed it was confronted with a Cuban- and Soviet-supported Marxist Nicaragua bent on toppling the pro-American governments of El Salvador and other neighboring countries by supporting indigenous leftist guerrillas. Had this happened in the days before the Vietnam syndrome, the War Powers Act, and the congressional penchant for simultaneous interference and timidity, the president need have only sent in a large Marine force or other shock troops to stabilize the situation, as American presidents had done in every decade of the twentieth century up to the 1970s. It quickly became apparent that American combat troops would have to be used if any significant change in the situation were to be effected.

But, denied that option, Reagan set about trying to restrain Nicaragua with a charade. An endless succession of massive naval, air, and land "maneuvers" were staged within gunshot of Nicaragua, especially within the range of the battleship *New Jersey*. All manner of bases, airfields, and other facilities were established in neighboring Honduras, which received generous helpings of military aid and large contingents of American military advisors. The United States also supplied and trained several thousand anti-Sandinista Nicaraguan guerrilla groups based in Honduras and, to a lesser degree, Costa Rica.

This failed to intimidate the Sandinistas, whose large army greatly outnumbered its opposition and at one point even fired on Costa Rican security forces. The Reagan solution was to put Americans into combat anyway—not American soldiers but CIA operatives running anti-Sandinista units in covert operations. Their commander in chief was CIA Director Casey, who turned with relish from clipping his coupons to indulge himself as he had in the good old days of World War II. Except matters didn't quite work out the same way.

In a typical operation in September 1983, a contra air force of two American Cessna business craft made a raid on Managua. One dropped two bombs, destroying next to nothing, and returned to base. The other, piloted by Agustin M. Roman, a former chief of operations for the Sandinista Air Force who had defected to the contras, made a pass at the Managua International Airport, cratering the runway with a bomb. Roman's plane crashed, however, killing him. The aircraft had been registered for much of the year to a company in McLean, Virginia, called Investair Leasing. Though the firm had been incorporated since July 1982, the sale of the Cessna to a Panamanian company in June 1983 was its only recorded transaction. One of the principal executives of Investair had exactly the same name as the secretary and treasurer of Air America, a CIA cargo airline. The Sandinistas filed much of this information with a protest to the United Nations.

The agency's covert units were somewhat more effective in blowing up some fuel-storage facilities, in a campaign of economic harassment aimed at making foreign nations curb their trade with Nicaragua. By 1984, this included an effort to strew the approaches to three Nicaraguan harbors with hundreds of noisy mines designed to damage but not destroy shipping. The goal was to make insurance and other costs of shipping to Nicaragua so prohibitive that the country would soon find itself with empty harbors.

Though nearly a dozen ships were damaged, including a Soviet freighter, this did not come to pass. The biggest explosion came in Washington, much of it contained in this 1984 letter to Casey from the Senate Intelligence Committee:

Dear Bill:

All this past weekend, I've been trying to figure out how I can most easily tell you my feelings about the discovery of the president having approved mining some of the harbors of Central America.

It gets down to one, little, simple phrase: I am pissed off!

I understand that you had briefed the House on this matter. I've heard that. Now, during the important debate we had last week and the week before, on whether we would increase funds for the Nicaragua program, we were doing all right until a member of the committee charged that the president had approved the mining. I strongly denied that because I had never heard of it. I found out the next day that the CIA had, with the written approval of the president, engaged in such mining, and the approval came in February!

Bill, this is no way to run a railroad, and I find myself in a hell of a quandary. I am forced to apologize to the members of the Intelligence Committee because I did not know the facts on this. At the same time, my counterpart in the House did know.

The president has asked us to back his foreign policy. Bill, how can we back his foreign policy when we don't know what the hell he is doing? Lebanon, yes, we all knew that he sent troops over there. But mine the harbors in Nicaragua? This is an act violating international law. It is an act of war. For the life of me, I don't see how we are going to explain it.

My simple guess is that the House is going to defeat this supplemental and we will not be in any position to put up much of an argument after we were not given the information we were entitled to receive: particularly, if my memory serves me correctly, when you briefed us on Central America just a couple of weeks ago. And the order was signed before that.

I don't like this. I don't like it one bit from the president or from you. I don't think we need a lot of lengthy explanations. The deed has been done and, in the future, if anything like this happens, I'm going to raise one hell of a lot of fuss about it in public.

Sincerely,

Barry Goldwater, Chairman.

A lot of fuss was made about the mining in public, in part because of leaks made to either members of Congress or the press from sources within the CIA, where the agency's role in the Central American follies was exceedingly unpopular.

"The CIA shouldn't be doing this!" said an agency veteran to one of the authors. "It's an intelligence-gathering agency. If the administration wants to fight a war down there, it should use the Green Berets or one of the covert military units!"

Clearly, it does the CIA little good to replace reduced funding and Admiral Turner with increased funding and William J. Casey. The agency must be reprofessionalized, and at once. Not simply with the maintenance of a career man in the Number 2 position, but by elevating the requisite qualifications for the top job to those now demanded of the director of the Federal Bureau of Investigation or the head of the General Accounting Office. The director of Central Intelligence should not only be the best man possible but he should be guaranteed tenure and protected against being made the scapegoat for White House mistakes or the instrument of White House political policy. The feeling for this within the agency, if not very public, is deep and strong. Senators like former intelligence officer Richard Lugar have long argued for the most professional agency leadership possible.

Military actions should be the province of the military. If Congress and/or the public will not support them, then, as General Meyer warned, the high command should not try to carry them out, even on the sly. When an operation gets to the point of exploding mines under Soviet ships in Central American waters, it is no longer covert anyway.

The expanding intelligence empires of the various armed services must be hauled back into line and confined to purely military functions, such as providing accurate maps for Caribbean invasion forces. The CIA should be able to devote its major effort to the gathering of the most accurate, dispassionate, objective, and nonideological intelligence possible. It should be given every possible resource to carry out this mission, including transferring most of the National Security Agency's operations to its jurisdiction.

Most important of all, the CIA should be *believed,* even when its intelligence product disagrees with Pentagon or White House policy. As Vice-President Bush observed, there is a need for competitive analysis, but not for competitive intelligence gathering, especially when the competition may be an American defense contractor evaluating Soviet weapons capability for its own profitable purposes. Never again should hard facts dug up by the United States's best intelligence officers be blithely disregarded because they contradict the policy that promotes generals the fastest. The future looms bleak enough without indulging such heinous mistakes.

chapter twenty-one

THE $300 BILLION AIRPLANE

"Why show me this, if I am past all hope?"
—EBENEZER SCROOGE,
IN CHARLES DICKENS'S *A CHRISTMAS CAROL*

Imagine a national defense budget that would be devoted entirely to the construction of a single airplane.

Norman Augustine, president of the aerospace division of Martin Marietta, made a projection of American defense spending trends and concluded that such a prospect is theoretically possible, and, barring a monumental change in the system, in some degree inevitable.

"From the days of the Wright brothers through the F/A-18, aircraft costs have been increasing by a factor of four every ten years," Augustine said. "In the year 2054 the entire defense budget will purchase just one tactical aircraft. This aircraft will have to be shared between the Air Force and Navy three and a half days each per week."

Starting with a cost of $1,000 for the Wright brothers' Flyer and ending with the original sticker price of $18 million for the computer-laden F/A-18, Augustine offered this arithmetic: The top-of-the-line airplane that cost $1,000 in 1908 cost $4,000 in 1918, $16,000 in 1928, $64,000 in 1938, $256,000 in 1948, $1 million in 1958, $4 million in 1968, $16 million in 1978, and would probably cost $64 million by 1988. According to his formula, that airplane should cost more then $300 billion by the middle of the next century.

Among critics of the defense establishment, this projection became known as Augustine's law, a development that may not have pleased Augustine, a corporate executive with impeccable establishment credentials. He served in the Ford administration as chief of Army research and development and held senior weapons designing positions at Douglas Aircraft and LTV Corporation, before taking over at Martin Marietta. Despite his pocket calculator jeremiad about the absurd horrors of future defense procurement, Augustine served in the Reagan administration as chairman of the Defense Science Board, helping to bring along vastly complicated and costly projects like the Stealth bomber and the President's "Star Wars" program.

Just as Augustine was able to examine sixty years of ever ballooning aircraft costs and extrapolate a ridiculous future, it is possible to forecast how the flawed American defense system will continue on its present disastrous course until Augustine's law or an annihilating war becomes reality.

Much of this book has dealt with the tremendous pressures that have arisen to drive the costs of increasingly unworkable weaponry ever higher and to render military policymakers impotent as they attempt to press American interests in an ever more unfriendly world.

If the political system continues to give immense procurement power to a relative handful of corporate-connected members of Congress, if defense contractors continue to build their business on false promises and artificially low bids, if profit margins continue to be set as a fixed percentage of final weapons cost and competition is kept to a minimum, if contracts and procedures remain incomprehensible, if Pentagon scientists continue to be told that price is no object and "anything for defense" continues to be the Pentagon's rallying cry, then the day of $1 billion bombers and $300 million fighters will shortly be at hand. The cost of the 25 cent Air Force plastic stool cap will go from $1,118 to $10,000. A whole new catalogue of costly weapons that don't work will be dumped on a shrinking combat force that will desperately need anything that will work and that may well prefer old M-1 rifles to the latest laser ray gun to come out of the Pentagon's Strangelove works.

If the elite priesthood that controls Pentagon research and development is not reformed by a military Martin Luther who knows that high-tech and ballooning budgets do not translate to strength, if military careers continue to prosper on the basis of program size and budget instead of effectiveness and efficiency, and if the individual services continue to combat each other instead of uniting to prepare the country to combat its enemies, the American economy is going to be severely damaged, the United States will fall farther and farther behind the Soviets, and it will likely lose its next war.

Kelly Johnson, head of the Lockheed Corporation's "Skunk Works," recalled a conversation he once had with Soviet aircraft designer Andrei Tupolev.

"You Americans build airplanes like fine lady's watch," Tupolev said. "Drop watch—watch break. We Russians build airplanes like Mickey Mouse clocks. Drop clock—clock stop. Pick up clock and shake— the clock work."

Defense Secretary Caspar Weinberger dramatically represented the difficulty facing those who would reform the system in an impassioned talk before the Air Force Association: "Critics who would have us do without this modern equipment—make do with cheaper, less sophisticated, easier-to-maintain technology—don't consider really the value of human life."

Directing his wrath at the reform groups who had done so much to publicize excessive weapon cost and inefficiency, Weinberger said, "Maybe it's easier for them to take these bookkeeping arguments, but I have a responsibility that doesn't permit that luxury."

From the dreadnoughts of World War I to the F/A-18, the advocates of expansive defense spending have justified their stupendous demands with the argument that no price is too high to pay to give America's soldiers the best possible weapons, the best possible chance to survive the horrors of war. Critics would be silenced with an all-encompassing "war is not cost effective!"

Indeed, the men and women in the defense companies who design the computer-guided, laser-firing battle tanks, the wire-guided missiles, and other wonder weapons are motivated by a genuine desire to give their users the best possible chance for survival. Their goal—laudable if costly and counterproductive—is nothing less than making the American fighting man immortal in combat.

After weapons specialist and reformer Pierre Sprey told a congressional hearing how miserably the expensive new F-15 had fared against the old but reliable little F-5, an officer angrily demanded, "Would you like your son to go up in an F-5 or an Eagle [F-15]?"

"I'd like to see him go up in something that worked," Sprey replied.

There is every indication that the quest for the immortal soldier has failed and that the actual result of this costly effort will be that the losses in future wars will be far greater than ever suffered in the past.

The high death tolls from helicopter mishaps in military adventures such as the *Mayaguez* rescue, the Desert One raid, and the assault on Grenada—not to mention the catastrophic losses suffered by helicopters in Vietnam—indicate that casualties would be enormous in a confrontation with an equally matched foe such as the Soviet Union.

The vulnerability of sophisticated F-15s to confusion when engaged with large flights of smaller fighters bodes ill for an air war in which the United States plans to rely on technology to overpower superior Soviet numbers. The heavy reliance on radar by Navy warships, particularly those assigned to guard carriers in each of the naval battle groups, threatens to betray fleet positions and actually guide enemy missiles to their targets. Though Navy secretaries and admirals choose to look the other way, the radar-heavy, big-ship Navy is threatening the United States with a missile-age Pearl Harbor that could see it suffering devastating losses from an attack by a relatively small foe. A recent congressional report on readiness found the Navy able to wage war at sea against the Soviets for only a week or less and vulnerable to attack by small powers that could render it "a disgrace." The lessons of the Falklands War may finally be learned in an extremely painful way.

Less obvious, but just as dangerous, are the threats that continuation of the present system poses to the civilian economy. During the last three decades, as the United States has progressively slipped from world dominance as an economic and military power, the Defense Department's budget has continued at high and stable levels, with notable steps up for Korea, Vietnam, and the Reagan administration's "rearm America" buildup.

As analyst Robert W. DeGrasse, Jr., noted, military purchases have come to represent more than 70 percent of all U.S. government spending for goods and services.

The huge increases in defense spending rushed through by the Reagan White House, coupled with the administration's irresponsible decision to cut income taxes and revenues by 25 percent at the same time, created almost overnight a continuing annual federal deficit of $200 billion or more that not even an economic boom could greatly diminish.

These deficits, piling up year after year, rapidly brought the national debt to almost double the $900 billion it had been when Reagan took office and threatened to triple it by the end of the decade. The accumulation of debt in turn required larger and larger portions of the federal budget to go for interest payments to the nation's creditors, some 12 percent of the budget in 1983 and as high as 15 percent by 1985.

This not only creates a huge new government mouth to compete with the Defense Department for taxpayers' money, it wreaks severe injuries on the economy. With the federal government borrowing one half of all loan money by the end of 1983, there's been an intense struggle for credit with private industry, which needs borrowed dollars to expand. The more the government keeps borrowed money out of the hands of industry, the less the economy can grow.

This credit competition also drives up interest rates, putting another brake on the economy, while increasing the sums the government has to pay out to attract investment money to finance its debt. The federal insolvency will ultimately have to be addressed with massive tax increases, creating another obstacle to economic growth. A continued military spending spree of this sort may also put a strain on the pool of savers and investors who at baseline supply the credit. The Reagan tax cut did not, as promised, increase the number of savers in the country. As a percentage of GNP, savings actually decreased. The loan money to finance the "rearm America" effort came in substantial part from foreign banks and private investors—especially those from Arab petrodollar countries—who wanted to take advantage of the high price of the dollar and the United States's supposedly stable investment climate. Should that climate become less stable or some political question intervene, as it did in the 1973 Arab oil embargo, the government could find its loan sources dwindling and itself with no recourse but to pay even higher interest rates.

A recurring argument made for these fiscally dangerous practices is that defense spending creates jobs. Computer models of the American economy have determined that for every $1 billion spent on defense programs only 28,000 jobs are created, compared with 32,000 jobs created when the money is distributed to education, public works, and other nonmilitary government activity. Military projects were found to create most of their jobs among the ranks of professional and technical workers—groups with much smaller unemployment problems than less skilled workers. Military contracts created far fewer jobs for the less skilled categories of worker—production workers, store clerks, laborers, and the like.

As military spending increases, the number of the hard-core unemployed will grow, even as large numbers of skilled technicians return to work. In December 1982, with the Reagan arms buildup well under way and the overall U.S. unemployment rate above 10 percent, only 3.7 percent of technical workers were unemployed. Some 20 percent of laborers and machine workers were jobless.

Pentagon budgets will increase costs by moving American economic activity from traditional centers of manufacturing in the Midwest and Northeast to the Sun Belt states, requiring a massive restructuring of the industrial plant—machine tool works, foundries, and the like—that traditionally has been concentrated in the North, amidst ample water and power supplies and transportation networks.

In 1981, ten states received 65 percent of all defense spending—California with 20 percent, Texas with 8.6 percent, New York with 7.4 percent, Massachusetts with 5.2 percent, Connecticut with 5.1 percent, Missouri with 5 percent, Virginia with 4.1 percent, Florida with 3.6 percent, Louisiana with 3.5 percent, and Washington state with 3.2 percent—seven of them in the South and West. While they prospered, the economy was dragged down by the collapse of "smokestack industries" in New Jersey, Illinois, Ohio, Michigan, Pennsylvania, and several other states.

Big defense spending also threatens to contribute mightily to the collapse of American dominance in world trade. In the mid-1960s, as the United States was expanding its force in Vietnam, it was exporting some 80 percent more manufactured goods than it was importing. By the time Reagan took office, the nation was a net importer of manufactured goods—many of them from allies like Japan, whose position in world markets was strengthened because it only needed to spend tiny fractions of its national wealth on defense—depending on American defense to do the job.

The Council on Economic Priorities (CEP) documented the role of the military burden in national productivity or "manufacturing competence" in a study incorporating two charts: one showing the amounts of defense spending by the United States and sixteen allied countries and a second showing the seventeen countries' productivity rates.

The United States, with 7.2 percent of its GNP dedicated to military spending, was at the top of the chart depicting defense expenditures. Japan, with less than 2 percent of its GNP going to defense, was at the bottom.

On the second chart, showing national productivity and economic health, Japan led the list with a 10 percent growth in manufacturing, while the U.S. was last with less than 4 percent. The West Germans, devoting slightly more than 3 percent to military spending, enjoyed a 6 percent productivity growth. Italy's productivity grew by nearly 8 percent while its defense spending shrunk to below 3 percent.

Analyst DeGrasse noted, "Our economy would have performed significantly better if the United States had reallocated a portion of the resources used by the military." He cited the example of mass-transit systems, a service heavily subsidized in Europe and Asia. DeGrasse said that without plowing wealth into arms which were used in large part to defend allies, "we could have sustained and expanded the now-failing American mass transit vehicle industry, reducing the need to import subway cars from Europe, Canada, and Japan to fill the needs of New York, Boston, and Philadelphia."

While the United States was moving its skilled work force from the North to the Sun Belt and sending them from manufacturers of consumer goods into arms plants, its allies were building their civilian economies by replacing older machines with more sophisticated equipment, expanding factory size, and developing new civilian technologies—activities that faltered in the American economy. Catching up with them remains a challenge to the United States for the rest of the century, perhaps an impossibility as defense spending consumes more and more of available capital and credit.

As military projects continue to weaken America's civilian industrial plant, they will absorb much of the scientific talent that could be put to work finding new and successful ways of competing commercially in foreign markets. By 1980, the Pentagon was financing roughly 40 percent of all research and development in the United States. Much of the technology developed for such projects had little application to the civilian economy.

A frequently cited consequence of tying up American scientific expertise with military pursuits is the overpowering Japanese dominance of the civilian electronics market, using many of the same technologies that had been developed in parallel research by U.S. R & D experts for solely defense purposes. As Congressman Aspin and other critics have pointed out, the United States led the way in developing microcircuits and computer chips, but then used them in weapons—ranging from the smart bombs of Vietnam to the fire-control computers of today's faulty DIVAD gun. The Japanese, however, developed parallel technology—often with U.S. assistance—and put it to work in the design of videotape recorders, small television sets, stereos, portable radios, Walkman portable tape players, and other high-profit items. As a result, the Japanese now dominate the American commercial electronics market.

In 1964, the CEP study noted, the Japanese did not export color television sets. By 1977, Japan had captured 42 percent of the world market and 37 percent of the U.S. color television market. By 1983, Japan's government-subsidized efforts to surpass the American computer industry were so intense that both the Pentagon and a separate consortium of private companies embarked on crash programs to keep the Japanese from taking over world computer sales.

The same disadvantage has occurred in the production of machine tools. While the United States concentrated so much of its milling and foundry capacity on military work, the West Germans and Japanese were able to grab increasingly larger shares of the world market for machine tools used in manufacturing automobiles, trucks, sewing machines, and other consumer items. In the 1960s, the United States accounted for nearly 35 percent of worldwide machine-tool production. By 1981, it had only 20 percent of the market. Western European companies, led by the West Germans, had captured 34 percent. Many of these tools were used by firms like Airbus Industries, which were in direct competition in the manufacture of passenger jets with American firms like Boeing.

The General Dynamics factory in Fort Worth, Texas, has been performing much of the high-tolerance machining work on F-16 air frames with robotic lathes leased to it by Japanese companies. There are strong indications that this will be the unhappy wave of the future—that the

United States will be compelled to buy the majority of the machinery and manufacturing technology it uses from foreign countries, so that it may continue to build the weapons needed to defend those countries.

In 1984, Japanese equipment was being used in 50 percent of all the computer-operated machining works in the United States, compared to just 4 percent in 1974. Much of the drain of American industry from its established facilities in the North to the new ones in the Sun Belt has been made possible by the purchase of Japanese and West German machinery.

On the way to building its $300 billion airplane, the United States faces the prospect of doing so as a second-rate civilian industrial power. As its economically debilitating defense burden grows with its consequent decline in employment levels, quality of life, and decreases in consumer goods production, the United States will become ever more like its nemesis, the Soviet Union, an awesome global military power whose citizens' wretched standard of living is the price of might.

Despite the inequity of this, America's allies are unlikely to prove receptive to U.S. entreaties to increase their share of the West's defense burden. In some cases, notably the widescale public protest in many European countries over the deployment of cruise and Pershing II intermediate-range missiles, it has become clear that the alliance is in some danger of disintegration and that many NATO nations are unwilling to bear much of a defense burden at all.

As noted elsewhere in this book, a major problem displayed by American defense and diplomatic leaders in trying to practice "alliance management" has been a failure to comprehend the depth and power of peace movements in allied countries throughout Europe and in the Western hemisphere and Asia as well.

The worst recent U.S. failure to anticipate problems with allies stemmed from President Carter's decision first to deploy the neutron bomb in Europe to counter Soviet tank attack—pressuring West Germany mightily to go along—and then deciding later not to deploy it. Opposition parties in West Germany and Britain seized upon the hysteria generated over this incident to make political capital out of local fears about hosting nuclear weapons.

The Reagan administration, seeking to meet the same threat of Warsaw Pact armored assault that had prompted Carter to order the neutron weapon in the first place, subsequently deployed both nuclear cruise and Pershing II missiles in Western Europe, with further political upheaval the result.

As deployment of the missiles proceeded, opposition parties were able to use the issue to thwart U.S. efforts to persuade its NATO allies to bear a larger share of the burden of maintaining alliance strength in Europe. It's been said repeatedly by General Bernard Rogers, commander of U.S. forces in Europe and supreme commander of NATO, the choice will be one of raising the nuclear threshold by reinforcing Europe with large numbers of American troops or lowering the threshold by relying on a larger nuclear force to pose against possible Soviet attack. The prospect is for a hollow NATO in which most of the frontline European troops will be Americans, and in which the nuclear lanyard may be yanked at the slightest indication of a Russian assault as the only available means of stopping them from overrunning Europe in a conventional war rout.

The NATO alliance may also be undermined by the Russian carrot. Nerve-racking experiences like the 1973 Arab oil embargo, the fall of Iran to the mullahs, and the desperate Iran-Iraq War have made Europeans long for the stable oil and gas supplies enjoyed but not shared by the United States and Canada. The Soviet oil and gas pipeline now being built across Europe could someday prove that source of supply. The Soviets have been supplying NATO member Iceland with oil for years.

The United States's global strategy is built on political, military, and economic realities that could change overnight—and some will. The violent overthrows of the Shah in Iran and Anastosia Somoza in Nicaragua, with all their dramatic consequences to U.S. policy, are possibly to be repeated—most particularly in the Philippines. A violent leftist revolution in Mexico is also a possibility, and would confront the United States with a massive political and military problem that would transform its global situation alarmingly.

Key U.S. military bases in Asia, the Middle East, and even Europe could be lost because of changes in political winds. Leftist parties in Britain and Iceland have threatened just that repeatedly. NATO allies Greece and Turkey remain disposed toward war with each other, a war that could disintegrate NATO's Eastern Mediterranean flank. The Mideast daily threatens catastrophes ranging from region-wide war to a pull of the nuclear trigger, especially as Israel continues to behave as one of the United States's closest friends and most unreliable allies.

But Europe remains the centerpiece. In version after version of the chilling Single Integrated Operations Plans (SIOPs) drafted to meet all contingencies dreamed up by the Pentagon's war-gaming bureaucracy, the final war is always fought in Europe. Frequently the SIOP scenarios begin at a flashpoint elsewhere in the world—North Korea invades South Korea, Iran or Iraq closes the Strait of Hormuz and cuts off European and Japanese oil, Israel attacks Syria or vice versa, Cuba attacks in Central America, Libya detonates a nuclear weapon in Israel, the Soviet Union occupies Pakistan, and myriad others. But in each case the SIOP planners must prepare for an escalation of the regional hostilities into a more widespread conflict reaching to where East-West tensions and war-making potential are highest—along the NATO/Warsaw Pact front line. The two alliances have prepared for war in their own backyard for the forty years that have passed since the last war there ended. And the grim, brutal realities of their plans explain much of why the peace movements have been so successful and such a problem for American alliance managers.

Dwight Eisenhower recommended to the newly formed NATO in 1949 that the countries deploy 96 divisions, plus some 9,000 aircraft, to oppose the Soviets along a defensive perimeter extending from Scandinavia to the Mediterranean. NATO ministers rejected Eisenhower's urgings, observing sourly that such a force approximated the size of the force the allies had put together to fight World War II itself. At a subsequent conference in Lisbon in 1952, they settled on an "ideal" NATO force of about half the size Eisenhower wanted—50 divisions and 4,000 airplanes.

Long before alliance members created that force, however, the ministers laid the groundwork for today's balance of terror by instituting the so-called nuclear fix, in which the United States supplied short-range nuclear weapons to take the place of 26 divisions and 2,500 aircraft. Instead of moving in troops, the United States agreed to supply an array of 15,000 nuclear weapons, ranging from Long Sam atomic artillery to nuclear land mines about the size of a milk can. According to analyst Tim Alexander Meyers, "All of those weapons were built. During the late 50s and early 60s, one new type of nuclear weapon was produced and deployed each [fiscal] quarter." A hard-liner, Meyers added, "Contrast that with today, when it is hard to get a new conventional weapon deployed every 10 years."

Although the United States produced the 15,000 "theater" nuclear weapons, only 6,000 were deployed in Europe. As "ban the bomb" marches led by notable figures like the late Bertrand Russell and Jean-Paul Sartre illustrated, the presence of all those nuclear arms and the near certainty that any U.S.-Soviet war would be waged in European cities, towns, and countryside has made it difficult from the beginning for the Americans to secure popular European support for the goals and methods of NATO. While Americans live with their recurring nightmare of sudden destruction from a blizzard of ICBMs with the hammer and sickle on their sides, Europeans are told to prepare first for days or weeks of conventional fighting, tanks rolling through their streets, jets strafing and pulverizing buildings, soldiers firing massively destructive missiles, machine guns, and automatic rifles. To many Europeans, an all-out conventional war on their continent would be every bit as bad as a nuclear one.

The most likely NATO scenario projects that the Soviets will attack in staggered waves or "echelons" with the first units storming over the border and across West Germany, as the Warsaw Pact armies attempt to engage NATO forces all along a Forward Edge of Battle Area (FEBA). The Soviet war plan calls for using at least three echelons—two now deployed in Eastern bloc countries and a third in the westernmost Soviet territories—the last two moving in as reinforcements to apply continuous pressure at the FEBA. For Europeans living from the North Sea to the Swiss border, this means total war around their homes.

The second part of the Soviet war-fighting plan is to use highly mobile exploitation forces to strike wherever the allies appear weakest along the FEBA. These exploitation groups are called Operational Maneuver Groups (OMGs), and one of their key missions is to knock out U.S. nuclear weapons before they can be used. Those living around Pershing and ground-launched cruise missiles would be savaged by Soviet shock troops even if no one reached for the missile-ignition keys.

But these missiles are at the heart of the NATO strategy for defeating a Soviet echelon attack. The NATO plan calls for using the intermediate-range nuclear missiles to destroy the second and third echelons if the alliance's conventional force fails to stop the first Soviet wave at the FEBA. Since the Soviet third echelon is positioned on Soviet territory, the Kremlin might reasonably feel compelled to use its several hundred intermediate-range SS-20s as a counter to the Pershings and cruises—or more likely, according to defector Victor Suvorov, to launch them first, along with their first echelon attack.

All this fuels doubts that a conventional war could be fought in Europe without snapping the nuclear trip wire.

In densely populated Europe, NATO war plans invariably stir a tremendous political controversy that American SIOP writers are spared in their own country. Typical are discussions involving a scheme to counter the Soviet FEBA plan by having NATO's divisions swiftly fall back from the front in order to spread, thin, and overextend the first enemy echelon and provide the opportunity for a decisive counterattack. This would mean abandoning the defenses of Bonn and Frankfurt and withdrawing to new positions as far back as Paris, allowing the Russians to swarm over much of West Germany and France. Debates over such options do little to win sympathy for U.S. pleas for more European spending on defense.

The widespread feeling is that war is more and more likely and that it will likely be a nuclear war. The feeling is not misguided. The stresses and strains of changing geopolitics are telling. As the Polish people become more and more combative, Romania grows more independent, and the ethnic minorities in the south of the Soviet Union increasingly assert their Moslem religion and latent nationalism, the Kremlin marshals will grow itchy and nervous. The two Germanys are feeling a kindred bond. East Germany, Russia's most vital industrial resource, is being tugged into de facto membership in the European Economic Community through its trade with West Germany. If the Soviets were ever to use brutal military force to suppress the East Germans as they did the Czechs in 1968, the West German military and the situation might be very difficult to control. Once the tanks of both sides started to roll, a terrible bloodbath would be inevitable.

U.S. planners still look to Europe as one of the least likely places for war to begin. Though the American public is only dimly aware of the dangers there, a much more probable place is the Korean peninsula.

During the four decades the United States has been preparing for hypothetical war in Europe, it has actually had to go to war twice in Asia, and a third war there is far from out of the question. It is one of the most dangerous corners of the earth. The United States, the Soviet Union, North Korea, South Korea, China, Taiwan, and Vietnam have more forces posed against one another there than the NATO and Warsaw Pact countries do in Europe. North Korea's nearly 800,000-strong military is a larger force than any in either NATO or the Warsaw Pact except for the United States's and Russia's. Its force of 2,675 medium tanks is slightly more than the United States has in Europe. Across the tense DMZ, the South Koreans have 520,000 troops and 1,000 tanks.

The Soviets have nearly 500,000 troops—including a great many crack units—posed across the Chinese border in its eastern military districts, along with several hundred SS-20 missiles aimed at targets in China, Japan, and South Korea. The Chinese have 3.1 million combat troops in a total military of 4 million. They also have four nuclear ICBMs and one hundred intermediate- and short-range nuclear missiles, as well as ninety bombers equipped with smaller "atomic" fission weapons. The Vietnamese army, backed by the Soviets and recurringly engaged in combat with the Chinese, is 1 million strong.

Analyst Anthony H. Cordesman pointed to several possible ways hostilities could erupt in Asia:

1. Soviet antagonism of its old enemy Japan or an outright attack on Japan over disputed territory like the Kuril Islands.

2. A surface battle between U.S. and Soviet naval forces in the Pacific arising from one of the frequent harassment clashes that continue to take place on the high seas.

3. A limited nuclear exchange confined to the Pacific in which the two sides attempt to close ports and destroy each other's ships.

4. War between North and South Korea that would instantly involve the United States—and either China or the Soviet Union or both—while compelling Japan to allow the United States to use its territory for staging its forces, as in the first Korean War.

5. A war between the Soviets and the mainland Chinese that could escalate quickly to a theater-wide conflict.

6. A sudden conflict over Taiwan.

7. Another large-scale war between the Chinese and Vietnam that could draw in the Soviets and other forces.

Any one of these could occur virtually overnight.

Vietnam, with its relentless adventuring in Cambodia and Laos, its crippled domestic economy, and its increasing reliance on the Soviet Union, will continue to be a flash point for years and years to come, always carrying the potential for sparking a war between the Soviets and China.

China, obsessed with Taiwan, both fearful and contemptuous of Vietnam, and a blood enemy of the Soviet Union, acts as a dangerous wild card with its crude but growing arsenal of nuclear weapons—enough already to take the world across the nuclear threshold not crossed since 1945.

American defense and intelligence officials have long warned that the Soviet Union has reacted to the superior American nuclear presence in the Pacific by adopting war plans that rely heavily on early use of nuclear weapons if battles begin at sea. This Soviet doctrine greatly increases the danger that a long-feared Sino-Soviet border war could rapidly expand into nuclear conflict between the Soviets and the U.S. Pacific fleet, which could lead quite directly to all-out nuclear war.

The Soviet megatonnage assigned to Asia is substantial. In addition to more than 200 SS-20s, it has some 250 out-of-date but still deadly SS-4s and SS-5s deployed in the region, missiles noteworthy for carrying the largest warheads on earth.

The Asian situation is changing—for the worse—because of the furious force buildups under way by both the United States and the Soviets. After the bloody but inconclusive war between China and Vietnam in 1979, the Soviets rapidly began to expand their Pacific fleet. According to the International Institute for Strategic Studies, that Communist armada grew from 56 major combat vessels in 1973 to 85 warships in 1983. Many of these craft are modern, heavily armed types, including Kashin-class guided missile destroyers and frigates and helicopter carriers like the *Minsk*. The Soviet fleet was also expanded to include 25 nuclear submarines, 95 attack submarines, and more than 300 support ships. But the U.S. Pacific fleet, with 206 major combat vessels, including carriers and nuclear missile submarines, is more than a match. To quickly turn the tide in their favor, the Soviets rely on nuclear weapons targeted according to U.S. ship movements.

As futurists like the late Herman Kahn have often noted, the great imponderable of "thinking the unthinkable" is how the hostile, heavily armed factions of the world will react once the first nuclear weapon is detonated in combat. The United States is the only country ever to use nuclear force in war. Though minor by today's potential standards, the attacks on Hiroshima and Nagasaki were so stunning that a bloody, intractable struggle that had threatened to drag on for another year was abruptly ended in days. Indisputably, the next detonation of a nuclear weapon in anger will also prove stunning. Questions that arise most readily focus on whether, once the trip wire is yanked for the first time, it will be easier to use a second nuke, and a third.

In 1956, Dwight Eisenhower wrote to a publisher friend concerning a column written by Joseph and Stewart Alsop on the Soviet military threat. Eisenhower said:

> Thank you for your letter, which brings up subjects too vast to be discussed adequately in a letter. Suffice it to say here that I doubt that any columnist—and here I depend upon hearsay as I have no time to read them—is concerning himself with what is the true security problem of the day. That problem is not merely against man or nation against nation. It is man against war.
>
> I have spent my life in the study of military strength as a deterrent to war, and in the character of military armaments necessary to win a war. The study of the first of these questions is still profitable, but we are rapidly getting to the point that no war can be *won*. War implies a contest; when you get to the point that contest is no longer involved and the outlook comes close to destruction of the enemy and suicide for ourselves—an outlook that neither side can ignore—then arguments as to the exact amount

of available strength as compared to somebody else's are no longer the vital issues.

When we get to the point, as we one day will, that both sides know that in any outbreak of general hostilities, regardless of the element of surprise, destruction will be both reciprocal and complete, possibly we will have sense enough to meet at the conference table with the understanding that the era of armaments has ended and the human race must conform its actions to this truth or die.

The fullness of this potentiality has not yet been attained, and I do not, by any means, decry the need for strength. That strength must be spiritual, economic, and military. All three are important and they are not mutually exclusive. They are all part of and the product of the American genius, the American will.

But already we have come to the point where safety cannot be assumed by arms alone. But I repeat that their usefulness becomes concentrated more and more in their characteristics as deterrents than in instruments with which to obtain victory over opponents as in 1945. In this regard, today we are further separated from the end of World War II than the beginning of the century was separated from the beginning of the Sixteenth Century.

Naturally, I am not taking the time here to discuss the usefulness of available military strength in putting out "prairie fires"—spots where American interests are seriously jeopardized by unjustified outbreaks of minor wars. I have contented myself with a few observations on the implications of a major arms race.

Finally, I do not believe that I shall ever have to defend myself against the charge that I am indifferent to the fate of my countrymen.

Asked whether he thought a country such as the United States could compete with the Soviet Union—maintaining strength, will, and reason enough to deter challenges that could lead to war—Vice-President Bush said, "My gut answer is yes. . . . I think in spite of all the problems out there the answer should be yes." He then paused, and expressed the basic point of this book:

"The answer better be yes."

EISENHOWER'S FAREWELL ADDRESS TO THE AMERICAN PEOPLE, JANUARY 17, 1961

My fellow Americans:

Three days from now, after half a century in the service of our country, I shall lay down the responsibilities of office as, in traditional and solemn ceremony, the authority of the Presidency is vested in my successor.

This evening I come to you with a message of leave-taking and farewell, and to share a few final thoughts with you, my countrymen.

Like every other citizen, I wish the new President, and all who will labor with him, Godspeed. I pray that the coming years will be blessed with peace and prosperity for all.

Our people expect their President and the Congress to find essential agreement on issues of great moment, the wise resolution of which will better shape the future of the Nation.

My own relations with the Congress, which began on a remote and tenuous basis when, long ago, a member of the Senate appointed me to West Point, have since ranged to the intimate during the war and immediate post-war period, and, finally, to the mutually interdependent during these past eight years.

In this final relationship, the Congress and the Administration have, on most vital issues, cooperated well, to serve the national good rather than mere partisanship, and so have assured that the business of the Nation should go forward. So, my official relationship with the Congress ends in a feeling, on my part, of gratitude that we have been able to do so much together.

We now stand ten years past the midpoint of a century that has witnessed four major wars among great nations. Three of these involved our own country. Despite these holocausts America is today the strongest, the most influential and the most productive nation in the world. Understandably proud of this pre-eminence, we yet realize that America's leadership and prestige depend, not merely upon our unmatched material progress, riches and military strength, but on how we use our power in the interests of world peace and human betterment.

Throughout America's adventure in free government, our basic purposes have been to keep the peace, to foster progress in human achievement, and to enhance liberty, dignity and integrity among people and among nations. To strive for less would be unworthy of a free and religious people. Any failure traceable to arrogance, or our lack of comprehension or readiness to sacrifice would inflict upon us grievous hurt both at home and abroad.

Progress toward these noble goals is persistently threatened by the conflict now engulfing the world. It commands our whole attention, absorbs our very beings. We face a hostile ideology—global in scope, atheistic in character, ruthless in purpose, and insidious in method. Unhappily the danger it poses promises to be of indefinite duration. To meet it successfully, there is called for, not so much the emotional and transitory sacrifices of crisis, but rather those which enable us to carry forward steadily, surely, and without complaint the burdens of a prolonged and complex struggle—with liberty the stake. Only thus shall we remain, despite every provocation, on our charted course toward permanent peace and human betterment.

Crises there will continue to be. In meeting them, whether foreign or domestic, great or small, there is a recurring temptation to feel that some spectacular and costly action could become the miraculous solution to all current difficulties. A huge increase in newer elements of our defense, development of unrealistic programs to cure every ill in agriculture, a dramatic expansion in basic and applied research—these and many other possibilities, each possibly promising in itself, may be suggested as the only way to the road we wish to travel.

But each proposal must be weighed in the light of a broader consideration: the need to maintain balance in and among national programs—balance between the private and the public economy, balance between cost and hoped for advantage—balance between the clearly necessary and the comfortably desirable; balance between our essential requirements as a nation and the duties imposed by the Nation upon the individual; balance between the actions of the moment and the national welfare of the future. Good judgment seeks balance and progress; lack of it eventually finds imbalance and frustration.

The record of many decades stands as proof that our people and their government have, in the main, understood these truths and have responded to them well, in the face of stress and threat. But threats, new in kind or degree, constantly arise. I mention two only.

A vital element in keeping the peace is our military establishment.

Our arms must be mighty, ready for instant action, so that no potential aggressor may be tempted to risk his own destruction.

Our military organization today bears little relation to that known by any of my predecessors in peacetime, or indeed by the fighting men of World War II or Korea.

Until the latest of our world conflicts, the United States had no armaments industry. American makers of plowshares could, with time and as required, make swords as well. But now we can no longer risk emergency improvisation of national defense; we have been compelled to create a permanent armaments industry of vast proportions. Added to this, three and a half million men and women are directly engaged in the defense establishment. We annually spend on military security more than the net income of all United States corporations.

This conjunction of an immense military establishment and a large arms industry is new in the American experience. The total influence—economic, political, even spiritual—is felt in every city, every State house, every office of the Federal government. We recognize the imperative need for this development. Yet we must not fail to comprehend its grave implications. Our toil, resources and livelihood are all involved; so is the very structure of our society.

In the councils of government, we must guard against the acquisition of unwarranted influence, whether sought or unsought, by the military-industrial complex. The potential for the disastrous rise of misplaced power exists and will persist.

We must never let the weight of this combination endanger our liberties or democratic processes. We should take nothing for granted. Only an alert and knowledgeable citizenry can compel the proper meshing of the huge industrial and military machinery of defense with our peaceful methods and goals, so that security and liberty may prosper together.

Akin to, and largely responsible for the sweeping changes in our industrial-military posture, has been the technological revolution during recent decades.

In this revolution, research has become central; it also becomes more formalized, complex, and costly. A steadily increasing share is conducted for, by, or at the direction of, the Federal government.

Today, the solitary inventor, tinkering in his shop, has been overshadowed by task forces of scientists in laboratories and testing fields. In the same fashion, the free university, historically the fountainhead of free ideas and scientific discovery, has experienced a revolution in the conduct of research. Partly because of the huge costs involved, a government contract becomes virtually a substitute for intellectual curiosity. For every old blackboard there are now hundreds of new electronic computers.

The prospect of domination of the nation's scholars by Federal employment, project allocations, and the power of money is ever present—and is gravely to be regarded.

Yet in holding scientific research and discovery in respect, as we should, we must also be alert to the equal and opposite danger that public policy could itself become the captive of a scientific-technological elite.

It is the task of statesmanship to mold, to balance, and to integrate these and other forces, new and old, within the principles of our democratic system—ever aiming toward the supreme goals of our free society.

Another factor in maintaining balance involves the element of time. As we peer into society's future, we—you and I, and our government—must avoid the impulse to live only for today, plundering, for our own ease and convenience, the precious resources of tomorrow. We cannot mortgage the material assets of our grandchildren without risking the loss also of their political and spiritual heritage. We want democracy to survive for all generations to come, not to become the insolvent phantom of tomorrow.

Down the long lane of the history yet to be written America knows that this world of ours, ever growing smaller, must avoid becoming a community of dreadful fear and hate, and be, instead, a proud confederation of mutual trust and respect.

Such a confederation must be one of equals. The weakest must come to the conference table with the same confidence as do we, protected as we are by our moral, economic, and military strength. That table, though scarred by many past frustrations, cannot be abandoned for the certain agony of the battlefield.

Disarmament, with mutual honor and confidence, is a continuing imperative. Together we must learn how to compose differences, not with arms, but with intellect and decent purpose. Because this need is so sharp and apparent I confess that I lay down my official responsibilities in this field with a definite sense of disappointment. As one who has witnessed the horror and the lingering sadness of war—as one who knows that another war could utterly destroy this civilization which has been so slowly and painfully built over thousands of years—I wish I could say tonight that a lasting peace is in sight.

Happily, I can say that war has been avoided. Steady progress toward our ultimate goal has been made. But so much remains to be done. As a private citizen, I shall never cease to do what little I can to help the world advance along that road.

So—in this my last good night to you as your President—I thank you for the many opportunities you have given me for public service in war and peace. I trust that in that service you find some things worthy; as for the rest of it, I know you will find ways to improve performance in the future.

You and I—my fellow citizens—need to be strong in our faith that all nations, under God, will reach the goal of peace with justice. May we be ever unswerving in devotion to principle, confident but humble with power, diligent in pursuit of the Nation's great goals.

To all the peoples of the world, I once more give expression to America's prayerful and continuing aspiration:

We pray that peoples of all faiths, all races, all nations, may have their great human needs satisfied; that those now denied opportunity shall come to enjoy it to the full; that all who yearn for freedom may experience its spiritual blessings; that those who have freedom will understand, also, its heavy responsibilities; that all who are insensitive to the needs of others will learn charity; that the scourges of poverty, disease and ignorance will be made to disappear from the earth, and that, in the goodness of time, all peoples will come to live together in a peace guaranteed by the binding force of mutual respect and love.

Notes

Introduction:
THE AMERICAN WAY

An excellent reference on the American military in the early days of the Republic (and its development through the first term of the Eisenhower administration) is *Arms and Men*, by Walter Millis (G.P. Putnam's Sons, 1956). A wealth of material on force levels over the decades and other comparative data is contained in *The Statistical History of the United States*, with introduction and guide by Ben Wattenberg (Basic Books, 1976). *Americans at War*, by William J. Koenig (G.P. Putnam's Sons, 1980) is a very useful history of American arms from colonial times through the Vietnam War.

For more detail on President Eisenhower's actions ending the Korean War, *This Kind of War*, by T. R. Fehrenbach (Macmillan, 1963) remains the definitive history on this conflict. Eisenhower himself deals with the subject in volume one of his presidential memoirs, *Mandate for Change: 1953 to 1956* (Doubleday, 1963). An excellent short biography of Eisenhower is *The Eisenhowers: Reluctant Dynasty*, by Steve Neal (Doubleday, 1978).

The bureaucratic flaws afflicting the American military were compellingly explained in "Why Our High-Priced Military Can't Win Battles," by Professor Jeffrey Record of Georgetown University's national security studies program, published in *The Washington Post*'s Outlook section January 29, 1984. *National Defense*, by James Fallows (Random House, 1981) remains a basic primer on the military procurement system and other failures of U.S. Defense.

An excellent translation of Sun Tzu's *The Art of War*, with an introduction by Chinese scholar Samuel B. Griffith and forward by British military historian B. H. Liddell Hart was published by the Oxford University Press in 1963 with subsequent editions published as recently as 1982.

376

Karl von Clausewitz's *On War,* first published in 1832, was most recently reissued in a Penguin Classics edition in 1982.

Chapter one:
DEATH IN A BRIEFCASE

Most of the material for this chapter came from interviews with Colonel Christopher I. Branch (USAF) and from the authors' firsthand knowledge of the Pentagon building and its operations. The Defense Department publishes a small pamphlet on the building, entitled *The Pentagon,* available from the information office.

Chapter two:
THE MEANEST SONOFABITCH IN THE VALLEY?

The data on troop strength, composition, and deployment was assembled from regular reports issued by the Defense Department's public information office in the Pentagon. These are summarized annually by DOD in excellent almanacs entitled *Defense 83, Defense 84,* etc. The annual Military Balance report compiled by the International Institute for Strategic Studies in London also provides a hard count of troop strength; numbers of divisions; quantity and deployment of strategic and tactical missiles, aircraft, naval vessels, armor, artillery, and other weapons; and an analysis of national defense spending. The IISS assessments are considered extremely accurate and are highly regarded by military leaders throughout the world, including those in the United States.

Data on defense spending and budgets was taken from annual Defense Department budgetary reports and analyses, which include breakdowns on the amounts paid the largest defense contractors, military spending, payrolls state by state, and weapons costs. *Defense Spending and the Economy,* a study prepared by the Congressional Budget Office in 1983, was used in discussing the impact of the military budget on the domestic economy. A more detailed analysis concerning the impact on jobs, *The Price of the Pentagon* (Employment Research Associates, 1982) shows how much less labor intensive the defense industry is compared to private industries aided by federal domestic-sector spending. *Arms, Men, and Military Budgets,* by Francis P. Hoeber, David B. Kassing, and William Schneider, Jr. (Crane, Russak, 1978) provides a helpful analysis of defense budgets during the Carter administration.

The most accurate, dispassionate but by no means least disturbing assessment known to the authors of the probable effects of a nuclear exchange is *The Effects of Nuclear War,* prepared for the Congress by the Office of Technology Assessment and published in hardcover by Allanheld, Osmun & Company in 1980. *The Day After World War III,* by Edward Zuckerman (Viking Press, 1984) contains disturbing if often hilarious documentation of the lack of reality that pervades government civil defense plans for coping with the aftermath of a nuclear attack.

Chapter three:
THE RED MENACE

Primary sources for this chapter included the four editions of *Soviet Military Power,* published by the Defense Department at the direction of Secretary Caspar Weinberger in 1982, 1983, 1984, and 1985 and its Soviet counterpart, *Whence the Threat to Peace,* published by the USSR Ministry of Defense in 1982. The IISS's annual *Military Balance* reports were used as the ultimate authority, however, especially in cases of discrepancies between Defense Department and USSR assessments.

The authors relied in substantial part on their own reporting in preparing this chapter (Michael Kilian has traveled in the Soviet Union), including interviews with knowledgeable individuals in the Defense Department, State Department, Congress, in Moscow and Leningrad, and at the United Nations. This partly involved articles and commentary written by the authors for the *Chicago Tribune.* The authors also valued reporting on the subject done by other *Tribune* correspondents, including Moscow Bureau Chiefs James O. Jackson and Michael McGuire. Leads, guidance, corroboration, and other help was derived from extensive reporting in a wide variety of articles on the Soviet Union published in *The Washington Post, The New York Times, The Wall Street Journal,* the *Toronto Globe and Mail,* the now-defunct *Washington Star, U.S. News & World Report, Time* magazine, *Newsweek, World Press Review, Armed Forces Journal, Air Force Magazine, Defense Week, Defense Daily, Defense Monitor, Security Affairs* (the newsletter of the Jewish Institute for National Security Affairs), *Foreign Affairs Quarterly, The New York Review of Books, Europe* (a publication of the European Economic Community), *The Economist, Washington Monthly, The Atlantic, Harper's, Soldier of Fortune, The Nation, The New Republic,* and *National Review.*

Reports by the Congress's Joint Economic Committee, Senate Foreign Relations Committee, House Foreign Affairs Committee, and the Foreign Affairs and National Defense Division of the Library of Congress were also quite helpful, as was participation by author Kilian in a 1984 Senate Foreign Relations Committee symposium on east–west trade and national security.

Important book-length sources on the capabilities, intentions, and historical interests of the Soviet Union include *The Threat: Inside the Soviet Military Machine,* by Andrew Cockburn (Random House, 1983); *Inside the Soviet Army,* by Viktor Suvorov (Macmillan, 1982); *Weapons and Tactics of the Soviet Army,* by David C. Isby (Jane's Publishing Co. Ltd., 1981); *The Cambridge Encyclopaedia of Russia and the Soviet Union,* edited by Archie Brown, John Fennell, Michael Kaser, and H. T. Willets, all of Oxford University (Cambridge University Press, 1982); *The Russians,* by Hedrick Smith, (Quadrangle, 1976); *The White Generals,* by Richard Luckett (Viking Press, 1971); *The Life of Lenin,* by Louis Fischer (Harper & Row, 1964); *KGB: The Secret Work of Soviet Secret Agents,* by John Barron (Reader's Digest Press, 1974); *Conventional War and Escalation: The Soviet View,* by Joseph D. Douglass, Jr., and Amoretta M. Hoeber (Crane, Russak, 1981); and *False Science: Underestimating the Soviet Arms Buildup,* by Steven Rosefieldc (National Strategy Information Center, 1982).

Chapter four:
THE COMMANDER IN CHIEF

Accounts of the difficulties besetting the Madison administration in the War of 1812 can be found in *The Oxford History of the American People,* volume two, *1789 Through Reconstruction,* by Samuel Eliot Morison (Oxford University Press, 1965 and 1972). The follies of the Battle of Bladensburg that preceded the burning of Washington are vividly retold in *The Dawn's Early Light,* by Walter Lord (W.W. Norton, 1972).

Two highly recommended histories of the Mexican War and the Polk administration are *The Mexican War,* by K. Jack Bauer (Macmillan, 1974) and *The Mexican War,* by Otis A. Singletary (University of Chicago Press, 1960). There are also *Polk: The Diary of a President,* edited by Allan Nevins (Longmans, Green, 1929) and a somewhat partisan contemporary work, *A Review of the Causes and Consequences of the Mexican War,* by William Jay (Benjamin B. Mussey, 1849).

The information concerning the "Gold Codes" cards and the mix-up involving the "football" officer after the shooting of President Reagan in March 1981 was drawn mostly from the authors' reporting.

For more on Eisenhower's military activities as president, particularly as concerns his brief and highly successful military intervention in Lebanon in 1958, the second volume of his White House memoirs, *Waging Peace: 1956 to 1961* (Doubleday, 1965) is a good resource. An amply detailed look at Eisenhower's command experience in World War II and an interesting perspective on Franklin D. Roosevelt's performance is to be found in *The Papers of Dwight David Eisenhower: The War Years*, volumes one through five (Johns Hopkins Press, 1970).

One of the best basic histories of the Kennedy administration, with ample discussion of the Bay of Pigs invasion and the Cuban Missile Crisis, is *JFK: The Presidency of John F. Kennedy,* by Herbert S. Parmet (Dial Press, 1983). *With Kennedy,* by Pierre Salinger (Doubleday, 1966) and *Johnny, We Hardly Knew Ye,* by Kenneth P. O'Donnell and David F. Powers (Little, Brown, 1972) provide an intimate "insider's" view of how Kennedy handled those crises. A thoroughgoing examination of his administration's misadventures in Africa is contained in *JFK: Ordeal in Africa,* by Richard D. Mahoney (Oxford University Press, 1983).

Because of his assignment to the 82nd Airborne Division in this period, author Kilian acquired a more immediate knowledge than most of the operations involved in the 1965 Dominican Republic invasion. Conversations in later years with those participating in White House command functions or otherwise familiar with President Lyndon Johnson's conduct during the emergency, including presidential assistant Jack Valenti and State Department Spokesman John King, added amply to this knowledge. *The Washington Post* published an excellent analysis on June 27, 1965, "Crisis Under the Palms," which occupied the paper's entire Outlook section, and an insightful retrospective, "A Distant Dominican Mirror," by diplomatic correspondent Murrey Morder, in the Outlook section on October 30, 1983.

A February 27, 1984, article in *U.S. News & World Report,* "Can't Anybody Here Run a War?," provided a useful summary and analysis of American military failures from 1970 through 1980 and the built-in Defense Department flaws that helped produce them. In a January 24, 1980, interview in the *Los Angeles Times,* Vice-President Bush made a prophetic critique of the Carter administration's defense policies that proved to be one of the harbingers of the Reagan administration's all-out defense build-up.

Two extremely revealing articles on Ronald Reagan's performance as commander in chief were "Reagan As Military Commander," by Richard Halloran, *The New York Times Magazine,* January 15, 1984, and the *Time* magazine cover story "How Reagan Decides: Intense Beliefs, Eternal Optimism and Precious Little Adaptability," December 13, 1982.

Reagan's foreign policy drift until the ascendancy of Secretary of State George Shultz was detailed in a well-reported two-part series, "Reagan and the World," in *The Washington Post* beginning November 20, 1983. Another *Post* article, "Foreign Policy or a Recipe for Disaster?: Reagan Won't Alter His Ideas to Fit the World's Realities," by Robert G. Kaiser, in the Outlook section, October 30, 1983, grapples well with the same subject. Hedrick Smith's prophetic article "Typically, Lebanon Strategy

Delegates Authority," *The New York Times,* September 20, 1983, discusses the command flaws that led to the disaster in Beirut a month later. Former undersecretary of the Navy R. James Woolsey produced a compelling hindsight view of the same problems in *The New York Times,* November 15, 1983.

One of the best book-length sources on the Reagan administration's conduct of defense policy is *With Enough Shovels: Reagan, Bush, and Nuclear War,* Robert Scheer (Random House, 1983). *On Reagan: The Man and His Presidency,* Ronnie Dugger (McGraw-Hill, 1983) is a very good reference, especially as concerns Reagan's own public comments on defense and other matters. *SIOP: Nuclear War from the Inside,* Peter Pringle and William Arkin (Sphere Books, 1983) discusses the nuclear war–fighting policies of the Reagan administration and its predecessors in rather unsettling terms.

Chapter five:
THE MEN IN THE MIDDLE

The essential reference for understanding the structure and workings of the National Security Council and the rest of the government's national security apparat is *American National Security: Policy and Process,* Amos Jordan, William J. Taylor, Jr., and associates (John Hopkins University Press, 1981). Assistant Secretary of Defense Lawrence J. Korb's 1978 paper, "National Security Organization and Process in the Carter Administration," published later as part of *Defense Policy and the Presidency: Carter's First Years* (Westview Press, 1979) offers an expert's perspective on the changes in the national security process that develop from administration to administration. "Making U.S. National Security Policies," a paper produced by the National War College in 1979, is another recommended reference.

Dom Bonafede's article in the October 15, 1977, *National Journal,* "Brzezinski: Stepping Out of His Backstage Role," proved prescient in terms of the rivalries and divisions that came to plague Carter national security policy. "The War Planners," by Jerrold and Leona Schecter, *Esquire,* January 1983, deals thoroughly with both the Reagan and Carter national security teams.

In an article in its August 1, 1983, issue, "Rolling Out the Big Guns," *Time* magazine reported how Henry Kissinger was brought in as head of a bipartisan commission on Central America in an effort to achieve a national consensus on Central American policy—the idea emanating from United Nations Ambassador Jeane Kirkpatrick. "The Influence of William Clark," Steven R. Weisman, *The New York Times Magazine,* August 14,

1983, relates how a California judge with limited foreign policy experience came briefly to function as the country's most powerful national security official.

The failure of successive administrations to give expert Sovietologists an important role in crisis management and national security policy-making is examined in an article in *The New York Times* by Leslie H. Gelb, March 12, 1984. In the March 28, 1984, edition of the *Times*, Gelb wrote an excellent profile of Reagan's most recent national security advisor, Robert McFarlane, considered one of the best appointments to that job in recent presidential history.

Additional book-length sources on the subject are *Power and Principle: Memoirs of the National Security Advisor, 1977–1981*, Zbigniew Brzezinski (Farrar, Straus and Giroux, 1983); *Hard Choices: Critical Years in America's Foreign Policy*, Cyrus Vance (Simon & Schuster, 1983); *Caveat*, Alexander Haig (Macmillan, 1984); and *International Security Yearbook: 1983/ 1984*, Barry M. Bletchman and Edward N. Luttwak (St. Martin's Press, 1983).

Chapter six:
THE GENERALISSIMOS IN SUITS

Secretary of State William Seward's role in bringing about the seige of Fort Sumter at the outbreak of the Civil War is fully discussed in *The Invisible Presidency*, by Louis W. Koenig (Rinehart and Co., 1960), which also deals with such highly influential presidential lieutenants as Alexander Hamilton, Martin Van Buren, Theodore Roosevelt's William Loeb, Jr., Woodrow Wilson's Colonel Edward M. House, Franklin Roosevelt's Thomas G. Corcoran and Harry Hopkins, and Dwight Eisenhower's Sherman Adams. A good companion work is *The President's Men*, by Patrick Anderson (Doubleday, 1968), which discusses the presidential aides of Franklin Roosevelt, Harry Truman, Dwight Eisenhower, John Kennedy, and Lyndon Johnson.

On Watch, by Admiral Elmo Zumwalt (Ret.) (Quadrangle, 1976) offers an intimate if military view of the service secretary system and the function of civilian command in both the Nixon and Ford administrations. *Thinking About National Security: Defense and Foreign Policy in a Dangerous World*, by Harold Brown (Westview Press, 1983) examines the system from the perspective of Brown's long career in the American defense establishment and may be viewed as probably the most rational discourse on the American military produced by the Carter administration.

Also recommended for further reading on the subject are these works mentioned earlier: Cyrus Vance's *Hard Choices: Critical Years in America's*

Foreign Policy; Alexander Haig's *Caveat;* Zbigniew Brzezinski's *Power and Principle: Memoirs of the National Security Advisor, 1877–1981;* Walter Millis's *Arms and Men;* and Herbert S. Parmet's *JFK: The Presidency of John F. Kennedy.*

For the passages on Navy Secretary John Lehman, the authors drew largely on their dealings with him and his office, which extended over several years, but were also helped by an informative and illuminating profile and interview published in the November 1983 *Armed Forces Journal.* The clash between Lehman and then–Deputy Secretary of Defense Paul Thayer was well recounted in an article by Richard Halloran in *The New York Times,* August 24, 1983.

The authors' familiarity with Secretary of Defense Caspar Weinberger derives from many years of press conferences, briefings, social conversations, and reporting dating back to the Nixon administration. Author Kilian was also a television writer and reporter in California when Weinberger was chairman of the Republican Party there and has discussed the secretary with mutual friends who have known him since Harvard.

An excellent, if partisan, profile of Weinberger by his friend, author Theodore White, "Weinberger on the Ramparts," appeared in *The New York Times Magazine,* February 6, 1983. A more dispassionate discussion of Weinberger and his conduct of office was Nicholas Lemann's article "The Peacetime War," *The Atlantic,* October 1984. A two-part series on Weinberger and his defense policy goals, "Caspar One-Note's Military March," by Martin Schram, began in the April 18, 1982, edition of *The Washington Post.*

Weinberger's beliefs about using military budgets to wage economic warfare are laid out in a speech he prepared for the Atlanta Chamber of Commerce that was reprinted in the Summer 1982 issue of *Aerospace Magazine,* the official publication of the Aerospace Industries Association. His position on nuclear deterrence was set forth in a speech at Fordham University April 28, 1983, and released by the Defense Department public information office.

An article by Dan Orberdorfer in the October 23, 1983, *Washington Post* detailed Secretary of State George Shultz's methods in gaining the upper hand over Weinberger with President Reagan on foreign policy matters.

Chapter seven:
THE HILL

The Iron Triangle, by Gordon Adams (Council on Economic Priorities, 1981) remains the basic reference on the incestuous *ménage à trois* of the

Congress, the White House, and the military-industrial complex. *Defense Dollars and Sense,* by Mark Rovner (Common Cause, 1983) reduces the military-industrial-congressional relationship to a simplified 90-page outline liberally augmented with charts, glossaries, and sidebar stories. It is a valuable primer for college students approaching military issues for the first time.

A more establishment source is *U.S. Defense Policy,* third edition, edited by Michael D. Wormser (Congressional Quarterly, 1983). Chapters written by staff reporters of this Washington-based news and analysis organization and by such senior Pentagon correspondents as Charles Corddry of the *Baltimore Sun* trace how eight Capitol Hill powerhouses worked their will on the foreign and defense policies of the Reagan administration in its first term.

Super Weapon: The Making of MX, by John Edwards (W.W. Norton, 1982) draws heavily from top Carter administration sources to describe how proponents of the missile worked their will on the dovish, unsure president through the Congress and other pressure points. *The High Priests of Waste,* by A. Ernest Fitzgerald (W.W. Norton, 1972) amounted to the first critical look at defense contractors since congressional commissions probed "war profiteering" in the 1930s and 1940s.

The disclosures concerning the Lockheed lobbying effort on behalf of the C-5B cargo jet were put into the public record by Representative Jack Brooks, chairman of the House Government Operations Committee, on September 29, 1982. He released a report by the General Accounting Office that included the controversial computer printouts taken from Lockheed and the Air Force. That report is entitled "Improper Lobbying Activities by the Department of Defense on the Proposed Procurement of the C-5B Aircraft" (GAO/AFMD-82-123). "Report on Double Dipping," by Sid Taylor (National Taxpayers Union, 1982) lists members of Congress collecting military pensions and otherwise tied to the military.

In a candid interview with reporter Judith Martin in the November 7, 1981, *New York Times,* Captain Ingolf N. Kiland discussed not only the size and makeup of the Pentagon's military liaison offices on Capitol Hill but outlined as well some of the techniques the military officers used to win and maintain favor among powerful lawmakers.

Throughout the 1970s and 1980s, the authors and many other newsmen have written on the well-documented junkets arranged and conducted by the 89th Military Airlift Wing. Two examples are "Pentagon: First-Class Travel Agent," *USA Today,* February 9, 1983, and "Congressman's Farewell: A Holiday in the South Pacific," an article by author Coates in the *Chicago Tribune,* November 28, 1976.

The authors made ample use of Federal Election Commission files listing all the legal political contributions made by corporations, companies, and allied interests to members of Congress.

Chapter eight:
THE HIGH COMMAND

The Pentagon's extensive public information establishment is extremely helpful to journalists who want to tour the Joint Chiefs of Staff (JCS) war room, the underground command bunkers at Strategic Air Command headquarters at Omaha, Nebraska, the subterranean North American Air Defense Command (NORAD) beneath Cheyenne Mountain in Colorado, and other high-tech showcases.

The account of Yeoman Charles Radford's spying on Kissinger and Haig for the JCS is based greatly on interviews with W. Donald Steward, chief Pentagon investigator for the Nixon administration between 1978 and 1980. The official Senate investigation of the Radford matter culminated in a report issued February 20, 1974, "Transmittal of Documents from the National Security Council to the Chairman of the Joint Chiefs of Staff." The report includes transcripts of testimony at hearings conducted by Senator John Stennis in which Radford alleged he had been ordered by Admiral Rembrandt C. Robinson to obtain information concerning the operations of the National Security Council and pass it along to Admiral Thomas H. Moorer, then chairman of the JCS. Moorer denied Radford's allegations that the spying was ordered by the chiefs in his own testimony, but acknowledged that sensitive White House information had indeed been passed to the Pentagon by Radford.

The earlier mentioned *On Watch,* by Admiral Elmo Zumwalt, provides an account of how the JCS reacted to the Radford affair and a bitter critique of chaos and confusion in the high command. Equally tough and candid was an article in the November 7, 1982, *New York Times Magazine,* "What's Wrong with Our Defense Establishment," by then-just-retired general and JCS chairman David C. Jones.

Also helpful was a 1978 seminar on the subject conducted by the American Enterprise Institute. Retired generals and JCS chairmen Maxwell Taylor and George S. Brown were participants, as was author Coates. At this session, Lieutenant Commander Watson recalled how Admiral Moorer had returned to the JCS "Tank" with the news that the President had placed the military on alert. General Brown confirmed Watson's account.

The disclosure that all five members of the JCS had advised President Reagan against keeping the Marines in Lebanon in their sorry situation was initially made by Representative Larry J. Hopkins. He was quoted by

The Washington Post in a December 21, 1983, article as saying that the House Armed Services Committee had been informed of the JCS opposition by JCS Chairman General John W. Vessey, Jr., in a secret session. "They didn't think it was a viable military mission," Hopkins said.

Lieutenant Colonel Tyrus W. Cobb's excellent critique of the command system, "Issue Brief: Reforming the Joint Chiefs of Staff System," was presented at the twenty-second Senior Conference held at West Point in 1982 and attended by Coates.

In testimony before the House Armed Services investigation subcommittee on October 3, 1978, former Defense Secretary Harold Brown offered an excellent insider's explanation of the bizarre alphabet soup bureaucratic process involved in formulating policy and developing weapons from the first DG to the actual firing of the bullet. *Defense Dollars and Sense* contains a more simplified depiction.

The account of the 1980 Desert One Iranian hostage mission, referred to in this chapter and elsewhere in the book, is based on a wide variety of sources and source material, but two are notable: the official May 6, 1980, report to Congress on the incident, JCSM-122-80, and the January 1983 issue of *Gung-Ho,* a magazine for combat aficionados, which contained the report of one of the troopers in the ill-fated C-130 transport. He observed that the mission collapsed when officers from the several service branches failed to communicate with one another.

An article in the October 3, 1984, *New York Times,* "A Runaway Pentagon," by David Evans, dealt thoroughly with the chiefs' inability to control the weapons acquisition process and consequent cost growth.

The earlier mentioned *American National Security: Policy and Process,* by Amos Jordan and William Taylor, contains a comprehensive explanation of the national command structure.

Thinking About the Next War, by Thomas Powers (New American Library, 1983) raises some of the qualms felt in applying Clausewitzian doctrine to modern warfare and nuclear war.

In addition to Clausewitz's own *On War,* two other works are strongly recommended: *Clausewitz,* by Roger Parkinson (Stein and Day, 1971) and *Clausewitz and the State,* by Peter Paret (Clarendon Press, 1976). *A Genius for War: The Germany Army and General Staff, 1807–1945,* by Colonel T. N. Dupuy (Prentice-Hall, 1977) has become the bible of advocates of a strong general staff system for the American military.

Sources on the superiority of the German military system and soldiery include *Six Armies in Normandy,* by John Keegan (Viking Press, 1982); *History of the Second World War,* by B. H. Liddell Hart (G.P. Putnam, 1971); and *Inside the Third Reich,* by Albert Speer (Macmillan, 1970).

Chapter nine:
A BROTHERHOOD OF RIVALS

Mentioned earlier, *SIOP: Nuclear War from the Inside,* by Peter Pringle and William Arkin, was one of very few works that documented the little-known but considerable impact of the Carter administration on the nuclear war fighting plans of the Pentagon. Though Carter was in many defense circles considered weak and vacillating—an impression little contradicted by his leadership of the Desert One Iranian hostage rescue mission—this book shows that he brought forth profound changes in the nation's war plans, including a major expansion of the numbers and types of targets designated for nuclear weaponry.

Pringle and Arkin interviewed Kistiakowsky before his death and learned of the Eisenhower administration's discovery that the service branches had failed to coordinate or even inform each other of their nuclear target schedule—all because of interservice rivalry. Kistiakowsky dealt with this subject himself in his book *A Scientist at the White House* (Harvard University Press, 1976).

The Army's tragic decision to develop its own helicopter air force—and the disturbing reasons for it—were compellingly detailed in Gregg Easterbrook's September 1981 *Washington Monthly* article, "All Aboard Air Oblivion," a groundbreaker that had tremendous impact with the press. Richard Halloran's June 12, 1983, article in *The New York Times,* "Why the Military Has Four Tactical Air Forces: A Case Study," shed a great deal of additional light on the subject.

L. Kim Smith's article, "JVX: Pentagon Alchemists Would Change Paper to Hardware," which appeared in the October 1982 *Government Executive,* quoted internal Pentagon memos to reveal the damage done by uncontrolled interservice competition.

J. I. Coffey's essay, "SALT and the Triad in the 1980s," which was published in *The Future of U.S. Land-Based Strategic Forces* (Institute for Foreign Policy Analysis, 1980) outlined the logic of the need for a common missile for the Air Force and the Navy.

Senator Mark Hatfield made a significant contribution to the MX missile debate with his article, "Should the United States Build the MX Missile?" published in the American Enterprise Institute's *Foreign Policy and Defense Review,* December 1980.

Chapter ten:
THE PROCUREMENT ELITE

Jeffrey Record's article "Our Academies Don't Teach the History of War," *The Washington Post,* April 20, 1980, stunned many supporters of the American defense establishment with its revelations of the nonmilitary curriculae of the nation's service academies. Once a military advisor to Senator Sam Nunn and later a private consultant, Record established himself as a leading proponent of using innovative fighting tactics as a counter to the alarming failures that resulted from implementation of war plans based on miracle weapons that broke down in the friction of battle. Among other things, Record viewed as feasible arming entire infantry batallions with machine-gun equipped motorcycles instead of having them fight in the traditional and predictable troops-behind-tanks formations.

Colonel Dilger's ingenious approach to cutting weapon costs while producing more effective weapons was outlined to author Coates in December 1981. A subsequent article on Dilger, "A Career Cut Short by a Mission Well Done," by Frank Greve, appeared in the November 15, 1982, *Philadelphia Inquirer* and attracted a great deal of attention among military reformers.

The serious flaws of the ill-fated Maverick missile were exposed by Morton Mintz in a series of articles in *The Washington Post* that began February 23, 1982. These were later combined and expanded as a chapter in *More Bucks, Less Bang: How the Pentagon Buys Ineffective Weapons,* edited by Dina Rasor (Fund for Constitutional Government, 1983).

The flaws in the costly Bradley armored fighting vehicle and the procurement process that gave it life were well documented in an article in "The $13 Billion Dud," by William Boly, *California* magazine, February 1983.

The first major critique of the grieviously troubled Sergeant York air-defense gun was made in an October 1982 *Atlantic* article, "DIVAD," by Gregg Easterbrook. In a series starting April 17, 1983, in the *St. Louis Post-Dispatch,* "The Defense Lobby: Reaching for Billions," writer Bob Adams laid open the revolving door syndrome and its costly effect on Pentagon procurement.

James Fallows's *National Defense,* mentioned earlier, was the first major book inspired by the "reformers," the group of patriotic defense-establishment figures fearful of a weakening of American military strength because of overreliance on costly and undependable high-tech weaponry.

Defense or Delusion?, by Thomas H. Etzold, mentioned earlier, is an insider's warning about the dangers of the wasteful, self-serving procurement bureaucracy. A professor of strategy at the U.S. Navy War College, Etzold outlined what he called a "malaise" in the American military "that in peacetime transforms warriors into bureaucrats."

Chapter eleven:
LIFERS

Of the hundreds of newspaper and magazine articles written on the flaws of the American military command system, perhaps the best summary of the counterproductive effects of the military bureaucracy, top to bottom, was made in a two-part series by Michael Getler in *The Washington Post,* "Big Bureaucracy Seen Hampering Missions," which began March 4, 1984. A companion piece appearing March 5, 1984, "Budget Not Helping Response Capability," by Fred Hiatt, detailed how, despite a three-year $632 billion arms buildup by the Reagan administration, there were 25 percent fewer Army units and 15 percent fewer Air Force units listed as combat-ready than there were in the last year of the Carter administration. Performance, manpower training, and supply had actually improved from the Carter days, but were at levels woefully shorter of need.

Hiatt's December 23, 1983, article in the *Post,* "Army Drops Plan to Boost Strength," provided a good explanation of why the military's true troop strength needs are never met despite continually escalating costs, as outlined in a companion piece by Hiatt, "Pentagon Aims at 5.5 Percent Raise for Military." The bad news for the Pentagon contained in the economic recovery of 1983 was made clear in a February 3, 1984, Hiatt piece, "Army Reports Downturn in '83 Recruiting." The drop was 22 percent for the last quarter of that year.

Phillip Kiesling's article on the underworked and probably overstaffed Air Force in the February 1984 *Washington Monthly* underscores the serious problem for the all-voluntary military posed by the superfluity of recruits attracted to the more glamorous and comfortable services, where they are not so badly needed.

The *Armed Forces Journal* dealt splendidly with the problem of reliance on machines rather than men for combat effectiveness in a November 1983 article, "Combat Veterans Ask 'Why?'," which attempted to explain the comparative weakness of today's ground forces to veterans of World War II and Korea.

General Bernard Rogers remarks on our overreliance on nuclear weapons in Europe and our need for more troops and tanks to raise the nuclear threshold were made at a closed congressional hearing in March 1983, but he has made the same point publicly many times since.

The Reagan administration's case for continuation of the all-voluntary military was made in the November 1982 Report to the President on the Status and Prospects of the All-Volunteer Force made by the White House Military Manpower Task Force, headed by Defense Secretary Caspar Weinberger.

Statistics on manpower recruitment and reenlistment for the relevant years were taken from such official sources as the Defense Department's quarterly manpower strength assessments, fiscal year departmental selected manpower statistics, and reports to Congress by Dr. Lawrence J. Korb, assistant secretary of defense for manpower, reserve affairs, and logistics, and other ranking department officials.

Representative Les Aspin's November 1976 paper, "Guns or Pensions: A Study of the Military Retired Pay System," remains a basic primer on how all-volunteer military retirement costs are eating away at the financial base of national defense. Former Representative John Erlenborn brought matters more up to date in a lengthy paper accompanying the August 3, 1983, introduction of his Federal Annuity and Investment Reform (FAIR) legislation aimed at reducing the burden of federal pensions. An excellent critique of the military retirement system was written by retired Army Colonel John B. Keeley in "A New Look at Military Retirement," in the August 1983 *Armed Forces Journal*.

Damning evidence of the bloat in the officer corps was presented in "Officer Inflation: Its Cost to the Taxpayer and Military Effectiveness," a Project on Military Procurement study prepared by Thomas Lawson and published June 1982. The Pentagon did not dispute the study's statistics but differed strongly with its conclusions. A more sanguine look at the officer corps was contained in "How Good Are Our Military Officers?" by Al Santoli, published in *Parade* magazine, November 28, 1982.

A thoroughgoing report on the role, recruitment, and performance of women in the armed services was the Defense Department's "Military Women in the Department of Defense," published in April 1983. The sarcastic memo on hand-held showers on board ships and their possible uses in coed showers was actually classified as secret. A copy was obtained by a crew member of one of the ships covered by the hand-held shower order and was subsequently made available to the authors.

Data on educational opportunities in the military and other recruitment inducements was obtained from the October 1982 issue of *Profile*, published by the Department of Defense High School News Service, headquartered at Norfolk, Virginia.

The Committee on the Present Danger's 1983 report, "Has America Become Number 2?" offers useful information on comparative Soviet and American troop strengths.

Book-length sources dealing with the United States's military manpower needs include *Strengthening Conventional Deterrence in Europe: Proposals for the 1980s*, prepared by the European Security Study (St. Martin's Press, 1983); *Changing U.S. Military Manpower Realities*, edited by Franklin D. Margiotta, James Brown, and Michael J. Collins (Westview Press, 1983); *Blacks and the Military*, by Martin Binkin and Mark J. Eitelberg with Alvin J. Schexnider and Marvin M. Smith (Brookings Institution, 1982); *Military*

Compensation Background Papers, Compensation Elements and Related Manpower Cost Items: Their Purposes and Legislative Backgrounds (prepared and published by the Department of Defense, 1982); and the earlier-mentioned *Arms, Men, and Military Budgets,* by Francis P. Hoeber, David B. Kassing, and William Schneider, Jr.

The Defense Department's *Defense 83* and *Defense 84* almanacs were also used as statistical and data sources.

Chapter twelve:
INSIDE BRAINS

Two books by veteran Pentagon journalist James Canan stand as the basic histories of the men who have served in the post of DDR&E: *The Superwarriors* (Weybright and Talley, 1975) and *War in Space* (Harper & Row, 1982). Despite the tremendous problems with military procurement and combat effectiveness, many of the new wonder weapons have enormous and unprecedented killing and maiming potential, and Canan does an excellent job of explaining how these weapons came to be.

An equally good treatment of the exotic projects at the labs in Natick, Massachusetts, was done by Clayton Haswell of the Associated Press in his article "Army Laboratory Marching to the Beat of Progress," published in the *Chicago Tribune* and elsewhere September 25, 1983.

The CIA's occult projects are described in "Pentagon Is Said to Focus on ESP for Wartime Use," an article in the January 10, 1984, *New York Times* by William J. Broad. Admiral Stansfield Turner made his remarks at an August 9, 1977, breakfast meeting with reporters hosted by Godfrey Sperling, chief Washington correspondent of the *Christian Science Monitor.*

The Boys Behind the Bombs, by Michael Parfit (Little, Brown, 1983) is a sensitive and entertaining book dealing with many of the personalities involved at the top of the Pentagon research and development establishment.

The question of major conflicts of interest in the Defense Science Board was raised in "Report on the Audit of Policies, Procedures and Practices for Operation of the Defense Science Board," by the Defense Department Office of the Inspector General, submitted July 7, 1983, and reprinted in the July 22, 1983, *Congressional Record.* Testimony by Comptroller General Charles A. Bowsher about the computer case was made before the House Committee on Government Operations on July 22, 1982.

Richard DeLauer's angry attack on Inspector General Joseph Sherick for making his reservations public was printed along with the entire text of the Sherick report in the July 22, 1983, *Congressional Record.*

Chapter thirteen:
OUTSIDE BRAINS

James Canan's earlier mentioned *The Superwarriors* contains a good account of the role Project Jason thinkers played in developing the "electronic battlefield" of Vietnam. See also "The Jasons" in the April 15, 1968, issue of *The Nation.* The "electronic battlefield" is also discussed, particularly as concerns the use of sensors, in Stanley Karnow's excellent book *Vietnam: A History* (Viking Press, 1983).

The Nuclear Barons, by Peter Pringle and James Spigelman (Holt, Rinehart and Winston, 1981) contains an insightful treatment of the feud between Robert Oppenheimer and Edward Teller. Pringle's earlier-mentioned *SIOP* outlines how the same tight fraternity of "nuclear barons" subsequently produced their plans for new strategies and techniques in nuclear war fighting.

President Truman's condemnation of Oppenheimer is cited in *The Oppenheimer Case: Security on Trial,* by Philip M. Stern and Harold P. Green (Harper & Row, 1969).

Richard Garwin frequently supplies those who interview him with a personal compendium called *Papers and Testimony and Talks by R. L. Garwin Since 01/01/47,* which includes some of his work for the Jason project. Dr. Garwin has long since moved from the inner circles of the establishment to the role of critic of such defense schemes as the MX missile "racetrack" basing plan.

Disclosures of the Jasons' role in Vietnam were printed in *Science,* July 23, 1971, and February 2, 1973.

Fred Kaplan's *The Wizards of Armageddon* (Simon & Schuster, 1983) provides some comprehensive insights into the enormous influence wielded by think tanks in driving U.S. nuclear war plans.

Government by Contract, by John D. Hanrahan (W.W. Norton, 1983) deals with the abuses of federal contractors throughout the government. The newspaper series we cite is "The Revolving Door," by Jonathan Neumann and Ted Gup, June 21–June 26, 1980, in *The Washington Post.*

The General Accounting Office study "Factors Influencing DOD Decisions to Convert Activities from In-House to Contractor Performance: The United States General Accounting Office Report to the Senate and the House of Representatives Committees on Armed Services," April 22, 1981, documented how military officers frequently retire to collect pensions while starting new careers as private consultants to their old uniformed colleagues.

The transcript of Rickover's fiery valedictory testimony is "Economics of Defense Policy," Admiral H. O. Rickover, Hearing Before the Joint Economic Committee, Congress of the United States, January 28, 1982.

For a compendious treatment of virtually every conventional weapon in the American military arsenal, complete with brief discussions of the companies that built the weapons and the foreign countries that have purchased them, see *Arsenal of Democracy II: American Military Power in the 1980s and the Origins of the New Cold War,* by Tom Gervasi (Grove Press, 1981). Also see *What Kind of Guns Are They Buying for Your Butter?* by Sheila Tobias, Peter Goudinoff, Stefan Leader, and Shelah Leader (William Morrow, 1982).

The current defense activities of colleges and companies alike are available in the annual publication *500 Contractors Receiving the Largest Dollar Volume of Prime Contract Awards for RDT&E,* published by the Directorate for Information, Operations, and Reports, The Pentagon, Washington, D.C.

Chapter fourteen:
ELECTRONIC BRAINS

"NORAD's Missile Warning System: What Went Wrong?" General Accounting Office, May 15, 1981, details the Wimex failures. Editorials on the subject in the June 5, 1981, and March 1980 issues of *Science* are also recommended.

A Senate Armed Services Committee investigation produced a disturbing report, "Recent False Alerts from the Nation's Missile Attack Warning System," released October 9, 1980. Senator Gary Hart was later to say during his 1984 campaign for the Democratic presidential nomination that the Wimex investigation continued to haunt him. At a session with reporters in New Hampshire, Hart said he thought the greatest threat facing the world was a "mistake attack" and that it would probably be launched by the Soviets because their command, control, and communications computers were "even worse" than Wimex. Hart's commentary on this subject was reported by Thomas D. Elias in a March 1, 1984, article in *Rocky Mountain News* of Denver.

The "mystery flash" in the South Atlantic received widespread media coverage, notably in such articles as "Officials Hotly Debate Whether African Event Was Atom Blast," by Thomas O'Toole and Milton Benjamin, *The Washington Post,* January 17, 1980; "South Africa Blast May Have Been Bolt," by Walter Sullivan, *The New York Times,* October 30, 1979; and "A-Blast Was No Lightning Bolt, Panel Decides," by Thomas O'Toole, *The Washington Post,* January 1, 1980.

Plans for the next generation of Wimex development were outlined in testimony before the House Armed Services Committee on April 1, 1983, by DARPA Director Robert Cooper and Richard DeLauer, Reagan's first term Pentagon DDR&E. Pentagon plans for giving Wimex added sophistication were detailed in a DARPA annual report, "Fiscal Year 1983 Research and Development Program (U) A Summary Description," published March 30, 1982.

The Bomb and the Computer, by Andrew Wilson (Delacorte Press, 1968) provides a dated and therefore extremely prophetic book about the ways the war gamers started using data processing machines to keep score in hypothetical combats and soon found themselves using the machines to plan their strategies as well as compute their scores.

Among useful popular magazine articles dealing with military computers are "Computers in Combat," by Christopher Simpson in *Science Digest,* October 1982, and "Can ADA Run the Pentagon?" by Sharon Begley with Robb A. Allan, in *Newsweek,* January 10, 1983.

The poll results in which a majority of officers said they distrust Wimex were printed in the October 9, 1980, Senate report on the false alarms.

Chapter fifteen:
THE MAKERS

An excellent account of the cost growth in the Wright Brothers' military Flyer is contained in "Aviation History Made in N. Va., Alexandria," an article by Jim Garamone and Liz Neblett in the *Alexandria Gazette,* January 18, 1983.

Conservative economist Murray Weidenbaum warned of the dangers of concentration of defense contracts with a noncompetitive handful of giant companies in "Arms and the American Economy: A Domestic Convergence Hypothesis," a monograph appearing in *American Economic Review,* volume LVIII, no. 2, May 1968. Lockheed President Roy Anderson candidly acknowledged his company had decided to devote virtually all of its attention to military business in an article by Charles Mohr, "Lockheed's Grip on Washington," *The New York Times,* October 17, 1982.

The entrenchment of the same companies in the arms business throughout the major wars of the twentieth century is illustrated strikingly in the Nye Commission report, "Report of the Special Committee on Investigation of the Munitions Industry," 1936, U.S. Senate, vols. 1–5, 74th congress, 2nd session. A book-length source is *The War Profiteers,* by Richard Kaufman (Bobbs-Merrill, 1970). Kaufman notes that much of the Nye Commission's concern focused on the turning over of government arms manufacturing plants to private companies for a fraction of their worth after World War I, a practice repeated following World War II.

Jacques S. Gansler warned about the continuing concentration of defense contracts in a few hands in testimony on October 31, 1981, before the Joint Economic Committee. He is also the author of *The Defense Industry* (MIT Press, 1981).

Sears executive Knox discussed his decision to abandon doing business with the Pentagon in a December 10, 1980, *Chicago Tribune* article, "Arms Spending Hike Bypasses Illinois," by James Coates and Bill Neikirk.

The Schwartz analysis of why and how the Pentagon was forcing small contractors out of military business was contained in a study by Dr. Gail Garfield Schwartz, "Small Business: Vital Links in the Defense Production Chain," published June 3, 1982. A transcript of Dr. Hans Mark's amazing speech was reprinted in *Security Affairs,* the newsletter of the Jewish Institute for National Security Affairs, Washington, D.C., in its December 1982/January 1983 issue.

Industrialist Peter Grace's hard-hitting critiques were published in his commission study "Status Report: The President's Private Sector Survey on Cost Control," released August 30, 1983.

Chapter sixteen:
THE REFORMERS

The goals and background of "The Reformers" were in many ways best defined by an opponent, Lieutenant Colonel Walter Kross, in a review of James Fallows's book *National Defense* that appeared in the Spring 1982 issue of *Air University Review.* Fallows had acknowledged substantial help and inspiration from the reform group in expressing themes that ultimately were taken up by the Congressional Military Reform Caucus.

Veteran fighter pilot Fay's first public warnings about the counterproductive trend to more costly and complex but fewer combat aircraft were made in an interview with CBS for the June 17, 1981, special series "The Defense of the United States," featuring correspondents Dan Rather and Richard Threlkeld.

Retired Air Force Colonel Everest Riccioni discussed the dangerous drawbacks of ultrasophisticated but fuel-hungry high-tech aircraft in an unpublished paper, "The Progression of Maximum Speeds in Modern High Performance Fighter Aircraft."

The devastating use of supposedly obsolete radar technology and out-of-date aircraft to defeat the almighty AWACS plane was revealed in a *Chicago Tribune* article by author Coates, "AWACS Jet Fails Crucial Defense Test," September 20, 1981.

Thomas Amlie's April 1982 article in *IEEE Spectrum,* "Radar: Shield or Target?" amply detailed the flaws of overreliance on radar target-finding technology.

Information on the failures of the Navy's Aegis system came in substantial part from congressional and other defense establishment sources. A rare interview with an Aegis project officer was contained in Michael Gordon's article "Aegis: A High Priority Naval Defense Project . . . But Will It Work When the Chips Are Down?" *National Journal,* July 24, 1982.

The first major information about the troubles with the Abrams M-1 battle tank was made public in an article in the April 26, 1981, *Chicago Sun-Times,* "M-1," by Patrick Oster and Bruce Ingersoll.

More Bucks, Less Bang: How the Pentagon Buys Ineffective Weapons, a compendium of magazine and newspaper articles prepared by Dina Rasor of the Project on Military Procurement, was a helpful resource for this chapter. Miss Rasor's group had provided much of the information used in the articles.

Chuck Spinney's original briefing paper, "Defense Facts of Life," was published by the Pentagon December 5, 1980, and given out in a limited distribution. This was the first of two major Spinney briefings. "The Plans/ Reality Mismatch" and "Why We Need Realistic Budgeting," a later version of Spinney's presentation, included data on the negative effect of the Reagan administration's arms build-up binge on the situation.

In his "What 'Quality vs. Quantity' Issue?" briefing, Pierre Sprey dramatically recounted the preponderance of cheap winners over expensive losers among weapons in military history—and in current U.S. and Soviet arsenals. A published version of Sprey's briefing appears in *The Defense Reform Debate,* edited by Asa A. Clark IV, Peter W. Chiarelli, Jeffrey S. McKitrick, and James W. Reed (Johns Hopkins University Press, 1984).

Chapter seventeen:
THE AGAINSTERS

Excellent sources on the congressional warhawks who pushed for the War of 1812 and the rancorous debate that divided the nation over that conflict are *John C. Calhoun,* by Hermann E. von Holst (Chelsea House, 1980); *Henry Clay and the Art of American Politics,* by Clement Eaton (Little, Brown, 1957); and *Daniel Webster and the Rise of National Conservatism,* by Richard N. Current (Little, Brown, 1955).

The widespread opposition to the Mexican War is discussed in the earlier-mentioned *The Oxford History of the American People,* by Samuel Eliot Morison, and in *Daniel Webster and the Trial of American National-ism:1843–1852,* by Robert F. Dalzell, Jr. (Houghton Mifflin, 1972). A wonderful work dealing with Abraham Lincoln's role in the controversy is *A. Lincoln: The Crucible of Congress,* by former congressman Paul Findley (Crown Publishers, 1980).

A comprehensive anthology of Randolph Bourne's works is *The Radical*

Will: Randolph Bourne, Selected Writings, 1911–1918, edited by Olaf Hansen with preface by Christopher Lasch (Urizen Books, 1977).

The incompetence, recklessness, conniving, and arrogance on the part of the then-aging general Douglas MacArthur during the Korean War is amply discussed in *MacArthur in Korea: The Naked Emperor*, by Robert Smith (Simon & Schuster, 1982), among other works. Author Kilian also participated in a U.S. Army training course in Korea on the failures of the American military during that conflict. The previously mentioned *This Kind of War*, by T. R. Fehrenbach provides additional material.

Stanley Karnow's earlier mentioned *Vietnam: A History*, remains in the authors' minds the definitive reference on the Vietnam War and deals thoroughly with the progress of combat during the period of the most intense domestic protests against the war. A worthy companion work is *The Ten Thousand Day War: Vietnam, 1945–1975*, by Michael Maclear (St. Martin's Press, 1981).

Both authors were heavily involved in coverage of the antiwar movement in the late 1960s and early 1970s as well as the political reaction to it. In addition to numerous personal interviews by both authors with such antiwar notables as Tom Hayden, Jane Fonda, Staughton Lynd, Jerry Rubin, Abbie Hoffman, John Froines, Joan Baez, and many others, author Coates covered the Chicago 7 conspiracy trial and author Kilian testified in it. Kilian covered all of the presidential and vice-presidential candidates in the 1968 and 1972 elections and the primary challenges of former senator Eugene McCarthy and the others. Both authors were involved in coverage of the riotous and divisive national conventions of that era. Coates has continued to deal with Jeremy Rifkin and other activists as a reporter on other issues.

Miss Fonda's contrite remarks about the hostility generated by her protest methods werre contained in an interview published in the April 1984 *Ladies' Home Journal*.

Some extremely solid reporting on the lobbying effort against the B-1 bomber was provided in "The B-1 Bomber: Organizing at the Grass Roots, from Interest Groups, Lobbying and Policymaking," by Norman J. Ornstein and Shirley Elder, *Congressional Quarterly*, 1978. Orr Kelly's "The B-1: When Pentagon, Politicians Joined Hands," *U.S. News & World Report*, July 11, 1983, is equally authoritative.

On the nuclear freeze issue, the June 1982 *Bulletin of the Atomic Scientists* contains a number of informative articles, including Milton Leitenberg's "The Numbers Game or 'who's on first?' " Christopher Paine's "The Freeze and the United Nations," and Jane M. O. Sharp's "Nuclear Weapons and Alliance Cohesion." Excellent summaries of freeze movement arguments were provided in "Nuclear Freeze: A Necessary First Step," in *The Defense Monitor*, 1982, volume XI, number 7, and in the *Journal of the Federation of American Scientists*, September 1982.

Other recommended writings include Leslie Gelb's "Is the Nuclear Threat Manageable?" *The New York Times*, March 4, 1984; Eugene Kennedy's "Debate on Doomsday," *Chicago Tribune Magazine*, May 1, 1983; and three pieces in *The New York Review of Books:* "The Missed Chance to Stop the H-Bomb," by McGeorge Bundy, May 13, 1982; "How Not to Think About Nuclear War," by Theodore Draper, July 15, 1982; and "The Bishops and the Bomb," also by Bundy, June 16, 1983. In an April 25, 1983, article in *U.S. News & World Report*, "Nuclear Freeze Crusade, Gaining or Waining?" James Wallace produced a valuable analysis of the effectiveness of the nuclear freeze movement.

Some worthy book-length sources typical of the freeze movement include *Freeze? How You Can Help Prevent Nuclear War*, by Senators Edward M. Kennedy and Mark O. Hatfield (Bantam Books, 1982); *Nuclear War: What's in It for You?*, prepared by Ground Zero, Roger C. Molander, executive director, and Earl A. Molander, deputy director (Pocket Books, 1982); and *The Disarmer's Handbook of Military Technology and Organization*, by Andrew Wilson (Penguin Books, 1983), which hawks as well as doves will find extremely useful.

The alliance of diverse opponents against the MX missile was incisively explained in a February 22, 1981, article in the now-defunct *Washington Star*, "Alliance Against MX Makes for Strange Bedfellows." Other pertinent references on the MX debate include Representative Bill Green's May 9, 1983, contribution to the *Congressional Record*, "MX: Four Fallacies"; Senator Edward M. Kennedy's statement opposing the MX missile on the Senate floor on July 26, 1983; the National Campaign to Stop the MX's barrage of statements in May 1982, including a macabre but hilarious list of proposed MX missile deployment modes; and the Committee for a Sane Nuclear Policy's (SANE) pragmatic September 26, 1983, polemic, "Ninety Percent of Congressional Districts to Lose If MX Missile Is Built, Texas, Illinois, New York, Biggest Losers."

Other worthwhile sources include the August 28, 1979, paper prepared by David Cohen, then-president of Common Cause, for the United States Army War College at Carlisle Barracks, Pennsylvania, Special Interest Groups and the Public Process; Laurence Grafstein's October 4, 1982, article in *The New Republic* dealing with Pentagon muckraking by the Better Government Association, "Wallowing in Waste"; and three pieces on Georgetown University's Center for Strategic and International Studies, "Lawrence Feinberg's Georgetown U. a Prime Source of Advisers for Campaign" and Don Oberdorfer's "Abshire to Aid Reagan Team," both appearing on November 9, 1980; and James Lardner's "Thick and Think Tank," September 21, 1982. Andrew C. Seamans, Sr.'s, article "Heritage Study Sets Firm Foundation for Reagan," in *Human Events*, January 10,

1981, dealt with the burgeoning institution that became the major fount of ideas for hard-core Reaganites.

Philip Taubman's July 31, 1983, article in *The New York Times*'s The Week in Review, "Despite Nicaragua Vote, Foes Seem Divided and Conquered," ably explained the difficulties posed to the peace movement after what the public came to view as a feckless and defeatist Carter administration.

A quintessential Pentagon counterattack against its critics was voiced in "Imagination Shapes the Future: The Nay-sayers Have Not Changed Their Tune Much Since the Day of the Wrights and the Foulois," by Defense Secretary Weinberger in the November 1983 issue of *Air Force* magazine.

Chapter eighteen:
BAD NEWS

Stanley Karnow's *Vietnam: A History,* mentioned before, was a very useful resource for this chapter as well. The authors also benefited greatly from many friendships with colleagues and others who both fought and reported the war in Vietnam, as well as firsthand knowledge of how journalism's elite in Washington and elsewhere dealt with the subject during the combat and in subsequent years.

The Pentagon's dealings with and attitudes toward the press are also recounted from personal knowledge. "The Pentagon Press: Prisoners of Respectability," by Timothy Noah, in the September 1983 issue of *Washington Monthly,* is a very informative if somewhat overwrought treatment of the subject with a polemic thrust that might better be directed at the White House press corps or some of the obviously incestuous political coverage that surfaces in election years. In fairness, the article does cite the high caliber of such Pentagon reporters as *The New York Times*'s Charles Mohr and *The Washington Post*'s Fred Hiatt.

George C. Wilson's "Is the Press Being Duped? The Tale of a Phony CIA Document Suggests the Dangers," in *The Washington Post,* September 25, 1983, revealed how forged papers and other devices may be used by the national security apparat to manipulate the press, much as the controversial Arnold de Borchgrave insists the American news media has been misled by highly orchestrated Soviet "disinformation" campaigns.

Richard Halloran's April 18, 1983, article in *The New York Times,* "The Problem of Keeping So Many Secrets Secrets," lays out the problems engendered by the Pentagon's mania for classifying seemingly every document in sight.

"Lehman Fires Blanks in His War on Congress and the Press," an article by Deborah G. Meyer in the August 1983 *Armed Forces Journal*, related the pitfalls of the blitzkrieg approach to media and legislative relations used by Navy Secretary John Lehman and others.

The constant temptations and pressures the Washington press corps is subject to from Embassy Row is revealed in "Foreign Governments Are Playing Our Press," an article in the October 1983 *Washington Journalism Review*, by James Buie, Maura Casey, Gregory Enns, Vandana Mathur, and Mark Williams of the American University School of Communications.

Also recommended is William Safire's October 30, 1983, column in *The New York Times*, "Us Against Them," which warned the Reagan administration of the Nixonian dangers of conjuring up the press as "the enemy."

Jerry Friedheim's remarks on the necessity of press presence during American military actions were published in the November 14, 1983, *U.S. News & World Report*.

The Washington Reporters, by Stephen Hess (The Brookings Institution, 1981) is an insightful examination of the Washington news media and how they are regarded by the government establishment they cover.

Chapter nineteen:
FRIENDS AND ENEMIES

Author Kilian's foreign affairs reporting and commentary has included especially the governments and international activities of Britain, West Germany, Canada, France, the Soviet Union, Korea, and the five Nordic nations, as well as coverage over the years of the Senate Foreign Relations and House Foreign Affairs Committees, NATO, and the United Nations. Author Coates has done substantial reporting on foreign arms sales and the influential reach of foreign governments through highly placed American lobbyists.

A good analysis of the stresses confronting the Western alliance was contained in James O. Goldsborough's article in the May 9, 1982, *New York Times Magazine*, "The Roots of Western Disunity." Lucy Komisar's piece in the March 25, 1985, *Chicago Tribune*, "East German Peace Movement Growing," ably summarizes the pressure from the left that continues to confound the fractured country that is the keystone of NATO. *U.S. News & World Report* published a thoroughgoing analysis of U.S. alliances in "Our Alliances—Are They Worth The Cost?" in its June 13, 1983, issue.

Canada's woeful lack of support of the NATO alliance is made clear in its own government publication, *Defense Estimates, 1983/1984*, published by the Ministry of National Defense, March 15, 1983. The April 4, 1983,

Time article "Testing Weapons and Friends" dealt with the seizure of the widespread Canadian peace movement on the issue of U.S. cruise missile testing on Canadian territory. This was under the policies of Liberal Party Prime Minister Pierre Trudeau. His Conservative party successor, Brian Mulroney, pledged to reverse Trudeau's antimilitary trend, but faced with the prospect of annual budget deficits far exceeding the United States's in per capita terms, Mulroney had to freeze military budgets.

British attitudes toward the United States were well expressed in an October 28, 1983, *Chicago Tribune* article, "Queen Is 'Immensely Displeased' with Reagan over Grenada War"; the May 1, 1983, *Washington Post* Outlook section article "Look Again: It's the West That's Strong, Moscow That's Weak," by Peter, Lord Carrington, former Thatcherite British foreign minister and subsequently NATO secretary general. He later opined that he saw NATO as a diplomatic institution rather than a military one. The dispatch of large segments of the Royal Navy on a show-the-flag cruise of far-flung waters was announced July 14, 1983, in the House of Commons by John Stanley, Minister of State for the British Armed Forces.

Eric Margolis, international affairs columnist for the *Toronto Sun*, outlined Israel's little-known role as an arms purveyor in the February 6, 1984, *Chicago Tribune* Perspective article, "Israel: Global Arms Merchant." *U.S. News & World Report* dealt thoroughly with the United States's concerns in the Mideast with its February 6, 1984, story "Arab World: Where Troubles for U.S. Never End."

The recent deployment of Pershing II and cruise nuclear missiles in Western Europe, a mixed success for American foreign and national security policy and a major defeat for the Soviets, was examined in a number of worthwhile pieces. These include "A Good Day for the Alliance," by Richard Burt, assistant secretary of state for European and Canadian affairs, *Washington Post*, November 27, 1983; "New NATO Missiles: One Small Step," by Drew Middleton, *The New York Times*, November 15, 1983; "Weinberger Tells Dutch Missiles Are 'Vital,'" by Fred Hiatt, *The Washington Post*, March 30, 1984; and a companion piece, "U.S. May Drop Limits of SALT at End of '85," by Don Oberdorfer, March 30, 1984. The *Post*'s "Weinberger Visit Had Little Effect on Dutch Missile Deployment Debate," by Priscilla Painton, April 5, 1983, further emphasized the difficulties the U.S. faced in European capitals, especially with Weinberger as secretary of defense.

Also recommended is Martin Tolchin's July 5, 1983, article in *The New York Times*, "The Role of 'Barnacles' in Foreign Aid," in which the powerful and learned Representative Henry Hyde is quoted as saying, "Everybody's a Secretary of State around here. It's an exercise in power. You get a kick out of meddling in foreign policy. It's an aphrodisiac."

The Washington Post's half-page map of the war front in the Iraqi-Iranian War in its February 24, 1984, edition provides a graphic explanation of that conflict that illustrates its essential dilemma admirably.

The menace posed by international arms sales has been examined in a number of comprehensive journalistic pieces. Anthony H. Cordesman's "The Soviet Arms Trade: Patterns for the 1980s," in the August 1983 *Armed Forces Journal*, is a must. So is the *Time* magazine October 26, 1981, cover story, "Arming the World." Other sources include the September 25, 1981, report of the Congressional Research Service to the House Foreign Affairs Committee Subcommittee on International Security and Scientific Affairs, "Changing Perspectives on U.S. Arms Transfer Policy." Another illuminating report of the Congressional Research Service was Richard F. Grimmett's April 11, 1983, study, "Trends in Conventional Arms Transfers to the Third World by Major Suppliers, 1975–1982." Also see "U.S. Is Becoming Arms Merchant of the World," by Bill Neikirk and James Coates, *Chicago Tribune*, December 11, 1981.

A dramatic illustration of the perpetually unpeaceful nature of the world was presented in the summary "Even in 'Peacetime,' 40 Wars Are Going On," *U.S. News & World Report*, July 11, 1983.

Two recommended book-length sources, in addition to the aforementioned memoirs of Alexander Haig, Harold Brown, Cyrus Vance, Zbigniew Brzezinski, and Dwight D. Eisenhower, and *Strengthening Conventional Deterrence in Europe*, are *Nuclear Weapons and World Politics*, by David C. Gompert, Michael Mandelbaum, Richard L. Garwin, and John H. Barton (McGraw-Hill, 1977); and the handbook *Everyman's United Nations*, published and revised regularly by the United Nations.

Basic to any study of U.S. alliances is *Barren Victories, Versailles to Suez: The Failure of the Western Alliance, 1918–1956*, by Basil Collier (Doubleday, 1964).

Chapter twenty:
SPOOKS

Admiral Bobby Ray Inman outlined the ills that beset American intelligence in a *Chicago Tribune* Perspective article, "The Decline of U.S. Intelligence," October 3, 1982.

Information on the clash between the Army and the Central Intelligence Agency on enemy order of battle counts in Vietnam was obtained by the authors from American intelligence officials then on the scene. An excellent account of the 1963 Diem assassination was made in the *U.S. News &*

World Report special section, "Untold Story of the Road to War in Vietnam," published October 10, 1983. Stanley Karnow's previously listed *Vietnam: A History* is a good reference on both of these pivotal aspects of the war. Charles Mohr's interview with former defense secretary Robert McNamara in the May 16, 1984, *New York Times,* "McNamara on Record, Reluctantly, on Vietnam," offers more details.

Thomas N. Bethell's article in the March 1980 *Washington Monthly,* "The Spy Who Went Out in the Cold War," deals with former Central Intelligence director Richard Helms's role in Vietnam and other activities.

Admiral Stansfield Turner's purges in the CIA were noted in "The Langley File: Turner Is in Trouble," by Joseph Goulden, in the Capital Comment section of the May 1979 *The Washingtonian.* A more positive view of Turner's performances was to be found in Tad Szulc's "Putting Back the Bite in the C.I.A.," *The New York Times Magazine,* April 6, 1980.

United Press International produced a good profile of Admiral Inman, "CIA's No. 2 everybody's No. 1," which appeared in the March 1, 1981, *Chicago Sun-Times,* among other places.

"America's Secret Warriors," an article in *Newsweek,* October 10, 1983, contained a good analysis of William Casey's performance running the CIA. Congress's clumsiness and frustration in dealing with the intelligence community was treated in a September 26, 1983, article in *The Washington Post,* "Hill Learns That Being Tightfisted Is Its Only Way to Collar CIA," by Joanne Omang.

Some interesting insights into American intelligence were provided in a paper, "Intelligence Management: Some Notes on the CIA," by the controversial Max Hugel, briefly Casey's deputy director of central intelligence and head of human intelligence, presented at the Defense '83 Conference on Defense and Foreign Affairs.

The very best single reference on the supersecret National Security Agency is *The Puzzle Palace,* by James Bamford (Houghton Mifflin, 1982). Other sources include David Burnham's "The Silent Power of the N.S.A.," an article in *The New York Times Magazine,* March 27, 1983. David Shribman's piece in the September 2, 1983, *New York Times,* "Side Effect: Peek at U.S. Intelligence Abilities," related how the Soviet's Korean jetliner downing that year helped make public the United States's electronic eavesdropping capability. Bamford's "The Last Flight of KAL 007," an article in the January 8, 1984, *Washington Post Magazine,* deals with the subject in greater detail.

Some of the flaws and failures of the American intelligence system are explored in a number of sources: "Soviet Arms—Guess Who Does the Guessing?" by Richard Whitmire of the Gannett News Service, April 25,

1984; "Intelligence in Beirut Reported Still Faulty," by Margaret Shapiro, and "Initial Accounts of Attack 'Misleading,' " by Michael Getler, both in the December 22, 1983, *Washington Post;* "Administration Said to Have Misjudged Soviet A-Arms Strategy," by Walter Pincus, in the December 18, 1983, *Washington Post;* "Grenada Highlighted One of DoD's Major C3 Problems, But Increased Funding Is Bringing Solutions," by Benjamin F. Schemmer, in the February 1984 *Armed Forces Journal;* and the earlier mentioned *False Science: Underestimating the Soviet Arms Buildup,* by Steven Rosefielde.

"The Secret Files of Mr. X," by Charles Fenyvesi, in the July 11, 1982, *Washington Post Magazine,* explains the State Department's apparatus for gathering and organizing knowledge about the Soviets. Fred Kaplan's "Pentagon Superweapon: The Hair-Raising Briefer" in the March 20, 1983, *Washington Post* revealed how Pentagon intelligence briefings are used to frighten members of Congress and the press into seeing matters from the Pentagon point of view.

"Boom Days for Political Risk Consultants," by Peter H. Stone, in the August 7, 1983, *New York Times,* told how Richard Helms, William Colby, and other former intelligence officials and operatives have swelled the ranks of private consulting firms influencing American decision-making and policy. Edward Jay Epstein's "How Badly One Man Hurt Our Nation," *Parade* magazine, September 18, 1983, discusses the serious problems posed by rogue intelligence agents.

John Barron's *KGB,* previously mentioned, is an excellent reference on Soviet espionage activities in the United States. William Hood's "Mole," *The Washington Post Magazine,* August 15, 1982, was also very informative. See also author Coates's "Soviets Walk Right In, Take American Technology Home," April 13, 1981, and the August 31, 1983, article by John Bennett of Scripps-Howard News Service, "How Tass Covers the News."

References on discussion of the intelligence community's role in the fighting in Central America included Joseph Shapiro's August 1, 1983 article in *U.S. News & World Report,* "The Showdown Over CIA's 'Dirty Tricks' "; Stansfield Turner's piece in the April 24, 1983, *Washington Post* Outlook section, "From an Ex-CIA Chief: Stop the 'Covert' Operation in Nicaragua"; Joanne Omang and Walter Pincus's "Security Experts Differ on Effects of CIA's Mining," *The Washington Post,* April 21, 1984; "CIA Views Minelaying Part of Covert 'Holding Action,' Stepped-Up Role Seen After U.S. Elections," by Bob Woodward and Fred Hiatt, *The Washington Post,* April 10, 1984; "Ex-U.S. Intelligence and Military Personnel Supply Anti-Nicaragua Rebels," by Jeff Gerth and Philip Taugman, *The New York Times,* November 8, 1983; Representative Lee Hamilton's piece, "The CIA and Nicaragua: Covert Action Is Not in Our National Interest," *The*

Washington Post, May 1, 1983; and *Time* magazine's "Uneasy Over a Secret War," May 16, 1983. The authors also drew heavily on private sources familiar with American operations in the Central American and Caribbean regions.

Senator Goldwater's letter to CIA Director William Casey was widely circulated on Capitol Hill. Admiral Inman's admirable role in preventing a Casey attempt to return the CIA to widescale spying on U.S. citizens was detailed in "A CIA Spy Ploy Backfires," in *Newsweek,* March 23, 1981.

Book-Length references include *Trouble in Our Backyard: Central America and the United States in the Eighties,* edited by Martin Diskin (Pantheon, 1984) and *The Report of the President's National Bipartisan Commission on Central America,* with foreword by Henry Kissinger (Macmillan,1984). For more on CIA operations in the 1970s and earlier, see *The Man Who Kept the Secrets: Richard Helms and the CIA,* by Thomas Powers (Alfred Knopf, 1979).

Useful book-length references on the subject mentioned previously include *American National Security: Policy and Process;* Walter Millis's *Arms and Men;* and Herbert S. Parmet's *JFK: The Presidency of John F. Kennedy.*

Don Gregg, national security advisor to Vice-President George Bush and a former corps area CIA chief in Vietnam was *not* a source for any information on operations or activities of the CIA or any other American intelligence unit.

Chapter twenty-one:
THE $300 BILLION AIRPLANE

The startling prediction that the 2054 defense budget would likely suffice to buy only one airplane was made in "They're Redesigning the Airplane," by Norman Augustine, *National Geographic,* January 1981.

Military Expansion, Economic Decline, by Robert W. Degrasse, Jr., Council on Economic Priorities, 1983, examines the kind of jobs created by arms spending, the impact of defense outlays on the nonmilitary segments of American business, and other aspects of military spending. Two major studies also dealing with the subject were *Defense Spending and the Economy,* by Alice Rivlin (Congressional Budget Office, 1983) and *Economic Choices 1984,* edited by Alice Rivlin (The Brookings Institution, 1984).

"The Army's New Fighting Doctrine," an article by Deborah Shapley in the November 28, 1982, *New York Times Magazine,* outlined current government views on the likely nature of prospective warfare. A more technical treatment was "NATO: Can the Alliance Be Saved?" by Dr. Tim Alexander Meyers (a pseudonym), in the November 1983 *Armed Forces Journal.*

The dangers posed to the United States in the Far East were powerfully stated in *The Military Balance in Northeast Asia: The Challenge to Japan and Korea,* by Anthony H. Cordesman, also in the November 1983 *Armed Forces Journal.*

Analyst Robert W. Komer outlined the drift toward nuclear warfare in Europe in *Rethinking Defense and Conventional Forces* (Center for National Policy, 1983).

Acknowledgments

The authors are particularly grateful to Vice-President George Bush for taking of his very valuable time to provide us with an overview of American national security as seen from the command pinnacle of the White House and from the perspective of his past experience as one of the nation's foremost diplomats and as a director of central intelligence.

We are also very grateful to Air Force Colonel Christopher I. Branch for freely allowing us a look at the life of a front-line missile commander and Pentagon officer, even though he may have a basic disagreement with the premise of this book and many of the assertions contained within it.

Former Ambassador and Brigadier General John S. D. Eisenhower (Ret.) has been an inspiration to us, both through the example of his long career of concerned and dedicated public service and by his advancing the notion that to criticize military wrongs does not necessarily mean a lack of patriotism.

The authors really acknowledge their gratitude and enormous debt to the *Chicago Tribune,* without which this book would not have been possible. This venerable American institution not only provided the authors with their journalistic careers but gave them the opportunity to deal with national affairs on a firsthand basis in Washington for many years.

It is important to point out that the positions taken in this book are not necessarily those of the *Tribune* or any other of its employees. The views are expressed strictly as the authors'. They take full responsibility for the accuracy of the reporting and the weight of argument behind its assertions. But the authors still must express gratitude for the assistance, support, guidance, inspiration, leads, and ground-breaking reportage of a number of their *Tribune* colleagues.

These include Editor James Squires; Chief Editorial Writer and former Pentagon Correspondent Jack Fuller; Managing Editor F. Richard Ciccone; Washington Bureau Chief and veteran War Correspondent Ray Coffey; Washington Correspondent and Columnist Bill Neikirk, who joined with author James Coates in producing a prize-winning series on military procurement; Foreign Editor and veteran Moscow Correspondent James O. Jackson; Washington Correspondents James O'Shea, George deLama, and Storer Rowley; and Washington Bureau Librarian Carolyn Hardnett.

Similar gratitude for the same reasons must be expressed to others in the Washington press corps, notably George C. Wilson, Morton Mintz, Michael Getler, Fred Hiatt, and Rick Atkinson of *The Washington Post;* Charles Mohr and Richard Halloran of *The New York Times;* Joe Volz of the *New York Daily News;* Orr Kelly of *U.S. News & World Report;* Rudy Abramson of the *Los Angeles Times;* Frank Greve of the *Philadelphia Inquirer;* Gregg Easterbrook of *The Atlantic;* Stephen Webbe of the *Christian Science Monitor;* Knut Royce of the Hearst Newspapers; Lance Gay of Scripps-Howard News Service; John Fialka of *The Wall Street Journal;* and Michael Gordon of the *National Journal.*

A similar debt is owed to fellow authors James Fallows, Fred Kaplan, Alexander Cockburn, Thomas Etzold, Tom Gervasi, James Bamford, Dina Rasor, A. Ernest Fitzgerald, Peter Pringle, William Arkin, James Spigelman, and James Canan.

The highest praise is due "reformers" Pierre Sprey, John Boyd, Franklin C. Spinney, Robert Fay, Thomas Amlie, George Spanton, Gordon Rule, Paul Hoven, Joseph Bernice, and so many others we can't name in the defense community, who risked their careers and more in a courageous effort to make the American public, the Congress, and responsible elements of the Executive branch aware of flaws in the United States military system that posed so many dangers to American national security.

Among these we include Dieter, referred to in the dedication, who contributed so much to revealing these dangers under a great stress—a stress that ultimately brought on his untimely death. We trust that those who loved him know to whom we refer and will rest easy that his secret is safe.

There is courage aplenty among elected officials as well. Though ideological opposites, Congressmen Denny Smith of Oregon and Les Aspin of Wisconsin made gigantic contributions toward uncovering horrific problems in the military and making the Pentagon do something about them. Also impressive have been the efforts of Senators Charles Grassley of Iowa, Nancy Kassebaum of Kansas, Alan Dixon and (former Senator) Charles Percy of Illinois, William Roth of Delaware, Gary Hart of Colorado, Ted Stevens of Alaska, Mark Hatfield of Oregon, Dale Bumpers of Arkansas, Rudy Boschwitz of Minnesota, Mark Andrews of North Dakota, and Barry Goldwater of Arizona. Many of them are conservative Republicans who stuck to their concerns and principles despite a reflexive Pentagon response that to question military policy and practices is unpatriotic. Also to be commended are Congresswoman Barbara Boxer of California and Congressmen Jack Brooks of Texas, Joseph Addabbo of New York, Tom Downey of New York, and Tim Worth of Colorado.

No member of the House or Senate can accomplish much without a skilled, effective, and dedicated staff. Among many staffers who deserve the nation's praise and gratitude for furthering the cause of making national security policy and military defense systems work are Warren Nelson of the House Armed Services Committee; John Heubush, Congressman Denny Smith's military aide; Alan Mertz and William Strauss, aides to former Senator Percy; Kris Kolesnik of Senator Grassley's staff; William Lind, Senator Hart's military advisor; John Maddox and Charles Osolin, press secretaries to Senator Roth; and, of course, Jeffrey Bergner, the highly regarded staff director of the Senate Foreign Relations Committee.

We should note that, though portions of this book are highly critical of the military establishment, much of the information it contains was provided by frequently helpful and always courteous representatives of that same establishment. Public affairs officers as high ranking as Assistant Secretary of Defense for Public Affairs Michael Burch and so lowly as the airmen who answer the phones at Offut Air Force Base were invariably forthcoming when asked for factual information. The United States remains the most open society in the world, and the military, for all its problems with the news media, remains respectful of that tradition.

We are also grateful for interviews and other conversations that have been granted by others in officialdom and the foreign affairs community over the years. These include former Defense Secretaries Donald Rumsfeld, James Schlesinger, and Elliot Richardson (who was extremely helpful with Law of the Sea matters); Undersecretary General Brian Urquhart of the United Nations; Admiral Bobby Ray Inman (Ret.); Ambassadors Max Kampelman and Patrick J. Lucey; State Department Counselor Edward Derwinski; former Chief of Naval Operations Admiral Elmo Zumwalt (Ret.); Donald Gregg, national security advisor to Vice-President Bush; Sovietologist Dr. Eberhard Heyken of the West German foreign ministry; Peter Hall of the British Foreign Office; Marc Lortie of the Canadian Office of External Affairs; and Hal Saunders, one of the most thoughtful and professional foreign policy experts ever to serve on the National Security Council.

We must discreetly omit the names of two former officials of the Central Intelligence Agency, who have maintained an interest in intelligence matters in retirement and who were most helpful in providing insights and background knowledge concerning intelligence problems. The country was never better served as when they were in office.

We are indebted to Martha Kinney, formerly of Penguin Books, for first seeing the possibilities of a defense book of this scope and thrust. We are extremely grateful for the sensitivity and skill of Viking Penguin Senior Editor Gerald Howard, and for the thoughtful encouragement and guidance of editor Alan Williams as well. The enthusiasm and professionalism of Victoria Meyer, Viking Penguin director of publicity, has been a wonder to behold and a rarity for which we are most thankful.

There is no limit to our gratitude to our wives, Kay Coates and Pamela Reeves Kilian, and our children, Marianne and Paul Coates and Eric and Colin Kilian, for their extraordinary patience, forebearance, and support in several years of coping with a demanding new family member named "book." May we somehow make it up to them.

A special note of thanks is due Bill Anderson, a former *Tribune* Pentagon correspondent, who was city editor when the authors were launching their newspaper careers as city-side general assignment reporters. In many memorable ways, he set us on this path.

Index

428   INDEX

Teller, Edward, 201, 209, 212
TEMPER (Technological, Economic, Military, Political Evaluation Routine), 230–231
Tenneco, 109, 219
Tercom guidance system, 146, 159
Terpil, Frank, 341
tests of weapons, 261, 275
Thayer, Paul, 86–87, 164, 170
Thieu, Nguyen Van, 115
Thinking About National Security (Brown), 123–124
think tanks, 215–218
   universities as, 217–218, 223–224
Third World, arms sales to, 327
Thomas, Norman, 242
Thor rocket project, 143
Threat: Inside the Soviet Military Machine, The (Cockburn), 44–46, 152
Thurmond, Strom, 100
Ticonderoga, 254, 259–261
Time, 307–308
Today show, 302
Tomahawk cruise missile, 151
Tower, John, 40, 92–93, 101–102, 111, 270–271
Townes, Charles H., 213
Transportation Department, U.S., 27
Treasury Department, U.S., 338
Tregaskis, Richard, 299
Triad, Strategic, 144–146
   Strategic Force suggested for, 150–152
Trible, Paul, 109–110
Trident missile, 146–147, 240
Trident submarine, 146, 237
Truman, Harry S, 126, 212
   Air Force and, 138
   NSC and, 75
TRW, 209
Tsipis, Kosta, 233
Tupolev, Andrei, 357
Turner, Stansfield, 200, 345, 347–348

underwear, air-conditioned, 200
Union of Automobile, Aerospace,

and Agricultural Implement Workers of America, International (UAW), 283–284
United Nations, 322–325
United States:
   arms exported by, 326–328
   European relations with, 55
   foreign policy of, 313–330
   GNP of, 47
   as reactive and defensive power, 54–56
   treaties of, 313–314
   UN and, 322–325
United States Military Academy (West Point), 153, 264
United Technologies, 240, 249
universities, as defense think tanks, 217–218, 223–224
U.S. News & World Report, 40–41, 289, 308, 348
Ustinov, Dimitri, 152

V-2 rocket, 142
Vance, Cyrus, 75–76, 84
Vandenberg, Hoyt, 136, 138
Vanguard rocket project, 143
Vela satellite, 227
Vessey, John W., 86, 120, 129
Veterans Administration, 27
Vietnam syndrome, 293–295
Vietnam War, 3, 55, 94, 278–283, 293, 332–334
   antiwar movement and, 278–283
   CIA and, 332–334
   Diem's overthrow and, 332–333
   escalation of, 333
   helicopter losses in, 136–137
   ideological and moral opposition to, 280
   Jasons and, 213–215
   "McNamara's Wall" and, 214–215
   Maverick missile in, 155
   military leadership and, 280
   news media in, 300–301
   nuclear weapons use suggested for, 213–214
   presidential control and, 64
Viking rocket project, 143